the Witch's fate

COLLEGE OF WITCHCRAFT BOOK SIX

ALICIA RADES

ONE

I'd been an interim priest for a week, and already it was apparent that our first order of business was to restore the coven's hope. I'd made a nice, fancy speech the night we drove the priestesses out of town, but it wasn't enough to get our people moving to rebuild the town. The coven had chosen my friends and me to lead them and restore what the previous Imperium Council had destroyed, but the priestesses had broken the coven far beyond its infrastructure.

These people were hopeless. It was up to us to show them that we could heal this community together.

Nadine and I approached the hospital doors at the clinic entrance. We'd spent the last week speaking with coven members and visiting public facilities to survey the damage and learn as much as we could about where we could help.

People needed us… everywhere. Buildings, businesses, and services all around town had been destroyed. It was already an overwhelming job, but I forced myself to stay positive. These people needed us, and I wasn't going to back down, no matter how desperate things seemed.

Nadine paused outside the hospital doors, and I stopped beside her. We were alone, because Talia and Grant were back at the house watching Marcus, and Chloe was at Miriam College, working with Verla and Warren on plans to reopen enrollment so that classes could resume in the fall.

Nadine kept her voice low. "Before we go in, we need to be prepared. Not everyone is going to be happy to see us. Some of these patients were members of Miriam's Chosen, and they won't want to speak with us after we drove their leaders out of town."

I took her hands in mine to reassure her. "For every person who's angry, there will be someone who's grateful to see us. We just have to go in, listen to their concerns, and take them all to heart—the good and the bad. We need to show these people that we're listening, and that we're going to get them the help that they deserve."

"How are we going to promise that?" Nadine shot a glance toward the front doors, though we were alone. "The priestesses completely drained the council's funds before they left. There's no money left to run this town. We can't give these people promises we can't keep."

"We'll find a way," I vowed. "The priestesses may have stolen our resources, but we aren't giving up that easily. We'll find a solution. We *have* to."

Nadine nodded in agreement, then took a deep breath to steel her nerves. "You're right. The priestesses have taken so much from us before, and it hasn't stopped us yet. We just have to keep moving forward. Let's go see what assistance we can provide."

Nadine and I entered the hospital. The registration area was packed, but it was eerily quiet. The only voice that could be heard was the single receptionist behind the counter checking patients in. Other patients sat and waited their turn, but there weren't enough seats for everybody. Some patients were standing in line. It was obvious the clinic was severely understaffed.

A nurse hurried through the room, and an elderly man with a cane tried to stop her.

"Excuse me," he said weakly. "I'm looking for the radiology department."

"Ask reception," the nurse snapped. "I'm very busy."

Onyx entered the reception area in her nursing scrubs. We were supposed to be meeting with her so she could lead us around the hospital.

The elderly man approached her. "Excuse me, can you point me to radiology? I've checked in for my appointment, but I can't find where I'm going."

Onyx gave the man a kind smile and pointed. "Radiology is on the first floor down that hall. I can walk you there if you'd like."

"I don't want to trouble you," he insisted.

"It's no trouble at all," she replied. "Would you like a wheelchair?"

The man nodded, and his eyes brimmed with tears. He looked like he'd been ready to give up seeking help only a moment ago. I wondered how long he'd been wandering the halls looking for his appointment office.

"You stay right here. I'll be right back," Onyx assured the man. She approached the entrance, where Nadine and I were standing. She offered us a bright smile, though she looked exhausted, and her shift had only started an hour ago. "Good to see you both. If you want to follow me, I have a patient to help, and then I can show you around from there."

Onyx grabbed a wheelchair that was sitting by the door, and she helped the man into it. We followed her down the hall.

He looked up to me. "Are you a patient as well?"

"No," I told him. "My name is Lucas, and this is my wife, Nadine. We're from the Imperium Council, and we've come to see how we can help."

"Hmph," the man huffed. "Can't say I've heard of a man on the council for ages. What happened to the other council members?"

Nadine and I exchanged a glance. It'd been big news that the priestesses left town and we took over the council. I was surprised he didn't know.

"They left town," Nadine answered simply. "Coven members asked us to stand in their place."

The man frowned. "I don't keep up with politics. If you think you can help, then you can start by staffing this hospital. My hip has been bothering me for months, and I'm still waiting for a diagnosis."

"We'll see what shows up on imaging today, and hopefully you'll walk out of here with some answers," Onyx encouraged.

"I doubt it," he said flatly. There was no emotion behind it—no anger or anything. He merely expected that no one could help him, and he had already resolved himself to his fate. "It's time to accept that my last good years are over. My body's given up."

I wished I could offer him words of encouragement, but what could I say? So many people in the coven shared the same sentiment.

We reached the end of the hall, and Onyx led us into a small waiting room. There were several patients there, including a middle-aged man with a beard and a mother with her young child. Nadine recognized the elderly woman in the wheelchair closest to the door.

"Rose!" Nadine exclaimed. "I didn't expect to see you here."

I'd never met Rose, but I'd heard of her before. Nadine used to spend time with her at the nursing home, and they'd put puzzles together to pass the time.

Rose reached out for her, though her hands trembled weakly. "Priestess Nadine. It's so good to see you."

Nadine knelt at her side. "How have you been?"

"I've been better," Rose said. She spoke slowly, like finding the energy to talk was taxing. "I've been experiencing some knee pain, and the doctors at the resident facility were unable to help. They sent me here for more tests. How are you? Last I heard, you left town."

"I'm back," Nadine said.

The bearded man scoffed from across the room, though he didn't say anything. I noticed the mark of Miriam's Chosen on his wrist. He was most definitely a part of the cult and was among those who didn't want us here. The man crossed his arms and shifted in his seat until he was turned away from us. He certainly didn't want to speak with us.

The woman with the child kept her gaze on me. She too bore the mark of the Chosen, but she didn't appear afraid of us. "Why are you here?" she asked.

I sat two chairs down from her so that I was at her level, but not so close as to make her uncomfortable. "We're here to speak to people and address their concerns. Is there anything we can do to help?"

I looked at her child, who was holding his arm. It appeared to be injured, though there were no visible external injuries.

"My main concern is getting my child proper medical care," the woman said. "We believe he's dislocated his arm, though we're waiting for imaging to confirm. We've been sitting here for hours. The staffing and resources at this hospital are severely lacking. What are you going to do about it?"

She wasn't angry; she was merely curious. She'd been part of Miriam's Chosen, but it didn't appear that she was going to write us off immediately. Her main priority was ensuring her family was safe and well cared for, and she was willing to wait and see if we could provide for them in ways the priestesses hadn't.

I wanted to give her specifics, but like Nadine said, we couldn't make promises we weren't able to keep. We were still trying to gather information to develop the best plan moving forward. I couldn't tell this woman we were going to fix everything when we didn't even know if that was possible.

"We're going to do our best to provide this hospital with more resources so that everyone is well taken care of," I answered. It was all I could promise. I only worried our best wouldn't be good enough.

"I truly hope you're right," she said, before dropping her head. "I've gotten that answer from the priestesses before, and they never came through."

It was disheartening to know that wasn't the answer I'd wanted to give her. I wished I could provide more, but I didn't know how we were going to do that right now.

"Lucas, Nadine." Onyx gestured us over, and we stepped out into the hall. "I ran into Dr. Tracey in the hall. She's willing to speak with you."

Down the hall, I saw a woman I recognized in a white lab coat. It was Dr. Anna Tracey, Nadine's nephrologist who we'd met during the kidney transplant. She reached out to shake our hands when we approached.

"Nadine, Lucas, it's nice to see you again," she said. "I only have a few minutes, but Onyx says you're here to listen to our concerns. I'd like to know what the Imperium Council plans to do to rectify the budget issues we've been facing."

"That's what we're here to figure out," I told her. "What would you say are your main concerns?"

Dr. Tracey pursed her lips. "My main concern is that this hospital won't be able to continue treating patients, and that it will completely shut down within the year. People are losing trust in us, and we aren't able to provide them with the level of care they deserve. They believe we don't care about our patients, but that couldn't be further from the truth. We want everyone to be taken care of, but we simply don't have enough resources to go around. We've already been forced to shut down several patient wards, because we don't have the staff or the medical supplies to keep them running. So many of our nurses and doctors left town to find work elsewhere, and we've used up everything trying to treat the patients here."

"What would be the most help to this hospital?" Nadine asked. "What if we sent volunteers?"

"We already have volunteers, but without proper medical training and licensing, they can only help so much," Dr. Tracey said. "What we need is money. In the last year, the priestesses diverted the bulk of our funding for themselves. We had to fire staff, as well as pick and choose which medications and supplies are a priority. Non-life-threatening illnesses have gone untreated, but we can't keep these people waiting around forever. We need you to restore our funding, so we can bring back our staff, purchase more medical supplies, and give these people the care they deserve."

"Thank you for the valuable insight," I told her. "We will do our best."

I heard the words come out of my mouth again, and I hated that it was the only thing I could say. I was a priest, and I was supposed to have power, but it was difficult to wield power without proper resources.

"What exactly do you plan to do?" Dr. Tracey cocked an eyebrow. We needed to give these people *specifics*, but we didn't have the money sitting around to simply hand over.

"We'll ask for resources and assistance from *Hok'evale*," I offered. "They've been willing to help us before, and I'm sure they will again."

It wasn't enough, and we all knew that. Assistance may help alleviate some of the burden, but it wasn't a long-term solution, and *Hok'evale* had their own people to provide for. Furthermore, they were on the other side of the country. I was the only person in the coven who could create portals to get our people to their healers quickly, and I could only transfer a few people at a time on days when my powers weren't affected by the Waning. We could ask for help with the worst of our injured, but *Hok'e-vale's* clinic was already full of refugees from supernatural nations across the world. They couldn't take care of themselves and a whole witch city on top of it.

Dr. Tracey left with a frown on her face. She'd obviously been hoping for a better answer.

I turned to Nadine and Onyx. "We need to come up with a real plan, because I can't keep promising these people our best and giving them jack shit in return."

"What can we possibly tell them?" Nadine asked desperately. "They're just so devastated. We thought people would react when we arrived, at least be angry or grateful—*something*. But it's like they've gone numb. They don't even *care* who's in power anymore, because it doesn't matter. They feel their lives are over. The priestesses sucked the life right out of them."

Onyx frowned. "It doesn't look good if you two are in the most powerful position in the coven and even *you* are completely helpless. If we can't change things in the coven, they'll throw you off the council."

"Worse than that," I muttered. "Things are still tense around here. It's a possibility people could get angry at the lack of progress and blame us for it. We could still hang."

"There have to be resources we can utilize that aren't reliant on money," Nadine insisted. "We can trade and barter with other supernatural societies to obtain resources. We can utilize volunteers, and we can provide incentives of some sort to get businesses back off the ground. Once our economy is going again, we can fund the hospital. We just have to move quickly."

"It sounds nice when you say it, but our best resource for trade is magical potions, and without access to ingredients, we aren't going to be able to trade anything," I pointed out. "Volunteers are nice, but people can't give their time when they're struggling to survive—"

Kaboom!

I was cut off by the sound of an explosion. My heart leapt as the ground shook beneath us. The blast sent us flying off our feet so fast that none of us managed to cast a shield in time. I landed hard against the floor as building materials rained down around us.

My ears rang, and it took me a moment to orient myself. Nadine and Onyx lay beside me, but the waiting room we'd just left had caved in. There was still some structure to the building, but the hall was covered in dangerous debris, and dust billowed into the air.

Nadine scrambled to her feet and shouted something, but I couldn't hear it. I shook my head, and the ringing in my ears began to subside. The sound of an alarm grew louder, and screams filled the air.

"We need to search for survivors!" I heard Nadine shout.

Onyx was already following her, and the girls climbed over rubble to get back to the radiology waiting room. I shook off the shock and quickly got to my feet. We'd been on the edge of the blast zone. If we'd been only a few more feet down the hallway, we'd have been crushed under the rubble.

"I'm right behind you!" I called over the sound of the alarm. I cast a shield around us, so that if any remaining debris fell, we wouldn't be injured by it.

The radiology department hadn't been far from where we'd been standing, but it seemed like a mile as we traversed the rubble. The alarm continued to blare, but the panicked screaming that we'd heard had faded. The hospital must've evacuated.

As we came closer to the worst of the blast, it became abundantly clear that we weren't going to find any survivors. There was too much rubble, and this waiting room had been too close to the explosion.

Then we heard it—a distant whimper. "Priestess Nadine?" an elderly female voice called out.

"It's Rose!" Nadine cried as she jumped over a pile of rubble to get to her.

I didn't see Rose anywhere. Then Nadine knelt next to a pile of debris, and I saw a wrinkled hand reaching out for her. Rose was pinned beneath pieces of concrete and building materials. I quickly came to her side to see there was a small hole in which we could see through. Rose was lying on her back, and a small but weak shield shimmered around her. She'd been quick enough to cast it so that she hadn't been crushed.

"I don't know how long I can hold it," Rose whimpered weakly.

"I'll hold the shield," I told her. "Onyx, go find as many Mentalists with telekinesis as you can. We need help moving the rubble! Call Chloe, too. We're going to need her."

Onyx took off immediately to go find help.

Nadine took Rose's hand in hers. "It's going to be all right. Lucas and I are here, and we aren't leaving."

I formed a shield around Rose. I tried expanding it outward to push the rubble aside, but it was so heavy that it required all my strength. The rubble shifted, and several pieces tumbled over each other, nearly knocking into Nadine and me.

"Lucas, stop," Nadine pressed. "Wait until the Mentalists arrive. We have to work together."

I'd be lying if I said I wasn't panicking. This was a deliberate attack, and unless we found out who did it, it was going to happen again.

Mere moments passed before Onyx returned with a team of doctors and other medical staff. They'd already been on their way when they heard the explosion, and they quickly surrounded Rose to help get her to safety. Mentalists used telekinesis to carefully remove the rubble, then they levitated Rose into the air and hurried off to another ward to provide immediate care. Other staff members looked for more survivors, but I wasn't sure we'd find any.

Onyx gestured us over, and Nadine and I went to her side. The worried look on her face scared me. "Did you get a hold of Chloe?" I asked.

"I did, and she's already on her way. There's something you're going to want to see," Onyx said hollowly. "You should both follow me."

Onyx led us back down the hall, and it seemed to take forever before we reached an area that wasn't covered by debris. Onyx took us outside into the parking lot, and she pointed upward. My stomach turned to stones, and Nadine grabbed on to me tightly. There in the sky was a message, written out in dark smoke—a spell obviously cast by whoever had caused this.

Long live our rightful priestesses!

I didn't know who was specifically responsible, but it was obviously someone within the priestesses' cult.

Tires squealed, and a black car with gold trim came screeching to a halt in front of us. It was Priestess Lilian's car, but Chloe had claimed it as her own once her grandmother left town. It was really fancy and belonged to the family trust, so Chloe technically had a rightful claim to it. Chloe jumped out of the car. She didn't even look up at the writing in the sky, as if she'd been watching it the whole ride here.

I still couldn't take my eyes off the smokey black words. "If they wanted to target Nadine and me, why take these other innocent people with them?"

"People like this don't care about the sick," Nadine said hollowly. "They think disabled people take up resources, and they surely believe the ill are the same people who put us in power."

Chloe marched up to us, looking ready to kick someone's ass. "Make no mistake, Lucas, this wasn't just an attack on you. It was an attack on us all, to destabilize the coven and create distrust in the new Imperium Council. I just received word from Miles. We know who did this."

"Miles has only been leading the police force for a week. He's already caught the guy?" Nadine asked.

"No, they've fled," Chloe replied. "The Executors that were locked up in jail are gone—every single one of them."

"What!?" I roared. "How could this happen?"

Chloe shook her head. "We don't know. Miles went on his lunch break, and when he came back to the station, the cell doors were unlocked, and the Executors had taken off. Miles is sheriff now, but other people stepped up to help him out with the police force. One of the volunteers must've helped the Executors escape."

It was the only explanation, because the Executors couldn't have gotten out by themselves. The jail cells were made of noxite bars.

"Miles received a call from a witness saying they saw the Executors heading toward the hospital. The witness watched them cast a spell to blow up the radiology wing," Chloe explained. "Miles and his team are patrolling the nearby streets, but the Executors are gone."

"Fuck!" I growled, kicking a rock so hard it skidded halfway across the parking lot. "We should've been more prepared! If someone on the police force betrayed the coven, that means there are more people inside the city *right now* willing to help the priestesses. Someone who was supposed to be on our side helped them escape. There are more people willing to turn their backs on us right now than those who are willing to help us!"

We knew we'd be met with backlash, but I didn't think the coven would continue the priestesses' torment of murdering innocent people. The reality was harrowing.

Anyone could turn on us at any time. We had no way of knowing who was already plotting their next move. Betrayal could come from anyone...

Even someone we trusted.

nadine

TWO

"The Executors couldn't have gone far," I insisted. "If we're fast, we can still catch them."

I was already on the move, marching around the outside of the building toward the wing where the blast had detonated. I was determined to keep our people safe, which meant making sure something like this *never* happened again.

"We can try following their trail, but you can't underestimate my grandmother, Nadine," Chloe said as she followed me. "With the Master Wand, she has the power to cast portals now. I wouldn't put it past her to use one to get those Executors out of town."

"We've followed portals before. It's how we tracked down Autumn at her cottage in the mountains," Lucas pointed out.

We rounded the side of the building, and I slowed as I took in the blast site. The whole wing had been devastated by a powerful spell. The outer wall had completely collapsed, and building debris lay scattered everywhere.

Nearby, Gregory and Brayden were taping off the crime scene, and Alex was snapping photographs of the evidence. They'd all joined the police force after the coven put us on the council, but they'd barely started their training. They weren't technically qualified to do this work, but we needed the manpower.

Professor Blackbird stood nearby in his police uniform, interviewing several witnesses. He was the town's new assistant sheriff and had resigned as the Wand Studies professor to take the job. He was in his seventies and probably shouldn't be out in the field, but he was ex-military and one of the highest qualified people in town to serve on the police force.

"Thank you for your time," Professor Blackbird told the witnesses.

Lucas quickly flagged him down. "Sheriff, what have you learned?"

Professor Blackbird flipped through a notepad. "As far as we can tell, the blast was caused by a battle spell, though we aren't ruling out potions or traditional explosives. Witnesses counted four suspects fleeing the scene."

"We heard it was Executors," Chloe said. "Any idea who let them out of their cell? They couldn't have gotten out by themselves."

"The security footage has been tampered with, but there was only one officer at the station when the Executors broke out," Professor Blackbird said lowly. "It was Lincoln, the guy who used to guard Octavia Hall for the priestesses. He showed up at the station after the priestesses fled town, saying he wanted to help. I can't say I wasn't wary of hiring him, because he worked so closely with the priestesses for so long. But he's one of the few guys we have left with any proper training, so we gave him a job."

"Have your team bring him in for questioning, if he hasn't fled with the others," Lucas ordered.

I carefully stepped over rubble to look at the blast from another angle.

Chloe nudged Lucas. "I think Nadine's on to something."

I kept my eyes on the debris as I explained, "If we look at the direction that the rubble's laying, we can reasonably estimate where the suspect was standing when he cast the spell."

I took a few steps back and planted my feet firmly in place. I was far enough away from the building that there was no rubble at my feet, but close enough to cast a spell. "Right here. The blast is spread out almost symmetrically from this spot."

"How does that help us?" Chloe wondered.

"I'm not sure yet…" I squatted down and closely inspected the ground around me. There were tiny bits of building material embedded in the dirt. If there were any clues here before, they were surely obscured by the blast.

Then I saw it—the tiniest hint of a muddy footprint left behind. It was only a partial print, and to the untrained eye barely looked like a disturbance in the soil at all. "I've got a partial print!"

"Good catch," Lucas said. "I never would've spotted that."

"Judging by the direction of the tread marks, the suspects went that way." I pointed to a line of trees. The hospital was situated on the edge of town, and I didn't think there was anything past that tree line but forest for miles.

Lucas carefully watched where he was stepping. He stopped several yards away from me. "I've got another print. It's a different tread pattern, but it's headed in the same direction."

I conjured the enchanted broom I kept in my stash. "Let's follow the trail."

Lucas and Chloe followed my lead, conjuring their own brooms. Chloe's wasn't enchanted like the ones we'd found at Wicked Alchemy, but she could use her telekinesis to fly on hers.

"Professor, you should stay here and continue to question the witnesses," Lucas suggested. "We'll let you know if we find anything."

"On it, Priest," Professor Blackbird said.

We mounted our brooms so we wouldn't disturb any of the footprints, then took off flying toward the trees. The trail was sparse at first and hard to follow. The dirt here was dry and hard, and didn't lend itself well to capturing prints. I wasn't surprised the police hadn't noticed the boot treads.

My heart raced, and the wind blew my hair back as we ducked branches and dodged around trees. The deeper we got into the trees, the more apparent the footsteps became. The ground became muddy, and upturned leaves made the trail easy to follow. We couldn't be far behind the suspects.

I caught movement up ahead. I signaled to Lucas and Chloe, and they both nodded back. I motioned for each of them to circle around to the sides, so that we could approach from three angles. They quickly veered off in either direction.

I leaned further over my broom, increasing my speed. I spotted four figures, and I was closing in on them fast. I didn't need to see their faces to know exactly who they were, because I recognized them from behind. They were our worst enemies right behind the priestesses—Ryan

Greyson, Frederick James, Cody White, and Leroy Benson. They were the cruelest students back at Miriam College of Witchcraft. They'd been among the worst of the Executors to perpetrate the most heinous crimes, having tortured and murdered innocent people.

I lifted my hand to cast a stunning spell. I didn't want to kill them, just slow them down. Lucas and Chloe did the same, but before we could cast the spells, the Executors sensed us coming. They whirled around and blasted spells that hit us mid-air. I went flying off my broom and landed flat on my back, gasping for breath. The trees swayed above me, and to be honest, I was shocked the spell hadn't taken my life. Not a single one of them would've hesitated to kill me.

Lucas and Chloe had been knocked off their brooms as well, but Lucas quickly jumped to his feet. He cast a shield around the four Executors, trapping them inside a small, shimmering dome.

I finally found my breath and pushed myself upright. Chloe stood beside me, wiping a bit of blood off her lip. Inside the shield dome, James, Cody, and Leroy all wore a matching stunned expression. Leroy reached out to touch the edge of the shield, as if he'd never seen one before in his life. He yanked his hand back like he'd been shocked.

"What are we going to do with them?" Chloe asked. "If we lock them up, then they'll just escape again, and we can't execute them. We promised the coven they'd stand trial."

"They will." Lucas took a step closer to the Executors. "First, I want them to talk. What's your plan, Ryan?"

Ryan simply stated, "We are the army. We will destroy you at harvest's end."

"Yeah, tough words, big guy," Lucas replied flatly. "We can do this the easy way or the hard way."

In unison, the Executors repeated Ryan's words, which sounded really creepy and ominous as their voices overlaid one another. It felt like they were mocking us, and that really pissed Lucas off. Lucas blasted a spell straight through his shield. It hit Ryan in the face, and he stumbled back into the others. It wasn't enough to cause any serious damage, but it sure looked like it hurt. Ryan grabbed his nose and then grunted—literally grunted, like a fucking caveman. I didn't know if he thought it was threatening, but it was merely comical.

"So I guess we're doing this the hard way," Lucas said as he conjured his scythe. I didn't think he intended to use it, but these men should know how powerful he was by now. They'd seen what he did to all the other Executors that night at Octavia Hall. Yet not a single one of them appeared afraid at all—like the mere concept of death eluded them entirely.

"Wait." I grabbed Lucas's arm as I observed the Executors. James didn't even look at me, which was strange, because he was always foaming at the mouth to kill me. They weren't casting spells or shouting obscenities like usual. I could feel magic coming off of them, but it wasn't quite *right*. "Something's very off about this."

"Nadine's right," Chloe agreed. She circled around them, but her proximity didn't arouse a single response. "It's like they've been enchanted."

Ryan dropped his hand to his side, and I gasped. His nose had completely flattened. In its place was a clump of dirt smeared across his face. It looked completely unnatural… *inhuman*.

"Fucking golems!" Lucas sneered. In the blink of an eye, he dropped his shield and swung his scythe through the air, slicing through the four Executors' abdomens all at once. The blade cut through their stomachs like warm butter. Their bodies instantly morphed into mud that landed in a heap at our feet.

I jumped back. "What the hell is a golem?"

Lucas ran his fingers through his hair and began pacing. "A diversion —that's what they are. The hospital bombing wasn't just an attack. It was meant to keep us occupied while the *real* Executors got out of town. These are just useless copies."

I crouched down to inspect the mud but found that all magical traces were gone. Lucas's scythe had broken the spell on these duplicates. "What is it? Some sort of illusion?"

"Basically," Chloe explained. "A golem is a being that's made from natural material—usually mud or clay—and brought to life by magic. They act as assistants to whoever creates them and do whatever the spellcaster tells them to. You can make them look like someone you know or give them fresh faces, which is useful either way depending on how you want to use them. It's a relatively simple spell that most witches and fae can cast, but it doesn't usually last very long or hold up well. Touch a golem wrong, and the spell breaks, reducing them to their original form."

"They seemed so real, though a bit brainless," I noted. "They could talk and cast spells."

"Golems can cast basic spells and communicate in simple sentences, but it's not at all convincing if you're trying to hold a conversation with them," Chloe told me. "I've never seen a spell like this hold so well. Usually a golem's spell *looks* real but doesn't have much oomph behind it. These golems were strong—dumb, as usual, but strong. We all felt their strength when they knocked us off our brooms."

"That's true, but their attack wasn't as strong as I expected," I admitted. "I was shocked they didn't kill us on the spot."

"The golems must've used up most of their energy casting the spell to blow up the radiology wing, and then writing that message in the sky… but they shouldn't have had that strength to begin with," Lucas said. "They're more powerful than they should be. The only thing that can make them that strong is the Master Wand."

"They were made with the Master Wand, all right," Chloe agreed. "Which brings up another problem. Usually, witches and fae can only sustain one golem at a time. But if all four golems were made with the Master Wand, that means the Wand can create and sustain multiple golems at once. We have no idea what its limit might be. The Master Wand could potentially sustain thousands."

"That must be what the Ryan duplicate meant when he said *we are the army*," Lucas mused. "The priestesses are going to make loads of them."

I noticed something as I inspected the dirt closer. "Check this out. The consistency of mud between each of the golems is different. The dirt from James's golem is dryer and more powdery than Ryan's, which is more clay-like. It's as if the James golem is older. Even if the priestesses can sustain multiple spells at once, I don't think they *create* multiple golems at the same time. It looks like it takes time."

Chloe crouched down next to me. "That tracks. Even though the Master Wand is strong, they'd still need to shape the mud for each individual golem. That's how they're made—you have to sculpt their bodies first, then the magic brings their features to life."

Lucas furrowed his brow thoughtfully. "If that's the case, it'd take them months to build a golem army that could take on all of Octavia Falls. Why not do something simpler, like using necromancy magic to raise an army of the dead?"

I tapped my chin. "Let's think from their perspective. The only reason Margaret and Lilian haven't returned to Octavia Falls is because they believe Santos is protecting us, and the gods are the only thing stronger than the Master Wand. Santos has power over the dead, because our necromancy magic descended from him."

"I see where you're going with this," Chloe said. "We borrowed the golem spell from other cultures. The fae used it first, so the priestesses must be building an army that even Santos can't control. Golems follow the instructions of their maker, and the priestesses have found a way to make them stronger. It's their perfect army."

I stood up straight. "The Ryan golem said they will destroy us at harvest's end. That can only mean that the priestesses plan to march on Halloween, which has historically marked the end of the harvest. We have time, but we have to be ready for them."

"Let's go tell the others what we found here," Lucas said. "The real Executors are long gone, but we have a better idea of what we're up against, and that might just save our asses."

When we returned to the hospital, the first responders had pulled all the survivors from the blast site. Mortana were on site to search for signs of life, but I could tell by the solemn looks on their faces that anyone else left in the rubble was already gone. Lucas gave a shudder, like he felt death in the air. I wondered how many voices he'd heard when the blast happened. He hadn't mentioned it, so I didn't ask.

The emergency room was on the other side of the hospital and thankfully hadn't been affected by the blast. The waiting room was in pure chaos when we entered. Staff rushed from one set of doors to another, barking orders, while patients crowded the room waiting to be seen.

Miles was there in his sheriff uniform, scanning the waiting room like he was looking for someone. His shoulders sagged in relief when he saw Chloe. He rushed over to her and swept her up into a tight hug, then planted a passionate kiss on her lips. She placed her hands on either side of his face and kissed him back with fervor.

Miles drew away from Chloe. "Thank Alora you're all okay! I'm sorry all this happened. I take full responsibility. My team is out searching for the suspects, but I'm afraid they may have gotten away for good."

"There's no use in blaming yourself," I said. "All we can do is keep moving forward and help these people."

"Call off the search, and get your team back here," Lucas instructed. "We need volunteers to help administer basic first aid. In the meantime, we have some business to discuss."

Lucas gestured for him to follow us down the hall. We found privacy in an empty exam room, where we told Miles about the golems we found in the woods.

He raked his fingers through his dark strands of hair. "I'm worried we don't have the means to hold the priestesses off. If Santos wants to help us, where is he now? We don't know if he's ever going to show up again."

"I'm not counting on it, to be honest," Lucas admitted. "It's rare for gods to meddle in human affairs. It's a miracle he showed up that night in the courthouse to protect us in the first place. Life is constantly teaching us lessons, and if he shows up to solve all our problems, we're bound to repeat the same mistakes. I don't think Santos is going to interfere. But I also don't think the priestesses are going to attack unless they're confident they stand a chance against any of our potential allies. That's why they're building this golem army."

"How do we defend against it?" Miles asked.

"Our priority is finding the Curse Breaker Wand," I said. "The night we faced the priestesses, they used the Master Wand to curse the four Oaken Wands in our possession to become powerless. The magic of the Seer, Alchemy, Mortana, and Mentalist Wands is locked down tight, and we can't use them against the priestesses or the Waning. But the Curse Breaker Wand is still out there and remains untouched by the priestesses' curse. If we find it, then we can use it to break the curse on the other Wands and unlock their full power again."

"Once we break the priestesses' curse and obtain the power of all five Oaken Wands, we'll be powerful enough to combat the priestesses' army and the Master Wand," Lucas added. "What's more, we'll have the power to end the Waning. We'll even be able to break the curse the priestesses cast on Marcus that night, which prevents us from using him to create another Master Wand, or from ever telling him he's a demigod."

"Where do we start?" Miles wondered. "You've been looking for this Wand for ages."

"We have full access to all the Imperium records now, which we never had before," I said. "I'm going to start there. We know that after my grandfather died, Grammy kept the Curse Breaker Wand until it went missing from her possession. We don't know who took it, but there could be clues somewhere in the records—connections the priestesses never thought to look for. Meanwhile, I'll contact our allies from other supernatural societies to see if they know anything about this Wand. Beau Blankard was half fae, and we learned about the Mortana Wand from him, which means there's a chance we could learn more about the Curse Breaker Wand from other societies as well."

"Say you do find the Curse Breaker Wand," Miles mused. "Couldn't the priestesses just cast another curse on the Oaken Wands the second you break it?"

"The Master Wand would have to overpower all five Oaken Wands," I replied. "These Wands are the most powerful weapon we have, and they're strongest together. Once they're all united, they'll be an equal match for the Master Wand, and the priestesses won't have the power to bind their magic again."

"That's *if* the Curse Breaker Wand chooses you," Miles pointed out. "The Wands can decide who to give their power to."

"If the Wand doesn't choose me, then I'll do whatever I have to in order to prove myself to it," I said. "The Seer Wand didn't choose Talia right away, but she was able to show it she'd use its power well. If it comes to that, then I can do the same. The Oaken Wands are the only thing strong enough to withstand an attack against the Master Wand. The Curse Breaker Wand is our only option."

"Why not just use Marcus's demigod powers against them? It worked last time," Miles pointed out.

"He's an infant, and his power is unpredictable," Lucas said harshly. "We aren't putting him in their path again."

"The Oaken Wands draw their magic from the coven, don't they?" Miles asked. "Why don't we just get the coven to combine their powers to defeat the priestesses? It'd save us a lot of time hunting down the last Wand."

"It's a good suggestion in theory, but there are too many hurdles there," Chloe said. "For one, we've agreed that these people aren't soldiers, and we aren't going to force them to fight for us. Even if we did, they'd have to willingly share their magic, and that's not a sure thing as long as the Waning's still depleting our powers at random. In that case, we'd still have to unite all five Oaken Wands, because the Waning isn't ending until all five Wands are found and we can actually do something about it."

"Isn't the Waning caused by the Protection Tree?" Miles asked. "Can't we just stop its spell?"

"You're right that the Protection Tree is causing the Waning," Lucas said. "Nadine and I learned that last year, when we discovered the tree was dying. The tree sustains the protection spell around the town by drawing magic from all of us, and by the coven dividing, our magic isn't working in harmony anymore. The tree keeps drawing more magic to try to keep up, but the more we divide, the worse it gets. But to end the spell, we'd have to overpower it, and the protection spell is far too strong for any one of us to break it—even Nadine. Even if we could do that, we'd open ourselves up to threats from outside the coven. We'd have a fae invasion on our hands, and they'd slaughter us before the priestesses ever got a chance."

"Lucas and Chloe are both right," I agreed. "Once we have all the Oaken Wands, we'll be able to redistribute magic to the coven, rebalance our magic and end the Waning, all while fortifying the protection spell to keep us safe. Until then, we need to navigate the Waning carefully. The priestesses can generate their own power from the Master Wand, but we have to be careful about expending our energy and using our crystals only on necessary spells, because the Waning is going to slow us down."

"All right, we'll focus on finding the Curse Breaker Wand. But if we don't find it by Halloween, when the priestesses plan to attack, then we need a contingency plan," Miles insisted.

"If we can't defend our people when the time comes, then we need to get them out of town," Lucas said. "We'll develop an evacuation plan and work with other supernatural societies to ensure our people have someplace to go, though I hope it won't come to that."

"It looks like we'll have to start building our own army in the meantime," Miles suggested. "We'll have to gather witches and warlocks who are ready to fight against the priestesses once they arrive."

"We can take volunteers, but we aren't exactly equipped to train an army, especially with the Waning draining our magic at random intervals," I admitted. "The Miriamic Coven has never had a standing army before, not even against the fae."

Lucas shifted his gaze thoughtfully. "We'll have to come up with an army another way. If witches can't fight, then we need to find those who can."

"Won't the priestesses be able to use the Master Wand to see what we're planning and how it will all play out? It's powerful enough to give them visions and read minds," Miles pointed out.

"In theory, but they'd have to know the technique and understand how to interpret their visions," I replied. "It takes years to learn how to control visions, and neither of them are Seers, so they don't have the training. Teleinsight alone took Talia and Chloe months to figure out with the power of the Oaken Wands. As for reading minds, Verla has been teaching us how to ward our minds since last Yule. As long as we keep practicing her technique, the priestesses shouldn't be able to get into our heads."

Miles reached out to take Chloe's hand in his. A black antique ring on her left hand caught the light. Miles had proposed to Chloe when we returned to Octavia Falls, and of course she'd said yes. A week ago when we'd driven the priestesses out of town, things felt hopeful. Now, we were faced with complete uncertainty.

"What does this mean for our people in the meantime?" Miles asked. "Do we put our lives on hold until this war is over?"

"Absolutely not," Chloe demanded. "I'm not letting my grandmother take what good is left in my life, and neither should any of you. We have to continue rebuilding Octavia Falls, because no one's going to want to fight for the coven if there's no coven left to save. I, for one, want to live as much of my life before my grandmother arrives and tries to ruin it."

"Does that mean you'll be planning a wedding?" I asked.

"Hell, yeah," Chloe insisted. "I've been planning my wedding since I was a kid, and I'm not giving that up just because my grandma wants to show off how big her wand is. Miles and I are getting married on the autumn equinox. Mark your calendars."

Chloe had clearly already made up her mind, and there was no changing it.

"All right," I agreed. "We've all got a job to do, and we keep at it."

Miles gave a firm nod. "It sounds like our new council knows what it's doing. Let's get to work."

We returned to the emergency room, where we found Onyx organizing volunteers. She placed me at registration to help check patients in, while Miles helped transport medical supplies. Chloe naturally stepped into leadership mode, carefully listening to coven member's concerns and reassuring them of their safety here in Octavia Falls. Chloe had an innate talent for articulating herself well, and she'd always been straight-forward and honest, so when she spoke, people believed her.

Lucas talked with families of the deceased, aiding them through their grief. He'd gotten really good at that and was extremely professional. It was obvious he took his job very seriously.

We stayed at the hospital for hours. Twice, Onyx brought me something to eat because the registration desk was so busy I hadn't been able to step away for any length of time.

Finally, well after sunset, we'd discharged enough patients that things started to settle down. I left the registration desk and went down the hall to find my friends. I passed my primary care provider, Dr. Yonker. He'd obviously been running around all day trying to help people, because his hair was disheveled and he had bags under his eyes. He didn't even notice me as he hurried to his next patient. I was glad he was here to help these people because he was a great doctor, but I could see that this was too much for even him. Even if we had the equipment to bounce back quickly from the devastation, the staff were already hanging on by a thread. One more calamity, and our healthcare system would surely collapse.

I continued down the hall. One section of the emergency room housed rows of beds that were separated by curtains. As I passed, I noticed one of the curtains was open, and a frail elderly woman I recognized lay propped up in bed. I was shocked to see that Rose was still here since this morning, as most patients had either been discharged or moved to a private room for overnight observation.

I approached Rose. She noticed me and gave me a kind smile. "How are you doing, sweetie?" she asked weakly.

I must've looked really tired. The fatigue had set in hours ago, but I was accustomed to pushing through it.

"Doing okay," I told her as I sat down. "I'm more worried about you. What did the doctors say?"

"I've got a clean bill of health," she said. "Just shaken up. Your quick response saved me from any lasting injuries."

"I'm so glad to hear that, but if that's the case, why haven't they discharged you?" I wondered.

"I can't drive myself, and there's no staff to transport me back to the resident facility. At least I have this bed for the night. The doctor says they'll find me a more permanent solution in the morning."

"Permanent solution?" I wondered. I did my best to mask my emotions. I didn't want her to know I was worried. "What happened to your room at the nursing home?"

"Rooms are hard to come by these days," Rose admitted. "Ever since the priestesses started shutting down nursing homes and shoving us all together in the same facility, things haven't been the same. It seems I get a new roommate every week. The priestesses wanted to conserve resources, but it has only led to a shortage. Nursing home staff were diverted here to the hospital today, and it sounds like they might need them permanently. I'm afraid they'll c-close my f-floor and I'll have nowhere to g-go—"

Rose burst into tears, and my heart shattered for her. I reached out to take her hand, and her whole body shook with sobs.

"I'm not going to let that happen," I stated firmly. "Rose, I promise I will work with your care team to make sure you have a place to go home to."

She wiped her tears with her other hand. "That's so kind of you, Priestess. I can't thank you enough."

"You don't have to thank me," I told her. "I'm here for you."

Rose gave my hand a weak squeeze. "The coven was right to choose you to lead them, Nadine. Now that you're here, we finally have hope."

I gave her a smile to mask the concern swirling in my gut. The priestesses had left a huge mess behind for us to clean up. I was more than up for the task. I just hoped my persistence was enough.

I waited at Rose's bedside until she fell asleep. I stepped into the hall and found Onyx speaking in a low voice to Lucas and Chloe. The hallway was otherwise secluded.

"We've done what we can to help these people today, but this attack has more than devastated our already fragile healthcare system," Onyx said. "There were over a dozen medical professionals working that wing who were killed today, and our most expensive imaging equipment is now gone."

"What do you know about the nursing homes?" I asked as I approached. "Rose is worried she may not have a home to go back to."

Onyx sighed heavily. "We're doing what we can, but things have changed a lot while we were in hiding. While the priestesses were in power, people were taking in the unhoused against occupancy laws, and doctors were providing services for free behind the priestesses' backs. In the months we were gone, the priestesses gutted one of our largest nursing homes to salvage supplies for the luxury apartment complex they wanted to build at the Catwalk."

"We can repurpose the material," I suggested. "The priestesses had other apartments built that are almost complete. We can convert those into temporary housing."

"It's a good start, but that's going to take a few more weeks of heavy labor," Onyx said. "In the meantime, many elderly patients are staying with family, but these families are overwhelmed with trying to care for complex medical problems they aren't trained to help with. One of the things I've been helping with is finalizing details for a temporary home-aid program that will support families who are helping provide basic care. It would allow certain patients to stay at home, while licensed staff would visit on a more part-time basis. It's far from a perfect solution, but it would help these families immensely in the meantime."

"We need to help Rose," I decided. "I've spent a lot of time with her during my visits to the nursing home, and I've never seen her so worried. We need to give her a home, so she has stability."

"Doesn't she have a family that can take her in?" Chloe asked.

I shook my head. "She has no one. Her husband's long gone, and her son doesn't live here anymore. It seems I'm the only one giving her hope right now, and if I can be that for her, then I'm happy to."

This decision wasn't just up to me, though. My friends and I were all living together at Lilian's estate, which now belonged to Chloe. If we were going to let someone else live there with us, we all had to agree.

"If you're all okay with it, I'd like to take Rose in until we find a more permanent solution for her," I suggested. "I know it's not ideal, but we have to do what we can, because she has nowhere else to go. I've said it before, and I'll say it again: We need to care for each individual, because there's no community without them."

"I agree," Chloe said. "We have an extra guest room, and Rose is more than welcome to stay."

"Any chance I get to help another patient is a chance I'll take," Onyx agreed.

Lucas nodded. "We'll take Rose in. It's not even a question."

He wrapped me in his arms and kissed the top of my head. I felt so much of my worry melt away at his touch.

I breathed a heavy sigh as I drew away. "What happened today was devastating, but if there's any good to come from it, it's shown us that our people will still come together in times of need. The priestesses may have the Master Wand, but we still have our coven. They can try to take this town by force, but they can't take the heart of the people."

They'd already laid this town to ruin. I'd sooner die than let them take what hope we salvaged in the aftermath.

THREE

Rose was elated when we told her we'd be taking her in. We got her settled into a guest room at the Olson estate, and the doctors said she'd been doing much better since then. I was grateful we were able to help her, because each individual we helped was progress toward a better community.

I didn't expect to rebuild Octavia Falls overnight, but I'd severely underestimated the amount of damage the priestesses had done. I'd seen with my own eyes the buildings they'd bulldozed to the ground, and I spoke with the families they'd left on the streets. Still, I was constantly learning new ways the priestesses had fucked the coven over.

For one, our justice system was in shambles. The priestesses' way of holding an execution without a trial wasn't going to fly with us, which meant restructuring a lot of processes. We'd arrested our suspected traitor, Lincoln, but we didn't have any hard evidence to try him with, so we were forced to set him free. He was still hanging around town, probably ferrying information back to the priestesses, but we couldn't exile him unless we could prove beyond a reasonable doubt that he was responsible for assisting the Executors' escape, and he'd done a good job covering his tracks. Still, Miles was keeping an eye on him.

While we hadn't heard anything from the priestesses or the Executors since the hospital attack, we were presented with a new crisis every day. Everyone was looking to us now for answers, and we had to make quick

—oftentimes heavy—decisions. There were so many problems that we couldn't fix them all, but we were damn well going to try.

First and foremost was making sure people were safe, which meant getting a roof over their heads and food in their bellies, as well as prioritizing their health. In the following week, we volunteered our time at the Octavia Falls annual blood drive and spent our nights serving food at the local soup kitchen.

We had no option but to take on debt from the United Supernatural Union. Once the funds arrived, we were able to implement grant programs to help businesses get off their feet to create new jobs, as well as provide a temporary health assistance program to help those who were currently unemployed. The money could only go so far, though. We couldn't pay everyone and had to provide tax incentives to recruit volunteers to undergo medical training so we could increase our healthcare staff numbers.

As soon as we could, we got to work contracting local construction crews to finish the apartment complexes the priestesses had started building. There were so many people who simply needed a place to live. Between massive layoffs, housing foreclosures, and forcing intercast families apart, the priestesses had left many families homeless. Not to mention there were dozens of orphaned children with nowhere to go after the priestesses had openly executed their parents. There weren't enough families in the coven qualified to take the kids in, because the approval process took so long. We'd had to make the tough call to send these kids to foster families outside the coven, even though the last thing we wanted was to take them away from their people.

In just a few short weeks, the coven had finished one wing of the new apartment complexes. It was a point of contention among the coven, as certain vocal members raised concerns at our town meeting about how we were going to decide who got to stay in the apartments rent-free and who was going to have to wait for housing. We couldn't delay housing people until all the apartments were finished, though, because these people needed a warm bed to sleep in *now*. It was the worst feeling in the world having to turn anyone away, but we did our best to help the most vulnerable first. We were still rebuilding and would open more housing as soon as possible.

The housing crisis was only the first of many problems. To aid in the food shortage, we converted several plots of city-owned land into community gardens. Teams of volunteer Alchemists were working around the clock to tend to the crops. Their magic made the plants grow faster, and they'd already made their first harvest. Still, we couldn't produce fast enough. I'd been to the food pantry to help pass out produce, and I witnessed people waiting in line for hours, only to be told there was nothing left for them and to come back tomorrow.

We were making progress, but there were still hundreds of people who weren't getting the help they needed. It wasn't enough.

Despite what we'd done in such a short amount of time, we couldn't undo everything the priestesses had damaged—including their own people's psyche. There were still coven members who called themselves Miriam's Chosen and claimed that what we were doing was all a manipulation tactic to gain power. Misinformation was at an all-time high, with members of Miriam's Chosen patrolling the streets claiming we were refusing item donations and confiscating people's belongings. They scared coven members into believing that if they accepted help from us, the Imperium Council had the right to take their land. Even if we *could* help everyone, some people wouldn't accept the assistance.

Nobody knew what was true or not, and there was little we could do to combat the lies. The priestesses had given a platform to idiots who no one would've taken seriously before, and now people believed them, which was a problem. Some radical members tried to burn one of our gardens, though the police department responded in time to arrest the vandals and save most of the crops.

The cult's response was inconsequential compared to the contention among the volunteers. Coven members had come together to help provide resources, and though they meant well, the hardest part was getting people to decide on a solution together and start taking action. It seemed that everywhere we went, people were arguing about details that didn't matter.

Every time I stopped by the community gardens, the two head gardeners were bickering about one thing or another. They couldn't get on the same page about which crops would produce the most food, and were constantly arguing about which plants to grow. Eventually, Nadine and I had to make an executive decision just to get them to put seeds in the ground. The radicals were easy to deal with, but regular people, who hadn't technically done anything wrong, were the hardest ones to handle, because their inaction led to big problems.

That left most choices up to us, to the point where we were making hundreds of decisions every day. Before becoming a priest, I understood that the Imperium Council was responsible for everything regarding town policies, budgeting, infrastructure development and regulation, and upholding citizen rights. However, I didn't understand how much negotiation and compromise that required.

We oversaw everything including public works; social services; maintaining roads, parks, and other local infrastructure; providing emergency medical services; managing property taxes, water supply, and sewage; protecting our local environment and managing waste; providing care to the animal shelter; managing the cemeteries; operating the food banks, shelters, and senior centers; planning for community events; and appointing officials to complete all these tasks. It was our job to stay informed on all of it, as well as make sure that each department was working in harmony and that our limited resources were allocated appropriately. Most of our days were filled with public appearances or meetings. When we had a spare moment, we volunteered where personnel was limited.

Every day was different for us. A whole month had passed since we were placed on the council, and it was already July. Nadine, Grant, Talia, and I spent that morning with city staff going over the town's budget. Chloe wasn't there, because we took turns staying at the house to watch Marcus and to be around in case Rose needed anything. Together, the council had approved a new tax rate that would provide relief for struggling families, but we were met with pushback from our staff.

"We don't have the money to be lowering tax rates right now," Jude Bennett said. We were on good terms, on account of having protected his kid, Travis, when the Gingerbread witches were kidnapping children. He worked in the city's accounting department, and though he was kind and willing to work with us, we had differing opinions on how to manage the city's funds. "The Waning has forced our syrup and cider producers to slow production, because we don't have the magic to infuse into the products. Alchemy magic is what makes our produce superior to others, and we now have a shortage of high-quality exports. The money's just not coming into the coven. Lowering tax rates means less money for the council to allocate to necessary programs."

"We have a starting point," Grant pointed out. "We've taken out loans from the United Supernatural Union, and *Hok'evale* has sent food and supplies to help us get back on our feet."

"It isn't enough," Jude argued. "*Hok'evale* is focused on sending aid to Kinpago and rehabilitating the Hawkei from the damage caused by their own civil war. They don't have the resources to send enough aid here. Taking on debt is only going to be bad for us later."

"We don't like it either, but there's no easy solution here," Talia said. "We need to take out these loans to help our people."

"We need to be thinking about the future of the coven. By taking out more loans, we're placing the burden of paying them back on the next generation," Jude pressed, before turning to me. "Do you want your son taking on this debt? Because he'll be the one paying these loans back when he's your age."

"If we use the money properly, then we can rebuild our economy and pay off the loans before our children are in our position," I replied. I understood that the coven didn't want to take on the debt, but no one had suggested any helpful alternatives. There really wasn't any other choice.

"You don't want to owe the United Supernatural Union. They'll come back and expect a favor," Jude insisted.

Nadine stood from the conference table. "We need to do this now, because if we don't, our people will continue to suffer. If we don't help our people today, there won't be a coven in the future."

The staff members continued to push back and complain, and by the end of our meeting, nothing got done. I wished that Chloe was here. It was difficult never having all five of us in a room at once, because Chloe would've been an asset when the city staff started pushing back. Nadine was pretty good at stepping in and setting them straight, but the priest-esses had spread so many lies about her that she was struggling to earn certain people's respect.

After our meeting that morning, we met with Judge Calloway and members of the police department to consult on new laws that would lower sentencing for first-time misdemeanors and provide more rehabili-tation resources to reduce the rate of second-time offenses.

Tension was high in the presence of the judge. She'd judged our trial and hadn't been kind, but she agreed to work with us because Mother Miriam declared us not guilty.

"That's not the way the system works," Judge Calloway insisted when we presented our idea. "If you're easy on criminals, they won't learn their lesson and will offend again. You're putting people at risk by giving these criminals a second chance."

"We *need* to give people a second chance at life," Nadine argued. "People commit crimes for a reason, and if we can get them the help they need, there's no reason for them to offend again."

"That may be the case for some, but not everyone can be helped," Judge Calloway barked back.

"We need to give that chance to the people who *can* be helped," Nadine pressed.

"This is ridiculous," an officer piped up. "The coven can't go soft on crime when we're at our most vulnerable. We need to be tough right now."

Several officers mumbled an agreement. Gregory and Brayden exchanged a wary glance. The other guys were all big muscles and broad shoulders, the kind of men to be out in the field taking down criminals. Gregory and Brayden, on the other hand, would surely be placed in the office pushing papers. That was fine, because we needed someone to do that work, but the poor rookies didn't know how to speak up.

Miles stood, his sheriff badge shining prominently on his chest. "My officers have a point. I agree with them, but at the same time, what we've been doing isn't working, so we need to try something else. I'll stick with the Imperium Council if this is what they think is best."

Judge Calloway sighed. "I'll endorse this new initiative because you're asking me to, but you have to understand that some of these people can't be rehabilitated. People are going to get hurt due to this policy, because you can't rehabilitate everybody."

That was really the best we could ask out of this meeting, but I worried the new policy wouldn't have the effect we desired because people didn't want to enforce it. They didn't quite seem to understand what we were suggesting, and miscommunication seemed to be the most difficult hurdle for us to overcome.

Later that day, we visited one of the town's residential construction sites and met with the foreman about their progress. Several more units were supposed to be ready for temporary housing, but they were running behind schedule.

"We're doing our best to get this done, but we don't have enough hands," the foreman told us. "Our crew is working seven days a week, and they're exhausted. I've got two guys out this week due to injuries, and another one's sick. It's not going as fast as we hoped, and we can't start letting people move in until these units are up to code. It's a public health hazard."

"We'll have to adjust our timeline," I suggested. I hated to say it, but I didn't see an alternative. If we made these people work too hard, they'd burn out, but if we didn't get these units finalized, our homeless population would suffer. It seemed there was no way to take care of *everyone*, and that totally sucked. "In the meantime, where do you need help? We'll do what we can."

Nadine, Talia, Grant and I spent the next two hours installing kitchen cabinets and countertops in one of the units. We were sweating by the time we had to rush off site for our next meeting.

After lunch, we stopped by the *Miriamic Messenger* to host a press conference. The newspaper wanted a report on our progress, but there were so many answers we couldn't give.

Where are the priestesses?

Have you found them yet?

What do you plan to do once they come back?

I had to carefully maneuver or downright ignore most of their questions, because I couldn't give them the answers they wanted. The journalists had more questions than we anticipated, so we stayed there an hour longer than planned.

That put each of us late for our following meetings. As members of the Imperium Council, each of us had the authority to represent the council at public functions. Nadine attended a meeting at the hospital, while Grant represented us at a presentation put on by the Planning and Zoning committee. Talia attended the school board meeting to keep us up to date on changes happening at Miriam College of Witchcraft. I met with constituents and left with twenty more problems to address.

We had only minutes to update each other on what we covered in each meeting. Nadine had to deal with the hospital board arguing about which patients to help, which really pissed her off. Several board members agreed they needed to help the healthiest patients first, because the sick people were already dying anyway.

Grant got caught in the middle of an argument with the Planning and Zoning committee about whether we needed more residential buildings to house our people, or if we needed to be building more businesses to stimulate the economy. Somehow, the former band members of the Wicked Warlocks, Clay and Carl, had ended up at the meeting—probably due to some connections their parents had. These two had been trouble for us before. I guess they thought they were some sort of experts because they worked in construction now, but they were just idiots intent on causing trouble. According to Grant, they kept shouting over anyone who brought up points in favor of focusing on residential housing. Grant managed to deescalate the situation, but no decisions had been made by the end of the meeting.

Talia had an even worse time at the school board meeting, which had been open to staff and school board members alike. Verla had invited several students to attend, in order to give the student body a voice in upcoming changes. She'd recruited the best of the best—Darcy, Samantha, and Alex. They were good people, and I knew if anyone had the rest of the student body's best interests at heart, it was these three.

Unfortunately, Camille got wind of it and showed up to bitch about how there weren't any student Mentalists in the meeting, and that she should be included to represent her Cast. It wasn't an unreasonable request, and one I'm sure could've been resolved easily if she hadn't brought along Gwen and Valerie to make a scene. Apparently, the three of them screamed at the school board until everyone was on their feet arguing. The way I heard it, the meeting ended with Professor Lewis slinging slurs at Professor Richards, until Professor Loren had to step in and use her telekinesis to force either side to opposite ends of the room. That must've been quite a sight, considering Professor Loren was old enough to be my great-grandmother. I was sure she was more than sick of everyone acting like children.

Talia complained that the meeting couldn't progress regardless of the controversy, because some people wanted to keep the curriculum as-is, and others wanted to change it. She was frustrated because the school was supposed to open back up in September, and the staff couldn't even get on the same page about what to teach. That was all between determining what to do with the limited space they had, and finishing construction on the school in the meantime. There wasn't room to house students in the dorms anymore, so they had to convert the rooms on the upper level into classrooms to accommodate enrollment. Students would have to travel to campus this year until we could find a better solution, because we just didn't have the magic necessary to restore the space-bending spell to hold that many people.

My friends and I wouldn't be enrolling this year, because our jobs were too important to be taking classes at the same time, but the school board needed to get moving on these plans if they wanted *anyone* to start classes in the fall.

I was more than worn out after addressing constituents' concerns. I just wanted to fix everyone's problems, and despite holding all this power, there was little to nothing I could do to fix everything.

We missed dinner to meet with the event committee about the Summer Harvest Festival, which was held in August every year to celebrate our farmers and the first harvest. The tradition was quickly approaching, and it required a lot of organizing ahead of time. Unfortunately, we couldn't even get started planning, because the coven couldn't decide if we should even *hold* the festival.

"You want to host a festival when we still have homeless people on the street? It's selfish to host a party when our people don't have food," Meredith balked. We'd encountered her before—once at her sister Monica's fake funeral, and once at the Festival of Santos, when she denounced her marriage and joined Miriam's Chosen on stage. I wasn't surprised her opinion differed from ours, but for once I could actually see where she was coming from.

"I understand it's a lot to ask the coven to plan for this, but it's important that the coven has community-wide events to look forward to," I said.

"This festival is an opportunity to bring the coven together, which makes it a priority," Nadine added.

"We shouldn't be wasting our time with *fun* stuff," Meredith argued. "People are dying!"

"Nadine and Lucas have a point," Talia stepped in. "People need to feel like a part of the community, and this is a sacred event. It's our religion."

"I don't care about our religion!" Meredith exploded. "I gave up my husband for my religion, and it was all a lie! Mother Miriam has done *nothing*. I don't care about worshiping her anymore, and neither should the rest of you."

"I agree with Meredith," Krista Thomas said. She was the mother of Caleb Thomas, one of the young boys who'd been killed by the Gingerbread witches. She volunteered on the program committee and had always been kind to us, but she didn't agree with our stance on this. "We don't need to worship Mother Miriam if she's not going to show up for us. We can be witches without following her."

"What good does that do?" Grant asked. "Our magic is tied to Alora. If we aren't following her, we won't *be* witches."

"At least we'd survive," Meredith pressed. "We're losing our magic to the Waning anyway. We'll inevitably lose our magic anyway."

That made me really sad to hear, because our magic was our identity, and if we didn't find a permanent solution to bring it back, we'd lose who we were entirely. Some days, it felt like we were fighting a losing battle. We'd fought so hard to stop what the priestesses were doing and to make the coven better… but we didn't realize how bad things really were. It was becoming clear that we weren't able to do this by ourselves.

As much as I hated to admit it, I was starting to understand why the priestesses had to put their foot down and control everything. I thought they were being dictators, but it occurred to me now that they had to be forceful, or no one was going to listen.

But that's not the way any of us wanted to lead the coven. We weren't going to take people's choices away, even if we had a difference of opinion. No matter how hard it was, we would continue to do everything in our power to rebuild these people's lives, while maintaining their autonomy.

The event committee eventually agreed that we *would* host the festival, but I didn't have high hopes that it would be anything like it was in years past. These people didn't seem very excited or motivated to make it anything special.

We were all exhausted. It didn't help that my parents had been blowing up my phone all day, as usual. I hadn't wanted to see or talk to them when we returned to Octavia Falls, but now that my contact details were public, they hadn't stopped trying to get in touch with me.

Dad was constantly sending messages to my work email with *ideas* for the council. He acted like he wanted to help, but it was obvious he was only interested in bolstering his own position, as most of his "suggestions" were completely insane. Last week, he'd emailed a massive rant about how we needed to start forcing *ungrateful college kids* into the workforce, even though they hadn't finished their degrees and didn't have the qualifications yet, not to mention there weren't enough jobs in Octavia Falls to go around right now. I stopped reading the email once I got to the part that said, *If these entitled kids don't get off their asses, people like me are never going to retire. We can't hand off these skilled jobs to morons.*

Dad thought his opinion meant more because he was employed. It baffled me that anyone would hire him, because he was a nightmare to work with, but he *did* get the job done. Dad was a functioning alcoholic who'd managed to hold down a factory job since I'd been away, but Mom had been laid off from the cider mill a few months ago. She sent multiple texts per day, trying to get me to visit her.

It was obvious what they were doing. My parents hadn't given a rat's ass about me when I was a broke, struggling college kid, but now that I had something to give them, they wouldn't let up. Dad thought because I was a priest I could change the laws to benefit him, and Mom only wanted to see me because I had a grandchild to give her.

By the time we got home that night, Marcus had already been asleep for hours, and Chloe was passed out on the couch. She hadn't been at work today, but she was just as tired as the rest of us. We'd made a promise to the coven, and we took that pledge to heart. We were working sixteen-hour days, and none of us had taken a day off in over a month. I didn't mind committing everything I had to the coven, so I hadn't realized the kind of toll it was taking.

I sat on the couch in our wing of the estate the following morning, cradling Marcus in my arms. Our wing was like its own mini apartment, with a small living room open to a kitchenette area and a walkway behind the couch leading to the bedroom and bathroom.

I fed Marcus a bottle while Nadine took a quick shower. Rishi was playing with a toy mouse, while Isa lounged on the back of the couch and Oliver groomed himself on the floor. We didn't usually take the cats to work with us, because we were constantly running around town, and we felt better leaving them home with Marcus.

The sun hadn't risen yet. We were up this early most days, and we wouldn't be in bed until long after midnight. Yesterday had been one of our longest days, and with Marcus up half the night after we returned home, I was running on less than three hours of sleep.

I rocked my son back and forth while he stared up at me with a curious expression. I sang him a lullaby.

The moon will come out
The owls will hoot
A cat catches a mouse
That runs over your boot

The bumps in the night
Are just soft lullabies
You're safe in your bed
Til the morning sunrise

A wide smile spread across Marcus's face, and it melted my heart on the spot. He was seven weeks old now, and it was the first time I'd ever seen him smile. It might've been the first time he smiled ever.

"You like the song?" I cooed in a high-pitched voice. "Daddy's a little off-key, but I can sing more if you'd like."

Marcus's smile had already faded, and he went back to sucking on the bottle—quite viciously, I might add. If I didn't know his feeding schedule, I'd have thought he hadn't been fed in days. He was a tiny little glutton and nearly ripped the bottle right out of my hands.

"Whoa, slow down, buddy," I teased. "You're a hungry fella, aren't you?"

Marcus crossed his eyes, and I tickled his toes to see if he'd smile again. He gave the tiniest of smiles and stared up at me like I was his whole world.

And he was mine—him and his mother.

It was a strange experience, becoming a parent for the first time. I couldn't shake this sense of detachment I felt from my own body. I loved my son more than anything. Being a dad was my greatest joy, but even after all this time we had to prepare—since the day I learned Nadine was pregnant—it still didn't feel real.

I always thought I'd hold my kid for the first time, and that'd be the moment I became a dad, but it wasn't instant like I'd expected. Becoming a parent was a process, and no one had prepared me for that. I was sitting here holding my own baby, and I couldn't believe that *I* of all people was a father. It was incredible really, but this moment felt more like a dream than anything. It didn't make sense that I could be a father when I was still a kid myself.

Nadine emerged from the bathroom, and I snapped my attention back to the present. I was here in the flesh, holding my baby boy, and I knew it was real. It had to be.

Nadine was already dressed for work, though her hair was still wet. She dried it with a towel as she walked across the living room. "How's he doing?" she asked as she leaned over the back of the couch.

The warmth of her skin was inviting. I tilted my head back to give her a kiss, then turned back to Marcus. "He's perfect. Watch this, Nad."

I tickled his feet again, and Marcus flashed a huge smile at both of us.

"Aww, you're a happy little boy!" Nadine tickled his belly, and he smiled wider. "Oh, that's the biggest smile I've seen yet!"

"You've seen him smile already?" I asked.

Nadine went over to the kitchen counter to prepare a pot of coffee. She pulled two mugs down from the cupboard. Neither of us had been coffee drinkers before now, but these days, we couldn't go without it. "Yeah, he was lying on his belly and lifted his head up. It was so cute. I clapped and we celebrated, and he gave the cutest smile."

"He lifted his head?" My tone had fallen flat. Marcus didn't have a lot of strength in his neck, on account of being born a preemie. He also had a really big head for his tiny body, which didn't help. The healing treatments he'd been given had made him so much stronger, but we'd been waiting for the day he could lift his head. It was a big milestone, and he'd come so far.

"Didn't I tell you...?" Nadine trailed off, then pressed her fingers to her lips. "Oh, Lucas. I'm sorry. You got home late that night, and I was going to tell you, but you were in bed before we got a chance to talk. We've just been so busy."

"Don't worry about it," I assured her. "I get it. We have a lot of responsibilities right now, and it's hard to keep track of all these things."

I was still sad I missed it. Marcus had only been in this world for a few short weeks, and he was growing so fast. At this rate, it felt like he was going to be off to college next week.

Nadine placed her mug on the coffee table and sat beside me on the couch. "Lucas, I'm sorry."

"I want to be a dad. I want to be here for him. And I'm realizing how much of his life I'm already missing—*we're* missing. We're working so damn hard, and it doesn't feel like enough."

"We're only getting started," Nadine encouraged. She snuggled into me and ran her fingers through my hair. "Maybe I can help. What's on your mind?"

I sighed, because I didn't even know where to start. "I just want to help people and fix all their problems. You and I, we're so good at problem solving, but I didn't realize how many problems we *can't* fix. This stuff is really hard to correct, because people are resistant to change and don't want to cooperate. They have a different set of values and beliefs, and if Mother Miriam isn't coming in to tell them what to do, they don't agree. It doesn't matter if we all worship Mother Miriam because everyone has a different idea of what that means. If we can't get people on the same page on what our religion and identity is, then we can't solve anything. If we don't have an identity, we don't have a coven. I didn't understand the scope and scale of what we were trying to do."

Nadine nodded in understanding. "These things take time. People are being difficult because their lives have been decimated, and they're just trying to survive, but once we get them back to a safe place, they'll see our good intentions and work with us."

"How do we convince these people they're safe?" I wondered. "We know that even when you're physically safe, your mind can still convince you you're in danger. Our life is better than it's ever been, and some days I don't feel any different than I did when our circumstances were at their worst."

Nadine curled her arms around me, until I was laying my head on her shoulder. The tightness in my chest eased, though my hands felt ice cold. Oliver rested his head on my leg and began purring.

"With time, things will get better, but everything we've been through is still fresh. We can't expect ourselves to just move on," she said.

"I feel like I have to," I admitted. "Because life is still moving forward regardless."

It felt like years had passed since we took our seats on the Imperium Council, and at the same time, the last month had flown by in the blink of an eye. Time seemed to hold no meaning anymore, and it was really starting to fuck with me.

I gazed down at our son, whose eyes were starting to droop. "It's strange. I'm holding Marcus in my arms, but it feels like a dream. Life can't be this good, can it?"

"It can, and it is, but that doesn't undo everything else you've been through," Nadine said gently. "Now that we're in a good place, we can finally work on healing ourselves in ways we couldn't before. I'm here for you. Whatever you need."

"I don't really know what I need," I admitted. Marcus had nearly fallen asleep again, so I placed him in his bouncer next to the couch. I strapped him in and turned back to Nadine. "I'm so used to going from one extreme to another. I've either got this impending feeling of doom, or I just can't be bothered to care. I feel like I'm in a constant war between my mind and my body. I want to feel *normal*, but I don't even know what that's like. I feel like I can't keep up. I'm slipping, Nad, and I want to catch it this time before it gets worse."

"You've already taken the first step by becoming aware of it," she pointed out. "We can use some of the tools Dr. Mack taught you to ground ourselves. You haven't written in your journal for a while, and that always helped. We can do meditations together, or come up with affirmations to bring us back to a better place when we start slipping."

I shook my head. "None of that is going to help. I was in a different place then. The stuff we've been through can't be undone by journal prompts and affirmations. I've sat down to try to journal it out, and I just get frustrated. I barely feel anything when I drink matus tea. Even music doesn't work anymore. I don't want to put you through this, and I'm sorry, but I wouldn't bring this up to you if I hadn't tried everything already to fix it."

"Asking for help is a really important step," Nadine encouraged. "It shows a lot of growth that you're able to do that."

"Thanks. I've found the good in my depression before. I know I can do it again. I'm just not sure where to start this time."

"It might help to go back to therapy," Nadine suggested. "You were doing so well with it last time."

"When am I going to find the time to do that?" I asked. "Not to mention the coven's going to have some big opinions about their priest going to therapy. They're going to question my capacity to help them if I can't even help myself."

"Or you can be an example to them," Nadine replied. "Therapy isn't anything to be ashamed of."

"*I* know that. Doesn't mean I'll convince other people."

"If you don't want to go back to therapy, I won't make you," Nadine assured me. "But I think it's important to explore alternatives. You said you feel like you're warring between your brain and your body, and maybe you're right. Your nervous system is very complex, and just because you consciously *want* to change it doesn't mean it's going to respond to that thought—not if the chemicals aren't there to elicit a change. Maybe you don't know what you need because you're trying to change your thoughts, when it's actually a biological response."

"Maybe..." I mused.

"When we were in *Hok'evale*, Dr. Metzi said that healing magic doesn't work on mental illness, because healing magic is limited by the body's own capabilities. Magic can't heal lupus because my immune system doesn't have the capability to cure itself, but that's going to be different for someone with a healthy immune system. Maybe your biology is different and your body doesn't make the chemicals you're supposed to make to stabilize your mood. Matus tea worked for you because it altered your brain chemistry. If it's not working anymore, perhaps it's time to try something stronger."

I hesitated. "Like... medication?"

"Yes, if you're willing to give it a try," Nadine said. "It's another tool we haven't explored."

I shook my head firmly. "I don't want to go on meds."

She ran her hand up and down my back. "It's not a moral failing. There's strength in calling out the bullshit society has led you to believe about your depression and finding what tools work for you. I think medication is at least worth a try. If it doesn't work, we'll try something else."

"If the meds don't work, there's nothing more to try," I pressed. "I need to find a way to work with my own mind and body, instead of trying to change who I am."

"I would never want to change you," she promised. "But there's so much of you underneath your pain, and I don't want to watch my husband suffer anymore."

"What if the suffering never goes away, and it's just a part of who I am? Are you okay with that?" I asked curiously.

"Yes. I will always be here, no matter what. But I still want to help in any way I can."

I pulled her close to me. "Having you here is more helpful than anything else. There's no guarantee that meds will always be there, and I don't want to develop a dependency on them."

"I don't think that's a fair way to look at it," Nadine insisted. "You're sick, Lucas. You would *never* say that I should stop taking my meds because I'm dependent on them. I need medication for my body to function, and maybe you do, too. I think antidepressants could be useful. We don't know until we try."

I was starting to get frustrated, because I'd already had this conversation with Grant and Miles over a year ago, and now Nadine was going to push this on me, too. "I'm not going to just slap on a band-aid and lean on a crutch. I need to really dig deep and heal myself, because that's the only way I'm going to get better."

Nadine scowled. "Meds aren't a *crutch*. It sounds like you're not interested in trying to get better."

"You're not listening to me. I'm saying there are other options. You want to throw all these solutions at me when all I really need is your support." I drew away from her and stood. All I really needed was Nadine to hear me, and I didn't feel like she was. I paced around the room. "A lot of my depression is circumstantial. Life is good, but we're overworked and stressed out. I think if I could solve some of these problems, I'd feel a lot better."

"A lot of these problems we either can't control or need to give it more time."

"There's got to be something we can control," I insisted. "The Imperium Council makes dozens of decisions every day, but we're being pulled in so many different directions that we aren't making the progress I hoped for. It doesn't help that all five council members aren't ever in the same room at the same time."

"Someone has to stay and watch Marcus," Nadine reminded me. "There's no way we're bringing him to work with us."

After what happened with the priestesses, the last thing we wanted was to put our child in the eyes of the public. That's why we'd come up with the solution to trade off days watching him. But to do so meant our council was running on fumes.

"I completely agree," I told her. "But there has to be another way."

"The only other option is to get someone else to watch him, but we've put our trust in so many people who have turned our back on us," Nadine said. "I wouldn't trust anyone but family to watch him."

That gave me an idea. One of my biggest problems was with my family. If I could fix my relationship with them, then maybe this stress would go away. I didn't really *want* to contact my parents, but maybe this was what we needed to get to a better place.

At the bare minimum, I needed them to stop contacting me, because it was interfering with my work. They'd never stop trying to contact me unless I reached out somehow. At some point, they were going to show up here, and a big blow out fight in front of Marcus and all our friends at the manor was the last thing we needed. If my family was better, maybe I wouldn't be so sad, and I wouldn't have to go on meds. At the very least, talking to my parents would make them stop bothering me, and that needed to happen if the council was going to get anything done.

"My mom could watch him," I suggested. She was the only family either of us had left.

Nadine crossed her arms. "Do you *really* think that's a good idea? I thought you'd decided to cut your parents out."

"Maybe that was never meant to be a permanent thing," I said thoughtfully. "We're here to bring the community back together, so it's fitting to extend an olive branch to my mom. How can we expect the coven to unite and forgive each other if I can't forgive my parents, and fix things with them? It's hypocritical to expect our entire town to get along if I can't mend the relationship I have with my own family. I have to take responsibility for my part, too."

Nadine hesitated. "I really don't like this."

"My mom isn't like my dad. She's more reasonable. She has experience with babies, and she keeps asking to spend time with her grandson. If we don't get help, we're going to keep missing work, and the council will keep struggling."

"We work long days," Nadine pressed. "We can't expect your mom to be here all day."

"We'll start with a couple of hours," I suggested. "My parents are driving me nuts blowing up my phone all day. If I don't give them *something*, they're going to show up at work and make things harder for us. Maybe this will help me, too. If I can't be around them without being triggered, then I haven't learned my lesson yet. I'd really like to get to a place where we're all at peace with each other. My depression isn't going to get better if this problem with my mom and dad isn't fixed."

"If we do this, your mom has to come here," Nadine demanded. There was no arguing with her on that. "I don't want Marcus anywhere near your dad."

"Me either," I agreed. "I'll fix things with my dad eventually, because I know I need to in order to heal, but I'm not ready for that yet. But Mom's a different story, because she'll be more considerate of what we have to say. Starting with her is a good idea. It's my day with Marcus, so my mom can come over this morning. I'll be home once our morning meetings are done. We need to get all five council members in a room again, because it just wastes time to constantly be updating each other. It'll only be for a few hours. If my mom can watch Marcus in the mornings, we'll be much more efficient as a council."

Nadine frowned. "I'm really not sure about this, but if you think it will help, then we can start with a few hours and see how it goes."

"I'll give her a call." I paced around the room as I waited for her to pick up. My heartrate quickened, so much that I could hear my pulse in my ears over the sound of her line ringing.

"Lucas," she answered. "Nice of you to finally return my calls."

She said it was *nice*, but she sounded less than pleased.

"Hey, Mom," I started.

I could feel the tension over the line. I'd kept my distance from my parents since returning to Octavia Falls, because if I went to see Mom, I knew Dad would be there. I felt bad for her more than anything, because she still had to deal with my dad, but I genuinely believed she didn't know any better and didn't have the tools to leave him. Maybe if I showed her there was another way, she'd finally see that she deserved better.

"What do you want?" she demanded.

"I know I haven't reached out in a while, but we could really use some help with Marcus. Would you like to watch him for a few hours, just so Nadine and I can get some stuff done? I promise it won't take up too much of your time."

"I thought you didn't want me to meet him," she replied rather harshly.

"I needed some space, but now that Nadine and I are back in town, I thought maybe you could get to know your grandson."

Mom's tone instantly brightened, because I was finally giving her what she wanted. "Well, okay. If you really need the favor, I'll be right over."

My mom seemed really excited to help out with Marcus. She arrived at the estate only twenty minutes later. Nadine gave her a hug when she stepped in the house, though the embrace seemed stilted from both of them.

"It's nice to see you, Margo," Nadine said kindly.

"Good to see you again, Nadine," Mom replied. She squeezed Nadine's hands, and her gaze darted down to Nadine's wedding ring. "It's been a while. I bet your wedding was so beautiful. I wish I'd been there to see it."

I ignored her passive-aggressive comment, but my voice still came out flat. "Thanks for coming, Mom."

"Of course! Marcus and I are going to have a great day together. Can I hold him?" Mom reached out for the baby in my arms. He was asleep now and wrapped in a bundle of blankets.

It was strange welcoming her back into our home, because back when we were living at the safe house, I was certain I'd never see my parents again. Now that we were back in town, it was inevitable that they'd be a part of our lives again.

I gently placed Marcus in my mother's arms, and he didn't even stir. She rocked him back and forth.

"Hello, Marcus dear," she sang. "Don't worry. Grandma Margo's here."

"All the supplies you should need are on the counter," Nadine instructed. "If he's still crying after changing and feeding him, he usually just wants his pacifier. His bassinet is in our room, but he gets really cranky when we set him down. He sleeps best when he's held."

"That's natural," my mother said. "All babies cry when you set them down. You just need to let them cry for a bit, and they'll eventually fall asleep. You can't go to them every time they fuss, or you'll train them to expect you to always be there."

Nadine frowned, though my mother didn't surprise me at all. A lot of people her age thought that way.

"I *will* always be there for him, so there's no harm in making sure he knows that," Nadine emphasized. "Studies show that you can't possibly spoil your child in their first year of life, and that creating a healthy environment for them where they know they're safe is important for their development."

"Lots of parents would disagree with you, and their kids still turn out fine," Mom stated coolly.

I quickly stepped in. "Mom, I understand that you're going to do some things differently than we are, but if you're going to watch Marcus, you need to respect our parenting style."

"I understand." Mom waved her hand like it was no big deal. "I didn't mean anything by it. If you want to spoil your kid, it's not my place to question it."

Nadine shot me a glance, like she was about ready to call off the arrangement. The last thing I wanted was to settle a fight between my wife and my mother in the first minute of this arrangement. My mom may not agree with us on everything, but she *was* harmless.

"There's no need to make a big deal out of small details," I said. "Just keep Marcus alive for a couple of hours. That's all we ask."

"One more rule," Nadine added. "We don't want Marcus around Jay."

Mom's features fell. She appeared very hurt by the request. Almost confused, actually. It's like she didn't know why we didn't want my dad to be a part of our son's life. She stared down at Marcus in her arms, ducking her face. "If that's what you *want*. I'll do my best to keep him alive."

We showed my mom where to find everything and introduced her to Rose. We didn't expect her to help with Rose, since Rose usually kept to herself in her guest room, but it was good to have my mom with her in case of an emergency. By the time we left the house, the others were already gone.

Octavia Hall had been destroyed the night we faced the priestesses, so the Imperium Council headquarters had been moved to a room in the courthouse. We met Chloe, Talia, and Grant there and got to work. It was good to finally work with all five of us at once, though our meeting stretched over two hours since we had so much to update Chloe on from the day before. Even though today's meeting felt cumbersome, I was positive that if we were able to keep up a morning schedule like this, things would start running more efficiently in no time.

Just as we were wrapping up our meeting, my phone rang. I quickly grabbed it, thinking it was my mom. Instead, it was Miles.

"Hey, we just got a call that there's a water main break on Oak Street," Miles said. "You guys need to get down here."

We hurried to respond quickly, and I called my mom on our way. "We might need you to stay with Marcus a little while longer," I told her.

"Not a problem," Mom assured me. "Take all the time you need."

The emergency response crews were already there when we arrived, but it was our job to direct everyone. We ordered the crews to block off the streets, which were flooding, and made sure the nearby businesses closed down while we worked on repairing the break. The crews worked for hours to excavate, inspect, and flush the pipe before we could reconnect it to the system. The sidewalk and road in the immediate vicinity were cracked and would need complete repair. This was devastating news because so many businesses were already shut down for good, and now many of those that still had their doors open were literally underwater or ruined.

After some investigation, we learned that the issue was due to old pipes, which the previous council had failed to replace years prior when it was needed. Now, we were the ones who had to deal with their oversight, and it was another problem we had to budget for. We stayed as long as we could to help and didn't make it home until after dinner time.

Marcus's loud cries came from the main living room when we arrived home. Onyx was already back from work, and I overheard her say, "It's a nasty bruise, but he's going to be all right. There are no signs of a concussion."

Nadine's features paled, and she rushed down the hall. We entered the living room to find Onyx rocking Marcus in her arms and my mother sitting across from her. My mom brought a teacup to her lips, though her hands shook. Her hair was a mess, and she appeared absolutely exhausted.

She looked like she hadn't slept in two days. I didn't realize how hard watching an infant would be on her, but it'd clearly taken its toll.

"What's going on here?" Nadine demanded.

Mom set her cup aside and shot to her feet, appearing stunned to see us. I didn't think she'd heard us come in over the sound of Marcus's screams. "Everything's all right."

I quickly took Marcus from Onyx's arms. My stomach dropped when I saw the goose egg of a bruise on the side of his forehead. Talia, Grant, and Chloe stopped in the doorway behind us, but they were all too stunned to say anything. Marcus began to quiet in my arms.

Nadine turned toward my mother. "What. Happened?"

"I'm *so* sorry," my mom started. "Marcus was in his swing, and I guess he didn't get strapped in properly. He wiggled himself down and fell out. He bumped his head on the floor."

"Is he going to be okay?" Talia asked in worry.

"Yes," Mom replied. "Onyx got home shortly after, and she looked him over. She says there's no permanent damage. It's just a bruise."

Grant eyed Marcus apprehensively. "That's one hell of a bruise."

He wasn't afraid to say what we were all thinking.

"Mom, you can't just brush this off," I said incredulously. "It's just a bruise *now*, but what if it was something more serious? If you'd have walked out of the room and he fell on his face, he could've suffocated! He can't roll himself over yet."

"I was right there, I swear. I picked him up and snuggled him immediately, and he's okay," she insisted.

Talia stepped between us. "Let's all calm down and talk this out. Guys, I know you're very protective because you're new parents, but it sounds like it was an accident."

I sighed heavily. "I was hoping we could get through day one without a catastrophe…"

My words trailed off when I realized there were two teacups on the coffee table. There was my mom's, which was half empty, and another that was completely gone. The empty teacup sat directly on the table, next to the saucer.

I didn't know how many times I'd heard my mother ask my dad to use a coaster. He never listened.

I became so enraged that I placed Marcus in Nadine's arms, because I couldn't hold him right now. I snatched the teacup from the coffee table. "You let *him* in here, didn't you!?" I growled. I didn't even need her answer, because I already knew the truth.

Mom's face drained of color. "Let me explain."

"What's there to explain?" I demanded. "We asked you for one thing only, and you didn't listen. You let Dad come see Marcus!"

It was so fucking obvious, and the room went dead silent. The betrayal cut deep—so much deeper than I ever thought a mother could inflict upon her child. She knew how I felt about my father. I'd *trusted* her with my own child, and she did the one thing I asked her not to do. I couldn't believe her.

Nadine took a step back, equally horrified. Our friends glanced between each other, like they wanted to help but couldn't.

"How could you?" Nadine asked in a broken tone.

"I promise I didn't plan this," my mother practically begged. "I was only trying to help. Your father hit his head this morning. I didn't know he was going to go see a doctor about it. They wouldn't let him drive home by himself, so he called me to pick him up. I was going to call you, but you said you had an emergency, and I couldn't take you away from your work. You're a priest now, and that's a very important job. I didn't want to stress you out, and I knew I could handle this."

"This isn't handled, Mom!" I cried. "Dad's the one who didn't strap Marcus into the swing, isn't he?"

I knew it didn't sound like something my mother would do. But my father, the careless fuck? Absolutely.

"Yes," Mom admitted.

"We told you he couldn't see Marcus," Nadine snapped, pulling our child closer to her chest.

"This was an *emergency*," my mom pressed. "I was only going to pick Jay up from the doctor and drop him off back home, but Marcus started fussing in the car, and I realized I forgot his diaper bag. Your house is on the way home, so we stopped here to get his diaper changed. While I put on some tea, Jay set Marcus in the swing, and he was *fine*."

"Until he wasn't," I bit sharply. "I wish you would've just called. There is nothing—*nothing*—that is more important than my family."

"Then why do you never come see us?" Mom demanded. "If we're so important, then why treat us as if we don't matter?"

My jaw clenched, and my voice shook as I said, "I wasn't talking about *you.*"

Mom's lip quivered. "If that's the way you feel, then I guess I know where we stand. If all I am to you is a free babysitter, then you can find yourself a new one."

She started toward the door, but I tried to stop her. "Mom, please. That's not what I meant."

She whirled toward me. "You never appreciated how hard I tried. I did everything for you boys!"

"You did your best," I stated, and that's really all I could give her. I *knew* she did everything she could, but my mother barely had the capacity to help herself, let alone two children.

"We both did!" she cried. "Your father made mistakes, but that doesn't make him a bad guy. You spend so much time focusing on the bad that you can't even recall the good memories. It's time to forget the past, so you can finally move on."

"This wasn't in the past, Mom. This happened today, to my son! I keep letting you in because I want to help you—I *want* you to be a part of my life. But I can't do that if you're going to keep making excuses for him. How many more times are we going to run around this circle? I'm so sick of saying goodbye."

Tears beaded in the corner of her eyes. "Then make sure the next time you say goodbye, it's for good."

Then my mother whirled around and stormed out of the house. The whole room went dead silent.

Nadine gently placed a hand on my shoulder. "Lucas, are you okay?"

I shook off my shock and turned back to my family. I didn't really have the energy to give to my mother right now. "I'm more worried about Marcus."

I stroked the top of his head, but he'd already fallen asleep in Nadine's arms.

Onyx stood from the couch. "Lucas, I'm so sorry. I didn't know your dad had been here. He must've left before I got home."

"You have nothing to apologize for," I told her. "Thank you for looking Marcus over."

"There's something else you should know," Onyx started. "I shouldn't be telling you this, because it goes against patient privacy laws, but I know what your relationship with your dad is like, because my mom's the same way. You deserve to know what's going on."

I didn't like where this was going.

"Your dad came into the clinic earlier with a huge bruise on his forehead," Onyx explained. "His employer must've sent him, because he made a huge scene about how he didn't need to be there. The receptionist was trying to explain that his insurance would cover the appointment, so it couldn't hurt to see a doctor. He went on this big rant about you guys, saying the new Imperium Council wanted to give everyone handouts, but that handouts were for lazy people."

I scoffed. "Why am I not surprised? We don't even have anything to do with his employer's insurance, yet we're the ones to blame."

"There's more," Onyx continued. "The doctors gave him a psych eval, and they were concerned by the results. They suspect some sort of personality disorder, though I didn't hear which one. They wanted to schedule him with a specialist to get him a proper diagnosis and treatment plan, but he refused. He went on and on about how he didn't want their handouts because he's a hard worker. He stormed out of the clinic."

"Honestly, I'd be surprised if he hadn't," I said.

"I saw the bruise on his head," Onyx admitted. "He said he hit it on the edge of the counter, but I knew he was lying. I've seen enough bruises to know he was hit by something flat and heavy. Then when I got home, your mom said something about having a rough morning. I think your parents got in a fight and your mom whacked him in the head."

I expected this day to come eventually. Mom had always sat back and let my father rampage around the house. She'd yell and fight with him, but never fought back physically. I knew one day she'd be done with his bullshit. What I didn't understand is why she went to pick him up at the hospital after all that.

"If I had to guess, I'd say she hit him with a frying pan," Onyx added.

Nadine turned to me. "I guess she got inspired by you."

"No kidding," I replied. "The last time I saw Dad, I whacked him over the side of the head with a pot of clam chowder. I bet he was mad Mom hit him, so he had to give our son a bruise to match."

Grant frowned. "That's fucked up. Marcus is just a baby."

"That's my dad for you," I said flatly.

"He never has to come near your son again," Talia promised. "We're all here for you, and one of us will be with Marcus at all times."

"I'd love it if that were true, but it's not realistic," I said. "We don't work efficiently if someone's always taking off to watch him. I'm not letting my mom watch him, but we need to find someone who can."

Chloe crossed her arms. "I don't get why you'd let your parents back in, Lucas. You should know better than this. You know how they are, but you let your mom have access to your kid anyway."

That was the last thing I wanted to hear right now. When you had narcissistic parents, people always found a way to blame you even when it wasn't your fault, because they didn't understand. Chloe didn't have the best parents, but hers weren't anything like mine. She thought you could just tell them off and they'd listen, but no amount of boundaries worked with my parents.

"We're stretched thin as it is, Chloe. What other choice did we have?" I demanded. "You want to fix the coven, but you're also demanding I completely cut out my parents, which doesn't fit what we're trying to do."

"The coven needs to be reunited; I get that. But we need to admit to ourselves that some people are never going to be able to be reunified with us no matter what, because they're shit people and they're always going to be," Chloe argued. "There's no reforming my grandmother, and there's no reforming your parents, either. Some people are going to have to be left behind in this new society we're building, because we can't take everyone."

"So we just take the people we like and leave the rest?" I asked incredulously.

"You're oversimplifying it," Chloe demanded. "I'm saying some people aren't going to work with us. You're insistent people can change, but can we really build our foundation on that?"

"I think it's worth trusting people to some degree," I argued. "I get that I shouldn't trust my mom, but it's a really fucking low blow to blame what happened on me."

Talia stepped between us. "I think everyone can acknowledge there's a problem here. Let's focus on solutions. We get that things are hard right now. Marcus wasn't planned, but you guys also chose to have him, and now we have to deal with the consequences."

"What are you saying?" Nadine snapped. "That we shouldn't have had

Marcus? I wasn't going to do what that stupid doctor said and have an abortion."

Grant sighed in frustration. "Come on, Nadine. You know that's not what Talia meant. We all love Marcus and we want him to be here, but we have to recognize that things are harder with a baby around. Tal and I got Plan B when we had a pregnancy scare, because we knew we weren't ready, but you guys went ahead with having a kid when you weren't prepared for one."

"We didn't know we'd be running an entire town and raising a newborn," Nadine insisted.

"But you knew you were on the run and in the middle of a war when you had him," Grant countered. "It's all difficult, but these were your choices. All Talia's saying is if having a baby was your choice, you need to figure out who you trust with him. Last-minute, irresponsible decisions aren't going to help you here."

"Thanks for the advice," I said sarcastically. "Our son just got hit in the head, and you've all been really fucking helpful. Nadine and I don't have to stand here and listen to this."

"We should all get some rest, and we can talk solutions in the morning," Onyx suggested.

Nobody argued with that, because we all knew this conversation was going nowhere after the long day we had. Nadine and I returned to our suite and got Marcus settled into bed. Rishi snuggled beside him in the bassinet. I trusted Onyx's medical assessment, but still, the nasty bruise on his head worried me.

Nadine paced around the living room of our suite, while I leaned against the bedroom doorway. "I said I didn't want Marcus anywhere near your dad, and this is exactly why!" she raged. "I don't condone hanging, but I understand why the priestesses hang people like that man."

I rubbed my hands over my face. I was angry, too, but that was a heavy thing to say. Didn't matter when it came to our child, though. "We're not going to hang him."

"Well, he sure as hell isn't going to see our son again!"

"We can try to protect Marcus from him, but we live in the same town," I pointed out. "We're bound to run into him."

"Being in close proximity to your parents doesn't mean they have to be a part of our lives. Why are you still trying?"

"I want to help my mom," I insisted. "She's not the same as my dad. She's a product of her upbringing. She's an abuse victim, too."

"That doesn't make it okay," Nadine snapped. "People have the choice to use that as an excuse or to learn and grow and do better. She failed us today, and there's no excuse for that."

"I wish I could say goodbye for good, but these things aren't easy." My voice grew louder with frustration. Chloe didn't understand, and neither did Nadine. "Ever since we've been back in Octavia Falls, they won't leave me alone, no matter how much I ignore their messages. How do you propose we fix this? Because if you think my family is going to stay away, you're delusional."

She placed a hand on her hip. "Delusional?"

"It's true. I can't control them, so tell me what you *want* me to do."

She crossed her arms. "You can start by cutting your parents out for good, because being around them puts our family in danger. Put up boundaries, block them, or do whatever you have to do. They need to know they aren't welcome in our lives."

"If I block them, they'll just show up at the house or to work," I told her.

"They need to know that isn't an option, because this has gone too far," she stated firmly. "Your connection to our family got our son hurt. Our son isn't going to be fucked up because you come from a fucked-up family!"

I reeled back. "You agree with Chloe that this is my fault? That's not fair!"

"None of this is fair, Lucas. I'm not blaming you for what happened. I'm here for you, and I'm going to help you through this, but to do that, we need to face this issue, and you're not facing it. We need to do *something* to put an end to this, because I don't want you to continue hurting like this."

"I don't want *anyone* getting hurt," I insisted. "Maybe my mom was right and dropping Marcus really was an accident. My dad's a broken person, but I know he can do better if he tried. We can get there with him, but we just need more time."

"How can you still give him the benefit of the doubt?" Nadine demanded.

"What else am I supposed to do?" I shot back. "Blocking them and burying my head in the sand isn't going to actually solve any problems. You act like it's easy, but you don't understand. Your parents were perfect. You don't know what it's like to be a child of an abuser."

"My parents are *dead*!" she yelled, as if she couldn't believe I'd bring them up.

"That doesn't change how good you had it," I countered. "I'd rather have a good childhood and have my parents be gone than to have them be alive and they treat me like shit. It doesn't matter if I go months without talking to my parents, because the second they're back in my life, everything's back to the way it was. Cutting them out, continuing to talk to them, it doesn't matter. There isn't a perfect solution. There isn't even a permanent one. You can't reason with these people."

"Maybe that's the problem—that you're trying to reason with them! Your need to please your parents and have them love you does not come before our son. I didn't really want your mom to watch him, but you pushed for it."

"You said you were fine with it!" I shouted.

"I wanted to support you, but at some point, I need to draw a line." Her voice cracked.

It took everything to make Nadine cry, and that's how I knew we had both reached a breaking point. The weight of the coven stood on our shoulders, and now we had a family to protect as well.

"You're putting your mom before Marcus, but her feelings aren't more important than our son," Nadine cried. "What if something really bad happened and Marcus was affected by it because you felt bad for your mom? As long as you keep letting them come around, he's in danger. It seems like you want to please your parents more than you want to keep him safe!"

I hated this. Nadine and I never yelled at each other, but the pressure of the last few months was finally catching up to us. I'd done a lot of fucked up things to piss her off, but Nadine had *never* been this mad at me.

I crossed my arms. I didn't know what to say to her, because everything she said was correct, yet my heart and my emotions told me she was wrong. I came back here to help people, and if I couldn't fix the family I came from, how could I be the dad Marcus needed me to be?

I tried to steady my voice, but it nonetheless came out sounding harsh.

"You can't put this all on me. My mom's not the greatest, but she'd never let anything terrible happen to Marcus. This isn't her fault. This is my dad's fault."

"That's not true," Nadine argued. "Your mom's an enabler, and as long as she's around your dad, she can't be around our kid. We already lost one kid. We're not losing another."

That really fucking hurt. It wasn't anybody's fault that Dean had died, but by her saying that, it felt like she was putting his death on me.

"I would *never* do anything to hurt our son," I said cruelly. "Don't act like I've forgotten about Dean, because I think of him every goddamn day. I'm sorry you can just go about life after a loved one dies, but I can't. I accepted my grief, but underlying it all is this ache that feels like it's never going to go away."

"You don't think I feel that, too!?" Nadine screamed. "I came back here to become the priestess I was born to be, and be a mom, and do it all, but I'm not Superwoman! I want to help these people, all while spending time with my family. There's just not enough hours in the day. I haven't even had a chance to look for the Curse Breaker Wand because we're working so much. Between all that, I'm supposed to find time to grieve our son properly!"

"I have things I want to do, too! I want to start writing a reaper guide, to pass on to my apprentice someday, and I want to finish my degree. I'm fine putting all that off for now because of what we're doing here, but I'm not okay with missing my son's life! I want to see him smile for the first time. I've barely held him all month. I've changed two diapers and given him a bottle a couple of times. You can't even breastfeed like you wanted because you're never with him."

"Yes, and that tears me apart inside!" she bellowed. "I want to spend time with my son, too. Please understand that I know what you're going through."

"Do you, though?" I asked. "You're so good at keeping it together. Meanwhile, I'm really struggling."

Tears leaked from her eyes as she shouted, "I *have* to keep it together, because if I don't, who will?"

If her words stung before, it was nothing like the knife to my gut now. The unspoken meaning in her words was clear. She didn't think I was capable.

I'd made so much progress these last few years. I didn't feel like the same person I was when we met, and Nadine had helped me through so much. But when she said that, it felt like she only saw the guy I used to be, and I needed her to see me for who I was now. Our lives were difficult at the moment, but I'd come to her to work through it before things got worse, and it felt like she was throwing that in my face. She didn't understand my struggle with my parents, and she didn't get this, either.

My shoulders slumped. "You don't have any faith in me, do you?"

Nadine's tone softened, like she realized she'd taken it too far. "That's not what I meant, Lucas. It's not about having faith in you. It's about how much you can take. You're so close to breaking again that I can feel it every day. I couldn't run a marathon when I was in the worst throes of my lupus, and you can't handle all of this, either. I know you can't because I'm watching you, and you're falling apart in front of my eyes. So don't blame me for trying to hold us all together."

"I'm sick of doing that to you, Nadine. I'm the man of this family, I'm the one who's supposed to be holding us together."

"I know. But you can't right now, so if I have to step up to do that, then I will."

That wasn't what I wanted. I'd wanted us to work together, but it was clear Nadine felt the emotional burden fall on her. The last thing I ever intended was to hurt her.

I slumped to the couch. "Forget it. I'll sleep out here tonight."

"Please don't," she begged. "Married couples should never go to bed angry at each other."

"Maybe we should," I suggested. "Perhaps we'll feel better in the morning. Maybe we're not angry at all, but just fucking tired. Nad, I'm so exhausted. It's been one thing after another, and we haven't had a chance to slow down."

My wife choked back her tears. "Let's table this for now, then. But please, don't sleep out here alone. Come to bed."

She reached out for me, and I reluctantly took her hand. I had nothing more to say, because if we kept this up, I didn't know if there'd be a marriage to save by the end of the night. I felt like a walking shell of a human being as I followed her into the bedroom. I went through the motions getting ready for bed. Nadine and I crawled under the sheets together, but for the first time in our marriage, we fell asleep with our backs to each other.

This issue with my parents went far deeper than I realized, because it was starting to affect my marriage, and that fucking sucked. I could deal with all these other problems, but I couldn't handle Nadine and me not getting along.

We'd come back here to rebuild the coven, but I feared saving our people might cost us our family.

nadine

FOUR

'd been so angry the night of our fight, but I hadn't wanted to hurt my husband. I wished we could talk things out, but I didn't think either of us knew where to go with these issues. If we tried to talk about it now, it'd result in a blow-up fight again, and neither of us wanted that. Instead, Lucas would tell me I was right about things, just to keep the peace. Meanwhile, he'd bury his feelings so deep inside I didn't know how to reach him. That was hard, because we'd always been able to solve problems together before. This time felt different.

Sleeping it off *had* helped us cool down. We were back to talking in the morning, but our conversations didn't go more than surface-level deep.

"Have you seen Marcus's pacifier?" I asked.

"No," he replied simply. "Do you need me to run to the store to get more formula?"

"Yes, we're almost out. How many meetings do we have today?"

I was certain we could both feel the energy shift, and I was waiting for Lucas to say something more, but he didn't. Several days passed, and neither of us brought up the fight. I could tell he was bothered we hadn't reached a conclusion, but I also didn't want to push him. Eventually, we'd find solutions to all these problems, but Lucas needed more time to get there. I resolved to let him come at his own pace.

I wasn't a very patient person, but for my husband, I'd wait as long as he needed. When we weren't at work, I kept myself busy by caring for

Marcus, tidying the house, or cooking meals. Lucas told me not to worry about all that, and that everyone else would help out, but I felt like if I slowed down, none of it was ever going to get done.

Obviously, the workload was starting to take its toll on all of us. We agreed we needed a day off, so we cleared our schedule on Saturday. Professor Warren had gotten his hands on some potion that mimicked snowfall, so the guys were taking it up to a trail in the mountains to go snowboarding. Meanwhile, the girls had planned an at-home spa day with aromatherapy potions and homemade face masks. We had plans to meet up with the guys this afternoon for a game night. Chloe had suggested playing Poker with a deck of Tarot cards and using caramel candies as our currency. It was going to be a lot of fun.

I woke that morning to Marcus's cries from the bassinet beside me. I shifted on the bed and winced as a shooting pain traveled down my shoulder. Every muscle in my body was stiff as a board, and I had to bite down on my lower lip to keep from crying out in pain.

I was used to adjusting to changes in my body, because every day was different for someone with a chronic illness. My body had changed a lot during pregnancy, and I was okay with the loose skin and stretch marks over my belly. It was a symbol of everything I went through to bring our babies into the world, and I wouldn't change that for the world.

But this? This was a different kind of change. I was still recovering from delivery, and we truly didn't know the lasting effect pregnancy would have on me. I hadn't felt this shitty since before the kidney transplant. Not good news.

Deep breath in, deep breath out, I told myself.

Marcus's cries grew louder, and Rishi started yowling to get my attention. The kitten jumped onto the bed beside my head and batted his sharp claws at my cheek. I rolled over and tried to reach out for my baby, but I winced at the pain in my joints.

"Lucas," I mumbled as I reached for his spot on the bed. "Can you get Marcus?"

No response came, and my hand met only sheets. I opened my eyes to see that the sun was already shining through the window. Lucas's side of the bed was empty. In his place sat a note.

I didn't want to wake you. Marcus has been fed and changed, and I put him down for his morning nap. I'm off to the mountains with the guys. Have a wonderful day!

Love, Lucas

I looked at the clock to see it was almost ten o'clock in the morning. I pushed past the aches and sat upright in bed.

"Mama's here," I whispered as I stroked Marcus's cheek. He only cried louder.

I reached into his bassinet and lifted him, but an intense pain shot through my wrist as his weight beared down on my joints. I gasped as I yanked him close to my chest, and thank the Goddess, he remained safe in my trembling arms. My racing heart took a moment to settle, because I realized I could have dropped him. It was the most terrifying feeling in the world.

When I became a mother, I'd chosen to share my body with another human being, and I was confident in that choice. I wouldn't choose anything less than to give my son my all. But at the same time, the physical limitations I'd learned to manage for myself now affected my child, and no amount of conscious effort could make up for it. I'd been able to brush off these worries before, but now I had no choice but to face them. I wanted to give everything to my son, and I feared it may not be enough.

I'd scared Marcus, and he began to scream. All I could do was hold him close to my chest, because I worried that if I shifted, I might not have the strength to support his weight. It seemed so fucking silly, because he was a tiny little peanut, but there was nothing I could do when my hands stopped working like this. I'd been here many times before, unable to open a water bottle or perform simple tasks, but those moments now seemed inconsequential compared to this. I'd been managing my pain so well this past year, and the thought of going back there scared me, because I wasn't the same person I was a year ago. I was a mother now. I didn't just need to stay healthy for myself anymore, but for him. I wasn't the kind of person to freeze up, but with my son in my arms, I did.

Footsteps sounded down the hall. "Nadine?" Talia asked with a light knock at the door. "Everything all right?"

"No," I cried in a trembling voice.

Talia threw the bedroom door open and rushed over to me.

"Take him," I begged.

She took Marcus from my arms, and I breathed a sigh of relief that immediately turned into tears.

"I—I couldn't do it, Tal," I sobbed. "I almost dropped him."

Talia cradled Marcus and swayed him from side to side. He stopped screaming, though he continued to fuss. "You *didn't* drop him, and Marcus is safe."

I drew in deep breaths to try to steady my sobs. It took a lot to get me to break down, but this had barely taken an instant. "He needs a diaper change and a bottle," I told her. I didn't like asking for help, but this was for Marcus, and he needed a caregiver right now.

"Don't worry, Nadine. I'm here," Talia promised.

"Thank you," I replied weakly.

Talia moved around our suite, quickly finding the diaper supplies and then mixing up formula to give Marcus a bottle. I was so thankful she'd come to check on us, because I didn't know what I'd do without her here. Marcus settled, and he seemed content once he had his bottle.

I tried calling Lucas. I really needed him here right now, but his phone went straight to voicemail. He obviously didn't have service in the mountains, and I had no other way of getting in touch with him. I got really frustrated that my husband wasn't here, but that only made me angry with myself, because it wasn't fair to take him away from something fun because I was having a crisis again. It didn't really matter either way, because the situation was out of my control. I couldn't contact him, and without service, he wasn't going to be able to reach out to me, either. I had to focus on what I could control, and right now that meant taking a shower.

I forced myself to go to the bathroom, because staying in bed all day wasn't an option. Talia was taking care of Marcus, but I had to take care of myself. Each task I performed that morning just to take care of my basic hygiene felt monumental. I came out of the bathroom feeling as if I'd already spent all my energy for the day—and more.

Chloe and Onyx had come into our suite, and they sat with Talia on the couch, all cooing over Marcus. Chloe sat in the middle, rocking Marcus back and forth, while Onyx shook a rattle at him and Talia sang him a lullaby. I nearly teared up all over again, because to them this was probably nothing, but to me, their friendship was invaluable.

"Aww, I want one," Chloe sang.

"Babies are sooo cute," Talia awed.

I leaned against the bathroom door to catch my breath, but my friends hadn't noticed me there yet.

Chloe sat up straighter, like she just had a great idea. "Hey, Tal, if everything works out with our men and we coordinate, we could both give birth at the same time. Our kids would be cousins, so it'd be perfect. They can grow up together."

Talia gave a nervous laugh. "Um… yeah. Someday."

"Oof," Chloe winced. "Sorry, I shouldn't have assumed you want kids."

"It's not that," Talia insisted. "I just want to wait. You saw what the priestesses did to Marcus, and I couldn't willingly bring a child into this situation. Not while *certain people* are still out there."

It was obvious she was talking about her ex-boyfriend Cody. He'd escaped with the Executors, and I didn't blame her for being scared of him. He'd manipulated her before. I wouldn't put it past him to use a child against her, too.

I'd been really angry at my friends the other night, but now that I had a chance to cool down, I had a better understanding of where they were coming from. I couldn't fault any one of them for waiting to have kids right now, because the constant fear that something bad could happen to your child was overwhelming. I wouldn't give Marcus up for the world, but if I could've delayed his arrival until after this was all over, I'd have done it in a heartbeat.

A silent moment passed before Chloe spoke. "Tal, can I ask you something? If it's too much, you don't have to answer."

Talia shrugged. "Sure, ask me anything."

"I saw the fear in your eyes when we told you Cody escaped," Chloe proceeded cautiously. "You never reported him for what he did. Did he threaten you so you wouldn't go to the cops?"

Talia sighed. "No. Though now I wish I had reported him. Maybe then he'd be locked up for different reasons, and he'd have never joined the Executors. But at the time, I didn't think anyone would take me seriously."

I recalled the night at the Dungeon when I learned that Cody had coerced Talia into things she didn't want to do. I'd sliced his face with a broken beer bottle and called him a rapist to his face. That'd unfortunately been the worst of his punishment, and I wished he'd been faced with a greater sentence.

The day she caught Cody cheating and broke up with him, I'd told her that if she needed anything, I was there for her. I meant it in every way. If she'd wanted to report him, I'd be the one driving her down to the police station that minute. I wanted to tell her to report him then, but she was already going through so much. It was a huge step just to break up with him, and I could tell then that she just wanted to move on. I would've rather seen her get away from him than watch her relive it all in a courtroom.

Society wasn't kind to women who'd been domestically abused, always twisting it back on the victim. I understood where Talia was coming from. I would always support my friend on what was right for *her*, and taking him to court would've fucked her up more than he already had.

"You've always been so sure of yourself," Talia told Chloe. "I admire that about you, but I wasn't like that. I don't think people can understand what goes through a person's head after being treated like that unless they've been through it themselves. People like Cody tear you down so hard you don't trust yourself. At the time, I thought I was to blame. I wasn't even sure I'd been abused, or that it wasn't all my fault. I thought I deserved everything that happened to me, that somehow I caused him to cheat because I wasn't enough. Nadine believed me, but I didn't think anyone else would. I didn't really believe I *could* report him. He would say that I consented to it, and technically I did say yes. By the time I saw it for what it was, it was too late. He was on the priestesses' side, and they'd do everything in their power to paint him out as the golden boy, while making me look like a psycho. They would've used the case to turn the coven even further against us."

Chloe placed a hand on Talia's. "I haven't *always* been sure of myself. Believe it or not, I understand and respect your decision. As women, everyone thinks we should just stand up for ourselves in situations like that, but it isn't that simple. Cody took your voice away, and speaking up was more dangerous than what he'd already put you through. If we ever find him and you want to take him to court this time, I'll support that."

Talia laughed. "If I ever see him again, I'm ripping his balls off."

"That's our girl!" Onyx exclaimed. She and Chloe exchanged a proud high-five.

Chloe became serious again. "He didn't take your voice forever, Tal. Clearly, you've already got it back, or you wouldn't be saying things like that."

Talia's shoulders fell. "I'm *finding* my voice. Truth is, I don't know what I'd do if I saw Cody again."

"Let's hope I find him first, then, because I'll fuck him up before he ever gets a chance to touch you," Chloe said.

Talia gave a light smile. "Thanks."

I winced as I shifted. The door creaked, and my friends turned to look at me. I would've really preferred to act as if everything was normal. Instead, they watched me intently like I was about to keel over and die.

"Girl, you're gonna have to fight me to see who gets to him first." I tried to crack a joke, but my tone fell flat.

Talia picked up on it, and she looked worried. "Feeling any better?"

I scoffed. "No."

I needed to give myself something to do, so I crossed the room and turned on the burner under the tea kettle, which Lucas had left full for me this morning. I didn't sit down, because staying in one place for too long absorbing all the pain and discomfort only made it worse. It was more comfortable to keep moving, even if it was exhausting.

"Why don't you tell us what happened?" Chloe asked gently.

"I woke up in pain. Normally, I just push through it," I admitted. "Marcus was crying, so I tried to pick him up, and my wrists gave out."

Saying it out loud made me feel worse, because it was really fucked up that I couldn't even hold my own infant. It made me wonder if maybe that angel doctor was right and I shouldn't have had kids. I hated thinking that way.

"This pain came on suddenly?" Chloe asked, sounding concerned.

"Yeah, for the most part," I said. "I mean, I've noticed I've been slowing down lately, and I'm more tired, but that's normal when you have a newborn."

Onyx frowned. "It sounds like it's more than that. You need to get in with your doctor as soon as possible."

"I'll be fine," I insisted. "I don't want to ruin all the fun we have planned for the day. This could go away in a couple of hours."

"If it's a lupus flare—which it sounds like it is—then you need to get on the front end of it," Onyx pressed.

No way. It was our first day off in over a month, and I didn't want to spend it at the hospital.

"What are your treatment options?" Chloe wondered.

"My doctor's probably going to recommend a steroid injection," I said. "It's supposed to take the edge off the joint pain." *If it even works*, I thought.

"How long will the effects last?" Talia asked.

"At least a couple of weeks," I answered. "A few months, if I'm lucky. Goddess, this fucking sucks. I don't want to go through with this again. I'm so sick of being poked and prodded by doctors, and not being well enough to perform simple tasks. If I can't even pick up my own child, what kind of mother am I?"

"Don't you dare say that," Chloe demanded. "You're a great mom, and your disability doesn't change that."

"It does, Chloe," I argued. "If I can't do a simple task like changing my son's diaper, then I'm not the same kind of mom everyone else is. I knew this was a very real possibility when I decided to continue my pregnancy, and I thought I could be okay with that, but I'm not. This isn't fair."

"You're right, it isn't," Talia agreed. "But it's important to get care. I'll drive you to the clinic, and Onyx and Chloe can stay here with Marcus and Rose. You don't know if this will turn into something worse, so it's better to get treated now."

"I'm okay," I snapped. I hadn't meant to be harsh with them, but I also didn't feel like they were listening.

My friends didn't understand. I wanted them to stop pushing this and leave me alone. Their insistence felt patronizing, because I was already aware of everything they were saying. I *knew* I needed to go to the doctor. I just didn't *want* to, so I wished they'd stop hounding me about it.

I'd been to the doctor a million times, and it was a miracle when they could do anything to help me. My friends had the experience where the doctor could just give them a pill and make it all better, but that didn't work for me most of the time. The steroid shot might work *now*, but who knew if it would keep working, or if it could make it worse? If going into the clinic today wasn't a waste of my time, I'd be shocked.

I was so medically burnt out. I couldn't stand the thought of going to the hospital again, let alone on my day off. Even a quick appointment turned into hours. Between traveling to the clinic and back and sitting in the waiting room, my whole day would be gone, and I'd be back to work tomorrow. I wanted to spend the day with my friends and snuggling my son. That wouldn't happen if I went in for treatment. Now I had to decide between them and my medical care, and it wasn't a choice I wanted to make. The collective experience of being disabled was exhausting, and my friends didn't get that.

I knew this was a big deal, and I wasn't downplaying the flare-up, but it was easier to ignore it than let it consume me. Just the thought of me going back to the hospital and enduring all that wore me out. I wanted to live a normal life, and to do that, I had to act as if this wasn't happening. I was going to spend the day with my friends and family, dammit. I wasn't going into the clinic unless it was a dire emergency, no matter how much pain I was in.

I softened my tone. "I appreciate everyone's help with Marcus, and that's really all I need right now. Does anyone want tea?"

I was *really* good at masking my pain, but today the three of them didn't seem convinced. I could see it clear as day on their faces. Talia and Chloe both shook their heads, but Onyx hopped up from the couch and hurried over to the teapot before I could get to it.

"I'll pour my own, thanks," she rushed to say.

I didn't want to be coddled. I should be able to do something as simple as pouring a cup of tea.

I reached into the cupboard to pull down a teacup. We had a beautiful collection from Grammy, which she'd hand-painted with purple and blue flower designs. This set was one of the few things I had left of hers.

My hands trembled, and I wasn't quick enough to react. One second the teacup was in my hand, and the next it had slipped from my fingers. The ceramic shattered into hundreds of pieces at my feet. I could swear the sound it made could be heard for over a mile. I felt detached from my body as an intense sadness entered my chest. We'd only had six matching teacups, and now we were down to five, which just wasn't enough when I had so little of my grandmother left.

The noise startled Marcus. Chloe soothed him, while Talia rushed over with the garbage can to pick up the largest pieces.

Onyx hurried to get the broom. "It's okay. We've got this."

My friends were trying to be kind, but I didn't *want* them to have to clean up after me. My body had taken another thing from me, and the devastation of losing another piece of my grandmother I'd never get back was all-encompassing.

Talia looked up at me from where she knelt on the floor. "I *really* think you should go in."

Obviously, I couldn't ignore this anymore. I couldn't even function enough to pick up a simple teacup.

"Fine, I'll go in," I caved. I didn't have to like this, but I needed help to get my hands back.

I called my doctor, and Dr. Yonker agreed to squeeze me in between his other appointments. I knew he was doing it because I was a priestess. It felt awful to use my privilege to get care when other people were going without it, but I couldn't help myself in this state, let alone anyone else.

I went to grab my keys off the hook by the door. With the unpredictability of the Waning, I didn't chance leaving important items like that in my magical stash anymore. "I'll see you guys in a couple of hours."

Talia quickly stopped me. "Uh-uh. You're not driving yourself."

"I don't need a babysitter," I protested. "I can handle myself."

"Nadine…" Talia frowned and looked at the shattered bits of teacup in the trash. Clearly, I wasn't going to be operating a steering wheel today. "I'm driving you. You can call me when you're done, and I'll pick you up."

I didn't really have a choice, so I followed Talia to her car and climbed in. Isa came along to support me.

I knew my friends were only trying to help, but I couldn't shake the resentment that I felt at my loss of autonomy. I couldn't even drive myself to my own doctor's office, and I needed my friends to give up their day off to help me. It was ridiculous that I had this big destiny to fulfill—that I had to lead our people, find the Curse Breaker Wand, and defeat the priestesses' Master Wand—yet I couldn't drive myself across town.

My friends were right, and I needed to see a doctor, but part of that didn't matter because I felt like my identity as a person was being stripped away from me. This wasn't my choice. My body and my friends were forcing me to do this, and I was angry at everyone, because I didn't consent to this at all. I didn't consent to waking up feeling like shit this morning, for my hands to betray me and not work, and for everything to fall apart on the one free day I had, a day I *desperately* needed for myself.

Talia dropped me off at the clinic entrance. I got checked in and went to sit in the waiting room. Isa hopped onto my lap and began purring. There was another woman there who looked to be about ten years older than me. I sat several chairs down from her. She shot me a few glances, but it looked like she was trying not to stare.

I finally locked eyes with her. If she wanted to say something, she needed to fucking spit it out, because I didn't have the time or energy for this game. "Can I help you with something?"

"I don't want to bother you, but um… you're Priestess Nadine. I'm Lucas's cousin, Jess."

Great. Another Taylor. Couldn't Lucas's crazy relatives leave me alone? I'd already had enough of his parents the other day.

Jess gestured to the chair beside me. "Would you mind?"

I didn't have the energy to decline. "Sure."

Jess didn't reach out to shake my hand, and I was grateful for that, because I didn't want to have to decline. People thought it was rude, but I didn't have the capacity for a handshake when my condition flared like this. As Jess sat closer, I noticed the mild redness in her cheeks and across the bridge of her nose. Most people wouldn't think anything of it, because hers wasn't obvious at first glance, but I was all too familiar with the butterfly rash that appeared in lupus patients. There was a reason she hadn't reached out for a handshake, and that's because she knew what it felt like. I realized Lucas had mentioned her before, years ago when I first told him about my diagnosis. He'd told me he had a cousin with lupus, just like me.

"It's great to finally meet you," Jess raved. "You're such an incredible inspiration to so many people."

I was shocked to hear it, because so often in my position I was told how I wasn't doing enough or helping enough people. "You really think so?"

"Yes. The way that you show up for this community—it's obvious how much you care. And you're doing it all as a brand new mom. That's more than anyone can ask for. You shouldn't have to do this, but you still show up to help people. I know what it's like, trying to manage your energy like that. I've got lupus, too. I'm sure what you're going through can't be easy, but don't overdo it."

I scoffed lightly. "Too late for that."

I didn't want to talk about my flare-up, so instead I asked, "Do you have kids?"

Jess shook her head. "No. My lupus is so advanced that I'm not able to carry children. My doctors and I agreed that the health risks were too great."

"I had a doctor who said the same thing." I was still bitter about it, too. I'd never forget that appointment with the angel doctor in *Hok'evale*. "I hadn't been trying to get pregnant, so when I found out, he wanted me to abort."

Jess wrinkled her nose. "He sounds awful."

"It was terrible," I told her. "He told me I was going to die if I chose to continue the pregnancy, even though I'd been in remission for months. On top of that, he tried to imply I was some sort of slut for sleeping with my husband."

Jess gasped. "He did not. Who was this guy? I'll give him a piece of my mind!"

I wasn't sure about Jess at first, but I was quickly warming up to her. "He doesn't work here, thankfully. It was at a clinic in another supernatural settlement. He got fired."

Jess chuckled. "Good. He got what he deserved."

"I'm glad I didn't listen to him, because he was wrong," I added. "I had preeclampsia complications, but now I have this amazing baby boy at home, and I wouldn't give him up for the world."

I didn't mention losing Dean, because I figured Jess already had to know about that—the whole coven did—and it was a really heavy topic to bring up to someone I just met.

"I ended up getting a second opinion, and my doctor was *so* good at taking care of me," I continued. "It helped that she had healing magic. Honestly, I'm not sure I would've made it through delivery without her. Have you ever thought of getting a second opinion from another supernatural clinic that might have more resources to help?"

"I considered it," Jess said with a sigh. "But honestly, healing magic can only go so far, and unless I was in a really good place with my health already, it wouldn't help me. I've never really been in a place where I could take that risk. I'm so glad that you were able to continue your pregnancy, but I made the decision a long time ago that that's not my path. I've got a husband, a great career trajectory, and two cats at home. We're really happy with the life we have."

"What do you do for work?" I asked.

"I'm an artist," Jess said. "I run my own business selling art prints of my paintings online. It's great for me, because I absolutely love what I do and it gives me the flexibility I need to take time off when I need to. See that painting there?"

Jess pointed to a large canvas hung on the wall in the waiting room. It was abstract, in all shades of green, with thick and thin lines that reminded me of tree trunks. It very much gave off a forest vibe, and I loved it.

"That's one of mine," Jess noted proudly. "The hospital commissioned three of my paintings a few years ago. I was going for a witchy coven vibe."

"It's spot on," I praised. "You're really good. The art thing is going well for you then?"

"Oh, yeah. My husband doesn't work, apart from helping in the business. He's living his dream as a house husband, which is great because I have high support needs, and he's literally the greatest."

"That's amazing," I told her genuinely. "I love that for you. I'm really glad I have children, but I don't buy into the rhetoric that you have to have kids to be happy and successful. It sounds like your family's doing great."

"We really are," Jess agreed. "And honestly, kids aren't for everyone. I've seen what some people can do to kids, and it's just… heartbreaking. You've met Lucas's dad, right?"

"Oh, yeah," I grumbled. "He's a charming guy."

"My father's the same way. Those brothers are cut from the same cloth. Our whole family has problems. My parents are narcissists just like Jay, and I didn't want to bring another kid into that kind of family dynamic. I know Lucas doesn't see much of his parents anymore, but mine are still around, and the way my family works, I can't really get away from them."

"You shouldn't have to deal with that," I said gently.

Jess shrugged. "We've all got our own ways of dealing with it, you know? It's not easy, but I do what I can to placate them and keep moving forward. When you're the child of a narcissist, it's a life-long endeavor. Even when your parents are gone, they leave you with a lot of baggage, and that's not something you can ever really be done with."

Jess was merely making conversation, but she didn't know the impact her words had on me. I thought of Lucas and everything he'd been through. I realized maybe I wasn't understanding him simply because I *couldn't*, the same way most people would never understand what it was like to live with a disability. They could try to imagine what it was like, and have sympathy for my situation, but they would never truly *know* without going through it first-hand.

It occurred to me that Lucas had pushed back when I suggested going on pills because even if it *could* be good for him, that didn't mean he *wanted* it. At the time, I thought he was declining because he didn't know how they could help him, but that wasn't the case at all. I was pushed by my friends to come to the doctor's today, even when I knew I should but didn't want to. Lucas was only trying to hold onto his autonomy, same as I was.

Jess was right. This kind of stuff was life-long, and that's why it kept coming up over and over again, because these weren't problems you could just solve once and be done with. We were constantly learning how to navigate these situations under new circumstances, and it was futile to expect them to go away permanently.

In the same way, the kidney transplant wasn't the cure I thought it was going to be. I thought it would fix all my problems with lupus, but it didn't. I was still having symptoms. Lucas's depression wasn't going to be fixed with a treatment either, because there wasn't really a cure for disabled people—only ways to manage it. You learned to live with your illness, because even if the treatments worked and you went into remission, it was never going to go away one-hundred percent. Your illness was always going to be a part of you.

I had to be okay with the fact that my disability was going to change over time. Sometimes it would get better, and sometimes it would get worse, but I had to work with what I had, not with what I wanted. I simply couldn't willpower my way through everything and wish things were different.

The *what if* didn't matter, because the fact was my son was here, and he was being raised by disabled parents, and there was no changing that. All I could do was be the best mom I could be with what I had. Some days that meant I *couldn't* show up for him and that I had to ask for help. I didn't get to be a mom one-hundred percent of the time. There would be days I had to step back, and while I didn't like it, that was our reality.

Lucas had a disability too, and it worked the same way. Sometimes, he was going to have worse days than others. He would always be this way, but it didn't matter, because I was going to stay with him and love him regardless. And to love him meant backing him up and supporting him on what *he* needed, not what I wanted or thought was best for him.

Maybe he still needed his parents in his life, but I couldn't understand that because I didn't know what it was like to deal with them. Perhaps it was like Jess said, and it was easier to placate them and move forward, rather than trying to fight against them. I'd meant well, and I wanted to keep our family safe, but it'd be foolish to assume Lucas didn't want the same.

But at the same time, Marcus *had* gotten hurt because of his parents' actions. There didn't seem to be a good middle ground.

"Thank you, Jess," I told her. "I appreciate you sharing that, because sometimes, it's hard to understand Lucas when I haven't gone through that myself."

Jess wore a look of sympathy. "How's he doing?"

"Better," I said. "Some days are harder than others."

"Keep fighting for him," Jess encouraged. "He's a good guy."

"The best," I agreed.

"I know you guys are really busy, but maybe we can get together soon," Jess suggested. "We're going to be moving, and I hope to see Lucas before we leave."

"Moving… outside the coven?" I asked.

"Yes. We're finalizing the details on a rental in Boston. Luckily, I can take my work anywhere, and my husband thinks this will be good for us. I've been seeing a lupus specialist in Boston, but it's a long commute, and I need to be closer to my health team. My lupus is getting to the point where I need a higher quality of care than our hospital can provide."

That was really sad to hear, because we'd been working so hard to get the healthcare system back up and running efficiently, and it just wasn't fast enough.

"I know the coven's healthcare system isn't as good as it used to be," I admitted. "When I came here, I was so impressed by the staff, but everything changed so quickly. I have faith we can get it back to where it needs to be. We've made so much progress, but we just need to give it more time."

"Please know this is no reflection on you or the Imperium Council," Jess insisted. "I know you're trying as hard as you can, but time isn't something I have."

It was clear what she was getting at. If she didn't get the help she needed on a consistent basis, she was going to die. Lupus wasn't usually fatal if managed properly, but it could cause organ damage, like what happened to my kidneys. Poor access to healthcare was one of the leading risk factors for complications.

"I understand you have to do what's best for you," I said. "But I hope that we can make improvements and one day you can come back. We shouldn't be losing coven members over this."

"Thanks, but coming back here isn't something I ever plan on doing," Jess admitted. "I need to build a life somewhere else, and my magic is basically gone already from the Waning. There's no point in being a witch anymore if I can't be in a place where I'm healthy and living my life. I need to start over and leave the supernatural world behind."

That was devastating to hear. While I respected her decision, I knew Jess couldn't be the only person making this choice. I was witnessing the coven dissolving before my eyes, and I worried how long it'd be until there was no coming back from this.

I swallowed the lump rising in my throat. "I understand."

A nurse came into the waiting room then and called Jess's name. Jess offered me a light smile before she left. "Take care of yourself, Nadine."

Coming from her, it wasn't just a pleasantry. She really meant it.

I was left alone with my thoughts, which were nothing more than melancholy. I was doing all I could to help people, but even my best wasn't enough, because people were still dying. No matter how hard I tried, or what I did, I couldn't control everything. This flare-up was the result of pushing myself so hard that my body was forcing me to slow down. I was actively hurting myself by trying to help these people, and it was a cold realization to come to terms with the fact that no matter how much of myself I gave, there were still going to be people left behind.

To do better, I had to take care of myself, because there wasn't any more I could do than what I was already doing. I wouldn't be here in the clinic today if I'd have slowed down, and now I couldn't help anybody, including myself, because I'd pushed so hard I couldn't function anymore.

I thought giving my all to the job would result in faster change, but really we were spinning our wheels thinking it would get us somewhere. We needed to do better for ourselves so we could give our best to our people.

That started with our family.

FIVE

Snowflakes whizzed past me as I sped down the side of the mountain. I hadn't snowboarded much before, but I found that I was a natural on the slopes. I shifted my weight from side to side, then jumped to do a full three-sixty rotation and landed it with ease. Snowboarding was the perfect activity for our day off, because it really took my mind off things. I hadn't been sure I wanted to come, but at this point we'd been at it for hours, and I'd lost count how many times I'd gone down the slopes. I was really glad Professor Warren had suggested this.

Warren had brought along a potion infused with fae illusion magic, which created isolated snowfall along a smooth slope. It was strange, because it was summer and the forest was green with foliage, yet the path ahead was nothing but ice and snow. The air was warm, and I was dressed in a t-shirt, but as I bent my knees and dragged my hand through the snow to steady myself around a curve, the snowflakes were ice cold on my fingers. The illusion would disappear in a couple of hours, but for now, it was as good as the real thing.

"Beat you to the bottom!" Professor Warren called from behind me.

I saw a flash of color, and then he was gone around another bend. "Not if I beat you first!" I called.

His laughter echoed behind him, and I bent my knees to pick up speed. Professor Warren used to be a competitive snowboarder and knew his way around the slopes. I would've thought his leg injury from the night Octavia Hall was destroyed would slow him down, but after being treated by a healer in *Hok'evale* a few weeks ago, he was doing much better. As I rounded the corner, I saw that I was catching up fast and the end of the slope was quickly approaching.

I caught up with him just as the ground evened out, and we reached the bottom of the slope at the same time. We slowed beside each other.

"Nicely done!" he praised. "Ready for another go?"

I smirked playfully. "How about this time we race to the top? You think you can keep up, old man?"

"Who are you calling old man?" he teased. Warren grabbed his snowboard under his arm and took off up the trail next to the slope.

I immediately raced after him and quickly passed him. The slope wasn't super long—it hardly made it a fraction of the way down the mountain—but it was perfect for a day like this.

By the time I made it to the peak, I was out of breath. I set my board aside and took a swig from my water bottle, which was sitting in a pile of snacks and supplies we'd left near a large boulder. I could see Professor Warren through the trees. He must've realized he didn't stand a chance, because he'd slowed down and was only halfway up the slope by now.

I sat on the boulder and breathed in the fresh mountain air. The sun had already dipped low in the horizon; we'd been here all day. The sound of Miles's and Grant's laughter echoed over the mountaintop as they sped down the trail. From this vantage point, beautiful greenery seemed to stretch on forever, interrupted only by the peaks of Gothic structures nestled in the valley below. Octavia Falls appeared so quiet and peaceful from up here, which was strange given everything happening in the coven right now. Looking at our town from this angle could really give a guy perspective.

I'd been sitting there alone for a few minutes when Professor Warren reached the top of the trail. "Whew. That was a close one," he joked.

"Yeah, I won by mere inches," I teased. "Thanks for doing this. We all really needed a break."

Warren obviously heard my tone turn serious. He set his snowboard aside and came to sit beside me. "You want to talk?"

I knew I could trust him with anything. "I'm just thinking about how big this town is—how big the *world* is—and why I choose to focus on little things that don't matter."

"But they do matter," Professor Warren countered. "Why do you wish to diminish your problems?"

He thought I was getting down on myself, but that wasn't what this was about.

Still, his question prompted me to really think about the answer. "I guess if I can see that these problems aren't as big as I'm making them out to be, then it's easier to find solutions."

"Does it help you to see things that way?" Warren asked curiously.

"Sometimes," I admitted. "When I get caught up in ruminating, a slap in the face can really wake me up. It's helpful to be able to separate the real problems from the bullshit. Losing your kid—that's a real fucking problem. Things like helping feed and house our people are real problems."

I gave a sigh. "But trying to gain my parents' approval when I already know they'll never give it is useless. I don't understand why I'm still trying."

"Because you care," Warren encouraged.

"It's just so silly to be sad all the time when all I'm really doing is just battling a voice in my head," I said thoughtfully.

"And why shouldn't that be treated as real as any other problem?" Warren questioned. "We filter the world through our own minds, so if we don't treat our minds right, everything else falls to pieces."

I propped my elbows on my knees and kept my gaze on the town below. "I guess so. But can't I just choose to make it easier? It's my own mind, after all. I've got control of it."

"Yes, but there are parts of life we can't control—things that happen to us that alter us forever. You cannot wrestle your mind out of feeling."

"But I can change *how* I feel," I replied. "It was an easy decision to leave my parents behind when we weren't living in Octavia Falls, because I didn't have to see or deal with them. Now that we're back, I've got to make things right. To feel better about my parents, all I have to do is forgive them. So why does that feel like the hardest thing in the world?"

"Just because it's simple doesn't mean it's easy," Warren said. "Have you considered that if you've tried to forgive them and it hasn't worked, perhaps that's not what you need? Sometimes, there are problems we can't fix, and so all we can do is move on, because the damage is already done, and trying to fix them isn't ever going to make it feel better."

I furrowed my brow. "How can you move on without forgiving people?"

"Forgiveness is a misnomer, because everyone has a different way of viewing it. For some people, forgiveness is not about accepting or excusing behavior, but simply releasing anger and resentment, even if the person who did them wrong doesn't deserve it. But for others, the anger and resentment is serving them, and so to release does them a disservice."

"How can anger and resentment be a good thing when it doesn't feel good?" I asked curiously.

"It only feels bad when you're resisting it and wallowing in it. If you're willing to accept your anger, it no longer has a hold on you, and you can use it to fuel yourself, until that anger dissipates without the need for forgiveness at all."

"Hmm…" I mused on his words. "Let me get this straight. I let my parents back in because I thought that was the path to forgiveness and healing. But you're saying if I accepted my anger, I could use that to uphold my boundaries, which would've protected my family. I don't have to sit in the anger, but just use it as needed?"

Professor Warren nodded. "That's it exactly."

I sighed heavily. "Does it ever end, Professor? I'm so sick of learning these lessons over and over again."

Warren chuckled lightly. "I'm in my forties, Lucas. I'm not an ancient wiseman. I'm still learning a lot myself. But I will say it does get better, as long as you put in the work. This is a lifelong journey. What worked for you yesterday may not work today. Life can't be solved by a single epiphany, but progress can be made, and you've made *so* much progress. But you don't have to do it alone. We're all here for you. Whatever you need, we're going to back you up."

"What does Lucas need?" Miles asked as he trudged up the trail. Grant followed closely behind him.

"A fucking happy pill—that's what I need," I cracked. It felt good to laugh about it, because I always took life so seriously, and it wasn't doing me any favors. "Nothing to worry about. Just the same shit, different day."

Warren wore a curious expression. "It's *not* the same, though. You're discovering new facets of yourself all the time. This problem with your parents is a new angle you haven't dealt with before, because you've never been the person you are now. You're a husband and a father now. You're not just dealing with your parents, but with your son's grandparents. Before, the decision was whether or not to let them be a part of *your* life. Now you have to decide if you want them to be a part of *your son's* life."

"I guess that's true," I said. "It's hard, because I want my kid to grow up around family, but I don't want him around my dad. But if they aren't around, he won't grow up with grandparents. I think my mom would be a really good grandma, but not if my dad's around. Nadine's already made the decision—as long as my mom's still with my dad, she doesn't get to see Marcus."

"Is that what *you* want?" Grant asked, sounding concerned.

"I don't think Nadine's wrong," I admitted. "My mom screwed up bringing my dad around, and I'm not about to give her a second chance on that. But I do think it'd be all right for my mom to come see Marcus if Nadine and I were there."

Grant frowned. "It sounds like Nadine gave you an ultimatum, which isn't fair. She's got to realize Marcus is your kid, too. If you want him to have a relationship with your mom, Nadine needs to support you."

Miles scowled. "I'm sure it's not that simple. Nothing's more important than keeping Marcus safe."

"Nadine's just trying to protect our kid, and I don't blame her for that," I said. "I think what's hard about this stuff is that there's so much nuance, and on top of that everyone's emotions are involved."

"Did you mean it—about the happy pill?" Miles wondered.

I scoffed. "Nadine seems to think I need one. I'm really not sure it's for me."

"It could be worth trying," Miles suggested. "Antidepressants really helped me by stabilizing my emotions. It's like all my life I've been on this emotional roller coaster—either climbing a mountain or standing at the edge of a cliff ready to fall off. Now it's like a weight has been lifted. This impending worry and rage that used to follow me everywhere has calmed down. I still feel like me, but it's like my mood swings don't control me anymore. The track ahead feels smooth. I'm telling you this because I resisted meds for a long time, thinking that I was weak to give in, but it's just another tool, and there's nothing weak about accepting help. Our brains don't work the same way *other* people's do, but that just means that our version of normal is different, and we need to find our own tools to operate effectively."

"You should've seen this guy a couple of years ago," Grant said. "Miles couldn't hardly operate a fork. He was all like, *What's the point in eating? Nothing tastes good anyway.*"

"It was bad," Miles admitted. "But I finally took control of my life, and now look at me! I'm the youngest sheriff Octavia Falls has ever had, I've got great friends, and I'm engaged to the hottest chick in the state! I'm finally in a good place, and I want that for you, too, Lucas."

Warren turned to me. "At the very least, it may be worth speaking to your therapist about your options."

"I've got to do something," I agreed. "The last thing I want is to let my parents affect my life any more than they already have. I just don't want to be a bad dad and make the wrong decisions for my son."

"You're a brand new father," Warren encouraged. "You haven't had the time to be a bad dad yet. So go say hello to your baby boy and be the best damn father there ever was."

"Yeah, you know what? I am a great dad," I said as I stood from the boulder. "I'd do anything for my son, and that's more than my dad could ever say about me. My child isn't going to be raised by a broken father like I was. I'll never be like him, because no matter what, I'll be there for Marcus. That starts with taking care of myself, so I can give him all of me."

"Yeah!" Grant cheered, throwing a fist into the air.

"That's the priest we know and love!" Miles exclaimed.

"What exactly is your plan?" Warren asked.

"I need to get my health back on track and go back to therapy," I said. "At the very least, I've got to start meeting with Dr. Mack again."

Warren offered a kind smile. "I'm proud of you, Lucas."

"Thanks, all of you," I said. "I know it's not easy listening to me whine."

"But we love Whiny Lucas," Grant teased.

I rolled my eyes. "Yeah, I'm sure I'm a joy to be around."

"No, you know what?" Grant stated firmly. "I'm serious! Whiny Lucas is a guy who's aware of his problems and determined as hell to find a solution. You're always looking for ways to make things better, and then you go out there and you *do* it, dammit. I'll take Whiny Lucas any day over some complacent warlock who's just going to sit inside their comfort zone and accept shit for the way it is. Does it get annoying sometimes? Sure, but you know what? You're *our* whiny, annoying little bitch, and goddess, we love you for it."

Everyone stared at Grant as his passionate speech echoed across the mountaintop. A silent beat passed, and then I broke into laughter—full body, clutch-my-stomach laughter.

"Fuck, man," I cracked up. "You just don't hold back, do you? Come here."

I pulled Grant into a hug and clapped him on the back. Strangely enough, he told me exactly what I needed to hear. "Goddess, you make me sound so emo," I joked.

Miles shrugged. "Well, I mean, if it quacks like a duck…"

I slugged him lightly, and he ducked away from me, laughing. "If that's what I am, I'll own it. I'll be the best damn emo dad there ever was."

Grant snickered. "You'll raise little emo babies!"

"Maybe I will," I challenged playfully. "At least if Marcus grows up to be a little emo kid like me, I'll know how to handle him."

Grant nudged me in the side. "You say that, until you realize you're just raising a carbon copy of yourself."

"Dear Goddess, no," I groaned. "I can't imagine."

"Marcus will be his own person, with his own set of interests and challenges," Professor Warren encouraged. "But no matter what happens, he'll have great parents to lead him in the right direction."

"Thanks," I said.

Professor Warren shot a glance at the setting sun. "We should gather our things and head back to town."

"One last race down the mountain?" Grant suggested. "The winner gets all the glory."

"You're on," I agreed.

We gathered our things, then took off down the slope one last time.

"Speed it up, Grandpa!" Miles trash-talked Warren.

Warren didn't say a thing as he passed Miles, spun one-hundred and eighty degrees to board backwards, and still out maneuvered us all.

We laughed all the way to the bottom. Warren had beat us all by a mile, and Grant came in second. He wouldn't let us forget it, either.

"Professor Warren used to snowboard competitively, so it doesn't really count that he won," Grant claimed. "So *technically*, I came in first place."

Miles clapped him on the back. "If that's what you want to believe."

Professor Warren had brought his own car, and we'd come in mine. We piled into our respective vehicles and descended the mountain, going our separate ways.

When we arrived home, the girls were in the living room doing their nails. The cats lazed around, all except Rishi, who was chasing a toy bat.

"Times have changed since I was young," Rose was saying. She sat in her wheelchair, holding her hands out in Chloe's direction. Chloe painted Rose's nails a deep red. "When I was a kid, my friends and I would sneak out of the house, strip down under the night sky, and perform séances in the woods!"

Chloe gasped playfully. "Rose, you naughty girl."

"Wasn't nudity more taboo when you were younger?" Talia asked. She wiggled a stuffed animal at Marcus, who was squirming around on the floor.

Rose scoffed. "I was a rebellious child and very in touch with my sexuality. Don't tell me you girls have never danced naked under the full moon."

"Never in a group, *but* I would not be opposed," Onyx said. She leaned over and painted polish onto Nadine's toes.

"It sounds freeing," Nadine agreed. She sat curled up under a blanket next to Onyx.

Miles chuckled as we stepped into the room. "Count me in!"

Chloe threw a cotton ball at him. "You weren't invited."

He kissed her on the side of the cheek. "I guess we'll have to schedule a ritual of our own."

"Oh, please." Chloe rolled her eyes, but she couldn't hide the blush rising to her cheeks. She wouldn't admit it, but she was totally smitten by him.

Grant went to sit beside Talia on the floor, and he tickled Marcus's belly. I leaned over the arm of the couch to give Nadine a kiss, but I immediately picked up that something was off. The kiss wasn't as soft as normal, and there was a hint of concern in her eyes.

"Did you have a good day?" I asked.

The girls went quiet, and all eyes turned to Nadine. She pulled the blanket off of herself, revealing an ice pack on her hands underneath.

My stomach dropped. "Nad, what happened?"

"A flare-up." She cleared her throat, because just saying that seemed to choke her up. "Everything's going to be okay. I went to the doctor, and I got a steroid injection. It should help."

"I should've been here for you," I insisted.

"There's nothing you could've done," she replied. "I tried calling, but you didn't have service. I had my girls here, and they helped."

Marcus started crying then, and Grant quickly backed away. "I didn't do anything! I swear."

"He's okay," I assured him. "He's just hungry."

"Tired, too, I'm sure," Talia said. "He missed his afternoon nap."

She went to pick him up, but Nadine cut in. "Lucas and I can put him to bed. You guys have helped so much already."

I took Marcus from Talia's arms and rocked him back and forth. "I'll start his bottle," I told Nadine. "Come to our suite whenever you're ready."

I wanted to hear all about her day, but I didn't want to rush her. I went to our room and changed Marcus, then fed him a bottle. He was out cold before he finished the whole thing. I set him in his bassinet and quietly closed the bedroom door behind me. Nadine was sitting on the couch in our living area, and the door to our suite was closed.

I sat beside her. A tear fell down her cheek, and I reached out to wipe it away. "Nad, I'm sorry I wasn't here. I should've checked on how you were doing before I left. I thought I was letting you sleep in, and Goddess knows none of us are getting enough of it lately. I didn't stop to think if there was something more going on."

"It's not your fault," she assured me. "There's no use in assigning blame. I'm not angry; I'm frustrated. But I gained some perspective today, and I don't want to keep fighting."

"Thank Alora, because I can't handle fighting with you, either," I said. "I came to you for help, but I should've realized you were struggling, too. I'm really sorry I put all that on you."

"I'm your wife, and it's okay to come to me if you need help," she countered. "I don't want you to ever feel as if you can't lean on me, because that's what marriage is for. I really wanted to help you, and I got frustrated when it felt like I couldn't. It wasn't right of me to take it out on you. When things get hard, we have to recognize where we're at and figure out what works for us at different times. Some days, I'm going to have to lean on you more, and others, you'll lean on me. Marriage isn't about never fighting, but navigating those disagreements together."

"I agree. I know you were just worried about our family, and I could've done a better job at trying to understand your perspective. I'd like to work together on this, and I'm willing to explore *all* our options."

"Maybe my suggestions weren't the best solutions," Nadine admitted. "I pushed when I shouldn't have, and I'm sorry. Your depression is like my disability. It doesn't ever go away, even when you get better, but we can work with it and find solutions. Ultimately, that means the decision is up to you. I will be here to support you whatever you decide, on the medication issue and with your parents."

She had no idea how much those words warmed my heart. "And I'll be here for you," I promised. "I want you to know how deeply I value your opinion, and if you don't want Marcus around my parents, we can take a step back from them for now. If we decide to change our minds in the future, we can talk about that, but we need to be on the same page and make that decision together."

Nadine sniffled. "I don't want you to feel pressured by my opinion, though. I want you to stay true to yourself, and then we come together and find ways that work for both of us."

"And I don't want you to ever stop expressing *yourself*," I insisted. "You weren't trying to push me—you were just offering options because you care. I thought about what you said, and I've decided to resume therapy with Dr. Mack. I'll talk to her about medication. I still don't know if it's for me, but the least I can do is get more information about it so I can make an informed decision."

"If that's what feels good to you, then I'll support that," Nadine replied. "I know we can take care of each other, but to do that, things need to change. Our work schedule isn't sustainable. We can only get so much done in a day before we crash, and anything after that is wasted time anyway, because our productivity plummets."

"Are you suggesting we cut back our hours?"

"I don't think we have any other option," she said. "My illness flared up and your depression is coming back because we're running ourselves into the ground."

I was apprehensive, but deep down, I knew she was right. "If we focus on ourselves, the community is going to suffer. There aren't enough hours in the day to focus on the coven *and* ourselves. If we make this choice to take time off, it's a selfish one."

"I know, but we have to do it even if we don't want to," Nadine said sadly. "I don't know about you, but I can't keep going like this. I'm not capable of working efficiently through this kind of flare-up. I need to heal, so I can give my all to the coven and fix these problems for everyone."

I chewed the inner side of my lip. "How can this be the right decision? Our people need us."

"And we'll help them as much as we can, but we need to know our limits." Nadine frowned. She clearly didn't like this any more than I did. "I thought we could help everyone, but now I'm not so sure, because so many people don't even want our help. We need to get our health in order before we face the priestesses, or we don't stand a chance. That's really the only way we can help everyone."

I took her hand in mine. "All right. We'll reduce our hours and focus on getting better."

Nadine let out a sigh of relief. "I really appreciate you being here, because even though we had a fight, I know we can come together and solve it. We just need to communicate."

"And we're improving," I agreed. "Nadine, I promise you that no matter what comes our way, I will never stop putting in the effort."

She wiped her eyes. "I will *always* be here, too, Lucas."

"I love you," I whispered as I caressed the side of her face.

I leaned in, and my heart lifted as my wife closed the space between us. I placed a gentle kiss on her lips, and she responded with a soft moan. She tasted so sweet. Desire for her ignited deep in my belly. Our passion was unmatched as our emotions ran high, tangling into one another and igniting a fervor between us.

"I love you, too." Nadine's hand traveled up my chest, then to the back of my neck, where she ran her fingers in my hair. She drew me closer. "I've missed this."

I tenderly kissed her again, intentionally being careful with her. She kissed me over and over, and my dick hardened. It'd been so long since we'd been intimate, because we'd been waiting for her body to recover from delivery.

I pulled away from her. "Nad, we should wait. I don't want to hurt you."

Her fingers tightened in my hair as she pulled me closer and parted her lips against mine. "So be gentle," she breathed.

She was deliberately trying to drive me wild, and it was working. My head spun as she leaned back, until she was lying on the couch. I was extra careful not to put any weight on her.

I had to practically wrestle myself away from my wife, and by the time I did, I was already panting in wanting. "We need protection."

She shook her head. "I'm not ovulating yet. We almost never get to do it without a condom, and I want to feel your skin on mine."

"Are you sure you want this?" I had to make sure we weren't getting ahead of ourselves.

Desperation flared in her gaze as she locked eyes on me. "I don't *want* it, Lucas. I *need* it. Being close to you like this… it helps. So please, Lucas… make me yours."

She dragged me close again, sealing her request with a kiss. My dick gave a jerk in my pants, and I wanted nothing more than to fill her up and show her just how much I loved her.

Carefully, deliberately, I began trailing soft kisses down her neck and across her collarbone. Nadine gave tiny moans of pleasure that turned me on even more. I helped her slip out of her clothes, then situated a pillow under her head as she laid back, fully exposed.

Her breasts had swelled during pregnancy, and they were still larger than normal, which was really fucking hot. She ran her hands over her chest in a sensual way, showing them off. Fuck it all if that didn't drive me absolutely insane.

I knelt beside her and kissed her belly, which was different now that she'd given birth. The skin there wasn't as firm as it used to be, and she had stretch marks that were still fading. I kissed each one of them, because honestly it was the sexiest fucking thing in the world. She'd carried my babies and given life to our children. So yeah, if I had the chance to kneel at her side and give her all of me, I was going to fucking worship this woman.

It felt more than appropriate, because Nadine might as well have been a goddess herself with the hold she had on me. I didn't mind falling to my knees and worshiping her. In fact, I found great pleasure in succumbing to her every desire. Nadine had always said she wanted us to stand on equal ground in the relationship, and for the most part we did, but when it came to moments like this, our primal nature emerged and I realized it was natural to submit to her—not because I put her on a pedestal for everything I thought she could be, but because I honored her for everything she already was.

Nadine closed her eyes and took in the sensations of my lips caressing every inch of her body. My tongue grazed her nipple, and I ached to take her in my mouth.

"May I?" I asked.

"Yes," she begged.

I drew her nipple into my mouth, and I nearly came right then and there. I brought myself to my full height on my knees, straining to withhold my burning passion as I drank her in. She tasted so sweet.

She moaned in pleasure. "Fuck, that feels so good."

I trailed my delicate touch up her legs, gently stroking her at the apex of her thighs. She let out a light sigh that begged for me to continue. I slipped a finger inside of her and worked her slowly.

I couldn't resist her intoxicating scent, and I climbed onto the couch between her legs to take her in my mouth. She gasped as my tongue rolled over her sensitive areas. I explored her body with my fingers and tongue for a long time. I didn't want the beautiful moment to end.

"I want you inside of me," Nadine begged.

I lifted my head from between her legs, my breath unsteady with a craving for her. Nadine kept her eyes on me as I unbuttoned my jeans and stripped down. She smiled at the sight of my cock, which was hard and ready for her. Carefully, I positioned myself above her. Nadine tilted her head back and closed her eyes. I slid my cock inside her gradually, deliberately drawing out the sensation. She was so warm and velvety, and she enveloped me completely. My heart hammered, and my breath wavered as I made her my own.

Nadine bit her lower lip as I filled her up. "Keep going," she pleaded.

I wrapped an arm around her waist, supporting her hips as they tilted upward into me. I drew myself out of her slowly, then pushed into her again in a steady rhythm. It felt so fucking good to be this close to her. I watched her facial expressions to make sure I wasn't going to hurt her, but she parted her lips and begged for more. I went deeper, but I didn't increase my speed. I wanted to make love to her, for her to feel safe and cared for, so I moved inside of her at a soft, tender pace.

Nadine's fingers tightened in my hair. "I'm going to go... Fuck, Lucas—"

Nadine reached her peak, and her body contracted around my cock. It was my complete undoing. I came inside of her, thrusting as deep as I could go as we spiraled into a beautiful orgasm together.

I sagged against the back of the couch, my head spinning. "Do you... feel any better?"

Nadine gave me a soft smile. "With you, I always feel better."

I climbed off of her and began cleaning up, then came back with a blanket that I draped over her. I put on a pair of shorts and sat beside her on the couch. Nadine cuddled close to me, and I wrapped my arms tightly around her. Her naked body felt wonderful against my exposed skin.

I kissed the top of her head and played with the ends of her hair. "Thank you for being here, Nadine. You don't have to be, but the fact that you chose me, and continue to choose me every day, makes me the luckiest guy in the world."

She entwined her fingers in mine. "It's easy to choose you when you're so kind and gentle with me. Even when things get tough, you come in and say, *I want to do better, and I'm going to.* Being able to grow alongside each other and build a life together means so much to me. If we were perfect, there'd be no room for growth, and I want to keep growing and experiencing life with you. As long as we keep working together, we'll make it through anything."

"We will," I promised—at least, I hoped so. Professor Warren was right when he said some of these problems didn't have solutions, and never would.

That didn't mean we'd ever stop trying to fix them.

SIX

Over the following weeks, we began to find a rhythm that worked better for us. The side effects of my treatment lasted for a few days, which mostly left me tired, but I found that the treatment helped. Lucas was seeing Dr. Mack again and attending weekly appointments, though he was still on the fence about starting medication.

Professor Wykoff had volunteered to watch Marcus while we were working, and it turned out to be a great arrangement. She had been with us the night the priestesses kidnapped Marcus, and she'd risked her life to protect him. We trusted her more than anyone else, and she was really great with our son.

Council duties continued to take up most of our time, but we were committed to being home before dinner and taking one day off every week. I'd spent the better part of the summer poring over Imperium records and meeting with our allies about the Curse Breaker Wand, but I had yet to stumble across a credible lead. The autumn equinox was quickly approaching, which meant Halloween wasn't far behind. I kept reminding myself that we still had time before the priestesses' arrival, and I was staying confident until then.

The Waning was only getting worse and slowing us down, though, and we were already running short on magically-charged crystal reserves by casting spells to help the coven. The first week of September arrived, and the Waning hit me so hard that I could barely even access my intuition, let alone any simple spells. Onyx and Miles didn't have any magic, either.

Saturdays were our day off, and my friends and I always planned a laid-back activity to help us unwind. It was less than two weeks until Miles and Chloe's wedding, and we agreed to help prepare party favors.

Talia and I had gone shopping with Marcus at a craft store after work one day, and we picked up supplies to make pendulum jars for the wedding guests. They were super simple. All we had to do was attach a pendulum to a cork, fill the small vials with crystals, leaves, or whatever else we wanted inside, then seal the corks on the jars. Then we could use them to commune with spirits, with the pendulum able to answer yes or no questions depending on the direction it swung within the jar. Miles thought they were the best wedding favors ever.

While we were shopping, we found shadow boxes at the craft store, which were like a deep picture frame meant to put memorabilia inside. I thought it'd be fun to make a display of keepsakes from Miles and Chloe's dates to put on display at the reception. Chloe loved the idea.

I bought extra shadow boxes for myself, because I'd always wanted to make one for Marcus and Dean with the hats and onesies from their birth, along with photos from our ultrasound appointments and the footprints we'd taken after they were born.

I figured if I was making one for them, I wanted to make others—one for our wedding, and one for my parents. I had all these keepsakes hidden away in a box, but it was time to stop hiding them. We had a home now where we could put all these things on display. My dad's collector's license plate and my mom's apron shouldn't be left sitting in a box somewhere. They should be hanging on the wall, where I could look at them every day.

My friends and I gathered in the kitchen that morning and spread our art supplies over the long dining room table. Talia, Grant, and Onyx formed an assembly line to begin crafting the pendulum jars, while Miles started on the shadow box.

Talia leaned over to Onyx to eye one of the pendulum jars she'd just finished. "Ooh, I like that one!"

"Here, have it." Onyx placed it in Talia's hand. "We have tons of extra supplies."

Talia beamed as she slipped the jar into her pocket.

"How can I help?" I asked.

Onyx glued one cork onto a vial before quickly moving onto the next pendulum jar. "I think we have this covered. I know you had some other shadow boxes you wanted to make. You and Lucas can work on those."

"Yeah, we're here to have fun," Miles agreed.

Lucas started on the kids' shadow boxes, while I brought out my parents' keepsakes and started organizing them for their display. Marcus sat beside us in his bouncer, appearing fascinated by the rattles and toys that hung above his head. The cats were batting around a marble that had fallen from our craft supplies. Rose had declined to join us, as she wasn't feeling well today.

Chloe plopped down next to Miles, smacking a thick binder on the table. "Now that everyone's here, we need to finalize wedding details."

We didn't have a lot of time for wedding planning, but we didn't really need it because Chloe had been planning her wedding her whole life, so all the details were already decided on. Booking a venue wasn't an issue, because Chloe wanted to have the wedding in the backyard under the garden arch. It was one of the most beautiful places in town. Miles didn't care about the details; all he wanted was for her to have the wedding of her dreams.

"Nadine, how did that adjustment on your bridesmaid dress work?" Chloe asked. "We're running out of time to make any more changes."

I pulled my collection of handwritten birthday cards from my parents out of their box. Luckily, they hadn't been destroyed when Lucas accidentally knocked my things into the sink a few months ago. "It fits great. Everyone's going to look really good."

Chloe had planned a black and white wedding, where all the guests would be in black and the bride and groom would both be wearing white.

"If you don't mind me asking, why the rush to get married?" Talia asked, sounding genuinely curious.

"Yeah, is there something you're not telling us?" Grant teased, wiggling his eyebrows at his brother.

Miles wrapped an arm around Chloe's waist. "We are not *rushing*. We're just excited! You never know what the future holds, and we want to make it official sooner rather than later."

Chloe planted a kiss on his lips. "We can't wait when we're this madly in love."

Talia dropped crushed petals into one of the vials. "There's no question you two are perfect for each other. It's just that marriage is a big step, and there are a lot of details to think about. What's life going to look like after the wedding? Things like that."

Chloe shrugged, keeping her eyes on Miles. He stared back dreamily. The two were absolutely smitten by each other.

"I guess we'll figure that out when we get there," Chloe said. "I know some people need to plan out their whole futures together to be comfortable moving forward with something like this, but Miles and I agree that we can't know what the future holds, so why not live life now?"

I understood where both couples were coming from. Chloe and Miles were the kind of people who were certain of what they wanted, and once they made a decision, you couldn't convince them otherwise. It didn't make sense for them to wait on the wedding, because to them, there was nothing to wait for.

Talia and Grant were a different story. They'd always taken their relationship slowly, and they had to map out every detail of their futures before they said *I Do.* Sometimes I thought Grant and Talia could be too rigid, because there would be things they couldn't predict that no amount of planning could prepare them for. But they also had to do what worked for them, and if they needed to agree on which color to paint the nursery before walking down the aisle, that's what they had to do.

"Nadine and Lucas planned their wedding pretty quickly," Onyx pointed out. "Do you guys ever wonder if you should've waited longer?"

Lucas shook his head. "I like the pace we took things, but every couple has their own timeline."

"Lucas is right," I agreed as I cut one of my birthday cards straight down the middle. I was going to arrange the cards in a way where the front image peeked out from behind the message written on the inside. When I was finished, it'd be a collage that covered the back of the shadow box. "I'm glad we didn't wait, because if we hadn't gotten married when we did, I might've never gotten pregnant, and Marcus wouldn't be here with us now. But I don't think everyone has to go at the same pace…"

I trailed off, and all eyes turned toward me. "Huh," I mused as I stared down at my parents' birthday letters.

"Everything all right?" Lucas asked.

"Yeah, it's just… hold on." I laid the letters out across the table, starting with the earliest date, all the way up to the card my parents had left me a few months before my nineteenth birthday. I noticed something strange about my mother's handwriting that I'd never caught before. The anomaly appeared in each card, all the way back to when I was born. It was sporadic and didn't seem to have any rhyme or reason to it.

I placed a hand on my hip as I looked them over curiously. "I can spot my mom's handwriting anywhere. She always writes in print. So... why are some of these letters in cursive?"

I pointed to an *S* at the end of a word, which swirled in a way that no other letter on the page did.

Lucas leaned over to inspect the cards. "Maybe it's some sort of code. Your mom knew you liked puzzles. There's got to be a meaning behind this."

I got really excited at the idea that my parents had left something behind for me. If it really was a hidden message, it'd be really fun to highlight that in the shadow box. It was like one last game with my parents.

"Let's work together to figure it out," I suggested.

Lucas found a pen and notepad in one of the kitchen drawers, then returned to the table. He started scribbling down each letter that my mom had written in cursive.

Everyone gathered around to hunt down the cursive letters together. By the time Lucas finished writing them down, he'd filled up the whole sheet of paper.

Lucas tapped his pen against the table. "These letters don't make sense in order. Maybe they mean something if you mix them up?"

"There's got to be fifty letters here," Miles pointed out. "You could make any combination of words with that if you wanted. Maybe you're looking too deep into it. It might not mean anything."

"Maybe it doesn't, but it *does* seem strange for my mother to do. If my parents left me a message, I want to know what it is." I picked up the oldest card. "Some of these have more cursive letters than others. Let's try treating each card like its own separate piece of a whole, instead of trying to interpret these letters all together."

Lucas tore off the top sheet of the notepad, giving himself a fresh piece of paper. "What letters do we have in the first card?"

"Just one," I told him. "The letter *I*."

He wrote that down. "The second card?"

"O. T. O. K," I listed out.

We continued on like this, until we'd organized each cursive letter by their respective cards. I looked over the list Lucas came up with. It became very clear that all together, the cards spelled out a full sentence.

"It's still gibberish," Miles insisted.

I shook my head. "No. The pattern's there, but each word is mixed up. Each card spells out its own word, and if we unscramble them individually, we can figure out the whole message. See this second card here? O. T. O. K. That can only be *took. I took...*"

Lucas started writing down the unscrambled version. "Let's keep going."

As we worked our way through the next words, my pulse began to quicken. I thought this was a fun game my parents had left behind, like the puzzles my dad and I used to solve together. But as the words started to form a sentence, I realized this was something else entirely.

I stared down at the sentence Lucas had written out once we reached the last card. *"I took the curse you seek from Octavia Falls and hid it in a place close to my heart,"* I read aloud in a shaky tone.

Onyx's gaze darted between me and the cards. "What does that mean?"

"She must be talking about Nadine's family curse," Grant theorized. "Except Nadine broke it."

"She says *the curse you seek*," I emphasized. "There's only one thing we're looking for. My *mom* took the Curse Breaker Wand."

I stepped back as the weight of the realization hit me.

Talia furrowed her brow. "Why wouldn't she just say that? Why call it a curse?"

"Because this message is meant for *me*," I said. "She didn't want to be too obvious in case someone else deciphered it. But these cards are written to me, which means this message is referring to me... the curse *you* seek. The curse I, Nadine, seeks. Which can only mean the Curse Breaker Wand. The word *curse* in this message isn't the item; it's a clue, for me."

"It fits everything we know," Lucas added. "Helena had the Curse Breaker Wand for years after Nicholas died, and then she lost it. She said someone took it from her house. Faith must've found it when she was living there and took it with her when she left town over twenty years ago."

"But how did she *know?*" I wondered. "This message took her nineteen years to write, and more than that, she wrote the last card *before* my nineteenth birthday, shortly before she died."

"You think your mom knew she was going to die?" Chloe asked.

I shook my head. "I don't think so. It's more like she knew she had to get the last of the message to me sooner than later. But I'm not sure she knew *why*. If she knew she was going to die, she would've left more behind for me, or hinted in some way that she wouldn't be around anymore."

"Why wouldn't she just tell you all this, instead of leaving a message in these cards?" Miles asked. "Haven't you seen your mother's spirit since she died?"

"My parents' spirits appeared at our wedding to give their blessing, but they were only there for a few seconds," I said. "She didn't have time to tell me any of this, even if she wanted to. Talia and I tried contacting my parents in a séance when I first moved to Octavia Falls, but the connection wasn't very good. We didn't get through to them. The only other time I've seen them since their death was in a vision during my Evoking Ceremony, but I don't think it was really their spirits. That vision was more like a projection of them from my own subconscious. So no, I haven't really spoken to her since she died."

"Clearly, your mom knew *something*," Chloe pointed out. "How she knew to leave you this message isn't as important as the message itself. If this really does refer to the Curse Breaker Wand, then we need to go find where she hid it. Any idea what this second half of the message means —*hid it in a place close to my heart?*"

"I think so," I admitted. "Mom always said home is where the heart is. I think she hid it in the house I grew up in."

"Any idea what might've happened to it when you moved?" Grant asked.

I racked my brain, trying to remember if we ran across anything that looked like a wand when we packed up the house, but I couldn't recall anything like that. "If we'd found the Wand while packing, Grammy would've recognized it."

"What if it's still there?" Talia theorized.

I shook my head. "Grammy and I completely emptied the house after my parents died."

"Unless she hid it somewhere you wouldn't think to check," Miles suggested.

I inhaled a sharp breath as I realized something. "When I was a kid, my mom and I were playing hide and seek, and I hid inside her closet. I found a hidden panel in the wall that led to a cubby space, just big enough to hide a few valuables. I don't remember finding anything there at the time, but I do remember Mom saying it was a secret. I forgot about it until now."

"You think that's where she hid the Curse Breaker Wand?" Lucas asked.

"It's got to be," I said. "We have to go check it out."

There wasn't time to waste. We quickly agreed that anyone who had access to their magic should come along with me. Chloe, Miles, and Onyx offered to stay back and watch Marcus. Lucas created a portal, and we stepped through it alongside Grant and Talia. Our four cats followed at our feet.

We emerged into a cluster of trees behind my childhood home. I could see the white siding and green shutters from here, and my heart ached for the home that once was mine.

It didn't feel the same, though. Various building materials and construction equipment were stacked in the driveway. The inside of the house was dark, and there weren't any cars parked outside.

The backyard was all torn up, with mounds of dirt piled in various places. My mother's bushes she tended to on the side of the house weren't there anymore, and her flower gardens were completely gone. The old car dad had parked out behind the garage hadn't been there since we sold it after his funeral. The swing set I used to play on as a child, along with the tall oak tree I used to climb, were both missing. The yard was completely unrecognizable, and that made me sick to my stomach.

We approached the back of the house, and I peered in through the sliding glass door. Ladders, buckets of paint, and various sheets of plastic scattered the house. Clearly no one was living here right now, as the house was undergoing a major remodel. I couldn't understand why the new owners would want to change something that was already so beautiful. It was really sad to witness.

Grant muttered an incantation, and his green magic swirled around the door handle before disengaging the lock. We entered the house, our footsteps echoing off the hardwood floor. The cats were silent as they slunk through the house beside us.

It was strange being here again, because it felt so familiar, yet so distant at the same time. This had been my home growing up, but I'd changed so much since I left this place. I'd made a new home now, and it was surreal coming to this place that was merely a memory.

I led my friends upstairs to my parents' old bedroom, which smelled of new paint but was otherwise empty.

"It's in here," I said as I entered my parent's old closet. I knelt beside a shoe storage shelf and reached for the hidden panel. I held my breath and popped the panel out of place.

My stomach sank. It was empty.

"I don't get it," I said. "I was so certain of what the message meant, but there's nothing here."

"Do you think the priestesses could've gotten to it first?" Grant wondered.

I shook my head. "I don't think so. They pushed me so hard to find the Curse Breaker Wand, and we never had a lead. I don't see how they could've learned that my mom had it."

"You could still be right about the message, but it's just not in *this* spot," Talia suggested. "Are there any other places in the house where she could've hidden it?"

"I don't have any ideas, but we should look while we're here," I said.

My friends and I scoured the whole house, and the cats sniffed around for clues. We searched under the sinks for hidden panels and inspected every floorboard in the house for potential hiding spots. We searched every nook and cranny of the basement, and even lifted Talia into the attic crawlspace, but we found nothing.

We met back in my parents' empty bedroom.

Grant sighed. "There's nothing here."

"There's got to be something. We can't use magic to track an Oaken Wand, but what if we can *feel* it's magic?" Lucas wondered.

"Maybe, if I had an ounce of magical access," I said. I lifted my fingers, but not even a spark appeared. I turned my gaze to Isa. "Any ideas, girl? You're the one who hid it."

Isa stared up at me helplessly and gave a small meow.

"She's not going to remember anything from a past life," Grant pointed out.

"But she would remember in the afterlife," I said, forming an idea. "That piece of her that's still in Alora knows where she hid it. I know we're not supposed to summon loved ones because it complicates the healing process, but this is different. We need to contact my mom and ask her where she put the Curse Breaker Wand."

"I think this is a valid exception," Talia agreed. She withdrew the pendulum jar she'd slipped into her pocket earlier. The crystal was contained within a small vial that fit in the palm of her hand. "I can lead the séance."

Lucas nodded in agreement. "Let's see what Faith can tell us."

We sat in a circle in the center of the empty room, and Talia placed the pendulum jar in the center. We joined hands, and the cats circled us to keep us protected as we performed the séance. Talia led us through a guided meditation, until she felt confident in our connection to the other side.

"Faith?" Talia called out. "We're looking for information about the message you wrote to Nadine in her birthday cards. You hid the Curse Breaker Wand, but we need more information to find it. Are you here with us now?"

I expected to feel something, but not so much as a breeze passed through the trees outside. The room remained completely silent.

Then, the pendulum gave the smallest shudder. We all noticed it, and Talia gave a start.

"I think she's here," she announced excitedly. "Faith, can you show us *yes?*"

The pendulum didn't move.

Talia tried again. "Can you show us *no?*"

The pendulum wiggled slightly, but in no discernable direction.

"Mom, please," I begged. "If there was ever a time for you to come through, now is it. This is our first lead on the Curse Breaker Wand, and we *need* to find it if we stand a chance against the priestesses. I know you had your secrets, and there was something you were trying to tell me in those cards, but to fully understand where to find the Wand, we need you here now. Is the Wand here in the house?"

Nothing happened. We must've sat there for minutes awaiting an answer, but the pendulum didn't move.

I leaned back. "I don't get it. Why won't my mom come through?"

Lucas looked to Isa. "Your mom's already reincarnated. That makes it harder to contact her, even though there's still a piece of her soul in the afterlife."

"Can we use Isa to amplify the spell somehow?" I asked desperately. "We could do a past-life regression on the cat or something. There has to be *some* way to get answers."

"There's no spell for a past-life regression on cats," Talia said. "But maybe your dad knew something. We could try getting through to him."

I agreed to give it a shot, and Talia began calling out to my father.

"Nathan? Are you here? Your daughter Nadine needs you now," Talia said. "We believe Faith hid an object from the Miriamic Coven here in your house. Do you know where to find it?"

For a brief moment, I thought that the temperature in the room dropped a few degrees, but I couldn't be sure it wasn't just my imagination. I kept my gaze firmly locked on the pendulum jar, willing my father to give us an answer.

The sound of shattering glass filled the room, and we all jumped as the jar exploded. The cats scurried in all directions. Lucas threw himself in front of me, but he wasn't fast enough. A shard of glass sliced the back of my hand. A line of blood quickly formed over my skin. I winced as I pressed my other palm over the wound to stop the bleeding.

Grant was so startled that he jumped to his feet and put his fists up. "What the hell was that?"

"I don't know. That's never happened to me before. The Waning must be affecting our spell," Talia theorized. She lifted her hand, but only a few sparks emitted from her fingers. "I must've overdone it, and my spell failed."

Lucas conjured a first-aid kit and placed a bandage over my cut. "Mine and Grant's magic should've been enough."

"Then maybe it wasn't the Waning this time," Talia said. "We can't force spirits to talk to us if they don't want to."

I sat back on my heels, heartbroken. "I don't get why my parents wouldn't talk to me. We need them to find the Wand, or the entire coven is going to die out."

"Maybe they didn't have any answers to give," Talia offered kindly as she picked up pieces of shattered glass. "We might've confused them. I can't say for sure why the séance didn't work, but I think this is a clear sign we can't try again."

I got to my feet, feeling wholly disappointed that we'd come here only to walk away with nothing. "I guess I was wrong. The Curse Breaker Wand isn't here."

"That doesn't mean your mom didn't have it," Lucas encouraged. "She must've hidden it somewhere else."

"Then we need to find out where that is," I stated. "If we hope to get any information about where to go next, then we need to talk to the one person alive who knew my mother best. We need to tell her about the message we found, and maybe she'll be able to piece together something my mother told her. We need to visit Headmistress Verla as soon as possible."

Lucas raised his hands. "I'll portal us there right away."

I hesitated, because I knew speaking to Verla about my mother was going to feel heavy, no matter how I approached it. When I'd lost my mother, Verla had lost a best friend, and the topic of my mother's passing was never an easy one for either of us. I needed my mother more than I needed answers about the Curse Breaker Wand, but she couldn't be here. Verla could provide comfort in a way my friends couldn't, because she knew my mom better than anyone else.

"I should go alone," I suggested. "I need to tell Verla about what we found on my own."

Lucas nodded. "We understand. Call me whenever you're ready, and I'll come pick you up."

Lucas portaled us back to Octavia Falls and dropped me off on Headmistress Verla's doorstep. It was Saturday, which was her day off, so I figured she'd be home. I knocked, and she answered right away.

"Nadine!" she greeted brightly. "Come in. I just put on some tea."

I entered her house and sat next to the fireplace in the living room. Odin lazed next to a faded carpet stain beside the coffee table, where it looked like someone had spilled tea long ago. Verla brought a tray from the kitchen with tea and tiny sandwiches on it.

She sat in the chair beside me. "To what do I owe the pleasure?"

"We have information about the Curse Breaker Wand, and I'm hoping you might be able to help us find it," I said.

Verla sat up straighter. She appeared genuinely shocked that we'd found something after all this time. "I'll help in any way I can."

I dove into an explanation about the message we'd found this morning, and then told her how we'd been to my parents' old house but didn't find anything. By the time I finished, tears had beaded in the corners of my eyes.

"Do you have any idea where my mom might've hidden the Wand—anything she might've said to you before she died?" I asked.

Verla noticed my broken tone, and she set her teacup aside. "I suspect that's not the main reason you're visiting me today, is it?"

Tears leaked from my eyes, and I dashed them away. "No," I admitted, my voice cracking. "She didn't show up, Clarice. I need her now—the *coven* needs her—and she wasn't there. I don't understand. My friends are some of the most powerful witches I know. The séance should've worked. If Mom wanted to send me a message, then why wouldn't she show up to provide clarity?"

Verla placed a gentle hand on mine. I gazed down at the long scars on her arm, which she'd obtained when trying to protect me from the questing beast on our way to the Abyss. Verla cared so much, but even her love couldn't fill the hole inside of me that formed without my mother here.

"Nadine, I am *so* sorry," she said genuinely. "I know it seems that magic can answer all our questions and solve all problems, but that is far from the truth. I'm certain your mother wanted to be there for you today, but even the most powerful of witches can't guarantee results, especially when it comes to tricky spells like séances."

"Séances are supposed to be easy," I said in a small voice.

Verla's features grew even sadder. "Even when we open that connection, we don't know which spirits might come through. I don't want you to think you and your friends failed, or that your mother didn't want to show up for you, because that's not true. Believe me, I know."

I noticed something in her eyes—something she'd buried so far down that only the deepest of sorrows could unearth. My gaze darted to a picture framed on the mantle. In it, Verla stood beside her sister on their graduation day. They looked so much alike that I wasn't entirely sure which one was her. The twins shared the same eyes and bright smile.

"You're not just talking about my mom, are you?" I asked slowly.

"No, honey." Verla followed my gaze to the photograph. "I tried contacting my sister many times after her death, but each attempt failed. She wasn't the kind of person to abandon me, so I know there are greater forces at play. Something, or someone, here or in the afterlife, has prevented us from meeting again. I am certain that is the case, because Nicole would *never* leave me."

Verla seemed sad, but with it came a spark of joy at the memories. She rarely talked about her sister, but I got the sense that maybe she was just waiting for someone to ask first.

"I can tell you loved her very much," I said. "Are you okay talking about her?"

"Of course," Verla replied. "You can ask me anything."

"What was your sister like?"

Verla drew a deep breath. "Nicole was my rock. She kept me grounded when I took life too seriously. She was always singing and dancing, trying to lift people's spirits. To others, she appeared to have no care in the world, but between you and me, I believe she acted the way she did to make people feel better. She couldn't stand to see people get hurt."

I picked up a deeper meaning in her tone. "Someone hurt *her*, didn't they? She didn't want anyone to feel the way she did. She sounds very noble."

"She was," Verla said fondly. "Nicole and I both grew up with a strong sense of justice. Our father was a lawyer, and we were both expected to follow in his footsteps. I loved and admired my father very dearly, but he wasn't always kind to our mother. When we were nine years old, we came home from playing in the woods with a tree branch we wanted to show him. It was twisted like his wand, and we thought he'd like it. When we entered the house, he was screaming at our mother. Nicole begged him to stop, and when he didn't, she stood between them. He smacked Nicole with the back of his hand, and she fell to the ground. My mother cowered, but I knew that he was wrong. I wasn't going to stand for it. I smacked him across the face with that tree branch so hard he fell to the ground. My father never dared to lay a hand on any of us again."

"I'm sorry that happened to you," I told her. "You were too young to have to stand up to a full-grown man."

"I did what I had to do," Verla replied. "It was that day that I became my sister's fierce protector. I was the older one—even if only by a few minutes. It was my job to take care of her, but at the same time, and in her own way, she became my protector as well. I stood up physically to my father, but Nicole found her own ways to fight back. She was always coming up with creative ideas on things we could build with sticks in the backyard or activities that would get us out of the house. My father wanted her to become a corporate lawyer like him, but her greatest rebellion was choosing to specialize in family law instead."

"It doesn't sound like she loved him the way you did," I noted.

"Our relationship with our father was... complicated. He loved in his own way, often buying us presents and praising us endlessly for our accomplishments. His love for his daughters was never a question, but he never should've married my mother, because he couldn't love her in the way she deserved. Once we were old enough to care for ourselves, my mother left my father. Soon after, she moved away from Octavia Falls altogether. My parents were right to get divorced, but things changed once they did. It seemed that when my mother left him, my father just... stopped caring. He threw himself so deep into his work that he didn't even show up for our graduation."

"I'm sure that wasn't easy for either of you."

"Nicole and I took it in different ways," Verla admitted. "I saw my father's grief, and I recognized his struggle. I did everything I could to show him I was still there, to be his little girl, to follow in his footsteps and become that great leader he wanted me to be. Nicole didn't understand why I was still trying to please him. She thought I was taking his side over my mother's, but I wasn't. My mother was happy for the first time in her life, and I was so grateful for that, but I wanted that for both of them. Nothing could excuse or undo the way he treated my mother, but I thought if I could be there for him, maybe he could have a second chance. Nicole didn't think he deserved it."

"Where is your father now?" I wondered.

"He died of a heart attack many years ago," she said sadly. "He left us with a large inheritance and willed the house to me before I became headmistress. The financial security is what allowed me to pursue a new career in teaching after working as a lawyer, although Nicole continued to practice law."

"What happened to her?" I asked. "I've heard bits and pieces of the story, but not the whole thing."

Verla dropped her gaze. "Nicole took a case prosecuting a man who had brutally beaten his wife. Despite all the evidence against him, the jury ruled him not guilty. That night, the wife drove her car off the road, presumably because she could not live with the ruling. Nicole took it personally and believed that if she'd done a better job presenting the case, the man would've been convicted, and the woman would've lived. We were both highly ambitious people, and we always had this saying that we were going to make this world a better place—*whatever it takes*. She took this one personally. She believed it was her fault that she couldn't convince the jury."

Verla let out a shaky breath. "Something within her broke after that trial. She quit her job, lost her apartment, and moved back in with me here in our childhood home. She started seeing strange visions after that. They say it's something that can happen to Seers—*disunion*, they call it. The night she died, she took an ax to the Protection Tree. The priestesses caught her in the act and hanged her for it."

"Did she ever tell you why she did that?" I wondered. It seemed like such a strange thing for her to do after everything Verla had told me about her.

"I believe it was my sister's final form of protest," Verla said. "She always held on to the faith that the coven would protect each other, but this trial that she lost proved otherwise. The coven had stopped protecting its people, and in her eyes, I don't think she believed we deserved protecting anymore."

"I heard she called the tree a *murder tree*, and no one knew what she meant," I said. "Could she have been referring to her client? The tree was a symbol of the coven protecting the wrong person, and she blamed the coven for her client's death."

"It has to be," Verla replied. "What people didn't understand was that my sister had no intention of harming anyone. She just wanted them to listen."

"I can understand that," I said. "It's hard getting people to listen. Sometimes it feels hopeless altogether. I just hope that's not ultimately the witches' fate."

"The what?" Verla's brow furrowed.

"The fate of our coven," I clarified. "It can't be hopeless."

Verla's shoulders relaxed. "Just because we're presented with challenges doesn't mean it's hopeless, Nadine. I tried so many times to contact my sister, but even though it didn't work, I've learned that if I still have these memories, that's good enough."

"It doesn't feel like enough when my mom has answers to the Wand, which we need to face off against the priestesses, and she's not answering us," I countered.

"There have to be answers somewhere," Verla encouraged. "But continuing to try contacting your mother will only distract you from the work that needs to be done."

"She never told you anything about the Wand?" I asked in desperation.

Verla shook her head regrettably. "I'm afraid not. But I know your mom wouldn't leave you hanging. That's not the type of person she is."

"I know you're right. I'm just not sure where to look next."

"I'm not your mother, but I knew her well enough to know what she'd say," Verla said. "Look within yourself, Nadine, because your heart already has the answers."

That was *exactly* what my mom would say. "Thank you."

Verla pulled me into a hug. It was so motherly, so comforting, that it was like receiving a hug from my mother herself. My mom had picked a really wonderful friend. I was so glad they never lost touch, because Verla was everything I needed in a motherly figure when my own mom couldn't be here anymore.

I drew away and wiped my eyes. "You're right. The Curse Breaker Wand is still out there, and I can't be wasting time on spells that don't work. My mom would've left something more for me. I just have to find her other clues."

I just hoped I could decipher her messages… before it was too late.

SEVEN

We finally had a lead on the Curse Breaker Wand, and Nadine was utilizing every spare moment she had looking for more clues, though she hadn't found any yet.

My cousin Jess invited Nadine and me out for coffee the following week. It was her last day in town, and she'd be leaving for Boston in the morning with a moving van.

"Lucas! It's been a while!" Jess said brightly as we entered The Cozy Cat café. "Nadine, it's good to see you again."

We exchanged hugs, then placed our orders at the counter. The café featured a large selection of paninis and specialty sandwiches. I ordered a chicken bacon ranch panini, which sounded really good. We gathered around a table near the window with our coffees as we waited for our food to come out.

I turned to Jess. "It really *has* been a while. I haven't seen you since that family reunion back when I was in high school."

"Don't remind me," Jess groaned.

Nadine glanced between us. "I take it things didn't go well?"

"Our dads tried to start a fistfight," Jess said casually.

Nadine sipped her coffee. "You say that like it's a regular occurrence."

"It is when you get those two men in a room together," I stated.

"Men? You mean *children*?" Jess cracked. "Goddess, those two never grew up. I don't want to talk about our family, though. How have *you* been?"

I cupped my hands around my mug, really contemplating the question. "Better," I said honestly. "I'm back in therapy, which has helped a lot, but we're talking about putting me on meds."

Jess's shoulders fell sympathetically. "I'm not going to tell you what to do, Lucas, but I went on antidepressants a few years back, and there are a lot of side effects they never tell you about. Just be sure you know what you're getting into."

"They didn't work for you?" I asked.

"That depends on your definition," she replied. "I wasn't as sad anymore, but I became numb to everything, so much that I'd say whatever I was feeling without questioning if it was appropriate or not. Sometimes, that could really hurt the people around me. All intimacy with my husband stopped, because my desire went away. I thought I went on meds for my own mental health, but I learned that it affected everyone around me. I thought doing it would make it easier on everyone else, but I realized that the way I treat my illness affected other people, too."

"How'd they make you feel?" I wondered.

"There was an emptiness inside of me, but it was a different kind of emptiness than I'd ever felt before," Jess explained. "In the worst of my depression, the emptiness felt lonely and all-consuming, like I could be swallowed up by a black hole, and I'd be relieved if I didn't wake up in the morning."

I understood that feeling far too well.

Jess sighed. "This wasn't like that. It didn't feel like I was on the precipice of a deep, dark hole that wanted to consume me. It was more like there was nothing there at all—no darkness, but also no light. Meds really *did* stabilize my mood, but it was to the extreme. There was no sadness like I used to feel, but those rare glimmers of joy were gone, too. It seemed I could only feel one thing, and everything else had gone foggy. If I didn't know better, I'd have thought my spirit had left my body and I was watching my life from above, because I didn't feel attached to my body at all. I didn't even notice until my husband pointed it out. I felt like I was just going through the motions, and I didn't like the way that felt."

"That's the opposite of how my friend Miles talks about his experience," I said.

"It's different for everyone," Jess replied. "I was angry about it for a long time. Antidepressants were helping my friends live better lives, but they were only making me feel worse. It felt unfair. I couldn't even be treated for my depression because the treatments weren't working. I did everything I was supposed to, followed all the doctors' advice, and even though I was doing everything right, I didn't see the payoff."

Jess wasn't trying to scare me. She was only sharing her own lived experience. But her story made me hesitate, because I didn't want this if my body was going to react the same way hers did.

"I'm sorry you went through that," I said. "It's hard to know what to do when some people have a great experience and others don't. I really appreciate you sharing your experience with me. Hearing from both sides will help me make a better decision when I'm ready."

"I'm sure whatever you decide will be the right choice," Jess assured me.

Our paninis arrived then. We didn't have a lot of time until she left town, so I changed the topic to something more cheerful. "Tell us about Boston. What's your new place like?"

Jess started talking about her move, telling us about the apartment she'd found and how it was so close to her treatment center, as well as an art gallery she wanted to get involved in. The way she raved about the neighborhood, it sounded like she was going to be really happy there.

Nadine's phone rang near the end of our meal. She looked like she was about to decline the call, until she glanced at the screen and her features fell. "It's Chloe. Sorry, I have to take this."

Chloe's voice was muffled from the other end of the line, so I didn't hear what she said, but it was clear as day by the look on Nadine's face that it was an emergency.

"We'll be right there," Nadine said quickly, before hanging up. She turned to me, her features ashen. "Grant had a diabetic reaction. He's in the emergency room."

I stood right away. "I'll drive. Sorry to cut this short, Jess. It was good to see you again. I wish you the best of luck in Boston."

"Thank you, and don't worry about me. Go visit your friend." Jess stood to give me a goodbye hug, and she squeezed me a bit tighter than normal. "And Lucas? I know you'll never hear this from anyone else in our family, so I want you to hear it from me. *You've got this.*"

"That means a lot," I told her. Jess and I weren't close, but she *was* family, and it was nice to know that she cared.

Nadine and I hurried out of The Cozy Cat café and drove to the hospital. When we got there, the nurses let us through to the patient rooms right away. We found Chloe and Onyx talking in the hall outside a private room with a glass wall. The curtains around the bed were drawn, and I could only assume Grant was inside. It looked like a private room, which the staff must've prepared just for him since he was a priest, because beds were limited now.

"How's Grant?" Nadine asked immediately.

"He's stable," Onyx assured us. "Talia's with him, and the doctors have hooked him up to an IV to help with dehydration. He got an insulin shot, which will help bring his blood sugar back to normal."

"What happened?" I asked.

Chloe looked shaken, which wasn't a good sign. It took a lot to crack her hard exterior. "Grant and I were having lunch together—just the two of us because Talia had gone to a meeting at the school. Grant's meeting got canceled, so I invited him to eat with me at headquarters. Everything was fine at first. We had our food delivered, he took his potion, and we started eating and chatting."

The potion she mentioned had to be the one Grant was brewing for his diabetes. He'd been taking it for over a year now, ever since the priest-esses cut his insurance and he couldn't afford his insulin shots anymore. I'd hoped he'd go back on insulin when we returned to Octavia Falls, but medical resources were already stretched thin, and he didn't want to risk being unable to fill his prescription. In my opinion, brewing potions was just as risky right now with the Waning getting worse by the day, but he had a large stock of potion that wouldn't spoil.

"Then Grant's breathing changed, and he started giving one-word answers," Chloe continued. "His face flushed, and when I asked him if he was okay, he said he was really tired and had a headache. I said something might be wrong with his medication, but he didn't even get a chance to respond before he was vomiting. I immediately called an ambulance."

"Can we see him?" Nadine asked.

"Of course." Onyx stepped aside, and we entered the treatment room.

Grant was lying on the bed, and though his features were a bit ashen, he was awake and coherent. Talia sat beside him, holding his hand. Bella and Gus were both curled up on the bed next to Grant.

"How are you feeling?" I asked him.

"Crappy, but I'll live," he admitted, before turning to Onyx. "What's the verdict?"

"The doctors are still working on getting you answers," Onyx said. "I've spoken to your care team, but really, I'm here as a friend. The doctors want to run more tests."

Talia dotted her eyes with a tissue. "Could this be a side-effect of the potion he's been brewing?"

"It *could* be," Onyx said carefully, like she was trying not to freak anyone out. "Symptoms like this aren't unusual in diabetic patients, but it usually takes hours or days to develop, and it appears this came on more suddenly."

"Why would Grant have a reaction now?" I asked. "He's been taking this brew for over a year now, and nothing like this has ever happened before."

Onyx frowned. I didn't think she wanted to say much without Grant's care providers in the room. "The thing is, there isn't any viable research on the potion Grant was brewing, so we don't know the long-term effects it might have. That's something to ask his doctors about."

Grant sighed. "You can say it, Onyx. I screwed up. Everyone told me I shouldn't be brewing my own medication, and they were right. But also, I didn't have a lot of options, and that brew kept me alive when the medical system couldn't. Sometimes, you've got to take these things into your own hands, even if it comes back to bite you in the ass later."

He leaned over to rub his butt. "And ouch… I bit myself hard."

I nudged him in the shoulder. "Good to see you still have your sense of humor."

He shrugged weakly. "Someone's got to. Eventually, you get so sick of seeing the inside of a hospital that laughing about it is the only way to get through it. Got to keep our spirits alive."

"You're going to be okay, then?" Talia asked, stroking his arm.

"I'm not going anywhere," Grant promised. "Literally. Not as long as they've got me hooked up to this IV."

We all chuckled, though it was uncomfortable laughter.

"In all seriousness, I let this go on too long," Grant admitted. "I should've sought out proper care in *Hok'evale*, or at the very least, checked in with my doctors when we returned to Octavia Falls. I'm going to get back on the right medication, and I'll be back to normal soon. I'm just lucky Chloe was there to help."

Chloe waved a hand. "It was nothing. Anyone would've done the same thing."

"Anyone can call an ambulance, but not just anyone can chew an EMT out the way you did when they didn't strap me in properly," Grant said.

"Oh, yeah. Our ride to the hospital was *fun*," Chloe replied sarcastically. "We'd have been here sooner if the driver hadn't taken a wrong turn."

"You guys should've seen her barking directions," Grant chuckled. "I mean it, Chloe. I'm glad you were there. I know things haven't always been easy between the two of us. I wasn't sure for the longest time that you could be trusted, or that you really meant it when you said you wanted to change. But after all this time together, I can honestly say I misjudged you. I'm lucky to call you my friend."

Chloe teared up, but she quickly cleared her throat. "After today, you don't have a choice. I saved your life."

"Trauma bond!" Grant joked in a high-pitched voice. He lifted his fist, and Chloe fist-bumped him in agreement. It was nice to finally see them getting along.

Shouts from out in the hall caught our attention. "Miss, you can't come back here," a nurse said loudly.

"It's okay. My daughter works here," a woman insisted.

Onyx went visibility rigid. "My break is over. I'll see you guys after work."

She raced out of the room like her ass was on fire. We all exchanged an uncomfortable glance. I went over to the curtain and peered out the door.

"I'll handle it," Onyx told another nurse, before turning to a woman who clearly didn't work here.

The woman was tall and wore business slacks with a black blazer. Her auburn hair fell in neat curls, and she looked like she'd just come from work at an office job. Onyx spoke to her in hushed whispers, so I couldn't hear her, but whatever conversation they were having appeared heated. The woman sneered something back, though she kept her features calm. All I could hear was the word *ungrateful*.

Onyx lost her cool, and her voice rose. "Mom, you *cannot* come into my place of work like this! This is the third time this week."

I'd heard stories of Onyx's mother before, and none of them were good. I remembered Onyx had told us her mom's name was Heidi.

Heidi took a step back, acting shocked. "I merely wanted to take my *only* daughter out for lunch, but you never showed up. Am I not worth the courtesy of an explanation?"

Onyx glanced up and down the hall. There were other nurses and patients there, and it was obvious Onyx was trying to keep the situation under control. "Mom," she stated in a calm but firm tone. "You need to leave."

Heidi didn't bat an eye. "I'm not leaving until I get an explanation."

"I've said all I need to say to you," Onyx replied. "You know why I wasn't at lunch. I told you last time I wasn't coming."

Onyx's mother grabbed her so hard by the arm that I could see her skin turning red beneath her mother's grip. "Keep your voice down," her mom sneered. "I will *not* have you embarrass me in front of other people."

Nope. I wasn't letting *this* happen.

I stepped out into the hall, and Onyx's gaze locked with mine. She wore a pleading expression, begging me not to get involved. I knew that feeling of sheer embarrassment all too well. Heidi didn't notice me as she yanked Onyx around the corner.

"You've been very distant lately, and frankly, your distance is depressing me," I overheard Heidi say. "What more do you want from me?"

"I want you to go to therapy," Onyx begged. "I've asked you to do that a million times, and it's like you don't hear me."

"I don't need to waste my time and money for some shrink to tell me how I feel," Heidi sneered. "I already know how I feel, and I know we could fix this if you'd work with me, but you won't do that, because it's always about *you* and what you think you deserve."

"I deserve a mom who's willing to work on herself," Onyx insisted.

Heidi scoffed. "I deserve a daughter who thinks I'm great! I did everything for you. I put a roof over your head and food on the table, yet the second you had a chance to go live with your little friends, you completely abandoned me. You've changed, Onyx."

"Good!" Onyx cried. "That's what children are supposed to do, Mom.

They grow up. I'm in my twenties. You need to stop treating me like I'm nine."

"You just love to make me feel worthless, don't you?" Heidi sneered. "You're such a little bitch, prancing around the hospital all day caring for your patients, but what about your mother?"

"I'm a nurse," Onyx said. "It's my job to care about these people."

"You're my daughter," Heidi shot back. "It's your job to care about *me*. If you think any of these people care about you, you're stupid."

"I'm not stupid, Mom," Onyx demanded. "You always said I wasn't smart enough to work in healthcare, but you were wrong. I got my nursing license despite everything working against me, and I'm a damn good nurse. I will *never* let you tell me differently."

Onyx stormed past me before her mom could respond. She ran down the hall and around the corner.

Our friends had followed me into the hall, but they looked confused. I didn't think they'd caught the whole conversation, and I was glad they hadn't. Onyx didn't need everyone to know the depth of her mother's abuse.

There was understanding in Nadine's eyes, though. I knew Onyx had confided in her about her mother before, but that had been Onyx's story to tell, and Nadine never mentioned much about it. I suspected Nadine knew more than I did up until today.

"I'll talk to Onyx," I told them.

Nadine lifted her chin as Heidi stepped around the corner. The older woman appeared horrified when she saw us standing there, and she knew she'd been caught. "We'll take care of *this*," Nadine told me.

Chloe crossed her arms and pursed her lips. I was already on my way down the hall, but I heard her say to Heidi, "Are you going to leave this building on your own, or are you going to make priestesses do it for you?"

"I'm going," Heidi snapped.

I followed Onyx outside and into the hospital gardens. A pathway cut from one entrance of the hospital to another and was surrounded by trees and flowers. A fountain sat in the middle of the gardens, along with a gazebo on the other end. It should've been beautiful, but the gardens appeared abandoned. Flowers were dying, and the fountain hadn't been turned on. The gardens were empty apart from the two of us. I found

Onyx sitting on a bench in the gazebo with her face in her hands. Her shoulders shook in sobs.

"Hey," I said lightly. "Mind some company?"

Onyx lifted her head and wiped her eyes. She moved over on the bench. "Sorry you had to see that."

"You have nothing to apologize for," I assured her as I took a seat beside her. "You don't deserve to be treated that way."

"I know, but I also don't know how to stop it," Onyx admitted. "Everyone wants to talk about setting boundaries and standing up for yourself, but it isn't that simple when people plow straight through those boundaries and keep on going. To act as if I'm just *letting* her step all over me is an insult to my character, because I *do* set boundaries. I *do* stand up for myself. And I still get shit on. It doesn't matter if I'm being nice to her or aggressively telling her exactly what I think, because nothing works. Some people will stop at nothing to break you. What she said in there isn't a fraction as bad as how she usually treats me."

"I understand," I said gently. "These solutions are nice in theory, but the chances of it actually working on people like this are slim to none."

Onyx wiped her eyes. "I try not to let her bother me, but her persistence is overwhelming. If I'm not answering her texts at all hours of the day, she shows up at my work and makes a scene. I can't get my work done efficiently or be there for my patients when I'm afraid she's going to be lurking around the corner. She shows up here almost every day to harass me. She wants me to be at her every beck and call, and if I'm not available, she has to do something rash to exercise control over me."

Heidi was a lot like my parents, but she seemed even more persistent and controlling. I had a good idea of what Onyx was going through, but there were aspects of her mother I'd never understand. It was hard to watch my friend go through this, especially someone so resilient and strong like Onyx. I didn't think I'd ever seen her cry, and that was sad, because there was a reason she always held it together. She'd had to from an early age, and it wasn't fair.

"I can talk to your mom," I offered. "If the only language she speaks is aggression, I can be so fucking mean she'll never show her face around here again."

"I appreciate the offer, but I don't want you to do that."

"I'm not going to hurt her," I promised. "But I can be so scary she'll have to listen."

I was already plotting on donning my reaper robe and bringing along my scythe to scare the living hell out of her.

Onyx frowned. "Has that ever worked on your parents?"

"No," I admitted. "But Heidi isn't my mom. She can't control me."

Onyx hung her head hopelessly. "You know as well as I do that's not going to work. There's *nothing* we can do that will make our parents listen. Lucas, I've tried everything. My mom never wanted a kid, and from the day I was born, she made certain I knew it. I was always an extension of her, instead of my own person. She was sick of beating herself up, so she found a new toy to play with. She wanted me to be as miserable as she was. I'm not a person to her, and I'm so sick of being her personal punching bag."

"I know this is hard," I told her. "We're all here to help you, and we're going to do whatever it takes to make sure you're safe."

"I know, and your friendship means the world to me," Onyx replied. "When I was growing up, my mom sabotaged every friendship I ever had. Every time I thought I found a friend, they'd meet my mom and go running off in the other direction. I was the luckiest girl in the world when you guys welcomed me in, because for the first time in my life, I felt like I had real friends—friends my mother couldn't touch. Our time together living at the safe house was the happiest time of my life, because my mom didn't know where I was and couldn't get in touch with me."

Onyx shuddered. "I thought she might've changed in the time we were gone, that she would realize her mistakes and commit to doing better, but if anything, she's been worse since we've been back. It's like all that time we were gone, she's been plotting new ways to destroy me. I'm *so* happy you guys are my friends, but friends alone can't solve this."

"We're going to do our damndest," I promised. "I'm going to start by talking to the hospital staff and making sure they know she's banned from the building."

Onyx shook her head. "That would help me at my job, but it doesn't solve the problem outside of work. She'll still be blowing up my phone, and if I block her, she'll track me down outside of work. We both know what I need to do, Lucas."

I really hoped it wouldn't come to this. We really enjoyed having Onyx around. She was one of the kindest, caring people I knew, and she always had creative ideas and suggestions that helped the team out. But I already knew what she was thinking, because I knew what it was like to be in her place. I didn't have to put myself in her shoes, because I was already there, and I shared her sentiment. Living in the safe house had been *great*, because for the first time in my life, I'd felt a reprieve from the constant humiliation and dehumanization. Onyx needed a safe house of her own now.

We heard a door open and turned to see Nadine, Chloe, and Talia stepping into the gardens. They looked apprehensive, like they didn't want to interrupt anything, but Onyx stood and waved them over.

"We got rid of that bitch," Chloe said harshly as the three of them entered the gazebo.

Onyx just looked sad. "I appreciate you're trying to cheer me up, but talking shit about my mom isn't going to help. I know what I need to do. I have to leave Octavia Falls. As long as my mother's here, I can't stay. I have to go somewhere where she can't find me or get in contact with me."

"That can't be the only way," Nadine said sadly. "We don't want you to leave."

"I don't want to leave, either," Onyx replied. "But I need to follow my gut, and this is what I feel I have to do right now."

"This isn't a permanent solution," I said gently, though I knew there was nothing I could say to convince her to stay. Her mind was already made up, and I couldn't fault her for her decision.

"I know leaving town isn't going to undo everything she's done to me, but at least I'll have a chance at a good life," Onyx said. "I know the coven needs help right now, and I committed to helping the council restructure our healthcare system, but as long as I'm around my mother, I can't do my job. I wanted to be a leader, and someday, I will be in that position. But to do that, I have to go somewhere where I can be of more service, and I truly believe I'm going to better help our community outside of it."

"Where will you go?" Talia asked.

"With permission from the council, I'd like to go to Malovia," Onyx requested. "I want to be a part of real change, and I think I have what it takes to begin fostering peace with the fae. I want to work on building diplomatic relations with the king and queen there. If I can't be here, that's what I need to be doing."

"It seems you've put a lot of thought into this," I remarked.

"I have," Onyx said. "I've stayed because I thought it was what was best for the coven, but I'm realizing that if I don't have the tools to thrive here, I'm never going to be able to help in the capacity I want to."

"You need to do what's best for you," I stated. "The coven needs you, but if your community can't take care of you and give you what you need, then it doesn't deserve to keep you."

"You come first," Nadine agreed. "Whatever you need to do, you have our full support. We're just really going to miss you."

Onyx choked back tears. "I'm really going to miss you guys, too."

We wrapped Onyx in a group hug and held her for a long time. It was sad and melancholy, because it truly felt like the goodbye hug that it was. This wasn't just some idea Onyx came up with in the heat of the moment. This was real, and we had to come to terms with the fact that one of our closest friends was leaving for good. I didn't know when or if we'd ever see her again.

We didn't want to see her go, but we also didn't fight to make her stay, because no matter how hard this was, we all knew this was what was best for her.

Didn't make it any easier, though.

Onyx finally drew away, wiping her eyes. "Thank you all for being here. I'm ready for this, and that means it's time to turn in my resignation papers."

"I'll come with you," Chloe offered.

Chloe and Onyx headed off in one direction, and Nadine and I followed Talia back to Grant's room.

"Do you think this is the right decision—sending Onyx to make alliances with the fae?" Talia asked as we entered the building.

"I'm not sure," I confessed. "But I do know that sometimes being there for a friend means giving them space, and right now, we have to support whatever Onyx decides."

Nadine sighed heavily. "I wish we could fix everything for our friends. Grant's sick, and Onyx is going through a crisis. Jess is leaving town. Everyone's having problems, and it seems there's nothing we can do about it."

"We can be there for them," I said. "That's all we really can do."

"We need to prepare better for these kinds of things," Nadine insisted.

"The priestesses are still out there building an army. We can't predict what kind of emergencies we might face in the future. If one of us gets sick, or we get separated, we need a way to stay in contact with each other —magical or otherwise."

"I agree," I said. "We've all been learning how to astral travel, and we can use it if all else fails. It's something even humans can do, which means we should be able to use it even if we're cut off from our magic. We need to agree on a place on the astral plane where we can meet if we ever get separated."

We didn't want to bother Grant with any heavy topics, so we stopped outside his room. Through the curtain, I could see that he had fallen asleep.

"We could meet at the Olson estate," Talia offered.

"That's too obvious," I countered. "If the priestesses found out we were on the astral plane, they could come looking for us, and we don't want them messing with our spirits while they're outside our bodies."

We all still wore our protection beads we'd received from Professor Ward after her death. They protected us from astral travelers and spiritual spies. I could still feel the magic pulsing through the beads, and we were protected, for now. Either the priestesses were too preoccupied building their army, or even the Master Wand couldn't break through this spell, because the protection charm hadn't been broken. But that didn't mean the priestesses wouldn't try if they got desperate.

"There's one place they don't know about," Nadine stated. "The abandoned mansion behind the school."

"Everyone knows that place is there," Talia said.

"They know it exists, but they don't know what that place means to us," Nadine pointed out. "They wouldn't think to look for us there."

"That's the perfect spot," I agreed.

"That mansion is protected by magic," Talia pointed out. "Will the spell prevent us from going there on the astral plane?"

Nadine wore a contemplative look. "We've never tried. We should test it out."

"Nadine and I can handle that," I offered. "You should stay here with Grant. We'll let you know what we find."

Talia nodded. "All right. I'll keep you updated on his progress."

Nadine and I left the hospital, and we drove home. The house was empty except for the cats, because Professor Wykoff had taken Marcus and Rose to story time at the library. It was nice coming home to a quiet house in the middle of the day, because we rarely had this time off work.

I kicked off my shoes, and Nadine put on calming music as we climbed into bed together. We had to lock Rishi out of the room, or he'd bat at our faces and wouldn't let us meditate. Isa curled up in Nadine's arms, and Oliver snuggled against my leg.

Nadine curled into me. "Meet you on the other side."

We fell into a deep mediation together, which was getting easier to do the more we practiced. I pictured my spirit melting into the mattress, imagining my body and mind separating. Soon, my body felt as if it was spinning, and I lost all sense of direction as I meditated to the astral plane.

As I became aware again, I found myself transported to the grounds outside the abandoned mansion. We hadn't been there all summer, and it was as beautiful as ever, with ivy growing up the side of the house. The stone steps leading up to the front door were cracked, but there was a charm beneath the layers of overgrown bushes and towering trees. This had been *our* place when we'd been attending Miriam College of Witchcraft, and I didn't realize how much I missed it until now.

The abandoned mansion was even more beautiful on the astral plane. Here, colors didn't quite match up with their shapes, so each ivy leaf glowed a rainbow of ethereal colors, displaying all shades of green at once. The house itself glimmered against the backdrop of a purple sky.

Nadine was already standing on the front steps, waiting for me. Isa's and Oliver's spirits prowled at her feet.

"You made it," Nadine teased.

"I wouldn't miss it," I said.

I was still staring up at the towering turret in wonder. This building was on the verge of falling down on the physical plane, but here, it seemed more solid. It felt like looking at two images at the same time—as if I could see the potential of what this house could be, overlaid against the dangling shingles. I couldn't tell which was real.

I took Nadine's outstretched hand, which was solid against my own, though my skin tingled where we touched. We approached the doorway, and together, we stepped straight through the wall. I got the over-whelming sensation that I was coming home.

Nadine paused in the entryway and looked back at the door. "It looks like the home's protection spell still lets us through on the astral plane."

"Then we can tell the others this is our official meeting place," I said. "Though let's hope we never have to use it."

The sound of a cat meowing caught our attention. Isa and Oliver were standing at our feet in spirit form, but it sounded like it'd come from down the hall. Curiously, I stepped forward.

"Here, little fella," I called, though I didn't know if the cat could hear me.

A cat poked its head out from behind a doorway, perking its ears and tilting its head at us. At first, I thought it was standing on a piece of furniture around the corner, but it leapt out from behind the doorway and appeared to be floating in mid-air. The cat somersaulted in the air, leaving behind a trail of colors. The cat had a solid gray coat of fur, but here on the astral plane, it glowed a bright purple and magenta.

The creature let out a happy trill, and Isa and Oliver leapt into the air to greet the cat, floating alongside it as ethereal beings. The cats sniffed one another, then started licking each others' ears in approval.

"Aww," Nadine cooed. "It's a spirit cat. He must be really lonely living here by himself."

"Technically, not living," I joked.

We stepped forward, and the cat let us scratch him behind the ears. He purred loudly, which seemed amplified in our spirit form. The sound was really comforting.

"I wonder how long he's been here," I mused. "If he was left behind by the previous owners, it's been over a decade."

"He's been here a while," Nadine stated with certainty. "Every time we've come here, I can feel a welcoming but lonely energy. I think this cat has been waiting for company."

"You don't have to wait anymore, buddy," I told him as I stroked his tail. "We're here."

The cat's ears perked up when I said the word *buddy*.

"Is that your name?" Nadine asked. "Buddy?"

The cat jumped, then spun around in a circle.

"Either way, I think he likes it," I said. "Don't worry, Buddy. We'll come to visit you as often as we can."

I scratched him under the chin, and Buddy pulled away to sniff my fingers. He must've decided he really liked me, because he started rubbing his cheeks over my knuckles and purring even louder. Buddy crawled up my arm, until he was standing on my shoulders and nuzzling against my face.

Then he bit me in the ear, and his sharp fangs pierced me as hard.

"Ow, Buddy!" I scolded.

Buddy jumped down from my shoulders and scurried over to the stairs near us. I held my ear, but the pain quickly subsided, like I'd only imagined it.

Nadine chuckled. "You must've done something he didn't like."

"I didn't do anything. I was only petting him."

Buddy cocked his head, and I realized there was intention behind his eyes.

"I think he was trying to get my attention," I said. "It looks like he wants us to follow him."

Buddy hopped down from the stairs and ran down the hall. Isa and Oliver chased after him, and Nadine and I followed. Buddy stopped in front of the door that led to the primary bedroom and pawed at the floor.

It'd been years since Nadine and I had been in this part of the house. Being back here made my heart skip a beat as I thought of the night we'd shared together in this very room. It'd been here that we'd gotten back together after our breakup, and here that we'd seen each other naked for the first time. That night had been a massive turning point in our relationship, and I would forever cherish it.

"I think he wants us to see what's inside." Nadine went to walk through the door, but she stumbled back as if she'd been shocked.

I caught her, though she didn't appear hurt. "You okay?"

She eyed the door curiously. "That's weird. This door shouldn't be solid."

Instinctually, I reached for the door handle to test it out, and my hand met solid metal. I twisted the handle, and the door swung open. I was surprised to see the bedroom I expected to find there was gone, replaced by what appeared to be a small, dark closet. It was filled with all kinds of odds and ends, some of them hovering in mid-air, like gravity didn't exist here. There were two items that stood out amongst the others—a black robe, and a scythe.

I reached out to run my fingers over the smooth fabric of the robe. "It's… mine. All this stuff is mine."

"Lucas, it's your stash!" Nadine exclaimed. "We found it, just like how we found mine back at my dorm room at school during our astral travel lessons."

"I wonder how Buddy knew."

"I think he recognized your scent," Nadine said.

I pulled my reaper robe out of the closet and slipped it on. It was completely solid, and I ran my fingers over the fabric to help make sense of it. "I don't understand why it's *here* of all places."

"You keep your stash wherever you feel safe and at home, right?" Nadine asked. "It makes sense that you would keep yours here, because this has always been a safe place for us."

"But I never came here until I met you," I pointed out. "I had my magic long before then."

Nadine shrugged. "Who's to say the location of your stash can't change? After everything that happened at the school, I'm certain my stash isn't in my dorm room anymore."

"Where do you think it is?" I asked.

Nadine pressed her lips together. "Probably back at the estate, though I'm not sure what door it's behind."

"We could go check," I offered. "It's good to know we can move our stashes, in case their safety is ever compromised."

Nadine bent down to scratch Buddy behind the ears, and he purred loudly. "Thanks for showing us this. We'll be back again to see you. We promise."

Buddy gave a cheerful meow, then bowed his head to say goodbye.

To get back home, all we had to do was visualize where we wanted to go. Our spirits materialized back in the main room of our suite. Isa and Oliver followed us in spirit form. Rishi noticed us right away, circling around our feet like he was happy to see us. I bent to stroke him on the top of the head, but I couldn't touch him in my spirit form.

"My *best* guess is that my stash is at the entrance to our suite," Nadine said, but when she tried the door, her hand went straight through it.

"Maybe the bedroom?" I suggested, only that didn't work, either. We went around the suite trying different doors, but nothing happened.

"The only door we haven't tried is the bedroom closet," I offered.

I stepped straight through the bedroom door, where mine and Nadine's bodies were soundlessly sleeping on the bed. Isa's spirit jumped onto the mattress, and she stared down at her body in Nadine's arms.

Nadine followed me into the bedroom. She tried the closet door, and she let out a gleeful yelp when the door swung open. "I found it!"

The door swung open to reveal a small closet with her things inside. A folded piece of paper floated by our heads.

"Oh, hey. I forgot I had this." Nadine plucked it out of the air.

"What is it?" I asked.

She handed me the piece of paper. "See for yourself."

I unfurled the paper to find my own handwriting on the inside.

Our hands entwined
Just like our fate
The day we met
You stole my heart away

I'm forever yours
I'll always be
Because you'll always have
This part of me

"It's one of the first poems I wrote for you," I realized. "I didn't know you'd kept it."

"Of course I did," Nadine said. "I keep all of them. They're really special. I love looking back on them."

"It means a lot that you keep them," I told her. My body stirred on the bed, and I realized I was starting to wake up.

Nadine noticed, too. "Looks like our time on the astral plane is over."

I held out my hand to give her the poem back, but before I could, the room around me vanished. My eyes opened, and I lay flat on my back on the bed. Nadine awoke beside me, and the cats both stretched as they came out of the meditation.

Nadine rolled toward me, and I curled her in my arms, but I paused abruptly when I heard the crinkle of paper. Nadine looked confused, and we both sat upright. I glanced down at myself to see I was still wearing the reaper robe I'd put on while we were astral traveling, and the poem I'd been holding was in my hands—just as solid as the bed beneath me.

Nadine stared down at the piece of paper. "Lucas, how are you still holding that poem?"

"I don't know." I ran my fingers over the robes, and those were solid, too. "I must've conjured it."

"But the poem wasn't in your stash to conjure," Nadine pointed out. She reached out for it, and it crinkled in her hand. "And if you'd have conjured your robes, you wouldn't be wearing them. This is different than conjuring magic. It's like you pulled objects straight from the astral plane onto the physical, but I don't know how that's possible. I've never heard of magic like that."

"It's got to have something to do with my reaper magic," I theorized. "The reaper plane is another level of existence that goes beyond even the astral plane, so it stands to reason I have some sort of influence on the astral plane that other people don't. If I can move souls between realms, then maybe I'm powerful enough to move objects between planes of existence, too."

"This could be useful," Nadine mused.

What she was getting at clicked immediately. "Do you think the priestesses are hiding something on the astral plane?"

"It could be possible," Nadine theorized. "They might have some sort of weapon that we don't know about hiding there, and if they aren't showing their hand, we don't know what's coming."

"Then I'm going to use whatever spare time I have to keep searching the astral plane," I decided. "We don't have enough information about what the priestesses are planning. We know they're building a golem army to attack on Halloween, but there could be information that we're missing. We could use astral traveling to learn more about their planned attack. We need to make sure, just in case."

We had to at least try, because if the priestesses showed up with even more surprises, we were done for. I needed to get ahead of whatever they were planning.

Otherwise, the coven wouldn't survive the outcome.

EIGHT

The autumn equinox arrived, along with the wedding. Chloe was the most beautiful bride I'd ever seen. We'd fashioned her black hair in a half-updo, and the rest lay over her shoulders in perfect curls. On top of her head sat an elaborate crown that made her look like a queen. Her wedding dress was super sexy, with long sheer sleeves that fell off her shoulders and crystals embedded all over the bodice. The skirt was made of layers of tulle that had a slit going all the way up to her hip. I'd never seen her smile as much as she did today.

Talia, Verla, and I gathered around Chloe in her bedroom that afternoon once our hair and makeup was done. Verla wasn't in the wedding party, but she'd come to help out and watch Marcus while we got ready. Chloe had invited her to stay for the Blessing Brew.

Talia and I were dressed in black off-the-shoulder gowns that Chloe had picked out. Chloe and Miles had kept their wedding party small, and Talia and I were the only bridesmaids. Chloe had wanted Onyx to be a bridesmaid as well, but she'd already left last week in a tearful goodbye, and she wasn't able to make it back for the wedding. Onyx was in Paris now, settling into a supernatural community there. It was the closest neutral settlement to Malovia. Last we heard from her, things were going well, and she felt she'd made the right decision leaving Octavia Falls.

I couldn't help but notice that our group continued to shrink. So many of our friends had left town because it was no longer safe for them here, and we had lost others completely. I found solace in knowing those who'd left were free from danger, but I still missed them.

While Chloe had been getting ready, I'd set up an altar with a cauldron in the center, just like my bridesmaids had done on my wedding day. She'd asked me to lead the ceremony, and I'd be lying if I said I wasn't touched by the invitation.

I took in the glamor as she spun around in her dress. "What do you think?" she asked, before touching her crown to make sure it was straight.

"You look amazing!" Talia raved.

"Absolutely beautiful," Verla agreed as she rocked Marcus back and forth.

"Chloe…" I was at a loss for words. If someone had told me when I met Chloe that I would be standing here on her wedding day, I wouldn't have believed them. I'd have been certain one of us would sooner kill the other than celebrate their love, but that was a poor assumption. Back then, I thought Chloe and I were polar opposites, but the more I got to know her, the more I found we were alike, and her headstrong nature I so much despised at first was actually what I admired about her most.

"You're stunning," I finally said. "But more than beauty, you radiate a regal energy, and I see so much strength, passion, and power in you."

I started to tear up, and I quickly dashed the tears from my eyes.

"It's okay," Chloe said gently. "You don't have to say anything."

I sniffled. "I want to. You deserve to hear it."

I reached for Chloe, and she took my hands. "Chloe, it is an honor to be standing with you on your wedding day. Since I've known you, you've exuded this strength that transcends any limitations or barriers set in place by others. You've always known what you wanted and gone for it, and I admire you for that. You're someone I can look to and say, *I want to be like her*. We were both a mess when we met, and we made mistakes that we can never take back, but to grow up alongside you has been one of the greatest privileges of my life. You've found the one person who has made you the happiest girl in the world, and it's amazing to witness you two come together and help each other grow into better people. I'm lucky to have been your rival, and even more fortunate to be your friend. I love you."

Chloe pressed her fingers to her eyes. "Bitch, I just did my makeup," she chuckled lightheartedly as she wiped away tears. "I love you, too. Thank you for being here."

She pulled me into a hug, and I squeezed her back tightly.

"I'll do my best not to make you cry," I said as I pulled away. "Everyone gather around."

Verla set Marcus in his play pen, and the four of us stood around the altar. Isa, Odin, Marley, and Gus jumped onto the table and began circling the cauldron.

I began to recite the prayer I'd learned. "Mother Miriam, we call upon you to bless this union so that we may celebrate the love between Chloe and Miles, and bring the coven closer together."

The cauldron began to bubble as we recited the Blessing Brew incantation together.

On this night,
this bride becomes a wife.
Through this potion,
take our blessings into a new life.
So shall it be.

Verla stated her blessing first. "Chloe, I gift you ginkgo to symbolize mental clarity. May you be clear in your intentions and communication with your spouse."

"I will be clear," Chloe said as Verla sprinkled the leaves from the altar into the potion.

Talia went next. "Chloe, I gift you ashwagandha, to symbolize energy and vitality. May you have the strength to face any obstacles that come between you and your husband, and the energy to overcome them."

Chloe nodded. "I will be strong."

I picked up my vial of herbs on the altar. "Chloe, I gift you chamomile to symbolize balance. May you find balance in your relationship—to see from both sides and find solutions that work for the good of all, to balance your own emotions, and to know when to remain calm and when to take action."

"I will have balance," Chloe promised.

"Together, our blessings will become one, that you may step into your marriage as a new witch with these blessings to guide the way," I said.

Talia, Verla, and I placed our hands together on a wooden spoon and stirred the cauldron. Our powers mixed, and the potion lit up with a white hue. It seemed a miracle that we were able to brew the potion at all, because we didn't have access to much magic these days. But this potion and this ceremony were an important part of our religion, so we used what we could to bless Chloe on this important day.

"The Goddess has accepted our blessing," I announced. I spooned a small amount into a cup and handed it to Chloe. "Will you accept our blessings as well?"

Chloe took the cup from me. "So shall it be."

She drank the potion and beamed as she set the cup aside.

"Now, we will don the veil, to ward off evil spirits," I said.

Talia and Verla went over to the bed with me, where we'd laid out Chloe's veil. Together we placed it into her hair. The veil was sheer and sparkly, and she looked absolutely divine in it.

"So shall it be," I whispered.

"So shall it be," Talia and Verla echoed in unison.

Chloe sniffled and fanned her face to keep from crying. "I can't believe it's actually happening!"

"Believe it, girl. You've been waiting for this day for a long time. You always talked about wanting to change your last name," Talia joked.

"It's funny you bring that up," Chloe said. "Remember when we started The Coven's Shield and we were all sitting around the Gravestone talking about me changing my name? Miles was like, *You should change it to Bryant.* I said it was a dumb idea, but deep down something about it felt *right*, but I didn't know how to tell anyone that, because it didn't make sense at the time. Looking back I can see that my intuition was telling me we'd be together all along, and I just needed my heart to listen."

"You've made the right choice," Verla told her. "We can all see that you and Miles are very happy together."

"Thank you," Chloe replied. "A lot of our relationship has grown in private. The flirting, the dates, the stories we share with each other—that all happened when other people weren't looking. Sometimes it feels like people don't get us, because they haven't seen the way he looks at me like I'm the only girl in the world, and they can't know that my heart skips a beat every time he enters the room. My parents have barely met him, and while they're here today to support us, they don't quite understand why we're getting married only a year into our relationship."

Chloe picked up her bouquet of white roses from the dresser and ran her fingers over the petals. "But they don't know that Miles is the funniest guy I've ever met, and that when I get too serious about life, he brings me back to a place of security and comfort. They haven't seen how he pulls a chair out for me every time I sit down, or that he opens the door every time I enter a room. Every other guy I dated always told me I was too much and overbearing. I didn't know if I'd actually get married one day, because I knew I'd never compromise who I was for a man. But Miles? He loves every part of me, and he honors the parts that I still have to work on. Through him, I'm truly becoming a better woman. It means a lot to know that our love is recognized. I appreciate you all being here to celebrate that."

Verla smiled. "Of course. Are you ready?"

Chloe took a deep, steadying breath. I'd never seen her so nervous before, but I knew it couldn't be cold feet, because she wasn't the kind of person to second-guess a decision. Chloe was excited, and we were all super happy for her.

"Ready," Chloe said confidently.

Verla picked up Marcus, and the cats all followed at her feet. "Then we'll see you out there shortly. Best of luck, Mrs. Bryant."

Chloe squealed at the sound of her new name. "Goddess, start the ceremony already. I can't wait!"

Chloe's parents arrived to escort her to the ceremony, and the rest of us left to prepare the altar. Outside in the gardens, we'd set up a circle of chairs that guests had already filled, all facing the garden archway that was covered in ivy. The wedding was small, but the guest list was large enough to warrant seating, unlike during mine and Lucas's wedding, where all guests participated in the ceremony. Both Chloe's and Miles's parents were here, along with Miles and Grant's younger brothers, who had traveled with their mom to attend. Several professors sat in the circle around the altar, including Professor Warren and Professor Wykoff, along with Hattie and her Familiar. Rose sat in her wheelchair next to the professors. There were a few other people I didn't know, who I assumed were members of the bride and groom's extended families.

It was late September now, and the ivy around the archway had started turning shades of red and orange. All around us, fall colors graced the landscape. Beautiful flowers bloomed in all different colors, and white and black candles lined the aisles. Chloe had wanted to get married at sunset, and the sun was nearly at the horizon now.

Talia and I stood on one end of the garden, while Grant and Lucas—who served as Miles's groomsmen—stood opposite us at another entrance. Lucas looked really good in his suit, and he caught my gaze and smiled. I noticed Grant and Talia making eyes at each other. It was really good to see everyone happy.

Music began to play over speakers. It was a beautiful melody Talia had written and recorded before the ceremony. The four of us began our way down the garden pathway, until we met beneath the archway at the altar. The couple had hired a professional photographer, and she snapped pictures as we entered.

Chloe and Miles wanted to do an equinox ceremony during their wedding, so they had selected offerings that were set in a bowl atop the altar. A collection of leaves, pinecones, two apples, and a small pumpkin filled the bowl, as a symbolism of the abundance of the fall harvest and their connection with nature. A small pot of dirt, along with a lily bulb, were on the altar as well. Beside the bowl was a candle, as well as four cedar bundles.

Each of us took one of the cedar bundles and lit them with a match, then cleansed the space around the guests. When we were satisfied that the space was clear and protected, we began singing the coven's traditional wedding song.

Hush, now
The time for vows
Is coming all so soon

Tonight we seek
Our mother's blessing
Underneath the moon

Protect this space
And hear our prayers
To bless this sacred union

The guests joined in on the song, but it was only Grant, Lucas, Talia, and me who formed the inner circle and danced with orbs in our hands, which was done to bless the ceremony space. Orbs were one of the simplest spells a witch could create, and still our lights didn't seem as bright as they should be. I only hoped the Waning wouldn't affect the rest of the ceremony. As we danced and sang, Chloe and Miles were led down the aisle by their parents.

Ahead of Chloe came the ring bearer, and my heart melted on the spot when Marcus appeared. Verla had helped strap him into a wagon, which had reigns attached. Kiki and Marley pulled the wagon as if they were tiny horses, which made it look like a miniature fairytale carriage. Talk about baby fever. I wanted another one right now. It was absolutely adorable. Everyone *awed* at our child.

When Miles spotted Chloe, he got the biggest goofy grin on his face. Chloe's eyes lit up, and she appeared impatient as she nearly ran down the aisle. Her parents had to hold her back and remind her to slow down.

Marcus reached the altar, and Lucas pulled the rings from a pillow inside the carriage. Verla helped wheel the wagon to the side, then held Marcus as the ceremony started.

Chloe and Miles met at the altar and joined hands. Talia and I stood on either side of Chloe and pulled her veil back. She glowed from the magic of the ceremony, a symbolism of the light and dark combining.

Grant lifted a hand, and the song faded as the guests took a seat. Miles had asked him to officiate the ceremony, so he stepped forward while Talia, Lucas, and I joined hands to form a circle around them.

"Welcome," Grant said loudly for all to hear. "The bride and groom would like to thank you all for being here, to celebrate and bless their union on this powerful day. The autumn equinox represents a time to reflect on the abundance the previous year has brought, while letting go of the old and welcoming the new."

Grant turned to the couple. "Chloe, Miles. You have chosen me to act as Mother Miriam's proxy, to facilitate this ceremony so that you may be wed in the eyes of the Goddess. Join hands."

The two couldn't seem to touch each other soon enough. They looked like they'd fuck each other right here on the altar if we weren't all watching.

Grant recited the traditional wedding speech. "We are gathered here tonight because you have asked your family and friends to bless your union, so that you may be bound together in this life and become one amongst the coven. We will begin by inviting the community to give their blessings."

Grant spoke to Lucas first. "Do you accept this union?"

"I accept this union and bless the couple with the sign of the wand, to cast your dreams into reality. So shall it be," Lucas replied.

"So shall it be," the guests murmured.

Lucas had chosen the same blessing Miles had given us on our wedding day, which seemed appropriate. It fit the couple well.

I went next and blessed the couple with the sign of the fox, to represent playfulness, so they always remembered to enjoy life and not let it pass them by. Talia blessed them with the sign of a cauldron, so they could alchemize their emotions into empowerment each time. Grant blessed them with the sign of the toad for abundance.

Other guests were welcome to join in the blessing ceremony, and they received blessings of wisdom, courage, communication, and joy.

"Goddess, gods, ancestors, and guides," Grant said. "Descend upon us to bless this union between this witch and warlock through sacred matrimony."

Spiritual lights appeared just as the sun was setting, forming into the image of ancestors I didn't recognize. The spirits seemed to struggle with the connection, though, because their forms blinked in and out of existence.

A few guests gasped, and the ceremony got really quiet as people looked around for an explanation. Chloe and Miles exchanged a worried glance, and Grant hesitated, like he wasn't sure if he should continue.

"Our ancestors aren't rejecting the union, are they?" Miles whispered to Grant.

Chloe quickly steeled her nerves. "It's just the Waning," she said under her breath. "Our magic's growing more unstable by the day, but the ceremony must go on."

Miles nodded. "Keep going," he whispered to his brother.

"Your ancestors will now bless you with a message," Grant announced. He withdrew a wedding deck of tarot cards, and together, Miles and Chloe selected a card from the deck. They pulled the Three of Wands.

"This is a card of foresight, one that shows that your partner is aligned with your goals," Grant stated. "Your relationship will thrive as you come together and share your ideas, plans, and goals to create something new. Lean on each other, and seek guidance within one another, because it is through each other that you will find your strength."

"It's perfect," Chloe whispered to Miles.

"*You're* perfect," he replied, and she blushed.

"And now, the bride and groom would like to perform an autumn equinox releasing ceremony as they express their gratitude and speak the vows they've written," Grant said. He stepped back and joined hands with Talia and Lucas.

Together, Miles and Chloe lit the candle on the altar.

Miles reached into his white suit coat and unfurled a piece of paper. His hands shook as he began reading. "Chloe Jane Olson. When we met, people warned me about you."

The crowd laughed, and Chloe added loudly, "And rightfully so."

"Rightfully so," Miles agreed with a chuckle. "But I was right not to listen. From the moment I met you, I knew you were special. You intrigued me as much as you terrified me, and I have so much gratitude in my heart that I didn't listen to fear. Through our friendship and our partnership, you have shown me a love that I never felt before, and passion I didn't know existed. I'm grateful for the space you hold for me in your heart, the secret moments that we shared when no one else was around, and the strength that you continue to show me every day that makes me want to be a better man. Today, I let go of all my fears, because through you I have learned that even fear can't hold me back, and *nothing* can stop me from loving you."

Miles held the paper over the flame, and the page burned to ashes.

Chloe choked up as she began reading off a paper she'd tucked between the offerings on the altar. "Miles, I cannot tell you how grateful I am to call myself your friend, your girlfriend, your fiancé, and tonight, your wife. There is no ceremony and no promise I can make to express my gratitude that you are in my life. Some days, I question if this is real, because I never truly thought we'd find each other—my best friend and partner, who will stick by my side through anything. I will always cherish the memories we've made, but more than that, I am grateful to have you with me right here right now, and in every moment after. I've never known a love like ours, and tonight, I choose to let go of the love I thought I knew, but was not serving me. Thank you for showing me what love can be. There is no love in this world greater than yours, and I'm beyond grateful to be taking your last name."

Knowing Chloe's background, her vows were obvious. She was leaving her old family behind and becoming part of a new one, though she didn't say it so blatantly in front of her parents. I'd wondered why she wanted them to walk her down the aisle, because it seemed so unlike Chloe, who was fiercely independent. She was the kind of girl to firmly say she could walk her own damn self down the aisle. But I understood it now. It was a symbolism of the family she was parting from, into the family that she'd chosen.

Chloe burned her paper, and I noticed her shoulders drop in relief.

"The couple has shared their gratitude for what has passed, and released what isn't serving them," Grant announced. "Now, they wish to honor their union by performing a *plant your prayer* ritual. The bride and groom will speak their intentions for their marriage, and plant them in the dirt to ground their prayers and give them life. They have chosen to plant their intentions alongside a stargazer lily, to represent love, commitment, prosperity, and the fulfillment of dreams."

Miles pulled another piece of paper from his pocket. "Chloe, today I promise you to always be by your side, to always communicate what I'm feeling, to open every door for you and pull out every chair, to always save you a seat at the table, and to always put the toilet lid down."

Chloe started laughing, but with it came tears that streaked her cheeks.

"My prayer for us is that no matter what hardships we face, and no matter what the future holds, we never stop loving each other. So shall it be." Miles folded his piece of paper and placed it in the pot of dirt.

Chloe sniffled as she began reading her own notes. "Miles, I promise to care for you always in sickness and in health, to work together as your equal in all things, to fiercely defend and protect you, and to always remind you to put the toilet seat down."

Everyone laughed.

"My hope for our future is that just like this flower we are planting together, we continue to grow and to blossom, and that our love may never die," Chloe concluded.

She planted her paper, and together the two placed the lily bulb into the pot, then covered it with dirt. They concluded the ceremony by kneeling beside an oak tree at the edge of the garden and forging their Wedding Wand from the trunk. I noticed they both held a crystal in their hands that they'd reserved specifically for this spell. We'd depleted our crystal stores helping the coven, but this was an important spell for their ceremony, and I wasn't sure they could pull it off without the extra help. A ten-inch wand appeared beneath their hands, with an intricate twisted blade and a heart at the end of the handle. They returned to the altar and exchanged rings.

"Your word is your intention. I now pronounce you warlock and wife!" Grant announced. "You may now seal this union with the show of your love."

Miles dipped Chloe into a kiss, and the magic surrounding their forms exploded upward like fireworks.

"Witches and warlocks, I present to you Mister and Mrs. Bryant!" Grant cried.

The guests cheered loudly, and an upbeat tune started playing over the speakers. The energy of the crowd was palpable, and the happiness I felt for my friends seemed like it could explode out of my chest. The struggles we'd been facing this past year seemed forgotten today, because all there was in this moment was joy.

Chloe and Miles went dancing down the garden path. I took Lucas's hand, and he spun me around as we followed behind them. My skirt swirled around my ankles, and I felt so carefree surrounded by family and friends. Talia jumped on Grant's back, and the two laughed cheerfully as he piggybacked her down the aisle. The photographer smiled brightly and quickly snapped their photo.

"Send me that picture," Grant told her. "We're framing that!"

"You've got it," the photographer replied.

We were all laughing as we left the gardens and made our way into a large white tent set up in the backyard. Lucas wrapped his arm around my waist, and I leaned into him. The sun had set now, but inside the tent were hundreds of candles that lit up dinner tables and a dance floor.

"That was beautiful," I said. "I'm so glad Chloe and Miles got the wedding they wanted."

Lucas smiled. "It brings back good memories of our wedding."

I noticed he added the *good* caveat. Our wedding night had been tainted with the arrival of the Executors at the safe house, but everything before that moment had been happy and joyful. I cherished those last few moments with my grandmother, and I'd never forget how happy we were during the ceremony. It was nice to revisit that joy and witness our friends celebrating their love.

But it also put me on edge. The priestesses had found a way to ruin mine and Lucas's wedding night. I worried that they might try to do the same tonight. Miles had recruited a bunch of guys from the police force to run security, though, so if the priestesses tried anything, we'd be alerted right away.

As the night wore on, I relaxed. We hadn't heard anything from the priestesses in months. It was unlikely they'd strike tonight. We deserved a night off from worrying about the future, to just enjoy this moment with our friends.

Lucas and I sat beside each other at the head table, and we traded off feeding Marcus throughout dinner. We feasted on tender pork roast, roasted potatoes and squash, braised corn, and the best apple cider in town.

After dinner, Talia's brother Tyler grabbed the microphone to shout, "Let's get this party started!" Music blasted over the speakers as he pressed a button on his computer.

Chloe had hired Tyler to DJ for the wedding. She'd wanted a live band, but seeing as the Wicked Warlocks had broken up, Tyler agreed to DJ the party rather than show up as a singular Wicked Warlock. She was willing to compromise, and I was glad she did, because Tyler was really good. He played a lot of fun songs and kept the guests entertained by telling jokes between songs.

"Hey, why aren't there any vampires at this wedding?" he asked the guests. "Because they suck!"

The crowd roared in laughter, and it felt great to let our guard down for once. Chloe and Miles shared their first dance, and they looked like the happiest couple in the world spinning around the dance floor. Professor Wykoff offered to hold Marcus while Lucas and I stepped onto the dance floor for a slow song. My husband pulled me close, and I felt warm and safe in his arms. He seemed relaxed as he swayed me back and forth, which was certainly a first in a long time. I leaned my head against his shoulder and sighed heavily.

Lucas noticed. "Everything all right, Nad?"

I turned my back to Chloe and Miles, so they wouldn't see the concern that I knew was plainly written across my face. "I'm just worried. Have you learned anything on the astral plane yet?"

Lucas frowned. "No. I've been astral traveling every day, but the priestesses have too many protections in place. I can't get through to see if they're hiding anything there."

"Maybe we're being paranoid and they don't have anything else planned," I suggested hopefully.

"If they do, the astral plane isn't giving us any answers."

I forced a smile on my face. "We don't have to talk about work right now. As long as the priestesses stay away tonight, we can enjoy this peaceful evening."

Lucas took in the wedding around us. "I suppose even in the worst times, life still goes on."

"You're right," I agreed. "We're still technically in the middle of a war with the priestesses, and rebuilding the town is a work in progress. It'd be so easy to feel like giving up right now, but we're *here*. In the midst of it all, we can still watch our friends get married and start a new life together, and that's so beautiful. It reminds me why we're doing all this, because love is most important. It gives me hope."

Lucas rubbed my back as we spun around. "I agree. This all makes me feel really good."

"Good enough to take this dress off me later?" I winked at him. We'd been so busy lately that we didn't have a lot of time for intimacy. Just being close to him was making me want to go back to our room right now.

Lucas smirked. "I'm sure that can be arranged."

"It's late," I said. "We should probably get Marcus to bed."

Lucas looked over to Professor Warren, who was shaking a rattle at Marcus. Our son grabbed it and stuck it in his mouth.

"He seems all right for now," Lucas replied.

Clearly, I had to be more direct, because that one went way over his head.

"Lucas, we should get Marcus to bed so that *we* can get to bed." I wiggled my eyebrows very obviously.

"Oh," Lucas dragged out the word. "Yeah, he's very tired."

The party was already winding down at this point. We said goodbye to everyone and returned to our suite with Marcus and our cats. It was late, so Marcus fell asleep in my arms before we even made it back to our room. We tucked him into his bassinet in the living room and left our cats to watch over him.

Lucas took my hand and pulled me into the bathroom. He playfully pinned me up against the back of the door and grabbed my ass as he kissed me. I melted beneath his touch, and my panties became wet at his masculine scent.

"Is this what you want?" Lucas asked, running his lips over my jawline.

"More," I begged breathlessly.

Lucas kissed me tenderly, and I nearly crumbled at his feet when he drew away. "Let's get you out of that dress," he whispered.

I turned around, and Lucas slowly unzipped me. My heart hammered as the fabric fell away. I stripped down completely, and he helped remove the bobby pins from my hair. He was so gentle and slow with me, which was driving me mad. I yearned to have him inside me already.

"I need to wash my hair," I said, touching the strands. "I have so much product in it."

Lucas kissed the top of my shoulder. "I can help with that."

He stripped out of his suit and hung it on a hook. I warmed up the water, and we stepped into the shower together. I stood facing away from him, leaning my back against his warm body. Lucas worked the shampoo through my hair tenderly, then rubbed the suds over the rest of my skin. I moaned as his hands traveled over my breasts, then down between my legs. It felt really nice to be this close to him.

I helped him wash up, too, then lowered myself to my knees and began pleasuring him with my mouth. If there was one thing that never failed to turn my husband on, it was my lips on his cock. I was really enjoying myself, and I got a thrill in my belly when he began to respond to my touch. I worked him with my tongue and pumped his dick with my hand until he filled my mouth completely. Warm water cascaded over us, and Lucas's fingers tangled in my hair.

"Take me," I begged.

Lucas picked me up, and my legs wrapped around him as his hands cupped my ass. He held me against him as I slid downward, his dick effortlessly gliding into me. I tilted my head back and moaned in pleasure as he thrust upward. Fuck, it felt so good.

Lucas leaned my back against the wall of the shower and pinned me there while he fucked me. I couldn't stop myself from panting, because it was so hot and sexy.

Eventually, he couldn't keep holding me upright, and we had to switch positions so he was fucking me from behind. My breasts pressed into the cool tile of the shower wall, and I enjoyed every second of the sensations.

We must've been in the shower for twenty minutes. The shower water was starting to cool, and Lucas drew away, panting. "Should we... take this to the bedroom?"

"Absolutely."

We got out of the shower and dried off. We made our way to the bedroom, and Lucas playfully tossed me onto the bed. I caught sight of his reaper robe hung on a hook by the door, and my eyes locked on it.

Lucas noticed. "You like my reaper robe?"

"Hell, yeah," I told him. "Your powers are sexy. You should put it on. I dare you."

Lucas smirked. "It's been a long time since we dared each other to do anything. I like that you're being playful."

Lucas pulled his robe off the hook and slipped it on. I chuckled as I reached out to pull the hood over his head.

"You like the dark and mysterious vibe?" he asked.

"Absolutely. You can keep the robe on. I think it's hot." I leaned over the side of the bed, shaking my ass at him. "Take me from behind, Lucas. Show me what a bad reaper can do to me."

Lucas smiled as he stood behind me and smacked my ass lightly. I moaned playfully when the sleeve of his robe touched my bare skin.

"Am I the bad guy, or have *you* been a bad girl?" he growled in my ear, which was really fucking hot.

"Oh, I've been a *very* bad girl," I giggled.

Lucas and I hadn't gotten much into role playing, and we certainly weren't the kind of couple to tie each other up and punish one another. We didn't really do the dominant-submissive thing, but it was still fun to joke around and get playful with it.

He grabbed my hair and tugged on it lightly, leaning over to whisper in my ear. "You know what reapers do with bad girls? They take them to realms they've never been before."

"Take me, then," I begged breathlessly.

He opened his robe, revealing his hard cock, then thrust into me firmly from behind. I moaned loudly as he buried himself deep inside of me.

I grabbed the sleeve of his robe and yanked hard on the fabric. "Harder, Lucas."

Lucas grabbed my hips and thrust his hips forward.

"Fuck!" I cried out desperately as his cock filled me up. Heat spread up and down my skin, and I had to bury my face in the pillow to keep from screaming out in pleasure. I was loving every second of this.

Lucas's moans filled the room as he pulled my hips into him with every thrust. Each sensation was stronger than the last. He leaned over me and bit my shoulder—gently, but oh so sensually.

As my passion grew, I slid my hand between my legs, but Lucas entwined his fingers in mine to stop me. "Allow me."

"Lucas," I pleaded. "I need my release."

"Don't worry, darling," he whispered. "You'll have it."

He began working my clit, and a glorious sensation built up inside of me. Stars burst across the back of my lids as I reached my peak. I contracted around his cock as I came, moaning loudly with the incredible climax.

I sagged to the bed, completely losing control of my body. I'd become so entranced by the blissful sensations. Lucas opened his robe further to press his skin against mine. I lay on my stomach as he fucked me from behind. That must've been his final undoing.

Lucas moaned as he emptied himself inside of me. He rolled over and curled me in his arms as I rested my head on his chest.

"That was amazing," he breathed.

"It really was," I replied dreamily. "We haven't gotten much time alone lately, and I cherish these moments of bliss."

"Me, too." Lucas gave a shudder, and I noticed his skin turn cold for a second before returning to normal.

"You alright?" I asked.

"Yeah, just a dying thought," he admitted. "Lately, the voices of the recently deceased don't come in as loud and clear as they used to, due in part to the Waning. This one seemed really melancholy, with tones of shock and regret. Those ones are always a bit louder."

"You seem to be handling it better," I remarked.

"I am." Lucas wrapped me closer in his arms and kissed the top of my head. "Thanks for being here and not giving up on me. It really means a lot."

"I'll always be here for you," I promised. "I know we've both been trying to hold ourselves together these last few months, and things haven't been easy. Taking time for ourselves isn't a luxury we have as new parents or Imperium Council members. But in the midst of it all, we still had this perfect day, and when I'm with you like this I see that we can still honor our connection even when we're trying to help everyone else."

I knew we both felt the strain in our relationship, but I didn't realize just how much of a toll it was taking until I said it out loud. Our relationship was suffering because we were putting all our effort into helping other people instead of ourselves. I didn't want to have to choose anymore. My people needed me, but so did my husband, and *I* needed *him*.

"Honoring our connection is really important to me," Lucas said. "I want to honor it in every way, both in the bedroom and out of it."

"We'll work on it," I promised. "Together."

A *bang* sounded as the front door of our suite burst open. My heart dropped, and the color drained from Lucas's face.

"Marcus!" we cried in unison.

Lucas leapt out of bed and shoved the gap in his robe closed as he raced into the main room where Marcus was sleeping. I threw on a nearby bathrobe and ran out behind him.

Talia stood opposite Lucas, panting like she'd run to get here. "Miles just got a call from the police station. They have an Executor in custody. Everyone else is already on their way downtown. They need you both down there. Now."

NINE

So much for a peaceful evening. Nadine and I got dressed in record time. Talia stayed with Marcus while we hurried down to the police station. Our tires squealed as I slammed on the brakes in front of the building. I shoved the car into park, and we ran inside.

Miles wrapped his arms around Chloe, while Grant paced back and forth with clenched fists. The newlyweds hadn't had a chance to change their clothes yet and were still in their wedding attire.

"This is bullshit!" Chloe cried. "Of all nights, he had to show up here on *my* wedding night! This bastard is going to pay!"

"Bring us up to speed," I demanded as Nadine and I marched into the station.

"One of the escaped Executors was found lurking around the perimeter of town—in the flesh. No golems this time. Three officers went after him, and unfortunately…" Miles choked up, but he took a deep breath to steady himself. "Unfortunately, Professor Blackbird was hit by a spell, and our assistant sheriff is no longer with us."

"Let me at him," Grant growled. "I'll kick his ass."

"Where's the Executor now?" Nadine asked.

"My officers immobilized him and brought him in," Miles replied. "It's up to the council what to do with him. We can start building the execution block the second you give the orders—"

"No!" I cut him off. "No more executions."

I shot a glance at my friends, and I could tell by the wary expressions on their faces that we were all in agreement. Chloe seemed particularly reserved, though I didn't know why.

"We agreed to run this coven differently than the council before us," I added. "I don't care what his crimes are. We'll find another way to handle this."

"Lucas is right," Nadine agreed. "We chose to lead with love, and that applies to *all* coven members."

"What do you want to do with him?" Miles asked.

"I want to talk to him," I said.

Miles gestured down the hall. "He's all yours."

Nadine and Grant followed me down the hall, and we entered the holding cell area. I could feel my energy drain immediately at the presence of noxite in the cell bars. Two officers stood guard at the entrance to make sure the Executor didn't escape again. A broad-shouldered man sat on a bench in the farthest cell with his back toward us. Although he wasn't facing us, I recognized him immediately.

It was Ryan Greyson, former leader of the Treacherous Tarantulas. He was the last of his little gang left, though by now I was sure he'd started a new gang with Cody, Leroy, and James. Those four were peas in a pod. Ryan had been one of the priestesses' loudest supporters and among the most ruthless Executors.

I now understood Chloe's hesitation earlier and why she hadn't followed us into the holding cells. Ryan was Chloe's ex-boyfriend, and though I didn't think she felt any love for him anymore, I wondered if there was a small part of her that still cared. It also made sense why Miles wanted to go trigger-happy on him. Ryan had broken Chloe's heart, and Miles didn't want anyone around who could hurt his wife. Ryan was going to be an absolute *joy* to talk to.

I held a hand up to Nadine and Grant, gesturing for them to stay behind me. Nadine wanted to lead with love, but I wasn't counting on that working here. I knew how Ryan ticked, and the only way to get him to talk was to rile him up, unfortunately.

"Well, well, well." I clicked my tongue as I approached his cell. "If it isn't Ryan Greyson. I thought the former priestesses would've gotten sick of your mouth running and taken out the trash by now."

Ryan scoffed, but he didn't turn to me. "Don't act so surprised. You'd know if I were dead. I'm certain you're just waiting for the day you hear my voice enter your head."

"The voices have been pretty quiet lately, actually," I stated coolly. "Funny how the death toll falls when you stop murdering your own people."

Ryan finally turned toward me, curling his lip up in disgust. "Don't act like you're better than them. *Former priestesses?* As if you can just sit in their place and call it your own? You're a fake."

"I assure you the work I'm doing here is very real," I said, though I didn't see any reason to try convincing him. He'd already made up his mind. "Where are your friends?"

"I came alone," he stated bluntly.

As if I would believe that. "Why would you do that?"

Ryan shot to his feet so fast that I jumped back a step. He lunged toward the bars like a rabid dog, shaking them violently. Spittle flew from his mouth as he shouted, "My friends are dead! Finn, Nolan, Declan, Corbin—all my brothers are fucking gone, and it's your fault!"

I hadn't been the one to kill his friends, but whatever. I could see where the priestesses would convince him it was my doing.

"Everyone I cared about had their lives ripped away from them, and the priestesses want to *bide their time,*" Ryan sneered. "I'm done waiting for my revenge. The priestesses are taking too long, so I came to finish the job myself."

"You really think you can walk in here on your own and just… take me on yourself?" I asked. Honestly, I was confused by his thought process. Probably wasn't thinking at all, I guess.

Ryan cocked his head toward Nadine and Grant, who were standing near the door. "Take on you, your weakling girlfriend, and your lame-ass sidekick? Yeah, I'd do it all in one night and feel no remorse."

"You really thought we'd have no security measures in place and you'd just walk into town unnoticed?" I demanded.

"If those officers hadn't spotted me before Professor Blackbird got there, yeah," Ryan said with a shrug.

The dying thought I'd heard earlier came back to me. *We were supposed to do this together.*

At the time, I thought the elderly man's voice expressed sadness about dying without his loved ones, but I'd completely misinterpreted it. It'd been Professor Blackbird's thought.

The pieces fell into place as the realization hit me. "You intended to reach Blackbird so he could escort you into town," I accused. "He's the one who let all you Executors out of the cells that day the hospital was bombed."

It was clear by his last thought that he regretted trusting Ryan and trying to help him. Professor Blackbird had suggested Lincoln had been the one to let the Executors out, even though we weren't able to find any evidence to pin it on him. Blackbird had accused the guy intentionally to thwart suspicion off himself. For once, I actually believed what Ryan was saying.

"Congratulations!" Ryan mocked. "You're so *smart*, Taylor. Couldn't see who was working for the other side when he was staring you right in the face, though, could you? You trust too easily."

Ryan wasn't exactly wrong, but he said it as if it was a moral failing. It was true that we'd put our trust in the wrong people far too many times, but the alternative was to trust no one at all. If we resorted to that, we wouldn't have any allies at all, and we'd never accomplish anything.

We'd thought Professor Blackbird had been one of those allies. He'd been friends with Professor Wykoff, who had stood up against the priestesses to protect us more than once, and Professor Daniels, who had been an ally to her dying day. He stood up against the Executors the night the space-bending spell on the school failed. I thought Blackbird was like our other allies, but I'd been wrong. If he'd been on our side at any point, he'd clearly changed his tune in the time we'd been away. Blackbird was ex-military, and he'd been hired as the assistant sheriff for his experience, but I realized now we should've been more cautious about that. Guys like him were trained to answer to the highest authority, and to him, that would always be the priestesses.

"If Blackbird was on your side, why'd you kill him?" Grant asked. "The police said he was hit by a spell when they brought you in. Were you afraid he was going to talk?"

Ryan gave a cold laugh. "Blackbird knew nothing. He only did as he was told. I didn't intend to kill him. I was aiming at the other guy."

It disgusted me how nonchalant he was about it, like Blackbird was merely a casualty he couldn't give a fuck about.

"You gonna hang me for it?" Ryan taunted. "Gonna execute me for my *crimes*? You can't wait to get rid of me, can you, Taylor? Might as well get it over with, or the priestesses will beat you to it."

"What game are you trying to play?" Nadine demanded. "The priestesses aren't known to kill their followers."

"Of course they would," Ryan said simply. "I went against their orders, and I have nothing to show for it. I failed, and now I'm done for. Either you're going to do the honors, or the priestesses will finish me off once they get here."

Ryan seemed resolved to his fate, because he slowly sank back down onto the bench in his cell, staring ahead at the blank wall in front of him. "It won't be long now."

I didn't like the ominous way he said that. "What do you mean?" I demanded.

Ryan didn't respond, which pissed me off.

I stomped up to the bars and got as close to him as I possibly could. "*What do you mean*? The golems we captured said the priestesses would be here at harvest's end. That's Halloween, which is weeks away."

Ryan merely smirked, clearly enjoying that he was getting a rise out of me, but he still wouldn't talk.

"Tell us, or so help me—"

"You'll what?" Ryan cut me off, finally turning his mischievous gaze on me. "You'll torture it out of me?"

He knew exactly how to toy with me. It was clear my friends and I had no intention of executing or torturing anyone, and Ryan was challenging us to go against our morals. It was a dare I wasn't willing to take, even for all the headache he'd caused us in the past. Resorting to such measures would undo all the progress we'd made in the last few months, and Ryan knew we weren't going to go down that road.

He didn't really seem to care, either, because he knew there was no way out of this. Either we killed him, or we would keep him locked in this jail cell, where the priestesses would find him and finish him off themselves. They wouldn't hesitate to make him an example to keep the rest of their followers in line.

"Ryan, if you don't tell us what the priestesses are planning, then they will come here and level the entire coven," I urged. "This isn't about us— this is about the thousands of people who will be caught in the crosshairs.

Frankly, my friends and I can handle death, but to let everyone else suffer for us? No. Not going to happen."

Ryan didn't move, as if he hadn't heard me at all.

"Isn't there anyone else left you care about?" I demanded. "Anyone you'd wish to save from the priestesses' wrath? Because if you don't talk and they bring their army before we're ready for them, then *everyone* is going to die. There won't be a coven left, and everything you fought for will be for nothing! They don't care about these people, Ryan. All they want is to be in charge, and if they can't have their way, then no one can."

Ryan was as stone cold as a statue, and I realized there was absolutely *nothing* I could say to get through to him.

"What happened to you?" I asked hollowly as I took a step back. "We used to be friends. You used to be a good person. Something changed in you when we went to college. I couldn't understand how you passed your Evoking Ceremony after getting into the drugs and treating people like a complete shithead. I thought one day it might make sense but… maybe you were never the person I thought you were to begin with."

I thought I saw a muscle twitch in Ryan's jaw, but still, he didn't respond. And he wouldn't. He'd said all he wanted to say, and now there was nothing left for him.

I turned away in frustration. "He's not going to talk. Come on."

Nadine and Grant followed me out of the holding cells, but both were seething once we made it to the end of the hall.

"We *need* Ryan to talk!" Nadine insisted.

"How?" I stopped before the door at the end of the hall. "For all we know, Ryan is screwing with us."

"He probably is, but right now, we know nothing except what the golems told us," Nadine pressed. "Getting Ryan to talk could give us a huge advantage."

"I'm telling you he's done talking." I pushed the door open, and we returned to the front of the station where Miles and Chloe were waiting.

Chloe had been pacing, but she stopped when she saw us. "Did he say anything?"

"He outed Professor Blackbird as the traitor who let him out last summer," I said. "Claims he killed him by accident tonight. That's about all we got, apart from some insults."

"Ryan also said, *It won't be long now,*" Nadine added. "That could mean the priestesses are on their way, but he didn't say anything more. He obviously knows something."

"I'll give it to him, that guy's got a thick skin," Grant said with a sigh. "Even if we *did* resort to torture, I don't think he'd crack."

"No, he wouldn't," Chloe agreed.

"Goddess damn it," I growled, smacking a hand on a nearby desk. "We're not going to torture anybody, but we have to do *something*. Our whole philosophy of ruling with love isn't working! Love only cooperates with love, and Ryan wouldn't know love if we shoved it up his ass. Now we have to make a difficult decision to throw him out of the coven, execute him, or let him continue hurting people, none of which are an option."

Nadine crossed her arms and pursed her lips. "There has to be another way. We can still operate with love. I know we can."

"I'm open to suggestions," I said, though anything other than letting the priestesses come for Ryan seemed futile.

Slowly, Nadine's gaze traveled over to Chloe. "Maybe he'll listen to you."

"If you think Ryan ever loved me, you're insane," Chloe said. "But... I can think of one person he loved."

I scoffed. "Did it happen to be the face in the mirror?"

Chloe frowned, clearly not amused. "I'm talking about his grandma, Lola. His parents split when he was a kid, and his grandma took custody. If there's anyone left he cares about, it's her."

"Let's get her here then," I demanded.

Miles quickly started barking orders, and several officers were already on the move to bring Ryan's grandmother in. They returned within half an hour.

Lola was a short, elderly woman with salt and pepper hair and cat-eye glasses. I'd met Lola many times before, back when Ryan and I were friends, but I hadn't seen her in years. I recognized the permanent purse of her lips, which was usually followed up by, *What trouble are you boys getting into this time?*

Apparently, Lola had dealt with enough of Ryan's shit, because she didn't seem at all shocked or worried when she entered the station. Instead, she merely sighed as she set her purse on one of the desks like she owned the place.

Her eyes landed on me instead of one of the officers. "Take me to him."

"I'll show you the way," I offered.

I led Lola down the hall, past the officers standing guard, and into the holding cell area. Nadine followed close to me, but the others stayed behind. Ryan obviously heard our footsteps, but he didn't turn toward us. Nadine and I kept our distance, while the heels of Lola's shoes clicked as she approached his cell.

Lola stood there for nearly a minute, waiting for Ryan to do something. He didn't move. Finally, she cleared her throat. Slowly, Ryan turned, like he wasn't sure if he was hearing things. His eyes went slightly wide when he saw her.

"Good to see you're back in town," Lola stated flatly, sounding wholly disappointed in him.

Ryan shot a wary glance my way, then turned his gaze back to his grandma. "Unless you're here to bail me out, you can leave."

"I don't believe bail's an option," Lola stated. "I heard you killed a man tonight."

"Accidents happen," Ryan said coolly. "You shouldn't have bothered coming, Gran."

"Why wouldn't I?" Lola's voice grew stern. "You're my grandson. I promised you long ago that I'd drop everything in a heartbeat to be there for you if you were in trouble. I don't intend to break that promise."

Ryan blew a hopeless breath. "You can't help me, Gran. I got caught, and now it's over. Now I just wait for my sentencing."

Lola tilted her head. "You think I came here to save you from *the authorities*? Ryan, you greatly misunderstand. I came to save you from *yourself*."

Ryan looked taken aback. "What's that supposed to mean?"

"Nobody made you come here and kill that man," Lola said calmly. "Your trouble is not with these people, but with what's going on inside of you. Nobody can help you and give you what you need if you are not willing to help yourself."

Ryan wore a confused expression, as if his grandmother was speaking another language.

"Do you recall the breathing exercises we used to do together when you were a kid?" Lola asked. "You loved meditating with me. Breathe with me now."

Lola inhaled a deep, audible breath.

"You can save your new-age lecture," Ryan spat. "Meditation's not going to fix anything."

"My dear, you're missing the point," Lola replied. "I'm not telling you to breathe to calm down. I'm reminding you of the lesson I taught you long ago. Love is like breathing, Ryan. We can breathe together, but I can't take your breaths for you. All I can do is lead by example and serve others by breathing in a rhythm they can follow. But you need to do your part and tune in. People can be by your side to help out, but no one has the ability to take your pain away but yourself."

Ryan scowled. "Fuck off."

Lola remained surprisingly calm as she closed her eyes to take another deep breath. "Breathe with me, Ryan," she pressed, her tone growing more urgent. Ryan just sat there. "You aren't breathing! *Breathe, Ryan. Breathe.*"

"I AM BREATHING!" Ryan screamed as he leapt from the bench and smacked his palms against the cell bars. The *clang* rang throughout the room. "You'd rather I suffocate?"

"I want you to see the lesson here," Lola replied.

"I've learned my lessons!" Ryan seethed. "I know how this world works, and I've seen first-hand that no one's going to watch out for you but yourself. I did *everything* for you, Gran, and at the end of the day, I'm still sitting in this jail cell with nothing to show for it. Who was the one who risked everything to raise the money to pay your doctor bills when you couldn't work anymore? That was *me*. Everyone wants to know how a guy like me passed his Evoking Ceremony. It should be obvious to every goddamn person in this town that I did it for you! I didn't get into dealing drugs because I needed the hit. I did it to keep you here, to keep you alive, to have more time with *you*, because *someone* had to pay the rent and put food on the table. I put my neck on the line for you and did everything the priestesses asked of me, because they promised me they could fix everything. You gave me the world growing up, and all I wanted was to give it back to you. And now you just want to tell me to *breathe*? To *just calm down* and get over it? What a fucking insult to everything I've done for you."

Lola took a step back. "I'm terribly sorry, dear. If you can't understand that I'm trying to help you, but I need your consent to do so, then there's nothing more I can do… no matter how much I love you."

Then she turned on her heel and started for the door, breezing past Nadine and me. I witnessed the anguish on Lola's face. She tried to hold it in, but tears spilled from her eyes before she made it to the door. She kept her back to her grandson so he couldn't see.

"Gran. Gran!" Ryan shouted after her, but she kept on moving.

She paused for a beat at the doorway, but she didn't turn back as she whispered, "Goodbye."

Ryan sagged against the bars of his cell, until he'd fallen to his knees. A mournful cry filled the room, and his shoulders shook in agonizing sobs. "Gran!"

I'd never seen Ryan shed a tear in his life—didn't know he was capable of it, to be honest. Despite the way he'd treated my friends and me throughout the years, and everything he'd done as an Executor, witnessing his breakdown was absolutely heartbreaking.

Ryan didn't understand what his grandma was trying to say, but I heard her message loud and clear. He never would. More than that, I didn't think he *could* understand her.

It occurred to me then as I watched Ryan sink to the floor of his cell, looking so helpless and drained, that he wasn't the terrible, heartless person I thought he was. Ryan was everything I could've become—what *any one of us* could've become. Hell, some of the decisions I'd made weren't so different from his. We both just wanted to protect the people we loved, though we disagreed on the methods.

Nothing excused the choices he'd made, but I realized that maybe from his perspective, he didn't have the means to make any other decisions. He didn't have the tools or resources, and he truly didn't understand how. He was merely a wounded person who never learned that he didn't have to settle with the hand he'd been dealt in life. It was wholly tragic.

I turned toward Nadine, who wore a sad expression as she watched Ryan's cold exterior fracture before our eyes. I took her fingers in mine as the weight of the decision fell over me. "I know what we have to do."

Her eyes glimmered as she looked up at me, and understanding crossed her features. "It's a huge risk that could undo all our progress."

"We need to," I told her.

"All right," Nadine agreed, before turning to the officers. "Unlock his cell."

"Priestess," the first officer protested. "He's a dangerous criminal."

Nadine lifted her chin higher. "Yes, and he's going to get his chance to answer for his crimes. Open his cell door."

The officer stepped forward to fit a key into the lock. Ryan just sat there on the ground, appearing completely defeated.

I stepped into his cell and grabbed him by the back of the collar. He was a big guy, but I managed to drag him to his feet. He didn't even protest. The officers aimed their wands at him in warning.

"Let's get this over with," I said, clapping him on the back.

Ryan kept his gaze down as I led him out of his cell and down the hall.

"How are you going to do it?" he asked hollowly. "Are you going to draw the execution out—make me *suffer*?"

We turned a corner, and power flooded through me again once we were far enough away from the noxite. "Who said anything about an execution? You and I are going to finish our warlock's duel."

My magic bloomed outward in an instant, and a portal opened beneath our feet. Ryan and I went tumbling through the portal.

We fell out of the treetops and into the middle of a dark forest far past the edge of town. I rolled on my side a couple of times, before coming to a stop at the base of a tree. I didn't give myself a second to catch my breath before I was on my feet.

Ryan was already moving in for the attack, and a deathly battle spell flew in my direction. I ducked, and the spell exploded against a tree behind me, making such a loud *boom* that it rocked the forest. I threw a stunning spell in his direction, but he jumped behind a thick trunk. The spell missed him.

Ryan gave a deranged laugh. "Of course you'd want to finish me off yourself!"

Tree branches snapped from overhead, and Ryan used his telekinesis to send sharp branches flying at me like arrows. I threw up a shield, and the branches splintered against its surface.

I thrust my shield outward, causing trees to bow and snap under my power. Tall, powerful maple trees that had stood for at least a century toppled over. Ryan jumped out of the way, until the two of us stood in a newly formed clearing under the stars.

Ryan thrust his hand outward, catching my ankle with his telekinetic powers. With the flick of his wrist, I was swept off my feet and left hanging six feet above the ground. Ryan drew his arm back, and the intense power of a killing spell crackled in his palm.

"Praeligo hostilis!" I shouted. The binding spell was a difficult one to pull off, and it nearly took all my strength, but I'd done it before and knew I could do it again.

Ryan's spell died in his hand. His arms pinned to his sides, and he collapsed to the ground.

I fell from the air, doing a flip that landed me on my feet in a crouch. I jumped upward, conjuring my magical scythe as I raced across the clearing. The scythe glowed bright with the power of its enchantment. Within an instant, I was standing over top of Ryan, the tip of my scythe pressing into the side of his neck. Just one swing, and this weapon could take his head clean off his shoulders.

It reminded me so much of the position we'd been in before, when we'd first declared a warlock's duel outside the Cat-fé all those years ago. Students had surrounded us and hyped up the fight before Professor Warren stepped in and called it off.

Ryan heaved heavy breaths. "Picking up right where we left off, eh? No one's around to save me now, so I guess that means you win."

My shoulders sagged in relief. "Finally. We can declare this duel over."

"Then what are you waiting for?" Ryan demanded. "Stop standing around and do it already!"

I took a step back and slowly lowered the scythe to my side. "I don't have to kill you to end this."

Ryan had declared my victory, which meant the duel was finally over. I knew it, because I felt an intense and powerful energy wash over me. I'd learned how to harness the power of Death magic, and just like the Death card in the tarot deck, Death was an energy of transformation. We had reached the end of a cycle, and a rebirth was already starting to take place with the power of one single decision. The magic pulsing through me now was more than enough to rip Ryan's soul from his body in an instant, to destroy his soul completely from the inside out. But there was only one thing I wanted to destroy—and that was all the malice, hatred, and resentment we'd chosen to carry with us until this moment. We didn't have to get along, but we didn't have to keep fighting, either.

I released the spell binding him, and Ryan pushed himself to his elbows, blinking incredulously. "W—what is this? Are you trying to prove you're better than me or something?"

I shook my head. "I don't think I'm better than you. I believe we all have our demons. That doesn't excuse or condone wrongdoings, but I think that can help us understand each other better. I don't believe we should ever use our demons to hurt each other, but I understand if you felt you didn't have any other choice."

"So… you're letting me go?" Ryan asked warily.

"I'm giving you the chance to make a choice," I said. "Your gran was trying to teach you back there that the path you walk is up to you. The question is, where are you going to go now, Ryan?"

I lifted my hand to conjure a small crystal. The transformational energy pulsing through the clearing began to concentrate as a pinpoint of light hovering above my palm. White light illuminated the entire forest, and Ryan had to shield his eyes from the intensity. The magic funneled into the crystal, until the power of our transformation manifested into physical form.

The light dimmed, and the magic pulsing through my body ebbed away, bound now into the crystal in my hand. I held the crystal out toward Ryan.

He hesitated. "What is it?"

"It's a new beginning," I told him. "I can't do this for just anyone. This is once in a lifetime magic. The magic within this crystal was forged out of a choice we made just now to stop fighting with each other. This power belongs to us both. Our past is over, and this is a symbol of all the potential you have in front of you. This crystal contains some of my Death magic, which will be just enough to open a portal anywhere in the world. It's a one-way ticket meant only for you. You can go anywhere you want, but you don't ever get to come back."

Slowly, Ryan got to his feet. "What reason do I have to trust you?"

"Trust isn't based in reason, Ryan," I said. "That too is a choice."

"If this magic is real, then I could use my one chance to run back to the priestesses," Ryan pointed out. "Why would you risk that?"

"Because I don't think you ever wanted to help them destroy our people," I answered. "You know they don't have your best interests at heart, or you wouldn't have been talking about them the way you did tonight. You followed them because you didn't think you had any other choice, but now you get to make your own decision. What will you choose?"

Warily, he reached out, and I placed the crystal into his hand. He flipped it around, as if trying to decide if it was dangerous or not. "I don't understand why you would do this for me, after everything I've done."

"I'm not doing it for you," I stated simply. "I'm doing it for all of us. I've got to take a breath myself so that others can, too."

Ryan closed his eyes and took a long, deep inhale, letting his shoulders sag when he breathed out. "You could've killed me," he said softly. "I had every intention of coming here and making certain you didn't make it until morning. You're a better warlock than I could ever be, in more ways than one. I never imagined you'd let me go. Didn't even cross my mind that it was an option. Perhaps there are more choices in front of us than I thought."

Ryan curled his fingers around the crystal. "Nadine didn't know you were going to let me go. She said I'd answer for my crimes."

"She knew," I told him. "And you *will* answer for it. One day, when you stand before your reaper, you will choose Alora or the Abyss, and that's when you'll know if the choice you make now was worth it."

Ryan looked deeply contemplative, like he couldn't think of a place in the world he really wanted to go. Then he closed his eyes, and a single tear streaked his cheek. A portal bloomed in the middle of the clearing as he made his decision, and the crystal he held was reduced to sand. I peered into the portal, curious to see where he chose to go, but all I saw was a forest much like this one.

I glanced between him and the portal. "What is this place?"

"It's a Midnighter settlement," Ryan said, sounding wholly at peace with his decision. "I spent a summer there dealing nightshade. I met a vamp who was trying to get me off the stuff. She said if I ever returned, she'd be there to help me. I know vampires are dangerous, but I also know Octavia Falls is no longer my place. There's nothing left for me here. If I'm going to find my place in the world, then I've got to go somewhere far away from here. The vampires will take me in."

"If this is the choice you really want to make, then I won't stop you," I told him.

"I know you won't," Ryan replied. "Maybe I don't understand what Gran was saying, but I'd like to try. I'm going to take my chance with the

Midnighters, and maybe one day it'll all make sense. Your power's enough to get me there, but it's your compassion that's going to let me actually go. I guess what I'm trying to say is… thank you for giving me another chance."

The transformational power we'd created had clearly been stronger than even I realized, because Ryan sounded *genuine* in his gratitude. Something glimmered in his eyes, a hint of the man he used to be before desperation dictated his descent into cruelty. For a brief second, I saw that guy who used to stand up to bullies in the hallways in high school, back before he became one of them. Beneath his cold exterior, there was still the kid inside of him who wanted to help people.

Ryan stepped toward the portal, but paused at its edge to turn back to me. "Before I go, you should know that the priestesses have been trying to read your minds to figure out when it's most advantageous to attack. Whatever spells you're working to keep them out of your minds must be powerful, because they can't see anything. They plan on moving in before you can make any big moves."

I furrowed my brow. "The golems we encountered said we have until Halloween."

Ryan shook his head. "Those golems only repeated what the priestesses told them. Their plans have changed. It's why I came here in a rage —I didn't want to wait any longer, even if it was only a couple more days."

My whole body tensed in panic. "How much time do we have?"

"Three days," he said. I thought I detected regret in his tone.

Three days wasn't enough time, but I didn't express my concern to Ryan. Instead, I offered a kind nod. "Thank you."

"You're giving me the option to start over. The least I can do in return is give you a fighting chance. Tell Gran I love her," Ryan requested, before turning to take another step. The portal encompassed him, until he had disappeared from the clearing completely. The portal vanished, and I was left standing in the dark alone.

I knew Ryan couldn't be changed by a single act of kindness. There was still anger and bitterness within him, and that would take time to shift. But when I had him under my scythe, poised to take his life from his hands, and I chose not to, I saw a spark of hope flicker inside of him. I had despised Ryan with every fiber of my being, but now I wondered if all he ever wanted was that fresh start, and I could understand that. Now he had the chance at it. I didn't know what choices he'd make from this point on, but I knew he'd taken a step in the right direction, and it was worth letting him discover who he could become from that decision.

Ryan had made the choice that was right for him. He'd taken a breath, and in turn I had to take my own.

I tried to create a portal to take me back to the police station, but not even sparks of magic emitted from my fingers. I'd exhausted everything I had with that final spell, and now the Waning had come back with a vengeance.

I started walking toward town. The police station was on the edge of the city, but it still took a good half an hour of hiking to get back. When I entered the station, my friends looked wholly relieved to see me.

"Thank goodness you're back!" Grant exclaimed. "We were about to launch a search party."

"What happened out there?" Chloe asked, though she sounded a bit scared to hear the answer.

"I let Ryan go," I stated simply.

"You let him go!" Chloe demanded. "After he *ruined my wedding*? That's some nice wedding present there, Lucas. I know you and Nadine left the party early to fuck, but I'm sure not getting any on my wedding night!"

"Sorry, but you've got to seize the moment when you've got some spare time, since we never have any," Nadine said with a shrug.

"Clearly, since you snuck out of my reception to screw around. I still haven't consummated my vows, and now I've got to deal with this bull-shit!" Chloe sneered back.

Grant quickly stepped in. "All right, we get it, Chloe. Your wedding was ruined, but you're not actually mad at Nadine and Lucas. You're pissed your ex showed up to crash your party. Let's get back to the topic at hand."

Miles crossed his arms. "Letting Ryan go is a big risk. He could come back to town, or run and get the priestesses. I know you all want to try a different way, but he's a threat."

"He won't be back," I promised. "Letting him go was the right call. We can't keep fighting our own coven members."

I told them about how Ryan had surrendered to the duel and declared me the winner, and how the transformational energy had created the spell to take him anywhere. I told them about the choice he'd made.

"I know my decision to set him free goes against conventional wisdom," I stated. "But I could feel it in my bones what had to be done. I'm glad I listened to my gut, because even though Ryan's my enemy, I got to give him the choice that everyone in the coven should have. In return, his decision made me realize that I'm done fighting who I really am."

I sighed. "I keep going back and forth about taking pills because people are giving me this blanket statement that certain tools help everyone, but I have to consider what *I* need. So often we make the safe choice because we can't see where our intuition will lead us, but I'm sick of not being in alignment with myself. Logically, it seems letting Ryan go is a bad decision, but I know it was the *right* choice for both of us. I have to do the same with my healthcare and my future. I can listen to other people's experiences to gain insight and understanding I didn't have before, but I can't keep looking outside myself for answers. In the end, I know what's best for me, and I need to start making the right decisions for myself. We're all built to do things differently, and I have to listen to my intuition and do things my way."

I expected my friends to protest, to tell me to give it more time and try new things, but they didn't. Nadine stepped forward and looped her arm through mine. "Whatever you need, Lucas. We're here to support you."

"Yeah, I'm proud of you, man," Miles added. "Pills are working for me, but they aren't for everyone. I never meant to push this on you."

"You didn't," I assured him. "You all meant really well, and I know you just want to see me get better. And I will, but I need to commit to my own process."

"We'll be here to support you the whole way," Grant promised.

"There's one more thing…" I added. "According to Ryan, the priestesses will be here in three days."

Everyone started shouting over each other at once that I couldn't make out what anyone said.

"The golems said we had until Halloween!" Nadine panicked.

"Ryan said their plans have changed," I told them.

"Is his information credible?" Chloe demanded.

I nodded. "I believe Ryan was telling the truth."

"That doesn't give us enough time!" Grant cried.

"Then we have to make every minute count," I said. "We need to find the Curse Breaker Wand, and we need to find it *now*."

nadine

TEN

The priestesses will be here in three days.

Lucas's words repeated over and over in my head, feeling like a bass drum pounding against the sides of my skull. I felt the blood drain from my face, and I steadied myself against an officer's desk. The Oaken Wands were our last line of defense, and their magic was locked down tight by the curse the priestesses had put over them. If we didn't find the Curse Breaker Wand now, we'd be completely defenseless once the priestesses arrived.

"Finding the Curse Breaker Wand is going to take a miracle," Grant said breathlessly.

We were all thinking it, but Grant was the only one brave enough to say it out loud. The rest of us went silent as the harrowing reality fell over the group. We had a mere three days to do what we'd spent years trying to accomplish. It wasn't enough time.

We knew my mom had taken the Curse Breaker Wand out of Octavia Falls and hidden it, but we didn't know where. The message we'd found in my birthday cards was our only lead, and I'd pored over my mother's belongings every day since, looking for clues. I came up short each time. I didn't know how we were going to find the Wand in the limited time we had.

Chloe cleared her throat. "We've pulled off miracles before."

"If we do find the Wand, what are we going to do with the priestesses if we win the fight?" Miles asked. "We can't just let them go like Lucas did with Ryan. I know you guys want to play nice, but compassion won't work on the priestesses."

We could stand around all night discussing possible outcomes, but that wasn't going to help us find the Curse Breaker Wand. We needed to get moving right away.

I stepped forward. "Every moment we spend talking about it is time away from pursuing the Curse Breaker Wand, and we aren't going to win this fight without it. We can figure out what to do with the priestesses once we destroy their army and seize the Master Wand. If we can pull that off, they'll be forced to surrender. In the meantime, we developed a plan months ago for this invasion, and it's time to move on it. I'll focus on getting the Curse Breaker Wand, and the rest of you need to implement the protocol and start the evacuations."

"The priestesses want a coven to control. It's not about Octavia Falls to them—it's about the people," Chloe pointed out. "Without the Oaken Wands, how can we ensure an evacuation will actually keep anyone safe?"

All eyes turned to me, which was the absolute worst feeling in the world. I could feel my friends giving up, and the little hope I had left was hanging on by a thread. It was tragic to witness, because we'd always been the kind of people to persevere through anything. I wasn't sure how things were going to play out this time, and I couldn't bring myself to give false promises.

"We can't say for sure that everyone's going to be safe," I answered carefully. "But we have to save as many people as we can. No matter how unlikely, and how much the evidence is stacked against us, we're going to find a way out of this. We always do. The Shield Squad has faced haunted mansions, demon possessions, and literal torture. The priestesses have thrown everything they can at us, and we've outwitted them before. I know we're at the eleventh hour, but even when I'm disconnected from my magic, my intuition is still there telling me we stand a chance. We have to persist down to our final moment, because that's what The Shield Squad does."

"Yeah!" Grant agreed. "Nadine's right. We've got to hold on to the team motto. *To hell and back, even if it kills us.*"

I wasn't sure I believed a word I'd said, but it got Grant excited, and that was all I could ask for. More than anything, I needed my friends to keep going, because if they gave up hope, then I would, too. If that happened, then we'd already lost.

"We're not going to just sit down and take this," I added. "We're going to continue following my mother's clues to the Curse Breaker Wand, and if we don't find it, then we'll die trying."

"I'll be by your side through it all," Lucas vowed. "Whatever you need, Nad, I'm here."

"I'm with you," Chloe added. "We're not going down without a fight, even if there's no magic left to fight with."

Miles nodded. "All right. You're in charge, Nadine."

"Miles, brief your officers and start the evacuation protocol," I ordered. "Evacuating this many people is going to take time, and we need officers directing traffic at all of the town's exit points."

"You've got it," Miles said.

"I'll hold a press conference and inform civilians of the evacuation," Lucas offered. "If they want to stay and fight the priestesses, they're more than welcome to, but otherwise they need to leave. I'll contact Verla and Warren on my way, and they can start transporting students out of town. Dr. Mack has connections down at the hospital, and I know she'll help us get as many patients out as we can."

I turned to Grant. "Call the bus garage. We need all public school buses working to get as many people out of town as possible. Send them to the nursing homes and anywhere else we can to pick up people who can't drive themselves."

I choked up a bit as I added, "The rest of us have to stay here to fight, but you make *sure* Rose gets on one of those buses."

"I will," Grant promised.

"Chloe, you're with me," I ordered. "We'll meet up with Talia at home, and the three of us will follow my mom's clues to locate the Curse Breaker Wand."

Chloe clapped her hands together. "All right, you heard the boss! Let's get to work."

We all got moving right away and went our separate directions. When Chloe and I returned home, Talia already had Marcus tucked in for the night. We quickly filled her in on what was happening.

"What do you need from me?" she asked immediately. "Whatever it is, I'm with you until the end."

"We need to decipher the clues my mom left behind," I told her.

The three of us gathered around the dining room table, and I spread all of my mother's belongings across the surface. I tapped my fingernails against the tabletop. "We're missing something, but no matter how many times I look at her things, I can't see it. I know my mom, and she wouldn't have spent nineteen years crafting a message for me only to lead us to a dead end. She would've left something else behind to guide me. We just have to find the missing piece and fit it all together."

We must've sat there for hours looking for coded messages like the one we'd found before. We tried decoding the first letter of every sentence in the cards, rearranging birth dates and other important numbers, but ultimately came up with nothing. Isa kept letting out heavy sighs at my feet, like she wanted to help but couldn't.

My head sagged into the palms of my hands. It was *my* job to find this Wand, and I had failed to do so at every turn. My mother left this message behind for *me*, and I felt like the worst daughter, because I couldn't figure out what she was trying to tell me. It didn't matter how many codes I'd cracked or how many complicated puzzles I'd solved in the past if I came up empty-handed here. If I couldn't figure this out, then the fate of the coven fell solely on me.

"Something's missing," I said through gritted teeth. As I stared down at my mother's things, I had to face the horrifying truth that perhaps I *couldn't* crack the code this time. I had so few things of hers left, and perhaps the message I was supposed to find just wasn't here anymore.

Chloe picked up a photograph that was only half visible. The rest of the photo had been ruined when Lucas knocked my things into the sink a few months ago. The edges were crumpled, and the ink had bled together into splotches that covered most of the image. Most of my photos had suffered some sort of damage in the accident.

"It's possible you're missing something that *was* here but is gone now," Chloe suggested.

"I've considered that, but there's nothing we can do to restore the images," I insisted. "I don't have any spare copies of these pictures."

"What if we could use magic to restore them?" Talia wondered.

"You don't think I've thought of that?" I asked hopelessly. I shoved one of the photos in her direction. "Touch it, Tal. Use your Seer powers to look into the past and tell me what this photo used to look like."

Talia frowned hopelessly. She'd barely conjured a spark of magic since our séance failed, and that'd been weeks ago. The Waning had drained so much of our powers that even she couldn't uncover what was lost.

"If we *could* use magic to reverse the damage, the Waning has made that basically impossible," I said.

"I could try using a Seer crystal," Talia offered.

"Where are you going to find one?" I demanded. "We've used up the last of our last crystal reserves helping the coven, and you can't just waltz into a crystal store and buy magically charged crystals anymore. Verla's been supplying us what she can from the Crystallary at school, but we've used all that, too. There's not enough magic to go around."

"Maybe your mom left something else behind," Chloe suggested.

"There's nothing!" I snapped.

I knew they were trying to help, but I'd already considered all these angles, and it killed me to admit that I had no answers to give them. If we'd found this clue months ago, maybe we could've used magic to learn more, but the Waning had never been worse than these last few weeks. We encountered spurts of magic here and there, and Lucas's powers were strong, but it was Seer magic we needed, and we didn't have any right now.

"Everything else I had left was destroyed in Grammy's house fire," I reminded them. "It's a miracle any of *this* survived. If the rest of my mom's message was in one of my other boxes, it's gone now. It *has* to be here, or we're done. We've failed!"

"There has to be something more," Talia pressed. "If it's not in her things, then it's in the message she left behind in your birthday cards. Is there anything else she could've meant by it?"

"I don't know!" I cried, smacking my palms against the tabletop. "Everyone wants me to have the answers because I'm the chosen one, but I don't have a plan! I'm supposed to be the leader here, but that doesn't mean I have an endless supply of answers. I'm not some savior born to redeem you all. I'm just a girl who wants to do right by her people, but I can't do it anymore. I've been at this for months, and I'm out of solutions. I wish I could say I knew what to do to take care of everyone, because I *know* it's my job to save them, but we're out of time and I have nothing to show for it. There's nothing I can say that can express how *sorry* I am, and even if I could, apologies won't find the Curse Breaker Wand."

Talia shot Chloe a nervous glance, looking desperate to help me. I'd completely broken down. I said I needed my friends to hold it together or I'd crack, but the truth was I was going to crack regardless, because no matter how much I tried to hold on, I'd already reached the end of my rope. There was nothing else I could give them.

"Nadine, I'm sorry," Talia apologized. "I never meant to imply you had all the answers."

"You don't have to do this alone," Chloe added. "Talia and I are going to figure this out. You go get some sleep."

I sighed, because that wasn't what I wanted. "I'm not giving up."

"You *need* a break, along with our help to provide a fresh perspective," Chloe demanded. "We said we were here for whatever you needed, so let us support you. Go to bed, and we'll let you know what we find in the morning."

"Chloe—" I started.

"That wasn't a suggestion," she pressed. "You're obviously frustrated and tired, and we need you at the top of your game. This is not optional, and it's not up for discussion."

Chloe knew how to get me to listen, because she was right. It was almost three o'clock in the morning, and I wasn't going to be much help here without sleep. If it was anyone else, I'd have protested more, but the great thing about Chloe is she knew how to take charge when the situation called for it. She could see what needed to be done even if I was too stubborn to admit it.

"All right," I agreed. "I'll see you in the morning."

I slumped to my bedroom, and though I was completely wiped out, I tossed and turned all night. Still, the morning came far too soon, along with a harrowing reality I wasn't ready for.

The priestesses' impending arrival required unthinkable preparations that Lucas and I hadn't had a chance to talk about last night. I knew the decision ahead of us was inevitable, but that didn't mean I wanted to go through with it.

I awoke to a quiet house, which felt oddly surreal following the chaos of the previous night. The cats slept at my feet, but the bed and bassinet beside me were empty. I could hear the soft sounds of Marcus sucking a bottle from the next room.

Slowly, I got out of bed. The air felt ice cold on my skin, so I grabbed my bathrobe and wrapped it around myself. It wasn't enough to ward off the chill—nothing could ever be.

I stepped into the main room, where I found Lucas sitting on the couch rocking Marcus back and forth. He stared down at our baby boy, stroking Marcus's nose with the tip of his finger a few times. It was like he had to remind himself that Marcus was really there and not just a figment of his imagination. I understood, because I did the same thing when no one was looking. When you'd had everything stripped from you before, it was hard to believe in miracles even when you held them in your arms.

I wasn't sure I could do this again. I sniffled, and Lucas looked up at me. He must've noticed the sad look on my face, because he quickly asked, "Do you want to hold him?"

I couldn't get the words out. I nodded, then rounded the couch to sit beside him. Lucas placed Marcus in my arms, and I steadied his bottle for him. My husband draped an arm around me, until the three of us were snuggled together.

"What time did you get back?" I asked. I'd heard him return home before sunrise, but I hadn't noticed him get up.

"Around six o'clock," Lucas said. "It's ten now. Grant and Miles are still evacuating citizens, but they sent me home so we could take turns sleeping. I'm not sure where Talia and Chloe are. They must've left before I got home."

Under other circumstances, their absence might've worried me, but right now I couldn't be bothered to care. My family had an immediate issue to address, and I was honestly glad Lucas and I were alone for it.

"Did you get any sleep?" I asked, though my voice was strained.

"A little," he replied vaguely. "It's hard to sleep knowing the evacuations that need to take place."

I stared down at Marcus, who was scrunching up his nose in the cutest possible way. He had no idea what was about to happen, or that my heart was already breaking into a million pieces. If I had one wish, it'd be to take all the pain from my child's life in every moment—past, present, and future. But no amount of magic could stop the agony from coming.

"I had really hoped it wouldn't come to this," I whispered.

Lucas pulled me closer, until my head rested on his shoulder. "We have to do it, Nad, even if we don't want to."

A tear streaked down my cheek. "I know. I just… didn't think it'd be so soon."

"You don't have to let him go until you're ready," Lucas promised.

I stroked the dark tuft of hair on top of my son's head. "I'll never be ready, but I know it has to be done. It's too dangerous for Marcus to stay here. He has to evacuate with the rest of them. We can't put it off."

Lucas kissed the top of my head, then started to stand. His tone came out sounding hollow as he said, "I'll call Professor Wykoff."

She was the obvious choice to care for our son and get him out of town, because she was the only person we trusted outside our closest circle. She'd promised us the night we rescued Marcus from the priestesses that she would always protect him. She'd said that if we ever needed her help, we just had to ask. This was a monumental request, but we had no other choice. The rest of us had to stay here and fight.

Lucas and I had been through so much together that we barely had to discuss the plan out loud. We just knew what we had to do, though I wasn't sure we *could* have a full conversation about sending our son away. Usually, we could open up and talk about anything with each other, but this was different. This wasn't just something that happened to us. It was a tragedy we were choosing, one that was happening right here in real time, and I feared that if we gave it too much consideration, we'd back out of the decision. That would be the worst possible thing for our son. I wanted him as far away from Octavia Falls as possible when the priestesses arrived. I'd sooner die than ever let them lay a hand on my son again.

I held Marcus closer than I ever had before. We got half an hour with our son. That was it before Professor Wykoff showed up at our doorstep with her bags packed. It was the shortest thirty minutes of my entire life, and I wanted every precious second of snuggling my son back. Mother Miriam could freeze our family in time right there for a million years, and it still wouldn't be enough.

"Marcus will be safe with me," Professor Wykoff promised. She stood in our suite awaiting the exchange, but I just couldn't bring myself to hand my son over.

"Where will you take him?" I asked as I rocked him. Marcus laid his head on my shoulder, which made it all the harder to let him go. Isa,

Oliver, and Rishi meowed at our feet, like they could sense the melancholy of the moment.

"Off to Paris," Wykoff answered. "I've already been in touch with Onyx, and she'll have a room ready for us when we get there. It's the safest place for your son, because even with the Master Wand, the priestesses will hesitate to get that close to Malovia."

"Marcus doesn't have a passport, and I don't have enough magic to portal you," Lucas pointed out. "How are you going to get him out of the country?"

"I have allies that can get me there," Wykoff said. "I've been researching demigods extensively since we rescued your son from the priestesses. I've heard whispers of a group of people who will protect your child. They're called the Demigod Guardians, and I'm in contact with one of them."

Marcus tugged on my hair, and I shifted uncomfortably, though for entirely different reasons. "How can we be sure we can trust these people?"

"Believe me, I've asked myself the same question," Wykoff said. "I too am cautious about anyone claiming to have information on demigods, let alone wanting to protect them, but in the research I've done, I know these allies to be genuine. They are a group I hope to join myself someday."

"Who are they, exactly?" Lucas asked.

"The Demigod Guardians are a secret organization made up of elder supernaturals who seek to protect demigod children from all around the world," Professor Wykoff explained. "Many of their members are like us and have personal experience with demigods. They believe that demigod children deserve a proper upbringing, and that a demigod's powers are not for others to exploit, but that their magic should only be used for good. Therefore, it is their mission to protect these children from being exposed to anyone who wishes to use their powers for their own gain. If they had to, members of the Demigod Guardians would step in to care for a demigod child, and raise them to do the best for the world."

I took a step back. I didn't like the way she was talking. "I don't want anyone else raising our child."

"Of course not," Wykoff said gently. "The Demigod Guardians believe in preserving a demigod child's family unit and wouldn't interfere with how you choose to raise him. I simply mean that if we were faced with the worst case scenario, your child would be taken care of."

Lucas quickly stepped in. "We don't know that it will come to that."

The thought of making plans for if we didn't make it was absolutely crushing. It was so unlike us to consider every possible scenario. But if we had to think about dying and leaving our son behind, I wasn't sure either of us would be willing to go through with this.

"Lucas is right," I agreed. "We don't know these people and can't trust them, but we trust you. You use your allies to get to Paris, and that's it. You don't take our son to these people unless we're dead. Right now, you just protect him and bring him back when it's safe."

"Yes, of course," Wykoff said. "You're his parents, and I will honor your wishes."

Lucas had already packed up Marcus's things, but I noticed his blanket with the cartoon kittens on it was still draped across the back of the couch. I reached for it and wrapped it around my son's shoulders.

"Marcus fusses when he's cold," I said with a sniffle. "Lucas, did you pack his teether?"

"Yes, all three of them."

"Including the one shaped like a wolf?" I asked.

Lucas nodded. "And the wyvern and unicorn."

"What about his pacifier? He can't sleep without one," I worried.

Lucas wrapped his arm around my waist. "He's got everything he needs. I packed the teethers, pacifiers, rattles, bottles, formula, diapers— it's all there, Nad. I promise."

I turned to Professor Wykoff, but I hesitated. I couldn't hand Marcus over. Instead, I handed him to Lucas. "You didn't get a chance to hold him yet."

Truth was, Lucas had been holding Marcus most of the morning. I only handed him off because I knew Lucas would be able to give him to Wykoff, whereas I never could.

Lucas pulled Marcus close and touched his forehead to our son's. "You're going to go on an adventure now, pumpkin. Professor Wykoff is going to keep you safe so Mommy and Daddy can build a better world for you here. When you get back, all will be better, and everyone will be safe. Don't worry about us. We've got an important job to do, and we'll do our best. We love you, nugget, and nothing will ever change that."

I choked back my tears. "There's one thing he's missing."

I hurried into our bedroom, then came out carrying mine and Lucas's Wedding Wand. It didn't hold any power of its own, and our magic was useless right now with the Waning, but once this was all over this wand would be as powerful as the magic caster wielding it.

"Momma and Daddy made this wand, just like we made you," I said, holding our Wedding Wand above Marcus. He reached for it like it was a rattle, then started chewing on the end of it. "If you ever need us, just hold this wand tight. Momma and Daddy forged this wand from our love, and it will always hold our love for you."

I kissed the top of Marcus's forehead. "Goodbye, honey. I love you so, so much."

"Goodbye," Lucas whispered.

Then he knelt down and strapped Marcus into his car seat. It was hard to watch, harder even than I imagined it would be. Rishi meowed mournfully and batted at the edge of the car seat. Carefully, Lucas lifted the kitten and placed him in Marcus's lap.

"Take Rishi with you," Lucas told Wykoff. "He belongs with Marcus, and he can help protect him."

"I will," Wykoff replied.

Lucas lifted the car seat by the handle. "We'll be in touch when it's safe to come back. Let us walk you out."

Professor Wykoff took the stroller, and I grabbed Marcus's bag. We loaded it all into the back of Wykoff's car, while Lucas strapped Marcus into the back seat. We must've said goodbye to our son a million more times, but it still didn't feel like enough. I reached into the car seat to take Marcus's hands, then leaned down to kiss his tiny little fingers. Marcus giggled like I was tickling him, and I wanted to keep that beautiful sound of my son's laughter with me forever. There was no amount of goodbyes that would be enough.

"I love you, honey. Momma loves you so much." I repeated it at least a hundred times, and it still didn't feel right to step back and let him go. Lucas grabbed my hand, and I knew I had to do it now, or I never would.

Professor Wykoff kindly shut the back door, then turned to us. "Thank you for trusting me with your son. I will protect him with my life —and more if the Goddess wills it. You are both very brave in many aspects, but rest assured your son will be safe. You have my number if you need anything."

"Thank you, Professor," Lucas said.

Then she got in the car and backed out of the driveway. Just like that... our son was gone.

Tears stung my eyes. That couldn't be it, could it?

Lucas wrapped his arms around me and whispered, "We did the right thing."

"I know, but that doesn't make it any easier," I replied bitterly.

"We'll see him again," Lucas said with a sniffle. He was sad, but *I* was pissed.

"We have to," I insisted harshly. "I won't let that be the last time we see our son. We've said goodbye for now, but it isn't forever."

"No, it's not," he agreed. "I know it feels like a bad thing right now, but we're saving our son. I'm willing to take on all this pain for him so he can live, because I love him, and that's what parents do. If I have to take on that pain for you, too, I'll do it in a heartbeat. No matter what it takes, I'll do anything to save our son and get him back, even if it kills me."

It was an admirable stance to take, but one I couldn't accept. I couldn't lose my husband, too.

Lucas's phone went off then, and he sighed heavily. "What now?"

He pulled out his phone, and I saw that it was his alarm for his weekly therapy session. He silenced the alarm and slipped it back in his pocket like it was nothing, then wrapped his arms around me again.

I shuddered under his touch. "You should go to your session."

Lucas shook his head. "We don't have the time. I mean, I saw Dr. Mack last night after I left the police station, and she said she was keeping her clinic operations going to help people who needed counseling through this time. She more or less said she hoped to see me at my session today, but I wasn't counting on it. There's too much work that needs to be done."

"Lucas, we just gave our son away," I insisted. "We can take one hour to process this. If there's any time you need a therapist, it's right now."

Lucas pulled away from me, searching my eyes for answers. "Do you want to come with me?"

He'd misinterpreted that I was speaking about myself. Truth was, we both needed to give each other permission to process this, because we sure as hell weren't getting anything done in the state we were in now. I loved Lucas and wanted him close to me, but at the same time, I needed to be completely alone now that we'd sent Marcus away. Last night, everyone was looking to me for answers I couldn't give, and now, my son was gone. I just needed a moment to pull myself together.

"No. I think you should go alone," I said.

"Nad, it's a waste of time—"

"Lucas, I need you to understand." I grabbed him by the shirt desperately. If there was ever a time I needed him to hear me, it was now. "We *both* need to be in the right headspace to face this, because we can't afford a mistake. I have lost my parents and my grandmother, everyone I ever loved before I knew you. You're my family now—you and Marcus. We've already lost one son, and I won't lose another family member. You talk to Dr. Mack and do whatever you have to do to get into the right frame of mind, because I won't let you face the priestesses with the intent to die. You promise that you'll stay alive, because I didn't go through all of this just to lose you both. We will *both* be holding our son by the end of this, or so help me Goddess, I will hunt you down in the afterlife and drag you back here myself!"

Lucas trembled beneath my touch. I must've really scared him, but he composed himself and spoke gently. "All right. We'll take *one* hour, and then we'll reconvene and get back to work."

Lucas left the house under my insistence. I was grateful to be alone so I could break down in private, but the seclusion didn't give me the reprieve I'd hoped for. There were no sounds of my son's coos coming from the next room, and that silence came with the appalling thought that I'd just said goodbye to my son for the last time. I said we'd get him back, but who knew if that were true? Lucas and I could promise each other to do everything in our power to make this right... but no one knew if our power was enough anymore.

I cried hot, angry tears until I couldn't cry them any longer. I thought this time was different because Lucas and I were sending our son away willingly, as a means to protect him, but the loss was devastating all the same.

I went to the bedroom and sagged into the mattress beside Marcus's bassinet. His swaddle from that morning was draped over the corner. I lifted it to my nose and inhaled the sweet scent of my child. I already missed him so much. I'd witnessed torture beyond what most people could ever comprehend, and none of that was as excruciating as this.

I gazed into the bassinet, and my eyes locked on one of Marcus's pacifiers that had been left behind. That was my complete undoing.

"Gah!" An angry scream erupted from my lungs. I flung Marcus's swaddle across the room and kicked his bassinet so hard it fell over. His pacifier bounced and rolled under the bed. Isa had been watching me curiously, and she jumped at my sudden outburst.

I couldn't torture myself like this. I'd been here a million times before, and I had enough experience to know that wallowing in this sorrow wouldn't get me anywhere. I could stew in this sadness and anger, or I could let it drive me.

I was Nadine Fucking Taylor. I wasn't the kind of girl to just sit around and take this. No matter how bad it got, I kept on forging ahead. I'd been through hell and back, and I could do it again.

This time *was* different, because the person I loved was still alive to fight for. If we couldn't find a weapon strong enough to defeat the priestesses for good this time, then my son wouldn't have a family to come back to. I knew what it was like to lose your parents, and I wasn't letting my son live through that. I'd been faced with death more times than I could count, and I wouldn't allow two bitter old ladies with a thirst for power to do me in. I was going to find the Curse Breaker Wand and defeat the priestesses, if not for the coven, then for my son, because we *would* see him again. When he came back to the coven, he'd come back to safety, and nothing and no one would ever threaten his life again.

Isa followed me into the kitchen. I sat at the dining room table and began arranging my mother's photographs in chronological order. To anyone else, they probably seemed like everyday pictures. There were photos of me as a child playing with my mom on the playground, and others of us traveling. To me, they meant everything because these photos and memories were all that was left of her life.

Isa jumped onto the table, and I stroked her fur. "I wish you remembered more from your past life. We're out of time."

I was glad Isa was here, but all she could provide was emotional support. She couldn't tell us where to find more clues—or if there even *were* any. Even an intelligent cat like Isa couldn't recall past life experiences. Everything my mom knew and remembered remained with a piece of her soul in the afterlife, and despite all our efforts, we couldn't contact her.

Isa purred under my touch, then pawed lightly at the corner of one of the water-damaged photographs. I picked it up. I must've been only four years old in this picture, because my mom was carrying me on her hip. I had my face scrunched up in a funny way and my hand over my eyes to block out the sun, while my mom smiled brightly in front of a red carousel. I remembered that day, because I'd fallen down and skinned my knee on the driveway. To cheer me up, my parents took me to a carnival and bought me ice cream. It was one of my earliest memories.

It'd been so long ago that the memory was fading right along with the picture. My mother's smile was only half visible, due to the other half of the photo being ruined. I flipped the picture over, but there wasn't anything on the back.

"There's got to be more to it," I muttered.

The front door opened, and I recognized the sound of Chloe's and Talia's footsteps coming down the hall. The soft pad of their cats' paws followed them.

"Do you really think it will work?" Talia asked Chloe in a hushed whisper.

"It has to," Chloe replied. "We're out of options."

I turned as they entered the dining room. The girls stripped off their coats and purses and hung them over the backs of the chairs.

"What has to work?" I asked.

"This." Chloe slapped a black draw-string bag onto the table in front of me. It made a *thunking* sound, like there were several heavy objects inside.

Talia pulled a leather-bound journal from under her arm and flipped it open to a marked page. "We found this hidden in the basement. It's one of Priestess Lilian's grimoires. There's a spell inside that can help."

She pointed to the top of the page, which read *Thoughtography Potion*. My brow furrowed as I opened the bag to find two crystals inside—a purple amethyst point and a rose quartz stone—along with various herbs.

I looked up at my friends standing on either side of me. "I don't understand."

"It's a thoughtography spell!" Talia exclaimed. "We can use it to restore the ink on the photographs and see what's beneath the water damage."

"I know how thoughtography works," I said. "I took a thoughtography class for my Cast diversity credit my second semester. But none of us have the power of thoughtography."

"That's what the crystals are for," Chloe stated proudly.

I withdrew the crystals from the bag, and I noticed they both pulsed with magic. "Where did you get these?"

Chloe waved her hand. "Not important."

They must've been out all night trying to find these ingredients for the spell, which meant procuring these items couldn't have been easy. Something told me the girls had stolen them from somewhere, but I didn't ask where.

"What's important right now is doing this spell and finding out what else your mom left behind," Chloe said.

"How are we possibly going to do this?" I asked. "None of us have any access to our magic."

"You're a Curse Breaker. You've got access to magic right here." Chloe reached for my fingers and curled them around the crystals in my palm. "We've got the magic we need, and all you have to do is manipulate it to create the spell. You've used Alchemy crystals to brew potions a million times. You can do this one."

I looked down at the spellbook. "How does it work?"

Talia plopped into the chair beside me. "This spell combines thoughtography magic with alchemy to briefly provide the person who drinks the potion with the powers of thoughtography. This rose quartz crystal is infused with thoughtography magic, and you can use the Alchemy magic in the other crystal to transform the power and make it your own. You took a thoughtography class. You know the technique."

My heart lifted in the hope that we could actually pull this off. We didn't actually know if these photographs contained any clues from my mother, but we'd be foolish not to try. "I'll do my best," I told them.

Chloe was already in the kitchen placing a cauldron on the stove. "Let's get to work."

The three of us gathered around the burner and began mixing the ingredients. Our cats jumped onto the counter to join us. Talia poured water into the cauldron, while Chloe sprinkled in the herbs. The cauldron began to bubble as I stirred it all together. In my other hand, I clutched the Alchemy and thoughtography crystals tightly. Magic began to swirl up my arm as I commanded the crystal energy to transfer into the potion.

My knees nearly buckled in relief as the magic filled me up, because it'd been weeks since I'd been able to access magic properly. It felt so invigorating.

Dark blue magic sparked from my fingers and funneled into the mixture. The potion began to glow with tiny pinpricks of light, as if a thousand tiny stars were being lit inside the liquid.

Poof!

The potion gave off a purple puff of smoke, making the three of us jump. The crystals in my hand grew cold, and I knew I'd used up all the energy inside of them. I set them aside.

"We did it," Talia said as she peered into the cauldron.

I leaned over to see the potion had turned black and inky. "Looks… tasty."

Chloe turned off the burner, then pulled a cup from the cupboard. "Bottoms up, girl."

I ladled the potion into the cup, though there wasn't much there. It was only enough for one of us, and since I was the one who'd taken a thoughtography class and knew the technique, it was all mine.

"Cheers," I said as I lifted the glass.

I threw my head back and drank the potion. It was thick going down, but it had a slight citrus taste that wasn't all terrible. As the potion settled in my stomach, I could feel the magic tingling up my body, all the way from my toes to my head. As soon as it came, I could already feel it fading.

"We have to move quickly," I instructed.

We hurried over to the table, and I sat next to the pile of photographs I'd left lying there. I laid the first damaged photo flat in front of me—the one of my mom holding me in front of the carousel. I closed my eyes, trying to recall everything Professor Clarke had taught me years ago. I set the intention to see into the past and bring forth what was lost. I pressed my hand to the photo paper, and as the magic tingled down my fingers, the ink began to form into clear images. The half of my mother's face that had been water damaged became clear again, and her smile was as bright as I always remembered it. The smudge of the carousel horses was gone, and the picture appeared as if it had never been damaged in the first place.

"Any clues?" Chloe asked as she leaned closer.

I shook my head. "No, it's just me and my mom—wait."

I caught sight of something in the background. It was a green street sign that was barely legible behind the poles of the carousel. "There might be something here…"

I squinted my eyes, but I couldn't read the tiny letters. Talia hurried over to the cupboard and returned with a glass that I used to magnify the words.

"Chamber Street," I read off. My heart surged in excitement, because I *knew* we were finally on to something.

"There's a Chamber Street on the other side of town," Chloe said thoughtfully.

"You think it's a clue?" Talia wondered. "It could be a coincidence."

I reached for another damaged photo. "After my mom's message in my birthday cards, I don't believe anything here is a coincidence."

"Does that mean she left the Curse Breaker Wand somewhere on Chamber Street?" Talia asked.

I shook my head. "It can't be. She said she took the Wand out of Octavia Falls. But it's got to be leading us there for a reason. There has to be more to it."

I pressed my hand to the next photograph, one of me holding a kitten in our living room when I was a kid. The damaged ink formed a clear picture at my command. In the background, I noticed the scattered bits of a wooden number puzzle that I recalled from my childhood. All of the numbers were flipped over, except for a prominent red seven.

"It's an address!" I realized. "My mom is leading us to an address. We have to hurry up, because the magic's fading."

Chloe shoved photographs at me, and I quickly worked the magic to restore them. Talia arranged the fresh photos, sorting them into a pile that contained any numbers or letters, and a pile that didn't.

I held my breath as I felt the magic fade from me completely the moment I restored the last two photographs. In the last one, my mother was pushing me on a swing. My hair was blown back, and my features were frozen into a permanent smile. Behind me, my mother held up three fingers. It was such a strange gesture; I couldn't believe I hadn't noticed it before.

"I've got a three," I said. "What else did you find, Tal?"

She laid out the picture of the carousel and the kitten, along with a photo of my dad and me standing in front of one of his collector cars. We stood blocking most of the license plate, but the last number peeked out from behind my leg.

"I found an eight in this photo," Talia said. "Which gives us seven, eight, and three."

Chloe stared down at the photos. "Nadine was right. It's an address. But how do we know which order the numbers go in?"

"I'm not sure." Talia tapped her chin. "We could start knocking on doors and try all combinations."

As my eyes roamed over the photos, the answer became immediately clear. "It goes in chronological order. I look roughly the same age in all these photographs, but I'm not. I remember this carnival picture was taken at the end of the summer, but this photo of me with the cat was earlier that year in January, right after Christmas."

I picked up the photo of me standing beside my father, searching for clues as to when that took place. The image with the car and the one with the swing could've both been taken in the summer, but I didn't know which came first. Then I noticed I was wearing different sneakers in each photograph.

I pointed to the photo with my father. "I remember getting these shoes right before I started school, because I was so excited that they lit up. I wore them all the time. The photo with my dad must come after the swing photo, because I'm not wearing these shoes on the swing. I must've not had them yet. No one else would know these little details, but this message is for *me*, so it has to go in the order I remember."

I arranged the photographs, revealing the clues in order: 738 Chamber Street.

Chloe grabbed her coat. "Looks like we have a lead! Let's go."

We hurried to Chloe's car, and she floored the gas. Talia hadn't buckled in yet and fell across the back seat. "Goddess, Chloe, slow down."

Chloe shrugged. "My husband is the sheriff. I'm not going to get a *speeding ticket*."

Talia straightened herself up. "Just try not to kill us, okay? Your grandmother's trying hard enough."

"You're safe with me," Chloe promised. "And if my grandma wants to show her face around here, I'll kick her ass—Oaken Wands or not."

A few minutes later, we pulled up in front of an old Victorian house at

738 Chamber Street. The lawn was overgrown, and there was no vehicle in the driveway. I wasn't sure anyone lived here.

Talia eyed the house warily as we stepped out of the car. "Are we sure this is the right place?"

Chloe didn't miss a beat as she started up the walkway. "I guess we're going to find out."

"What are you going to do, just knock on the door?" Talia hissed as she followed.

"It's only *polite* to check if someone's home first," Chloe said.

The street appeared eerily quiet as we approached the house. We climbed the stairs to a large wraparound porch. Instead of a turret, the house had a gazebo attached to the corner of the porch. Inside the gazebo sat a small table surrounded by metal chairs with intricate floral designs. I knocked on the door, but no answer came.

I turned to Chloe. "Think your husband will let you off on breaking and entering charges, too?"

"He's going to have to, because we have to find out what clue your mom left behind here." Chloe leaned down to inspect the door handle. "You know how to pick locks, right?"

Before I could answer, the door swung open. Chloe jumped back, straightening her spine. An elderly woman stood in front of us, and though I'd never seen her before, she appeared to recognize me.

She held her chin high, almost regally, as her gaze traveled over me. "I've been waiting for you for quite some time. Your mother didn't believe you'd come."

"You… knew my mom?" I asked warily.

The woman nodded. "Yes. I knew Faith for a brief time. You're Nadine, aren't you?"

"Yes," I said. "These are my friends Chloe and Talia."

"It's nice to finally meet you," she replied. "Please, come in."

She opened the door wider, revealing a dark, ominous hallway beyond. The hair on the back of my neck stood, but while my body was screaming danger, my mind was totally at ease. I'd interpreted my mother's message correctly, and I knew I'd ended up at the right place.

I went to take a step forward, but Chloe shoved her arm in front of me. "Hang on, Nadine."

Chloe sniffed the woman—actually *sniffed* her, like a dog. "This is a trick. You're a fae!"

"I *knew* something about this felt off," Talia agreed. She scratched her arms, like she too felt her hair standing upright.

The old woman took a step back, as if to reassure us she wasn't dangerous. Before our eyes, insect-like wings appeared to grow out of her back. At the same time, she pulled the collar of her shirt over her shoulder to reveal an eye tattoo identical to Talia's.

"It's true," the woman said. "I am fae, but I'm also a Seer. I mean you no harm."

I didn't have to question it. I could feel the truth of her statement in my bones. My mother wouldn't have led me here if it was going to get me hurt. "I believe her. We've encountered part fae, part witch allies before. Most of the coven's magic is gone, but our protection spell around town hasn't failed yet. She wouldn't have been able to make it into Octavia Falls if she were our enemy."

"If Nadine trusts you, then so do I," Chloe said. "But I'm still not falling for any fae tricks. We aren't coming inside."

"I understand," the woman replied kindly. "We can talk out here."

The four of us gathered around the table in the gazebo. I knew fae maneuvered with grace, but this woman appeared very frail and moved slowly. She coughed a few times as she settled into her chair.

"How did you know my mom?" I asked once we were all seated.

"I was a fae professor who taught Enchanting at Arcanea University— Professor Calliope is my name," she said. "I've lived most of my life in Malovia, but I spent some years on and off studying in Octavia Falls to learn more of my witch heritage. I met your mother during one of my sabbaticals here in the states."

"You said you *were* a professor," Chloe pointed out. "Not anymore?"

Calliope sighed. "I'm afraid things aren't as they used to be in Malovia. The fae queen has been missing for a while now. No one knows where she is. The rival monarch is going to win the war, so I came to say good-bye. I had hoped to move to the Malovian countryside with my daughter after my retirement, to live out the rest of my days. I only have so many now."

"What do you mean?" Chloe asked.

"A terrible illness, I'm afraid. There is no cure," Calliope replied. "I am living on borrowed time. I wish to spend the rest of my life with my daughter, but I had to come here first. There's still work to be done."

"What kind of work?" Talia asked.

Although my best friend had asked the question, Calliope's eyes fell on me. "Work with the Demigod Guardians, of course."

A sharp inhale passed my lips. "You're Professor Wykoff's contact, aren't you?"

Calliope nodded. "Yes. I sent her and your son off in a portal this morning."

I was stunned, but Chloe spoke up before I could. "What are the Demigod Guardians?"

"They're a group of people whose mission is to protect demigods. Professor Wykoff told me about them," I explained, before turning back to Calliope. "If you wanted to help us, why didn't you contact us?"

Calliope cocked an eyebrow. "Would you have trusted me?"

Not a bit. This woman was a fae, and while I liked to believe the best in people—and I knew we had allies throughout all supernatural societies —I'd have never handed my son off to a faerie who approached me. Professor Wykoff had warned us of people who would use our son's demigod power for their own, much like the priestesses had done in forging the Master Wand. I wouldn't have let a stranger get close enough to touch my son, let alone a fae known for their trickery.

"No, I wouldn't have," I told her honestly. "The only reason I'm trusting you now is because my mother left me a message. She wanted me to come find you."

"I trusted she would do as I told her," Calliope said with a fond smile. "I knew it would only work if you came to me yourself. You wouldn't trust me otherwise. You and your son are the reason I came back to Octavia Falls now. I don't have much time left, and you are one of the few visions I've had that has yet to be fulfilled."

"What vision?" I asked. "What did you tell my mom to do?"

"While I was in Octavia Falls last time, I performed readings part-time. Your mother came to me to ask me about her future," Calliope explained. "She had found an object of great power, though she never shared with me what it was. She wanted to know what to do with it. When I looked into the future, I saw that this object would one day end up in your hands some time after your mother had passed."

"So, she knew she was going to die?" I asked.

"We all die eventually," Calliope pointed out. "Your mother did not know she would die young. I'm sure she assumed this would all happen after she died of old age. I told your mother to hang on to the object, that one day, her daughter would need it, but that it had to be passed down at the right time. To ensure you'd find it, I instructed her to leave clues behind that only you could decipher. I told her which clues to use and where to place them. I gave her this address so that one day, you could find me."

This had to be what my mom's last thought meant. *The coven's in danger. Stay safe, Nadine. I love you.* I'd never been able to figure out what danger she knew of, but if Calliope had told her I'd pursue the Curse Breaker Wand after her death, she must've known something bad was coming and that I'd be involved.

"Why couldn't she just tell me this?" I wondered. "Why leave all these puzzles for me to solve?"

"In my visions, I could see that there were other people looking for this object. Knowing what I know now, I can only assume that refers to the Miriamic priestesses. I knew that if your mother handed it down to you too soon, the object would end up in the wrong hands," Calliope said. "However, the vision I had so long ago is coming true now. Your time has come. You are free to pursue the object she kept for you."

My eyebrows pinched together. "I don't understand what good this vision is if I don't know where to find it."

"My dear, it's as I said. Your mother kept this object with her at all times. *Keep it in your stash,* I told her. *Your daughter will come for it when you're dead.*"

I gasped. It was the answer we'd been looking for all this time. "Her stash? I can access that even though she's dead?"

I couldn't believe it hadn't occurred to me. The thought of the Curse Breaker Wand being in her stash even after her death seemed so outside of the realm of possibility that I hadn't considered it.

Calliope wore a light smile. "Your mother asked the same question. *Just trust me,* I said. *This is what you need to do.*"

"How do I access it?" I asked desperately. It wasn't something my friends and I had ever done before.

"I can't say for sure," Calliope answered. "Usually, if a person dies with items in their stash, those things are forever lost. But I know from my visions that in this case, that is what needs to be done. I can't say for sure if your mother followed those instructions to her dying day, but that is what I told her. My fae identity was discovered, and I was chased out of Octavia Falls soon after. I never spoke to her again."

I stood quickly, ready to follow this clue through to the end. "Thank you very much, Professor Calliope. I don't know how I'm going to get into my mom's stash, but I'll find a way."

"My grandmother ordered the Executors to perform stash searches," Chloe said. "I bet there's a spell for it in the grimoire we found in her house."

"We have to tell the guys," Talia added urgently.

"We can't thank you enough," I told Professor Calliope. "If there's anything we can do to return the favor, please let us know."

Calliope grabbed my wrist, and desperation filled her eyes. "You see this through to the end, Nadine. I told you, I didn't come back here for you. Demigods are being born in supernatural societies from all across the world, and my visions led me here. My work here with the Demigod Guardians is to confirm the presence of a demigod child, so that we may protect him. I am not here to interfere; it's not his time yet. There are other young demigods like your son, and one day, they all will be important to the future of the world. The Demigod Guardians will do what we can to protect him in the meantime. There's nothing you need to do now, except defeat the priestesses so your son has a coven to grow up in. We'll reach out when the time is right."

A shiver traveled down my spine. The last thing I wanted was some cryptic prophecy about my son, but she didn't tell me anything I didn't already know. Talia had similar visions earlier this year at our baby shower. There was no denying that Marcus was destined for great things. As much as that scared me, it was more terrifying to think he may never get a chance to fulfill his destiny if I failed. He wouldn't be raised under the priestesses' tyranny.

It was time to finish this once and for all.

Nadine wanted me to talk to Dr. Mack about sending Marcus away, but that was the *last* thing I wanted to talk about. Dr. Mack couldn't change my mind about laying my life down for my family. Nadine didn't understand that I'd do everything in my power to stay alive, but if it came down to her and Marcus versus me, it was them every single time. I didn't have to question that.

But Nadine *was* right about one thing. I had to get in the right head-space. The priestesses would be here soon, and the only way I'd be able to get my son back was if these witches were dead. The last thing I should be doing was going about my day as normal, but I needed to get the bullshit off my chest just to think straight.

I entered the clinic with Oliver following at my feet just as Gregory Walker was leaving. I was surprised to see him, considering I'd told him years ago he needed to see a psychologist and he'd refused. He looked different than normal. The frizz in his wild curls had been tamed, and his skin looked clearer and healthier. I'd never seen him look so put together.

Gregory ducked his head, then quickly tugged at the end of his sleeve to cover up the Chosen tattoo on his wrist. His cheeks turned bright red in embarrassment. I felt really bad for him, because Gregory had received all kinds of false promises from the priestesses and joined their cult, only to leave later on, yet he was clearly still struggling because of it. I didn't want him to think being here was at all shameful, because he was doing the right thing by getting help.

"Hey, Gregory. Good to see you." I nodded kindly as I passed him. I didn't intend to stop him for conversation, because I didn't want to make him more uncomfortable than he was. I just wanted to give him a bit of encouragement, because we could all use that every now and then.

"Hey, Lucas…" He fidgeted with a loose thread on his sleeve. "I, uh, should probably tell you thanks. You once mentioned that you were seeing Dr. Mack, and I figured if she could help you, maybe she could help me. She's been… really helpful. So, thanks."

"Of course. No problem," I said. "I'm glad to hear she's helping."

Gregory tugged on his sleeve again, and though he'd fully covered the tattoo on his wrist, he seemed really self-conscious about it. "Don't judge, okay? Brayden and I are both getting them removed once we have the funds."

"I'm not judging," I promised.

Gregory took a deep breath. "Sorry, that's something I'm working on with Dr. Mack. I feel like I made a huge mistake joining Miriam's Chosen, and I'm anxious that I have to justify it with everyone."

"You don't have to justify anything with me," I told him. "Being aware of your feelings is a big step. You're doing great, Gregory."

"Thank you," he replied genuinely. "I like Dr. Mack a lot… enough to say goodbye. That's why I had to see her this morning."

"Goodbye?" I asked. "Aren't you on the police force? I thought you were all staying to get people out of town."

He sighed. "Brayden and I quit a week ago. We wanted to help, but we're just not cut out for this kind of work. I want to be an artist, not chase down criminals on the street."

"You're an artist? I didn't know that about you."

Gregory shrugged. "I've had such a shitty life, I just wanted to use my necromancy magic for good, you know? I taxidermy mice and dress them up in costume. They make great displays. I know it's weird, but people love them. Not that my necromancy magic is much use anymore, but I can continue my art without it. Brayden and I are evacuating today. We're going to get as far away from here as we can, then maybe we'll settle down and start a business. He's great with numbers, so I'll make the art and he'll manage the business. Maybe in a few years if things do well, we'll be able to get married and adopt a kid."

I felt bad for Gregory, because he'd been thrust into this conflict when it wasn't his battle to fight. He'd done a lot to help us, but in the end all he wanted was a quiet life with his boyfriend. I didn't blame him for wanting to leave.

"If we manage to win, I'll pull whatever strings I can as a priest to save you a shopfront," I said. "I'll be your first customer."

Gregory offered a shy smile. "Thanks, Lucas. I really hope you do win. I guess I'll let you get to your appointment. It was nice seeing you."

I really hoped Gregory found what he was looking for outside of Octavia Falls, because despite the differences we'd had in the past, I truly wished him the best. Gregory left the clinic, while I went to check in with registration.

"Lucas," Dr. Mack greeted brightly when I stepped into her office. "Have a seat. How are we doing today?"

I sat on the couch across from her. "I wasn't sure I was going to come in. It was my wife's idea."

She leaned back in her chair, looking curious. "I understand Nadine is a headstrong woman, but I also know you, and you wouldn't have come if a part of you didn't want to be here. What made you come in today?"

I didn't tell her about Marcus because we'd end up talking about that the whole session, and I wasn't worried about sending him away—only concerned with getting him back.

I leaned forward, resting my elbows on my knees. "You know the priestesses will be here in two days' time. We've been in charge for a while now, and even though we've made plans, we aren't accurately prepared for an attack. I need to be ready. We know there's a weapon out there that we can use to stand against them, but we have yet to find it. I worry that we've wasted our energy trying to rebuild the coven when we should've been defending it first and foremost and rebuilding in the aftermath."

"You can't discount the progress you've made because you're afraid of losing it," she encouraged.

"If the priestesses have their way, they'll undo all the progress we made."

"And if you hadn't done anything, there'd be no coven left to save," she replied. "This new Imperium Council cares deeply about its people, and you're getting the coven back on their feet. People are happy to be working again and going back to school. Because of the health assistance program *you* implemented, I'm able to see patients who need me but otherwise couldn't afford care. People are starting to believe we can thrive again. The priestesses can't take that away, because the progress is within the people, not in the policies."

"They could break these people all over again," I said. "I'm not going to let that happen. I came to see you today because I need to be at the top of my game to face the priestesses. I want to try a new type of treatment."

Dr. Mack furrowed her brow. "What type of treatment? We've talked about medication, but that can take months to adjust to."

I shook my head. "I've decided I don't want to go on meds."

She set her clipboard aside, appearing sympathetic. "There's no shame in trying different things."

"I'm actually not ashamed at all. I used to think medication was a crutch or a band-aid for mental illness, but I have such a respect for it after listening to other people's experience. I know pills are super helpful and a tool a lot of people need, but I also don't think they're right for me. I want to come back to myself, and I realize the medication is just one road there but not the final destination. Our therapy together has worked for me before, and I want to go deeper into that and try new modalities we haven't used before."

"I respect that," she replied kindly. "The choice is entirely up to you, and I will be here to support you the whole way. Is there a certain treatment you have in mind?"

"You wouldn't happen to be able to look into the future, would you?" I joked.

She frowned, though she looked more amused than upset. "Lucas, you know my visions can be unclear, and I don't tell my patients what I see. That's on days when the Waning isn't affecting my powers, which means my visions are few and far between these days. It's my philosophy that healing comes from within you. While I can use my visions to guide you in the right direction, I can't give you the answers, or it would negate the role your experience plays in your growth."

I sighed. "I thought you'd say that, though it was worth a shot. But this isn't about me. It's about the entire coven."

"I'm afraid I don't have knowledge of the outcome. I can see the potential within people, and sometimes I get visions of what they *could* become to help guide my practice, but I can't give concrete answers. However, there is something we can try that may help. I think you're ready for it. I'd like to lead you through a shadow meditation."

I hesitated. "That sounds... almost demonic."

"Quite the opposite, actually. Shadow work is about shedding a light on the parts of ourselves that we're hiding. Those parts aren't bad or malicious—you merely aren't consciously aware of them. You've been doing this kind of work for years, though you may not have used this terminology. You've brought so many pieces of yourself to light and made so much progress, but through this meditation, I believe we can go even deeper and perhaps find areas that you haven't yet acknowledged or embraced. This can be very intense work that can be too overwhelming for many patients, especially those starting out on their healing journey, but you've been doing this work long enough that I think you can handle whatever comes up, if you're willing."

"I am," I said. "I know what it's like to be afraid of myself, so I'm sure whatever comes up won't be a surprise to either of us. If it helps, I'll do it."

"I can't promise results," Dr. Mack warned. "You may not see anything at all, or you may not like what you see. What comes up may not be at all what you expect, but if you let the meditation unfold, you may find the answers you need."

She made it sound scary, but I wasn't nervous at all. I was serious about doing this work, and I was ready to take it to the next level. "I'm open to anything."

Dr. Mack gave an agreeable nod and stood. She went over to the cabinets behind her desk and opened a drawer. She withdrew a bundle of herbs, a miniature ceramic cauldron, and a lighter. "To perform this meditation, I will be putting you into a dream-like state using specialized Seer herbs. This will bring your subconscious to the surface, with the hope that you may reveal some of those deeper layers of yourself to provide clarity. You will still be consciously aware, but you will be unable to influence the events in your dream. Do I have your permission to do that?"

"Yes." I laid back on the couch, propping my head up on a pillow.

Dr. Mack placed the mini cauldron on the end table near my head, then sat in a chair on the other side of the table. I closed my eyes to relax into the cushions, and Oliver curled into my lap. Linda's lighter clicked, and the sweet aroma of the burning herbs filled the room.

"Inhale deeply, and feel your breath fill every cell in your body, all the way from the top of your head and deep into your toes," Dr. Mack started.

She continued guiding me to relax, and I thought I heard her mutter an incantation. I didn't process what she'd said, as the Seer herbs started to take effect quickly. I found myself drifting off.

☽

I STOOD ALONE in the middle of the street in downtown Octavia Falls. It looked like it had years ago, before the priestesses had torn down some of the older buildings. It didn't register that anything was out of place, though. The sky was dark, and a thick layer of clouds blocked out all the stars. Nearby, a singular streetlamp flickered. The bulb appeared to be dying out, because it cast a dull blue hue around the street.

I didn't remember what brought me here. I thought I'd been looking for something, but I couldn't place my finger on what it was.

Movement out of the corner of my eye caught my attention. I whirled toward a nearby alleyway, but it was completely deserted. I told myself it must've been a cat, but a shiver traveled up my spine, indicating something far more sinister.

I started walking down the street, and the sound of my shoes on the pavement seemed to echo off the empty buildings. The hairs on the back of my neck stood, and though I listened closely for the sounds of anything following me, I heard nothing. Still, I couldn't shake the feeling that something had its eyes on me.

I picked up the pace, and my heart started to pound to the rhythm of my footsteps. I heard the scratch of something behind me, like claws against one of the shop windows. I shot a glance over my shoulder, and that's when I saw the creature following me. I couldn't make it out clearly in the shadows, but it looked like a man, only taller and slimmer, and it had long, spindly fingers. The creature's silhouette wasn't clearly defined, as if he wasn't entirely solid but made up of some sort of dark, thick gaseous material instead.

The creature was there one second and then gone in the blink of an eye. The streetlamp flickered, and I was once again alone on the street, but I didn't slow my pace. I could still feel the creature lurking, though I had no idea where he'd gone.

I shot nervous glances up and down the street. The light flickered once more, revealing a second creature standing on the sidewalk ahead of me. This one was bipedal like the other, but not as tall. It appeared to be made from thousands of thin threads. The creature's form looked chaotic and disordered, like a child had scribbled across the outline of a man and the drawing had come to life.

My pulse pounded in my ears, and sheer panic sent me searching for the closest exit. I spotted an alley to my right, and I took off running to escape from the terrifying creatures. They were hunting me, and I was certain that if they caught me, they'd consume me entirely.

The creatures raced after me, following me down the alleyway. With every footstep I took, they came in closer. Their shadows seemed to loom over me, and I felt the whoosh *of the wind as their claws swiped out at me, just barely missing my skin.*

I broke out of the alleyway and onto the next street. I quickly veered left and grabbed the handle of the nearest shop door. The door wasn't locked, so I ducked inside. I crouched behind the window display, curling my knees to my chest as I covered my ears and squeezed my eyes shut tightly. It was something a child would do when they were afraid of the monsters in their closet. If I couldn't see or hear them, they didn't exist.

It's all in your head, *I told myself.*

Slowly, my heart rate began to stabilize, and I opened my eyes. I scanned the shop for signs of the monsters, startling when the shadows of a clothing rack appeared too life-like. I lowered my hands and listened for movement, but I was alone.

I got to my feet and peered out the door, but the street was empty now. When the coast was clear, I stepped outside and back onto the street. As I started walking down the road, I noticed the hairs on my arm rising again, and that familiar sense of being watched overcame me. I glanced around the street, but the monsters were nowhere in sight. I was scared to look behind me, because everything in my being told me that's where they'd be, and I feared facing them again.

You're ready to face them, *I heard a voice within me say. It sounded like my own, though I didn't know where it'd come from. Somewhere inside of me, I knew that voice was safe to listen to.*

Slowly, I turned, my body trembling with each micromovement. The two creatures stood side by side in the middle of the street, but they didn't pursue me like I expected. Surely, I was merely their prey, and they wanted to harm me... so why were they just standing there?

I wished I could say facing them eased my fears, but it did the exact opposite.

I felt myself contracting, and every cell within my body became alive with discomfort. I wanted to run again, but I didn't, because running away wasn't going to get rid of them. It'd only wear me down, until they finally captured me.

"What do you want?" I called down the street.

The tall one with the spindly fingers slowly stepped forward, and I noticed he was clutching his stomach. I hesitated, nearly breaking out into a sprint again, but I forced myself to keep my feet grounded. As he came closer, I realized something about him seemed familiar, but I couldn't quite define it.

He stepped under the light of a streetlamp and slowly opened his arms, revealing his full torso to me. In the pit of the creature's stomach was a swirling vortex. It looked like gray smoke funneling into the depths of a black hole that took up the entirety of the creature's abdominal cavity.

Then I realized what was so familiar about him. It was the energy he gave off. I sympathized with the creature, because I too knew what that dark swirling vortex in the pit of your stomach felt like. Such an affliction could suck the life out of you, until you became nothing more than a shell of a being.

This monster seemed to be even less than a shell. With his smokey outline, it appeared like he was fading away.

"You're hurt," I realized.

The creature nodded, then pointed down the street. I turned to see a man slumped over a large desk. He had his head in his hands, appearing hopeless as he looked over mounds of paperwork. He drew a long, deep sigh and dropped his hands, revealing his features under the light of the desk lamp next to him.

It was me, *an exact copy right down to the shoes I'd worn thin. Only, there was something different about him, too. He had bags under his eyes and looked like he hadn't slept in days. His hair was unkempt, and the distress in his features was impossible to miss. A sandwich sat next to him on the desk, though it'd gone completely untouched. He appeared to be working so hard he wasn't even eating. I didn't understand how he'd let it get that bad.*

The other Lucas scribbled a few things on a piece of paper, then began to drift off. His head sagged, and he jolted awake suddenly. Sighing, he set down his pen and stood from his chair.

A bed appeared nearby, along with the distant grunting of a baby. The infant wasn't in distress or in trouble, but the other Lucas also didn't seem to hear him. Someone was already sleeping in the bed, but I couldn't make out who, because they had the blankets pulled up around them. The other Lucas didn't acknowledge the sleeping figure as he collapsed into bed and was out in seconds.

I realized the other person was Nadine, and it bothered me that this man hadn't even acknowledged his family.

The monster swiped his hand through the air. The scene washed away in a smokey mass, like the creature had erased it before my eyes. In its place, two men appeared in the street. One was a mirror image of myself, and the other was my father.

"All you ever do is disrespect and disobey me!" my father raged at my duplicate. "You'll amount to nothing!"

The other Lucas cowered under my father's insults. I didn't understand why he would do that, and my heart broke to witness it.

"Stand up to him," I told my other self. "Why aren't you fighting back?"

But the duplicate didn't hear me. In an instant, the figures vanished.

I didn't understand. I turned back to the creature, hoping he could explain, but the one with the pit in its stomach had stepped back. The shorter, chaotic-looking one stepped forward, pointing toward the sidewalk.

I followed its gaze and noticed a man sitting beneath one of the shop windows, his knees curled to his chest. He was muttering something under his breath, though I couldn't hear him.

Curiously, I stepped toward the man. In just a few paces, it became apparent that it was another version of me.

"I can't do it," he muttered. "It's all on me, and I'm bound to amount to nothing."

A pang entered my chest, because it hurt to watch him suffer. I didn't understand how he could think like that. We'd left behind that kind of thinking long ago.

I knelt at his side and placed a gentle hand on his shoulder. "Hey, Lucas."

My duplicate looked up at me, and I realized he wasn't a perfect copy. His hair was a little shorter than I wore it now, and his face was a bit smoother, without the bit of stubble I'd grown out. This version of me must've been at least three years younger than I was now.

I sat at his side and wrapped an arm around him. "I know what it's like to feel like you won't make it," I told him. "It's a valid fear, because you've been there before, when you lost everything and all seemed hopeless. I know you're afraid of going back there. But you never have to go back to the past—ever. That time in your life is over. Even if the circumstances look the same in the future, they won't be, because you aren't the same person who experienced them the first time. I'm here for you now, and I'm going to take care of you."

The younger version of myself didn't say anything, but I felt his shoulder sag beneath my arm.

"I know it's hard to believe in your destiny, because the future is a place you've never been before," I said. "You're afraid you won't fulfill your promises, because you can't be sure of how it's all going to play out. But one thing I know to be true—you've already put in the work, and there's no amount of doubting your power that could ever stop your momentum. One way or another, your destiny will be fulfilled, and we can't stop it now. Whatever happens, I am here for you. We are a whole, complete being, and whatever happens on this physical plane can't damage who we are at our core. You can do this, and you are capable."

The crease between the other Lucas's brows deepened. "Can I trust you?"

"Yes," I promised. "I accept you for all you are, and I'm going to take care of you."

"Thank you for acknowledging me," he whispered.

Younger Lucas leaned into me, and I pulled him into a hug. As I did so, I felt his energy melding into my own. He faded away, until we became one being. I could still feel him there deep inside of me, but it was like he'd stepped aside to allow me to take control.

I stood and faced the monsters. "I know why you seem familiar now. I've met you before. Even though we've worked together, there's still a part of me that's running from you. And maybe I'll never stop, but perhaps I can slow down and listen closer."

The two creatures bowed their heads in unison as a sign of respect. They agreed with me.

"That's the part I've been missing about this whole thing, isn't it?" I asked. "I don't have to get to a point where these old pieces aren't a part of me anymore. I just have to listen, because all they want is to be acknowledged, just like the two of you. And I can do that, while still knowing that my past is not where I'm going."

I'd picked up on bits and pieces of this healing process before, but it was one thing to have the information and another to truly know it and be able to put it into practice.

I addressed the taller figure with the pit in his stomach. "I know who you are. You're my depression. You're here to show me where I'm not being true to myself, and I thank you for showing me that."

I turned to the other creature. "And you're my anxiety. You're here to show me where I'm not trusting myself."

Both of the creatures nodded.

All the caution I felt before vanished, and I stepped toward them. I reached my arms outward and wrapped them both in a hug. Depression rested his head on my shoulder, and Anxiety pressed his heart space into my side. I could feel Anxiety's racing pulse, and I sensed the darkness of Depression's pit, but within my own body, I felt neither. It was a profound feeling to witness each of them without taking them on as my whole truth.

"Thank you for being here," I told them. "Maybe you are in my head, but that doesn't mean you aren't real. I don't need to run from you, because I see you're trying to work with me and not against me. You'll always be a part of me, but now I know you aren't my enemy, but my ally. All you ever wanted was to be heard. Even though it's going to take some practice, I can do that for you."

Anxiety and Depression began to fade away, their energy becoming my own just as I'd done with Younger Lucas. I was left standing on the empty street, only this time, I knew I wasn't alone, and I never would be. I would always have these pieces of myself guiding me.

All I had to do was listen.

☽

I awoke in Dr. Mack's office, not quite sure how much time had passed. Something within me felt profoundly different, though I couldn't explain it. Something had clicked that I'd known all along, but hadn't understood until this moment.

"How do you feel?" Dr. Mack asked as I pushed myself upright.

I looked into the bowl of Seer herbs and saw that they were burning their last embers. "I feel like I'm learning new layers to this journey every day," I admitted. "I can know something for years, but then it all changes when I see it from another angle or put a different lens on it. I can't put it into words, because to someone else it may look exactly the same, but to me, it's like opening my eyes to a whole new world. Thank you for doing that for me, Dr. Mack."

"Anytime, Lucas," she said with a kind smile. "Did you get what you needed?"

"Yes, and perhaps even more," I replied.

My phone rang, and I quickly pulled it from my pocket to see Nadine was calling. "It's my wife."

"Take the call," Dr. Mack said approvingly. "Our session is over, and I'll see you next week."

Dr. Mack knew exactly what she was saying. I'd just told her there was a chance the priestesses could destroy the coven in two days, and she was acting as if we'd all be here in a week. It was her way of showing me she believed in me.

Oliver and I stepped out of her office, and I answered my phone. "Nad, everything okay?"

"Lucas, we know where the Curse Breaker Wand is," my wife replied urgently. "You need to come home, because we're going after it. Today."

TWELVE

e rushed home and got there the same time Lucas returned.

"I called Grant," Talia said. "He's on his way."

"Tell me everything," Lucas urged as we entered the house.

"The Curse Breaker Wand is in my mom's stash!" I told him. "We were right. She had it all this time."

We hurried into the dining room, where Chloe had left her grandmother's grimoire laying on the table. She flipped through it quickly while I told Lucas about the clues we'd found.

"We think this grimoire could contain the spell the Executors used to force stash searches," I said. "We can go to my mom's grave, do the spell, and we'll finally have the wand. Lucas, we're *so* close."

"This is great news but… how are we going to pull this off?" Lucas wondered. "I'm out of magic since last night. Does anyone else have access?"

"We have enough." Talia grabbed her purse off the back of one of the chairs and plopped it on the table. The contents *thunked*, and crystals of all sizes and shapes spilled out of the bag.

Lucas's eyes widened. "Where did you get all these? I thought we'd used up our stores."

"We did," Talia said. "Chloe and I went looking through Lilian's boxes in the basement last night, hoping she had information we could use.

That's how we found the grimoire. We also discovered records of a storage unit she rented out. We went there and found these crystals. We're pretty sure it's all that's left of what the priestesses had."

Lucas picked up one of the stones—a Mortana crystal, by the looks of it. "All right, how do we cast the spell?"

Chloe's features fell as her eyes traveled over a page in the grimoire. "I, uh, found the spell, but there's a caveat… To pull it off, the subject has to remain conscious so we can look in their stash, which clearly doesn't apply in this case. It's not going to work."

I didn't understand. I was so certain we were moments away from finding the Curse Breaker Wand. It didn't make sense for my mom to lead us this far if we couldn't actually obtain it.

I leaned my hands on the table, scanning all the clues that were scattered there. "My mom sent us to Calliope for a reason. We just have to find another way to access her stash. What do we know about witches' stashes?"

"They're individual pocket universes set on the astral plane," Talia rattled off. "A witch can manipulate the space around themselves to conjure and subconjure items out of their stash, though there are limitations. Your stash is only so big, and you can't subconjure a living being."

"The astral plane…" Lucas said thoughtfully. "Talented supernaturals like Nadine and I can access our stashes when we're astral traveling. We just have to know where your mom's stash is, and we can get to it on the astral plane."

I picked up one of my birthday cards, my eyes roaming over the sporadic cursive letters my mom had left behind. I reread the piece of paper where we'd written out her clues.

I took the curse you seek from Octavia Falls and hid it in a place close to my heart.

It was back at home. It *had* to be. There was no other place she'd have left it.

"I wasn't wrong about where she hid the Wand," I realized. "A person's stash is kept wherever they feel safe, somewhere that feels like home. The Curse Breaker Wand *is* in the closet! It has been this whole time. We were just looking on the wrong plane!"

"If that's correct, how do we access your mom's stash?" Chloe asked.

Lucas tapped his chin. "Good question. When I tried to access

Nadine's stash on the astral plane, I was blasted backward. She couldn't get into mine, either."

"If my mom knew I was coming for the Wand, she must've found a way to unblock her stash for me," I said. "She left all these other clues behind leading me here. She wouldn't do all that if I couldn't get to it… right?"

Lucas looked unsure. "We won't know until we try."

"You guys are forgetting something," Talia said. "Even if we found the Wand in Faith's stash, how do we get it back here? Wouldn't it be stuck on the astral plane?"

Lucas and I exchanged a glance. I thought back to that night we astral traveled to the abandoned mansion, where we met the spirit cat and found Lucas's stash. He'd been able to draw things from my own stash onto the physical plane.

"As a reaper, Lucas has power over the realms, which includes the astral plane," I said. "He can move items from the astral plane onto the physical. I've seen him do it before."

Lucas lifted the Mortana crystal he'd been holding. "I've got the magic to do it. Let's get to work."

Lucas and I gathered blankets and pillows from the linen closet, while Talia closed the drapes in the living room. Chloe lit a few candles and started burning cedar to cleanse and protect the space.

"Talia and I will stay here to facilitate from the physical plane and ensure your safety," Chloe said. "Take as much time as you need."

Lucas and I laid our blankets out in front of the fireplace, and Talia turned on soothing music. Our cats gathered around as we began our deep meditation.

The familiar sensation of separating my spirit from my body came over me. We'd been practicing astral travel for years now that it came easily to us, even without use of our magic. My skin tingled, and my spirit seemed to fly through space a hundred miles from my body.

When I opened my eyes, I found myself standing in my mother's old bedroom. It looked different from the last time we were here. The builders had made progress on the house, and a bed, nightstand, and dresser stood in the room now. All the furniture was white, and there was no artwork on the walls. My mother would've hated it. She was the kind of person to lay a colorful quilt over her bed and hang pictures on every wall. I bet she was rolling over in her grave at the lack of character the house had now. Even the astral plane appeared duller than normal. The new owners had stripped this house of all its wonder. Every memory we'd had here was gone.

Lucas appeared beside me, the outline of his ethereal shape glowing. He must've sensed my sadness as I looked around the room. "You okay?"

"It's just… hard being back here," I admitted. "Her stash is like a piece of herself she left behind when everything else has been erased."

"Your mother can't be erased, Nad," Lucas said gently. "She may be gone from this house, but you took her with you when you left. Even though she's not here in person, she's been with you all this time."

I turned toward the closet door. "My life as a witch seems completely separate from her. She wasn't here to watch me come into my power, but in a way, you're right. She still got to be a part of it, because in the end, she led me here. Everything she did to set this up was to protect me this whole time, and now my mom gets to be a part of this final stage. I'm ready."

I stepped forward and reached for the doorknob. The second I touched it, a sting like an electric shock darted up my arm. My shoulder lurched backward like I'd been punched. I stumbled back a few steps, clutching my arm.

Lucas was at my side in an instant, helping me stay upright. "Nad!"

"I'll be all right," I assured him, though I winced as I stood taller. "I don't get it. She went through all the trouble leading me here. She would've found a way to let me through. Unless…"

A horrifying thought hit me then, and even my spiritual legs became unsteady. "Unless she thought she had more time. Maybe she never got this far before she died."

Lucas shook his head, refusing to believe it. "We didn't come this far for it not to work."

"We've never been able to access someone else's stash before," I reminded him.

"I can give it a shot." He lifted his hand, and wisps of purple magic rose from his palm. "I'm still holding the Mortana crystal back at the estate."

"What are you going to do? You can't just barge down the door. We're on the astral plane—things work differently here."

"I'll use my reaper magic. We know I have influence over realms that other people don't. Maybe *I* can get inside."

I took a wary step to the side. "Please don't hurt yourself."

"I'll be fine—" he started to say, but the moment he touched the door, a blast of blinding protection magic exploded through the room.

The blast sent my spirit reeling backward. My heart leapt to my throat, and the floor beneath me failed to catch me. I felt like I was tumbling off a cliff, diving hundreds of feet head-first, before my spirit slammed back into my body.

I gasped as I jolted upright, my pulse racing. I clutched at my heart, yanking on my shirt. For a moment, I feared I'd been sent to a different realm entirely. Hands landed on me, and I heard the muffled sound of Talia's voice.

"You're back at the estate on the physical plane," she said reassuringly.

After a beat, my surroundings came into focus. I sat in front of the fireplace exactly where I'd left my body. Isa nudged her nose into my arm.

My whole body shook as I turned toward Lucas, only he hadn't awoken like I had. He lay perfectly still at my side, oblivious to my urgent awakening. He must still be on the astral plane.

"What happened?" Chloe asked.

"My mom's stash backfired on us," I replied through ragged breaths. "It wasn't too bad when I tried to get in, but it hit us like a freight train when Lucas did. It was like the first time was a warning, and when we tried again, the spell freaked. I don't know how Lucas didn't wake up from it. He was closer to the blast than I was."

Instinctually, I reached for my husband, but Chloe stopped me. "Wait. He might've gotten inside her stash. Give him a minute…"

I held my breath, waiting for my husband to wake, but the hair on the back of my neck stood straighter with each passing moment. Ten seconds turned into thirty, which dragged into a long, agonizing minute. Oliver slowly approached Lucas with hunched shoulders. He sniffed him, then batted at the back of his hand. Lucas still didn't wake. Oliver turned his nose to the sky and let out a mournful cry.

"Something's wrong," I insisted as panic set in. "Lucas!"

I shook my husband *hard*, but he didn't respond. He was a light sleeper, and usually just shifting beside him would wake him up. Even on the astral plane, I should be able to break through his meditation and get him to hear me. He didn't so much as flutter his eyelids.

Out of the corner of my eye, I witnessed Talia and Chloe exchange a desperate glance.

Chloe hunched over my husband. "Lucas!" she called as she smacked the side of his face. She was gentle at first, before smacking him so hard his head wrenched to the other side. "Wake up!"

A red welt formed on Lucas's cheek, but his head fell limply against his pillow. Even Chloe's aggressive assault couldn't wake him.

"Give me every crystal you have," I stated firmly, rolling onto my back again. "I'm going back."

Chloe scrambled to her feet and ran to the kitchen. She came back a moment later with the bag full of crystals, along with her grandmother's grimoire. She handed me the bag, then started flipping through the spell book. "Watch over them," she ordered Talia. "I'm going to see if there's any answers here."

I clutched the bag of crystals tightly to my chest. I needed every ounce of power I could get. It wasn't easy getting myself back into a state of relaxation, but for my husband, I'd do anything. The tingling sensation of separating my spirit from my body came over me, and I imagined myself traveling back to my mother's old bedroom. In the distance, I could hear Talia's and Chloe's hushed whispers, though I couldn't tell what they were saying. My connection to the astral plane was unstable, but I pushed myself to focus more on my spirit and less on my body.

My mother's bedroom appeared before me, and the closet door remained latched shut. I nearly sling-shotted back into my body when I realized my husband was nowhere to be found. The room started to fade, but I forced my breath to stabilize, willing my spirit to remain in place.

"Lucas!" I called out desperately.

"Nad?" a muffled voice answered back.

Relief flooded through me—both here in spirit and back in my body. "Lucas, where *are* you?"

I couldn't tell where the voice had come from. Dear Goddess, had his reaper powers transported him to some other realm adjacent to this one?

"I don't know." His voice remained steady, though a hint of panic bled through his tone. "There was a bright light, and I felt like I was blasted into some other place… It's dark here. I'm trying to get back to my body, but I can't connect with it."

As he talked, the direction of his voice became clear. Slowly, I stepped toward the closet door, and his voice grew louder.

"Nad, where are you?"

"I'm in my mom's bedroom on the astral plane. Lucas… are you *inside* my mom's stash?"

"Um… maybe. That would explain the tight space."

A knock rapped at the closet door. I closed the last few feet in an instant. I knocked back, and I heard Lucas sigh in relief from the other side.

"How did you get in there?" I asked.

"I touched the door handle, and the magic must've blasted me through the doorway. I can't get out. Nad, I'm stuck."

"Try opening the door from the inside," I suggested.

The door handle rattled, but it appeared to be magically locked. "I'm trying, but I can't."

Even in death, my mom's stash was still magically protected.

"Let me try something." I closed my eyes and tuned into the power of my mother's spell. I could feel the power pulsing throughout the room. I tried to siphon the magic for my own, to dissolve the protection magic around her stash. The power shuddered, but with it I felt the entire spell tremble. I had the horrifying realization that if I tried to dismantle this spell, I could very well destroy her stash completely, effectively wiping out everything inside—including my husband.

That wasn't a risk worth taking, so I had to try something else. I didn't want to demolish the whole spell, only break through the protection magic standing between Lucas and me. If I couldn't siphon the magic, perhaps I could overpower it with force.

"Stand back," I ordered, though I wasn't sure how much room Lucas had in there.

I pedaled back a few steps. Magic from the crystals I held back at the estate swelled through my body and funneled into my spirit. I formed a battle spell that surged throughout my whole being. Aiming my palm at the doorway, I blasted the spell forward like a firehose. The power blazed brighter than any spell I'd created before, slamming into the doorway so hard it would've leveled the whole house on the physical plane.

Here on the astral plane, it did nothing but bounce off the doorway, like it was hitting into a shield. The spell took everything I had in me, and it was like I hadn't cast it at all.

I tried again, desperately commanding my spell to break down all barriers around my mother's stash. I ordered the spell to shatter the protection magic in place and blast through the doorway. I gave it my all… and still the results were of no consequence at all. No matter how hard I tried, my desire to achieve the spell wasn't enough.

I dropped my arms, gasping as the magic ebbed away. It wasn't adequate. We simply didn't have the magic to break through this.

Pure devastation twisted in my guts. It was one thing to come this far and lose the Curse Breaker Wand. It was another entirely to lose my husband along with it.

"I can't get through," I told Lucas in a broken voice. I stepped toward the doorway again, splaying my hand over its surface. I imagined Lucas doing the same from the other side. "Years ago in one of my first lessons at Miriam College, Professor Carlisle said that snooping into someone else's stash could have dire consequences. This must be what he meant."

"We'll find a way out of this, Nad," Lucas pressed.

I sniffled. "I can try opening the door again, but there's a chance I'll get stuck in there with you."

"Don't!" Lucas demanded. "We'll try something else."

"I'll think of something," I choked out.

The promise felt entirely hollow. I didn't have enough information on how this magic worked, or whether or not this entrapment was permanent. We were told not to mess with this type of magic, and we didn't listen. I'd had no idea the weight of the consequences our professors had warned us about, and now I wasn't sure how to fix it.

I dropped to my knees in front of the door. My parents had raised me to solve puzzles, a skill that my mother knew one day I'd need. This was just another puzzle to solve. I just had to be clever.

Only this time, I feared that my ingenuity had run out. I tried to hold back the tears, but they were already welling in my eyes. I could even feel the warmth of their sting on the physical plane.

We'd gone against the rules of the game. My husband had tried to use his magic to solve a puzzle that was built for *me*. We cheated, and now the broken bits of that puzzle lay scattered out in front of us with no solution.

Lucas's spirit could very well be trapped here, unable to return to his body, and his physical form would remain a shell until his organs gave out. He'd be taken from me just as everyone I ever loved had gone before. My parents and beloved grandmother were gone, along with my children. Now it was my husband's turn.

It was a sick, twisted reality we lived in. I'd begged my husband not to die, and his ending wouldn't come with death, but I may very well lose him anyway. Although he said I didn't lose people—that I brought them with me—his memory could never compare to having him with me in the flesh. How could he be so foolish to say my mother was still with me, when her absence was the reason we were here in the first place?

Tears leaked from my eyes. I needed her here right now in a way I never needed her before. In the past, it was the little girl inside of me that craved her company. I just wanted to be cradled and protected, for her embrace to heal a part of myself stuck in the past.

Now, I needed her here for the sake of my future, because a life without Lucas was not one I wanted to live. We always promised each other we'd move on if we lost one another, but I wasn't sure anymore that I could actually go through with that. I couldn't walk out of here without him and return to a broken coven alone. I couldn't raise our son on my own. He was my light, my rock, and my *family*. When all felt wrong in the world, he was there to show me the good.

Lucas and I could always pull each other out of a hole. When he was having a hard time, I could wrap him in my arms and assure him everything was going to be all right, and he believed me. When I felt hopeless, he'd cling to the final threads of hope that I couldn't hold on to myself and drag them back to me. Together, we had discovered who we were and supported each other through every painful step of our growth. All I ever wanted was to keep on growing with him. Even though there were parts of me that could stand on their own, the *best* parts of me were the ones I shared with him.

I wished I had an answer to give him, but this time, I didn't know how to tell him that I couldn't see a way out of this.

"Nad," Lucas called softly from the other side of the door. "You still there?"

"I'm here. I'm not going anywhere," I promised.

"Do you believe me when I say your mom's still with you?" he asked.

"I wish I did."

"Ask her what to do," Lucas encouraged.

I scoffed. "She's not going to answer. I've tried to contact her a million times."

"She may not show up in a séance, but she'll show up in your heart," Lucas said. "Magic or not, you've still got your intuition. If your mom left you any solutions, then they're inside of you."

I wanted to believe Lucas so *badly*. I wanted to trust that my mom was still with me in ways I couldn't understand. I knew her spirit was still out there, but she remained realms away, and I couldn't reach her.

We'd been caught in a bind more times than I could count, and each time we'd found a way to pull miracles out our asses. Lucas wanted me to turn inside of myself, but this time, we were playing with volatile magic beyond our current capacity. There were no creative spells to pull off, no loopholes to play with. My mother's stash was inaccessible, and even if I could overpower it, I didn't have the magic to do so. She had protected the Curse Breaker Wand from the priestesses all these years. To get to it now, and reach my husband, I needed *her*.

"There's nothing inside of me, Lucas." My voice squeaked as I tried to hold back the sobs and failed. I sank all the way to the floor, my back pressed against the closet door. I curled my arms around my knees and dropped my head. "I have no answers."

A brief silence settled over the room, then Lucas breathed a solemn sigh. "I'm not asking *you* to have the answers."

I didn't understand what he meant. It'd always been up to me to find the Curse Breaker Wand. If there was one last clue to uncover, then it was for *me* to figure out. I had to pull myself together like I had every time before this, because no one else was going to save me.

I tried to recall how I'd dragged myself back from desolation before, how I'd clung desperately to my faith to defy the odds time and time again. I needed to find that strength within me now, because I couldn't let myself give up.

Turbulent memories invaded my mind, some so fresh I still hadn't had a chance to process them. I thought back to earlier this year when I'd experienced a bad flare-up. I remembered how helpless and out of control I felt because I couldn't just make it go away on my own. Then I thought of my desperation when I couldn't solve my mother's clues on my own, how I'd exploded at Talia and Chloe in the heat of the moment.

I realized then that I hadn't pulled myself out of that on my own. My friends had been there the whole time. When I'd had my flare-up, my girls had rallied around me and got me the care I needed. It'd been my friends who figured out the thoughtography spell to uncover the last of my mother's messages.

And when I'd sent my son away, I'd begged my husband to leave me be in the devastating aftermath of the heartbreak. It hadn't helped, because I'd *needed* Lucas to be there for me, and instead, I pushed him away.

It was a recurring pattern of mine, and I didn't realize until now how deep it went. I had no problem working with others on large-scale tasks like running the council, but when it came to *my* duties—anything deemed my job or responsibility—I still felt ashamed if I couldn't carry the burden and solve the problem myself. I kept telling Lucas there was no shame in asking for help or seeking assistance from the tools available to him, but I hadn't realized how much I struggled with that myself. Despite my fierce independence, I still needed my community. They were everything that drove me forward, and it's why I couldn't stand the thought of losing Lucas now.

Lucas's words echoed in my mind. *I'm not asking you to have the answers.*

I felt like I had to be on the top of my game all the time and to be strong so everyone else didn't fall apart, because I was a leader. But great leaders didn't work alone. Their job was to coordinate the group, to know each individual's strengths and delegate tasks effectively. My greatest strength wasn't in solving these mysteries all on my own, but in bringing people together to work it out as a group.

I'd been so upset last night because I didn't have answers to give my friends, but they'd never been asking me to spell out the solution. They'd only been seeking guidance, which I'd failed to provide. Chloe had been forced to step up and take control when I'd lost it. At first, I thought that was a failing on my part, but perhaps it wasn't a bad thing at all. That was how we operated, because we were a team who stood on equal ground. When one of us fell, everyone else was there to pick us back up. I'd been so afraid to fall all this time, but I realized it didn't have to hurt if I let others catch me.

The truth was, I *didn't* have answers on how to get into my mother's stash. Lucas said I didn't need them, and he was right. I couldn't expect to put the solution on my shoulders all the time. It was okay to hand this over to someone else, because even though I didn't have a solution, that didn't mean there wasn't one.

I rose to my knees and folded my hands in front of my heart. Closing my eyes, I bowed my head. It went against all logic, but deep down I knew what was required. I'd said I needed my mom here, and I meant it. I knew how impossible it sounded, because she couldn't cross realms to be here with me, but somehow, someway, I had to believe she'd find a way to answer my prayers.

"Mom," I prayed. "You've been here every step of the way to guide me to this point. You may not be here in the flesh, but your memory, your letters, and your pictures have brought you to me through time. You left me clues so I can finish what you started, but I'm stuck at the final stage. If there's anything else that can bring us together, then I'm open and ready for it. I realize now that this isn't just my puzzle to figure out. It's *ours*. Even if you can't come back, I have to believe we can still do this together."

A calmness washed over me, but the room remained dead silent. I wasn't sure what to expect. She hadn't responded to any of my pleas before. How could I expect her to answer me now?

I peeled my eyes open, hoping to find something profound—perhaps not my mother, but a way for her to communicate with me regardless. A glowing key under the floorboards would be *great* right about now.

But there was nothing… no glowing magic, no voice calling to me from beyond.

I didn't understand it, but I didn't have to. I wasn't the one who held a key to this door—*she* was. I just had to be ready to receive it.

"Help me, Mom," I whispered. They were some of the hardest words I'd ever uttered, but at the same time, the most comforting. "I can't do this without you."

A soft *mew* met my ears. It was so quiet that I wasn't sure I'd actually heard it. Slowly, I turned my head to see an ethereal black cat with green eyes padding toward me.

"Isa!" I cried.

She jumped into my arms, meowing happily and nuzzling her head into my neck. My heart filled to the brim with gratitude, overflowing with great happiness and comfort as I pulled her close. My tears of despair morphed into those of joy as I scratched Isa behind the ears.

"Of course." I laughed in pure relief. "You don't remember the clues you left behind for me, and you can't give me answers, but you're still here."

Isa licked my tears, then pressed her forehead into my third eye. The sorrow that had been coursing through my veins ebbed away, and a deep feeling of love swelled through me. I was still sad my mom couldn't be here the way I wished. I couldn't see her or speak to her in flesh or spirit, and she wouldn't come back the way I remembered her. But she had shown up in her own way. I realized then that my mother *had* found a way to cross realms to be here with me. She'd known years ago when she died that one day I'd end up here, and she'd come back to be a part of it. She never intended for me to do this alone.

"Nadine, what's going on?" Lucas asked.

"It's Isa," I told him. "She must've heard me calling out for her. She's here!"

I could hear Lucas's sigh of relief. "Nad, she's a piece of your mom's spirit, which means this stash is *hers*."

I gasped as the monumental weight of what Lucas was suggesting hit me. It was never my job to break through the protection spell and get into my mother's stash, because *Isa* could. The spell would respond to her.

I set Isa on the floor and got to my feet. She bowed her head to me respectfully, her emerald eyes glinting up at me like she understood. Then she turned to the door and placed her paw on it. The door swung open with ease, as if it hadn't been latched in the first place, let alone locked.

Lucas stood behind the door. His gaze landed upon me, and his face lit up brighter than I'd ever seen. Before I had a chance to say anything, he stepped out of the closet and took a long stride in my direction. I rushed to close the distance between us. His hands came to the side of my face, and he leaned down to plant a deep, passionate kiss on my lips. Warmth pooled in my belly. I threw my arms around his neck, but before I could drag him closer to me, I was falling again.

My pure elation at having my husband back in my arms sent my spirit spiraling back into my body. My eyes sprang open, and the intricate swirling patterns carved out on the ceiling at the estate became clear in my vision.

I sat upright to find Isa purring in my lap. She had already awoken and was kneading at my leg with her paws. Talia and Chloe were still gathered around us, and they went silent as I woke up. Chloe paused mid page turn as she frantically searched her grandmother's grimoire.

"Lucas!" I gasped. I whirled toward him, practically flinging Isa off my lap. I grabbed for him to shake him awake, but he was already stirring. His eyes fluttered open. I threw my body over his chest, squeezing him tightly. "You're back."

"I'm here," he assured me as he ran a hand—a very real, solid hand—down my back.

I planted a kiss on his lips. "I'm so glad you're safe."

I drew away from Lucas, and we finally got to our feet.

"Where's the Curse Breaker Wand?" Talia asked.

Her question stalled me in my tracks. I'd been so worried about Lucas, I'd barely given a thought to why we'd been there in the first place. "We didn't get it. We woke up too soon."

A smirk crossed Lucas's features. His eyes sparkled in a way that instantly sparked hope in my chest. "Who says we didn't get it?"

He lifted his hand, and in it he gripped a beautiful wand with a honey oak finish, nine inches in length and a crescent moon carved into the end of it.

"Lucas, you got it!" I cried.

"It was there, just like you said." Lucas unfurled his other hand to show that the Mortana crystal he'd held had turned to sand. He must've used all its energy in one go to pull the Curse Breaker Wand onto the astral plane —so much that it shattered the crystal completely.

Lucas held the Curse Breaker Wand out in my direction. "Are you ready to end this?"

Determination filled my chest. My mother had answered my prayers. She was here, and had been all along. Together, we'd accomplished what she set out to do decades ago, and I knew that if we continued working together, *nothing* could stop us. "Hell yeah. Let's claim our power back."

I took the Curse Breaker Wand from his outstretched hand. It fit perfectly in my grip, like it'd been specially crafted for me. Immediately, powerful magic surged through my body like a tidal wave rising up from my feet. It was so strong I stumbled back a few steps, nearly falling over at the Wand's impressive energy. My friends backpedaled, their mouths agape as they witnessed the Wand work its power.

The Wand glowed a blue magic to match my own, and tendrils of magic reached out to swirl around me. The power circled me like a vortex lifting me upward. My feet never left the ground, but my spine straightened, and I pushed my shoulders back as the Wand filled me with a confidence I hadn't felt in months. More than that, I could feel all the Curse Breaker magic in the coven pouring into me. Such extreme power would kill me under normal circumstances, but I didn't have to harness it all on my own. The power of the Curse Breaker Wand steadied the magic, which I could feel flowing through me from Alora. I'd never felt a connection to our afterlife so strong before. The Wand energized me in a way I never knew, as if together, the two of us could immediately restore cities that had previously been leveled.

It was a strange thought, I realized—one that certainly had come from the Wand. Usually, people described power like this as destructive, something that could destroy whole civilizations, but the Curse Breaker Wand didn't think that way. It wanted to build and restore, and it'd chosen *me* to be its companion in that endeavor.

The Curse Breaker Wand glowed white on the end and sang a beautiful chord as its power reached a peak, filling my body all the way from my head to my toes. I could sense her magic edging its way deep into my soul, but she hesitated a moment, as if asking my permission.

Yes, I told her.

My heart gave a mighty jolt as her power latched on to me completely, sealing our agreement to work together as one. She didn't speak, but with her power came a deep *knowing* of what she wanted, and in turn, my own desires influenced hers. We were bound together now, until one of us chose to sever the connection. Something told me we never would, because my soul resonated with her song, like she was a missing piece of my ancestry that had been calling to me all throughout time and space. She *wanted* to be mine, and I desired to be hers.

I could feel through our connection that the Curse Breaker Wand was an honest, benevolent being who desired to pursue the good of all. There was a calmness about her, but beneath that a fierceness brewed. Like me, she wasn't afraid to do what she had to do, and that made us the perfect pair.

The spell ebbed away, though I could still feel her power pulsing through my veins. My friends stared in awe from several paces away.

"Thank the Goddess the Wand chose you!" Talia cried happily. "How'd you convince her?"

"I'm not sure," I admitted. "I wasn't trying."

"You didn't have to try," Lucas said gently. "The Wand would know if you were lying or trying to force it. All you had to do was be yourself and show the Wand who you are. At your core, you're amazing. Anyone can see that."

My cheeks warmed at his compliment. "I can feel something within her that desires connection. I don't know if this makes any sense, but I think I convinced her by asking for help."

"It makes perfect sense," Chloe replied. "Curse Breakers are most powerful when they're working with others. You showed the Wand that you won't lead with pride, but will consider other people's expertise and assistance instead of taking all the credit for yourself."

The Wand's intentions resounded through me like her song. She'd been designed for the purpose of sharing power, and it saddened her to witness what had happened to the coven's magic. Above all else, she wanted to be reunited with her brothers and sisters, so that together we could all restore what was lost.

The front door burst open, and we all turned to see Grant rushing into the house. He wore an urgent expression and wiped a bead of sweat from his brow. "I got here as quickly as I could."

"What took you so long?" Talia asked. "I called you a while ago."

Grant's breathing slowed as he stepped further into the room. "You said you were going after the Curse Breaker Wand. I figured you'd want all the Oaken Wands together once you found it, so we could finally break the curse the priestesses put on them and get their power back."

Grant lifted his hand to reveal the Alchemy Wand, with its spiral handle and a bulb on the end. "We were all tasked with keeping track of our own Wands, so I hid mine to keep it safe. I kept it in the locker room at the pool and used what magic I had left to cast a protection charm on its locker. Everyone else got theirs?"

"Mine's right here," Talia said. She walked over to an end table near the couch and opened the drawer. "I modified this table as soon as we moved in and gave it a false-bottom drawer. I thought it was best to keep my Wand close at hand."

Talia piled the contents of the drawer atop the table. With a soft *thunk*, she dislodged the false bottom to reveal the Seer Wand lying below. She held up the delicate Wand with swirls all over the blade.

Lucas reached into his pocket and pulled out a white wand carved with a rib cage at the end. "I kept mine on me. The Mortana Wand's bound to a reaper's soul, so I figured it was safest with me anyway."

"I hid mine, too," Chloe said.

"How far do we have to go?" Grant asked. "Knowing you, you hid it somewhere far outside of town."

Chloe smirked. "I thought of that, but that's what everyone would expect of me, including my grandma. I had to fool her and make sure it was somewhere close so I could get to it first if she came after it. It's out in the garden."

We followed Chloe outside. The air was cold, and the sky overcast. All the plants in the garden had wilted in preparation for the upcoming winter. Chloe knelt beside a brick-lined flower bed and pressed on one of the bricks. I was astonished to see it move beneath her touch, because I'd have never guessed it to be loose. It blended so perfectly with the others.

Chloe wiggled the brick free, revealing a deep crevice behind it. She reached inside and withdrew a textured old wand. Her fingers curled tightly around the branching handle.

"Let's break the curse on these Wands for good," I said.

The five of us gathered in a circle and pointed our Wands toward the center until the ends touched. With all the power of the Curse Breaker Wand, I could feel the deeply horrible curse the priestesses had placed on the other Wands. I knew it had to be bad if it could influence these powerful objects to such a degree, but I hadn't anticipated the depth of their abhorrent spell. I hadn't been able to feel it before because the Oaken Wands' power far exceeded my own, but now that I had the immense power of the Curse Breaker Wand at my fingertips, I could perceive the curse in its entirety.

It was repulsive in a way that made me want to drop the Wand immediately and run far away from here. To feel the vile hatred the priestesses used to create this spell made me want to never stop running. But I held on tight to the Wand, knowing the only thing keeping me here was the hope that I could end this.

The curse felt like sludge over my skin, weighing me down in a way that seemed like it might drag me to the Abyss. It tasted like rot, leaving a terrible bitter tartness on my tongue. Beneath that, though, I could sense glory like a sunrise, though it remained untouchable. It was like someone had forced the sun to remain beneath the horizon, never able to shed its light on the surface of the Earth again.

I realized it was the power of the Oaken Wands, begging to escape the chains of this curse. On their own, they couldn't break through. The Oaken Wands seemed to *scream* for their freedom. I could hear it—a high-pitched wail somewhere in the distance. It wasn't quite *here* on this plane of existence, but their desperate pleas reached me. The devastation of the Curse Breaker Wand constricted my airways as she screamed for the torment of her brothers and sisters.

Her infernal anger matched my own. The end of the Wand glowed as I ordered its magic to curl around the evil curse. The curse fought back, and this time, the high-pitched scream was real. My friends and I jumped and covered our ears as the blaring sound of an alarm echoed across the town. Black smoke billowed from the ends of the four cursed Wands, swirling into a vortex between us all.

"The curse is resisting!" I shouted over the deafening noise. "Keep your Wands together so we can finish this!"

My friends quickly stepped closer together, and we joined the Wands again at the tips. The black smoke swirled more violently, and dead leaves whipped all around the garden. The trees at the edge of the property groaned.

A gust of wind swept by us, and Talia grabbed Grant's shoulder to keep from falling over. "We're not going to make it!" she cried.

"We will!" I insisted. "I'm almost there. Everyone hold on."

I placed my left hand on Chloe's shoulder, while my right aimed the Curse Breaker Wand into the center of our circle. Chloe did the same, clinging to Talia. Talia held tight to Grant, and Grant grabbed Lucas. On my right, Lucas wrapped an arm around me, squeezing me close to his side.

"We do this together," I said, speaking to both my friends and the Wands.

Magic surged out of my body. The more I pushed, the more the curse shoved back. The dark smoke encompassed us from all angles, closing in on my friends and me. In our hands, the Oaken Wands shook.

The curse's effect on me intensified. It felt like slimy fingers slithering down my throat, taking home in my stomach until it seemed to solidify into heavy stones. I was so repulsed by it that I gagged.

"You've got this, Nadine!" Lucas shouted over the roar of the wind. "You've taken on the hardest job known to the coven—not as a priestess, but as a mother. You're incredible at it, and if I've learned anything from watching you, it's that you're capable of the extraordinary. I know that's hard to live with sometimes, because everyone's got expectations for you, but meeting those expectations isn't what makes you incredible. It's your tenacity to take on any challenge *knowing* you're capable. You started this because you know deep down inside of you, you have what it takes to finish it. But you don't have to do it alone. We're by your side the whole way."

"You can do it," Grant agreed. "Any time one of us decides it's too hopeless, you're there to pull us out of the dumps. Whenever we hit a wall, you're always telling us there's got to be another way, and then you show us how to do it. We've gotten this far because of you. Now let us do the same for you."

"I love you!" Talia cried. The smoke was so close now that it blocked out the daylight. I could barely see Talia across from me. "I had no one when I met you, but you became my greatest friend to depths I didn't know friendship could go. Before I met you, I was a shy, meek girl who couldn't stand in front of the class without toppling over in embarrassment. You taught me how to stand up for myself, and I learned how to find my voice through you. You gave me a power that magic can't, so *fuck this curse*, because no matter how strong it is, it isn't stronger than *you*."

"Talia's right!" Chloe added. "I've known a lot of strong witches, but it's not a witch's magical aptitude that makes them powerful. It's their fortitude. You've stood against the greatest of our enemies with the intent to win no matter the cost, and you've beaten them time and time again. This curse was cast with powerful magic, but it was cast by *my grandmother's* intent. You're stronger than her, Nadine! We all are."

Tears streamed down my cheeks. I knew my friends loved me, but their faith in me was astounding. We'd been through so much together, and I'd promised them that if we had to walk through hell and back again, we could. But we didn't have to this time, because we had everything we needed right here.

"I love you guys!" I shouted back.

Instead of directing my magic down through the Wand, I sent it through our circle, filling my friends with power. By the time the magic circled back around to me, it felt stronger than ever before. My friends didn't have access to their magic, and their Wands couldn't break through the curse binding them, but it didn't matter because together we were still stronger than we were alone.

My power wedged its way into the heart of the curse, and upon my command, the spell shattered. The Curse Breaker Wand gained control, and the black smoke surrounding us spiraled into the end of the Wand in a swirling vortex.

Around us, the wind died down, until fallen leaves merely tumbled across the stone pathway. The siren-like scream that filled the skies moments ago went silent. The magic the curse contained remained within the Curse Breaker Wand, lying dormant for a time we deemed it necessary to use again.

I took a ragged step back. Before my eyes, the end of each Oaken Wand glowed a glorious white light. My friends and I lifted our Wands in unison, and the light magic streamed upward in tendrils that wrapped together. I could feel their power binding together, committing to collaborating as one to reach our goals. The Oaken Wands had never been stronger. The lights exploded above our heads like a beautiful fireworks display.

"We did it!" Grant cried. He whirled around to test his Wand. Green magic swirled around a flower bed, settling into the dirt there. Grant alchemized the soil as some sort of magical fertilizer, and the wilted plants immediately grew color before our eyes.

Lucas tested his Wand, and the skeletal remains of a mouse that had died in the garden came skittering from beneath a flower bed. "We've got our magic back!"

In his excitement, he conjured his reaper robe and slipped it on.

"I feel so powerful!" Talia cried happily. She lifted her Wand, and a vision of party confetti raining down on us flashed through my mind, like an image of a daydream layered upon my eyesight. It wasn't real, but it might as well have been.

Chloe used the Mentalist Wand to lift herself into the air, performing a front flip with her telekinesis. "Ooh, yeah. I'm back, baby!"

She landed gracefully, with a big smile on her face. "So, when do I get to beat my grandmother's ass?"

"Soon," I promised. "The priestesses will be here in two days. Once they arrive, our goal is to immobilize them and get our hands on the Master Wand. Without it, they'll be as powerless as the rest of the coven."

"Then they'll stand trial," Grant said. "Though, it's not looking good for them."

"That depends on what the coven decides," Lucas replied.

"Lucas is right," I agreed. "Their crimes of openly executing coven members and embezzling their tax dollars are not against us. We can give them a fair trial, but we'll hand their sentencing over to the coven."

"In the meantime, we've got to keep getting these people out of town," Lucas said. "We've moved a lot of them, but it's going to take all the time we have left to get everyone else out of Octavia Falls."

Just then, blaring thunder rumbled across the sky. We whirled in the direction of the thunder, and my stomach dropped as I witnessed inky black storm clouds churning in the distance. They weren't there a moment ago. Already the clouds covered the horizon, and they were moving toward Octavia Falls *fast*.

"That isn't any ordinary storm!" Grant cried.

Chloe flicked the Mentalist Wand, and her telekinesis raised her high into the sky, giving her a vantage point above the tree line. Her voice took on a troubled edge as she shouted down at us. "You guys are going to want to see this!"

Quickly, I conjured the enchanted broom I kept in my stash. It'd been a while since I used conjuration, but with an Oaken Wand in my hand, it was as easy as breathing. My friends did the same, and we mounted our brooms and kicked off.

We flew higher than the rooftops, giving us a clear view of the sky miles ahead. Beyond the peaks of Miriam Mansion on the far side of town, storm clouds rolled across the Appalachian mountain range ahead of us, raging forward like a tidal wave. Lightning struck the sky, and a loud crack of thunder reverberated throughout the town. It reminded me of the battle at Octavia Hall, when Lucas's power grew so strong it caused a storm to roll in. That meant something powerful was coming—something so strong even a witch couldn't contain its power.

Then I saw it—a dark mass moving through the trees down the side of the mountain. At first, I thought it was the shadow from the storm, but this maneuvered differently, like soldiers marching in for battle.

"It's the priestesses," I said hollowly. "And they've brought their golem army with them."

"Ryan said we had three days!" Grant cried. "He must've lied."

I shook my head, feeling the truth resonate through my Wand and deep in my soul. "No. We miscalculated the effect of breaking the curse. The priestesses must've sensed that I broke it, and they know we have the power of the Oaken Wands now. They've moved up their attack to try to catch us by surprise."

Chloe gave a chilling laugh. "Oh, it's not just a surprise. If it were, they'd have surrounded us from every angle. No, this is a *show* to leave us quaking in our boots. They've got enough magic to portal hundreds, if not thousands, of soldiers right to our doorstep, and they want to march them into town in one big brigade to show off just how powerful they are."

"That's magic beyond anything we've ever seen!" Talia panicked.

"Tal, see if the Seer Wand has any insight," Lucas ordered. "How's this going to play out?"

She closed her eyes, but winced at the overwhelm of what she saw. "There are too many possibilities. Anything could happen."

"Then all we can do is press forward," I said. "We've prepared for their arrival. Everyone in position."

"Are we sure the Oaken Wands stand a chance?" Talia asked.

I leaned over the end of my broom, narrowing my eyes at the incoming storm. "We're about to find out."

THIRTEEN

Nadine took off on her broom to speed over the treetops. The rest of us followed closely behind, leaving our cats back home. The bitter chill of the wind whipped by my face as I ordered my broom to fly faster. We had to stop the priestesses before they made it into the city, or the casualties would be catastrophic.

Below us on the streets, civilians panicked as they turned their gazes toward the oncoming storm. We'd evacuated thousands of people last night, but there were so many more still in the middle of leaving. From this vantage point, I could see far across town to the roads leading out of Octavia Falls. So many citizens were trying to vacate the city at once that traffic was backed up for blocks. These people were stuck here, and if the priestesses made it town, they'd make sure there was no one left to save.

The inky black clouds reached the edge of town. At the same time, the wind picked up and vehicles began to shake. Heavy raindrops splattered the street, covering every surface in seconds. People screamed as they abandoned their vehicles and ran into the nearest buildings for cover.

The priestesses' army was closing in fast, and they'd almost made it to the base of the mountain. There were so many golems, far more than we could've anticipated. The lines of soldiers spanned acres upon acres, moving as a singular unit through the forest. We were severely outnumbered, and even with the Oaken Wands, I feared we were in over our heads. We'd seen what golems made by the Master Wand could do the day of the hospital bombing. These weren't any old mud puppets that would turn to mush at the touch of a finger. They had the power to fight back, and we were going to have to take out hundreds in each blow if we hoped to stand a chance.

I caught sight of the priestesses far in the distance, leading their army. Their black cloaks billowed behind them, as if mimicking the ominous swirling of the dark clouds above. Three men marched beside them, closer than the others. They had a swagger about them that wasn't quite as ordered as the swarm of golems. Those three must be what was left of the Executors who'd escaped town after the priestesses fled. I couldn't see faces from here, but I'd bet anything it was James, Leroy, and Cody. The shorter of the priestesses—Margaret—lifted a wand into the air, and lightning cracked through the sky.

The peaks of Miriam Mansion towered over the trees ahead of us. A large crowd gathered in the parking lot below, since we'd designated the college as a meeting point to bus people out of town. Citizens shoved each other as they ran into the school. Professor Warren and Headmistress Verla were there, shouting orders to usher people safely inside.

In the middle of the parking lot, I spotted Miles. He noticed us flying overhead and waved his arms in a wide arc to get our attention.

"Keep going and make sure the priestesses don't make it to town!" I told the others. "I'm right behind you!"

I swooped downward to land beside Miles. I couldn't see the priestesses' army from here because the school blocked out most of the mountain, and the rest was obstructed by trees.

Miles hadn't slept all night, and it showed. His black hair was in complete disarray, and he had bags under his eyes. Didn't seem to faze him, though, because he was just as panicked as the others.

"What's *happening*?" he demanded. "We heard some sort of siren, and now this freak storm is rolling in."

"It's the priestesses," I quickly explained. "They've come with a golem army thousands strong."

Warren and Verla weren't that far away, and they rushed over when they heard me.

"Where's Nadine?" Verla worried.

"She's on her way to face the priestesses. They're coming from that way." I pointed. "We'll hold them off the best we can, but you have to get these people out of here. If this army makes it to town, the school will be their first stop."

Miles raked his fingers through his hair. "That's it. We're done for!"

"Not yet," I promised. "We found the Curse Breaker Wand, and Nadine broke the spell on the other Oaken Wands. That was the siren you heard. We have the power of the Oaken Wands now, so we stand a chance, despite the Waning. The priestesses sensed us break their curse, and they stepped up their plans. We've got to move fast."

Verla's eyes widened in panic at the news that the priestesses were back. "What's your plan?"

"Only the Oaken Wands stand a chance against the priestesses, so we're going after them," I said. "The rest of you need to stay here to get these people somewhere safe. Miles, inform your officers so they can get civilians out of here."

"We're out of time to evacuate all these people," Miles insisted. "Anyone left is going to have to face this army and defend our town. Waning or not, we're going to have to find a way to fight."

"We have a few stores of potions left in the school," Verla informed me. "Jonathan and I can set up a trap to hold off any golems that make it this far."

"We'll handle the golem army. The rest of you do what you have to in order to protect these people." I mounted my broom, facing toward the cemetery.

Professor Warren stopped me. "Wait, Lucas. The golem army is that way."

"I have a job to do first, Professor," I told him. "As it stands, we don't have the manpower to fight the priestesses' army—not without putting our people in severe danger. So I'm going to make one of our own."

I kicked off the ground and flew high above the town. Then I sped toward the cemetery and flew past the gates.

The ends of my reaper robe billowed around my ankles as I landed on solid ground. Determination surged through my chest as I aimed the Mortana Wand to the dirt. A pulse of magic hit the earth, causing dust to rise into the air. An eerie sensation settled over the cemetery as Mortana magic sank into the graves.

Moments later, the earth began to shift. Thousands of soiled hands shot out of the dirt in a singular, collective motion. Some were merely made of bone, while others still had the flesh of old cadavers clinging to their gaunt frames. Zombies and skeletons climbed out of their burial plots under the command of the Wand's necromancy magic.

"A threat looms on the edge of Octavia Falls!" I shouted. "A golem army marches toward our home, led by priestesses who have hung and burned members of the coven. They have already razed whole neighborhoods to the ground, and if they reach town, they will destroy the homes of your children and grandchildren and force them to comply with their will. We're outnumbered, and I'm calling upon you to help. If you don't wish to participate, you may return to your graves and rest in peace. But if you're willing to help protect this home that was once yours, I ask you to join me!"

The zombies were nothing more than shells of their former selves—their spirits had long since moved on. But defiling their resting place was not a decision I took lightly, so I used my magic to give them a choice. From beyond the grave, their souls could make the decision for them, and if they so desired to fight with us, they could.

Several skeletons rolled back into their graves, but hundreds of others stepped forward. At the front of the group, an old woman limped toward me. Her skin sagged on her form, but her body had hardly decayed. She couldn't have been dead for very long—a year at most. Her eyes appeared glossy, but she stared straight at me.

It took me a few moments, but recognition set in. Though her features weren't quite the same as I remembered, the silver bun tied neatly at the base of her neck was a dead giveaway. It was Professor Willa Poppy, who'd taught Crystal Studies and Astral Travel back at Miriam College. I recalled that she'd died of a respiratory infection during the time we'd been away from Octavia Falls. The priestesses had sucked the coven dry of so many resources that she hadn't been able to get the care she needed.

Beside her, another man stepped forward. He was old and wore all kinds of rings on his fingers. I'd only met him once, very briefly. It was Theodore Knox, the man who'd owned a jewelry store downtown. I'd run into him before we fled town. He'd been one of the few business owners to welcome all Casts into his store, and because of that, coven members had robbed him. I'd found him in his shop crouched behind one of the counters after the robbery. He said he believed in us, and he'd gifted me a ring to remind me of it. That was the same ring I'd used to propose to Nadine.

It seemed Theodore's support for us had never wavered, because there was a dark line around his neck—the unmistakable mark of the priestesses' noose. They'd executed so many people, but I'd never known he'd been one of them. They tried to silence our supporters then, but now he'd come back to stand beside us one final time.

In unison, Professor Poppy and Theodore placed a hand over their hearts, then bowed their heads at me. Behind them, the others mimicked their gesture. Their message was clear as day: *We're with you, Lucas*.

"Thank you for your support." I bowed my head back at them, then mounted my broom and kicked off the ground. "Follow me!"

Zombies weren't particularly *fast*, but they moved quicker than I anticipated, their motions amplified by the power of the Mortana Wand. I flew above the trees, low enough so my army of reanimants could still see and follow me, but high enough to gain a vantage point.

From here, I could see that the priestesses and their army had stopped their advance. Through the trees, bursts of light in all colors flashed as spells whizzed through the forest. I witnessed dozens of golems levitate into the air at once, appearing to be attached to the sky by strings. It was powerful telekinetic magic, no doubt—Chloe was already putting the Mentalist Wand to work. Green battle magic blasted upward, slamming into the golems all at once. Their bodies exploded into muddy messes that splattered across the treetops.

"Behind you!" I heard Talia's distant scream, followed by the collective battle cry from the golems. The sound of their attack was quickly silenced by an explosion so strong it seemed to rock the skies. My friends had wasted no time slaughtering the priestesses' army.

The cemetery wasn't far from the edge of town, but the storm hadn't quite reached the graveyard yet. As I flew closer to the priestesses, the wind picked up, and rain began to pelt me so hard I nearly fell off my broom. I clutched the handle tighter, flying faster to reach my friends. The zombies I'd raised followed righteously on foot, though I was much faster than they were.

As I flew over the forest, I caught glimpses of the army below. My friends worked in a unit casting spells, but the golem army quickly advanced between them, forcing my friends apart. The golems blasted battle spells that exploded at my friends' feet. Alone, the spells weren't particularly impressive against the Oaken Wands, but with hundreds of spells coming from all angles, it was enough to kill any one of us if we let our guard down.

Chloe levitated into the air to dodge an attack, while Grant used battle magic to topple trees to create a barricade against the invaders. He retreated until he and Talia stood back-to-back, casting spell after spell to slow the army down. Golems surrounded them from all angles, but they didn't move in for the attack right away.

"Tal, what are they doing?" Grant shouted.

"They're mindless!" she screamed back. "I can't read their thoughts."

In unison, the battalion targeting Grant and Talia lifted their hands to the sky. I threw a shield around my friends a split second before the golems' spell came slamming down on them. With all the golems working together, their spell was strong; its energy reverberating up through my Wand.

The spell dissipated, and Grant and Talia were already on the move again. I circled around to get a better view. Up the slope on an outcropping of rock, Lilian and Margaret were mere silhouettes through the storm as they looked down upon their army. They stood with their shoulders back, looking proud of the battalion they'd brought upon us.

With my eyes on them, I could finish this once and for all, but a strong wind caught the end of my broom, knocking me sideways. I flipped through the air, but never let go of my broom. I quickly righted myself and looked around, but I didn't see the outcropping. I'd been completely disoriented. I shook my head, then did a one-eighty to find that outcropping was behind me now. Only the priestesses weren't there anymore.

Below me, the sound of Nadine's war cry caught my attention. I gazed through an opening in the trees to see her running head-first into a group of approaching golems. She lifted her Wand, but instead of blasting a battle spell outward, tendrils of magic flowed from the golems *into* her Wand. As the magic left their bodies, they melted into piles of mud.

As soon as that group was gone, another came flooding in from the other direction. Nadine whirled on them, blasting the magic she'd just siphoned from the other golems toward the newcomers. The spell slashed through them like a sword, slicing twenty golems in half all at once. Nadine was using her Curse Breaker powers to turn their own magic against them. The golems turned to piles of dirt that quickly washed away in the rain.

She tossed her wet hair out of her face and gasped to catch her breath, but she didn't have the time. Behind her, a lone golem sprinted in her direction.

"Nadine!" I screamed. A crack of thunder rang out at the same time, and she didn't hear me. Swooping downward, I reached the top of the treetops and subconjured my broom. I fell through the air several feet before landing on the golem and pulling him to the ground. I half expected him to turn to mud underneath me, but he remained as solid as I was.

Nadine whirled toward me. "Good work!"

"Look out!" I shouted as another dozen golems charged her. She spun around to take them out.

Meanwhile, the Mortana Wand had fallen from my hand and lay several yards away from me. The golem I'd tackled shoved an elbow into my face, and blood spurted out of my nose. I grabbed him by the shirt and slammed my fist into his face three times. I'd hoped to fuck him up the way I had with the golem the day of the hospital bombing, but the priestesses had clearly improved their golem-making skills since then, because his nose remained completely intact. His features appeared human, but they were very plain, like a guy I wouldn't notice if I passed him on the street. The last time we encountered the priestesses' golems, they'd made duplicates of our enemies to fool us, but the rest of their army were mere pawns, their features unfamiliar to me. I guessed it was easier magic, and that's how they'd managed to create so many so fast.

The golem spotted my Wand and scrambled to his feet. I raced after him, but he reached the Wand before I did. He bent to grab it, but he couldn't get his fingers around it, like the thing weighed a thousand pounds.

I laughed as I raised my hand. The Mortana Wand flew into my outstretched palm. "Sorry to let you down, but this Wand belongs to *me*."

That was one of the greatest perks of being a reaper. No one could take the Mortana Wand from me, because it was bound to my soul.

Unlike me, the golem had no soul, and he wasn't exactly *living*, so my Death power had no influence over him. I figured the priestesses had considered that when building their army, along with Talia's inability to read their minds, and Chloe's inability to control them mentally. That's why the priestesses had gravitated toward golems, on the off chance that we had magic when they faced us.

But my battle magic still worked just fine, and I summoned a powerful spell that slammed into the golem's chest and blasted him to bits.

Golems continued to race out of the trees, casting battle spells from all directions. I scurried backward until Nadine and I stood back-to-back. I threw up a shield, but the second their spells hit, my shield shattered. I did this over and over again, working in a pattern where my shield deflected their spells for a moment before shattering, I took the opening to cast powerful killing spells, and then immediately conjured a shield again.

A spell whizzed by my shield and slammed into my shoulder. I was blasted off my feet and landed flat on my back twenty yards from where I'd been standing. I gasped for breath, but I didn't have a second to catch it. I leapt to my feet again, pushing through the pain of what I was certain was a dislocated shoulder.

I'd been lucky. Had the spell hit me in the head, or I'd landed against a tree, I could've easily been knocked out, and it wouldn't take much for another one of these spells to kill me. I shot streams of magic back at the golems, slashed them in half with all my power, and blasted shields at them so strong trees cracked in half. It seemed that for every golem we killed, ten more were there to take its place. If they couldn't defeat us by sheer power, then they were going to wear us down until we couldn't fight back any longer. It was the priestesses' plan, I was sure—get their army to tire us out until they could come in with the Master Wand and kill us once and for all.

There were so many golems that they started climbing on top of one another. They seemed to move as a singular unit, climbing higher and higher until they were layers deep in bodies. The motion mimicked that of a tidal wave, until the wave crested and collapsed over top of us. I grabbed Nadine, and we crouched down. Our magic surged together into a singular spell, and we conjured a shield at the last second. Our shield bowed and bent under the weight of hundreds of bodies, but it thankfully kept us from being completely crushed.

The golems rolled to the side, and together, we thrust our shield outward to shove them back.

"Lucas, there's too many of them!" Nadine shouted. "We can't keep up!"

"We've got to get to the others!" I yelled back over the roaring wind. I blasted a bunch of golems back again, but others were already approaching from the opposite side. "Then we can go after the Master Wand together. We still stand a chance if we combine our powers! The golems are a distraction, but if we get the Master Wand, we can take them all out in one go."

"All right, let's move!" Nadine continued casting powerful spells that turned the golems to mud. She blazed a trail through the woods, while I aimed magic behind us to take out the army gaining on us.

I shot a glance ahead to see that Grant, Talia, and Chloe were surrounded. Talia held a shield to protect them, while Grant alchemized puddles of rainwater into vats of acid. The second a golem stepped in one, the creature sizzled and liquified into a pile of sludge. Meanwhile, Chloe used her powerful telekinesis to topple over trees, squashing dozens of golems all at once.

Nadine cast a spell that blasted into the dirt and sent a bunch of golems flying. Her spell created a clear path between us and our friends. Chloe had toppled so many trees that they stood in the center of a clearing, surrounded on all sides by massive logs and tons of wood splinters. Nadine and I leapt over a huge fallen tree to reach the others.

"We've got to get moving!" Nadine shouted. "We can end this if we get the Master Wand."

Chloe ducked an attack, then shot another spell outward. She lifted her hands to command wood splinters into the air, then sent them spiraling in all directions to pierce through the golems' chests. "I can levitate us all out of here, but what do we do about the golems? They'll go into town, putting our people at risk. We have to hold them off!"

"Reinforcements are on their way," I said as I conjured my scythe to swing at an incoming attacker. The blade sliced through his middle like warm butter. I winced as my shoulder screamed in pain.

I wasn't equipped to fight with a heavy weapon in hand. Instead, I funneled my Death magic into the scythe, charging up the Death enchantment I'd put on it months ago. The weapon glowed with purple magic, and it remained floating mid-air when I released my hold on it.

"Protect us!" I ordered my scythe.

As if it had a mind of its own, the blade went spinning through the air, following my command to keep the golems at bay. My scythe took out three golems in a single swing, then sliced through six more within seconds. The enchanted weapon continued slashing through the horde of golems to take them out in quick succession.

Still, it wasn't enough. Golems continued to pour out of the trees, and my friends and I blasted off battle spells to slow the army down.

Just then, the army of zombies I'd summoned reached the forest. Their grim moans filled the mountainside, which could be heard over the storm. Golems turned their heads to follow the sound, only to come face-to-face with an army of the undead that wanted to rip them limb from limb.

Golems attacked with battle spells that tore the zombies apart. Body parts went flying everywhere. But the golems couldn't kill them, because the zombies were already dead. Dismembered hands crawled up the golems' legs, taking them by surprise. Fingers dug into the golems' eye sockets, and the mud puppets screamed. Blinded, they ran straight into trees so hard that they killed themselves instantly.

Decapitated zombies picked up their own heads and threw them at the golems, then used their teeth to bite off their ears or fingers. Various zombies reconstructed themselves with other corpses' body parts, in order to take the golems in hand-to-hand combat.

The zombies who hadn't been blasted apart charged the golems. Skeletons detached their own arms and used them as clubs or swords. They swung their bones at the golems' heads to knock them out, or shoved them straight into the creatures' guts to kill them. In the blink of an eye, my army of the undead took out hordes of golems.

Talia waved the Seer Wand through the air. Moments later, white wisps of magic rose from the town, gathering together in a foggy cloud that sped toward our battle on the mountainside within moments. The cloud dispersed in all directions, and that's when I realized it wasn't a cloud at all. It was *ghosts*—all the souls of coven members who hadn't moved on. They'd heard Talia's magical cry for help and came running. There must've been hundreds of them.

Ghosts swept through the golems' bodies, using their ethereal energy to knock the creatures to the ground, where the zombies stomped the golems to mud beneath their shoes. Golems tried to fight back with spells, but their magic merely soared through the ghosts, never once slowing them down.

Our army had distracted the golems long enough that I was able to pop my shoulder back into socket. Hurt like a son of a bitch, though.

We barely had a second to catch our breath before another group came marching in our direction. They were mere silhouettes through the rain, but they moved forward with such confidence that I realized it couldn't be golems. One of the figures lifted a hand, and magic whizzed from their palm.

The spell spun straight at my head. "Duck!" I shouted to the others.

We crouched down the same time I cast a shield. The spell smashed into my shield so hard that my arms trembled as I struggled to hold it. The attack was far more powerful than any singular golem could cast. I figured it had to be the priestesses.

Then lightning streaked across the sky, and I caught a glimpse of their faces. A woman led the pack, her red curls flying wildly around her face as she stared us down with a look of vengeance in her eyes. It was Judge Calloway.

Hers wasn't the only face I recognized. She was flanked closely by Professor Clarke and Professor Lewis. I recalled seeing them both at the Festival of Santos a year ago. They'd been handing out fliers trying to convert people to Miriam's Chosen. They obviously still fell in line with the priestesses—nothing had changed there.

Behind them, Gwen, Camille, and Valerie stood with their hands on their hips, tossing battle orbs into the air and then catching them in a threatening way. Even Clay and Carl, the Wicked Warlocks' ex-band members, had joined the troops.

I didn't understand how they had any magic. Even if the Waning hadn't taken it away, we should be able to control their magic with the Oaken Wands.

"You're making the wrong choice," I told Judge Calloway. "The priestesses will kill you—"

Calloway waved her hand, cutting me off. She had the power to silence people, which worked great in managing the courtroom. Wasn't so great out here on the battlefield, though.

The judge's voice boomed across the clearing. "I tried to give you a chance, but you never were meant to lead this coven. I pride myself in being an impartial judge, but I've seen enough to determine your sentencing. I should've condemned you to the noose while I had the chance. You promised us you'd fix the coven, but you've done nothing of the sort."

Now wasn't the time for arguments. I could beg her to try to understand that we couldn't fix the coven overnight, and that we'd made progress but needed more time, but it'd do us no good. Judge Calloway had always leaned toward the priestesses' side, but now, she'd committed to it. There was no changing her mind now.

She may be able to silence me, but she couldn't stop my magic.

I readied myself for a powerful spell, and a powerful explosion rocked the mountainside. Only it hadn't come from me. Something swept through the trees so fast that I couldn't tell what it was, but it sure as hell packed a punch. Golems fell in a straight line, following the trajectory of the mysterious projectile. A moment later, a passionate battle cry rang through the storm. Judge Calloway and the others whirled in the direction of the attack.

A large group of people charged out of the trees, swinging all kinds of medieval weapons at the golems—crossbows, longswords, spears, halberds, and axes. At the front of the group, Miles swung a mace at a nearby golem, spattering him into a thousand bits of dirt.

"Ready the cannon!" someone yelled. That solved the mystery of the strange projectile. They'd brought a *literal* cannon.

Another *boom* sounded, and the priestesses' supporters went scattering in all directions. A cannonball shot through the trees right where they'd been standing, reducing multiple trees to splinters.

The golems continued closing in, and my friends and I whipped out spells in all directions to hold them off. It didn't seem to matter how many we took out, because there were so many, we couldn't keep up.

"Cover me!" Talia ordered. "I'm going to use the Seer Wand to predict their attacks."

The four of us surrounded her at all angles, our backs turned toward one another. I cast a portal across the forest floor that sucked multiple golems into its depths at once, where I sent them tumbling straight into an active volcano on the other side of the world. As I forced the portal larger, my magic shuddered. Sending one person through a portal at a time was hard enough. I was already pushing the limits of what witch magic could do, and I couldn't keep the portal open. I slammed it shut, but not before catching several other golems in its edges and slicing them in half when it closed.

Miles raced past us, his sheriff's badge glistening against a streak of lightning.

"Miles!?" I shouted. "I said we'd handle this. What are you doing here?"

He gave a maniacal laugh. "Joining you, of course. You didn't think this was your fight alone, did you? We've got beef with them, too."

"On our right!" Talia shouted as the end of the Seer Wand glowed bright.

A swarm of golems closed in on us, but Chloe levitated a fallen log and used it to knock them all to the side. They fell like dominoes. She'd slowed them down long enough for Nadine to finish them off with a spell so large it boomed louder than the thunder.

Chloe whirled toward her husband. "You don't have the magic to defend yourself!"

Miles twisted the mace around in his hand. "That's why we've got these. We raided the torture devices archives. It's the same stuff they used at Nadine and Lucas's trial, and boy, is she a beauty."

I spun to the side to deflect another attack. Beside me, Grant waved the Alchemy Wand at a charging squadron. He must've used his magic to alchemize the mud they were made of, because the golems stumbled forward as their legs began to crumble beneath them. The skin on their faces sagged, and their eyes popped out of their sockets. It appeared their faces were melting in the rain. They fell to the ground in human-shaped clumps of mud.

"You're supposed to be getting these people to safety!" I demanded of Miles. "Not bringing them into battle."

"I couldn't convince them to leave, so we came to help," Miles said.

I quickly assessed the newcomers, and I realized I recognized so many faces. Our friend Alex was among those wielding a sword. It seemed he'd bulked up a lot while training on the police force, because he swung the weapon with ease, slicing through the guts of multiple golems at once.

I spotted Lincoln, the guard we'd suspected of letting the Executors out before we learned the truth of Professor Blackbird's betrayal. He'd been honest in choosing our side, and that was evident by the way he used a dagger to gut three golems in quick succession. The guy was well trained, and the golems didn't even see him coming before they were mud.

Beside him, Jude Bennett from the city's accounting department swung an ax that decapitated every golem that got too close. I was surprised he was here. Jude was a family man who'd already been through so much, back when we thought the Gingerbread Witches were going to kidnap his kid, Travis. I expected him to evacuate with his wife and child, but he'd come to fight.

"That's for trying to come near *my* family!" Jude growled at the muddy masses he'd already slaughtered.

Professor Anthony Richards marched up the mountain, holding a large vial in his hand. Beside him, Professor Nina Loren poured various substances into his glass. Richards tossed the mixture at the golems, and they disintegrated at the smallest drop. Richards was an Alchemist, and they were using what little alchemy supplies they had left—and the remnants of magic within them—to create potions. It was badass for a couple of elderly professors who spent most of their time poring over textbooks in their offices.

Behind them, Darcy and Samantha used all their strength to wheel a cannon through the forest. Tyler Murphy stood on the backend of it, one foot propped up on the barrel.

"FIRE!" he screamed as he lit the fuse. The cannon exploded, sending a cannonball careening through a swarm of golems. The golems were powerful, but they were also stupid. There were so many attacks coming from different angles that they didn't know who to fight first.

A mere second passed as I took it all in.

Miles waved his hand at us. "These guys can hold their own. Besides, Verla and Warren have the town covered."

Just then, an explosion like dynamite shook the ground. It was louder than the thunder, and the flash of light that came from near Miriam College was nearly blinding.

"And they're doing a pretty good job of holding off any golems that slip past us!" Miles exclaimed proudly. "They're putting their potions to good use."

Two more people emerged from the forest. They charged forward with spears aimed at the golems' middles. In an instant, they stabbed four of our enemies at once. The golems became a muddy mess at their feet, which cleared a path from them to continue charging forward, piercing through one abdomen after another. The men's features became clear through the rain, and I realized it was Gregory and Brayden.

"Gregory?" I balked as they passed close to us.

They saw us, then ran to our side. I was pretty sure they thought we'd protect them, because despite their courage to shish-kabob the priestesses' army, they both trembled in fear.

"Lucas, good to see ya," Gregory said as he crouched down, aiming the spear out in front of himself. He pointed it one way, then the other, like he was on high alert hunting a lion. Brayden stood bravely beside his boyfriend, spear at the ready.

A powerful spell shot out of the end of my wand and reduced golems to mud, before I turned back to the couple. "I thought you were leaving town."

"We were, but we couldn't do it," Gregory admitted.

"You guys needed us!" Brayden agreed.

"I've been running all my life, always scared of what the next shitty day will bring, but I figured I'm going to be scared either way. Might as well make myself useful," Gregory said. "And Brayden wouldn't leave without me, so here we are."

I applauded their bravery, but these two were going to get slaughtered out here if they weren't careful. Couldn't exactly tell them to turn back now, though. I quickly cast a shield around the couple, leaving the point of their spears poking out of the simmering dome.

"Good work, both of you," I said. "This shield will follow and protect you. Just stick together and don't get hit by any powerful spells."

Gregory stood upright, throwing his shoulders back confidently. "You heard the boss, Brayden. Let's whoop some golem ass."

Brayden gripped his spear tighter. "Let's show them what we're made of."

The two charged back into the army line, taking down golem after golem.

I spun around, looking for the priestesses' allies, but they'd fled somewhere into the forest.

"What the fuck is going on?" Grant demanded. "How'd Judge Calloway get her magic back?"

"The priestesses have to be feeding them magic from the Master

Wand," Nadine said as she landed a spell to twenty golems at once. "I tried siphoning their powers, and they resisted me."

"If they can give their supporters magic, then so can we!" I lifted the Mortana Wand. All the Death magic of the coven pulsed through me. I directed it toward my allies and felt my power fill them up.

Gregory stopped in his tracks, and Samantha gave a cry of relief. The two Mortana cast battle spells at the same time, and their magic exploded against the golems.

"I'm back, baby!" Gregory shouted with glee.

My friends followed my lead, and our allies cheered in a collective chorus as they felt their magic return.

"Go!" Miles shouted, shoving my shoulder—which really hurt, damn it. "You've done enough here. We'll slow these chucklefucks down. Find the priestesses, and finish this!"

"Tal, can you use the Seer Wand to see where they went?" Grant asked.

She shook her head. "The Master Wand is blocking me from seeing them."

"I saw the priestesses up the mountain. They can't be far," I said as I lifted my hand and ordered my scythe to fly back in my direction. My scythe sliced through a few more golems before coming to a stop in my palm. I subconjured the weapon and turned to start moving up the mountain.

"Wait!" Chloe cried. She ran forward, then grabbed Miles by the side of the face and pulled him into a passionate kiss.

Nadine grabbed her by the wrist and yanked her sideways. "There's no time! Get us into the air!"

"I love you," Chloe told Miles desperately.

Then she whirled toward us and lifted her arms. Her power levitated us upward. Her magic was strong, and I felt as stable as if I were standing on solid ground.

Chloe guided us up the mountain, close to the treetops so we couldn't be easily spotted. Abruptly, she let out an agonizing scream and fell out of the air, spiraling into the trees below. I wasn't quite sure what had happened until I felt an ungodly pain cinch my guts. Grant, Talia, and Nadine must've felt it, too, because all five of us shared a collective scream of torture. Chloe's spell failed, and we fell out of the sky. Tree branches scraped my face and tore my reaper robe as I tumbled to the forest floor.

My friends landed with heavy *thuds* beside me. The Mortana Wand fell from my hand, and the other Wands scattered across the forest floor. Grant tried to crawl for the Alchemy Wand, but he couldn't reach it. Nadine clutched her stomach and curled in on herself. I wanted to go to her, but the pain in my body intensified, rooting me in place. I managed to push myself to my knees, but even that was too much.

My body felt as if I'd just been dunked into a vat of acid. Every muscle seemed to be separating from my bones, and my skin felt as if it were melting, even though every part of me remained perfectly intact. I could do nothing but scream.

It was a gruesome but familiar pain. I'd felt it once before—the night I'd questioned James about nightshade and he used his Mentalist powers to trick my mind into thinking I was dying. I knew it wasn't real, and I still couldn't convince myself otherwise.

"James," I rasped out to warn the others.

Three shadowed figures emerged from the trees. I didn't have to see their faces to recognize the sound of their gloating laughter. James led the pack, flanked by Leroy and Cody. These three had been nothing but bullies during our time at Miriam College of Witchcraft, and they'd been the primary perpetrators of our torture during our trial.

James paced back and forth, wearing a twisted smile. "Look at what we have here. The priestesses will reward us well for our capture!"

"Perhaps they'll make us priests," Leroy suggested. "The Mortana position's about to open up for me."

If my jaw wasn't clenched in ungodly pain, I'd have scoffed. Leroy was the furthest thing from a leader. He'd sooner exercise his Death magic and kill citizens at the touch of his hand than help them.

I tried to lift my palm to call the Mortana Wand back to me, but the pain was so unbearable I couldn't unclench my fists.

"The only reason I haven't killed you yet is because you've got our buddy prisoner," James said. "Where's Ryan?"

Their performance was comical. All this for Ryan? He didn't give a shit about any one of these three. Ryan had mourned the loss of his closest pals, and not one of these guys made the cut.

I sucked a pained breath between my teeth. "Ryan doesn't… care about you."

"Shut up!" Leroy spat.

"You're the ones who… asked the question," I gasped between shallow breaths.

Leroy broke into boisterous laughter so loud it echoed through the storm. He knelt to my level, laughing in my face as he watched me writhe. "You think you're a priest who can just walk in here and stand in *their* place. Look who's laughing now!"

What a fucking loser. These three clearly weren't on the same page, because James was worried about Ryan while Leroy just wanted to mock me. Nobody even tried to take our Wands. They were more concerned with toying with us than ending this.

"How's it feel?" Cody growled. He walked straight up to Talia and grabbed her by the hair, yanking her head back to force her to look at him.

Her eyes glistened, and it wasn't from the rain. It was obvious Talia had hoped to never see his face again, because it was the face that haunted her dreams. Cody had caused her more pain than I could ever imagine while they'd been dating. He'd been a senior her freshman year of college and knew how to target and manipulate younger girls. She'd given him all of herself, only for him to treat her like trash. He was covert about it, always framing his insults as jokes—or worse, as *compliments*. He'd broken down her spirit until he could coerce her into things she didn't want to do. He'd been very calculated about it. Talia hadn't been able to report him because he didn't physically force her, but it still made him a predator.

"You thought you could just walk away from me, like you were better than me?" Cody spat. "You hurt me, Talia."

Ha! As if he wasn't the cheating bastard.

Beside her, Grant tried to stand, but he couldn't move under James's spell. He gritted his teeth and spat out, "Leave. Her. Alone."

Cody scoffed as he eyed Grant up and down. "I don't know what she sees in you. But I guess you losers are better off together. She was a lousy lay anyway."

Talia let out a pained groan. "Hard to practice… when it lasts less than a minute."

"Fuck you!" Cody spat. "I faked it because you were so boring I just wanted it to end."

"Is that why you… stayed with me for so long?" Talia winced. Her eyes darted in our direction for a second, and though our enemies missed it, her message was clear. She was distracting them.

"Please," Cody scoffed. "We barely dated."

Beside me, Nadine reached out for me, and I pushed past the pain to stretch my fingers in her direction. She took Chloe's hand on her other side, and I reached for Grant. James's spell was merely a mind game, and even without magic, we should be able to break through it. We just had to convince ourselves the pain wasn't real. With my friends' hands in mine, I reminded myself that *they* were what was real—not this silly charade.

Grant's fingers trembled as he reached out for Talia, but her attention was laser-focused on Cody.

"You thought… you owned me," Talia gasped. Her arms spasmed under the weight of James's spell.

"Tal," Chloe urged past gritted teeth. "Castrate… him."

I didn't know what she was referring to, but it must've meant something to Talia, because she began to sob. It wasn't from the pain, though. It was more like relief… or perhaps an unleashing of courage.

Her sobs turned to screams. Talia's chin turned toward the sky as she let out a grueling cry of pain. "Fuck. You!" she cried. "You were never the one… in charge. I was the one who… gave myself to you… and you abused me. You never deserved me. I will not… remain silent any longer."

An invisible force blasted outward from Talia, so strong the rain around us paused for the briefest of moments. At the same time, Talia lunged for the Seer Wand several feet away from her. She caught Cody off guard, and he dove for it, too, but she was faster than him. Talia grabbed the Wand and scrambled to her feet.

"What the hell!?" James shouted. He shook his hands, like he couldn't understand why his spell wasn't working on her.

Terrible pain continued to course through my veins, but I understood now what the blast had been. It was James's spell backfiring. Talia had broken through it, though the rest of us were still trapped.

Leroy ran toward Talia. If he got her hands on her, he could kill her in a second. But Grant kicked his leg out to trip Leroy. The fucker landed flat on his face.

James hesitated, shooting a glance between Talia and the rest of us. For a beat, his pain spell faltered, but it came back full-force a second later. He'd lost control of Talia and couldn't focus on her without losing his grip on us.

Talia aimed the Seer Wand straight at Cody. "I get it now, why you had to convince me I was nothing and that my feelings didn't matter. You couldn't handle that my magic was stronger than yours. You're a Seer with empathic abilities, but I never saw you use them. It's because you can't, isn't it? Not because your magic doesn't work, but because you don't know how to feel for someone else. Instead of caring for people, you break them down until they feel as shitty as you do. You take people's voices away because you can't handle what they'd say about you if they spoke up. You played with my head for too long, but now I'm the one in charge. I know what you did to me, and I've seen what you've done to other girls. Now you're going to see it from my perspective."

The end of the Seer Wand glowed. Cody clutched his head and scrambled back until he stumbled into a tree. Talia must've been projecting a vision into his mind, because he squeezed his eyes together and shook his head violently, like he could rid his mind from everything she showed him.

"You bitch!" he screamed.

"I'm not showing you anything you didn't do yourself!" Talia shot back. "You know what you did, and now you're going to know the pain it caused."

Cody dropped to his knees as veins bulged in his face. He stared blankly into the forest with a look of horror permanently etched onto his face. Whatever she showed him next caused him to sag forward and spew vomit across the forest floor.

Cody couldn't handle it. He scrambled to his feet and took off down the mountain, running and screaming like a maniac.

Leroy pushed himself to his feet and turned on Talia. "You're going to pay for that."

Black tendrils of magic danced out of Leroy's fingers. I'd seen his magic at play before and knew that if he got close enough to her, his spell would kill her instantly. He could've achieved the same effect with a battle spell, but it was clear he liked to show off.

"Leroy, the priestesses wanted us to—" James started.

"Shut up!" Leroy spat. "The priestesses aren't here. I'm going to handle this my way. And when the priestesses put me on the council, *this* is the way we're going to deal with people like her who step out of line. She thinks she's so powerful, but I'll show her what power looks like."

Fuck that. It didn't matter if the pain tearing my body to shreds right now was real or not. I could be burning in hellfire and still wouldn't let him touch my friend. I squeezed Nadine's and Grant's hands tighter, then something within me snapped.

James recoiled as his spell broke its hold on me, blasting outward like it had with Talia. I lifted my hand, and the Mortana Wand flew into it. Leroy reached Talia, but his killing spell had died on his fingers.

"You won't touch her!" I growled as I got to my feet.

Mortana magic pulsed through me, so powerful that I didn't even have to think about cutting off Leroy's magic. The Wand merely responded to my will.

I felt his connection to Alora snap as the Mortana Wand overpowered him completely. The tendrils of black magic swirling out of his fingers drifted away in the wind as I severed his control of power.

Leroy's eyes went wide. He touched Talia again, but nothing happened.

"You're right, Leroy," I said. "You are powerful. But it's not your power that matters—it's how you use it. You could've used your power for good, but you didn't even try. Instead, to prove to everyone how strong you were, you chose to use it in the most horrific of ways. You tortured us and tried to drown me at my trial. I've watched you use your power to kill innocent people. You were a bully because you couldn't figure out how to be great without harming others. Your streak is over. I have all the magic of the Mortana Cast now, and I'm going to take your power so you can't keep hurting people."

"No!" he panicked.

"I don't want to do this," I said honestly. "I'm not in the business of taking people's power. But if I can prevent you from stealing one more innocent life, it's worth it. I'm not doing this to punish you. I'm doing it to protect all your future victims, because you've made it damn clear you won't stop hurting people unless someone stops you first. You won't hurt my friend, or anyone else ever again."

He backpedaled a few steps, though he kept his arms lifted like he was trying to overpower me. But the Wand had already damned him, for the spell was so strong that even if I wanted to give his magic back, I couldn't. Death was a transformation, and I had transformed his magic entirely. Leroy's connection to his magic had been severed, and his power to kill was forever gone.

"You can't do this!" Leroy protested.

Energy rippled through my entire form as I conjured powerful reaper magic. The chill on my skin disappeared as my magic turned me into something otherworldly. I appeared as nothing but a skeleton—my full reaper form. My scythe appeared in my hand, and I crossed the distance between us in a split second. The empty sockets of my skeletal face stopped mere inches from his nose.

"You want to bet?" I threatened.

Sheer terror crossed his features, then Leroy whirled around and took off running the way Cody went. I didn't know where he would go, but it was sure as hell somewhere far away from Octavia Falls. Leroy would never show his face around here again, that was for certain.

"Nobody move!" James warned. He still had a hold on Nadine, Grant, and Chloe, but his arms shook, like he was struggling to hold the spell. "Try anything, and I'll hurt your little Curse Maker girlfriend."

"No… you won't!" Nadine snarled.

Her proclamation was enough to break the last of his spell. His power ricocheted in his direction, sending him flying off his feet. Grant and Chloe sagged to the ground, letting out a collective sigh of relief as the pain ebbed away.

Nadine grabbed the Curse Breaker Wand from beside her and got to her feet. James trembled as he scrambled back on his elbows.

Nadine aimed her Wand at his face. "It's over, James. You called me a Curse Maker because you were afraid of people who were different than you. It's our differences that make us a coven, but you were so intent on causing pain to everyone else around you so you never had to feel it yourself. You wanted me to make curses—fine. I'll give you a curse. I want you to walk in the shoes of your victims. Get on your feet, turn around, and start walking. Walk until your feet bleed. Don't stop until you know what it's like to suffer like all the people you've hurt."

James whimpered as he got to his feet. Then he did exactly as Nadine ordered. He started walking, disappearing into the trees with the gait of a man who would never be seen or heard from again.

I breathed a sigh of relief, and my magic subsided to bring the flesh back to my bones. I rushed over to Nadine and swept her into my arms. Grant hugged Talia so hard he picked her nearly a foot off the ground.

Chloe bent down to grab the Mentalist Wand from the ground. "You guys, that was totally badass!"

"Scared me there for a bit," Grant said as he set Talia down. "I thought we were going to break the spell together, but when you guys started breaking it on your own, I worried I was going to have to do it by myself."

"We *did* break the spell together," Nadine said. "Maybe not at the same time, but we gave each other the courage to do it."

Chloe walked over to Talia and placed her palms on her shoulders. "Tal, I am so, *so* proud of you."

Then she wrapped her in a tight hug, and Talia squeezed her back. "Thank you. I never thought I could do it, but now I know I can—and nobody will *ever* silence me again. Certainly not some asshat like him."

Chloe pulled away beaming proudly. "How'd it feel?"

Talia couldn't help but smile. "Really fucking good. Now let's go kick some priestess ass."

"We've got to get a vantage point," I said.

Chloe lifted her hands, and her powers raised us into the air once again. We quickly flew upward, until Chloe deposited us all gently onto the outcropping of rock I'd seen the priestesses standing on before. There were no signs of them now.

We stood at the top of a steep cliff that towered over the treetops below. It gave us a clear view of the battlefield that had been carved out in the forest at the base of the mountain. So many trees had toppled over that the clearing was bigger than ever before—at least twenty acres now. Shadowed figures ran from one end of the battlefield to the other, and screams could be heard over the storm. Explosions sounded in the distance, and flashes of magic lit up the clouds. It was impossible to tell who was winning the fight, because we couldn't see much else through the rain. I figured our side must be holding up well, because I hadn't heard a single dying thought since we arrived.

Then it occurred to me that James's spell very well could've distracted me long enough to not hear a thing. We had no way of knowing what was going on down there.

Chloe spread her arms to the sky. "All right, we're here! Come and get us!"

No answer came except the rumbling of thunder overhead.

"I don't get it," Grant said. "Don't the priestesses want to kill us? Why aren't they coming for us?"

"Because they don't know where we are," Talia realized. "Cody, Leroy, and James took power from people because they didn't feel they had it themselves, and the priestesses are no different. That's why they're blocking me from seeing them—because they don't know how to use their visions effectively. The priestesses don't know how this is going to end any more than we do."

I wiped rainwater from my eyes. "Good. We can use that to our advantage."

Nadine tore her gaze from the battlefield. "Tal, you said the Master Wand was blocking your visions of the priestesses. Can we get around that somehow? If we use the Seer Wand to target other people on the battlefield, maybe they have eyes on them."

"Good idea," Talia said. "Let's work the spell together."

We ducked into the cover of the trees. The five of us formed a circle and created a powerful shield around ourselves. As we joined hands, magic began to pulse around us like a spinning wheel. Talia's visions invaded my mind, and we seemed to be transported down the mountain, looking over the scene.

The vision gave us a clearer view of the battlefield. All across the clearing, mounds of mud were piled high from the remains of hundreds of golems. The golems still fighting hid behind the mounds, aiming powerful spells at our allies who came too close. Our people hid in the trees, blasting magic and cannonballs over the clearing.

Bodies lay sprawled across the battlefield. Some were corpses of the undead, who had been beaten down so hard their magic couldn't sustain them any longer. Others were coven members who had come to support our cause.

The vision zoomed in on the battlefield. A line of blood left a trail to an injured man at the edge of the trees. Three people dragged him to the tree line and laid him down gently. The Seer Wand took us closer, until we could see him reaching out with a shaky hand.

"Tell my wife and son I love them," he choked out.

I saw his face in my mind's eye a second before his hand went limp. Jude Bennett had a hole ripped through his stomach so wide his intestines were spilling out. Samantha was beside him, her hands bloody as she tried to shove his guts back into his abdomen. But it was too late. His features went pale as life drained out of him. My Mortana magic fused with Talia's Seer powers, and together, we all felt the void of death permeate the battlefield.

Jude's voice entered my mind. *I did this for them. Protect my family like you protected them before, Lucas.*

Jude had used his last thought to send me a message—a plea from beyond the grave to do everything in my power to help.

The vision lingered on Jude a few moments longer, until Nadine said, "We have to keep going."

Talia cleared her throat. "Right."

The vision flew us over toward the other end of the battlefield. We witnessed the golems gathering a spell together, forming it in the blink of an eye. Instinctually, I went to throw up a shield, before realizing I wasn't actually on the battlefield and my shield wouldn't reach that far.

The spell exploded toward our allies, and they scrambled out of the way to dodge the attack. But one person wasn't so lucky. Professor Loren was an old, frail woman, and she couldn't get out of the way in time. She lifted her hand to cast a shield, but the golems' spell blasted straight through it. She was hit in the shoulder and fell to the ground, panting.

"Nina!" Professor Richards screamed. He'd been among those who dodged the spell, and he'd landed on his hands and knees. He crawled over to her. Richards reached into this pocket and pulled out a tiny vial of white liquid. "I brought this just in case. It's the only one I have left. Take it."

Professor Loren pushed his hand away. "Save your healing potion, Anthony," she rasped. "I'm prepared to go. I've been ready for a long time."

Tears welled in Professor Richards's eyes. "Nina, no. Fight with me. We promised to fight together."

Professor Loren took his hand in hers. "We did, and we fought *well*. I'm ready to be with my Autumn again."

"You were the best colleague I could ask for," Richards told her.

Then her hand went limp in his.

The fight has been worth it, her voice echoed through my mind.

A shiver traveled down my spine.

"Tal, keep going," Chloe pressed.

Our vision took us into the trees, where we caught sight of Cody tearing through the battle, trying to escape the horror of the visions Talia had given him. From out of nowhere, a crackling spell whizzed through the trees and hit Cody in the back. His form went rigid, and black veins spiderwebbed up his neck.

Mother Miriam, forgive me. His voice echoed through my mind as he collapsed to the ground.

The power of the killing curse seemed to shudder through the trees. This wasn't just any rogue spell. Whoever had cast it had done so with a vengeance.

The vision shifted its angle, and we saw Tyler standing several feet away from Cody, his chest heaving. "That'll teach you to mess with my sister," he sneered. Then he spat on Cody's corpse and walked away.

"I—I can't believe he did that for me," Talia whispered.

"I didn't see anything," Chloe said innocently. "Keep going. We need to find the priestesses."

The vision shifted again, flashing from face to face on the battlefield to hunt the priestesses down. The Seer Wand settled upon Professor Lewis. She didn't look as angry as the others engaged in battle. Instead, she appeared desperate.

"Priestesses," Professor Lewis groveled.

Footsteps sounded in the background of the vision, but the spell resisted changing angles. I witnessed the flash of a black cloak, but nothing more.

"I saw the traitors heading up the mountain," Professor Lewis said.

The vision turned hazy as a muffled voice responded, but we couldn't hear what they said.

Professor Lewis stumbled to the side, like someone had shoved her. "Wait! Don't I get a reward for helping you?"

Another muffled voice came, and then a sinister flash of light. I didn't comprehend what happened until Professor Lewis's voice came into my mind.

I was loyal. Her final thought was melancholy, almost regretful, but it all occurred so fast I wasn't sure she fully understood what had happened to her.

Talia yanked her hands away, and the vision ended. "I'm sorry… that was too much."

"Why would the priestesses kill their own follower?" Grant asked hollowly.

Chloe shifted uncomfortably. "Because she outlived her usefulness. She was only going to slow them down."

"That means they're on their way to us." Nadine turned her gaze skyward. "We obtain the Master Wand at all costs, agreed? Everyone get ready. We do this together."

I nodded firmly and placed my left hand on her right shoulder. "Together."

Grant did the same to me, and Talia and Chloe joined us on either side. We formed a line and lifted the Oaken Wands to the sky. I could feel our magic pulsing as one. The Wands' power spoke to us, and we didn't even have to speak aloud to know which spell we wanted to cast. I could *feel* the intention of my friends, and I knew the desires of each Wand as if it were my own. The Wands weren't just one—but *we* were one.

I didn't shrink down to become something else. I was still a whole and complete human being on my own. But together, by standing united with each other and the Oaken Wands, we each became something bigger than ourselves. We were no longer five individuals working toward a common goal. We were *one* people made of five different parts.

Two ominous silhouettes appeared through the treetops above us, their cloaks billowing against the backdrop of flashing storm clouds. Margaret lifted the Master Wand above her, while Lilian kept her hands outward to control her levitation powers.

Before they could spot us, my friends and I blasted our magic outward simultaneously. Beams of light burst from the ends of the Oaken Wands, becoming one as the massive spell enveloped the priestesses entirely. It was a spell unlike I'd ever seen before—the kind so strong it made the earth shake. Above us, our spell was so bright it lit the dark sky like the sun. The forest quieted as the thunder halted at our command. My ears rang as I urged my Wand to push harder. Rocks tumbled down the mountainside, and trees fell over as our spell intensified. It felt as if we were pulling magic from the core of the Earth itself. All the magic of the coven flowed through us, and it was enough to drain the priestesses of their power for good. They should never be able to cast another spell again, for our magic was so strong it would forever refuse their desires.

The massive ball of light in the sky became brighter and brighter, expanding outward as if it were a star about to go supernova.

Then it stopped. From out of nowhere, the magic simply halted. There was no explosion, no backfire… the magic just vanished, like it was never there to begin with. The sky turned dark again, and thunder returned with a vengeance. Lightning cracked three times in a second. Around us, the wind picked up heavier than before, whipping through the trees at least sixty miles per hour. Now the earth wasn't rumbling in response to our spell, but because of the storm. A funnel cloud began to form overhead, and I realized we'd made the storm even worse.

"Did it work?" Grant shouted.

A loud, wicked cackle rang through the sky. I shielded my eyes from the rain and looked up to see the priestesses descending upon us. They landed in the forest with ease, like our spell hadn't even shaken them.

"What a sad attempt at exhibiting your power!" Lilian mocked. "Too bad all that determination will go to waste."

We didn't let her finish. Together, my friends and I blasted out another spell, but Margaret had already flicked the Master Wand. The two spells rushed through the forest like tidal waves speeding toward each other. They slammed into one another, creating an echoing *crack* louder than any thunder. It must've been audible a hundred miles away. I threw up a shield to protect us from the deafening noise.

The magic from our spell shot upward toward the sky, sending light beams into the clouds. Margaret's spell had stopped ours, and its power had nowhere else to go.

My friends and I held our ground, pushing with all our might to overpower her magic. I could feel her spell resisting ours, and as we touched it, her intent was clear. She wanted to strip us of our magic, the same way we intended to do to her. The only way to win this was for one of us to weaken the other, and it was obvious the Master Wand and the Oaken Wands were equally matched.

"We've got to try something else!" Nadine shouted over the roaring wind. She flicked the Curse Breaker Wand, and her magic rippled through us all. We could feel her intent and instantly agreed to help her.

Basic magic alone wasn't working. We had to try something darker, something sinister. If we wanted to win this, we had to put our morals aside, because we weren't playing by our rules anymore—we were playing by *theirs*. It wasn't a route we wanted to take, but if we didn't stop the priestesses now, they would continue their rampage across Octavia Falls and stop at nothing to bring every last coven member under their tyrannical control.

Together, the five of us cast a curse through the earth. The magic sent black goo bubbling up from the ground at the priestesses' feet. Just one touch, and they would be cursed to surrender. The two of them merely laughed, like our attempt at dark magic was comical. Margaret swished the Master Wand, sending the black goo melting back into the dirt. Our spell recoiled, and the five of us were blasted into the air in all different directions.

Dynamite might as well have gone off at our feet. My back slammed into the massive trunk of a tree behind me, and I felt something crack. I was fairly certain it was a rib or two. I was so disoriented I couldn't see where my friends had gone.

I forced myself to lift my head, but it pounded so hard I could barely see a thing. I caught sight of Nadine lying on her side not far from me. Her features swam in front of me, and my heart ached to reach out for her. I tried, but she was too far away to touch. Her eyes fluttered open, then closed again. She appeared to be drifting in and out of consciousness.

Chloe's voice rang out from my right. "You're going to pay for what you've done to the coven!"

My vision cleared to see Chloe standing in front of her grandmother. She lifted the Mentalist Wand, but at the same time, the funnel cloud touched ground. The colossal winds of an enormous tornado swept her off her feet. Leaves spiraled upward into the air, and I was dragged across the forest floor by an invisible force. Trees groaned and cracked as they were uprooted. I grabbed a hold of a large tree root to avoid being swept up in the swirling twister. My legs lifted into the air. My broken ribs screamed in protest, and I struggled to breathe. It took everything I had to hold on for dear life without losing the Mortana Wand to the storm. I heard Nadine scream, but I couldn't be sure of where she'd gone.

Chloe's frightened cry ripped across the mountainside as the tornado yanked her across the landscape and out of sight. The cyclone careened off across the mountain, but the windstorm continued to whip leaves and debris across my face. I sucked in a greedy breath as my feet returned to solid ground.

"No!" Grant cried. He came running through the forest from behind me, the Alchemy Wand at the ready.

The rain above the priestesses' heads lit up a bright green, reminiscent of glowing potions from the Alchemy classrooms back at school. He'd alchemized the rain into a mighty spell. The rain came down on the priestesses in a sheet, but Margaret quickly retaliated. Grant's spell backfired, and green magic spiraled back into the end of his Wand. The magic lit up his entire form for a second, and then… he vanished.

I gasped, and the shock sent pain rippling through my torso. Grant had only been standing a few feet away from me, and now, he was gone. I didn't understand what had happened. Then I spotted the Alchemy Wand in the dirt where he'd been standing. A fat, warted toad hopped toward the Wand.

The toad was Grant! I scrambled forward on my elbows, pushing past the searing pain in my side, and grabbed the toad and the Alchemy Wand before the priestesses could aim another spell. I shoved Grant and his Wand into the pocket of my robe to keep them safe.

It had all happened in a second, but Talia was already on the move. I spotted her stumbling to her feet twenty yards from me. She lifted the Seer Wand and aimed it at the priestesses. Our Wands were still connected, and I could feel her intent. She was going to cast a spell like the one she'd put on Cody, to show the priestesses what harm they'd caused. She hoped to change their minds.

No sooner had she lifted her Wand did Margaret cast out a shield. Talia's spell backfired on her, sending her spinning through the air. She lay still on the forest floor, knocked out by the power of her spell.

I got to my feet, but the priestesses had already anticipated my attack. With a flick of the Master Wand, Margaret created dozens of portals all at once. The dark depths of the Abyss stared back at me.

Then monsters came running. At least twenty hellish beings jumped out of the portals all at once, all salivating with the thirst for human blood. There were so many of them I couldn't take them all in. All I saw were endless gnashing teeth and sharp claws that could gut me in one swipe.

One of the monsters appeared as a skeleton-like canine—almost hyena-like with mangled ears and ashen skin hanging off its bones. It had big sharp teeth that it snapped at me as it crossed twenty yards in a single leap.

I cast my magic outward, and it was so strong that I didn't even need a portal to send the beast back to the underworld. The creature vanished the second my magic touched it.

A tall, bipedal monster with lava for skin lashed fat fingers out at me, but I sent him back to hell in the blink of an eye. I did the same to the others in quick succession.

In my attempt to defend myself, the priestesses had successfully distracted me. The second I sent the last of the monsters to hell, another spell blasted straight into my chest. An invisible force dragged me backward, binding my arms to my sides. The Mortana Wand dropped from my hand, and I was yanked backward another ten yards until my spine slammed against a tree. Fucking hurt, too. I thought the blow might've fractured another rib, but I couldn't be sure that it wasn't already broken.

Lilian laughed maniacally as she flicked her wrist upward. I was yanked off my feet and into the air. Her spell was like magical ropes tying me to the tree trunk at least six feet off the ground.

I knew my magic was still working, because I could feel my power still pulsing into my zombie army down the mountain. But when I tried to command my Wand back into my hand, I couldn't do it. Lilian had used some sort of curse fused with her Mentalist abilities to keep me from moving. I was frozen in place, unable to cast my magic. Lilian wanted me to watch as they ripped the rest of the coven to shreds.

Nadine stumbled out from behind a tree. She was the last one still standing... but barely. She had cuts all across her face, and bruises mottled her arms. She didn't waste a second casting a spell—only this time, Nadine didn't aim for the priestesses. She went after the Master Wand.

Battle spell after battle spell erupted from the end of Nadine's Wand. But the second she cast the spell, the Master Wand was already gone.

Priestess Margaret formed a portal that she tossed the Master Wand through, only for another portal to open above Lilian's head. Priestess Lilian caught the Master Wand with an evil laugh. Nadine aimed for her, but she'd already tossed it through another portal back to Priestess Margaret. The two were playing a sick game of Monkey in the Middle, cackling as they taunted my wife with their games. It was two against one, and Nadine couldn't keep up.

Margaret caught the Master Wand again, but instead of tossing it back to Lilian, she spun on Nadine. An intense spell shot through the forest, so fast Nadine couldn't respond. I tried to call out for her, but Lilian's spell had forced my jaw tightly shut.

Margaret's magic hit Nadine, and my wife collapsed where she stood. I watched in horror as cuts opened up all over Nadine's body. It was torture to be unable to stop it. Blood the color of ink oozed out of the wounds.

Nadine's agonizing cry seemed to unravel the very fabric of reality. I'd never heard such a heart-wrenching sound in all my life. We'd been through so much, and not even the worst of it could compare to this harrowing sound. It was the kind of pleading cry that could summon the gods down to Earth, because no one in any realm, throughout all eternity, should ever encounter such evil. Even the demons down in hell would have trouble stomaching it. Tears streamed from my eyes as I was forced to helplessly watch my wife convulse as the wicked curse bled her dry.

Then she did the most marvelous thing. Nadine clutched the Curse Breaker Wand tightly in her hand, and by sheer will and determination, the inky black substance reversed course. The drips that had been trailing down her face turned backward, sinking into the wounds. The cuts healed themselves as she drew the curse inward.

Then magic exploded out of her, barreling toward the priestesses. It swept through the forest in a millisecond, and the priestesses were caught off guard. Nadine turned their curse back on them, and the powerful magic caused both priestesses to fall to their knees. Their eyes took on a blood-shot appearance, and their jaws dropped open as their bodies shook uncontrollably. Deep red blood streamed from their eyes.

I thought for sure Nadine had gained the upper hand, but Margaret pushed back with the Master Wand, and the spell broke with the power of a shockwave. The ground between us and the priestesses cracked, splitting the mountain apart. A deep cavern formed that must've stretched hundreds of feet down into the earth.

Nadine moved quickly. Magic swelled through the forest, and I witnessed tendrils of magic stream out the end of the Mortana Wand and into Nadine. They were soft, white wisps that were hard to see through the darkness of the storm. I didn't think the priestesses noticed it, but I did. Nadine was siphoning power from the other Wands to use their magic against the priestesses.

In quick succession, Nadine cast a spell from each of the other four Casts. These weren't spells she could normally create on her own. In fact, every attempt she'd ever made to use magic from other Casts had failed. But this wasn't like the magic she'd used before. With the Oaken Wands working together, they created spells unlike any of us had ever seen. Through cooperation, Nadine was able to funnel their magic through her own Curse Breaker Wand.

A smoky black substance in the shape of a skull zoomed through the forest, until it became solid—like the dismembered floating head of a mythical giant. The skull hinged at the jaw like it was going to swallow the priestesses whole. Margaret swished the Master Wand, and the creepy skull turned to ash.

Before the priestesses had blocked her spell, Nadine was already casting the next one. The smoke from her Wand transformed into the shape of a massive cauldron above the priestesses' heads. It solidified into cast iron as it tilted, sending a sizzling black substance to pour over the priestesses like a waterfall. Margaret barely had to move her Wand before the poison alchemized into snow. Harmless snowflakes drifted down around the priestesses, then got carried away in the wind.

Then an image invaded my mind, one so real I forgot we were in the middle of a battle altogether. Instead, I stood on the edge of the outcropping not far from here, looking over the remnants of Octavia Falls. Storm clouds brewed above the city, as if they'd never left after the fight, but it had to be years in the future. The fallen trees in the battlefield below had rotted away to nothing. The town below appeared desolate and forgotten. Far off in the distance, a lone figure in a dark cloak walked the streets, their lonely, mournful cry carrying all the way up the mountain.

The scene shifted abruptly, and the lone figure grew to tower hundreds of feet above the city. They lifted their hands, and the gothic turrets of the forgotten town grew to the size of skyscrapers. The powerful being seemed to be creating a fortress for their town. Lightning streaked across the sky as wicked laughter filled the air.

Thunder cracked, and I was yanked from the vision and back to the present. The spell recoiled, and Nadine was knocked to the ground, panting on her hands and knees.

I realized the vision had been Nadine's interpretation of what the future held if the priestesses had won. She'd combined Seer and Mentalists powers to make it appear more real than the battle we currently stood in. She wanted to show the priestesses what would come of them if they achieved their goal—that they'd have no coven left to go back to, and by winning at all costs, they'd be left as nothing more than queens of their ashes. She wanted them to *feel* what winning for their side would cost them, in the hopes that they'd give up.

If anything, it only motivated them. The priestesses had turned the vision against her, shown her how much they relished in their victory. It didn't matter to them what was left of the coven as long as they didn't have to hand it over.

"You think your silly visions are going to stop us?" Margaret spat. "You thought you could beat us with *ideas* alone, that if you just told the coven to *think positive* and *work together*, all would be fine and they'd *listen*? This war only ever had one outcome, and it was always going to end in your defeat, Nadine, because you've been wrong about giving people choices all this time. You're too young and inexperienced to get it; it took me decades to figure it out. If we're going to follow our goddess, we have to *think* like goddesses, and you've been thinking too small all this time."

"Your ideas are going to die with you," Lilian spat in agreement. "You'll learn soon enough that no one ever wanted to listen to you in the first place."

A spell shot out of the end of the Master Wand. I wanted to scream as a stream of black magic connected with Nadine's chest, but I couldn't make a sound. The spell hit Nadine so hard and fast that she went flying backward, spinning through the air until she landed with a heavy *thud* on the forest floor below me. Her head smacked against the tree I was bound against, and she lay completely still.

Then her voice entered my mind, and with it the most agonizing heartbreak imaginable. *I'm with you until the end, Lucas.*

I wanted to scream, but I was trapped within my own body. That made it a hundred times worse, because my grief wasn't provided an outlet as simple as a scream. If I could let out a wail right now, I was certain the whole coven would be able to hear it—perhaps even feel the grim despair ripple through their bones.

Forget about defending Octavia Falls. The whole damn world was collapsing all at once.

Nadine was gone. We'd lost.

Margaret merely laughed, like this was some friendly game of chess and she'd just declared a checkmate. "The chosen one is down. We won!"

"Now we can finish this!" Lilian cried in delight.

Through my tears, I witnessed a smirk cross Margaret's features. She whirled on Lilian, the Master Wand pointed at her companion. "I'm afraid only one of us can continue from here," Margaret said with a tone of fake regret. "There's only one Master Wand, and it was built only for a single magic user."

Lilian raised her arms and dropped to her knees in surrender. I never thought I'd live to see this powerful woman grovel at someone else's feet. "Please, sister. You don't have to kill me. I have followed you all this time, and that hasn't changed."

"That's why I have to do this," Margaret spat. "Sometimes, being a leader requires you to make tough choices, even if you don't want to. It's not easy running a coven. People question you at every turn. Everyone wants to have it *their* way, but they're not smart enough or knowledgeable enough to know what it takes to manage all these moving parts. I've been a priestess for over three decades, and if there's anything I've learned, it's that people have to be told what to do, or nothing will get done. You can give them the world, and all they'll do is *whine* about it. They didn't appreciate what we gave them, so we had to take it away so they'd listen. We aren't built to share power. I'm going to rebuild the coven, but this time, I'm going to do it *my* way. You had the right ideas, Lilian, but you and I have always been in competition. You were always trying to assert your dominance to show who was really in charge, and at times I let you believe it. You were more than happy to show off your power, and I was pleased to use it to my advantage. But your usefulness has run out, and I'm done sharing power. I can't run the risk of you betraying me."

"So you would sooner betray *me*?" Lilian asked as tears filled her eyes.

"I did this all for you. I don't need the power of the Master Wand. You should be the one running the coven. It was your destiny all along."

"Of course it was!" Margaret yelled. "Witches believe in caring for the individual, but I tried all these years to care for these people, and the minute I couldn't fix their problems, they turned on me. What about me? When do I get the credit I deserve? When will I be respected for my rightful power? Mother Miriam sanctioned me as a priestess all those years ago, but she put me through these lessons and hardships to show me how it *should* be done."

"I agree," Lilian urged. "The coven doesn't understand how to manage under the division of power. They used their power to put my husband in prison, and I worked my whole life to change things. We need someone like you who will fight for what's right. Let me be there to help you."

"I really wish you could," Margaret said in a condescending way. "But you're too much of a liability."

Margaret flicked the Master Wand the same time Lilian lunged forward. She shoved Margaret's wrist toward the sky, and the killing spell Margaret intended to use on Lilian shot into the clouds. Lilian yanked the Wand from Margaret's hands and blasted a spell straight through Margaret's chest.

It had all happened so fast, it seemed surreal. But this wasn't some trickery or vision. A sizzling hole sat where Margaret's heart used to be. In the blink of an eye, Lilian had turned Margaret's betrayal against her and took her fellow priestess's life.

Lilian hadn't meant a word she'd said. She'd only been distracting her rival to give herself time to gain the upper hand.

Priestess Margaret's body slumped to the ground. The void of death made my stomach lurch as Margaret's last thought rang through my mind. *I sought power for nothing.*

Mere milliseconds had passed. Lilian's arm was still raised when a spell slammed into her wrist. I wasn't sure where it had come from. If I had to guess, Margaret had somehow enchanted the Master Wand to backfire on other spellcasters if she lost control of it. Lilian screamed as the sound of breaking bone filled the forest. Her hand appeared completely mangled. The Master Wand flew from her grasp, then spun across the forest toward me.

A hand reached up from below me, catching the Master Wand. I looked down to see Nadine had gotten to her feet, and my heart filled with immense joy and relief. *She'd* been the one to cast the spell, catching Priestess Lilian off guard.

I didn't get it. I'd heard her last thought. I could've sworn she was dead...

Then I realized the void of death I felt with Margaret hadn't been present with Nadine. I'd been too wrapped in my grief to realize it. I hadn't heard Nadine's *last* thought. She'd been communicating telepathically with the power of the Oaken Wands. She was trying to tell me she was still here, and I'd taken it the wrong way.

Lilian's eyes widened in horror as she realized Nadine now held the Master Wand. She thrust her hands outward to attack, but her magic didn't come. She stumbled back a step. "That's not possible! Margaret cast a killing spell on you!"

"Yes, she did," Nadine said as she paced forward, keeping the Master Wand trained on Lilian. "And I shielded myself from her attack. The spell did hit me, but not with full force."

Nadine has faked her death to trick the priestesses. What a clever girl.

"It's over, Lilian," Nadine said.

She lifted the Master Wand, and the storm calmed to a light drizzle. The crevice that had been spliced through the mountain merged together, leaving a scar behind in the earth.

Lilian's spell on me gently loosened. I slowly lowered to the ground like I was attached to a harness. I landed beside Nadine, then pulled the toad from my pocket and placed him in the dirt.

Grant instantly turned back into himself. He ran his tongue over his teeth. "Yuck. Being a toad tastes funny... although I'm really hungry for some flies right now."

"You can have all the flies you want later," I said as I handed him the Alchemy Wand. Then I raised my hand, and the Mortana Wand flew into it.

Nearby, Talia lifted her head and blinked a few times, before pushing herself to her feet. "Fuck, that's going to leave a mark."

A shadow passed above us, and Chloe levitated herself down from the clouds. She kept the Mentalist Wand trained on her grandmother.

"You should've died in that storm!" Lilian spat.

"Please, Grandma," Chloe scoffed. "I have telekinesis; I can fly. That tornado pulled me off course for a bit, but I found my way back. I always do."

Lilian's knees trembled. I'd never seen her look so frightened. Earlier when she groveled at Margaret's feet, it was all an act, but the fear I witnessed in her eyes now was genuine. She'd been too sure of herself to ever think she might lose.

"What are you going to do now, Chloe?" Lilian spat. "Kill me?"

Chloe took several steps forward.

"What's she doing?" Grant hissed.

Nadine held out a hand, signaling for the rest of us to stay back. "Let Chloe handle this."

Chloe tilted her head. "You think I would kill my own grandmother?"

"Wouldn't you?" Lilian asked coldly. "You know I'd do the same to you."

Chloe stopped just a few feet in front of her grandma. "I don't understand how you could be so cruel. I'm your flesh and blood. Does that mean nothing to you?"

"Of course it does, my dear grandchild. But there are things that are bigger than us, and you continue to get in my way. I'm a motivated woman, and I'll do anything to get what I want."

"Even kill innocent people?" Chloe asked sadly.

"If their existence obstructed my mission, then yes," Lilian stated, sounding almost *proud* of such a horrendous crime.

"How many innocents did you kill?" Chloe demanded.

Lilian scoffed and rolled her eyes. "You expect me to keep count? Let's stop this ridiculous charade. You have the power now. Are you going to be a coward with it, or are you going to step up and be the powerful witch I raised you to be? At least if you're going to kill me, make it great."

Chloe stared down at the Mentalist Wand in her hand, twisting it around like she was caught in indecision. "I'm sorry, Grandma, but I can't be the powerful witch you raised me to be. You taught me to be cruel, to push people down to get where I wanted to go. I tried that for a while, and I learned it's not the kind of witch I want to be. I'm not going to kill you. But that doesn't mean I can't be the damn powerful witch *I* choose to be."

Chloe placed the Mentalist Wand into Lilian's hand. My friends and I just stood there watching, trusting Chloe to know what she was doing.

The instant Lilian took the Wand, she aimed it at Chloe. She flicked her wrist to deliver a deadly spell… but nothing happened.

Chloe scoffed. "You think I'd just hand you power, after everything you've done? Grandma, I'm showing you *my* power. You always thought I'd follow in your footsteps and become some sort of prodigy you could mold to your will—as if your power could keep on living through me. You never saw me as my own person, but as an extension of yourself. I have power of my own, though. I always did."

Lilian's eyes widened, and she took a wary step back.

Chloe shook her head in disgust. "You weren't the one who hunted down this Wand and learned how to utilize its magic. *I* did that. And everything I do with this Wand is greater than anything you've ever accomplished, not because I need its power to make me great, but because I choose to use it to *help* people. That's something you can never say. You think I'm fighting you because I'm some rebellious college kid who doesn't respect her elders, but that couldn't be further from the truth. Everything I've done to bring about your demise is in the name of bringing power back to the people."

Chloe gave a chilling laugh. "The Mentalist Wand likes to play games, and it wants me to play this one with you. We've been playing together long enough that this Wand is loyal to me. You wanted to control me, and control the coven. Now I have control over you. I'm giving you the Mentalist Wand to show you that even though you have all this power in your hands, you can't use it."

Lilian's hands trembled as magic swirled out of the end of the Mentalist Wand. Horror filled her eyes as she tried to resist, but the Wand overtook her mind, controlling her to its will.

"Confess what you did, Lilian!" Chloe shouted. "Tell us all what your real intentions were."

"I intended to rule the coven," Lilian admitted. Her arms shuddered as she tried to resist the spell, but the Mentalist Wand was far more powerful than her own will. "When the Waning started, I got scared. We weren't equipped to deal with something like this, because it had never happened before. Nadine was right—we had to unite the people. But you can't unite people who think differently than you!"

"You can! It's called compromise and respect. Ever heard of it?" Chloe demanded.

"People didn't respect me, so why should I respect them?" Lilian spat.

"Respect is earned," Chloe shot back. "You tried to force people to respect you, and it can't be done."

"I did what *had* to be done!" Lilian sneered. "The Waning was a sign that the coven would fail unless we fixed our problems. If I had to sacrifice half the coven to keep around the ones who agreed with me, then I was willing to do it."

"That's thousands of lives lost at your hands," Chloe accused.

"It was either thousands, or all of us," Lilian insisted. "Which would you choose?"

"I'd choose another way," Chloe replied. "Things aren't always black and white, Grandma. Did you ever even stop to consider what Mother Miriam wanted?"

"I knew what Mother Miriam wanted!" Lilian shouted. "Her teachings are clear. *Protect the coven.* I did that by eliminating those who threatened our cause."

"You truly believe Mother Miriam sanctioned everything you did—the hangings, the burnings, the Chosen, all of it?" Chloe asked.

"The Chosen was a sham!" Lilian sneered. "It was all made up to get people to fall into line. Mother Miriam didn't tell us to make the Chosen, but we had to. People wouldn't listen to us unless they believed our orders came from Mother Miriam herself."

Chloe took a step away from her grandmother, like she couldn't stand to be near her. "So you knew all along that you really had no power? You had to defile Mother Miriam's good name to claim it for yourself."

"People wouldn't give up their power to me, so I had to take it," Lilian confessed. "If you and your friends hadn't been causing trouble, I wouldn't have had to kill so many innocent people."

Chloe scoffed in disgust. "I've heard enough. How about the rest of you?"

Chloe turned around, and at first, I thought she was talking to us. Then coven members started to emerge from the trees. I recognized people from both sides—Judge Calloway, Professor Clarke, Gwen, and Camille, along with Lincoln, Professor Richards, Alex, and Gregory. There were so many coven members that I couldn't take them all in at once. It appeared everyone was here.

"Oh, remember when I was carried off in that tornado?" Chloe asked innocently. "I brought some friends back with me."

Judge Calloway pointed a finger at Lilian. "You lied to us! We followed you because you claimed it was what Mother Miriam wanted, and all this time it was to fool us!"

"You had a responsibility to uphold!" Professor Clarke demanded. "Your word was the law of the land, and you abused it!"

"You take us for idiots, but you were stupid enough to get caught red-handed," Gwen added.

Lincoln limped forward. He must've hurt his leg in the fight, but he pushed past the injury to face Lilian. He curled his lip up in disgust. "I worked for you long enough to know you witches were morally corrupt, but I never imagined you'd go to this length. I joined the other side to end the hangings, but it looks like there's one last execution in order."

"You wouldn't," Lilian said in a shaky tone.

Chloe wrenched the Mentalist Wand out of her grandma's hands. "You thought I alone was going to decide your fate, Grandma? No. I'm going to let the coven enact justice, because that's exactly what you deserve. This is the worst way for you to go."

Chloe turned to the others. "Here you go. Have her."

The coven rushed forward in an angry mob. Rage-filled screams echoed across the mountain range as they carried out their revenge. They grabbed Lilian and dragged her toward the cliff that overlooked the battlefield.

Beside me, Nadine shuddered, and I wrapped her in my arms. Everyone seemed to be holding their breath. I wasn't sure any of us knew whether we were making the right decision, but none of my friends moved to stop it.

Lilian's scream filled the air as the coven tossed her over the edge of the cliff. It was the worst way to go—a Mentalist with telekinesis thrown to their death without the power to levitate themselves and stop it. We were lucky enough not to witness her fall, but I knew the moment she made impact, because Lilian's voice filled my head.

I hope the coven receives the miserable ending it deserves.

"It's done," I told my friends flatly. It was strange how little I felt at her death, but honestly, I was just relieved.

"How can we be sure they're gone for good?" Grant asked. "Not everyone leaves with their reaper."

I used the Mortana Wand to search out their spirits, but I found nothing except the remnants of reaper magic in the air.

"They're gone for good," I confirmed. "Whether by their choice or by force, they're in another realm now. We don't have to worry about the priestesses any longer. Now, we can finally put this conflict to rest. With the Oaken Wands and the Master Wand, we have more than enough power to end the Waning. It's time to finish what we started."

nadine
FOURTEEN

The immense relief I felt when we defeated the priestesses was surreal beyond words. I'd spent so much of my life fighting that it didn't feel real for the fight to be over.

I fell into Lucas's arms, letting my guard down for the first time in years. "Lucas, I was so scared," I whimpered.

"And you were *so* brave," he said softly.

"I knew they were going to turn on each other," I told him. "I just needed to wait for them to start arguing so I could take my opportunity. I realized in the middle of the fight that aggression wasn't the answer. They were going to be their own downfall, and I just had to let them."

He pulled away to push a strand of hair behind my ear. His green eyes sparkled. He didn't show it, but I could see he'd been afraid, too. "You succeeded beautifully."

"We all did," I said. I turned to my friends, and Grant, Talia, and Chloe joined Lucas and me in a group hug.

Grant's shoulders sagged. "I can't believe we did it."

Talia sobbed. "The war is over. We can rebuild the coven now without worrying if it's going to be destroyed again."

"We can get started right away," Chloe said.

I nodded in agreement. "We should get to the Protection Tree. That's where the Waning is originating from."

My friends and I started down the mountain. The clouds continued to swirl above us, but the rain had let up. Night had already fallen, so the forest was dark. We moved slowly, because everyone was battered, bruised, and tired. The rest of the coven members were already far ahead of us, and I could hear them cheering for our victory.

We came upon the battlefield. Most of the forest had been destroyed, and mounds of dirt covered fallen trees. Every last golem had been reduced to mud.

A few people milled around the battlefield. Lucas approached one of them, and as we came closer, I realized it was Gregory. He wiped tears from his eyes.

"We're… um… looking for survivors," Gregory stammered.

"Don't bother," Lucas said sadly. "I can feel life and death, and there's no one else out there. It looks like even my zombie army returned to the graveyard."

Gregory sniffled. "We lost some good people today."

I didn't want to ask, but I had to. "Brayden…?"

"No, no," Gregory said quickly. "Brayden's fine. He's back at the school helping the recovery team. A couple of necromancers stayed behind. Samantha and I were going to move the bodies to a better place, but… the Waning. We're out of power."

"Already?" Lucas asked. "I just used the Mortana Wand to give you magic."

Gregory shrugged. "It worked for a bit—helped us win the fight, honestly. But we used up what we had. Whatever is causing the Waning is stronger than your Wand. You're going to have to pull off some fancy magic to overpower it if you want to give our magic back for good."

"We will," I promised.

"In the meantime, I hope this helps," Lucas said as he waved the Mortana Wand.

Gregory inhaled a deep breath, then lifted his fingers. Sparks came out the ends of them. Lucas swished his Wand across the battlefield, distributing power to all the Mortana there.

"We'll use this magic well until it's gone," Gregory said, before addressing the others. "Let's get these people to the funeral home!"

He turned back to us. "You should go to the school. They've got EMTs there caring for the injured. I'm sure there are a lot of people who want to see you."

"Thanks, Gregory," Lucas said. "You fought well."

We continued toward the school, where red and blue lights flashed across the parking lot. The coven's entire fleet of ambulances were there, and anyone with medical training was rushing to help. A siren blared when we reached the school, and an ambulance took off in the direction of the hospital.

Gwen, Camille, and Valerie sat in the back of an open ambulance, huddled together under a blanket. Gwen rubbed at the Chosen tattoo on her wrist, like she was trying to get rid of it.

"It's not going to rub off," Camille said.

Gwen scowled. "I can get rid of it with Alchemy magic. I'll alchemize the ink and dissolve it. I don't want anything to do with the Chosen anymore. It was all a lie."

Valerie stared forward, her eyes completely glazed over. They'd been there to witness Lilian's confession and were clearly shook by it. "I committed everything I had to the Chosen. The Mentalist Wand must've forced Priestess Lilian to say all that. It can't be true."

"Believe it, Val," Camille said. "We've been following the priestesses blindly for too long. Does it *really* make sense that Mother Miriam would want us hanging our own people? We did a lot of bad things in Mother Miriam's name, and it's time we start seeing our history for what it really is. I, for one, believe Lilian's confession, and I'm disgusted we were lied to for so long."

Gwen's gaze flickered in our direction, and the girls quieted when they noticed us.

Nearby, a medical station had been set up to care for the most severe injuries. I witnessed Patty, a nurse who worked in the school's infirmary, attending to a long gash across Alex's face.

"Do you think it'll scar?" Alex asked her as we passed them.

"Most likely," Patty told him regrettably. "But with the right care, we can reduce its appearance."

"Awesome!" Alex exclaimed. "Scars are cool. Girls like scars, right?"

Patty sighed as she dabbed cream over the wound. "I can give you medical advice, but I'm not the person to ask what kids these days like."

At the next care station, my nephrologist Dr. Tracey administered first-aid to Lincoln's leg. She used scissors to cut his pants, revealing a red, blistering wound filled with pus. It looked like he'd been hit by a nasty battle spell, because his skin was starting to rot off the bone.

"Ah!" Lincoln gasped. He was a tough guy, so for him to show his pain meant it must be really bad.

I hurried over to them. "Here, let me help."

Dr. Tracey stepped aside, and I aimed the Master Wand at the wound. Its power was strong, vibrating through me from head to toe with an intensity that was difficult to steady. The Master Wand could create power out of nothing, and I willed it to heal.

Nothing happened.

Lucas gently pulled me aside. "Nad, I admire that you want to solve every puzzle, but this isn't something you can fix. Witches don't have the ability to heal that quickly."

"Why not? We have all kinds of healing potions. The Master Wand is more powerful than any other magic the coven possesses."

Lucas kept his voice low, for only me to hear. "It's still witch magic. Even demigods have their specialties—they can't do *everything*. This Wand was made with our son's power, and if he can't heal on his own, the Master Wand can't, either."

I turned toward Grant. "Can we start alchemizing healing potions for these people right away? I know it can't fix everything, but it could help the process along."

"That's going to take time," he replied. "It'll be hours before even the simplest salves can be ready."

I sighed as I turned back to Lincoln. "I can't heal it, but I can stop it from spreading."

Lincoln winced. "Anything that will stop the pain."

I used the Curse Breaker Wand to siphon the lingering magic from the spell. When I finished, I subconjured my Oaken Wand, along with the Master Wand. They were too valuable to leave out in the open.

Lincoln gave a sigh of relief. "Thank you, Priestess."

"You're welcome."

As we continued walking, I spotted a girl with wild red curls lying on a stretcher. An EMT wrapped a bandage tightly around her ankle, which was severely swollen and bruised.

I went over to her, and my friends followed. "Darcy, how are you doing?"

Her voice was strong as she said, "I might have a broken ankle, but I actually feel really good. I'm glad I came to help, because it was worth it to win."

Darcy had always been one of our meeker classmates. She'd been taken hostage by the priestesses the night of the Burning my sophomore year. We'd rescued her and gotten her pardoned for the so-called *crimes* the priestesses accused her of—even though she'd only been trying to put out the fires. After that, we asked her to fight with us, and she'd been too afraid to join us. She appeared so different now, with an air of confidence about her that I hadn't ever witnessed before.

"You didn't want to fight with us before," I pointed out. "What changed?"

"*I* did," Darcy said simply. "I used to be so scared that if I spoke up or brought any attention to myself, I'd become a target. But eventually things got so bad that I realized it was more painful to stand around and do nothing than it was to take the risk."

"You didn't have to do that," I told her. "But thank you for standing up for what's right."

She offered a kind smile. "I'm not afraid to do the right thing anymore, and I know I made the right choice this time."

I looked around the medical station and was amazed by how many people here were just like Darcy—people who we never asked to fight, but showed up anyway.

"I don't get it," I said to my friends. "These people have no magic of their own, but decided to defend the coven anyway. Defeating the priestesses was up to us because we're the ones with the Oaken Wands, but all these people stayed regardless, even though there was a threat."

"That's what community does," Talia said simply. "We help each other."

For so long the coven had been divided, but so much of it had just been a spectacle run by the priestesses as a power-hungry display. In the end, regular people just wanted to live their normal lives and help one another.

"Council," someone called.

We turned to see Professor Warren approaching. His hair was a mess, and he had dirt on his face. His brown suitcoat was torn, but he appeared unbothered by it. He carried a large cardboard box with him.

"I heard what happened up the mountain—the Golem War, people are calling it," he said. "You must all be very worn out. You should all eat something."

He withdrew bottles of water and energy bars that he handed to us.

Lucas took a swig of water. "What happened here in town?"

"We got most civilians to the other side of town before a golem squadron reached us, though some people chose to stay behind and help," Professor Warren reported. "We set a trap using our last potion stores just before the army got here. It was the biggest explosion I've ever seen— took out a good chunk of the forest, too. Luckily we had enough magic to take them on, because I wasn't sure it was going to be enough. Not a single golem got past us."

"Good work, Professor," Chloe said. "By chance, have you seen my husband?"

"Miles is over there." Professor Warren pointed toward a big van. "He's helping hand out supplies we brought from the Community Center. They've got blankets and dry clothes."

"Where's Headmistress Verla?" I looked around, but I hadn't seen her anywhere.

"She went to help civilians across town before the attack ended," Warren said. "They had no idea what was going on, and someone needed to get them to safety. I stayed here so she could help the others. She's still out there taking care of the evacuees and looking for survivors."

"Now that the threat is gone, these people can return to their homes," I said. "Can you get in touch with Verla and let her know we're rescinding the evacuation order effective immediately? She'll be able to help these people back into town."

Warren nodded. "You've got it, Priestess."

We were still wet from the rain, and I shivered in the cold.

The professor noticed. "You should all get into something warm."

It was clear it wasn't a suggestion. We approached the van he'd pointed out earlier. The back doors were open, and Miles sat there with a bundle of blankets in his arms, staring ahead with a blank expression.

"Miles?" Chloe approached him slowly.

He snapped out of his daze and looked up at her. "Chloe, thank the Goddess you're safe."

"What are you *doing*?" she asked.

"Trying not to fall asleep, honestly. I've been going since last night. I haven't slept at all."

"All right, hun. You need to get some sleep. You can help out when you're feeling better—" Chloe cut off as she reached out for him, and he drew the blankets away to reveal an unnatural twist in his left arm. "Miles, your arm is broken!"

He shrugged, like it barely bothered him. "It only hurts a little. There are people with worse injuries, and we're short volunteers. The doctors will see me when they're done with the others."

Chloe shot him a pointed expression. "Honey, I love how much you care. It's why I married you. But you're in no shape to volunteer right now. You can't carry anything."

"I can carry blankets." Miles shook them at her.

Chloe took them from his hand and placed them back in the van. "Right now, the best person you can possibly help is yourself."

Grant stepped forward. "Tal and I will hand out blankets."

"Come on," Chloe encouraged her husband. "I'll walk you over to the medics."

She turned back to us. "I'll meet up with you guys once things settle down here. Our main priority is making sure everyone is safe."

Miles didn't protest as Chloe guided him away.

Talia dug through a box of clothing donations. She handed a pile to me, then another to Lucas, before giving us each a pair of dry shoes. "These should fit you both. Go get cleaned up inside, and then you can get back to council duties. We'll take turns. Grant and I will start by getting these blankets to people in need."

We were drenched from the storm and caked in mud, so it was nice to have a chance to quickly change. Lucas and I turned to head into the school and found our way to the locker rooms near the pool. No one else was around, so I followed Lucas into the men's room.

Lucas gritted his teeth as he lifted his wet t-shirt. I gasped when I saw the deep purple bruises splayed across his entire torso. It looked incredibly painful. I reached out to lightly run my fingers over his sides. I could feel huge bumps where the bruises had swelled his skin. He definitely had a couple of broken ribs.

He turned his head to the side, like he couldn't look. "How bad is it?"

"Pretty bad!"

"I thought so. I've broken ribs before, but this feels worse."

"You need to go to the medic station," I insisted.

"I will. Could you help me?"

Lucas couldn't lift his arms very high, so I helped pull his wet t-shirt over his head. I felt awful watching him wince with every micromovement. I helped him dress, then tossed my dry clothes on.

"Do you need help walking?" I asked.

"No, I can handle that. Just stay with me, all right?"

I carefully wrapped an arm around his waist. "Always."

I walked Lucas to the medic station, where we found my primary care physician, Dr. Yonker, arguing with Talia's brother. Tyler sat in a chair where patients with less severe injuries were waiting to be seen, but he was waving Dr. Yonker off.

"Mister Murphy, I'm telling you, you need to let me look you over," Dr. Yonker insisted. "You're looking very pale, which could point to something severe. We won't know until we take your vitals."

"I'm fine," Tyler told him. "I'm just hungry. There are people far worse off than me. Take care of them first."

"Dr. Yonker!" Professor Richards came rushing over. "Your team should have this."

Richards held up a glowing potion—the same one we'd seen him try to administer to Professor Loren before she passed away on the battlefield.

"It's not much, but it's the last of the healing potions I have left," Richards told him. "If it helps just one person, I'm happy to give it up."

"That's very generous of you," Dr. Yonker said as he took the vial. He looked it over to be sure it was legitimate, but I personally wasn't worried about anything Professor Richards brewed himself. "This will be very helpful to one of our patients, I'm sure."

Dr. Yonker saw us standing there then. "Nadine, how can I help?"

"Lucas needs medical attention," I told him.

Lucas lifted his shirt to show the doctor what we were dealing with. Tyler's eyes went wide. He gagged, then looked away, like he couldn't stomach the bruises.

"Give the potion to *him*," Tyler insisted. "That looks like a bitch."

Lucas lowered his shirt again. "It's definitely not fun."

"Come sit at my station," Dr. Yonker offered kindly.

I helped Lucas get situated on a stretcher next to a table full of medical supplies. Dr. Yonker put on a pair of gloves, but he really didn't need to examine Lucas to determine if his ribs were broken. Anyone could see that just by looking at him. Even so, Lucas lifted his shirt, and Dr. Yonker looked him over.

"Six broken ribs, by the looks of it," Dr. Yonker said. "Four on your right side, two on the left. You'll need X-rays to confirm. Usually, these types of injuries heal in about six weeks. You'll want to limit your activity so you don't worsen the injuries. That said… I think Mister Murphy is right. You should take this potion. It'll help you heal faster and ensure there isn't damage to other organs."

Lucas pulled away. "I want that to go to the person who needs it most."

"*You* need it most right now," Dr. Yonker pressed. "I've known your wife for years now, and if you're anything like her, you'll be back to work tomorrow. I know it sounds like we can't do much, but that doesn't mean these injuries aren't severe. When I say take it easy, I mean it. But you won't… so you're going to take this potion to prevent it from getting worse. You may have won the war tonight, Priest, but these people still need you."

Lucas scowled. "It's not fair to use my own compassion against me."

"Maybe it's not fair, but is it working?" Dr. Yonker cocked an eyebrow.

"It's good enough for me," I cut in. "Dr. Yonker is right, Lucas. If you don't take this potion, you'll be back in his office tomorrow with a punctured lung. I'd rather see you get better than make it worse."

"Fine, I'll take it," Lucas relented. He took the potion from Dr. Yonker's outstretched hand and drank it. "What's my recovery time look like now?"

"Three weeks," the doctor replied. "*If* you take it easy."

Lucas pushed himself upright. "I'll take it easy. I promise."

Commotion on the other side of the medic station caught our attention. "Who's in charge here?" a woman demanded. "I want to speak to someone who knows what the hell is going on! They told us to evacuate, but I'm not going anywhere until I get some answers!"

It was Meredith, who'd been absolutely *lovely* to deal with in the past. She might as well have spat on Monica's grave at her funeral—a fake funeral, but Meredith still didn't know that. I had no intention of telling her, either. Even though the priestesses were gone now, I respected Monica's right to keep her whereabouts a secret, even from her own sister.

That wasn't the worst of Meredith's wrongdoings. She'd denounced her marriage in front of the whole coven at the Festival of Santos. But she'd admitted her regret about that, so I didn't think she'd be too devastated to learn the priestesses were gone now.

I started walking toward her, and she did a double take. "Oh, *hell* no," she protested.

"Meredith, please," I said calmly. "There's no reason to fight."

"What, you're afraid of causing a scene?" Meredith demanded. "I wouldn't have to do that if you fulfilled your promises when you and your little friends took over the council all those months ago. You said you were going to fix the coven and end the Waning, and look how far that's gotten us."

"We *are* going to end the Waning," Lucas said from behind me.

I turned to see he had followed me. Chloe, Grant, and Talia had just finished cleaning up inside. They heard the commotion and came to Lucas's side. Miles was notably missing, along with one of the ambulances, so I could only assume Chloe had pressed for him to be taken to the hospital for his injury.

All eyes had turned to us.

"Oh, *really?*" Meredith rolled her eyes. "*You're going to end the Waning.* And when exactly do you plan on doing that?"

"Right now," Lucas replied simply. He raised his voice to address the others. "Gather your friends and family. You all deserve to see your magic restored. We're bringing it back to the people *tonight*. We'll meet you all at the Protection Tree in fifteen minutes."

Meredith turned her nose up, looking skeptical. "All right, then. We'll see if you can truly fulfill your promise."

She hurried off in another direction to spread the news.

Lucas sighed heavily and kept his voice low. "We're all ready for this, right?"

"I'm ready," Chloe said confidently. Grant and Talia both nodded in agreement.

"We need to move fast," I insisted. "The priestesses may be dead, but the Master Wand is powerful enough for its spells to outlive the spellcaster. The priestesses used it to cast a curse on Marcus, which prevents us from telling him he's a demigod, but also ensures he can't create another Master Wand."

"Isn't that kind of a good thing, though?" Grant wondered. "You don't *want* anyone using Marcus to create another Master Wand."

"You're right, but a curse isn't the right way to protect him from that," I said. "I know what it's like to live with a curse inside of you, and I won't let my son grow up with that for another day. Even though Marcus is on the other side of the world right now, I need to find his curse and free him from it. Once that curse is broken, we can cast a protection spell on him so no one can ever use his magic the way the priestesses did. That way, he'll be safe, but we'll still be able to tell him what he is and prepare him for his future. We have to do this now, because even though the priestesses' curse prevents anyone from creating another Master Wand, that doesn't mean someone won't try to hurt Marcus in some other way once they have their magic back. It's imperative that we break Marcus's curse and cast a protection spell on him *first*, and *then* we can end the Waning. I'm not restoring the coven's magic just for someone to come after him again."

"Do you think you can break his curse, even if he isn't here?" Lucas asked.

"With the Wands? Absolutely," I said. "This isn't just for Marcus and us, but for the whole coven. If his powers get in the hands of someone else, we could see another repeat of this war. We need to keep anyone else from using his powers against him again, and we're doing that before anyone has enough magic to do anything about it."

Lucas glanced around. "We can't do it out in the open. I don't want anyone knowing our son is cursed, let alone a demigod. Let's get to the Protection Tree and do the spell before anyone gets there."

My friends and I hurried off the school grounds and sprinted down the trail that led to the Protection Tree. It wasn't far from the school, but the trail ahead seemed to stretch into an eternity. Chloe got sick of running and levitated us into the air, flying us through the forest faster than we could run. She deposited us in the clearing at the Protection Tree.

I heaved for breath, and my heart hammered. Dead leaves littered the ground, and above us, the gnarly branches of the ancient oak appeared dry and cracked. The tree had so little life left and was taking every last bit of magic it could in its struggle for survival.

"Cover me," I told the others. "Let me know if anyone's coming."

I gripped the Curse Breaker Wand in my hands and closed my eyes.

My magic reached outward, through the center of the Earth and across the globe. It was the furthest I'd ever taken it, but I was determined as hell to reach my son, no matter how far he was away from me.

Finding him amongst billions of other people was as easy as calling him up on the phone. I had carried this child in my womb for seven months—my magic *knew* his intimately. There was a loving familiarity there, a unique connection only shared between mother and child. I knew him like I knew my own heartbeat.

Then my magic brushed up against the darkness of his curse, and I gagged at the vile sensation. I immediately commanded the Curse Breaker Wand to draw the curse out of him... but the curse wrenched away from me. I could see the dark, chaotic energy of it in my mind's eye. It appeared to react with outrage, howling and hissing at me like a hostile monster infuriated at the disturbance.

I tried again, but the curse came at me at full force. When my magic touched it, it was like slamming my entire body into a brick wall.

"How's it coming, Nad?" Lucas asked urgently.

"It's not working!" I cried. "The curse is fighting me for its survival."

"Forget the curse and just cast the protection spell," Chloe pressed. "We can break his curse later."

"No!" I protested. "If I protect him from other spellcasters now, I could block myself from breaking his curse later. This curse prevents us from ever telling him what he is. We won't be able to prepare him for his future, and the curse will eat away at him like our family curse did—only this one is stronger, so it'll be worse. I can't risk my son growing up this way. I need to break it now."

I pushed the Wand to fight his curse, but no matter what I did, I couldn't break through. This curse had been cast with the Master Wand, and its power was too much for the Curse Breaker Wand to reverse.

Instead, I subconjured the Curse Breaker Wand and exchanged it for Master Wand. The Master Wand should be able to break its own spell. I clung to my connection with my son, and I ordered the Master Wand to break that curse. Immense power pulsed through me, more powerful than anything I felt with the Oaken Wands. If the Curse Breaker Wand could expand my power across the globe, the Master Wand spanned galaxies. I was everywhere and nowhere all at once.

My son's curse became enraged, seeming to grow to epic proportions as it fought against me. It lashed out, delivering a magical blow that rever-berated through the Master Wand. I stumbled back, gasping. I quickly drew back my power, because I feared I was only fueling the curse with this magic.

Only, the power didn't stop like I commanded it to.

"Nadine, what's happening?" Talia cried.

The ground began to shake, and the forest trees twisted and groaned. I struggled to maintain my footing.

"Stop the spell!" Grant demanded.

The Master Wand shuddered violently. I gripped it tightly with two hands, and my heart slammed against my rib cage in panic. My whole body convulsed as I tried to claim control of the spell again. I didn't know if I *could.* I'd never lost control of a spell like this before.

"I'm trying!" I shouted. "I can't control it. It's not working!"

Chloe threw her hand up to shield herself from a falling tree branch. "The Master Wand is too strong!"

Lucas withdrew the Mortana Wand. "We've got to work together to get this spell under control."

My friends met me in the center of the clearing. I struggled to hold on to the Master Wand in one hand as I took the Curse Breaker Wand in the other. We each extended an Oaken Wand outward until the tips touched. I commanded their power to steady the Master Wand's magic—but I never finished the spell.

A huge blast of energy shot out of the end of the Master Wand, sending my friends and me flying in different directions.

For a beat, I found my mind floating in empty space, then slowly I came back to myself. I lay flat on my back. The ground was steady now, but my ears rang. Tiny white dots filled my vision, and it took me a moment to realize they were stars. I pushed myself to a sitting position, wincing at the aches and pains in my joints. Around the clearing, my friends groaned as they sat upright. Lucas clutched his side and sucked a pained breath between his teeth.

I looked around to see the Master Wand lying several yards in front of me. I'd been so disoriented I hadn't even realized it'd flown out of my hand, though I still held the Curse Breaker Wand tightly. I crawled to the Master Wand on the ground and carefully reached out, as if I were testing the heat on a hot stove.

The Master Wand appeared perfectly benign. My fingers curled around the handle, and I could feel its magic pulsing, awaiting instruction from a spellcaster.

"Wh—what happened?" Grant asked warily.

"The Oaken Wands must've overpowered the Master Wand," Talia said.

I shook my head. "No, I never cast the spell. This was Marcus's curse. Even the Master Wand couldn't handle it."

"How's that possible? The Master Wand *cast* the curse," Chloe pointed out. "Its spell can't be more powerful than the Wand itself."

"Well, it was," I bit harsher than I meant to.

"So… did the spell work?" Lucas asked. "Did we break our son's curse?"

"I—I don't know," I admitted. I was too afraid to use my magic to check, because I feared making it worse. Instead, I conjured my phone. "I'm calling Wykoff. I need to make sure Marcus is okay."

I stood and began pacing around the clearing. I put the phone on speaker so my friends could hear. The phone rang three times before Professor Wykoff answered.

"Nadine—"

"Is Marcus okay?" I demanded before she could get another word in.

"Yes, what's going on? You sound very worried."

"Are you sure?" I pressed. "Check if he's breathing."

"He's perfectly all right," Wykoff promised. "I'm holding him right now. He was fussing for a bit, but I calmed him down."

I heard the soft coo of my son's voice over the line, and I began to sob in relief. It was a sound I knew so well, one I could easily distinguish from any other child. My son was alive and well, seemingly unaffected by the spell we'd just performed.

"We tried to break his curse," I told Professor Wykoff.

"That may be why he was fussing," she replied. "But he's perfectly fine now. Did you succeed?"

I swallowed the lump rising to my throat. "I haven't checked…"

Lucas slowly approached me. "Nadine, we have to. We need to know for sure."

I knew he was right, but I was afraid of what provoking the curse might do to our son. Still, we had to know. Hesitantly, I lifted the Curse

Breaker Wand and reached across the globe for my son again. I found his magic easily, and with it came the sickening gut-punch of his curse. On the other end of the line, Marcus began to scream. I gasped and yanked my magic back before I could do any more damage.

My jaw trembled. "It didn't work. Marcus is still cursed."

Lucas furrowed his brow. "Professor Wykoff, could this have something to do with Marcus's demigod powers?"

"Certainly," she replied. "His curse was cast with the Master Wand, which is just as strong as he is. Nadine's Curse Breaker powers wouldn't stand up to such a spell."

"We tried using the Master Wand to break it," I told her. "*And* the Curse Breaker Wand. Neither worked."

A silent beat passed, and I could sense Wykoff's panic from the other end of the line. "Not to worry," she forced out in an even tone. "I will look into this for you. I'll dedicate all my time to this mystery. I *will* find answers. I promise."

I wanted to believe her, but until we had answers in our hands, I wasn't convinced we'd find them. The stakes were far too high to rely on hope this time.

Voices approached in the distance.

Chloe shot a glance through the trees. "Wrap it up, Nadine."

"Thank you, Professor," I said. "We'll talk soon."

I hung up, then turned back to my friends. "I *know* we should be able to pull this off. If we combine the power of the Oaken Wands and the Master Wand, we should be able to overpower the curse."

Chloe's gaze darted toward the trees again, where the voices were growing louder. "We're out of time."

"No, we can still do it," I insisted. "This should've worked. The only explanation is that the Waning is screwing with our spell somehow, which means we have to end the Waning first."

"That puts your son at risk, once everyone has their magic back," Grant pointed out. "We don't know what the priestesses told people and who might already be plotting something."

"We're going to do the spells all at once," I said. "I did the same thing the night in the courtroom, when the priestesses kidnapped Marcus. I just had to time everything right to get him back. One spell to fix it all—end

Marcus's curse, cast a protection spell over him, and rebalance and restore all our magic, all at the same time."

"That's a lot of power," Lucas pointed out.

"We have power," I said, holding up the Master Wand. "We can end the Waning with just the Oaken Wands, but combined with the Master Wand, we can do anything. We need to use all the power that's available to us."

"If you think this is the right thing to do, then I'm on board," Grant said.

Talia nodded in agreement. "We set out to heal the coven, so let's heal *everyone*."

"Agreed," Lucas said.

Chloe tore her gaze from the trees. "All right. Let's do this."

Hordes of people flooded out of the trees. I recognized so many faces —Tyler, Dr. Yonker, Judge Calloway, and Professor Warren. There had to be a hundred people here, and far too many to name. The coven stared back at us expectantly, so I could only assume the earthquake that had occurred moments ago had been localized and the others hadn't felt it. Coven members surrounded us until the clearing was completely full.

Meredith stood at the front of the group with her arms crossed. She tapped her foot on the ground. "Well, are you going to fix this or what?"

"Lay off them," Tyler defended. He didn't look well and should've stayed back at the medic station. His face was really pale, and his body was covered in a sheen of sweat. "They're waiting for everyone to get here. This isn't just about you, you know."

Meredith scowled at him. "You really should learn to respect your elders—ah!"

Meredith screamed as Tyler stumbled forward and collapsed in front of everyone. Everyone closest to him jumped back in surprise. My friends and I rushed to his side, along with Dr. Yonker. Talia reached her brother first, and Dr. Yonker knelt beside him.

"I told him he needed to let me look him over," Dr. Yonker muttered. He pulled a small flashlight out of his pocket and shone it into Tyler's eyes.

"Is he going to be okay?" Talia asked desperately.

Tyler groaned as he came to. He pushed Dr. Yonker's hands away. "Easy on the light, Doc. You're going to blind me."

His voice was groggy and didn't quite sound like his own.

"Tyler, you lied to me," Dr. Yonker stated sternly. "You're sick."

"Yeah, Doc, I'm injured," Tyler moaned. "Couldn't hide it from you long enough, could I?"

"What's wrong with him?" Talia demanded.

"Hit by a rogue spell, sis." Tyler winced as he lifted his shirt.

If I thought Lucas's bruises were bad, Tyler's were ten times worse. His entire abdomen was a sickly purple color. The internal bleeding was severe. I didn't know how much longer he had left.

"Tyler, you should've taken the healing potion!" Lucas demanded. "Your injuries are far worse than mine. Why would you refuse help?"

"I knew I didn't have long left," Tyler rasped. "A measly witch potion wasn't going to help fast enough. I didn't want the doctors wasting time on me."

"We can still help you," Dr. Yonker insisted. "We'll get you to the hospital right away."

"It's too late," Tyler insisted. "I can already feel my reaper coming for me."

"*No!*" Talia screamed. "I only have one brother, and I'm not losing you. You stay with me. There has to be something we can do! Nadine?"

When Talia begged me, my heart shattered. The thought of losing someone else, someone we *loved*, made my insides shrivel up. I wished I could take Tyler's place, because I never wanted Talia to feel the loss I'd felt when my family died.

"Witches don't have healing magic, Tal," I whispered regrettably.

Tears streamed down her cheeks. "We have to be able to do it! We have more power than witches have ever had before. You're going to cast a spell to heal the tree—to heal the *coven*. Use it to heal *him*. That's healing magic isn't it? Even if it doesn't heal him completely, won't it give him a chance?"

I wanted to tell her yes, to give her every reassurance in the world that her brother would make it, but this kind of spell had never been done before. We couldn't know for certain.

"Tal, you have to let me go," Tyler requested. "I knew the risks. I'm happy to die so you can build a better coven."

I couldn't do this. I was sick of losing people all in the name of a better coven. There was no point in continuing to let people we love die in the name of our cause if they weren't here to be a part of it anymore.

"Lay him next to the tree," I stated firmly.

Grant furrowed his brow. "Is this going to work?"

I wasn't sure. "Talia said it best. *We set out to heal the coven, so let's heal everyone.*"

Talia squeezed her brother's hand. "Stay with me, Tyler. We're going to fix you."

A few muscular guys stepped forward to help move Tyler closer to the tree. He was a bit out of it when they laid him down. "I don't know if I should go through with this…" he slurred.

"Let us *try*," Talia begged.

Tyler's eyes focused for a second on his sister. "All right, Tal. For you, I'll try."

"Everyone stand back," Chloe ordered the coven.

My friends and I gathered around the Protection Tree, and we formed a circle around Tyler's body. I clutched both the Curse Breaker Wand and the Master Wand in my hands.

"We do this all in one go," I told my friends in a shaky tone.

"Group spells work better with an incantation," Lucas suggested. "*Through unity and these wands of oak, we pray to the Goddess to restore what's broke.*"

I nodded firmly. "Lend me your magic, and I'll do the rest."

My friends lifted the Oaken Wands and spoke the incantation in unison. Power rippled through me like a shock wave, but I forced my feet to remain grounded. The Master Wand responded to me this time, tangling its magic together with the power of the Oaken Wands. There was so much power that I had to force some of it back. If I allowed it all to be unleashed at once, it would rip through us like a tidal wave, tearing us to pieces in one fell swoop.

I wasn't a demigod—I didn't have the ability to harness that much magic all at once. But I *was* a talented supernatural, and I had my friends at my side, along with the Oaken Wands and the Master Wand to stabilize the power. It was more magic than the Miriam Coven had ever possessed before, and I knew that whatever we willed the Wands to do, they would follow our command.

The ground began to shake beneath our feet again, and wind whipped the Protection Tree's branches back and forth. The tree groaned from beside us. Coven members screamed and backed away.

"Keep going," I ordered my friends. "We've got this."

The stars that twinkled above us moments ago vanished as another wave of storm clouds rolled in. Only this time, they were worse than anything the priestesses had conjured. Lightning bolts cracked in quick succession, never pausing for even a moment. The rumbling of thunder was so strong it sounded like an animalistic growl coming from a massive, angry beast. Lucas instinctually conjured his scythe and glanced around frantically, ready to protect us all in the face of an attack. The wind was so strong I had to fight against it to stay on my feet. Coven members huddled in large groups or clung to trees to avoid being knocked off their feet.

"What are you doing?" Meredith shouted, though her voice seemed distant against the roaring wind. "Cast your spell!"

"Nadine, we're ready when you are!" Grant shouted.

When I pushed our magic outward, it didn't go anywhere. "I'm trying!"

"Have you lost control again?" Lucas asked.

"The magic's responding to us, but it's like it's trapped!" I told them. "Something's pushing back."

"The curse?" Chloe asked.

"No! I haven't even touched it," I said.

"We have to keep going!" Talia insisted. It was clear she'd do anything to save her brother.

Furthermore, we'd promised these people to restore their magic. We weren't about to turn back now.

I tried extending the spell outward again, but it was like I was hitting up against the solid walls of an impenetrable box. Moments ago, my magic could cross continents, and now, it was like it couldn't even leave Octavia Falls. It didn't make any sense.

"We distributed magic to other people when we were fighting the golems," Grant pointed out. "Why isn't it working now? We should be able to end the Waning."

I didn't have an answer. My body became electrified with incredible power. I knew my friends felt it too, because in unison, our bodies began to glow with bright white light, like we were made of magic ourselves. Our arms shook violently as we tried to steady the spell. I didn't know how much further I could push. With every ounce of energy my friends and I gave to the spell, that power seemed to push back on us. Even so, I was willing to take this as far as we had to if it meant the coven got their magic back.

A deafening *snap* filled the air, and everything changed in an instant. My body slammed into the dirt, and the breath left my chest in a violent blow. Though I maintained consciousness the whole time, I couldn't be sure I hadn't somehow skipped forward in time. The lightning came to a sudden halt, and the clouds vanished. The earth stopped rumbling, and the wind died down. It was like none of it had happened in the first place.

Only when I lifted my head, I found my friends sprawled out in the dirt. Lucas's scythe lay on the ground between us, and Tyler was still lying next to the Protection Tree. Coven members filled the clearing, clutching one another as they looked around in confusion.

It was far too quiet… the kind of silence that made my skin crawl. I'd never encountered anything quite so eerie.

I sat up and sank back on my heels when I lifted the Master Wand. The object of immense power fell into two pieces in my hand, sliced straight down the middle. I tried to search for the magic inside of it… but it was gone. My stomach became hollow as I realized the Master Wand was nothing more than a useless piece of wood now.

"I don't understand how this happened," I said breathlessly. "The Master Wand is destroyed."

"Uh… Nadine!" Chloe cried.

Her panicked eyes focused on something behind me. I looked up to see that everyone all had their eyes on the same thing.

Slowly, I spun around to look at the Protection Tree. My heart wrenched when I realized the Master Wand wasn't the only thing that had shattered. Before us, the Protection Tree had split in two. It looked like it'd been hit by lightning, with a crack straight through the center that left a three-foot gap in its trunk. Each side of the tree sagged, its branches hovering only inches off the ground.

Except I knew lightning hadn't been the culprit, because the crack was far too perfect… like something only magic could create. Frantically, I reached out with my magic to feel for the protection spell around the town, but I felt… *nothing*.

I gripped the Curse Breaker Wand tightly in my hand, searching for magic I could use to reverse this. But the Wand responded only briefly to whisper a final farewell. The Curse Breaker Wand wept, and the last of its magic faded.

It hit me with the most horrifying clarity that the protection spell around our town had fallen… and with it, all of our magic was gone.

If my stomach had hollowed a moment ago, my entire being seemed empty now. I witnessed the truth right before my eyes, and I still didn't quite believe it. I didn't understand how this could happen.

I had the horrible thought that I'd fucked this up, that in my selfish attempt to protect my son, I'd used too much power and cast a spell I couldn't reverse. But my theory was unsound. We weren't demigods, and we couldn't harness such power alone, but all the Wands we possessed should be able to make up for that. We hadn't pushed them hard enough to cause such a calamity. If we had, we'd all be dead.

My friends looked down at their Wands in confusion, stunned to find they didn't respond. The Oaken Wands could access all magic in the coven, and if they weren't working… that meant there wasn't any magic left for them to use.

"My magic… it's gone," Lucas said breathlessly.

"No!" I cried. I shook the Wand in my hand, like that would force its magic to come back. I tried to create a spell, but every ounce of magic inside of me had vanished. The void was all-consuming.

This wasn't like the Waning. Then, I could still feel the smallest hints of magic lingering in my chest, even if I couldn't cast a spell. Now, there was nothing. It was like losing one's own heartbeat—you never really paid attention, because it was constant, but once it was gone, you felt the agonizing desolation of emptiness.

We hadn't restored our magic at all. Somehow, in the midst of trying to save everyone… we'd lost it.

It was nonsensical and went against everything I knew. I tried to make sense of it, but instead of coming up with an answer, my mind went blank in pure and utter shock.

The excruciating silence was broken by the sound of Talia's heart-wrenching cries as she threw herself over her brother's body. His lifeless eyes stared at the sky, and there was no denying it from even a distance. Tyler was dead.

I got to my feet, though I barely felt them move under me. The ache of failure in my gut seemed to devour me. "Tal…"

"You said this spell could save him!" she snapped. "You said it would work, Nadine!"

Tears pricked at my eyes. "I said we would try. We did the best we could."

"*That* was your best?" Meredith spat. All around us, coven members started to whisper. They'd felt the void of their magic disappearing, too. "You promised us our magic, but instead you've destroyed it. We should hang you!"

Professor Warren quickly jumped in front of Meredith. "Nobody's hanging anyone! Have you considered that maybe this isn't the council's fault? It's *ours*! Think about it! We killed the priestesses to win this war, but we didn't win anything. We had a chance to make things right, but we chose the same path the priestesses did that started all of this. It's been our own choices that doomed us. Isn't it obvious? Alora doesn't want us anymore."

Professor Warren had to be right, because it was the only explanation. Something had been fighting to contain our spell. Whatever it was it had to be stronger than the Master Wand and Oaken Wands combined—and power that strong could only come from the gods.

The Waning was happening because the coven divided, and killing the priestesses had been our final undoing. Our connection to Alora was lost, and that meant we didn't have magic anymore.

We'd failed.

Meredith's lips curled back into an angry sneer. She stomped forward several paces, but before she could reach us, she doubled over and started to retch.

She wasn't the only one. All around us, people started to heave. Several people collapsed, groaning in a sickly way. Soon, everyone except my friends and me were doubled over in pain.

I stumbled back and grabbed Lucas's arm. "What's happening?"

"It's got to be some sort of side effect of the spell," Lucas theorized. "We aren't affected because we were the ones casting it."

Meredith dropped to her knees and reached out toward me. "Save us!"

Tears rose to my eyes as I whispered, "I can't."

Never had that heartbreaking reality been more true.

Dr. Yonker clutched his stomach and stumbled into the center of the clearing. "Everyone stay calm. This appears to be some sort of side effect of our magic. It *should* pass. If we just stick together, we can figure this out."

"*Together?*" Judge Calloway scoffed as she stepped forward. She clutched her stomach but spoke through the pain. "When are you people going to learn that none of us are ever going to agree on anything? If we don't have Alora, then we aren't witches, and there's nothing that connects us anymore. Perhaps Mother Miriam was right to take our magic away, because we aren't a coven. We haven't been for a long time. Octavia Falls is already in ruins, and if there was any hope of fixing it before, there's no hope now. I suggest you all take what you *do* have left and leave this place with your families."

Judge Calloway whirled toward my friends and me. "As for you five, we're not going to kill you and make the same mistake we did with Lilian. You're better off being left alone here in the ashes of your ruins."

"We never intended this to happen—" I started, but the judge cut me off.

"Intention or not, you're still responsible," she snapped. "You wanted to take over this coven—have what's left of it!"

Then she turned and stumbled down the trail. Others went to follow. After the Imperium Council, Judge Calloway was the next authority. People would listen to her. They would leave town like she suggested, and with no one left to build this town up… it would crumble.

We hadn't just lost our magic. With it, we lost our town. We'd lost our coven.

All I could do was stand there as the townspeople abandoned us. Professor Warren was the only one who stayed. He winced as he stepped forward.

"Professor… I'm so sorry," Lucas struggled to say. We were all at a loss for words.

Warren cleared his throat as he knelt at Tyler's side. "I'll, uh… get him to the funeral home."

Even Professor Warren had nothing to say, which was absolutely devastating. Usually, he had some sort of insight or pep talk to give us. This time, he couldn't offer any of that. All he could do to help was the one thing a necromancer knew how to do—move dead bodies.

Only this time, he had no magic to do it. He went to lift Tyler in his arms.

"Wait," Talia begged. She staggered forward and grabbed Professor Warren by his coat collar. "Did his reaper come for him? Will he make it to Alora!?"

He wore a sad look of regret. "Wherever he is, I'm sure he's at peace."

Warren wouldn't say the obvious aloud. For all we knew, Tyler was stuck here now that Alora had closed her doors to us. It was a cursed existence to live in a world you couldn't *live* in—watching and observing but never *experiencing*. Usually when ghosts got trapped on Earth, it was by their own choice, often due to some unfinished business.

But we'd done this to Tyler, and to every witch who died after. We'd lost our religion, our goddess, and our way to Alora. Every witch and warlock still living who eventually died would be stuck here as a ghost, unable to cross over to the afterlife.

Perhaps the people who'd died in the battle were lucky. At least their souls still had the chance to make it to Alora. The rest of us never would.

Talia sobbed as Professor Warren lifted Tyler's corpse and carried him away. The five of us were left completely alone in the clearing.

Talia turned her tear-filled gaze to Lucas. "What was his last thought? I have to know."

Lucas choked back tears, but he couldn't bring himself to answer. His tragic silence was answer enough. Lucas hadn't heard him. "Tal, I'm so sorry."

Talia's whole body convulsed into sobs. Grant wrapped her in his arms.

"I don't understand how this happened," Grant said hollowly. "How could the Oaken Wands lose their magic?"

"They draw their magic from the coven, and our magic comes from Alora," I rattled off without feeling. It was easier to compartmentalize, because I couldn't make sense of any of this myself. "The Oaken Wands have got to be able to access Alora's power to work. They can't generate their own magic like the Master Wand can."

"Then how did the Master Wand break?" Grant asked.

"Because something overpowered it," Chloe answered sadly. She'd made the same calculations I had. "The Master Wand is only as powerful as the demigod who created it, which means anything demigod level or more can break it."

"There's got to be a way out of this… right?" Lucas asked desperately. "We always find one."

I shook my head. "Not this time."

"Not all magic is gone," Lucas insisted. "We may not be able to access Alora, but the power's still in our blood! Nad, you've manipulated fae magic before. The fae's power isn't connected to Alora, so their magic is still operable. All we need is a little spark, and we can work with it. There must be something we can do to get back in touch with Alora."

"Not if Mother Miriam doesn't want us there!" I cried. "If I try this spell again, then Tyler might not be the only person to die! That spell took what was left of Tyler's life, and we made *everyone* else sick. If we try that spell again, more people are going to perish. How many more people are going to die for this? We keep acting like the five of us can just come in and fix everything, but this isn't some singular enemy like the priestesses that we're fighting against. Professor Warren was right—this was caused by the entire coven. We can't fix something that everyone else has given up on. Even if I could do this spell, I'm the *only* one who can, and if I try it, I risk killing every other witch on the planet. That leaves me. Alone. To start the coven all over again. And Lucas, I don't know anymore if it's worth saving."

"Nadine, if you don't want to pursue this, then we won't," Chloe said gently. "The choice is up to you, but you need to make sure you're okay with the alternative. Without Alora, our religion and our faith will die out. We won't be witches anymore, and when we die, there won't be an afterlife waiting for us. We might find somewhere else to go—someplace in between worlds, but our people won't be together anymore. Mother Miriam won't be waiting for us on the other side."

I wiped my eyes. "If the spell doesn't work, then the result is the same, and I'll have just expedited these people's damnation. If I don't do it, then at least they get to live out the rest of their lives in peace."

"Can any of us really be at peace if we give up who we are?" Grant wondered. "Do we really want to keep on living if we don't have magic?"

I shrugged hopelessly. "I grew up without magic. People live like this every day. Maybe our people won't be happy, but at least they'll be safe. No more conflicts… no more threats… no more war. Lucas and I were prophesied to end the coven's suffering, but maybe it never was about bringing magic back. Perhaps this is how it ends… no one's ever going to use witch magic to hurt each other ever again."

"If that's what you want, then I'll support your decision," Lucas said.

That really fucking hurt, because if my husband was ready to stop fighting, there was nothing more we could do.

"It's not what I want, but what choice do we have?" I bit angrily. "The coven doesn't want us to fix this anymore, so why are we still trying? We got the Oaken Wands, and we defeated the priestesses. *That* was our mission. We can't force these people to unite when *we're* our own worst enemy."

Talia sniffled and wiped her eyes. "So… what do we do now?"

My heart sank with the weight of unbearable misery. "We say goodbye."

The Miriamic Conflict was done. This wasn't the way we wanted things to end, but the only thing we ever really had control over was our own choices—not the outcomes. We kept saying we needed to unite the coven, and in a way, we *had* come together… but together we'd repeated the same mistakes. Professor Warren had been right. We brought this upon ourselves.

"I don't know where any of us will go from here, but we can't stay," I said hollowly. "That's what the Waning has been about this whole time, hasn't it? It was a message to move forward, to change our ways or lose our magic for good. But we didn't learn our lesson, and now we have to face that. We'll survive, but we'll lose ourselves, and that's the choice we made together."

This wasn't the kind of speech I normally made, and every word I uttered cut me to the core, but there was no way out of it. This is what our choices had led to.

I had no pep talks to give this time, nothing to tell them. We'd persisted until the end, and now it was over.

FIFTEEN

Nobody tells you how hard it is to say goodbye to your home even when there's nothing left for you there. It makes all the sense in the world that one would bemoan the end of joyful circumstances, but leaving Octavia Falls wasn't like that. This town had beaten us to the bone, and any greatness it once exhibited had been stripped away. We should've been ready to run away as fast as possible, toward something better, because anywhere was better than here.

And yet... walking away was tragically difficult.

Fleeing town sounded quick and simple, but this wasn't an abrupt evacuation with a threat looming on the horizon. People were mourning, and if anything kept us from moving forward, it was the grief of everything we'd lost. My friends and I had faced grief more times than we could count, and we knew now how to handle it, but there were other townspeople who couldn't let go, and I didn't blame them. I too wanted to cling to every last bit of home I could, because leaving behind everything I knew and braving the ordinary—yet strange—world beyond Octavia Falls was more frightening than anything we'd ever encountered here... even if there were memories here worth running from.

Thousands of people had evacuated the night before the priestesses arrived. After our magic vanished, there was no point in them returning. Remaining townsfolk found that they had nowhere to go. My friends and I agreed to stay a few more weeks to use what scarce resources we had left to help people find housing outside Octavia Falls. Professor Warren and Headmistress Verla had offered to stay and help as well, and Professor Wykoff had returned with Marcus from Paris. She'd vowed she wouldn't leave town until we did. Dr. Mack was still running appointments at the clinic to help townspeople through their grief. We'd all gone in to see her a couple of times, and her therapy had been really helpful for all of us. Everyone else we knew had left.

We kept in touch with our contacts in *Hok'evale*. We got a few people placed into houses there, but they couldn't take in everyone. We knew we couldn't fix this anymore, but we still couldn't give up the responsibility. We all shared the unspoken understanding that a captain goes down with their ship, and we'd been the captains who'd steered our people into the iceberg.

In a way, I supposed it was a distraction from the very pressing reality that we were going to have to leave soon ourselves.

No one could stay, that was for certain. So much of Octavia Falls had been destroyed in this war, and without its people, the entire infrastructure of the city fell apart. The cider mills and syrup farms had shut down all operations, and all imports and exports had completely halted. Our government was in complete shambles. Though we technically still held our seats on the Imperium Council, all other essential personnel had evacuated. Once the last of the food on the shelves were gone, the final people still holding on to this town would be forced to move on. Octavia Falls would become a ghost town, and our history would be forgotten.

My friends and I gave ourselves the following week to mourn. We'd held a memorial for the people we lost, but it felt strangely hollow. It was different from any grief we'd experienced before, because in the past, people's deaths had pushed us forward and driven us to make change. This time, we couldn't really be bothered to feel anything at all, because if we couldn't save anyone anymore, what was the point?

I tried to focus on everything we still had with us instead of ruminating on what we'd lost. The coven was no more, but we still had our family. Marcus was home with us again, and Nadine and I spent every second we could cherishing precious snuggles with him. Once we found housing for the last of the townspeople, we were going to take our child far away from here and start over.

Nadine and I would go to *Hok'evale*. Our friends all had other plans. It was too painful to stay together after everything we'd gone through. It wasn't the fresh start we'd wanted, but maybe there was hope in that anyway.

Hope was a heavy word these days, but we had to hold on to *something*, because we wouldn't let our family fall apart again. We had each other, and that's what was most important.

We had no way of knowing if Marcus's curse was still active, or if somehow he'd maintained his connection to magic even though the rest of us lost it. As a demigod, he should be able to create power out of nothing, and he didn't need a connection to Alora to do it. But without magic of our own, we could no longer feel his. Even if Nadine could harness remnants of magic as a Curse Breaker, demigod powers far outweighed her own and could easily overpower her ability to sense them. For all we knew, all witch magic was gone for good, and with it, Marcus's curse and his demigod powers had vanished, too. He smiled and laughed and burped and cried just like any normal kid. If there was still any remains of magic within him, there were no signs of it.

Nadine and I tried to maintain some semblance of normality, because despite everything that happened, life was still moving forward. It didn't feel like it should, and that was the hardest part of all of this. We decided to cook a nice meal together as one of our final goodbyes to our home.

Nadine fed Marcus a bottle while I cleared off and set the table. The Curse Breaker Wand sat on top of a stack of paperwork we'd brought home from the council offices weeks ago. It struck me how obsolete these things were now. The Imperium paperwork that seemed so pressing not that long ago didn't need to be filed anymore, and without magic flowing through it, the Curse Breaker Wand was useless. We'd fought so hard for these two things, and now, they were merely unnecessary clutter. What really mattered was this time with my family.

Slowly, Marcus's eyes grew heavy, and he started drifting off. Nadine secured him in his bouncer when he finished eating, then went over to the sink to wash her hands. The water was still running, and we were still getting electricity at the estate, but our utilities would eventually get shut off, along with the rest of the town's.

Something outside must've caught her attention, because she leaned forward and peered out the window.

"Everything all right?" I asked as I dished up our plates with mashed potatoes.

"Someone just pulled around the side of the house," Nadine said warily.

"That's weird. I don't know why they wouldn't park out front."

The estate had a long driveway that curved around the side of the house toward the garage, but we never used it so we wouldn't park each other in. I looked out the window, and my stomach dropped. I recognized the vehicle, but it wasn't one of our friends like I assumed. I'd gotten so used to our home being protected from unwelcome guests that I hadn't thought about how our wards had fallen.

My teeth gritted. "That's my mom's car."

"Do you want me to send her away?" Nadine asked. "I'll rip into her if I have to."

"No. I don't want to start a fight," I said gently.

"What are you going to do?"

I paused for a beat, because I knew what I *wanted* to do, which was to make her go away. But I also didn't think that would solve anything. I had to assume my mother had come to say goodbye, which meant this was my last chance to resolve the animosity between us before I lost my chance for good. I didn't know where Mom would go after this, but I truly wasn't sure I'd ever see her again. I didn't want to do this right now, but if I desired to heal, seeing her one last time was necessary.

My mother had already gotten out of the car and was heading toward the side door just outside our suite.

I turned back to Nadine. "If you're okay with it, I'd like to invite her inside for dinner. It'll be good to say goodbye."

Nadine nodded. "If that's what you really want, then she can eat with us."

"I think it's what needs to be done," I said, more to convince myself than my wife.

Nadine reached into the cupboard to pull out another plate, while I went down the hall to greet my mother.

"Lucas!" she said brightly when I opened the door. "I hope you don't mind me stopping by."

She damn well knew I cared, but it wasn't going to stop her. I really didn't want to fight with her, though. I caught myself in the middle of the thought and resolved to approach my mother with kindness.

"It's fine, Mom." I opened the door a bit wider. "Nadine and I were just sitting down for dinner. Would you like to join us?"

Mom smiled, which was a rare occurrence. "Of course we'll join you."

Mom was already entering the house and taking her shoes off at the entrance, making herself perfectly at home, when I stopped in my tracks.

"We?" I asked.

She waved her hand like it was nothing. "Your father's just getting something out of the car."

Heat flashed through my whole body, but I did my best to keep my cool. "I told you he couldn't be around us anymore."

"He wanted to come. What would you rather I do? Tell him no?"

She could've, but then Dad wouldn't have let her come, and if he had, she probably would've shown up with a bruise.

As angry as I was at my mother for what happened last time, realizing this made me really sad, because it occurred to me that perhaps I'd been too harsh on her, and she really didn't have a choice when it came to my father.

I still had that choice, though, and maybe if I did things right this time, things would be different. If Ryan could choose to do better, then anyone could, including Jay Taylor. He just needed a nudge in the right direction.

Nadine stepped into the hall, though she didn't bother with fake pleasantries. Nadine *hated* inauthenticity, and she thought we'd all get along better if we just told the truth. She wasn't going to be *mean*, though. She'd host my parents for dinner, but she wouldn't bother putting on a mask to make them feel more comfortable.

Nadine simply nodded at my mother. "Can I take your coat, Margo?"

"That's so kind of you," my mom practically cooed. It made me uncomfortable, to be honest. Nadine wasn't going to be fake, but my mom had no problem with it. "Lucas, get the door for your father."

I must've looked like a statue, because it felt as if my blood had turned to ice. Nadine's eyes immediately went wide, but my mom missed it, because she was already headed into the suite.

"I didn't know he was here," I whispered.

"He better behave himself," Nadine hissed, before turning to hang my mom's coat in the closet.

I opened the door to find my dad carrying a huge box that blocked out his face. The box was wrapped in colorful paper and had a big red bow on top.

"Uh… what's this, Dad?" I asked.

He peered around the edge of the box. "Can't you recognize a birthday present when you see one, son?"

He wasn't being malicious, though it rubbed me the wrong way. He was trying to make a joke that clearly fell flat. No one had ever called my dad funny, that was for certain.

"Yeah, um… who's it for?" I asked.

Dad struggled to get through the doorway with the big box. "You, of course. You're turning twenty-two soon."

I was actually turning twenty-three, but I didn't bother correcting him. "My birthday isn't for another few weeks."

Dad handed me the present. "I had to gift it a few weeks early this year. That way, you can't accuse me of forgetting your birthday again."

Like he had literally every other year of my life. I wasn't sure what made this birthday so special, until I realized maybe this was his way of saying he was sorry. My parents must be leaving town very soon, and they wouldn't be seeing me for my birthday.

"Thanks, Dad," I said genuinely.

He chuckled lightly. "Don't thank me yet. You haven't even opened it!"

"It's the thought that counts. It means a lot."

Dad turned toward the suite. "Don't get sappy on me now. You know I hate it when people cry."

His response irritated me, but I could see that he was *trying*, and that mattered for something.

I led my dad into the suite, where Nadine had already set out another plate for him. I noticed she'd moved Marcus's bouncer *very* close to her seat, on the complete opposite end of the table from my father's empty plate.

Isa took one look at my father, and her hair stood on end. She scooped Rishi up by the scruff—which was hilarious to see because the kitten was pretty big now—and ran off into the bedroom. Oliver followed.

Dad plopped down in his chair and started piling his plate full. "So, how's everyone been? We hardly hear from you anymore."

"We've been busy." I internally cringed that my immediate response was to make up an excuse to keep Dad from going off the rails. It wasn't exactly a lie, but it wasn't the full truth, either. I decided that if I really wanted to make a change here, I had to be fully open with them. "To be honest, it's been rough. We were making a lot of progress, in the coven and in our personal lives. But things didn't turn out the way we expected, and now, we're all just trying to figure out where to go next."

Dad shoved a pile of food in his mouth. "It's hard being the man in charge."

I thought I detected sympathy. Even Nadine looked surprised.

"I know what it's like to supervise people," Dad rattled on. "I took over for my supervisor for a few weeks at work when he was on sick leave. I tell you, I've never seen a batch of kids as *dumb* as the ones working the mills these days. Can't get them to listen to a word you say."

"Honey, please," Mom whispered under her breath.

I kept my composure. "It's been hard for everyone, for sure. A lot of students had to find jobs while the school was closed last year and their parents were out of work. The mills took whoever was willing to work for the lowest pay and had to rush their training. I'm sure it wasn't easy."

"Of course it's tough for these kids," Dad said. "I'm not saying it isn't. These manual jobs aren't for the weak. These kids don't get to sit in a cushy office, that's for sure."

Nadine narrowed her eyes at him, and I could tell if I didn't keep this conversation going in the right direction, my wife wouldn't hesitate to put my father in his place.

"I've been going to therapy," I blurted. If my dad wanted to know what was going on in my life, then perhaps I could convince him to go to therapy, too.

Dad chuckled. "What, like a shrink? What would you need one of those for?"

My palms became clammy, and I hid them under the table. "I have a couple diagnoses that I need a therapist for, and it's been really, *really* helpful."

"You didn't tell us you were sick," Mom said gently.

Dad narrowed his eyes skeptically. "Is a shrink really qualified to *diagnose* you? It's not like a therapist is a real doctor."

"Actually, most psychiatrists hold an M.D. My therapist is a doctor specializing in mental health," I emphasized. "She's more than qualified to diagnose me."

"What kind of *problems* does she think you have?" Dad asked.

I didn't like that he was asking like that, but I also thought that if I shared it with him, maybe he'd see that he had symptoms of his own to address. Life would be a lot better for everyone if my dad sought a diagnosis and got the tools to help him out.

"PTSD, for one," I started.

Dad cut me off with a laugh, as if the diagnosis was ludicrous. "Isn't that what you get in the military? Son, you haven't been to war."

Nadine and I exchanged a wary glance. She cocked an eyebrow at me, as if to ask, *Are you going to tell him, or am I?*

"Actually, Dad, I have," I told him. "What do you think the entire Miriamic Conflict has been?"

Dad wiped his napkin over his face. "Well, you've put an end to that, haven't you?"

Mom noticeably nudged him under the table. To be honest, I was shocked it took him this long to bring it up, but it was clear Mom convinced him beforehand not to talk about it.

Before Dad could go on, I said, "It's not something that's going to be fixed overnight. But my therapist *has* been helping—a lot, actually. She's been helping us *all* through this difficult time. She's put me on a good treatment plan, and I know it's going to be difficult with everything that happened and adjusting to this new reality without magic, but I'm going to put in the work and it'll be worth it. I think everyone should see a therapist at least once in their lives. You may find that it will give you a better outlook on your future."

"The future's already here, my son," Dad stated proudly, like he hadn't heard anything I said. "Open your present, and you'll see what I mean."

Dad liked to change the subject anytime things got uncomfortable, so his comment wasn't exactly unusual. If opening his present made him happy, then I could do that, and I'd find a way to circle back to this therapy conversation later.

I dragged the box across the floor until it was next to my chair, then ripped off the wrapping paper. I flipped the top of the box open and was entirely perplexed by what I found inside. My birthday present was merely a couple of plastic buckets, some thick tubing, and a big metal pot.

It looked like he'd thrown together a bunch of random stuff he'd found in his storage shed last-minute.

"Thanks," I forced out. "I'm sure we'll find a use for all of this."

"Don't you realize what it is?" Dad sounded quite pleased with himself. "It's the new era of distillery! Without magic, our cider mills have gone belly-up, but it doesn't have to be the end of commerce for the coven with *my* idea! We can sell alcohol anywhere, whether it's infused with magic or not. And *you* can be part of the revolution, son. Put these babies in every home in Octavia Falls, and we can work together to rebuild our economy."

I furrowed my brow. He couldn't be serious. "It's an at-home distillery kit? Dad, these things have been around forever."

"And without magic, we'll be forced to go back to the basics," Dad insisted. "I've already ordered enough to get the ball rolling. I just need a salesman to market these babies. You're a priest, which means you could order every house in the coven to buy one and participate in building our economy back up from the ground. It's the least you can do after everything you've done."

"What's that supposed to mean?" Nadine demanded, finally cracking. We'd barely been entertaining my parents for five minutes, and already, neither of us could take it anymore.

"Lucas claims he's done *so much* as a priest," Dad said. "If that's true, the failure falls on his shoulders. He couldn't end the Waning, despite his promises to restore our magic once he got rid of the priestesses. Someone has to come in and clean up his mess and get the coven back on their feet. I'm used to cleaning up after him, so it's only natural that the burden would fall on me. If our magic's gone for good, then the least we can pursue is money."

I sighed heavily and pressed my fingers to the corners of my eyes. I always knew my dad liked to hear the sound of his own voice, but I didn't realize until now that my father didn't actually listen to what he was saying. He had no idea he was being mean. How could he, if he really thought I'd help him after this?

"Is that all you came here for?" I asked. There was no emotion in my tone, because to be honest, I didn't care anymore. "You want to take advantage of our coven's darkest moment so that you can make a profit? You think because I'm a priest I can make you *rich*?"

"You're putting words in my mouth," Dad insisted. "I never said that. *You* did."

Though his accusation seemed benign, it was anything but harmless. With his words came every allegation that came before it. I felt that familiar hole in my stomach open up, and I seemed to shrink to three feet tall. I was a kid again, being yelled at by my father about everything I'd ever done wrong.

All I could do was shake my head incredulously. Any hope that I ever had for my father died in that moment. As I sat there listening to him, it became very clear to me that I *never* wanted to do this again. It wasn't even that—I *couldn't* do this, because I wasn't the same guy who'd sat through this bullshit before.

Professor Warren had been right. This thing with my parents never changed because they couldn't change, but I realized then that neither had I. This time was different, because *I was different.*

I could never explain to anyone why I let my father into my house after all that happened, because they wouldn't understand. When you're the child of a narcissist, you're taught from day one to never trust reality.

As I stared back at my father now, though, I saw him for who he truly was. I'd seen glimpses of it before. I'd always known he wasn't a good person, but I never truly understood how bad it was, because he'd conditioned me since birth to believe that everything I felt about him was wrong—that nothing bad ever happened, that I was making it up, and it was all in my head. It came with such an immense feeling of relief to acknowledge that everything I knew to be true about him wasn't just some fantasy I'd fabricated.

I thought I could show my father kindness and he'd recognize the error of his ways, but he wasn't the same as Ryan. I didn't have him under my scythe blade, giving him a second chance at life. And even if I did, it was abundantly clear that he wouldn't take it. He'd proven that months ago when the hospital tried to send him to a therapist and he refused.

I used to think my dad was a broken person who just needed to be shown there was a better way, but now, I saw that he wasn't broken at all. He made complete sense.

My father had been wounded, but instead of letting people help him, he kept on tearing those wounds back open, because somewhere deep inside of him he didn't know who he was without the pain. He had to lash out at everyone around him to make them feel as pitiful as he did, just so he felt a little less alone in his agony. I'd given him chances time and time again, but each time he showed me exactly who he was. It was time I started believing him.

I thought of the vision I'd had in Dr. Mack's office and the younger teenage version of myself I'd seen and embraced. Somewhere deep in my subconscious was an even younger version of myself, a child who appeared each time I was in my father's presence. I saw that little kid now, screaming to be heard, begging me to protect him in ways I couldn't when I was his age.

I thought of the scene from the vision where the present version of myself just stood there and took my father's harsh words. I didn't understand it then, but I understood now that there was a part of me still allowing this to happen. I'd stood up to my father before, but each time it came with conflict I didn't want to bear, so I backed down to keep the peace.

I'd embraced my younger self in the vision, along with my anxiety and depression, but doing so once wasn't enough. This work was on-going, and to embrace it fully, I had to put it into practice—not just inside myself, but in my physical reality.

As my father ranted on, I took a beat to acknowledge that pit in my stomach, thank it for showing me what wasn't working here, and let the moment pass. Then I conjured up an image of that small child within me calling out for help.

I'm here for you now, I told him, just as I'd said to the teenage version of myself in my vision. *I'm going to take care of you.*

The last time I cut my parents out of my life, I'd done it from a place of anger. Though their absence was a welcome reprieve to the stress of dealing with them, it couldn't heal the deep wounds left behind. I welcomed my parents back into my home because this time, I was ready for that healing. I thought that by showing my father love and mentioning my therapy, I could lead by example and he'd behave differently, but it wasn't my responsibility to alter his behavior. I had to do this differently for myself this time.

It became clear to me then that healing didn't look the same for everyone. It was like trying to find treatment for my depression; what was right for others wasn't necessarily right for me. Similarly, what worked for me in the past might not always work as I continued to evolve. There wasn't one singular answer, because I was always changing the way I saw the world based on where I was in the present moment. Even if something helped me in the past, it could be harming me now, and I had the opportunity to change it.

People thought healing meant being able to stand up and take the hit without getting hurt, but healing was complex and didn't look the same in every situation. Sometimes, healing looked like recognizing harmful patterns and choosing to no longer participate in them, even if ending the cycle hurt like hell. It was about looking toward the future and knowing that even if it was painful now, you were better off in the long run. It was about trusting yourself to do what was right for you and those you loved, even if sometimes that meant letting those people go.

I let my dad hang around this long because even though I hated how he treated me, there was still a part of me that loved him. I didn't understand how I *could* after everything he'd done, but I did. Deep down, there was a part of me that still wanted my dad to care, and I felt sorry for him that he couldn't. I wished I could show him the kind of love I shared with my own son, but my father wasn't me, and I couldn't expect him to be. He would always show up as the version of himself he chose to be, not the one I wanted.

Some people could heal from their childhood trauma and keep their parents in their life, but I realized that even if my father changed and did his own healing, I didn't *want* to be there for it.

Before, I'd have torn into him, exploded with anger and *tried* to make him see, but I didn't have to do that anymore. I felt no sadness or remorse in the decision I was about to make, because for the first time, I truly trusted what I needed to do. I'd known it in my heart for a long time, but I never quite understood how healing could exist in a place where I'd left him behind. It took a level of courage and bravery I never had before, and I was finally ready to make this choice for good—not from a place of anger, but from a place of absolute peace.

It occurred to me then that I didn't need my father in my life to prove that I'd overcome the trauma, because not having him here at all in itself was a healed decision. There was so much nuance and gray areas to healing. For every three steps forward, it was two steps back. For all the years I put into healing, I was still learning more about it every day. Healing wasn't about being able to sit in the abuse without it affecting me. It wasn't about learning to handle the trauma, pain, and depression. I already knew how to live with that. Healing was about learning to live in the joy, peace, and happiness that I never had growing up. I couldn't do that if he was still around.

I'd wanted to lead with love, but it was clear to me now that the greatest act of love was to end the cycle of pain. I didn't have to keep welcoming my father back in and hurting myself or my family. I thought we had to work this out together, but I realized that some people just didn't have the means to work together. Sometimes, the best thing to do for your community and yourself was to not be involved with certain people, because there was nothing you could do for them. I'd spent so long hoping that one day he'd figure out how to work with me, but it just wasn't going to happen, and I didn't have to force it any longer.

I stood calmly and walked over to the door. The room fell silent as all eyes followed me. A huge weight lifted from my shoulders as I twisted the handle.

"What are you doing?" my father demanded.

"Showing you the door," I stated.

"I know what a fucking door is," Jay replied sarcastically—and rather harshly, I might add.

It didn't bother me in the slightest, which was really strange, because everything that came out of that man's mouth got on my nerves. If he wanted to be a jerk, then so be it. To truly love my father, I had to let him be the person he chose to be, to accept him for all that he was and let him make his own choices, mistakes and all. I didn't have to change him, but that didn't mean I had to be around him any longer.

"You got what you came for," I said. "You can leave now."

"You can't kick me out!" my father protested.

"I live here, so yes I can," I stated matter-of-factly.

A proud smile touched Nadine's lips. She was clearly glad I was standing up to him. I was proud of myself, too. After all this time and everything I'd gone through, I could truly say I was done for good this time. Even if he tried to force his way back into my life, it wouldn't be the same. There was no coming back from this.

That really pissed my dad off, because he shot out of his chair and pointed a finger at me. "You think because you're a priest now that you can just turn your back on your family!? You owe me!"

I shook my head in disbelief. At this point, his outburst was comical. Nadine looked like she was trying to hold back a laugh, while my mother sat frozen in her seat.

"What could I possibly owe you for?" I asked.

"Mitchel and I were best friends back in school, and you got him killed!" Dad yelled.

"Mitchel?" I furrowed my brow, though my tone remained surprisingly calm. "You mean Sheriff Baker? Dad, he tortured me and my wife."

"I'm sure he had good reason," Dad seethed. "Mitchel always had my back. When my coworker got pissed off for goddess knows what, he cursed me with an itch behind my elbow that hasn't gone away for the last nine years! Mitchel was the one to bring the rat-bastard in and charge him with unauthorized spellcasting."

Nadine started laughing so loud it caught my dad off guard. "That's it, Jay? That's the curse you wanted me to break a year ago? Hm… I wonder how you pissed this guy off. Maybe by being your *delightful* self."

"Don't you start with me, you entitled little bitch," Jay snapped.

My mother gasped, but honestly, I felt more sad than anything. I didn't stand for anyone insulting my wife, but Nadine clearly wasn't bothered. All she could do was laugh at him, and it *was* funny, in a way, but tragic, too. My father really didn't know any better, and it was heartbreaking to acknowledge the fact that some people went their whole lives feeling bitter about the world around them. Worse, no amount of love, compassion, or resources anyone could provide would ever help, because people like my dad wouldn't accept change, even if it was for the better.

"You can leave now, Dad," I stated calmly.

Dad stomped his foot—actually stomped his foot like a child. "I'm not going anywhere until you stop misbehaving. If you weren't such a brat, we could be a family again!"

Marcus stirred awake and started fussing. Nadine quickly unstrapped him from his bouncer and cradled him in her arms. She shrank to the corner of the kitchen, because she had nowhere else to go. She'd have to walk past my dad to get anywhere else in the house.

"You think I'm such a bad guy, but you're the one hurting me and your mother!" Jay shouted.

I didn't even care to address the comment about being a family, seeing as we'd never been a real family in the first place. I had no interest in giving him any of my energy any longer. "I'm fine being the villain in your story if that means I'm the hero in mine."

Jay scoffed. "Hero? That's rich coming from a guy who failed the entire coven!"

Marcus started shrieking, and my dad raised his voice even more to be heard over my son's cries. "You're just mad I didn't give you everything you wanted as a kid. Everything is always about *you*!"

"I'm not mad at you anymore," I said, and I meant it. I wasn't here to judge my father and question his choices, only to acknowledge that I needed to walk away for my own healing—not because I was making him out to be bad or wrong, but because choosing to stay only perpetuated an unhealthy pattern that was hurting me and my family. It wasn't about him or anything he'd done. I'd spent so long trying to please my father, always backing down to keep the peace. In this singular act, I was done people pleasing, and I was putting my family first.

"You're an entitled little brat who doesn't know how good he had it!" Dad sneered. "You think I treated you so poorly, but my father was worse!"

"I'm sorry you were abused," I told him calmly. "You didn't deserve that. I appreciate your honesty, because it helps me understand you better. I can forgive you, Dad, but I can't excuse what you did to me. I know you treated me the way you did because you didn't have the tools to do better. But just because I understand that doesn't mean I have to be a part of it anymore. At some point, the cycle has to end, and it ends here with me, because I'm not going to be this kind of father to my son. You deserve compassion, and compassion for all of us means going our separate ways. I can feel bad for you and still know you're not good for me. I'm not doing this to punish you. I'm doing this for me and my family, because I can't keep hurting myself by being around you. What you do now is up to you. This is your chance to do better, but we will never speak again, and I'm okay with that."

"*Do better?*" he repeated. "You think you're *soo* much better than me."

My father hadn't listened to a word I said, and there was nothing I could say to communicate my feelings. He was never going to get it, and I had to be okay with being misunderstood. I was done trying to convince him of anything.

Marcus's cries pierced the air, but no matter how much she tried, Nadine couldn't soothe him. My wife rocked our son back and forth desperately, all while my mother sat in her chair hopelessly glancing between everyone else.

"Would you shut that child up!?" my father bellowed as he pressed his fingers to the sides of his temples. He looked like he was trying to prevent his head from exploding. Pretty sure my wife would've cursed him to cork off by now if she had any access to her magic, but she was helpless to defend herself without it.

"He'll be fine once you leave," Nadine spat. "So help me, if you don't walk out that door right now, you'll live to regret it."

Jay acted like he hadn't even heard her. Instead, he stomped toward her screaming, "SHUT UP!"

I reacted instantly and grabbed my scythe I'd left leaning by the door, but I was all the way across the room. My father reached Nadine first and yanked Marcus out of her arms.

"BE QUIET, YOU LITTLE SHIT!" Dad roared.

Then he did the unthinkable, an act so vile it made my heart feel as if it was falling out of my chest. My father *shook my baby*.

My mother gasped in absolute horror. Nadine shrieked a heart-wrenching cry as she lunged out for our son, but my father shoved her back forcefully. His elbow hit her in the eye, and my wife fell to the ground.

It all happened in a split second. I reached my father and tore my son out of his hands, but Marcus was screaming louder than ever. Nadine was already back on her feet, and I quickly handed over our son as I planted myself between my father and my family.

Nadine sobbed, and she *never* cried in the face of violence. She was always head-strong and ready to fight, but what my father had done tore her to absolute shreds.

If there was ever a moment that called for violence, it was now, because *nobody* touched my family like that and got away with it. I'd been angry at my father many times before, but I had never felt as much rage toward him as I did at that moment.

I swung my scythe at my father, but he jumped backward out of reach.

Jay stumbled into the dining room chair behind him and tripped over it. He crashed to the floor. As he lay there on his back, I noticed a small cut had broken open on his cheek, and a single drop of blood dripped down the side of his face.

Good. I still managed to nick him with the tip of the blade.

"You bastard!" Nadine seethed. "Do you have any idea what you've done!? You could have caused permanent damage!"

"Nad, take Marcus and get out of here," I instructed firmly. My main priority was making sure my wife and child got someplace safe and far away from my father. "Call Dr. Mack and meet her at the hospital. Have her do *every* imaging test to confirm if any damage was done. I'll handle this."

Nadine didn't have to be told twice. She grabbed the diaper bag and ran for the door. I finally took a breath once I heard her car leave.

My father hadn't moved from where he lay on the floor, because I had my scythe aimed at him. Mom was still sitting at the kitchen table, trembling. She couldn't even bring herself to look at my father.

Jay curled his upper lip back as he stared up at me. "You want to get rid of me? Why don't you go ahead and kill me."

I shook my head as I took a step back. "I'm not going to kill you. I'm going to leave you with the community you chose. You chose to be alone. You were given all these tools and opportunities, and people tried to help you, but you did nothing with them. Working with your community goes both ways. You didn't let people help you, and you've chosen to become this. Together means *together*. I'll meet you where you're at, but I won't participate."

Slowly, my father got to his feet. He never took his eyes off me, as if he thought I might take another swing if he turned his back. He practically scampered out of the room.

I followed him out of the suite and to the back door, to make sure he actually got in the car and left. My mother trailed behind me, but she paused at my side in the middle of the open doorway.

Dad stopped at the passenger side door when he realized my mom hadn't left the house yet. "What are you waiting for, bitch?" he snarled at her. "Get your damn keys and drive me home."

Mom trembled at my side, appearing indecisive.

"You don't have to go with him," I assured her. I really hoped she didn't. My dad had made his choice long ago, but I still had hope for my mother. She'd always followed my father's every beck and call before, but now was her chance to step away from him for good.

My mother reached into her pocket and withdrew her car keys. Her gaze dropped to her hand, where I noticed a small scar. I recalled the night a few years ago when I'd walked into the house to visit, only to find her cleaning up the remaining shards of a casserole dish my father had shattered.

Finally, Mom curled her hand into a fist and lifted her chin to look at my father. "No."

Jay was so shocked that he had to steady himself against the side of the car. "What did you just say to me?"

"I said no," my mother repeated, more firmly this time. "I'm done cleaning up your messes. I won't do it anymore."

Then my mother tossed the keys to the ground. They landed several yards away from us in front of the driver's side door.

Immense pride washed over me as I witnessed my mother stand up for herself for the first time. It was all I ever hoped for her, and there was a deep wound inside of me I didn't even know was there that I felt heal in that moment—not because of anything I'd done, but because I got to be here to witness her incredible transformation.

My father started moving toward her, and I knew he'd drag her home by her hair if given the chance. Mom shrank behind me, and the second my father noticed the scythe still clutched tightly in my hand, he backed off. He played it off as if he was just moving around the vehicle to get into the driver's seat.

Jay snatched up the keys on the ground and threw open the door. He whirled back toward us before getting into the driver's seat. "If you want to be difficult like your dead-beat son, go right ahead. You'll come crawling back like you always do."

Mom shook her head. "Not this time, Jay. What you did to our grand-child is unforgivable."

"If you want to leave now, then I'm not giving you another chance," Jay threatened. "I'll take the house, the cars, our savings, all of it!"

"All of what, Jay?" I asked in complete disbelief. His name felt strange on my tongue, but I realized then that I'd already stopped thinking of him as my dad. "You're living in a rental, and don't act like you haven't drank all your money away already. Now leave, before I make you."

Jay huffed and slammed the car door, before the engine roared to life and he tore out of the driveway, running over the flowerbeds on his way out. Only when he'd disappeared down the street did my mother finally turn to me and break down in sobs of relief. I dropped my scythe and wrapped her in my arms. Her whole body rocked with the weight of her tears. She felt so fragile in my arms.

"It's okay, Mom," I promised. "I'm not going to let him hurt you ever again. What you did here was very brave. I'm proud of you."

Mom drew away to wipe her tears. "I couldn't have done it without you. What you said about being able to understand him without participating in his madness made me realize that even though I care deeply about your father, that doesn't mean I have to put up with him anymore. I'm sorry about what he did to Marcus. I wish I'd never brought him with me."

"We can't change what happened, but we can move forward and do better," I said. "I need to go be with my wife and child now. You're welcome to stay here for as long as you wish."

Mom's form went rigid. "I can't be here alone if he decides to come back. I'll come to the hospital with you."

"All right," I agreed. "My car's out front."

I grabbed my keys, and we drove to the hospital. We found Nadine with Dr. Mack in the pediatric ward, but the rest of the hospital was deserted. Dr. Mack was just finishing up an imaging test. She didn't usually work with medical imaging, but she was the only doctor around to help us. My shoulders sagged in relief when I saw that Marcus had quieted down, though I wasn't sure if that was good or bad.

Nadine cradled Marcus in her arms. I rushed over to my family immediately and stroked Marcus's cheek. He wiggled in Nadine's arms and looked up at me, which was a good sign. He was alert.

"How's he doing?" I asked.

Nadine pursed her lips, appearing on the edge of tears. Her voice cracked as she said, "He'll be all right."

"Your son has a mild concussion, but it should heal on its own with rest," Dr. Mack reported. "But shaking a baby can have permanent consequences. You two should be on the lookout for any psychological conditions in Marcus's future, because now he'll be predisposed to them."

Mom's hand went over her mouth, and she seemed entirely devastated by the news. Nobody was shocked but her, and I didn't understand how she was still surprised by the monster my father was.

My hands shook at my sides, but I took a steadying breath, because the last thing we needed was for me to lose it and go teach Jay a lesson. There were better ways to deal with him. "Anything else?"

"No," Dr. Mack said gently. "You did the right thing by calling me. Your father could've broken Marcus's neck or caused retinal detachment, but I don't see any evidence of severe damage. I'm going to add these images to his medical file and get you a physical copy so you can take them to another hospital if you ever need them. I can drop the records off at your house later. You all take care."

"Thank you, Dr. Mack," Nadine said kindly.

Dr. Mack walked away, and Mom gave a huge sigh. "I guess Marcus got lucky."

I pulled my phone from my pocket. "He's not severely injured, but Dad still hurt him. We have evidence against him to build a case on child abuse. I won't let him get away with this. I'm calling Miles, and we're pressing charges. I don't care if we have to get another police department involved from a neighboring town."

"Lucas, you can't!" my mother protested.

I couldn't believe her. "After what he did, you're still taking his side?"

"I'm not defending him," Mom insisted. "But you're taking this too far by trying to get him arrested. It's an abuse of your power as priest to use your friends and status to punish your father. This is a family matter."

I was so stunned that I had to take a step back. "You said what he'd done was unforgivable, and you were right. You're just going to back down now?"

"I meant what I said to him at your house. I'm leaving him, and I'm going to file for divorce," Mom replied. "But that doesn't mean he deserves to be in prison over this."

"Mom, he deserves to be in prison for a lot more," I said. "For all the times he hit you and all the terrible ways he treated you. Isn't it better if you're safe from him? The cops can't arrest him for being an asshole, but they sure as hell can try him for shaking a baby. I don't understand how after everything he's done you're shocked he'd do this, too."

"I never imagined he'd do it again!" Mom cried.

My jaw hung slack, and I'd gone completely breathless. I had a hard time processing what I'd just heard, because I didn't want to believe what my mom had just admitted to. "You… let this happen before?"

I could barely get the words out. I kept wanting to believe the best in my mother, kept giving her the benefit of the doubt. But in that moment, all hope I had left for her collapsed. My father had shown her the kind of person he was over and over again, and she still defended him.

Beside me, Nadine already had her phone to her ear and was talking to Miles. She went down the hall while I handled my mother.

"When did this happen?" I demanded. "This summer, when you let him see Marcus without our permission?"

"No," Mom insisted. "This was decades ago."

The rest of her explanation was clear in her silence. I felt sick to my stomach, and I had to steady myself against the armrest of a nearby chair. "He did this to *me*? I can't believe you'd let that happen!"

"It was an accident," Mom pressed. "Your father suffers from *depression*—"

"I don't give a flying fuck what excuses you want to give," I growled. I had really wanted to believe my mother was better than this. "I have depression too, and it's never driven me to abuse people. This could be one of the reasons I'm mentally ill and have been suffering my whole life, and why I'll *continue* to need treatment. You realize this could've happened to Eric, too, and we *lost* him, Mom. Now dad's done the same thing to Marcus."

"You don't understand what your father has been through," she insisted.

I couldn't believe she was still defending him. I searched her gaze for one last shred of hope, but I didn't find it. "You are never going to be the person I need you to be, are you?"

Mom's mouth bobbed open, then closed. There was nothing she could say to make this better. "I'm sorry I'm not the mom you wanted. I tried so hard, but I don't know where I went wrong—"

"Stop," I interrupted. "If you can't be genuine with me, then I don't want to hear it. I know when you're trying to manipulate me. You want me to tell you that you're wrong, that you were a great mom and none of this is your fault, but that would be a lie. You weren't as bad as Dad, but you're just as wounded, if not more."

Mom sniffled. "Please, Lucas. Forgive me."

She reached out for me, but I took another step back. "I don't want your apologies. I don't need them. *You* do. Every apology you want to give me is an apology you need to give yourself. You stayed with Dad long enough to let this happen again, despite him showing you what kind of person he was the first time, and *you* need to be the one to sit with that. You're not the one who hurt Marcus, and I'm never going to place that blame on you, but you're a victim too, Mom. Until you acknowledge that and start to forgive *yourself*, you will never be free of him."

I hoped she could understand this, but this was no longer about what my mom chose to do. This choice was about what *I* needed to do.

"I'm done with him, I swear," Mom insisted.

"I'm glad you finally had the courage to leave him, but I can't be a part of your life anymore. We need to go our separate ways now."

The harrowing heartbreak of losing not just one parent tonight, but two, tore me to pieces. On the one hand, this was what I had wanted—to finally say goodbye and never see either of my parents again. But it came with a grief I hadn't anticipated, because even though I knew it was best, it was still difficult to let them go.

Mom took a wary step back. "For what it's worth, Lucas, I really am sorry."

It took a lot to believe her, considering she'd told me she'd *lost me just like Eric* many times over when I stopped visiting. She'd told me to leave all those years ago. Now she was finally getting her wish.

It didn't really matter if she meant it or not, though, because her apology was something I needed for my own healing. To accept it was not to do her any favors, but to show myself the love I desperately needed from my mother for so long. She couldn't give me that anymore, but I could still choose it for myself.

So when she said she was sorry, I chose to believe her.

Nadine hung up the phone and returned to my side. "Miles is going to pick up your father right now. He'll be facing serious criminal charges."

Mom seemed to shrink in on herself. She looked positively terrified. "I don't know where to go from here."

"Go be happy," I told her. "That's all I want for you, even if I can't be a part of your life anymore. We'll give you a car and enough money to make it across the country. You can go to Kinpago. There's a women's shelter there, and they'll take in any supernaturals who need help. *Hok'evale* isn't far from there, either. He won't find you in California."

"I—I'll gather my things," Mom stammered.

Then she turned and left the hospital, walking out of my life forever. I felt immense sadness at the same time I relished in profound relief, because it was finally done. I'd never have to do this ever again.

That reality was just as heartbreaking as it was freeing.

Nadine gazed up at me with tears in her eyes. "Are you sure this is what you want, Lucas?"

I wrapped an arm around her waist, pulling her and my son close. "None of this is easy, but I know in my heart it's the right thing to do. Mom needs to lose both of her kids so she can start over and completely redo her life. As hard as it is, I need to lose my parents, too."

Perhaps that's what losing the coven was about, too. We didn't have to keep trying to save what we once had, but move on and make something better. It was time to move on and start anew...

Even if we lost ourselves in the process.

nadine

SIXTEEN

Saying goodbye to Octavia Falls once was hard enough, when we'd been forced by the priestesses to flee town. We'd spent a year living in the safe house, and while I cherished our time there, I'd always known it wasn't permanent. Back then, we all had an understanding that we would one day return to Octavia Falls, to either defeat the priestesses and live out the rest of our happy lives here, or die trying. Either way, I always assumed I'd be put to rest somewhere in this town. Never did I imagine that we'd leave forever. Once we fled Octavia Falls this time, there'd be no coming back.

We'd overstayed our time in this town. We told ourselves it was to help get everyone else out, but in truth, we hung around a few weeks longer because we didn't want to say goodbye for good.

We couldn't put it off any longer. By Monday, our bags were packed and ready to be loaded in the cars. We had plans to meet Headmistress Verla and Professors Warren and Wykoff tonight for dinner to say our final goodbyes. Then we'd all go our separate ways.

Lucas and I were headed across the country with Marcus, where our allies in *Hok'evale* had a room for us to stay in temporarily. We didn't know how long we'd be there, but we hoped it wouldn't be more than a few weeks before we found something more permanent. It was certainly going to take some adjusting to, because I couldn't imagine a permanent solution, honestly.

Talia and Grant were headed to New York, where they could follow their dreams. Grant would find a job at a restaurant there, working his way up to become a chef, while Talia would pursue her music career. I was glad they still had the chance to pursue their dreams, but it didn't make it easier to say goodbye.

Miles and Chloe planned to travel to other supernatural communities, taking odd jobs and living a nomad life. I knew it wasn't what either of them wanted. They were both leaders, but they needed the time and space to figure out where they belonged after this.

Professor Wykoff was headed back to Paris. Even though she had no magic, her knowledge of magical societies was extensive, and she wanted to find a teaching job somewhere within the supernatural community there.

Professor Warren said he needed some time to himself for introspection. He was going to take a few months to backpack the Appalachian Trail, with the hopes that when he finished, he'd know where to go next.

Headmistress Verla had found a job at a law firm somewhere in the Midwest that specialized in domestic abuse cases. We'd invited her to come to *Hok'evale* with us, but she was very attached to this job offer. It was a good, high paying job, and Clarice Verla was the kind of career-driven woman who needed to throw herself into her work to process things. I recalled what she said about her sister, and how Nicole had been a lawyer who prosecuted similar cases. It was clear this was Verla's way of connecting back to what she'd lost and trying to do good in the world despite everything else.

I was happy for her, because I knew she'd be good at it and make a positive impact. She'd been so wrapped up in her career for so long that this could be the fresh start she needed to put all this behind her. I hoped she found someone to settle down with, who admired her ambition and perseverance, because I didn't want her going through this alone.

I trusted she would find her healing, as we all would. She just had to go about it her own way.

Apart from our closest friends, there were still a few hundred townsfolk who still hadn't evacuated. I didn't know what they'd do once we left, but sooner or later, they'd all have to move on as we did. We'd done all we could to help relocate townspeople, and now, it was time to say goodbye.

"Everybody ready?" Talia asked as we gathered in the living room that morning.

I strapped Marcus in his stroller, then slipped my leather jacket on. Lucas tucked a blanket around our son, making sure his feet were covered to keep him warm. It was our last day in Octavia Falls, and we were going to make the most of it before we bid farewell to our former mentors tonight.

"We're all set," Lucas said.

Grant cupped his hands around his mouth and shouted to the other side of the house. "Miles, Chloe. Time to go!"

When they didn't respond, Lucas cocked an eyebrow. "Pretty sure they're fucking again."

"Hey, *hermano*," Grant called. "Wrap it up."

Miles and Chloe appeared around the corner. Chloe ran her fingers through her hair to straighten the strands, then hoisted her purse further up her shoulder. Yep, definitely fucking.

Miles wiggled his eyebrows. "You don't have to remind me. I always *wrap it up*."

Grant groaned. "Not what I meant."

Miles nudged his brother playfully with his good arm. His broken arm was in a cast, which we had all signed as soon as he got it. Grant had drawn a penis near Miles's elbow, and he still hadn't noticed.

"Wrapping it up *is* important, though!" Talia piped up.

"Though not always effective," Lucas joked. "Marcus is proof of that."

Marcus let out a big belly laugh. I'd never heard him laugh so hard, and it made my insides melt. His laugh was full of pure joy, which made the day easier to face.

"That's the sound of a guilty child," Miles cracked. "He might as well be saying, *Te he, I escaped your latex prison. Look at me now!*"

"I for one am very glad to be harboring a fugitive," I said proudly.

"If Marcus is an escapee, then I consider it to be fate," my husband added cheerfully.

Marcus laughed again, and I placed my hand on my heart. "Aw… Lucas. I want another one."

Miles pretended to check an imaginary watch on his wrist. "It'll make us a few minutes late."

Everyone roared in laughter, and it felt *good* to be laughing again. Even

Lucas chuckled at the jab. I swore I'd never heard a sound more beautiful than my friends' collective laughter. That's what today was about—finding the beauty in the midst of our melancholy goodbye.

Our friends turned toward the door, but Lucas paused for a second. He wrapped an arm around my waist and leaned in to whisper. "We'll start planning our future again soon, Nad. I promise."

I leaned into him, enjoying the warmth of his body next to mine. "I like the sound of that."

We followed our friends outside, and our cats prowled along at our feet. It was a mild autumn day, warm for this time of year. Orange leaves tumbled in the soft breeze, and the sun shone down on us to warm our faces. It was certainly a day to remember here in Octavia Falls. We walked the deserted streets, breathing in the crisp air as we shared our most treasured memories with one another.

Miles pointed to a run-down shop on Main Street. "Grant, remember the Halloween I dared you to go inside that old wand shop? You nearly pissed your pants!"

"Yes, you remind me of it often," Grant said flatly. "There was a real ghost in there!"

"Oh, there's Starlight!" Talia exclaimed, pointing out the local performing arts center. "Grant took me there all the time. They were the *best* dates. Once, after we saw a musical review of *Wicked*, he took me home to put on his own rendition of *Dancing Through Life*."

"I bet the Ozdust Ballroom got a little *freaky* that night," Chloe teased. "Less of a ballroom and more of a… club?"

"Of the *stripping* variety," Miles added.

Talia cocked an eyebrow. "Yes, Miles, I know what she meant. And she is… *not* wrong."

"Oh, The Pie Shack!" I pointed to the abandoned restaurant. "Lucas took me there on Halloween one year. Their pies were delicious."

Grant rubbed his belly. "The best. Do you think there's some leftovers in their freezers?"

Talia frowned at him. "Is that how you plan on saying goodbye to Octavia Falls—in a diabetic coma?"

Grant smiled proudly. "It'd be a great way to go!"

Talia gasped and stopped in the middle of the street. "Winefred's! They have the cutest dresses. Would it be wrong to see if they have any left in stock?"

"Clearly I'm dying of a diabetic coma, and you will suffocate in a pile of fabric," Grant joked.

Talia's shoulders slumped. "I'm really going to miss shopping here. We had Cornerstone Antiques and Hallowed Harmonica. Those were my favorite hang-out spots."

"Don't forget The Jolly Pumpkin," I added. "Hattie's little shop was the cutest."

We hadn't seen Hattie since the wedding, as she had evacuated town and moved on with the others.

"I liked that shop on the next block that Everly Hall owned," Chloe said. "She was a really talented Seer. She let me stay there for a bit after my grandma arrested me for protesting. That was awesome!"

Everly Hall had been the one to write my prophecy, the one that foretold the witch hunts.

By fire and noose
The coven will fall
Division and suffering
Destruction to all

Great power of the chosen
The coven be made whole
By the only witch of her kind
And a reaper bound to her soul

At the time, the outcome seemed so certain. The coven *would* fall, and Lucas and I were supposed to be there to make it whole once again. But that phrase could be interpreted in so many different ways. At the time, I thought it meant we would be the ones to restore people's magic. Now I realized that *wholeness* was something meant to exist without our powers.

Lucas and I were never meant to bring magic back to the coven. Our job had been to fulfill the first half of the prophecy, in which the coven would be destroyed. All along, we were fated to let our magic fade so that people could learn who they were without it.

It was a somber, twisted reality I didn't want to accept, but one I had to. This was how things were now, and at some point, I had to admit that I couldn't do anything more to change it. I could wallow in the failure, or pick up the pieces of our shattered hope and mold it into a new mosaic. It wouldn't be what I'd hoped for, but I had to believe it would be its own kind of wonderful.

We continued through the streets of Octavia Falls until we reached Miriam College of Witchcraft. My friends and I stopped on the grounds of the school. I pulled a blanket from the basket at the bottom of the stroller and spread it out in the grass. Lucas unstrapped Marcus and placed him on his belly for tummy time. We gathered on the lawn for a picnic underneath the peaks of Miriam Mansion.

We'd brought along the last of our fresh apples from Blossom Orchards, along with a bottle of non-alcoholic cider. Talia had made popcorn trail mix with pretzels, roasted nuts, and candy corn mixed in. Chloe had brought maple candies and passed them around to everyone. They were like creamy caramels that melted in my mouth.

Our cats spotted a chipmunk running up a tree and went chasing it across the lawn. Isa climbed the tree to the first branch, while Oliver whined from the ground and watched her tail swish. Bella and Gus got distracted by a bug in the grass and started fighting over it, while Marley challenged Kiki to a wrestling match. Rishi rolled around, nipping at long blades of grass.

"Rishi, stop it," I scolded. "You're going to puke that up."

Rishi started gagging, because he shoved a grass blade so far into his mouth it hit the back of his throat. That humbled him real quick, and he came to sit beside us on the blanket.

Talia leaned back on her hands, letting the sun beat down on her face. "I'm going to miss this place. I loved Miriam College of Witchcraft. My favorite thing to do was go to the music room, where Professor Warbright had this piano that displayed colorful streams of magic with every note you played. It was really fun coming up with new songs and coordinating them to the colors."

"Coach Campbell did something similar during swim practice," Grant said. "If you beat your time from the last meet, he'd put a potion in your lane that made the water sparkle different colors depending on the stroke you swam. It was always a fun motivator. Sometimes, if I knew I was in the lead, I'd *just barely* beat my last time so I didn't have to compete so hard against myself at the next meet. I was always getting the potion in my lane."

"So the pineapple-printed Speedos weren't fun enough for you?" I teased.

"I like to swim *in style*," Grant laughed.

Chloe rolled her eyes. "You guys were all so *academically motivated*. My favorite thing to do was send unexpecting freshmen to the basement when they asked me for directions. Once you passed the Alchemy labs, that place was a labyrinth. I used to sit in a study area at the top of the stairs and see how many hours it took for them to find their way out."

Miles frowned, appearing disgruntled. "That prank cost me over an hour. I missed my first class!"

Chloe ran her fingers through his hair. "Yours was the record, hun. Most kids took at least three hours."

Miles puffed his chest out. "The record, huh?"

"That's what you want," Lucas quipped sarcastically. "The record for finishing the *fastest*."

We shared a collective laugh, and Miles rolled his eyes. "Ha ha," he said dryly. "Though, I suppose I deserved that."

The two shook hands to call a truce.

"My favorite place at school was the astrology classroom," I said. "There was something about that tower that was just... magical."

"Yeah, because that's where you lost your virginity!" Talia snickered.

"It was a beautiful experience," I insisted.

"Is this all we talk about now, is sex?" Grant asked.

Lucas shrugged as he tossed some popcorn in his mouth. "It was college. You were either in classrooms sitting at a desk... or in classrooms boning on a desk."

Chloe laughed. "Dear Goddess, how many classrooms did you and Nadine fuck in?"

"A couple," Lucas said nonchalantly. "You guys are the ones who wanted to walk down memory lane, and those happen to be *my* favorite memories of this place."

Chloe took a bite of apple. "My favorite memory is when I jumped off the balcony in the Main Foyer and made it look like I'd been hanged. It was pure art."

Miles gave a fake pout. "You mean, that time in the Gravestone when you *accidentally* tripped and landed on my dick isn't your favorite memory?"

We all started laughing, and Chloe's jaw dropped. "It's *not* what it sounds like! I *did* trip and fall in his lap, but we only made out."

"A *lot*," Miles bragged.

"It was a forbidden, sexy love, and I wouldn't have our love story any other way," Chloe said.

We must've sat on the lawn in front of the school for hours, sharing memories of our favorite classes and trying to one-up each other on how many places we'd slept with our significant other inside the school.

Marcus drifted off, and we strapped him back into his stroller as we continued our walk. The Black Circle Trail, which looped through miles of Octavia Falls, wasn't far from here. We followed the trail to the cemetery. The dirt path was smooth from decades of foot traffic. We had to push the stroller over a couple of small rocks and roots, but Marcus seemed perfectly content with the bumpy ride.

Lucas approached the iron gates surrounding the cemetery. There were several upturned graves from the bodies he'd reanimated during the Golem War. A number of zombies had been too damaged to return to their graves, but most had been reburied, and now those coven members could truly rest in peace.

"A lot happened to me here at this graveyard," Lucas said softly. "Those things seemed bad or insignificant at the time, but I didn't realize how many memories I was making."

"What are some of your favorite memories?" Talia asked gently.

Lucas drew a deep breath. "That's complicated, because each one of them has something good *and* bad about it. Like the night of my Evoking Ceremony. It was the night I lost Eric—worst night of my life, honestly. But when I look back on the ceremony itself, I see Grant, Chloe, and me joking around and having a good time."

Chloe burst into laughter. "That's right! I almost forgot about the tramp stamp."

"Wait, hold on. I haven't heard this story," Miles said.

Lucas sighed and reached for the hem of his jacket. He lifted the fabric a few inches to show Miles the skull tattoo located on his lower back. All our magic had vanished, but our tattoos indicating our Cast hadn't faded. They were permanent reminders of what we once had.

"Oh, wow. That *is* a tramp stamp!" Miles joked.

Lucas looked back over the cemetery. "I thought being the Reaper's Apprentice was so awful at the time, but then I think of the night of the Reaper Moon, when I summoned Edgar Nowak right here in this cemetery. That was the night I saved Nadine's life… put her spirit right back into her body. I couldn't have done it without my powers. That night sucked, but it was beautiful, too."

I grew sad watching Lucas peer over the graveyard. While this place was sentimental to him for many reasons, I also witnessed pain in his eyes. But he didn't seem bothered by that, and I realized maybe it didn't have to be one or the other.

I glanced toward the small oak tree at the edge of the cemetery, where we'd placed a memorial stone for Grammy and Dean. As the inscription on their memorial read, *Grief and death are ephemeral, but love lasts forever.*

It was something Grammy once said, and what a wise woman she was. This town and coven weren't permanent, either, but we could take the love we found in it with us wherever we went.

Watching Lucas now, I saw so much growth in him, which I greatly admired. He'd been able to walk away from his parents, even though he still cared for them and wanted the best for them. It took an immense amount of strength to do that. Perhaps our coven was like Lucas's family —Mother Miriam loved us, and we would always be her children, but maybe stepping away from one another was the best thing for all of us. We didn't have to suffer in this parting from our home, but thank it for all the love and joy it provided us.

I laced my fingers through his. "There really was so much beauty here."

"Easy for you two to say," Talia said. "Didn't you screw on a gravestone somewhere over there?"

"You two fucked in a graveyard!?" Chloe cried. "You nasty, kinky sluts. Miles, I want to fuck in a graveyard."

Miles's eyebrows shot up approvingly. "Sure, I'll try anything once. So did you guys do it like on the grave itself or on the *gravestone*."

"We weren't technically *here*," Lucas admitted. "We were astral traveling."

Talia looked impressed. "I hear astral sex is quite good."

Chloe frowned skeptically. "Like you two haven't tried it."

"A couple of times," Grant admitted. "But never in a graveyard."

"What *have* you done in a graveyard?" Chloe asked.

"We fought off a zombie once," Talia said. "But you knew that, because it was *your* dumb prank. I've always meant to ask—who'd you get to reanimate the body?"

Chloe furrowed her brow. "I didn't do that."

"Of course it was you. It was Halloween our freshman year," Talia prompted. "We came to do a séance for one of Lucas's classes, but you sent a zombie to scare us. It was a classic Halloween prank."

"A classic, maybe, but not mine," Chloe said.

"Huh," Talia said thoughtfully. "Must've been Ryan trying to sabotage Lucas's assignment."

"It's strange how many memories I have here," Lucas said fondly. "It's a graveyard—not exactly a place meant for the living."

"Well, you are a Death warlock," Chloe pointed out. "It's kind of your thing."

Lucas dropped his gaze, then turned away from the cemetery. "Not anymore."

Everyone kept quiet as we continued down the trail. For every memory I wanted to leave back here and forget, there was something good in each of them—stolen moments of passion with Lucas, nights of laughter with my friends, and heart-pounding thrills of solving mysteries and casting powerful spells. Even the worst of times held moments of beauty.

My friends and I found our way to the edge of Lake Santos, to a tiny secluded beach only a few yards from the forest. From here, we could see the decimated remains of the Catwalk in the distance, as well as the debris that used to be Pinewood Manor.

That evil, horrible place had been where Chloe and I broke our family curse, where we planted the seeds of the friendship that we shared now. The Catwalk had been where Lucas and I broke up, but it was also where Grant's ear got pinched by a zombie crab, and where my friends and I had indulged in sweets and took home magical potions.

Grant sat down in the sand, looking over the water. The sun had dipped low in the sky, and its light shimmered beautifully off the soft waves. "Do you guys remember this beach? We brought Nadine out here to *initiate* her when she moved here. She got tipsy off my Fizzy Bubbly."

"Yeah, and we went skinny dipping!" Talia exclaimed.

"Good times." Lucas wrapped an arm around my waist and lowered his voice. "I remember that night, when you dragged me into the water. I wanted so badly to be close to you. I was really stupid back then. I wish I never pushed you away."

"*I* was the idiot," I said. "Thinking back on it makes me cringe. I did and said a lot of really dumb things. But some of those dumb things really, *really* made me happy."

"I have an idea," Chloe announced as she plopped onto the ground. She pulled a deck of cards out of her purse. "Who wants to pull tarot cards?"

"Are we sure that's a good idea?" Grant asked.

Chloe shrugged. "Why not? We keep saying we're not going to be witches anymore because we don't have our magic, but you know what? There are parts of this town that we get to keep—all these memories that have made us who we are today. Losing our magic doesn't undo everything we went through. And I say that still makes us witches. We may not be able to cast spells and perform enchantments anymore, but we're still *us*, and we should take as much of ourselves with us as we can. We still have tarot cards and our intuition. Hell, we don't even need magic to astral travel—even a basic non-supernatural can do that. I may have to give up this town, but I'm not giving up who this town made me."

She shuffled her deck while she spoke, then spread the cards out in Grant's direction. "So pull two cards, and tell me what you're taking with you… and what you're leaving behind."

Grant drew two cards from the deck, then held them up for everyone to see. "Temperance and Ten of Wands. I'm leaving behind a burden, taking the weight of the Ten of Wands off my shoulders. I don't have to be a priest who's worried about taking care of anyone anymore, because that time of struggle is over. I'm going forward into the next chapter having learned how to approach life with balance, patience, and purpose. Maybe once we get settled I can start a bakery and teach nutrition classes, because I think culinary arts is where my purpose really lies."

"That's really insightful," Talia praised.

Grant stared down at his cards a moment longer. "The Ten of Wands can stay here."

He tossed the card into the lake, letting the waves carry it from shore, before it sank beneath the surface. He placed the Temperance card in his pocket, to take it with him once we left.

Talia drew her cards next. "Eight of Pentacles and Five of Cups. I'm walking away from disappointment, so that I can start new and work toward goals that really light me up. In the Five of Cups, the figure is focused on the three cups that are knocked over, not looking to see the potential in the other two cups still standing at his feet. I know we failed at our goal, but there's still hope in these two standing cups. I was glad to step in and be a priestess when I needed to be, but it's never been my calling. I want to make music and fill people's lives with joy, and with the Eight of Pentacles—a card of mastery and skill—I can do that now. And I get to take everything we learned along the way to make people's lives better through my music."

Talia tossed the Five of Cups into the lake, keeping the Eight of Pentacles with her.

Miles picked two cards from the top of the deck—The Hierophant and the Knight of Wands. He clicked his tongue, not quite sure what to make of the pair.

"The Knight of Wands is a card of impulsiveness, while The Hierophant is a card of spiritual wisdom," Talia offered. "Maybe this means you're leaving your impulsivity behind to gain a deeper spiritual understanding of yourself."

Miles shook his head. "I think it's the other way around, actually. The Hierophant isn't just spiritual wisdom. He's a religious teacher, and with that comes tradition and conformity. I never had a problem following Mother Miriam, but I wasn't the kind of person to do stuff the way everyone else did. I couldn't, not with a chronic illness like rheumatoid arthritis. I always had to get creative to get things done my way. But in the midst of conflict, you sort of have to fit this certain mold, especially as a police officer, and then as sheriff."

Miles furrowed his brow thoughtfully as he stared down at the Knight of Wands. "But this Knight... he's spiritual too. He has to be, because that's what the Wands suit represents. But he has this more young, carefree nature about him. He's ready to fight, but in a more energetic, passionate, and adventurous way. I did enjoy being sheriff, and I think I'd like to continue pursuing law enforcement, but I want to make it fun. I want to be the cop who's cracking jokes and dripping donut jelly on his badge. Life can be so serious sometimes, and there's gotta be someone in the station to laugh at. I want to be that guy who's ready to jump into action, but who also gives people something to smile about when life gets too serious."

Chloe stared at her husband fondly. "If I could fall in love with you any more than I already have, that just did it."

Miles threw The Hierophant into the lake, before turning to Chloe. "What do your cards say?"

Chloe picked the King of Swords and the Two of Wands. "The Two of Wands is all about future planning and foresight. I spent so much of my life focusing on what I could become in the future, what I could plan for and how I could make progress. All I ever wanted was to be a priestess, but even when I was, I never really sat with it. I was still so focused on where we were going that I was never really present with where I *am*. The King of Swords is confident on his throne. He knows he's made it, and he doesn't have to keep trying to get somewhere else. He represents mental clarity and authority, and if I just trust my inner guidance, I can progress from a place of truth and in knowing myself, rather than from a place of trying to control the future. I don't have to know where I'm going yet. I just have to be this king who trusts that it's all going to work out."

She tucked the King of Swords into her purse, then tossed the Two of Wands into the lake. Then she held the deck out to Lucas.

He stepped forward and withdrew two cards—the Page of Wands and Justice. He stared down at the cards for a long time, before finally deciding on his interpretation. "I'm leaving behind Justice. For so long we fought for what we thought was just and right. Justice *was* served in the end, but we were never the judges of it. I need to leave behind this rigidity I have about what's right and wrong, and step into the free spirit and limitless potential of the Page of Wands. He's just standing there with his wand, ready to move in any direction, and I need to be willing to get curious about the paths before me, knowing there isn't one singular right and just answer, but so many possibilities. I don't have to make any decisions yet, but I can be excited about anything that may come my way."

Lucas approached the edge of the water, then set the Justice card into the lake with reverence. The waves carried it away from shore, before it disappeared beneath the surface like the others.

Chloe held the deck out to me last. I withdrew the Six of Wands and

The High Priestess. The Six of Wands depicted a man on horseback, riding through a crowd with his head held high. It was a card of success, progress, and self-confidence. The High Priestess sat in front of two columns, one light and one dark to represent the duality of darkness and light. Hers was a card of intuition, divine feminism, and the subconscious mind.

At first, I thought I was going to let The High Priestess go. She was, after all, a representation of my place on the Imperium Council, which simply didn't exist anymore. I could step into the energy of the Six of Wands, knowing that I learned many lessons of self-confidence here in Octavia Falls.

But instead, I found myself dropping the Six of Wands into the water. "The Six of Wands is a card of success and self-confidence, but it also represents public recognition. I fought so long for the coven to see me for who I really was, to prove to them that the lies that had been told about me weren't true. I wanted people to see me for my authentic self, but I never needed to prove myself to anyone. I just needed to accept my own authenticity."

My breath shuddered as the resounding truth of my statement settled into my bones. "The High Priestess is not a position on a council, or a seat in government. She's simply a master of intuition and sacred knowledge. Even though I won't be a high priestess of the Miriamic Coven anymore, I can take the woman I became through that experience with me. She's a guardian of hidden mysteries, a message that things aren't always as they seem. She's the card that encourages you to look within yourself for answers and attune to your own inner wisdom. I don't have to keep looking outside of myself as with the Six of Wands. I just have to trust that I know myself and where I'm going."

I placed the card to my heart, and though there was no real magic in the tarot deck, my heart gave a jolt as if there was. Maybe in some way, it was Mother Miriam's final message, showing me that even without her, we could still find magic in our lives. It wouldn't come in the form of alchemy or levitation, but it still existed in some form as love, gratitude, and peace.

I placed the card in my pocket, beside my phone. We sat on the rocky beach until late in the afternoon. Marcus was asleep in his stroller, and the cats lazed around in the sand. Talia and Grant skipped rocks across the lake, and Chloe and Miles went looking for mussel shells to take with them. Lucas sat beside me near the water with his arm draped around me. I rested my head on his shoulder and stared over the calm water.

"I don't want to leave," I whispered.

He dragged me closer and placed a kiss on the top of my head. "I know, but maybe this isn't such a bad thing. Our family can find happiness anywhere. It doesn't have to be here."

I appreciated that he was trying to lift my spirits, but it didn't make me any less sad. Lucas could walk away happily because he still had hope for greener pastures. I couldn't, because I'd already lived outside Octavia Falls and knew there was nothing out there for me. Everything I loved had been here. I'd leave because we didn't have any other choice, but that didn't mean I wanted this.

"I must sound like a lunatic," I said. "Who else could go through everything we have and still want to stay? I know what happened here was awful, and people were absolutely horrendous to us, but this is where we fell in love and built a family. It's where you stood on stage and shook your ass in my dress because you wanted to give some asshole something to talk about. You didn't care if they made fun of you, as long as they stopped picking on your friend. It's where Chloe got Talia her birth control when the school wouldn't fill her prescription, and where Talia came barging into the courtroom at the end of our trial with final evidence that saved our lives. Octavia Falls is the place where Grant rescued you and the other hostages the night of the Burning, and where Miles infiltrated the Executors to funnel us information. Bad things happened, but through it all, we stuck by each other and became a family."

I sighed heavily. "A part of me enjoyed the haunted houses even when we were being chased by a ghost with a knife. I didn't love the part where I got possessed and our friend was stabbed, but I loved astral traveling the halls of Miriam Mansion with you and dancing with skeletons at the Midnight Formal. I made love to you in the Penthouse Suite, and these last few months, as stressful as they've been, have been wonderful making crafts with our friends and performing wedding rituals. I loved all the potions we brewed and all the puzzles we solved."

I chuckled lightly. "Call me crazy, but I *liked* tracking the Tarantulas down to their drug hideout and running away from them in the woods with Grant. It was thrilling, stealing all their supplies and returning them to the Alchemy lab. I loved investigating crimes with you, and I know you loved writing your news articles. Caesar Peppertrine is a legend!"

Lucas laughed. "Yeah, he is."

"I'm sad that we never got to experience all Octavia Falls had to offer without the threat of a noose. We have to give up a future we fought for but will never have. I'm *so* glad I get to take you all with me, but I don't get to take this place."

"We still have a bit of time left," Lucas said gently. "We can enjoy it for as long as we have."

I splayed my fingers in the sand and closed my eyes. There was no more magic pulsing through this town, but this town was magical all the same. I was really going to miss it.

Talia walked over to us, shaking lake water off her hands. "We should get going soon. It's time to start on dinner."

"We're right behind you," Lucas said.

Talia must've noticed the sadness in my gaze, because she gestured toward the stroller. "Do you want me to take Marcus?"

"Sure, Tal," I replied. "We'll catch up with you."

Talia unlocked the stroller wheels and pushed Marcus back toward the trail. The cats followed, along with the rest of our friends.

"You two be *quick* about it!" Miles cracked, before they all disappeared into the trees.

I turned my gaze back toward the water. Lucas caught a strand of my hair in the breeze and tucked it behind my ear. "I'll stay with you as long as you'd like," he offered.

"I'm just… not sure I'm making the right choice," I mused. "Once we leave, there's no coming back. Even if I found a spark of magic to fuel a spell—something that could bridge our connection to Alora again—it'd be useless once the coven forgets about this place. People will find new homes, and they'll start their own families. They may never want to come back. Am I being selfish by not even trying because I don't want to lose everyone I have left… or am I doing what's right for everyone?"

Lucas squeezed my hand. "I believe that whatever you decide *is* the right choice for everyone. I know this is a massive decision to put on your shoulders, but we've never had to go at it alone, and you don't have to now, either. You've been there for me through everything, and now, I can be there for you."

I curled into him, burying my face in his chest. "My choice is to keep you with me. I don't care where that is, as long as we're together."

"Then that's what we'll do," he promised. "We'll leave Octavia Falls in the morning, and wherever we go, we go together."

I lifted my chin, and he slowly leaned down to press his lips to mine. Sorrow and devastation swirled in my gut, but with his kiss also came immense passion and desire. He must've felt it too, because his hands tangled in my hair as he dragged me onto his lap. We kissed each other over and over again, desperately clinging to the one thing we couldn't bear to ever give up. We were losing Octavia Falls, but *Lucas* was my real home, and I was never going to let him go.

He reached for the zipper of my jacket and slowly pulled it down. I shrugged the sleeves off my shoulders. The air was cold, but the red-hot passion surging through my veins kept me warm. There was a strange comfort in the chilly autumn air biting at my skin. The cold kept me grounded in the present. I didn't have to think about what would happen when we left town, because right now I wasn't living in the future. I was here in my body, taking in the sensations of the cold air on my skin and my husband's lips against mine.

His touch contained something enchanting that could whisk all my worries away. I wanted this so badly, because this final moment together was the last bit of magic we'd ever get before we left, and we both needed something magical to take with us. I was taking him, he was taking me, and together, we would take one last cherished memory from this place.

Lucas's hands inched up my shirt, and mine teased the button on his trousers. Heart pounding, I slid my hands past the fabric and curled my fingers around his cock. Lucas gasped in elation. He grabbed me by the ass and dragged me even closer. Neither of us said a thing, and we didn't have to. We knew each other's bodies so well by now that we moved in a beautiful, synchronous rhythm.

Lucas undressed me, then I helped him out of his clothes. My nipples hardened in the cold, and I found that I enjoyed the sensation. He took my hand and slowly led me toward the water. The setting sun glittered off its surface, and I paused for a moment just to take in the shadows of his abs and the impressive length of his cock. He smiled at me, then playfully yanked me into the water, just like I'd done to him the first time we'd been to this beach all those years ago.

I landed on top of him. The icy chill of the water splashing into my face turned out to be immensely pleasant. Lucas thrust upward. With no effort at all, he slid inside of me. I gasped, my heart hammering wildly as he filled me up. The lake was cold, but it didn't matter once our bodies were bound together, because the passion that blazed between us was enough to warm the entire lake for miles.

Lucas kissed me all over my body like he craved my taste, and I rode him until the sun disappeared below the horizon. The stars came out and twinkled above us, shining down on us like magical sparkling orbs.

We found ourselves drifting away from shore, descending deeper into the depths of the lake. My legs wrapped around Lucas's middle as the water reached our shoulders. One hand cupped my ass, while the other cradled the back of my neck. His tongue slid in and out of my mouth with every thrust of his hips. I panted in fervent wanting.

This moment was every delirious daydream I ever had of kissing him here in Lake Santos where it all started, only immensely more passionate and delicious than I ever thought possible. The water might as well have swelled into waves that crested over us and submerged us beneath the lake's depths, because I found myself gasping for breath. Lake Santos swirled around our bodies to envelop us in a safe, erotic embrace where time itself seemed to stop, pausing briefly for just the two of us.

Lucas rolled my nipple between his fingers, and that was my undoing. My cry of ecstasy echoed across the lake as my intense desire swelled to a marvelous peak. I contracted around him, feeling as if I was melting into the lake itself—becoming one with the water and sand—before the wave of euphoria receded, gently bringing me back to myself.

"Fuck, Nadine," he moaned irresistibly.

He buried himself deep inside of me one last time as he reached his own peak. His eager gasps of wanting as he came inside me filled me with complete bliss.

As we came down from the high, I rested my head on his shoulder and placed a soft kiss on his neck. He tilted his head back to welcome in my affection. I sighed happily as I felt his pounding heart sync with mine.

"What a way to tell this place goodbye," he whispered.

I smirked lightly. "We aren't the kind of people to go out without a bang."

Lucas smiled, and to hear him laugh made me giddy all over again.

We emerged from the lake shivering and put our clothes back on. Lucas wrapped me in his arms, bringing warmth back to my skin. Being in his arms brought tears to my eyes, not of sorrow this time, but from an immense outpouring of love.

"Thank you for showing me that I don't have to do everything by myself," I whispered. "Like my mother's stash, not every door is meant for me to open. Sometimes I need to ask for help getting there, and that's okay, because the people who love me will show up to support me when I can't do it myself."

He pushed wet strands of hair over my shoulder. "Of course, Nad. I'm not going anywhere… not unless it's with you."

Then I closed my eyes and whispered one final prayer to the ether. Perhaps like my mother, our goddess couldn't be here for me anymore, not in the way I wished. But that didn't mean she wasn't still out there somewhere watching over us. The door on Octavia Falls had closed. Whatever came next was not my door to open… I merely had to find the door that had already opened for me and step through it.

Mother Miriam, show me where to go next, I prayed.

My phone rang then, and I pulled it out of my pocket to answer. The High Priestess tarot card I'd tucked in there fell out and fluttered to the ground.

"Hello?" I answered, leaning down to pick up the card.

"The Oaken Wands are gone!" Chloe barked into the phone.

All the warmth that had risen to my skin at Lucas's touch disappeared in an instant, and an icy chill akin to a ghostly haunting crept over me. Lucas heard Chloe, and his features paled in panic.

It didn't make any sense. The Oaken Wands were useless without witch magic. I couldn't imagine who would possibly want them now.

"What do you mean the Oaken Wands are gone?" I demanded.

"I'm telling you, we arrived home and the Wands are gone," Chloe insisted. "Someone broke in and took them."

"They didn't get them all." Lucas pulled the Mortana Wand from his pocket. "I always keep mine on me. Whoever did this must know they're useless now, though."

"But are they?" I wondered. "If someone wants the Wands, that means they intend to use them, and we have no idea what for."

"They can't use them, right!?" Chloe questioned.

My fingers froze against The High Priestess tarot card I'd bent to pick up. "They can't… unless they know how to access magic we don't."

I stood and showed Lucas the card. "My tarot reading told me something isn't as it seems. The High Priestess is a card of intuition. I said I didn't want to leave, and I need to trust my gut on that."

"What are we going to do?" he asked.

"We're going to figure out who took the Wands and what they intend to do with them," I stated. "Then we're either going to help them… or stop them."

Until we identified the culprit, there was no telling if the thief was trying to help our people… or bring the cataclysm of our divided coven to its bitter end.

SEVENTEEN

Nadine and I rushed home to find our friends frantic with worry. Grant had dragged his bags into the living room and was unpacking everything. He tossed clothes everywhere.

"The Wands have to be here!" he insisted. "We must've misplaced them."

"*All* of them?" Chloe demanded. "I *know* I left the Mentalist Wand in my room next to our bags. It's gone, along with the rest of them."

"Grant, the Alchemy Wand isn't in your suitcase," Talia pressed. "I packed it with the Seer Wand in my backpack, and they're not there anymore."

Nadine and I entered the living room, and Oliver scurried over to me and meowed in distress. Marcus started crying in his stroller, and I quickly went over to cradle him in my arms.

Chloe looked relieved to see us. "We went looking for the Curse Breaker and Mortana Wands, but we couldn't find them."

I rocked Marcus, and he quieted. "I have the Mortana Wand."

"I left the Curse Breaker Wand here." Nadine started down the hall toward our suite, and we all followed. "After we lost our magic, I assumed the Oaken Wands were useless. I didn't see a reason to protect it anymore."

She stopped in our suite and knelt next to our bags near the door. She unzipped the front pocket of her duffel bag… but it was empty.

Slowly, she stepped back. "The Curse Breaker Wand is gone, too."

"Nadine's right, isn't she? The Oaken Wands *are* useless," Grant said, but even he didn't sound like he believed himself. "Perhaps someone wanted to keep them as a memento."

"That'd be one serious collector," Miles mumbled with a curious expression on his face. It was the same look he got whenever he was on sheriff duty. I could see in his calculating eyes that he was already thinking of this as a crime scene.

"Someone must've waited until we left home and taken them for a reason," Nadine insisted.

Talia frowned. "We don't know what this thief could use the Wands for, but it can't be good. If they knew the Wands could still help us, they would've come to us directly."

Nadine tapped her foot thoughtfully. "Only if they trusted us, and we've made a lot of enemies."

"Yeah, but who's left? The priestesses are all gone, and everyone who doesn't like us has already left," Grant pointed out.

"Maybe the Wands are worth something to other supernatural societies, even if they're useless to us," Miles theorized. "Someone might've taken them thinking they could sell them off to the highest bidder."

Nadine didn't seem convinced. "Something's not adding up. Did you guys notice anything else missing, or anything out of the ordinary?"

Chloe shook her head. "Everything's in its place—everything but the Wands."

"Show me where you kept them," Nadine requested.

Chloe led us to the other side of the house and into her room. Her bags and a few boxes were piled near the door.

Chloe smacked the top of the dresser. "I left the Mentalist Wand right here. I know I did."

Nadine carefully examined the dresser's surface, then started opening and closing drawers. She got down on her hands and knees to look underneath the furniture—first the dresser, and then the bed. She found nothing. Chloe kept her room spotless.

"What are you looking for, exactly?" Grant asked.

Nadine leaned back on her heels. "I'm not sure yet, but I feel... something. I can't put my finger on it."

She started to stand, but as she pushed her knee against the floor, she winced. "Ow!"

Nadine picked something out of the carpet, so small I couldn't see what it was at first. She stood and held a small pink rock in the palm of her hand. It was raw rose quartz, barely an inch long.

"Um… that's nothing," Miles said quickly.

"It's definitely *something*," Nadine countered. She peered closer at the crystal, like there was something inside she couldn't quite make out. "I think the thief dropped this."

"Miles is right," Chloe said. "We used rose quartz in an intimacy ritual we did a few weeks ago. It wasn't a spell, exactly, but we mixed a bunch of rose quartz with herbs and essential oils while we—"

"They don't have to know the details," Miles cut her off.

Chloe sighed. "We must've dropped it during the ritual. It's ours."

Nadine furrowed her brow. "Then why do I sense it contains magic?"

The room went dead silent for several beats. We were all equally baffled.

"That's impossible. Can I see?" Miles held out his hand. Nadine placed the crystal in his palm, and he peered closely at the rock. "I don't feel anything."

"I do, because Curse Breaking is in my blood," Nadine said. "As long as there's magic for me to access, I can feel it."

Talia tilted her head. "All witch magic is gone, though. So… what's this?"

"It's gotta be fae magic," Miles theorized. "Which means the fae were causing the Waning all this time and this isn't some punishment from Mother Miriam, but an act of war from the Arcanea."

"But the fae helped us find the Wands—Beau Blankard, Professor Calliope, and the fae we met in Malovia," Talia pointed out.

Miles cocked an eyebrow. "Yeah, they put us through hell to find the Oaken Wands so they could eventually get their hands on them. Professor Calliope's looking like our prime suspect."

"How are the Oaken Wands useful to the fae?" Grant wondered.

"It doesn't matter if they can use them themselves, as long as they prevent *us* from using them," Miles said. "The Oaken Wands were built to protect our magic from the fae, but if they've got their hands on them, that leaves our magic completely vulnerable."

"It's not fae magic." Nadine took the crystal back. "I can feel that it's witch magic, but it's different, too. I can't identify one singular Cast. That's why Miles doesn't feel anything, because it doesn't quite resonate with him. But this is my specialty, and I've been working with sensing magical signatures for years. It's faint, but it's there."

"So our magic isn't *completely* gone like we thought," Chloe said thoughtfully. "The Waning never drained our crystal stores, so severing our connection to Alora must've not affected them, either. If there are any charged crystals still left in the coven, then there's still witch magic here, and it's magic we can access."

"If that crystal doesn't contain the magic of any witch Cast, then what *is* inside of it?" I asked.

Nadine swallowed audibly. "I said any *singular* Cast. This crystal contains magic from all of them."

Nobody knew what to make of that. I hadn't been aware witches *could* infuse a crystal with magic from multiple Casts.

Chloe appeared perplexed. "How did it get there? I mean, this crystal is ours. Miles and I never put any magic into these crystals during our ritual, and it's impossible for us to infuse them with magic that isn't our own."

"It may be your crystal, but this is the thief's magic," Nadine said. "Remember when we found those Executors dead near the safehouse? One of their wands had a crystal embedded in it that had absorbed Autumn's Mortana magic. It's how we tracked the reaper down. The same must've happened here. Your crystal absorbed some of the thieves' powers without them realizing it."

"So we're looking for a team of witches," Grant realized. "There's no other way to use the Oaken Wands but together."

Talia appeared wholly confused. "How's this possible? No one should have access to magic anymore."

"Unless they've got enough crystal stores," Chloe pointed out. "Someone must've been planning this for a while. The only question is… what do these thieves want to do with this magic?"

"Can we use the magic in the crystal to track them down?" I asked.

"It's our only shot." Nadine stepped forward and placed the crystal in Talia's palm. "Tal, we need your powers right now. Use the Seer magic in this crystal to see who's been here."

Talia pulled her shoulders back. "I'll see what I can get."

She curled her fingers around the crystal and closed her eyes. I squeezed Marcus close to my chest, holding my breath as we awaited Talia's vision.

Talia frowned. "I'm trying, but there's not enough magic here."

Nadine's eyebrows pinched together. "There should be. I can feel it."

"Then it's resisting me," Talia said. "I can't connect with the magic. It's like it's stronger than me, and I can't overpower it."

"Let's work together," Nadine suggested gently.

She curled her hands around Talia's fist, and the girls closed their eyes. A long, arduous minute passed. With each second we waited, the thieves got further and further away with the Oaken Wands.

Talia's eyelids fluttered. "I hear footsteps, but I can't see anything."

"How many pairs?" Nadine asked.

"One," Talia answered.

"The thieves must've split up to look for the Wands," Miles muttered.

"Shh…" Grant hissed. "Let her concentrate."

Talia squeezed her eyes shut tighter. "There's nothing here. I can only trace objects, and this crystal didn't see enough."

"Instead of tracing the crystal, can you follow the magic back to where it came from?" Nadine suggested.

"I've never traced magic like that before, but I can try," Talia offered.

Her eyelids fluttered faster, and she inhaled shallow breaths. "I think it's working."

"What do you see?" Chloe urged.

"It's more like a feeling," Talia explained, her tone growing in intensity. "I'm moving backward in time, feeling the magic in reverse. It's moving from the crystal to… someone's chest? It's a strange perspective. I can't see their face."

"Keep going," Nadine encouraged.

"It's coming in flashes," Talia said desperately. "I'm moving across town! I see houses… so many streets. I can't read the street signs. It's going so fast! I—I…"

Abruptly, she dropped to her knees on the floor, letting out a defeated sigh.

Grant rushed over to her and placed a hand on her shoulder. "Tal, it's okay. You're here with us."

Chloe took a wary step forward. "Did you get anything?"

Talia blinked her eyes open. "Not much. I saw a flash of something, but I can't quite make it out. All I saw were crystals *everywhere*—all shapes and colors stacked up on the walls."

"The Crystallary at school?" I wondered.

Talia shook her head. "This felt like it was outdoors somewhere… like some sort of crystal cave."

When she said that, something nudged at the back of my mind. I furrowed my brow, and Nadine wore a matching look of contemplation. I could've sworn I'd heard that somewhere before, but I couldn't recall where.

"We don't have much for caves around here," Miles pointed out. "Maybe a cavity in the bedrock, but that's hardly a cave."

"I'm telling you that's what I saw," Talia insisted. "I don't know where it was or how big, but that's where the magic led me."

Nadine tapped her chin. "So to find the thieves, we need to find the crystal cave."

I gasped as it hit me, and Nadine inhaled a sharp breath at the same time. *"Find the crystal cave!"* I cried.

"Lucas, the haunted house!" Nadine exclaimed. "We need to go back!"

Nadine was already headed toward the door.

"Wait!" Chloe demanded. "What are you two talking about?"

"When I first moved here, Lucas took me to Old Man Keller's house," Nadine explained quickly. "He was an old man who had recently died from tripping and hitting his head on a rock somewhere on the Black Circle trial."

"I remember Old Man Keller," Chloe said. "How's this relevant?"

"I heard his last thought," I told her. "Professor Warren gave me an assignment to look for the good in my gift, so I went to Keller's house to see if I could help him cross over. I brought Nadine along thinking she'd enjoy a séance. We summoned him, but all we got was him repeating his last thought—*Find the crystal cave.* He was a violent spirit who knocked Nadine out. I thought he was talking nonsense."

"Clearly not," Chloe said. "He obviously knew something."

"How much Seer magic is left in that crystal?" Miles asked.

Talia bit her lower lip. "A tiny bit. I used most of it up."

Miles smirked. "A tiny bit is all I need to talk to him. We're going to have to cancel dinner, because we need to go find this ghost and see what he knows."

I strapped Marcus in his car seat, and we took two cars since we couldn't all fit in one. We sped across town, coming to a screeching halt in front of Old Man Keller's house.

The house was different from the first time I'd been here. Back then, it had all the creepy feels of a haunted house—rickety front steps, peeling paint, and dust everywhere. But that had been years ago, and the house had been sold since then. Now, the front steps had been replaced, and the house had new siding. The porch light was on, but there wasn't a car in the driveway, so I could only assume the family had evacuated town.

The cats jumped out of the car and raced up the porch steps. Instead of going to the door, the cats circled around a porch swing that swayed lightly in the night breeze. I carried Marcus in his car seat and followed Nadine up the walkway. The others trailed closely behind.

When we reached the house, I realized the porch swing wasn't swaying in the wind at all... it was being rocked by a *ghost*. We didn't need Miles's Seer powers, because Old Man Keller was sitting there waiting for us. His form was ethereal, but that confused, crazed expression I recalled the first time we'd encountered him all those years ago was gone. Oliver jumped onto the cushion to lay beside the old man, and the ghost gently petted him.

"I've been waiting for you for a long time," Old Man Keller said. "I hoped one day you would come back."

"I understand better," I told him. "You just wanted to be heard, and I'm here to listen now."

Miles's jaw hung slack. "You guys are seeing him, too? I didn't even use my powers."

"You don't need to," Old Man Keller said. "I'm strong enough on my own."

Nadine took a careful step forward. "If you don't mind me asking... where are you getting your power from? Alora's magic has been lost to us."

"The magic is still out there," Old Man Keller replied. "You just can't access it because something is overpowering you."

"Does it have something to do with the crystal cave?" I asked.

Recognition glinted in Old Man Keller's eyes, but a second later, it was gone. "A crystal cave?"

"That was your last thought," I reminded him. *"Find the crystal cave. You said the same thing when I summoned you during a séance years ago."*

Old Man Keller stared out at the empty street. "Yes... there was a crystal cave. Forgive me. I remember very little of my death. It was traumatic, wasn't it? That's why I don't remember."

"You passed very suddenly." I didn't want to tell him too much, because triggering his trauma could put him back into that wildly confused state I first found him in. "What can you remember of this crystal cave?"

He tilted his head thoughtfully. "I remember it's why I died."

When he didn't elaborate further, I asked, "You wanted us to find it. Do you know why?"

"I saw something there... something you need to stop," he said distantly.

"Do you recall where this cave was?" I prodded.

He shook his head. "Not far. I was chased."

Nadine got a worried expression on her face. "Mr. Keller, are you saying you were murdered?"

"I... think so," he admitted.

The air seemed to drop several degrees. The police had ruled his death an accident.

"So we're not just dealing with thieves. We're dealing with murderers." Grant crossed his arms. "Could it be the priestesses' supporters continuing their work—trying to gain power to get people to submit to their will?"

Old Man Keller didn't look like he'd heard Grant. "Someone is trying to bring back what they lost."

I didn't know what that meant, but the ominous way in which he said it made my skin crawl. "Mr. Keller, is there anything else you can tell us that might help?"

Finally, he tore his distant gaze from the street to look at me. "It's all connected—this thing you call the Waning, the crystal cave, all of it. There are whisperings from the other side, rumors of a missing boy."

We all exchanged a wary glance, but Talia was the one to ask, "Could he be talking about Issac Miller and Caleb Thomas, the two kids murdered by the Gingerbread witches?"

"An infant," Old Man Keller said simply.

I didn't understand. "There were never any reports of a missing infant. Mr. Keller, do the rumors say whose child this is?"

"I don't know his name, but they say he works at the school," Keller said. "That's all I've heard."

Miles stepped forward, holding the crystal out toward the ghost. "With more power, could you connect to the other side to get more information? We need to know who's behind this."

"I can try to get you his name," Keller offered.

Miles placed the crystal on the porch swing, and Keller put his ghostly hand over it. His fingers went through the crystal, but I witnessed tendrils of magic swirling up his arm. He closed his eyes as he worked a spell that went far beyond my understanding. He'd been a Mentalist with telekinetic magic during his life, but in death, there must've been other spirits helping him, because his features started to change.

The wrinkles on his face smoothed out, and his hair turned from gray to dark brown. Stubble sprouted across his jawline until a familiar face I knew far too well stared back at me. The details were perfect, even down to the brown suit he always wore.

Professor Jonathan Warren.

My friends must've let out a collective gasp, but I couldn't quite hear past the ringing in my ears. I stumbled back a step, catching one hand on the porch banister. This couldn't be right. Professor Warren was my mentor, a better father to me than mine had ever been. He'd *helped* us through everything, even lived with us in the safe house for months. He couldn't be behind this.

Keller's features became his own again.

"A—are you sure?" I stammered breathlessly.

Keller nodded. "There are those on the other side who know better than me. I'm afraid that's all the information I can provide. I've used up all the magic in your crystal."

I steadied myself on my feet. If I weren't holding Marcus and didn't want to drop his car seat, I was certain I'd have fallen over.

"We'll find the crystal cave," I promised him.

For the first time, Old Man Keller smiled. "Then my unfinished business is complete, and I can move on now."

He stood and stared at something near the edge of the porch I couldn't see. I had to assume it was his reaper, but without access to my powers, I couldn't see them.

Keller turned back. "Thank you for hearing me."

"You're welcome," I told him.

Then he vanished. The street became eerily silent, and a shiver traveled down my spine as I turned back to my friends.

Nadine looked particularly troubled, like she was sad for me. She knew how much Professor Warren meant to me. "It can't be him, can it?"

My voice broke. "Keller said someone's trying to bring back what they lost. He's talking about a resurrection spell. Professor Warren's wife Roberta died of cancer years ago. He must be using some sort of dark magic to bring his wife back from the dead, and his kid is involved."

"I didn't think Warren had any kids," Talia said. "You think he and his wife had a child they never told anyone about?"

"If she was already sick when she got pregnant, and he thought he could use the kid to bring his wife back after the cancer took her, then I'm sure he'd hide it." I didn't want to believe a word I said, but it all added up. "Roberta was already too sick to go out, so he could've kept her pregnancy hidden. He told me once they went through fertility treatments. He claimed they all failed, but maybe one actually took. He told me he didn't go to therapy after she died, and perhaps that's because he had something to hide."

Nadine frowned deeply, appearing puzzled. "Old Man Keller said it was all connected—the Waning, the crystal cave, and the infant. If this is truly a resurrection spell, then Warren must be causing the Waning to steal our power so that he can sacrifice his kid, do a black magic spell, and raise his wife from the dead. He's been stealing the coven's magic for years."

"He's a necromancer," I replied hollowly. "He's already halfway there, but to actually get Roberta's spirit to bond with her body again... that would require the power of the whole coven. He *had* to steal our magic, or he couldn't complete the spell."

"But he shouldn't be able to handle that much power alone," Talia countered.

"That's where the crystal cave Old Man Keller found comes in," I said. "It's where Warren is storing the power he stole, and where he plans on doing the ritual."

"Does this ritual sound familiar to anyone else?" Nadine asked warily. "Two children were already murdered, and the Gingerbread witches said they intended to raise the dead the night they dragged Chloe and me to Pinewood Manor."

I felt the blood drain from my face as the pieces fell into place. "Professor Carlisle said he was receiving payment to do the ritual. We never found out who was the head of the operation. Those other kids must've been trials, to see if he could actually pull it off before getting his own kid involved."

Chloe placed her hands on her hips, looking *pissed*. "Professor Warren's behind all of it!"

"How could he possibly be causing the Waning?" Miles asked.

"I don't know, but it's got to involve some sort of dark magic," Chloe said.

"The Waning *was* concentrated at the school, where Warren spent most of his time," Grant pointed out.

"And he was there the night the Protection Tree was destroyed, when the last of our powers vanished," Talia added. She looked like she was going to be sick.

Nadine's hands shook. "He gave that speech to the coven that night, about the Waning being all our fault. He was trying to throw suspicion off *himself*."

I swallowed the lump rising to my throat. "And now everyone's left town, leaving him free to take all our magic for himself. He's not planning to go backpacking the Appalachian Trail—that's just an excuse so we can't contact him. He's going to stay here and use the Oaken Wands, along with the power he amassed, to bring his wife back."

"Who's he working with?" Miles asked. "Who would help him with something like that?"

"Dark magic doesn't work the same as our standard spells," Chloe said. "He could very well be working the spell alone."

"We don't know what consequences this dark magic could have. We need to find him, before he does something to destroy witch magic for good," I stated firmly. "We still have a chance to stop him."

"How are we going to do that?" Miles asked. "He's got all our magic!"

"We're going to have to find a way," I insisted. "We can't let another kid die."

The thought of giving up a child for *anything* made me want to hurl. Nadine could cork off tomorrow, and sacrificing my son to get her back would never cross my mind. I'd gone down some dark roads, but to go there was absolutely horrendous. I couldn't believe this man I'd admired so much had it in him.

But we'd been betrayed so many times. I was more pissed off that I hadn't connected the dots earlier. I was getting really sick and tired of putting my trust in the wrong people.

"Where do we start?" Grant asked.

"We know this crystal cave can't be far from the Black Circle trail, but it's fifteen miles long and circles the whole town," I said. "We need to narrow it down. We should start at Professor Warren's home and see if he's left any maps or research behind that could lead us to him—anything that could point us to where he plans on doing the ritual. He's got the Wands he wanted, so we have to assume he's not going to wait."

"I know where he lives," Chloe said. "I dropped off some council paperwork at his house over the summer."

"All right, let's get moving," Nadine ordered.

I hoisted Marcus's car seat up. "You go in Chloe's car. I'll drop Marcus off at Professor Wykoff's. Her place isn't far from here. Marcus can't come along for this. I'll be a few minutes behind you. You're our best detective, and you need to be there to decipher the clues."

Nadine nodded. We didn't have time to talk about it, because we didn't know how far Warren already was ahead of us.

My friends rushed to Chloe's car, and the cats followed them. They took off down the street while I strapped Marcus into the back of my vehicle. I quickly rounded to the driver's side. As I opened the door, an object tinkered across the pavement at my feet.

I thought I'd dropped something, but I looked down to find a tiny golden bell rolling to a stop against my shoe. It was spherically shaped, with tiny holes at the bottom like Christmas bells. I barely had a chance to process it before purple gas abruptly hissed out of the openings. I jumped into the car, but I didn't get the door shut before the gas reached my lungs.

The hex overtook me, and everything went dark.

EIGHTEEN

"This is insane!" Talia cried as Chloe sped down the street. "I know the Shield Squad has been through a lot, but we're in over our heads here. We can't just expect to waltz in and stop the most powerful warlock we've ever faced with no magic of our own."

"We can't sit back and do nothing, either," I insisted.

"Nadine's right, but we're going to need a plan." Chloe reached into her purse on the middle console and pulled out a small canister. "We may not have magic, but I do have pepper spray."

"I like the idea of weapons, but we're going to need something more powerful than that," Grant said.

Miles reached into his coat and pulled out a pistol. "How about this?"

Talia's eyes widened. "Are you suggesting we *kill* Professor Warren?"

"I'm suggesting we have the means to defend ourselves," Miles said. "And yeah, if I need to, I'll put a bullet in his chest."

"Why do you have a gun?" Grant asked.

"I'm the sheriff," Miles stated simply. "I've been training with guns since the day I joined the Executors, considering wands were no longer a reliable weapon."

"What else do you have?" I asked.

"We have some tools in the trunk," Chloe said. "I'm sure we can find something for everyone."

Chloe parked a block away from Professor Warren's house. We got out of the car, and she opened the trunk. It was mostly empty, apart from a few standard tools found in most vehicles.

Grant picked up a tire iron and spun it around in his hands. "This will work. Warren can't exactly cast magic if he's unconscious."

Chloe handed Talia a big, heavy wrench, while I grabbed a ratchet strap.

Talia eyed my weapon. "What are you going to do with that?"

I shrugged as I unraveled the strap and swung the heavy ratchet around. "Don't know yet, but it seems like it'd hurt."

Talia jumped back a few feet so she wouldn't get hit. "I see your point."

I turned to the others. "We stay together, keep quiet, and stick to the shadows. We'll do a perimeter sweep to make sure the coast is clear, then head inside to look for clues. Everyone ready?"

The other four nodded in unison.

We snuck through the darkness of neighboring back yards, until we reached Professor Warren's property. His home was small compared to the other houses in Octavia Falls—only one story, though it still had the gothic charm of other homes in the neighborhood. The lights were off, and it didn't appear that anyone was home.

Chloe pressed an index finger to her lips. She crept forward, but Miles stopped her.

"Allow me." He readied his grip on his gun, then started across the lawn toward a window that faced the backyard. The rest of us followed, keeping low and quiet.

The window was a good five feet off the ground. We huddled beneath it, then carefully peered inside the house to find an empty kitchen. A pot sat on the counter, and various items scattered the table, though I couldn't make out what they were in the darkness.

"Is that a cauldron?" Miles asked, gesturing to the pot. "Looks like he's planning on brewing a potion."

"I don't see any movement," Grant whispered. "He must be gone."

"We can't be sure until we check out the rest of the house," Chloe said.

We craned our necks to see into other rooms, but they were too dark.

"What are we looking at?" a voice hissed from behind us.

My heart lurched, and the five of us spun around in unison. Talia screeched as we came face-to-face with Professor Warren. He'd crept up behind us and crouched down low, whispering like he was part of our investigative group.

Talia reacted on instinct and threw her wrench at him, which hit him square in the gut. At the same time, Chloe sprayed her pepper spray into his eyes.

Professor Warren slapped his hands over his face, screaming in pain. I rushed forward and threw the ratchet strap around his arms. Chloe quickly grabbed the other end, and we circled him to pull the straps as tight as we could.

"Don't move!" Miles warned as he lifted his gun.

He didn't need to use it. Grant was already swinging the tire iron. The heavy end smacked Professor Warren on the side of the head, and our professor's screams died on his tongue. He slumped to the grass, unconscious.

My pulse began to slow, and I sighed a heavy breath as the adrenaline rush subsided. Thank the Goddess we got him before he could use his powers on us.

Chloe stared down at Professor Warren's unmoving form. "Great. What are we going to do when he comes to?"

This was definitely not how I pictured this going down, but it was too late now to change strategy. "Let's get him into the house and immobilize him the best we can," I suggested. "Miles, keep that gun on him. We're going to want to ask some questions."

Chloe and Grant each took one of Warren's shoulders, while Talia and I took his legs and carried him inside. It wasn't easy. Professor Warren was tall and muscular and weighed a lot more than I thought. Luckily, he was still passed out when we hoisted him onto a dining room chair. We used the ratchet strap to secure his hands at his sides. It wouldn't *stop* him from casting magic, but the threat of Miles's gun would certainly make him hesitate.

"Look for clues," Miles ordered as he kept the barrel of the gun aimed toward Professor Warren.

We scattered around the house. I hurried over to the kitchen table to find that the items I'd seen scattered there were various bags of all sizes. As I started digging through them, I found a small tent, a compression sleeping bag, and tent stakes. It looked like he really was preparing for a backpacking trip.

Grant went over to the counter and hopelessly held up the pot we'd seen. "This isn't a brewing cauldron. It's a camping pot."

"There's nothing in here!" Chloe called from the living room.

"Nothing in the bedroom," Talia added.

"Check the basement," I ordered. "There's got to be signs of a kid living here."

Grant ran into the basement, but he came back a few moments later. "There's nothing down there but storage."

"We're missing something," I insisted. "He must own another property. He's got to be hiding his kid and a cave full of crystals somewhere."

Professor Warren groaned, and we all jumped behind Miles. Our professor looked absolutely horrible, with a goose-egg bruise swelling on the side of his forehead and blotchy red skin from the pepper spray.

"Try anything and I'll shoot!" Miles spat.

Professor Warren squinted his blood-shot eyes. "Wh—what is this? Miles, is that a real gun?"

"You want to fuck around and find out?" Miles warned.

"Is this your idea of a joke?" Warren asked in a groggy tone. "I was just headed over to your place for dinner like we planned. I saw you sneaking across my lawn. If you would've rather said goodbye here, all you had to do was say so."

"You can rot in the Abyss for all we care!" Chloe snarled. "We'll send you there ourselves unless you answer our questions. Where's your son?"

"My... son?" Warren winced as he moved against the restraints. "You must've hit me harder than I thought, because I can't be hearing you right."

"You know what she's talking about," Grant growled. "We know everything. We know how you've been stealing people's magic and storing it in crystals to collect enough power to raise your wife from the dead—and you plan to sacrifice your son to do it!"

"That's impossible," Professor Warren stated.

"We don't know how you're doing it…" Grant admitted. "But we know it's you!"

"Tell us where to find this crystal cave, or so help me, I'll shoot," Miles demanded. "You're not going to get away with this."

Professor Warren's jaw hung slack. "I don't know what you think I'm involved with, but I'm telling you it's impossible to raise my wife from the dead!"

"You wouldn't know that unless you've tried," Talia alleged in horror. "You've already gone through with it, haven't you?"

"I haven't done anything!" Warren insisted.

He looked so helpless and desperate tied up like this. I didn't think Professor Warren wanted to hurt us, but with the magic he'd amassed by stealing the coven's powers, he should be able to break free from his restraints.

"Where is your wife?" I asked curiously.

Warren's shoulders dropped, and he gave a defeated sigh. It was like he'd completely given up. "She's in the living room."

"Bullshit!" Chloe sneered. "I was just in there. There's nobody there."

I narrowed my eyes at Professor Warren. There was so much sadness in his tone when he said that, but it wasn't the sound of a man who was desperately holding on. He appeared more like a man who regretted that he ever had to let go.

"I'll go check," I offered.

"Nadine, he's trying to trick you," Chloe objected.

I didn't listen to her. Instead, I walked out of the kitchen and to the small living room just a few paces down the hall. Sitting on the mantle at the center of the room was an urn. I picked it up to find it was heavy with ash.

I returned to the kitchen and held up the urn to show everyone. "You can't exactly bring someone back to a body that doesn't exist anymore."

"I told you it's a trick!" Chloe demanded. "How can we be sure that's his wife? Furthermore, we don't know the full extent of what dark magic can do! He could be using the spell to reconstruct her body from nothing."

"What spell?" Professor Warren begged.

"The revival spell," Grant said. "The one where you're sacrificing your son to bring back what you lost, just like you tried with those other kids! Don't act so innocent. The magic doesn't lie. We know *your* son is involved. Your wife has been dead for years. How long have you kept your child hidden from the coven?"

A crease formed between Professor Warren's eyebrows. "I don't know why you would think I'm hiding a child. Roberta and I couldn't have kids."

We'd been betrayed so many times before, but never had a traitor been so persistent once we caught them. I expected some hint of recognition in his eyes when we mentioned his son, but there was nothing there.

I'd been wrong about so many people before, but I was certain this time. We only had half a picture, and when I realized that, more pieces began falling into place. We hadn't been wrong about our clues—only wrong about who they pertained to.

"It's not him," I stated hollowly.

Chloe's eyebrows raised incredulously. "What do you mean it's not him!? Old Man Keller showed us his face. You think Keller lied to us, after all these years of trying to get someone to listen to him?"

"No," I choked out. "I think Keller was right, but I know what it's like to hold your child in your arms for the first time. It's one of the most profound experiences of a lifetime. Even the most diabolical people would show a shred of remorse to give that up. I can see it in his eyes—he doesn't know what that's like, because Professor Warren never got to experience it... he doesn't know his child exists."

"What are you talking about...?" Professor Warren started, but he trailed off as realization dawned. Warren went completely speechless as he began to process what I already suspected.

If I needed any more confirmation of my theory, the shock on his face said it all.

"If Warren isn't behind this, then why would Old Man Keller show us his face?" Grant asked.

I never took my eyes off Professor Warren as tears beaded in my eyes. "Because we were asking the wrong question. We asked whose child had gone missing, but every child has two parents."

Professor Warren may be this child's father, but this child had a mother, too. And there was only one woman I knew of in the coven who was missing a child.

"Lucas said there were never reports of a missing infant, but there *was* a baby—one no one ever thought to go looking for," I pointed out.

Tears streaked Professor Warren's cheeks as he stared blankly forward in shock. "She—she said the baby wasn't mine. I believed her."

The recognition in his eyes told me everything.

"Professor, it's not your fault," I assured him in a broken tone. "We all believed in Headmistress Clarice Verla."

The room went immensely silent, the kind of shocked silence that sent shivers up and down my spine. No one wanted to believe it, but now it was obvious. Everything that had pointed to Professor Warren were clues leading directly to Headmistress Verla. Warren wasn't the only person who had lost someone he might desire to bring back. Verla had lost her sister... a sister whose body was never recovered after the priestesses hanged her.

And then a stillborn child—her son, Allyn.

Only he wasn't stillborn like she'd said. It had all been a lie to keep anyone from looking for him.

I'd had so much sympathy for Verla. I thought her story was one of resilience, in which she used what she'd lost to fuel her rebellion against the priestesses. I'd been able to relate to her in so many ways. The loss of her sister made me believe she could understand what I'd gone through losing my parents. She'd been there for me when Dean died, providing guidance from the experience of losing her own child, but it wasn't even true. I thought these things had brought us closer together, but now I felt the agony of a chasm form in our relationship. To think of what she had planned for her son made me physically ill. I was utterly horrified, because I couldn't comprehend how anyone would perform a ritual with their own child.

Verla was more wounded than I ever thought, and she was going about healing that damage in the most horrific ways. There wasn't just a child to protect...

We needed to save Verla from *herself*.

"It can't be Verla." Chloe's voice trembled.

Miles lowered his gun slowly. "I don't believe it, either."

"She was so good to us," Grant agreed.

Talia shook her head, refusing to accept it. "She wouldn't."

"But she did," I whispered. A sob broke from my chest as those words twisted the knife of betrayal straight through my heart and out the other side. I didn't want to accept it was her.

I knelt to Warren's side and began untying his binds. "Professor, I am *so* sorry for what you've been through. We're going to stop her, and we're going to get your son back."

Professor Warren's tear-filled gaze shifted to mine. "How?"

"We need to find her," I said. "We believe she's planning to perform a dark magic ritual to raise the dead."

"Nicole…" Warren mused as his restraints dropped free. "Clarice and her sister were so close. They were twins. Clarice was devastated when she lost her."

"We think she's going to perform this ritual in a crystal cave," I said. "Does that mean anything to you?"

Warren appeared contemplative, but he shook his head. "No. I don't recall anything about a crystal cave."

"Is there *anything* you remember?" I asked. "The smallest details could help us find her and stop her before this dark magic does permanent damage."

Professor Warren rubbed his wrists. "Clarice and I dated several years ago, long after Roberta passed. We only loved each other for a short time before she called things off. We kept our relationship a secret because it'd put our jobs in jeopardy if people knew. There were times I tried to express how I truly felt about her, even after she broke my heart. I asked her to dance at the Midnight Formal when we were chaperoning one year. She wouldn't even look at me the rest of the night, because she was certain someone would suspect we'd been more than friends. I always sensed there were things she couldn't open up to me about, and I respected that. I see now she hid it all *very* well. If there's something she didn't want me to know, she did a good job of keeping it a secret."

"Maybe that's a clue itself," I realized. "Is there any place she was particularly secretive about?"

Professor Warren's eyes shifted in a calculating manner. "She didn't let me into her personal life much. Most of our time together was spent here… Although, she didn't like it when I visited her in her office at school. She said it would raise suspicion, but perhaps there was more to it."

"Let's start there. We might find valuable information that could lead us to her." I pulled my phone from my pocket. "I'm calling Lucas to tell him what we found. He can meet us there."

Grant glanced at the clock on the stove. "He should be here by now. What's taking him so long?"

The line rang, but it went to voicemail. My pulse quickened, and my mouth went dry in worry. "Lucas didn't pick up."

"Has he shared his location with you?" Chloe asked. "Check it—he might be driving."

I pulled up Lucas's location on my phone. "That's weird. It says he's still at Old Man Keller's place."

"He must've found something and is investigating another clue," Grant suggested.

"Then he might need help deciphering it," I said. "We should split up."

Professor Warren got to his feet. "I have access to the school. I can check Clarice's office."

"You shouldn't go alone," Miles insisted. "You could have a concussion and shouldn't be driving. I'll come with you."

"Call us if you find anything," I said, before we split off in different directions.

Miles followed Professor Warren to his car, while Chloe, Grant, Talia and I returned to Chloe's vehicle. We hurried back the way we'd come until we reached Old Man Keller's street.

Only, there wasn't a vehicle in sight. Lucas's car was gone.

Grant peered out the window curiously. "We must've just missed him."

I stared down at my phone screen. "This doesn't make any sense. GPS tracks him here."

Chloe parked across from Old Man Keller's house, and I stepped out of the passenger side. I looked up and down the deserted street, wondering if Lucas had dropped Marcus off at Professor Wykoff's, then come back for some reason and had parked somewhere else. But there was no car in the driveway—or anywhere, for that matter.

I brought up Lucas's contact again and tried calling him. The sound of his ringtone filled the night air, and a soft glow emanated from near the curb. My heart leapt into my throat as I raced across the street. Lucas's phone was lying on the pavement where his car had been parked. The screen was cracked in the corner.

My friends surrounded me. "What happened here?" Chloe demanded.

"I—I don't know," I stammered. I quickly punched in another contact.

"Hello?" Professor Wykoff answered on the second ring. My pulse pounded in my ears so loud I wasn't sure if she said anything else.

"Has Lucas been to your house tonight?" I panicked. "Is Marcus with you!?"

"No, I wasn't expecting anyone," she replied. "Nadine, is everything all right?"

I lowered the phone from my ear as the horrifying reality came crashing down on me. My husband and my son were missing.

Someone must've taken my phone from my hand, because I staggered to the curb. My knees buckled as I sank to sit in the grass. This couldn't be happening again.

The world swam in front of me, and I barely processed that Chloe was holding my phone and giving Professor Wykoff some sort of explanation. I didn't hear it past the ringing in my ears.

Talia came to sit next to me, gently placing a hand on my back. "We're going to find them, Nadine."

I shook my head, shaking off my shocked panic. "We have to," I agreed in a shaky tone. "I won't let Verla get away with any of this."

"You think Verla has them?" Grant asked.

I swallowed the bile rising to my throat. "She must. Lucas wouldn't take Marcus somewhere without telling me, and he never made it to Wykoff's. She stole the Oaken Wands to do her ritual, but she never got the Mortana Wand because Lucas still had it on him. Now she's stolen my family to finish the job."

Chloe hung up the phone. "How are we going to find him? We can't find Lucas with technology, and we don't have the magic to perform a tracking spell."

My head sagged into my hands. "There's got to be another way…"

I thought of all the times we'd faced the impossible, yet the Shield Squad had always managed to find a solution and defy the odds. We'd lost our son once before, and we'd raised hell to get him back. I'd go to the ends of the earth and beyond for my family. Even if it took me a hundred years and I had to haunt this town after I died—searching one building at a time to find them—I'd do it.

I inhaled a sharp breath when I realized something. "We don't need magic to track him, because we already know how to find each other when we're in trouble."

"How?" Chloe asked.

I was already on my feet, hurrying back toward her car. "I'm going to haunt this damn town, that's how. Keep an eye out, and protect my body while I'm gone. I'm astral traveling to find my husband."

Once I did, I'd make Clarice Verla beg on her knees for mercy. Nobody touched my family and got away with it.

Not even someone I cherished dearly.

NINETEEN

My head swam as I slowly came to. I could hear shuffling nearby but couldn't make sense of it. I tried to move, but panic hit me when I realized I was completely paralyzed from head to toe with some sort of binding spell. I couldn't remember where I was or how I'd gotten here.

I racked my brain for the last thing I remembered. I recalled going to Old Man Keller's house to get information, and then the memory of the purple smoke came rushing back. Someone had hexed me and brought me here… but I didn't know where *here* was.

I was aware I was lying flat on my back on a cold, hard surface. I could feel that the Mortana Wand was still in my pocket, pressing against my thigh. I didn't feel my phone, which meant I couldn't call for help. It must've fallen out of my pocket shortly after I'd been hexed. Cool air brushed against my skin, though that was all I could discern of my surroundings.

Slowly, I forced my eyes open. It was the only movement I could make, and I found it absolutely terrifying to be so disconnected from my own body that I couldn't even wiggle my fingers.

A stone ceiling came into focus. As my eyes swept around the room, I noticed a crack in the ceiling, which a ray of moonlight shone through. The moonlight shimmered a rainbow of colors over the walls. As I focused on the colors, I realized they were crystals in all shapes and sizes, stacked all around the room. They were everywhere—on shelves, tables, and all across the floor. There had to be thousands of them.

Looks like I'd found the crystal cave.

I strained my eyes to peer in my peripheral, but I couldn't move my head. I could barely make out the bottom end of a cot… then I noticed feet. They were covered in socks, so I couldn't tell if they might belong to someone I recognized. Clearly, I wasn't the only person who'd been captured. I tried to look upward to see the other person's face, but I couldn't move my eyes that far.

I looked as far as I could across the room, and the sight of a cradle made my heart jolt. It was an old wooden one, something a child might use for dolls. Inside, blankets had been wrapped in a bundle. I recognized the kitten blanket I'd put in Marcus's car seat earlier, then I saw a tuft of dark hair sticking out of the bundle. Dear Goddess, I prayed he hadn't been harmed.

Movement across the cave caught my attention. A cloaked figure stood at a table with their back to me, though I couldn't tell what they were doing. It had to be Professor Warren. He'd gotten to me before Nadine and the others could find him.

The figure turned, and I quickly shut my eyes before he could notice I'd awoken. My pulse pounded in my ears, and I was certain he'd catch the unsteadiness of my frightened breath. But he left the cave without turning back to me. The soft sound of a cat's meow followed.

Now would be a *really* great time to gain control of my body. I'd grab Marcus and run… but as I struggled against my own muscles, it became abundantly clear that I wasn't getting out of here by sheer will. I needed help.

I needed Nadine.

Keeping my eyes closed, I found my consciousness drifting. It wasn't difficult to fall into a sleep-like state, because I was still half asleep from the hex. As I fell into an intentional slumber, I willed my spirit to separate from my body.

The relief of gaining motion back to my limbs felt immensely freeing. I sat up in spirit form and looked around the room. Finally, I got a good view of the crystal cave. It was small, nothing more than a single room made entirely of stone. As my gaze traveled over to the other captive, my spirit nearly fell straight back into my body in shock.

It was *Verla*. She must've been hit by the same hex I had, because she looked pale and sickly, and she lay completely still. I had to move quickly to save us both.

I scrambled to my feet in spirit form, rushing over to the cradle. Immense relief washed over me when I stared down at my son's face. Marcus's chest rose and fell slowly. Instinctually, I reached out for him, because I wanted nothing more than to get him as far away from here as possible, but my fingers went straight through him.

Right. I was astral traveling. I couldn't interact with the physical plane. I looked back to my solid form lying on the floor. It was always eerie looking at myself from a different angle, and tonight was the most chilling of all. If I didn't get a message to Nadine right away, I may not live long enough to see her again—and neither would my son.

I had to figure out where we were so I could lead her to us.

I stood to see the four stolen Oaken Wands were laid out on the table. Alongside them sat a mortar and pestle full of herbs. That must've been what I'd seen Professor Warren doing—crushing the herbs in preparation for his black magic ritual.

I hurried out of the cave to find myself standing in a forest. The cave was set into an outcropping of rock, formed by the way the rocks leaned against one another, rather than being carved out by water. I'd never seen this particular outcropping before and didn't know where in the forest I was. I could be miles from Octavia Falls.

My spiritual feet levitated off the ground, and I started flying through the forest. I crossed several acres, but it wasn't long before I came upon an iron gate. It was exactly what I'd been looking for—some sort of landmark to lead Nadine to my location.

As I came closer to the gate, stones began to take shape in the moonlight, all spread evenly throughout an expansive lawn. *Gravestones.* It was a cemetery—not just any cemetery, but Octavia Falls Cemetery.

I had a location. Now I just had to get that information to Nadine.

I closed my eyes again, and when I opened them, I was standing in the entryway of the abandoned mansion we'd set as our meeting point. An ethereal feline circled around my ankles, yowling in a distressed manner. It was Buddy, the spirit cat we'd met here weeks ago when Nadine and I had practiced astral traveling to the mansion.

"Lucas!" a voice called across the house.

"Nad?" I cried. "I'm here!"

I ran toward the sound of her voice. Nadine's spirit turned a corner, and relief flooded her features when she saw me. She raced down the hall and fell into my arms. When our spirits touched, she felt solid. I squeezed her as tightly as I could.

Nadine drew back to look me over, as if searching for injuries that might've imprinted onto my spirit. "Are you hurt? Is Marcus with you?"

"We're not hurt. We were knocked out by a hex, and we're still asleep."

"Do you know where you are? Is there another child there with you?"

"I didn't see one. We're in the crystal cave. It's right next to the cemetery, near the entrance but deeper into the forest, close to Monica's fake grave."

Nadine's eyes widened. "It's on her property... Lucas, have you seen Verla yet?"

"She's here with me, but she's been knocked out, too. She must've been hit by the same hex Marcus and I were. Professor Warren's got her on a cot in the cave. How did you know she'd be there? Is he planning on hurting her?"

Terror filled Nadine's features. "Lucas, that's not Headmistress Verla. That's her *sister*."

I thought of her pale complexion, how I'd noted that she looked ill. It only occurred to me now that she didn't look sick at all... she looked *dead*. Only, she looked like she'd only died hours ago, not years.

"Professor Warren isn't trying to raise his wife from the dead!" Nadine exclaimed. "It's *Verla* trying to raise her sister! Keller pointed us to the father of the missing infant, but Headmistress Verla is the mother. The child Old Man Keller spoke of is Verla's son, Allyn. We can only assume she's been hiding her child all these years to use in this ritual—"

I cut Nadine off with a horrible gag. A burning sensation filled my nose, like I was inhaling water. I clutched my belly and dropped to the ground on my knees.

Nadine took a frightened step back. "I'm coming for you, Lucas!"

Then the mansion and my wife disappeared from view. My spirit snapped back into my body, and the appalling sensation of choking on something intensified.

My eyes shot open, and my heart slammed violently as I shot upright. I doubled over, spewing liquid all over the stone floor. Whatever it was tasted disgustingly bitter and smelled as vile as sewage. I gagged and spit across the ground, then wiped my chin.

"Welcome back, Lucas," a sinister voice said from beside me.

Slowly, I turned to see the cloaked figure crouched next to me. They held a potion vile in their hands, and it sizzled with a gross-looking green liquid. Surely that's what they'd shoved down my throat to wake me up. It was probably some counter-potion to the hex.

The figure lowered their hood, and the sliver of moonlight filtering in through the rocks met the eyes of Headmistress Clarice Verla. Beside her, Odin stepped forward and meowed.

I shot a glance to the cot, where the corpse of her sister lay. The two of them looked so much alike, with the same chestnut brown waves in their hair, straight nose, and high cheekbones. Only, as I peered closer, I noticed Nicole Verla had a dark freckle on her neck that Clarice didn't have. It was hard to tell beneath her pale features, but Nicole's skin was slightly smoother, and she appeared several years younger than Clarice. I didn't understand how her body had been so well preserved after all these years.

"Don't look so frightened," Headmistress Verla said calmly. She stood and walked over to the table, where she placed her potion vial. "If you simply do as I say, you and your son will walk out of here unharmed."

The second she had her back turned, I was already moving. I lunged for the cradle the same time I tried to get to my feet, but my legs failed to move under me.

Verla whirled around and thrust her palm toward me. I was dragged across the floor by an invisible force. She brought her hand downward, and her power pinned me to the ground.

"You think I'd capture you and then just let you walk out of here?" Verla demanded. "Your legs are bound, and there's no breaking free of my spell."

As I desperately fought against her magic, my gaze darted toward my son.

Verla noticed. Slowly, she walked over to him and began rocking his cradle. She stared down at him fondly, but every move she made sent a shiver over my skin. She was being deliberate, to show me how vulnerable my child was. It was a threat that made me sick to my stomach. She'd already touched him when she laid him into the cradle. She must've. I'd make sure that was the last time she ever laid a finger on him.

"Don't worry," she said. "I've cast a slumber charm on him. He'll be asleep for hours."

"If you wanted to keep me bound, why'd you wake me up?" I gasped under the weight of her magic.

"Because I need you awake for this, Lucas."

She released her magical grip on me. I sucked in a greedy breath as I pushed myself upright again. I'd regained control of my upper body, but my legs felt like they were tied together by ropes.

"How did you do that?" I asked warily. "You don't have telekinesis."

Verla gestured around the cave to the hordes of crystals. "I have access to all witch magic now. I can perform whatever spells I want."

I pressed my palms to the stone floor and dragged myself a foot away from her. "That's impossible."

Verla gave a wicked laugh. It was strange, because she appeared so much like the caring mentor I always knew, but there was a crazed expression in her eyes I'd never witnessed. "I assure you it's very possible under the right circumstances."

"You've been behind the Waning all this time," I accused. "How are you doing this?"

"It doesn't matter, as long as I get what I want." Her gaze flickered toward the corpse on the cot, and I noticed a familiar sadness in her features, one I'd felt myself far too many times.

"You want your sister back," I said gently. "I get it. I lost a brother, too."

"You have no idea what I've lost!" Verla spat. She appeared unsteady as she placed her palms on the table next to her. Her tone dropped to a near whisper. "I've lost more than you could ever know."

While I kept her talking, I slowly inched my hand behind myself to reach for a crystal. If I could just access a bit of Mortana magic, I could cast a defensive spell to buy myself enough time to get Marcus out of here. I just had to keep her talking.

"I'm sorry for your loss," I told her genuinely. "But turning to dark magic isn't the answer."

"You wouldn't know the first thing about dark magic," she snarled. At the same time, heartbreak flashed in her eyes. It was a bit terrifying, because I had so much sympathy for her that it was hard to wrap my head around the evil she planned to do.

My fingers inched closer and closer to a nearby crystal. "I don't understand how you could be stealing our magic all this time. You fought so hard to end the Waning with us."

"I fought to destroy the priestesses," Verla countered. "The Waning won't end until I get what I want."

Verla turned toward the Oaken Wands on the table. It was like she couldn't bear to look at me, because if she did, she'd have to face what she'd done. When she wasn't looking, I lifted my hand to grab the nearest quartz point.

Before my fingers could curl around it, Verla whirled toward me. My arm reacted like it was attached to an invisible string. My palm slammed into the sharp point of the crystal, and I cried out in pain as the rock pierced my skin. Blood sprayed across the stone floor.

I yanked my hand back to see there was a deep, jagged wound in the middle of my palm. My fingers trembled as I pressed my hand to my hip to slow the bleeding. Warm blood soaked into my jeans.

"Don't make me hurt you again, Lucas," Verla warned darkly. Her piercing gaze made me shudder. As much as it terrified me, I preferred she kept her attention on me rather than Marcus.

It was true that Verla had lost so much, but I couldn't let my sympathy for her cause me to underestimate her. She'd been behind the Waning all this time, which meant she didn't adhere to the moral compass I thought she did. As much trust as I'd put in her in the past, it was clear I didn't truly know what she was capable of, and I couldn't be sure of what measures she'd take to be with her sister again.

"You didn't bring me here to play games," I stated coldly. "If you can cast any witch spell you want, then what do you need me for?"

"Raising the dead isn't any typical witch spell," Verla stated. "I need the Oaken Wands. The others were easy to obtain, but the spell the Reaper Order put on the Mortana Wand has bound it to the reapers. As much as I've tried to pry it away from you while you were passed out, the spell that's binding it to you is not one I can break. I'm incredibly powerful, but so is the Reaper Order."

I slid my bloody hand down toward my pocket, feeling for the Mortana Wand there.

Verla picked the other Oaken Wands up from the table. "These Wands can amplify my power, and I couldn't let you leave town without them."

"Bullshit," I growled. "The Wands wouldn't respond to you. They choose who they work with."

Verla chuckled viciously. "They'll work with me if I make them."

I thought of how the Oaken Wands had stopped responding once the Waning had taken over for good. That could only happen if Verla had completely overpowered them. I didn't know how she did it, but somehow, she'd grown more powerful than all the Oaken Wands combined.

"However," she continued, "without the fifth Wand and the one I need most, I cannot complete the spell."

"You can't expect me to hand it over," I told her. "The Reaper Order bound the Mortana Wand to the reapers. You'd have to be one yourself for me to give it to you."

"Then you'll do the spell with me," she demanded harshly. "I have all this power, but reaper magic is specialized, and without proper training, I've failed to utilize it properly. I need reaper magic to move my sister's soul across realms. You've raised the dead before. Do it again!"

I shook my head in defiance. "This isn't the same. I've never brought back a spirit that has already moved on. You're asking for power that transcends witch magic entirely, something only the gods can accomplish. You still have a chance to restore the magic you stole, but once you do this, you can't take it back. You don't know what consequences this could have. It could destroy the coven completely."

"The coven has already been destroyed!" Verla shouted. "I don't care if I have to destroy you, too."

"So kill me," I said. "I won't do the spell."

Verla scoffed. "Killing *you* won't do me any good, but perhaps the blood of a demigod would…"

Verla pointed an Oaken Wand at Marcus, who still lay soundlessly in the cradle.

"No!" I shouted. The broken tone of my voice seemed to shatter my heart completely. "I'll do it!"

Verla smirked as she lowered her Wand. "Very good, Lucas. I see we *can* work together."

"I—I don't want to kill anyone," I stammered.

"Why would you assume we'd be doing that?" she asked innocently.

"Because you've tried this ritual before. We've already figured you killed Caleb Thomas and Issac Miller to raise your sister, but it didn't work. Why should this time be any different?"

Verla scoffed. "I abandoned that ritual a long time ago, as it proved ineffective."

"Then where's your child?" I demanded. Old Man Keller said it was all connected, so she must plan to involve her kid somehow.

"I don't need one. I'm stronger now, stronger than I've ever been, *and* I have the Oaken Wands. Do you understand how much power it takes to siphon the entire coven's magic before they can even *feel* it for themselves?"

I thought back to what Old Man Keller said, about how magic was still out there and we were being overpowered. We'd never lost our connection to Alora like we thought. It was all *her*.

"You weren't there that night at the Protection Tree, after the Golem War," I realized. "And you certainly weren't getting people to safety like you said. How'd you cut us off completely like that? You're draining us like batteries before we even get a chance to recharge."

"You wouldn't understand. It's power that even a demigod would struggle to manage." Verla shot a glance at Marcus. "Luckily, I have access to one, should I need him. But I do hate involving children."

"You aren't going to touch him," I snarled.

"Not if you behave," she assured me.

Verla flicked her wrist, yanking me to my feet like a puppet on a string. My toes dangled, scraping along the rock as she dragged me across the cave toward her. She grabbed my hand forcefully, and blood dripped across the ground.

Verla clicked her tongue. "We can't work like this."

She conjured a potion vial, then popped the cork and poured it into my palm. A stinging pain like fire seared my hand, and my scream filled the cavern. I could hear my skin sizzling. I didn't want to look at the damage she'd caused, but I forced myself to anyway. In the center of my palm was a tender red wound that was missing layers of skin. The bleeding had stopped, as if Verla's potion had cauterized the skin shut. It hurt like hell, but I'd stopped dripping blood over her precious cave.

"Now, take the Mortana Wand out of your pocket," Verla ordered, like I was some child who needed explicit instructions.

I shot another wary glance at Marcus, and the fear trembling through me was the only thing that got me to comply. I withdrew the Wand, and a greedy smirk crossed Verla's features.

"We're going to do this together," Verla stated.

"How? I can't cast a spell, even with the Wand. You're overpowering it. It can't access magic."

"I will share my powers with the Wands, and you will direct the power of Death magic into my sister. If you try to do anything but what you've been instructed to do, your son will die."

She was so cold about it that I had to assume she wouldn't hesitate. She'd already killed other children, and even Marcus's demigod powers wouldn't save him now. Verla was already just as strong as he was, if not stronger.

"Come now. We'll bring her back together." Verla picked up her bowl of herbs and carried them over to the cot where her sister lay. In her other hand, she clutched the four Oaken Wands.

She dragged me over beside her, then lowered me to my knees next to the cot. It was eerie staring down at the pale face that looked so much like Headmistress Clarice Verla, but wasn't her at all. Her sister had been dead for years, but Nicole's corpse appeared remarkably preserved.

Verla sprinkled the herbs over her sister's body, then lined the Oaken Wands from Nicole's sternum and down her torso, each point touching the end of the next Wand in line. Verla grabbed my hand *hard*—which really fucking hurt—and forced me to place the Mortana Wand above the others, over Nicole's heart.

"Don't move," Verla warned.

A chill spread throughout the cave as Verla stood and planted her feet in the center of the cavern. She raised her hands and began chanting a spell in Latin. *"Sub luna et in hoc antro, sororem de sepulchro suscitabo."*

Her power was so immense and strong that the earth immediately responded to her command. The ground shook, and crystals rattled against one another as dust rained down from the rocks overhead. A distant, animalistic hiss filled the air. I couldn't tell where it was coming from, but the chill tingling over my spine told me it was exceptionally evil.

Verla repeated her incantation again. I wasn't fluent in Latin, but we used it enough in our spellwork that I caught the rough translation. *"Under the moon and in this cave, I raise my sister from the grave."*

All around us, crystals began to glow with intense power. All colors of the rainbow lit up the cavern and shimmered off the stone. Verla's chest emitted a bright white light, and tendrils of magic swirled out of the thousands of crystals to connect to her body like powerful ropes. It was so magnificent and bright that I had to shield my eyes.

Her power pulsed through the Oaken Wands. I could feel it because my fingers were still tightly wrapped around the Mortana Wand laid over Nicole's chest. The power reverberated through the Wands so strongly that if I weren't already on my knees, I'd have collapsed. I wasn't the one working the spell, but magic still pulsed through me from head to toe. It was more magic than I'd ever felt at one time, as if someone had shoved a high-voltage powerline straight into my chest. Every muscle in my body contracted against my will, and my limbs shook violently. An ungodly pain rippled down to my bones.

It was more magic than a single person should be able to handle, and if she didn't stop now, it would tear me apart from the inside out. I didn't understand how she managed to control such power without killing herself.

I wasn't able to give it much thought, because the power of the spell seemed to turn my brain off completely. I couldn't be sure what was going on around me, because all I saw was the blinding glow of the crystals. All I heard was the evil hiss growing louder in my ears. The only sensation on my skin was pain like a thousand needles piercing me from every direction. It felt as if the magic was trying to rip my soul out of my body.

Then I felt Death magic—a power so familiar to me, but entirely different all the same. I knew the chaotic tingle of Mortana magic that flowed through me daily, and I was familiar with the void of death I so often sensed. But this power was deeper and more intense than any spell I'd ever cast before. The void of death seemed to open like a chasm in the earth, splitting so wide the fissure of the emptiness spanned entire realms... realms in which evil existed on the other side. The hiss filling my ears turned into an evil growl, like that of a monster that wished to claw its way through the chasm.

"Verla, stop!" a voice shouted.

It was so far away. I couldn't be sure I hadn't imagined it to disconnect myself from the agony tearing through my body.

Something seemed to snap within me, and a deafening *crack* filled the air. Throughout the cavern, hundreds of crystals fractured simultaneously, and many crumbled into pieces that skittered across the stone floor.

All at once, the magic ebbed away. I gasped as I sagged back on my heels. The glowing crystals around the cavern dimmed, and the earth stilled. I looked down to see I was still holding the Mortana Wand. Horrified, I yanked my hand back, tossing the Wand to the ground at my feet.

"Nadine," Verla said in a shaky tone. "You shouldn't be here."

My whole body shook as I turned toward the entrance to the cave. I thought I must've died and gone to Alora, because Nadine was standing there. I couldn't be sure of how she found me, until I remembered I'd told her where I was while astral traveling. It'd only just happened, but the memory already felt distant. Verla's spell had really fucked with my head.

"Verla, please, you have to stop this!" Nadine insisted. She was alone, and I didn't understand why she'd come here without backup. She had no magic to defend herself, no weapons, and no reinforcements. She was going to get herself killed.

Then I heard a soft meow outside the cave, and I realized our friends were here with her, but they'd let her approach Verla alone. Nadine believed she could talk Verla down.

"You have no idea what you're dealing with, Nadine," Verla growled. "Leave, before I make you."

"I'm not going anywhere," Nadine stated boldly.

While Nadine kept Verla talking, I quietly gathered the Oaken Wands. Nadine had interrupted Verla, and her spell had failed, but Verla was still more powerful than they were. If she got distracted, however, we might be able to claim some of our power back with the Oaken Wands.

"I don't want to hurt you, Nadine." Verla's voice wavered. It was strange to witness, considering the powerful threat she was. She was willing to risk all of witch magic and let hundreds of people die—hell, she'd started an entire war with the Waning—but deep down inside, there seemed to be a part of her that still cared. I didn't know what she could possibly care about as much as her sister… until I realized the only other person she ever loved was *Nadine*.

Verla had stopped her spell because she didn't want Nadine getting hurt. As she stared at her, Verla's shoulders sagged. Her hands shook in hesitation, like she wanted to bind Nadine too, but couldn't bring herself to do it. She had loved Nadine like a daughter, and even now, that was clear as day. All these years she'd spent away from her sister, she'd found another precious bond in Nadine.

"I know you're hurting," Nadine said gently. "I understand the pain of loss—"

"You understand *nothing*!" Verla shouted.

"I know you don't want to hurt Allyn," Nadine replied. "The way you talked about him after Dean died, I know you love him. You can't kill him."

Verla gave an evil—yet tragic—laugh. "You're right. I can't kill him, because Allyn is already gone. How do you think I amassed such power?"

Nadine's eyes filled with horror, and the final pieces fell into place. I saw the moment she accepted Verla for the truly vile being she was. She had loved Verla as if she were her own mother, but now, she had to face the reality that she never truly knew her at all. Nadine always saw the best in people, and it was something I loved dearly about her. But she had so much compassion that she couldn't recognize evil when it was staring her in the face. Nadine thought she could talk Verla down because she knew what it was like to lose someone, but Verla had already made her choices, and no amount of sympathy could undo them.

"You already killed him," Nadine accused hollowly. "When? How long did you let him live!? Tell me the truth!"

Verla's bottom lip trembled hopelessly. I thought she'd do anything to raise her sister, but clearly, Nadine had an impact on her even I couldn't comprehend. "You want to know the truth, Nadine? The truth is I'm sick of lying to you. If you want to know what happened, you can have the truth."

Verla waved her hand, and we were all sucked into a vision that pulled us several years back in time.

clarice

TWENTY

"*Beware the witch's fate, for her death shall mark the beginning of the end.*"

My sister sang the chilling phrase as if it were a nursery rhyme, repeating the words over and over again. There was no emotion behind it, as if she was nothing more than an empty shell speaking a warning from beyond.

I'd arrived home that night to find Nicole sitting in my living room, looking anything but herself. She sat on the couch, her hair a tangled mess atop her head. It looked like she hadn't showered in days, though she'd been fine when I left for work this morning. Our cat Odin sat beside her, meowing mournfully. Sometime in the last few hours, Nicole's eyes had taken on a wide, crazed appearance. She wrapped her arms around her middle and rocked back and forth.

Nicole was a Seer, though her visions rarely made any sense. I'd learned to put little stake in her predictions, but this one was different. I'd never seen her like this before; she didn't even make eye contact.

I knelt in front of her and spoke gently. "Nicole, I understand that you've had a vision. Why don't you tell me about it?"

Over the last year, Nicole had said a lot of things like this, but she usually brushed them off. Oftentimes, Seer visions were cryptic and difficult to decipher, and sometimes didn't mean anything at all. Nicole had always been a free spirit, never bothered by any sort of inconvenience.

She could always see the bright side to any situation, even in the worst moments that would surely crush anyone else. She wasn't the kind of person to be affected by her visions, no matter how dark. I never thought I'd live to see my sister's descent into madness.

And that's exactly what this was. Madness.

"Beware the witch's fate, for her death shall mark the beginning of the end," Nicole repeated.

"Who's the witch you're talking about?" I asked softly.

"The *witch*, Clarice!" she insisted, without looking at me. "She's going to die!"

Nicole gave a mad laugh, and I quickly drew away from her. My sister was sitting in front of me, but she didn't feel like my sister at all. I'd known her all my life, and we'd been best friends for nearly forty years. I knew every line on her face and every fleck of color in her eyes. Nicole and I were identical twins, and in the Miriamic Coven, that meant that we shared a soul. We were each one piece of a whole, a singular soul meant to live two separate lives alongside each other in this incarnation. We shared a connection unlike any other, but this was the first time I felt I couldn't get through to her. Usually when I looked at her, it was like looking into a mirror. Tonight, I hardly recognized her.

I wasn't the kind of person to fall apart *ever*. I'd always been the serious one, the one to hold us both together when our parents had been fighting. I always knew the best corners of the house to hide in to drown out their screaming. I'd become a lawyer to right the injustices of the world, and then turned to teaching to give back to the coven—to help raise the next generation of great witches and warlocks.

Something had changed. I could feel it. Deep down, a piece of our soul had fractured, and I didn't understand why or what had happened.

It was this vision. It had to be. Whatever she saw—whatever she *knew* —appeared to break her beyond repair. But she still had me, and I was going to fix this if it was the last thing I did.

"Nicole, tell me what you saw," I ordered.

"Fire!" she cried. "I see fire. I see a noose. There shall be a murder!"

I shuddered. I knew what she had to be talking about. The thought of the coven burning or hanging their own people never sat right with me, but it wasn't my place to judge the priestesses, as they knew Mother Miriam's will best. Our Imperium Council did what was necessary to protect the coven and please our goddess, and like any member of the Miriamic Coven, I would honor my goddess no matter what she desired.

Executions weren't particularly *common* these days, but they still happened from time to time. Nicole's prediction made it clear there was an execution just around the corner.

"I'm sure whatever happens is Mother Miriam's will," I assured her, though I hesitated. I couldn't help but wonder why Nicole would receive this vision unless she was meant to do something about it. "Did you see the witch who is to be executed?"

She continued rocking back and forth, like she never heard my question. Her wide-eyed gaze appeared unfocused as she continued rattling off the phrase. "Beware the witch's fate, for her death shall mark the beginning of the end."

"The beginning of what end?" I wondered aloud, but Nicole didn't respond.

I wasn't getting through to her, and though I had an extensive educational background, none of it could give me the understanding of a Seer when I myself was an Alchemist. I needed help from an expert.

"How about I put on a pot of tea?" I asked calmly. "Chamomile peppermint—your favorite. It should help calm the nerves."

Nicole didn't acknowledge my offer. Slowly, I retreated from the living room and into the kitchen. I filled the teapot with water and placed it on the stove. Then I drew my phone from my pocket and found a number in my contacts.

He answered on the first ring. "Clarice, how are you?"

"Not well, Emmett," I admitted as I paced around the room. I kept my voice low so that my sister wouldn't hear from the other room. "Something's wrong with Nicole, and I'm certain it has to do with her visions. I need your help."

If anyone could help her, it was Emmett Carlisle. He was a professor at Miriam College of Witchcraft, decades older and wiser than me. He was one of my closest colleagues and sat as head of the Seer department, while I was head of Alchemy. He was a mentor to me as much as a friend, and though we were both being considered for the headmaster position in the fall, he'd told me he was secretly rooting for me to get it, even though he had seniority. He was approaching retirement soon and thought the school was better off with a long-term headmistress. Truth be told, I didn't think he wanted to leave the classroom. He loved it too much.

"Of course, Clarice," Emmett said. "I'll help in any way I can. What seems to be the problem?"

I described what was going on as I placed the herbs into a tea ball.

"Is she responsive?" Emmett asked.

"Barely," I told him. "She responds in simple phrases, then goes right back to repeating the same words. It's like a prediction, but I've never seen her lose it like this before. She's unrecognizable."

"It sounds like a condition we call *disunion*," Emmett explained. "It's rare, but happens when a Seer becomes overwhelmed by their visions and resists them. This causes a divide inside their mind from what they know to be true, and what they *want* to be true. It happens most often with visions that could cause cataclysmic change."

"So there's really something to this prediction?" I wondered.

"We can't know for sure what it means or how impactful it may be, because this condition occurs due to her *interpretation* of her visions, whether they truly point to cataclysm or not."

"She's foretelling a woman's death," I said. "That's tragic, but is it truly enough to cause her to become unstable like this?"

"Disunion is never the result of only one vision," Emmett told me. "Likely, she's been resisting her visions for some time now, and this vision was merely the last straw."

I'd noticed she'd been pulling away over the last year, but she'd never been so disconnected as she was now. To be honest, I thought she might be seeing someone and didn't want to tell me. We were both unmarried and had joked our whole lives that we would become old maids surrounded by cats, because we didn't need anyone but each other. We had friends, and Faith was nearly as close to me as my own sister, but it wasn't the same.

Nicole and I were in our late thirties. We'd tried living apart for a while, but after Nicole lost her job a few months ago, she came to stay with me in the house our father had left me after his death. She'd been acting strange ever since. I figured she worried about leaving me behind for a man, though that could never happen. We would always be sisters, whether we lived together or not. Regardless, the promises we made in childhood still stood. We would be together forever, and that didn't change no matter the distance between us. I would be there to support whatever made her happy, no matter where that left me. And so, I'd resolved to let her come to me at her own pace.

I was starting to think that was a very grave mistake.

I should've seen the signs, but it happened so gradually that I never would've thought it'd culminate into something like this. She'd always told me about her visions before, and it never occurred to me that she might be hiding them, especially if it was something this serious. It appeared she wasn't the only one hiding from the truth, as I had refused to see reality as well.

"How do we help her?" I asked Emmett. "Do we need to figure out the meaning behind her vision and prevent this woman's death?"

"Without understanding her interpretation, it's nearly impossible to decipher the meaning until we're able to remerge the parts of her mind back together," Emmett said.

"So there's a cure?" I asked desperately.

"Through therapy or the proper ceremonies, yes, she can overcome this disunion, *if* she is willing to work with us," Emmett said. "In the meantime, disunion can be a very dangerous condition, as Seers who are afflicted by this ailment may act out in treacherous ways to try to prevent their vision from coming true."

The last thing I wanted was to see my sister get hurt. Something like that would surely break us both.

I pulled the steaming kettle from the burner as I whispered, "What do we do, Emmett?"

"All will be well, Clarice," he said gently. "I'm on my way to your house now. Keep a close eye on her until I get there."

"I will," I promised. I hung up and quickly poured the hot water into the teacup I'd prepared. I funneled my Alchemy magic into it to enhance its relaxing properties.

"Everything's going to be okay, Nicole—" I started, but I cut off when I entered the living room to find it empty. It hit me then that several minutes had passed since I last heard her utter those terrifying words.

I felt the blood drain from my face. Emmett said her condition was dangerous, and I could only imagine what dangers he spoke of. I slammed the teacup to the coffee table, but I barely afforded it a glance as it teetered on the edge and splashed across the carpet. I was already racing out of the room.

"Nicole!" I called up the stairs. The old house remained eerily silent. Even Odin's cries had vanished completely.

I wasn't sure where she had gone, but one thing was for absolute certainty. Nicole wasn't herself right now, and I didn't think she was aware of whatever she planned to do.

A cold breeze spread across my arms, and I whirled toward the front door to see it had been left open a crack. I raced outside into the dark of night. It was the end of May, and the spring days had grown warm, but the air tonight seemed to chill me to the bone. The trees surrounding our house swayed, their leaves rustling overhead. I could've sworn I heard the howl of a coyote far in the distance, but as I listened for my sister's footsteps, I heard nothing over the sound of my own pounding heart.

"Nicole!" I called out again.

A *mew* came from behind the house, and I hurried around to the back, where I found Odin staring into the forest. He meowed helplessly, like he too was looking for Nicole.

There was only one place I could think of where she would've gone. It was our hideout as kids, a place I hadn't been to in ages, but it had always been our greatest safe haven. I tossed a witch light into the air and trudged through the forest, until I came upon an outcropping of rock far from the house. Within the rock was a narrow opening that led into a small cavern no larger than our living room.

My witch light floated ahead of me, lighting my way as I squeezed through the opening. It seemed much smaller than when we were kids.

"Nicole, are you in here?" I called out.

I entered the cavern, but it was completely empty. There were a few odd items scattered around, like a blanket covered in dirt that we'd dragged out here as kids to use as a rug, and a few sticks we'd carved to look like wands when we played magic. An old leather-bound book we used to pretend was a grimoire lay on the ground. There was even a cot we'd set up ages ago, in case we ever needed to sneak out of the house at night when our parents' screaming got too loud.

Several baby dolls still lay in a wooden cradle, completely undisturbed for the past twenty-five years. It made me sad to look at, because we'd always talked about becoming mothers, but here we were at nearly forty years old, our biological clocks nearly at their end. Everyone else our age already had children, and it seemed a little too late for the two of us. Nicole and I rarely spoke about it, but I knew deep down in our soul that we were both afraid of becoming parents… becoming *our* parents.

We only needed each other. And Nicole needed me now more than ever.

I looked toward Odin. "We need to track her down before she gets herself hurt."

Nicole had a good five-minute head-start, and she could've gone in any direction. I couldn't waste any time guessing where she'd gone. I hurried back into the house and frantically searched cupboards for Alchemy supplies. My cauldron sat ready on the stove, and I began pouring herbs and magic together to brew a tracking potion. I went into her bathroom and pulled a strand of hair from her brush. The cauldron bubbled fiercely when I dropped it in, alongside a Seer crystal.

I spoke an incantation. *"By Santos's love and Miriam's light, show me my sister's path tonight."*

I finished the potion and quickly dipped a ladle into the liquid. I took several gulps, though the potion burned my tongue. My vision instantly began to blur, and I sank to my knees in the middle of the kitchen.

Soft footsteps sounded nearby, and the wind whistled through the woods. A cold chill surrounded me, and I saw only the outline of trees in the dark night. A woman's voice muttered incomprehensible words, and something heavy sounded like it was being dragged through the dirt. As my vision adjusted to the darkness, I witnessed movement. Nicole stumbled through the forest in her bare feet, dragging a wooden handle behind her. Moonlight glistened off the metal end, and I realized what it was.

An ax. It was ours from the shed, though I hardly remembered we'd had it. Nobody had used it in years.

I glanced around, looking for any clues as to where she might be headed. Through the trees, I spotted the tall turrets of Miriam College of Witchcraft. My sister seemed oblivious to the mansion, though, and kept on walking past the school. It didn't seem that she had any direction at all.

Then I heard the words she'd been muttering under her breath. "Protection, protection, protection," she repeated.

I knew exactly where she was headed.

Hands landed on my shoulders, and someone shook me. I was pulled from the vision and found myself back on my knees in my kitchen. An old gray cat pawed at me.

Emmett Carlisle's familiar gray hair and glasses came into focus. "Clarice, tell me everything."

I shook off the chill from my vision. "Nicole left the house while I was on the phone with you. I've tracked her down. Emmett, she's headed for the Protection Tree."

"Did you see anything else?" he asked as he helped me to my feet.

A shiver traveled down my spine. This all seemed so unlike Nicole. "An ax," I admitted.

Emmett's features paled. "Surely she's not in control of her own actions right now. We don't have much time. We must get to her."

Emmett and I raced out of the house, and our cats followed. We jumped into my car, and the tires spun as I hit the gas. I sped down several streets until we came to the nearest parking lot closest to the Protection Tree.

I didn't bother turning off the engine as I hurried out of the car and into the trees. There was a path from the parking lot to the clearing that held the Protection Tree. Tonight, that path seemed a mile long.

"Nicole!" I called out, but no answer came. Behind me, Emmett huffed as he tried to keep up.

A heavy *thwack* sounded in the distance. She was already here.

I broke out into the clearing. The gnarly oak branches of the Protection Tree rose above my head. The tree pulsed with the magic that held the town's protection spell in place.

Nicole stood beside the tree and lifted the ax above her head. The whole clearing seemed to shudder as she swung the blade toward the thick trunk. It connected with a heavy *thwack*. Bark separated, and splinters flew in multiple directions. There were already several cuts in the tree, and they were only growing bigger the more she swung.

I couldn't wrap my head around what could possibly possess her to do such a thing. This tree was sacred to the Miriamic Coven. To defile it in any way was a serious offense. Even if she wasn't herself, she had to understand that cutting down this tree would take hours. If she didn't stop now, the priestesses would be here to stop her by any means necessary. I was certain the priestesses could already feel Nicole's attack against their spell.

"Nicole!" I yelled. Odin wailed at my feet.

She paused for a moment as she lifted the ax above her head. Slowly, she turned to look at me standing near the tree line. Her eyes locked on mine, and I could've sworn I saw her features soften, as if she'd broken through the madness of her vision.

Then her face hardened, and she snarled, "You don't understand, Clarice! This tree is going to kill! It is a murder tree! You have to let me stop it!"

She swung the ax another time. It made contact with the trunk, and several more splinters flew across the clearing.

"It's only a tree," I pleaded. "It can't hurt anyone."

She lifted the ax above her head again, and I raced across the clearing. I came up behind her and grabbed her hands before she could swing it another time.

"Please," I begged. "Let me help you."

"Let me help you," she repeated, as if mocking me. Nicole yanked on the ax handle, but I held on as firmly as I could. In a wild attempt to wrestle the ax from my hands, she threw her shoulder backward. The heavy metal butt of the ax smashed into my eye, and I stumbled hard to the ground. My eye swelled shut within moments.

"Clarice!" I heard Emmett call from behind me, though his presence barely registered.

Before Nicole could make contact with the tree again, I threw a shield around the Protection Tree. Her ax clanged against my shield, but didn't splinter the wood.

"It is a murder tree, a *murder tree*!" she cried frantically, like it would help me understand something I never would.

Emmett reached me, and he dragged me several feet backward. "You can't reason with her," he protested.

"I can try!" I insisted. "Would you rather I hurt her, because that's our only alternative, and it will help nothing!"

Screams tore through the dead of night. "Someone is trying to break our protection spell!" a woman yelled in the distance.

"They will suffer Mother Miriam's wrath!" another shouted.

Emmett gasped. "It's the priestesses!"

Nicole whirled toward us. "You have to go!"

She lifted her hand, and a shield blasted out of it so fast that Emmett and I were both sent flying backward. We landed flat on our backs in the trees, alongside our cats. My head spun as I struggled to sit upright.

Through the trees, I witnessed Nicole lift her ax one last time. Four priestesses swooped into the clearing on flying broomsticks, surrounding my sister at all angles. Their hooded cloaks billowed in the wind.

"This is a murder tree, and I must save—" Nicole started.

She was cut off as the priestesses blasted battle spells at her from all angles. Nicole's eyes rolled back in her skull, and she slumped to the ground unconscious. The ax landed at her feet.

One of the priestesses stepped forward and lowered her hood. She was one of the older priestesses, at least twenty years older than me, with dark curls around her face. It was Priestess Lilian.

"Alert the coven," Lilian ordered one of the other women. "Tell them of the horrific crime that has been committed here tonight. We must ensure they know such attacks upon the coven are unforgivable. We must ready the gallows immediately. She will hang tonight."

My whole body quaked in horrified tremors as I scrambled to my feet.

Lilian lifted her hands, and her powers levitated Nicole into the air. The priestesses mounted their brooms and took off to the skies in the blink of an eye, carrying my sister's limp body with them.

"No!" I wailed. My heartbreak seemed to echo through the forest, but the priestesses never turned around, nor responded.

I ran into the forest, following the direction the priestesses had gone. I knew where they would be taking her. There was a hill not far from here that housed the gallows. I couldn't recall the last time they'd been used—a few years, at least—but the coven would certainly put them to use tonight.

I couldn't let that happen. Not to my sister. Not to *us*.

Something within my chest seemed to stretch, as if there was a rope tethering me to my sister. Our connection strained against the distance that grew between us. Each passing second, the priestesses dragged her farther away from me. It felt that at any given moment, our soul might snap.

"Nicole!" I called out, even though I knew no answer would come. Whatever had broken inside of her was slowly bleeding into my own heart, because I felt like a madwoman racing through the woods.

I tripped. My hands sliced open against sharp sticks, and my knees smashed into rocks that left them bloody and bruised. Footsteps followed behind me, and I thought they were Emmett's, but he couldn't keep up with me. My heart raced as I pushed myself to my feet and continued running.

By the time I broke through the trees at the top of the hill, at least a hundred coven members had already gathered. I witnessed in horror as a man in a hooded cloak walked my sister across a wooden platform and placed a noose around her neck.

"NO!" I screamed so loud that it echoed across the hill.

The crowd turned to look at me. I stumbled forward, pushing past townspeople to get to the front of the group. The priestesses stood at the base of the gallows, staring up at my sister.

"What is the meaning of this?" Priestess Margaret sneered.

"Priestesses, please," I begged. "She had a vision. Professor Carlisle believes what happened here tonight is a result of a condition called *disunion—*"

"The cause does not matter, only that she has angered the Goddess," Lilian snapped. "Stand back, Clarice, or you will join your sister."

"You don't understand," I pleaded. "None of this was her intention. You can't do this without a trial!"

"A trial is not needed, for we caught her in the act. No one may defile the Protection Tree and live," Lilian hissed.

I gave it one last try. "Nicole, tell them you didn't mean it!"

I stared up at my sister, hoping she would say something to plead her innocence. Instead, she merely stared down at me with the most intense gaze.

"Beware the witch's fate, for her death shall mark the beginning of the end," she repeated one more time. Her voice came out surprisingly steady, like she had no idea what was about to happen to her.

My heart dropped. I felt like a helpless little kid again, not a full-grown woman with decades of life experience. For the first time, I didn't know how to hold us together.

That's when I realized I couldn't... not anymore.

I waited around for someone else to speak up, for my fellow coven members to protest that this wasn't right, that Nicole was ill and needed help. I expected the crowd to rise up, for someone to come to our aid and demand that Nicole be given some sort of mercy. I wanted—no, *needed—*

my community to come through for us and do the right thing, because I knew in my heart I would for them. The coven had to take a stand against this. If not a group of people, at least one person... *anyone.*

These selfish bastards... they did *nothing.*

"I won't go alone." Nicole uttered her final words.

Then the executioner pulled the lever, and the platform beneath Nicole's feet fell open. The sickening snap of her neck echoed across the hilltop. Her bare feet just hung there inches from the ground.

Time stopped, and I couldn't make sense of what happened next, because nothing seemed to matter. The fissure that had opened up in our soul completely shattered, until I lost all sense of self entirely. I could've been standing there for hours watching my sister's body sway in the wind. Nothing felt real, and I wasn't sure there were any pieces of our soul left to pick up. The two of us had never been apart, and now, we'd been separated across entire realms. I might as well have crossed realms with her, because here in body, I felt wholly empty.

And they just... left her there—her body swinging on a noose in the wind, like some sort of symbol to the coven of what would come of them should they commit a similar crime.

But I didn't see my sister as a criminal, no matter what she'd done. She'd been trying to tell us something—something important—and instead of listening, the priestesses had chosen to silence her.

Footsteps sounded beside me. I couldn't fathom where they were coming from, because this world felt so empty now I was certain I was the last person living in it. I was on my knees at the base of the gallows, and the rest of the coven had left.

Left my sister to rot.

I looked up to see Emmett slowly approaching me. Odin mewed softly at his feet.

"Clarice, I'm so sorry," he whispered. "Take as much time as you need. I've brought the car around whenever you're ready."

I felt a flare of anger rise against him. He was useless, too. He had remained silent when I needed him to raise his voice. He could go to hell with the rest of them. Yet, still, I needed his help now, worthless as it was.

I wiped my eyes and got to my feet. "We need to get her down from there. It's going to get cold tonight. She always sleeps with her socks on, or she gets too cold."

Emmett gave a gentle nod. Together, we loosened the noose from around her neck and pulled her body from the gallows. We laid her gently in the grass. I knelt at her side and pushed her hair out of her face. It was easy to believe she was merely sleeping, because I didn't think I'd survive in a world where she wasn't in it. Odin nudged her hand, though she didn't respond.

She always was a deep sleeper.

I didn't cry because I just… couldn't. I didn't feel anything at all. I wished I could've said that emptiness saved me from the grief, but in truth, there was no feeling in the world worse than that numbness. At least if I was angry or sad, I'd have something to fight for. Instead, life felt wholly meaningless. I couldn't even tell if my heart was still beating.

My sister was gone… and I'd lost myself with her.

Emmett laid a hand on my shoulder, though his voice seemed distant. "There is nothing more you could've done. We didn't get to her in time."

"There's got to be more," I said hollowly. "It can't end like this."

"All we can do is lay her in a grave and—"

"*No!*" I cut him off. He was about to suggest a funeral, but to do so would be ludicrous. I could never say goodbye to my sister. "I won't bury her."

"Clarice, she must be laid to rest," Emmett insisted.

"Then we shall place her in a tomb," I said. "There's only one place she was ever safe."

Emmett helped me transfer her body to the car, then into the woods behind my house. We laid Nicole's body on the cot inside the hideout we'd used as kids.

Emmett stepped back and stared down at Nicole's unmoving form. "This isn't a proper resting place, Clarice. She's too exposed to the elements. Her body will rot."

I leaned down to pick up one of the sticks we used to pretend were wands. I twisted it around in my hands. Back then, it felt like anything was possible if we had magic. I'd seen so many witches perform incredible spells, and I couldn't wait for the day our magic awoke. We'd done our Evoking Ceremonies together. It was a beautiful thing to be placed into two separate Casts, because it meant we could accomplish far more together with our magic working in harmony. When we got our powers, we both agreed that *nothing* could stop us.

We were sorely mistaken. There was one thing that could stop us… our coven, the very people who'd sworn to protect and help us.

I'd given Nicole so many promises that were now broken. We'd promised we would be together forever, no matter the distance between us, but I never imagined she'd be ripped from my life and trapped realms away. I felt immense guilt that I couldn't stop the priestesses. The promises I'd made felt wholly empty now, because despite our sentiments, we *weren't* together. I had failed her.

"I know a potion that will preserve her body for many years," I told Emmett flatly. "We use it sometimes for Mortana Studies, to preserve cadavers for students to study on. All I need is some Mortana crystals, which are easy enough to come by."

"Nothing about this is easy," he replied. "If you need anything at all, let me know."

I stared down at Nicole's pale features. "I need my sister back, but that isn't going to happen, now is it?"

Emmett dropped his gaze. "No. I'm afraid not."

There was nothing he could do to help, so I told Emmett to leave. We agreed not to tell anyone about what we'd done with Nicole's body, because we didn't want anyone to come looking for her. I brewed and administered the potion to preserve Nicole's body that night, all while Odin pawed at her like he expected her to get up and start moving.

"She won't," I told him. "Not anymore. Not ever."

I'd heard the phrase *deafening silence* before, but there was no piercing quiet that could compare to returning to the house alone that night. I was so used to hearing the sound of my sister's spoon clinking against her teacup before bed, and the pad of her feet down the hall when she retired to her room. Tonight, the silence was as all-consuming as the empty hole that had opened up in my chest.

I lit candles and called out to my sister. She wasn't here anymore, but she wasn't *gone*. If I could contact her, maybe all of this would make sense. I needed it to make sense, because without her, nothing had any meaning at all.

The lights flickered, but the séance failed. That night and the next. And the next after that.

We shared a soul, but I couldn't get through to her. It was the curse of having a twin flame. Because we shared the same soul, reaching out to her merely meant I was reaching out to myself, and the piece of my soul that remained on Earth was already here. My power couldn't make sense of where my half of our soul ended and hers began. She could be lost amongst the many realms of the afterlife, for all I knew. I certainly felt as if our soul had lost all sense of direction.

Days faded into weeks, which became months. Each passing day turned out to be more meaningless than the last. I'd had most of the summer off, and while I'd been offered and accepted the position as head-mistress, I couldn't bring myself to care.

Nicole would've wanted to celebrate. I was the youngest headmistress in Miriam College history, and she'd have hyped me up to the whole town and never let them forget it. She'd have thrown a big party and told every-one, "That's my sister!" all night long. She'd have been proud I accomplished my life-long dream, but now, I had no one to share it with.

Even my best friend Faith couldn't help. She'd left Octavia Falls long ago, and though we kept in touch, she couldn't *be* here, and she'd never return. Besides, she had a daughter to take care of, and I didn't want to burden her family with my woes.

I sat on the edge of the tub one day, watching the ripples across the surface of the water as the tub filled. I pulled the belt on my bathrobe tight around my ribs, so much that I limited myself to shallow breaths. Sitting in the discomfort was the only way to remind myself I was still alive. Otherwise, I didn't feel like I was in my body at all.

I hated every second of it. Either my mind was somewhere else entirely and I lost hours at a time, or I was trapped in my own body. Both options felt like a prison.

I wondered what it'd be like to set my spirit free. I could be with her again. My soul would be whole once more, and I could start over in a new incarnation. It was that, or request my reaper destroy my soul, because going on living like this was no longer an option.

I didn't know what I was still doing here, to be honest. There was nothing here for me anymore. If I couldn't share my life with my sister, I didn't want it.

I didn't let myself think about it. I sank into the tub, bathrobe and all. The water was scorching hot on my skin, but it barely registered. I let my head dip beneath the surface of the water, and I just laid there... waiting for the water to take me away to another place.

Pressure built up in my lungs. I heard the splash of the water over-flow over the side of the tub, and Odin cried loudly from outside the bathroom door. Darkness pressed in from all sides. In the distance, I thought I heard my name. I imagined it was Nicole calling me home to Alora. For the first time in months, I felt wholly at peace as I began to drift away—

The bathroom door burst open, and hands landed on me and dragged me upward. I gasped as my head broke the surface of the water. Someone dragged me onto the cold tile, and water splashed everywhere. I heard the faucet turn off. I heaved for breath and blinked the world back into focus.

Emmett Carlisle knelt beside me, panting. His features appeared pale. "Clarice! Thank Alora I got here just in time."

I pushed him away. I was angry that he'd stopped me. "You shouldn't have come!"

He'd checked on me a lot in those first few weeks, but slowly his visits grew more and more infrequent. I hadn't seen him all month.

"What are you doing here?" I spat.

"I came to see how you were doing," he said. "I heard Odin crying, so I let myself in the front door. I knew something was wrong. The bathroom door was locked, but you didn't answer. I broke it down with a battle spell."

"You shouldn't have," I sneered. "If you saw this in one of your visions, you should've just let it happen."

"I didn't see it. I came because I was worried."

"You can stop worrying," I snarled as I got to my feet. "I know how to save myself now."

"Clarice, you can't!" Emmett pressed. "There must be a reason I was prompted to come today. Mother Miriam must have a divine plan, which means you still have a purpose here."

"Mother Miriam doesn't care, or she'd have answered my prayers!" I shouted.

"Perhaps she did," he replied softly.

If he was suggesting his presence was somehow an answer to my prayers, he was sorely mistaken. All I wanted was to be with my sister again, and he had prevented me from doing that.

"You're here by chance, and there's nothing more to it than that," I said.

"There must be," he argued. "Nicole would've wanted you to keep going."

I froze at the mention of her name. Nicole certainly would've been disappointed in me, that was for sure. I didn't like that he was using her against me.

Emmett grabbed a towel off the shelf. "Here. Dry off and let's chat."

He wasn't giving me any other option. Didn't matter, though. I'd just try again once he left. What was another few minutes in this cursed existence compared to the last three months of it?

"All right," I agreed as I took the towel from his hands.

I dried off and changed, then joined Emmett in my living room. He remained silent.

"Well?" I was less than friendly, but I didn't care. I just wanted to get this over with.

He spoke slowly, like he was choosing his words carefully. "What you were about to do in there breaks my heart, Clarice. I need you to understand how precious life is, because you never know how much time you have left."

"I know," I stated flatly. "My sister's death taught me that."

"I don't think you *do* know," he urged. "This isn't about Nicole. This is about you."

"What's the difference?" I scoffed. "The night Nicole died, I died with her. My reaper just forgot to come for me. I'm stuck here until I decide to do something about it."

"Even witches don't have the power over death that you think we do," he argued. "You go when it's your time, whether you want to or not."

"You will *never* convince me it was Nicole's time to go. It wasn't fate or destiny that took her life—it was the priestesses."

And then they'd just… left me here to pick up the pieces alone. No apology. Nothing. I had to pretend as if what they'd done was justified, in order to prevent myself from suffering the same fate. Though, I didn't think that'd be a terrible way to go anymore.

"We don't know if Nicole's fate was predetermined," Emmett said. "But I do know that you're sitting here in front of me with a life and a purpose. Why would you want to throw all that away?"

"There's nothing left for me. All I had was taken away," I replied hollowly.

"You're choosing to see things like that when you still have time to make another choice," he growled, clearly getting upset with me. It was cruel, honestly. "You have a whole life ahead of you, and you're letting yourself be defined by one moment instead of allowing it to push you forward."

"You don't get it!" I snapped. "My sister *died.*"

"We all die eventually!" Emmett shouted. "All we can do is make the most of the time we've got. Giving up defeats the whole purpose."

"And what if there is no purpose?" I shot back.

Emmett gritted his teeth. "Then I guess you'll just waste away, all that work and all your accolades gone. You won't make the mark on the world you hoped for, and everyone will forget you."

I reeled back. "I thought you came to help. How can you be so callous?"

"Because you're not the only one who's lost something!" he shouted. Emmett threw his hand over his mouth, looking regretful at his words. Tears beaded in the corners of his eyes, and he sounded defeated as his shoulders sank. "The truth is, I came today to say goodbye. I'm dying, Clarice."

That was certainly news. My temper melted away, and my tone softened. "Emmett, I had no idea."

"I haven't told anyone. It's cancer, and I'm afraid even magic can't provide a cure."

"How long have you known?" I asked.

"A while," he admitted. "It's why I advocated for you to become headmistress. I don't have much longer, and the cancer has progressed to the point I can't continue to hide it."

I'd noticed he appeared pale when he arrived, but I'd taken it to be distress. The closer I looked now, the more I realized how unwell he looked. He'd lost weight and moved slowly, when he used to be so vibrant and full of life.

"There are treatments," I offered. "Alchemists have potions that can help slow the progression."

"And how is someone like me supposed to afford that?" he demanded. "I'm a *teacher*. I barely have enough for retirement, let alone medical treatments. There was so much more I wanted to do. I haven't finished my research. There were books I wanted to write—knowledge I'm to pass on to the next generation! I know that you have dreams, too. You're the youngest headmaster in Miriam College history. Think of all the good you can do! It offends me that you would give up on that. I no longer have a choice, but you still do."

He thought he was helping, but I honestly never felt more alone. I needed someone to understand. Instead, I was met with anger, because once again, I had failed to meet expectations. It didn't matter how much work I put in or what I accomplished. It was never good enough.

"I'm not you," I said. "All those dreams I had—they mean nothing if I can't share them with her."

Emmett went silent for a beat. "I see. You need something to fight for. You need to find your joy again."

I scoffed. "I can't do that without her. She was my only joy."

"You can't bring her back, so there must be something else for you here."

His words made me stop. I glanced over to the mantle, where I'd set the toy wand I'd found in our hideout that night. I'd brought it back to the house, and it hadn't moved since. As kids, magic meant limitless possibilities to Nicole and me. Somewhere along the way, limits had been imposed, and I'd forgotten how wide open the world felt as a kid—back when anything was possible.

"Why *can't* I bring her back?" I asked slowly.

Emmett adjusted his glasses. "As I said, even witches don't have power over death."

"Yes, but there are others who do," I pressed. "There is magic beyond our own limitations, supernaturals and demigods who have defied death before. Perhaps *this* is the reason I'm still around."

"You think you're destined to find a way to raise your sister from the dead?" Emmett wondered.

"I don't know if I believe in destiny," I admitted. "But why wouldn't I at least *try?*"

"What purpose would that serve?"

"Research," I offered. "You said it yourself; I have dreams of making an impact. What better way to leave my mark on the coven than to expand our knowledge and understanding of just how far we can take our magic?"

The truth was, I didn't really care about all that. But Professor Carlisle did, and so, I had to speak his language. All I knew was that my soul had been torn across realms, and my sister was beyond my reach. I didn't know where she had gone, and I feared that even in death, I may not find her. The afterlife was a big place, after all.

But if I could bring her back here, we could be united again, and the empty hole inside of me could heal. Emmett told me to find my joy, and the thought of being reunited with my sister again was the only spark of joy I'd felt in the last three months. If there was anything that gave me direction and made me want to keep on living, it was this. It'd become abundantly clear over the summer that no one was going to save me. Even Emmett was only here as a formality. If no one else was going to help me, I was going to have to save myself.

"You really think you can raise the dead on your own?" Emmett asked skeptically.

It'd be an understatement to say what I was asking for was monumental. As far as I knew, no witch or warlock had ever done it, but that hadn't ever stopped me before. I couldn't do it alone—that was for certain—but it didn't make it impossible.

"No, I can't. Not by myself," I admitted. "But perhaps together, we can find a way."

Emmett shook his head firmly. "Magic of this level could have dire consequences. I won't participate."

"Not even if it could advance your research?" I questioned.

He dropped his head hopelessly. "I'm afraid I'm out of time."

"Not with the proper treatments," I proposed. "I can brew you the potions, Emmett. It could prolong your life another ten years."

A spark of intrigue entered his eyes. "I don't doubt your ability to brew the potion, but the ingredients alone are quite expensive. Surely such an offer doesn't come out of the goodness of your heart."

I leaned back in my seat. "The money is not a problem, and I'm in a position as headmistress to gain access to any ingredients I wish. Help me find a spell to raise the dead, and you'll get your treatments."

"What if raising your sister doesn't work?" he wondered. "It could take years to perfect such a ritual."

"Then it takes years," I told him simply. "You wanted me to find meaning, Emmett. This is it. I'm going to raise my sister from the dead. Whatever it takes."

It was something my sister and I had always said. Once I made the decision, it was a promise to Nicole to see this through to the end. If Emmett wasn't going to help me, I'd find someone who would.

He contemplated my offer, then stood. "All right, Clarice. As long as you keep supplying me with treatments, I will do as you ask."

We sealed our agreement with a witch's vow. When I said whatever it took, I meant it to the very core of my being. I'd burn this coven to the ground to bring my sister back.

I returned to work that fall with a renewed sense of vigor. I had a purpose and a direction, and *nothing* could stop me.

I visited Nicole in her tomb often, to keep her company and tell her about the research Professor Carlisle and I were doing. I was cleaning one day, because she deserved a nice tomb. I picked up the leather-bound book we used to pretend was a grimoire. I had so many fond memories of playing magic with Nicole here in this cavern. Sometimes, when our parents weren't home, we'd invite Faith over and she'd pretend to brew potions with us here.

I flipped open the book to find all kinds of drawings of a cauldron, along with scribbles I couldn't quite read. We'd found the book in Faith's attic when the three of us were playing up there one day. She'd said it belonged to her father—a man named Nicolas who had died before she was born. We all agreed it'd make the perfect spell book, so we'd brought it here to play with. We'd been so fascinated by the intricate crescent moon design on the front, but as children, we'd never given much thought to what was inside.

As I flipped through the journal, I realized it contained powerful spells and valuable information about lost coven relics. I remembered Faith's father had been a Miriamic priest before he died. That hadn't meant much to me as a kid, but now it occurred to me he possessed secrets of the Imperium Council.

I pored over that journal for weeks, searching for any information that could point to a revival spell the council kept hidden. I took notes of my own and added entries to Nicolas's journal. He wrote extensively of a special cauldron and drew all kinds of pictures of wands, but ultimately, his entries lead us nowhere.

It took years of research before Professor Carlisle and I found anything promising. We'd tried endless rituals, incorporated as much

Death magic as we could, and none of it was enough. With each ceremony, our efforts grew darker and darker. It was clear we had to go to lengths no other witch or warlock would attempt, but even animal sacrifices couldn't get the job done.

We'd descended so far into the darkness, I wasn't sure there was any ritual dark enough that we wouldn't try. I'd do absolutely anything.

"I found something," Emmett reported one day in my office. "But it's not a ritual we could ever go through with. Perhaps there are ways to modify it so we don't have to hurt anyone."

"People are going to get hurt, Emmett," I said. "We knew that when we agreed to go down this road. Whatever it takes, remember?"

"Yes, but not like this. The ritual requires the life of a cursed child."

I shrugged. "So we cast a curse."

"It's not that simple," he said. "The longer a child has been cursed, the more potent the magic. A curse we cast on our own wouldn't be strong enough to perform the ritual, unless we waited many years for the curse to mature."

"There are plenty of children in the coven," I said. "I'm sure we can find one who's been cursed."

Emmett gaped. "You can't really mean that."

"I do," I stated simply. "My sister is lost out there—she's all alone. I don't care who or what I have to sacrifice to get her back. We've dedicated years to this. Are you going to turn back on your witch's vow now?"

Emmett appeared horrified. Without the treatments I was providing him, he wouldn't survive long. "Even if we found a cursed child, we don't have the magic to pull this off. We'd need the power of a demigod, or magic of equivalent magnitude. I daresay demigods are difficult—if not impossible—to come by."

I tapped my pen on the desk. "So find a way to make it happen."

"Where are we possibly going to find that kind of power, let alone contain it?" he asked.

"We can always find help for the right price. Perhaps a demon will strike a deal."

Emmett's eyes widened. "There are lines we can't cross."

I didn't see it that way. "Lines are only drawn to keep you playing small, Emmett. Neither of us are small players."

"To do so would have dire consequences," he pressed. "Clarice, you know witches don't make demon deals anymore. The cost is far too high."

I smacked my hand on top of my desk, causing Professor Carlisle to startle. "*No cost* is too high to save my sister! I will do whatever it takes, and I don't care who gets in my way!"

He took a step back, though he appeared contemplative. "It would cost your very soul. You and your sister share a soul, and to sell your soul to a demon would destroy the very soul you're trying to save. There's no way around it, Clarice. Not unless…"

He trailed off, and I cocked an eyebrow. He cowered beneath my gaze. It was clear Emmett was terrified of what I'd become, but I held his life in my hands, and he cherished that above all else. It didn't matter what I asked him to do, because after all these years of working with him, I knew there was nothing he wouldn't do for his treatments—just as there was nothing I wouldn't do for my sister. We were the same in that sense, and to be honest, I wasn't sure if he was afraid of *me*, or afraid of how far *he* would go to get what he wanted.

Emmett shuddered. "A demon *could* take the soul of your kin as payment. But seeing as you have no kin, you'd never be able to make the deal. Not unless you were able to create kin of your own."

It was horrible to suggest—no, worse than horrible. To put your own desires above the wellbeing of your child was the worst thing anyone could do. The only person capable of such a vile thing had to be broken beyond repair. They had to be so empty inside they couldn't feel a thing at all, because any ounce of empathy would stop that person in their tracks.

They had to be like me.

"Whatever it takes," I repeated.

He took a cautious step back. "I—I'll handle the ritual so that it is ready whenever you are, when a demon can provide his assistance. But I can't do it alone. I'll need help."

"I'm sure we can find someone. Demons aren't the only ones who will make an exchange for the right price."

Emmett seemed horrified, though I didn't know why. I merely went about my day. It didn't quite register what I was suggesting until I passed the large window above the Main Foyer. I caught sight of my reflection in the glass, and I had to do a double take. I didn't know the last time I looked at my own reflection. It was too hard, because every time I looked at myself, I saw *her*.

I no longer recognized myself. I was well put together, in a clean black pantsuit and my hair tied into a bun at the base of my neck. I held my head high with my shoulders back. I looked all the part of the confident academic leader I was. It'd take one hell of an empath to notice how deeply I was suffering inside.

And yet… there was a darkness in my eyes that wasn't there before. I knew when the light had left them—the night my sister was murdered. I wondered how no one else had noticed. I looked like an entirely different person.

It's surreal, really—looking at your own reflection and not seeing yourself there anymore. How had I gotten to this point, where I was not only considering letting others suffer, but fully willing to go through with it?

I suddenly couldn't breathe, and it felt as if the school walls were closing in on me. I tore my gaze from the window and began racing down the hall, pushing past students and faculty. I must've looked like I was late for a meeting, but the truth was, I was trying to outrun myself.

I turned a corner down a secluded hallway and slammed straight into someone. I stumbled back a step, and the man caught me.

I stared up into the soft eyes of Jonathan Warren. He was my age, a Mortana professor here at Miriam College of Witchcraft. We'd worked closely for years, but we'd never been *this* close. I didn't think we'd ever exchanged more than a kind handshake.

"Headmistress, what's wrong?" Jonathan asked. Goddess bless his heart, he was so genuine. He had no idea what kind of monster he'd just stumbled into.

"I—I," I stammered. I *never* broke down, but in this moment, I just couldn't bring the words to come. Part of me wanted to tell him—tell *someone*—what was on my mind. He needed to stop me, because I wasn't sure I could stop myself. I wasn't scared when Emmett told me what had to be done, but now… I wasn't so sure.

Jonathan noticed the distress in my features. "Let's talk," he offered.

He wrapped an arm around my shoulder, guiding me through his classroom and into his office. The moment the door shut, I caught sight of my reflection in the window, and I completely broke down. I yanked the red drapes closed, and tears streamed down my face. I gasped for breath that didn't come.

"Headmistress," Jonathan said gently as he guided me into a chair.

"Call me Clarice," I insisted through sobs. I tried to make them stop, but the more I resisted, the harder I cried. I was wholly embarrassed and ashamed.

He knelt beside my chair. "Take all the time you need. I'm here for you."

I wiped my eyes. "It's ridiculous, isn't it? Your boss, crying in your office. You shouldn't see this."

"We all need a good cry every now and then," Jonathan encouraged. "This room's a good place to cry, really. Alora knows I've shed enough tears here after Roberta passed."

I barely remembered his wife died, to be honest. I'd heard of it in passing, but it seemed insignificant at the time. Now as I looked at him, I had the thought that maybe he could understand me, because he'd lost someone, too.

"How long has it been since you had a good cry?" he asked gently.

"Too long," I admitted. "Not since Nicole died, at least."

Jonathan took my hand in his. "Oh, Clarice. I'm so, *so* sorry. It's okay to let it out."

Nobody had ever given me permission like that before. Alora knew my father would've berated me for such a display of emotion. Jonathan was different. When I sobbed in front of him, I couldn't stop. There was something about him that allowed me to be vulnerable, when I never could before. Jonathan wrapped me in his arms, and my shoulders shook as tears soaked his suit coat. I was crumbling into a million pieces in front of him, but somehow, Jonathan was picking up the pieces and putting me back together again. I had no idea there were any pieces left to hold together anymore.

"If you want to talk about it, I'm here," he offered.

It was so kind and unexpected. I'd have thought he would throw me out of his office and tell me how disgusting I was for the person I'd become. But he didn't. He accepted me—broken pieces and all.

I thought about telling him, about laying it all out on the table and just being done with it. Jonathan was level-headed enough to do something about it, even if that meant locking me up so I wouldn't hurt anyone.

Somehow, that terrified me more than actually going through with my plan, because if I didn't, then my sister's death meant nothing. Jonathan couldn't know… *ever*.

My gaze traveled down to his lips, and Goddess, the only thing that kept me sane was thinking of what he might taste like. "I don't want to talk."

I drew him close, and we both paused at the precipice. For the first time in years, I could feel my heart beating in my chest. If I couldn't bring myself to talk about it, then maybe there were other ways to drag myself back from my descent into madness.

Jonathan didn't pull away. Our lips connected, and the world seemed to spin around me once more, vibrant with colors I forgot existed. I'd forgotten what it was like to *feel* something. And Alora, it was magical.

Jonathan and I couldn't get enough of each other after that. Months of passion rooted me in sanity. We agreed to keep our romance a secret, because it put both of our jobs at risk to admit we were anything more than colleagues. And that made it all the more thrilling for both of us.

The moments I was with Jonathan, he brought me back into my body —grounded me here so I didn't feel quite so broken. I shared the most vulnerable parts of myself with him, both in the bedroom and out of it. We had so many deep conversations, and I opened up to him about my parents and how empty I felt following my sister's death. He listened, and he validated me with every admission. We shared the deep connection I so craved.

And despite all that, I could never open up fully. I tried so many times to tell him about the rituals and ceremonies I'd tried to raise my sister from the dead. I'd wanted to tell him what Professor Carlisle and I had talked about that day I broke down. But I couldn't.

One night, after hours of passionate love making, I laid in his arms and asked, "Do you ever wish you could bring your wife back?"

I'd wanted to ask that question so many times, but I'd always talked myself out of it. It was out there now, and I nervously awaited his response.

"I did for a long time," Jonathan admitted as he kissed the top of my head. "But not even Death magic can bring her back. I find peace in knowing she's all right in Alora."

"What if she isn't?" I asked. "We don't really know who makes it to Alora or if they get stuck someplace else, do we?"

"I have to believe she's there," Jonathan said gently. "I understand why you're asking. You'd bring Nicole back too if you could, and that's completely valid. But we don't have the power to do that, so we've got to find ways to keep going. If you're not ready yet, it's okay, but I'll be here every step of the way to help you."

I scoffed, though I tried to make light of it. "Believe me, you don't want to stick around that long."

"Why wouldn't I?" he asked incredulously. "I'll be here until we're old and gray, if you'll have me."

I stiffened. I never really thought of where we were going with this, or how far we'd take it. Jonathan made it sound like he'd go to the ends of the Earth for me, and I realized then that I couldn't let this go that far. Jonathan was perfect in every sense of the word, and there was this innocence about him that I would destroy if we let this continue.

Goddess, I never realized it before. I was *in love* with Jonathan Warren.

That was more terrifying than any dark road I could go down, because I knew if I let myself love him hard enough, he just might fix me. I didn't want to be fixed, because if I healed from this gaping wound inside of me, then there'd be nothing left to push me forward. Above all else, my sister came first.

Before even my love.

I drew away from him, my naked body still on full display. I'd allowed myself to strip away the layers, to be vulnerable with him in ways I couldn't with anyone else. I realized now that was a terrible mistake.

"I'm sorry, Jonathan," I said in a trembling whisper. "I can't do this."

I fled from his house that night, and every stitch he'd sewn up inside of me burst at the seams, until that empty hole in my chest gaped wider than ever before. All those pieces of me he'd picked up and held together shattered into smaller pieces, leaving me more broken than I'd ever been.

Two weeks later, reality came crashing down on me in the face of a positive pregnancy test.

My life had fallen into complete shambles, and I'd gone so far beyond rock bottom that I seemed to exist in an empty abyss. I couldn't imagine hell could be worse than this. If bringing my sister back didn't save her piece of our soul, then I had to do it to repair the fractured bits of my own.

I didn't plan on telling anyone about the baby. I scheduled an appointment and resolved to be done with it—to be done with it all. Professor Carlisle was right. There were lines we couldn't cross. I'd break my witch's vow, even if it killed me, because if I was being honest that's all I wanted anyway.

I knelt beside Nicole's body in our hideout. The potion I'd administered all those years ago had preserved her body, so she looked no different than she had the night she died. Her cheeks were pale, but I'd spent so much time visiting this tomb that I'd nearly forgotten what she looked like otherwise.

This was how I remembered her now. For years, I'd been coming here daily, having one-sided conversations with my sister, telling her of all my plans to bring her back. I felt the madness seeping into my psyche. I talked to her all the time, even outside this tomb, because even though she wasn't *here* with me, she was the only thing that felt real.

I took her icy cold hand in mine. I wanted to tell her I was sorry, that I couldn't keep going and that I'd failed her.

But as I stared down at my sleeping sister, I couldn't bring myself to utter the words. Without me, she was wholly alone.

"I'm not going to give up on you," I promised instead. "Everything I do now is for love. I don't care if I tear apart the priestess's coven if I can restore what I lost, because their coven is not one I wish to live in anyway. We vowed to make this world a better place, and I won't break my promises. I'm going to make things better by bringing back what I love. Whatever it takes."

Even if that meant becoming a monster I no longer recognized.

TWENTY-ONE

I didn't go to the doctor's appointment.

Months passed, and eventually, I started to show. I couldn't hide the pregnancy any longer, and was forced to announce it.

Jonathan and I had only spoken once since the night I left his house—just long enough for me to break his heart. We hadn't talked after that, until he cornered me outside my office one day.

His gaze traveled down to my belly. I'd been hiding the bump the best I could, but now that he knew the truth, it was obvious. "We need to talk," he stated firmly.

I shot a glance down the hall. "Step into my office."

Inside, I took a calm seat behind my desk, though Jonathan remained standing. His fingers curled around the back of the chair opposite me.

"I wish I didn't have to hear the news from other faculty members," he said. "You should've told me."

"Why would I?" I asked. "You and I haven't spoken in months."

He hesitated. "Because it's mine… isn't it?"

"Goddess, no," I laughed. It was insanely easy for me to lie to him. I half believed it myself.

Jonathan furrowed his brow. "I heard you're due this summer. The dates add up."

"As they do with other men," I replied nonchalantly. I didn't care what lies I told him, as long as he left me alone.

Jonathan gaped, as if he wasn't sure he heard me right. I could see the moment he processed it, because he raked his fingers through his hair and collapsed into the chair across from my desk. "You… cheated on me?"

"I wouldn't say that, as you and I were never officially *together*," I said.

Jonathan's features appeared calculating. "I suppose we never defined it, and that's on me for making assumptions. I've been wondering for so long where I went wrong, and now, it makes sense. I took things too far that night—it got too real. I was moving too fast. I see now that it was too much for you."

He stared into my eyes. "I never meant to hurt you. I should've known better, and I'm sorry. I want you to know that whatever you decide moving forward, I will be here to support you. Whether we're together or not, I will always love you, Clarice."

Poor thing. Jonathan was such a pure, innocent soul that he couldn't see the monster staring him straight in the face. Outwardly, he appeared to be taking the mature approach, but inwardly, he was merely naive.

Things couldn't have ended any better. He was kind enough to take on all the blame, and I was more than happy to let him. I preferred he get out of the way regardless, because I knew if I let him back into my life, I wouldn't be able to resist the urge to keep him there.

My child arrived at sundown on a Friday night. It was a boy. He was so tiny.

I gave birth alone in my own home. I lay in bed for seven hours straight, and though my body felt everything, I couldn't remember a single sensation. He cried, but I'd already forgotten the sound.

I couldn't remember how Emmett got there. I must've called him. I answered the door.

"Where's the child?" he asked.

"In the bedroom," I told him. I turned and led him down the hall. The baby was crying. There was blood everywhere.

Emmett wrapped the baby in a blanket and lifted it into his arms. The child continued to cry. "We have everything we need to summon assistance. Where would you like to perform the ceremony?"

"In the tomb," I told him. "She should see what I've done for her."

I led Emmett outside in my bare feet and nothing but a thin, bloody nightgown.

We entered the room carved out in the rock, and I knelt beside

Nicole's body. "Don't worry," I told her. "I'm going to take care of every-thing. Nothing will stop us from being together again."

"Here, you must take the child," Emmett told me.

I gazed down at the baby, and something within me recoiled. "No. I can't."

"You *must*," he pressed. "Only you can make the exchange."

Reluctantly, I took the child in my arms, and for the first time, he settled. The baby gave a contented sigh and curled into me. I was stunned as I stared down at his delicate features. His chest rose and fell, and it hit me that I was holding a living, breathing person. Somewhere inside that tiny little body was a soul… an innocent soul that I was just going to give up.

It shouldn't have been this easy. I didn't really care what the demons did to him. That should've concerned me, but it was of no consequence if it meant having my sister back.

"It's time," Emmett said.

As I'd been studying the baby's features, Emmett had drawn a sigil on the ground with chalk. They were old, ancient runes that predated the coven and had come from hell itself. The runes would serve to summon the demon, as well as bind him in the spell so he couldn't cast magic that would hurt us. In the center of the sigil stood a bowl of foul-smelling herbs.

Emmett gestured me forward, and I knelt in the middle of the chalk circle. He held out his hand, and I offered him mine. Emmett conjured a knife, and in one quick motion, he sliced it across my hand. I winced as the blade cut deep. Blood poured out of the wound and into the bowl of herbs. The baby remained quiet.

"Speak the incantation," Emmett said.

"*In noctis tenebris, cum hac sanguinis oblatione, scelestum daemonem voco,*" I spoke. It was an old, ancient incantation that surely hadn't been uttered in over a thousand years. *In the dark of night, with this offering of blood, I summon the wicked demon.*

The herbs within the bowl erupted into flames that touched the ceil-ing, and a strong gust of wind swirled around the cavern. A blinding red light shone from all angles around us. I shielded my eyes with one hand.

The wind died down, and I opened my eyes to see a ghastly beast standing before us. He was at least nine feet tall and hunched over with his spine against the ceiling. He stood on two legs like a man, but had a skull-like face with empty eye sockets that glowed bright red. His teeth were razor-sharp, and he had no skin—merely bloody muscle covering his entire body. Four sharp, straight horns protruded out of the top of his head.

The sight of such a beast should've turned my blood to ice, but I felt a sense of relief in his presence. He was a Scelus demon, one of the most vile and powerful kinds. He was bound by no moral values. I knew he could give me what I wanted.

Emmett was struck with such terror that he screamed and scurried out of the tomb. Pathetic fool. He had no spine.

The demon stared down at me and gave a low growl. He spoke in a deep, ethereal voice. *"You have summoned me to this wretched realm. Speak your intentions."*

"I wish to trade one soul for another," I told him, holding out the child. "This child is my kin. I will give him to you, if you can raise my sister from the dead."

I gestured to Nicole's body lying on the cot.

The demon followed my gaze, then turned his red eyes back on the baby. He wore a hungry expression, like he would do anything to take this baby's soul for his own.

"I cannot do as you ask," he said. *"Power over death is not as simple as it may seem."*

"You must!" I begged. "We have a ritual ready, one that uses a cursed child to raise the dead, but we need *your* power to pull it off. Please, I will do anything."

"I'm familiar with such a ritual, but it requires more than power. You will need perfect timing," the demon said. *"Perhaps you would be satisfied with an alternative agreement."*

"Anything to bring her back," I urged.

"I can give you strength," he proposed. *"I can make your soul a vessel for power unlike you've ever experienced before, and give you the ability to shape magic to your will. If you wield this ability properly, you can amass the powers of a demigod, and under the proper circumstances, achieve that which you desire."*

I glanced between my sister and the baby, and I found myself hesitating. "What will you do with him?"

"I will take him to a demonic realm and raise him in the ways of a demon."

At least the child would know an existence of some sort. The demon would enslave him, but he was better off in this other realm than to be raised by a broken mother. I would only destroy him.

I knew what it was like to live amongst the ruins of a shattered soul, and it was not an existence I wished upon anyone. I could keep the child and give up my sister, or fulfill the promises I made long ago. Either way, there was no turning back.

I had reached the point of no return, and no matter what choice I made now, there was no redemption for my soul. The only choice I had now was to save this child I'd known for mere minutes, or resurrect the woman who had been at my side throughout lifetimes.

There was no decision to make.

"Done!" I agreed. I held the infant out toward the demon. "His soul is yours."

The demon took the child. The baby began to scream, his piercing wails echoing throughout the chamber.

The demon's spell was already underway. He lifted a hand, and red magic swirled around me. Heat like fire seared every inch of my body as his powerful magic lifted me into the air. I cried out as the magic permeated deep into my bones, vibrating with a frequency that seemed to tear my body apart at a cellular level, before knitting me back together again.

My body crashed to the ground, and though the pain ebbed away, I could feel power pulsing through me unlike ever before. I would never be the same again.

I expected the demon to be gone by now, but as the world came back into focus, I found that he was still standing above me, holding the baby.

"*What do you call him?*" the demon asked.

I was stunned he would bother to ask. "It doesn't matter."

"*If I am to raise this child, he must have a name,*" the demon pressed.

I didn't give it any thought. "Allyn."

"*Very well,*" the demon said. "*Our agreement is complete. Use your power well.*"

And then he vanished, along with my baby.

Silence permeated the cavern, and with it came the harrowing truth of what I'd just done. I'd made a terrible mistake, one I could never take back.

"Allyn," I whispered, as if my child could hear me… could come back to me.

It didn't seem real until I gave him the name. Moments ago, giving up the child seemed inconsequential. He was a completely blank slate, with no memories to speak of and no one to love him. Now he had a name, and with it, a future that was now lost.

If there was anything worse in this world than monsters, I'd just become that.

I stumbled back toward the house. I was *so* tired, and if my regret didn't consume me, the power buzzing within my body would. I wondered if I just laid down if it would take me… turn me to dust and bring my pitiful existence to an end once and for all. The demon had made me powerful, and now I wasn't sure I wanted this power at all. It didn't matter what I could gain at the cost of what I'd already lost.

Emmett was waiting for me in the woods.

"It is done," I stated as I continued toward the house.

"Where's your sister?" Emmett asked.

"Still waiting. This is just one stage of many."

"W—what do we do?" Emmett stammered.

"Continue our work," I replied. "The demon gave me power, and I must learn how to use it to achieve our final goal. We have a cursed child awaiting us in Pinewood Manor. When it is time, we will finish the ritual, and I will have the power to get the job done. Clean this mess up. No one can know what happened here tonight."

"Very well," Emmett agreed. "But Clarice… what will we tell people?"

I hadn't thought that far ahead, and my voice came out hollow as I answered. "We tell them he died, because it's the truth. Allyn isn't with us anymore. He never was."

The phone rang after Emmett left, and I picked up. I lay in bed, but I didn't say a word as I brought the phone to my ear. I could hear the sounds of a running vehicle in the background.

"Hello, Clarice?" Faith's voice came over the line. "Are you there?"

"I'm here," I said in a distant tone.

"I called to tell you the deal with the Midnighters went well," my best friend said. "We were able to sell off enough potion to pay off a significant portion of Nadine's medical debt. I can't thank you, nor my mother, enough for your help in arranging these meetings."

I remained silent, because nothing she said seemed to hold any meaning.

"Clarice?" Faith prodded again. "Did I lose you again?"

"You're a good mom," I stated. My voice was so hollow, it didn't sound like my own.

Faith seemed stunned by my response. "Oh, uh, thank you."

"It's not a compliment," I said without any emotion. "It's a fact. You put your daughter above all else. You love her. I wonder what it's like to love a child like that. I named him after my father. In so many ways, I hated that man. I thought it'd make it easier to let him go. It didn't."

Panic entered Faith's tone. "Clarice, what happened?"

"You don't want to know."

"I do," she insisted. "That's what friends are for."

If I could tell anyone anything, it was Faith, but I'd kept so much from her for so long. She wouldn't understand.

It didn't seem to matter anymore. I'd done the unthinkable, and I deserved every ounce of retribution the most evil powers in the universe could rain down upon me.

"I traded my son for my sister," I admitted, though it barely felt like an admission at all. There was no weight lifted off my shoulders, no feeling of relief. Just remorse that would forever haunt me.

"I'm coming to Octavia Falls," Faith demanded.

"You can't come back," I reminded her. "You're cursed to never return."

"Then meet me on the outskirts of town, past the protection spell," Faith urged. "We need to get you help."

"Nobody can help me now." I was already in too deep.

"I'll go to the priestesses. Surely they can send someone—"

"No," I interrupted. "They're the ones who started this. If they learn what I've done, I'll be hanged."

"We won't let that happen."

Something within me broke, and I spat, "They hung Nicole! What makes you think they won't hang me, too?"

"So stop what you're doing," Faith begged.

She didn't know the half of it.

"I took a witch's vow," I told her.

"Witch's vows can be broken," she argued. "Clarice, tell me everything!"

"Why?" I snarled. "So you can turn me in to the priestesses?"

"So I can *help* you!"

"Nobody can help me, Faith, least of all you. You don't know what it's been like without her! You haven't been here! Nobody knows how I feel. I'm so fucking alone, and she's out there Goddess knows where, a fractured bit of a soul that's trying to find its way back home. I can't do this without her! You have a husband and a daughter, and you know *nothing* about what it's like to have *no one*."

My voice shuddered as I continued to rant. "I haven't seen you in years. You only call when you want help for your poor sick child. Forgive me if I can't find the fucks to give to continue helping you, because *nobody* has been here to help me. I have to keep going at it alone, because that's what I've done all these years. If I don't finish what I've started, then it's all for nothing—then I sold my son to a demon for *nothing*."

The silence that hung in the air was deafening.

"Clarice…" Faith started, but she was at a complete loss of words. She knew now what a horrible monster I'd become, and it was obvious that moment had changed everything she ever once thought of me. I heard her husband mumble something in the background.

"I keep making one mistake after another," I said. The damage was already done beyond repair. "I've told you too much. I'm sorry, Faith, but you can't stop me. I need to see this through."

"Please, Clarice—!"

Faith's words were cut short at the sound of screams.

Casting the curse was far too easy with the power that was now pulsing through my veins. It took a mere intention and the wave of my hand, and it was done. I cursed the brakes on their car to fail, and then hung up before they'd finished screaming.

Nobody would stop me, not even my best friend. I'd already sacrificed so much to get to this point, and if she had to go as well, then so be it. There was nothing I could do now that was worse than what I'd already done.

I cast another spell that would silence the couple from beyond, so they couldn't reveal what they'd learned from me. If anyone tried to bring them back through a séance, it wouldn't work. No one, Seer or otherwise, would be able to communicate with their spirits. It wasn't magic just any witch could cast, but the deal I'd made with the demon had made me more powerful than any witch ever before.

Now all I had to do was pick myself up, dust myself off, and finish what I started.

Demons were tricksters, and it became abundantly clear over the following weeks that I'd been sorely misled. The demon hadn't exactly *lied* about the power he'd given me, but he hadn't been clear, either. The power I'd felt that night quickly faded, and I found that I was unable to generate that kind of energy on my own. He *had* made me a vessel for unmatched magic, but I could merely manipulate it, not generate it as a true demigod could. I had little control of my newfound abilities, and learned quickly that while I could supply myself with power from other witches, stabilizing and directing that magic required skill beyond my comprehension. It was going to take time and practice to master such a gift.

It began with the crystals. It was easy to overpower other witches and steal their magic. Each time I did, I funneled that power into a crystal, where it would remain dormant until I learned to manipulate it properly. I started small. I practiced stealing a bit of magic here and there, and no one noticed. My crystal stores grew more and more abundant. It was obvious I was going to require a large collection of crystals to contain the power I was stealing. I kept my crystal stores hidden away in the tomb with my sister, until the room became so filled with quartz, amethyst, fluorite, and other minerals that it was covered in them. It had transformed from a tomb into a crystal cave. I figured that here, no one would find my collection.

Until somebody did.

I was performing a ritual in the tomb, trying to funnel Death magic from my crystal stores into my sister's body. Her fingers twitched, and I gave a laugh of delight as I saw the necromancer powers I was manipulating were working. I couldn't generate Death magic on my own, but I could take it from other witches, place it inside the crystals, and then use it for my own spellwork. The magic responded to my command, and I just needed to find the right spell to get it to work for my purposes. My sister's body rose from the cot, though her eyes stared ahead lifelessly.

I cried out in glee. Finally, we were getting somewhere.

A stick cracked near the doorway. "Is everything all right?" a gruff voice asked.

I whirled around to find an old man standing there with a cat at his feet. I recognized him from town. Henry Keller—or Old Man Keller, some called him. He was an old, retired man who volunteered at the Historical Society. Sometimes, he appeared for guest lectures at the college. He was a nice man. It was a shame what he'd just stumbled upon, really.

"You shouldn't be here!" I sneered. "This is private property!"

He gazed around at the crystals covering nearly every surface. Hesitantly, he took a step back. "Forgive me. I wandered off the Black Circle trail and got lost. I will be on my way."

It was evidenced in his eyes that he knew he stumbled upon something he shouldn't have. Surely he would go running to the priestesses to report what he'd seen here.

"I can't let you do that," I stated. He'd seen too much.

The old man spun around and took off through the woods. As if he could outrun me. My sister's body slumped to the cot as I abandoned my spell in pursuit of the man. His cat had scurried away through the trees, and I didn't know where it'd gone.

Didn't really matter—the cat wasn't the problem.

Old Man Keller was a Mentalist. I could feel that from dozens of yards away. He had telekinetic powers. Just one twist of my wrist, and I could easily draw his magic into me. He shot a terrified glance over his shoulder. He withdrew a wand from his coat and aimed it at me, but nothing came out. I'd already drained his power. At my command, a telekinetic spell burst out of me, and he tumbled to the ground. His head hit a rock, and the forest went silent.

This had gotten messy, and I didn't like making messes.

I hadn't touched him, and no one knew what power I possessed, so there was no way to trace his death back to me. I used the telekinesis I'd stolen to levitate his body back onto the Black Circle trail far away from my house. It was better to leave him there where others would find him, because a missing person would only launch an investigation. This way, the authorities would write it off as an accident, and they wouldn't go looking for a killer.

I couldn't be making silly mistakes like this. I had immense power, and I had to use it to my advantage.

I returned to the tomb and cast a strong protection spell around it. The ward would only let through those whom I wanted to be there. Then I placed a powerful spell over myself. I was so strong now, stronger than any witch I knew, that if anyone tried to sense my power, they'd feel nothing beyond my own Alchemy magic. My wards would keep them from sensing anything deeper, and it would work every time, because there wasn't a witch powerful enough to break through them.

I knelt down and pushed my sister's hair out of her eyes. "I won't make a mistake like that again. I've got it all under control. I promise."

And I did… I was in full control.

I took my research outside the coven with the Omnimotus Curse. I sold my services to a group of Elementai in California. Their tribe was in the midst of the war, and I knew the right group would be willing to work with me. The curse couldn't be used on other witches, and it was best to keep my research outside of Octavia Falls anyway so that my own people would remain unaffected. The last thing I needed was to draw any attention to what I was doing. We already had one cursed child in captivity, along with a dead witness. The priestesses would undoubtedly launch an investigation if strange things continued to happen. I had no such reservations about causing mayhem amongst another group of supernaturals.

The Omnimotus Curse was an ancient one used in times of war. It acted like a virus, traveling from one person to the next, though in the Elementai's case, I focused the curse on their Familiars. It infected one's magic until it became poisonous to the victim, resulting in death. Once a Familiar died, its bonded partner could no longer go on living, which made it the perfect spell for the Hawkei to get their hands on. Witches had used the Omnimotus Curse in ancient times to steal the magic of other supernaturals, and that's exactly what I needed to learn how to do, so I could figure out how to better control my powers. In exchange for the curse I cast, my contact funneled back information about how the spell interacted with the population.

I thought I understood the mechanics. Emmett and I, along with the witches we'd hired to assist with the spell, went through with the ritual. A young boy died.

The spell didn't take. I had all this power, but we hadn't timed the spell right.

Didn't matter. We could try again.

I continued my research with the Omnimotus Curse, but the Elementai learned how to reverse the effects of the magical virus before my research could be completed. I had no choice but to continue stealing magic from my own people, learning how to manipulate it to my will to complete the spell Emmett and I set out to perform all those months ago. I stole a bit of magic here and a bit more there. People knew *something* was up, but there was no way to know I was the one draining their powers.

Meanwhile, Nadine Evers had shown up in town, and I was completely thrown for a loop. I hadn't given any thought to what would happen to her after I cursed her parents. She was an adult now, so I figured she'd be off at some college this fall. I just never thought it'd be *my* college—the very school I ran.

I felt an obligation to take care of Nadine, because I was the reason she was here in the first place. The poor girl knew nothing about magic. Her mother had never told her. I figured if I took her under my wing and mentored her, then perhaps I could make up for cursing her parents. It was the least I could do, after all.

Nadine was persistent and headstrong, a bit like me, to be honest, but she didn't give me any trouble. There was one night I thought she and her friends *might* be on to something, but they suspected nothing.

I'd dug up the grave of a recently deceased woman—Emily, I think her name was. Didn't matter the name. I just needed a body to practice a spell on. I'd nearly damaged my sister's body with the failed ritual we performed, so Professor Carlisle and I agreed that we needed to *perfect* our rituals before performing them on Nicole. A fresh body was the best option, because I could disturb the earth without anyone noticing. We were trying all different kinds of spells, and we were getting so close.

I reanimated Emily's body through necromancy magic on Halloween, when the magic would be stronger. Then Nadine and her friends had *summoned her*. Why they had to summon her of all spirits, I didn't know. Her body was called toward their spell. I turned my back for *one second*, and she was gone. Then Nadine comes knocking at my door speaking of a zombie. I thought I'd exposed myself then and there, but I'd played my part of the headmistress so well they couldn't see the evil staring them in the face.

I'd told them I'd handle it, and I did just that. I ended the spell and put Emily back in her grave. Nadine and her friends wrote it off as a Halloween prank.

I didn't give Nadine much credit then, but as the months passed—along with another failed ritual and a second dead child—I realized I was sorely mistaken. I was powerful enough now to send my magic across a distance, so that I could stay at the school while my colleagues performed the ritual, giving myself a rock-hard alibi. But Nadine had quickly befriended another student, Lucas, who'd been investigating the missing children Professor Carlisle had taken. The two of them couldn't stop digging. It was difficult to get away with something so outright bold, but it was necessary, and I had the power to cover it up. The authorities hadn't been able to trace anything back to us, and so, I didn't think Nadine and Lucas could, either.

Then the two of them showed up at Pinewood Manor the night we were to perform the ritual a third time. We'd learned from the first two failed attempts, so we were confident we'd get it right this time. I'd been mostly hands-off on this one, as I'd hired Professor Carlisle and a group of witches to handle it all for me, but I would *not* let another trial go to waste. We'd already killed two kids trying to get this perfect, and the circumstances had to be just right.

I regretted blowing up the mansion that night, but when I saw Lucas and Nadine outside the manor when I arrived, I knew I had to cover my tracks. If they dug any further than they already had, I would be exposed. Professor Carlisle and the other witches were identified as the perpetrators of the crime, and I was heralded a hero for getting there just in time to call for help.

No one knew I had anything to do with it, or that I had any connection to our waning magic. My powers were growing, and with the destruction of my operation, I had become desperate. I was trying to do it all on my own now, and to do that, I needed more power than I had ever stolen before.

As my power grew, it became more and more unmanageable. Magic flooded into me at all times, and I had to constantly be funneling it into my crystal stores to keep it under control. I couldn't stop it now. The effects of my power became so apparent that the coven gave it a name—the Waning, they called it. Every bit of magic that a witch lost to the Waning was magic they lost to *me*.

Amongst the chaos came the unveiling of the truth of Nadine's powers. She was cunning like me, and she'd spent a semester convincing everyone she was an Alchemist. Even I had fallen for it. I hadn't thought to examine her magic with my own, because there was no reason to do so. It was clear that Nadine and Lucas were going to do whatever it took to bring the Waning to an end.

So I kept them close. Nadine's Curse Breaker powers were similar to the abilities I'd obtained from the demon, only I could handle more power than she could. I could manipulate and cast spells with the power I stole, whereas she couldn't. My issue was regulating how much magic I took at any given time. I'd been researching Curse Breaker powers for months now, trying to understand the mechanics of magical manipulation. I'd taken all the Curse Breaker books from the school library to pursue my research. Nadine nearly caught me, as she'd been looking for the books herself. At the time, I thought perhaps she was considering raising the dead, as I was. Couldn't put it past her, after what happened to her parents.

Once I found out what she was, I wanted to know more. I'd never had access to a Curse Breaker like I did now. I continued mentoring Nadine and pushing her to the limits of her power, on the off chance that her magic was enough to finally raise my sister. If nothing else, she could teach me how to master my own craft. All those lessons—pushing her with transference, and making her transfer necromancy power into a dead mouse—was all to learn more about her magic so I could use it for myself.

Nadine was in control of her magic, but I had completely lost control of my own. No matter how much I tried to contain it, my power continued to grow and become more unpredictable with time. I could no longer control whose magic I stole or how much. It no longer took any conscious effort. Magic simply flowed into me, and I drained witches to the point where they couldn't regain their magical stores for days on end. The coven looked for reasons their magic was disappearing, but so many people were pointing fingers that no matter where they searched, they couldn't trace it back to me. I continued my work, and the Waning grew worse at my hand.

Nadine had the power to sense magical signatures, but she couldn't feel my power past the spells I'd put in place to ward off witches like her. She'd almost seen it once, the night of the Burning. Things had gotten out of hand, and I was going to stop this horrible witch hunt the priestesses had started. I funneled the magic of other witches into me in an attempt to stop them. The magic was so strong that my chest began to glow. I could still recall the fear I felt when that happened, because I thought for certain someone would notice what was happening and I'd be identified as the culprit behind the Waning. The priestesses wouldn't hesitate to burn or hang me like the others. I heard Lucas call my name near the tree line that night. He wanted me to escape with him and his friends. I didn't turn in their direction.

I wanted to help—I really did. Even with the monster I'd become, there was a part of me that still cared. I didn't want the priestesses to do to others what they'd done to Nicole, and though I had hidden intentions of my own, I still wanted to stop them.

I'd gotten close to Nadine. She was the child I never got to have. Even though I wished to use her powers to my advantage, I never wished to hurt her in the process. There was no reason I couldn't raise my sister *and* a child. I was a powerful woman, and I could easily have it all—my sister, a daughter, and perhaps one day, even a lover.

Nadine trusted me when she told me of her pursuit of the Oaken Wands, and about the Nex demon lurking inside the school. There was no reason she shouldn't. If anyone wanted to keep the Oaken Wands out of the priestesses' hands, it was me. The closer I was to the Oaken Wands, the better, because they were the only items in the coven that I knew of that were stronger than me. In the hands of the wrong person, the Wands could expose me completely.

But in my hands? I could use them to stabilize my power and finally cast the spell that would bring my sister back. If Nadine and her friends wanted to risk their lives for these Wands, then I'd let them, if it meant I could get close enough to use the Wands for myself when the time was right. Then, after I raised my sister, they were free to use the Wands to end the Waning and drain me of my power. I wouldn't need it anymore once Nicole was with me again.

There were steps I had to take and strategies to consider. I couldn't control how much magic flooded into me these days, but I *could* direct it. I targeted my powers at the priestesses' supporters known as the Executors. I kept their magic drained as much as I could, in order to slow the priestesses down.

At other times, I had to thwart suspicion off myself. It was my understanding that Nadine and Lucas's operation called The Coven's Shield had taken a witches' vow, but that was before I discovered what they were doing. They trusted me so dearly that they didn't ask me to do the same, which worked out in my favor, because I certainly couldn't keep their vow. I could, however, get past the ward to their secret hideout, because I *did* intend to help them beat the priestesses, but at the same time, I had to take calculated measures to protect myself. When I joined their operation, I agreed to assist Nadine in searching for patterns within the Waning. I knew she'd look to fit the pieces together either way, and as long as I was watching her closely, I could divert her attention and lead her in a different direction.

I was having to do that more and more these days. When the demon known as Professor Leto showed up at the school, I could tell immediately that something was off about him, though I couldn't put my finger on it. His magic just wasn't the *same* as other coven members. Then I learned of what he was, and I knew if anyone was powerful enough to sense what was going on with me beneath the surface, he'd notice my magic went beyond this realm. He'd sense the demon magic in my blood sooner than anyone else, and so, I kept my distance. Making an enemy out of Professor Leto was not an option.

Time and time again, I had to twist the truth to keep anyone from suspecting me. I convinced Nadine to brew a potion with me to wipe out the priestesses' magic, because under normal circumstances I'd never be able to brew such a potion on my own. With Nadine's magic involved, it appeared legitimate. I changed the formula, though, and together, we brewed a poison that would kill the priestesses. It was necessary, after all the lives they took and the pain they caused.

But the priestesses suspected poison, and they forced Hector Lawson to taste-test the wine we'd planted. My poison killed him instantly.

I thought Nadine had caught me. Then she told me the priestesses suspected William Connor of planting the poison. He was our ally who'd placed the wine in the Imperium headquarters to begin with. I knew the second they confronted him, he would know the truth—that I had been the one to brew it.

I had to take him out before he could speak to the priestesses. Furthermore, I had to blame the poison on him, as Nadine wouldn't believe any other explanation. I went to his house that night, and he was dead from a broken neck before the priestesses even arrived. It looked like an accident, and even the priestesses couldn't cast a spell to reveal that I'd been there.

The more out of control my magic became, the more the lies grew. The night in the town square, when the coven had tied up Nadine, Lucas, and our ally Everly Hall to torture them, I had truly come to help. I brought the three of them back to my home, only to discover the next morning that Everly had been hit by a curse that was quickly spreading throughout her body.

Nobody else had access to their magic. At that point, my power was so out of control that I siphoned the powers of anyone who came near me. They still hadn't picked up on my connection to the Waning—it was centered around the school, where I spent most of my time, and always affected people after they'd spent time around me. Still, no one suspected a thing that night when I announced my magic was still working, and that I could brew an antidote to Everly's curse. I intended to help her, but then I discovered I was missing the proper ingredients.

My fingers curled around the edge of the counter. "Everything is out of control, Nicole," I whispered. I was so used to talking to her now. "I can't contain this power. You should be here right now, because you'd know how to help."

"Everything all right in here?" Lucas asked, startling me as he came into the kitchen. "I thought I heard you talking to someone."

"I—I'm out of scaleweed," I told him. "It's the main ingredient in the brew."

He shrugged. "So we'll get some more."

I forbade him to do that. It was time to leave Octavia Falls, and if any of us returned to town, there was no telling what the priestesses would do. Everly's life was of no consequence in comparison to Nadine's. I'd already killed so many people. I was willing to let Everly die to keep from exposing ourselves. I had to get Nadine out of town, and I couldn't do that if I had to go into town for supplies.

Then Lucas defied my orders and went into town anyway, where he was arrested by the Miriamic Police Department. Nadine followed after him, and she was locked up as well. I couldn't believe they'd be so stupid.

I'd retrieved the ingredients Lucas had stolen and returned home to brew the antidote... but while I'd been gone, Everly had been snooping around. She'd found Nicolas's journal, in which I'd taken notes and added entries about my research. Everly discovered I was trying to raise the dead and confronted me about it.

"This is dark magic," she accused. "You can't do this, Clarice!"

I gave a wry laugh. "I assure you I can."

I really didn't want to kill her, and I didn't have to. She was nearly gone anyway. The curse she'd been hit with in the town square had almost run its course. It would be only a couple more hours before it took her life, and I would let it, because as long as I didn't cast the spell myself, her death couldn't be blamed on me.

I'd miscalculated the timing, though. Nadine and Lucas were put on trial after their arrest, and when we returned to my house afterward, Everly was crawling across the floor, trying to call for help. She died in Nadine's arms, and nearly exposed me to Lucas with her last thought.

Don't trust anyone.

"Obviously we can't trust the coven," I said, because once again, I had to divert suspicion off myself, and someone else had to take the fall for this. It was all too easy to accept this was the coven's doing, as they had already intended to kill her that night in the town square.

The lies didn't end there. When Nadine and Lucas were brought to court, it was revealed that the *potens crepitus* spell was used to explode Pinewood Manor the night our ritual failed and my associates were killed. It was a powerful spell that historically could only be cast by multiple Cast members. I was so powerful at that point, and had access to magic from multiple Casts, that it wasn't difficult to perform the spell on my own. But no one could possibly know that. I carefully curated my questions and coached my witnesses to divert any suspicion away from myself, convincing the coven that the attack was the result of a fail-safe spell my employees had cast on their own.

All the lying was getting exhausting. It seemed that no matter what I did, cataclysm followed. The night following the court trial, the school was attacked by angry coven members. I tried to help by siphoning magic from the mob, to stop the assault, but I couldn't control the flow of magic. My choice to fight back triggered the Waning on the student populace, and I began siphoning power from within the school itself. I'd completely fucked up the space-bending spell that expanded the school on the inside, and the rooms began to fold in on one another. It only got worse the more I tried to fix it.

As I walked the school halls in search of a solution, I came upon Nadine and her friends, though I couldn't reach them. They appeared to be trapped inside a mirror, though from their perspective, I was the one who was trapped.

"The mirror itself may not even exist. We're simply communicating from two spaces at the same time," I determined. Space-bending magic was tricky that way.

"How do we fix it?" Nadine demanded.

I was horrified she would suggest such a thing, because if she tried to fight against my power, it could destabilize the spell completely, and the whole school would collapse in on itself.

"Nadine, I beg of you. Don't try to fix this. Fixing it will only make it worse!" I warned.

"Then what do we do!?" Nadine yelled.

"Get to a stable room and stay there," I instructed. "I'm working on finding us a way out."

The mirror shattered, and Nadine and her friends were lost from me.

There was nothing more I could do but let the space-bending spell die completely. Students would die, but I could no longer save them. I used what power I could to get myself out of the school.

I was relieved when I discovered that Nadine and her friends had found a way out as well. I got them to the safe house outside Octavia Falls like we planned, and thanked my lucky stars that they were still alive. Despite everything that had happened and all the lives that were lost, I still loved these people.

But I feared I was doing more harm than good. I agreed to visit the Midnighters over the summer, because I thought the vampires might have insight on resurrection that could further my research. I secretly returned to Octavia Falls often to check in on my sister and test rituals that I hadn't tried before. None of them worked.

I'd hoped to gain more insight into the location of the Mortana Wand on my travels, because if any of the Wands were going to prove useful to my mission, it was the one that could control Death magic. I wanted that Wand above all else, though I desired them all. The more Wands I had, the better I could control my power. I learned nothing of the Oaken Wands while I was gone.

I clearly hadn't learned much of anything at all, because the moment I returned, I was right back to telling lies and hiding secrets.

Nadine and Lucas gained a lead on the Oaken Wands in *Hok'evale*, and they requested my help in casting a spell to learn more. I had to decline, because my magic was so out of control that I knew it would only fuck up the spell. Then they'd start connecting the dots.

"I won't be of any help," I lied. "I had to use magic to cover my tracks when I went to meet up with Hattie earlier today, and I haven't been able to cast any spells since. I took every precaution to prevent being followed, and it drained my reserves."

We'd known for a while now that there were Oaken Wands in the Abyss, but I'd urged Nadine and Lucas to ignore the Abyss and pursue the Mortana Wand instead. When I learned that we might find a lead to the Wand I desired in hell, then I was more than willing to get on board with the plan.

It was during that spell—which they used to track down the reaper Edgar Nowak—that I learned Lucas had raised the dead once before. I watched the scene play out in the crystal ball, replaying the night of Nadine's Evoking Ceremony. Lucas had fought off a reaper that had already claimed Nadine's soul, and he'd brought her back to life. I realized I didn't just need the Oaken Wands. I needed a reaper like Lucas.

No one seemed to realize this was the first I was hearing of what happened that night with the reaper, as they all appeared to know already. I kept quiet, as to not give myself away. I had to be careful with my plans, because it was becoming increasingly more dangerous to return to Octavia Falls. I would wait for Lucas to obtain the Mortana Wand. I hoped that by the time we defeated the priestesses, I could convince him to raise my sister by his own volition.

I'd slipped under the radar so long, I didn't think anyone would notice.

But Nadine's grandmother did. The more time I spent with Helena, the more wary she became around me. Helena never said it, but I could see it in her eyes that she was starting to worry. I didn't think she *suspected* me of anything just yet, but it was only a matter of time before she'd put the pieces together.

It killed me to get rid of her, because she'd been like a mother to me all these years. I loved Helena, but I loved my sister more.

I was the one to send Helena outside the boundaries of the safe house's ward. I hadn't cast the spell that killed her, but I'd convinced her to walk into danger, and she had died just as I intended.

She didn't know what I'd done, for I had been so cunning that even she hadn't caught on. I didn't think she was even aware yet of what was amiss with me, just that something was off. Even if she came back in a séance, she didn't know enough to tell anyone anything. I was almost certain she'd already spoken to Nadine about it, though they'd written it off as something else. I intended to keep it that way.

I'd said all those nice things about Helena at her funeral to gain more of Nadine's trust. Most of it was true. The bit about Helena standing next to me while I gave Nicole's eulogy was nothing more than a bold-faced lie, seeing as Nicole never got a funeral. I didn't even know why I said it. I supposed I was so used to telling lies now that it was second nature. It made Nadine cry, so I guess it worked.

As long as no one extracted the information from my mind, I could keep up this ruse, and no one would be the wiser.

Chloe and Talia developed a technique called teleinsight, but I had already prepared for this. The Midnighters worked in mind manipulation, and I had spent months learning from them how to ward my mind so I would remain undiscovered. I let Chloe and Talia try to read my mind, in order to convince them I had nothing to hide. But I didn't let them see anything. I convinced them it was all for their benefit, and that I could teach them the same technique.

I let Nadine and her friends hold on to the Oaken Wands while I bided my time for the Mortana Wand, when I could use the Wands and a reaper to raise my sister... until time ran out too soon. Lucas obtained the Mortana Wand from the Reaper Order, but we didn't get a chance to return to Octavia Falls before the priestesses kidnapped Marcus. By the end of that night, the Oaken Wands were cursed, and their powers were useless.

I was powerful, but I couldn't control it well enough to combat the power of the Master Wand. Once again, I had to wait until Nadine found the Curse Breaker Wand to restore the power of the Oaken Wands I'd waited so long for.

My plans kept falling apart, and like my magic, it felt as if I was constantly forcing shattered pieces back together. I tried my best not to take powers from Lucas, even though there were times I couldn't control it. His powers had to be ready when I needed him.

When the priestesses arrived in Octavia Falls with their golem army and Lucas revealed they'd found the Curse Breaker Wand, I panicked. I hadn't anticipated how quickly everything would move once the final Wand was located. I worried that together, the Oaken Wands would be strong enough to steal my power, so I had to use everything I had to raise my sister that night before Nadine could end the Waning.

I told Jonathan I was going to help across town, but in truth, I returned to my sister's tomb. I used everything I had—all my research and all my power—in a desperate attempt to bring her back with one final spell. It would be stronger than anything I'd ever done before, because *I* was stronger than ever before.

Then I felt the Oaken Wands opposing my power. Nadine was already trying to cast the spell to end the Waning. I couldn't let them do that, because without this power, bringing my sister back to life was hopeless. While Nadine and her friends cast their spell to end the Waning, I was fighting against them.

And I won. It was simple.

The Oaken Wands couldn't overpower me, because I had overpowered them first. Nadine assumed they were useless now, but in reality, they were just as strong as always… I just happened to be taking all the power of the coven before the Wands could cast the spell. The coven's magic was mine now…

And it still wasn't enough.

Nadine and her friends planned on leaving town, but I couldn't let them take the Oaken Wands with them. If my power alone wasn't enough to bring my sister back, then I needed the Oaken Wands to do it. I was the most powerful witch that ever lived, and the Oaken Wands were our strongest relics. The Scelus demon had promised that if I used my power properly, I could achieve my desires. This *had* to be the answer, because there was no more powerful witch magic than the Oaken Wands in the hands of the strongest witch in history. When used together, the Oaken Wands could stabilize the coven's power, and it was exactly what I needed.

I really didn't want Nadine getting involved, so I waited until her back was turned. Then I stole the Oaken Wands, along with the reaper who would make all the difference.

I prayed that was the last deception I had to make. Years of pursuing my sister's revival had really weighed me down, and I was ready for it all to be over. I was sick of fighting the priestesses and trying to keep power from their hands. I was done with the heartache that came with deceiving the ones I loved dearly. I didn't *enjoy* killing people to keep my secrets.

So many people had died at my hands—Faith and her husband, Henry Keller, Hector Lawson, William Connor, Everly Hall, Helena, and so many unnamed faces. Hell, I'd even given up my own son.

And I just... let it happen. The coven had broken me, but they couldn't stop me. It was as my sister's prophecy foretold, and the priestesses refused to listen.

They should have heeded her warning. The witch's fate my sister spoke of had been her own, for her death had marked the beginning of the end.

And now, the end had finally come.

TWENTY-TWO

I staggered back into the wall of the cave as the vision ended. I'd come in here with no magic or defenses, because I thought I could talk Verla down. I'd told the others to stay outside because I figured she would listen to me. If I couldn't fight with magic, I had to turn to the power of my words. The headmistress I knew would never use dark magic, but I realized now that she wasn't the headmistress I knew. She never had been, because that woman didn't exist. It'd all been a *lie*.

Horror shuddered through my whole body, and I had to press my palms against the rock to keep from falling over. I stared incredulously at Verla, and that darkness she'd succumbed to became apparent. I didn't recognize her anymore. She'd masked it so well, but now that the mask had come off, I could never look at her the same.

Grammy had told me a light had left Verla's eyes. I thought it'd been a shadow of grief. I never imagined it to be the complete and all-consuming darkness of wickedness.

"You… killed my parents?" I stammered breathlessly. I didn't want to believe it. Their death had been an accident. My mother's best friend would never…

But she had. All this time, my parents had been murdered. Of all the evidence that pointed to her as the culprit of these deplorable acts, that was one I couldn't quite wrap my head around.

"I had hoped you'd never learn the truth," Verla said softly, as if I might still forgive her.

She took a step forward, but I backed further away. My feet knocked over crystals, which clinked together and scattered across the ground.

"Stay the fuck away from me!" I cried. I'd never been more repulsed by anything in my life, and I'd seen torture in hell. "I should've figured it out. You weren't at my mom's funeral. The first time I met you was the day I moved into the dorms. If you and my mom were *such* close friends, why weren't you there? I always figured you were so busy being headmistress that you couldn't make it, but you didn't come because you couldn't handle the guilt!"

"You of all people should understand," Verla said. "We're not so different. We've both lost so much."

"We are *nothing* alike," I sneered. This woman I once so highly revered morphed into the most horrifying of monsters in an instant. I couldn't relate to her at all, and I despised every second I'd ever spent in her presence.

I shot a wary gaze across the cave toward my husband. He was crouched down with the Oaken Wands in hand, slowly inching his way toward our son. Lucas gave me a subtle nod, and I read the message in his eyes. *Keep Verla talking.*

Not hard to do, considering all the horrific things I wanted to say to her.

I eyed Verla up and down in disgust. "Do you know what my mom's last thought was? *The coven's in danger. Stay safe, Nadine. I love you.* She *knew* you were going to destroy it, and she tried to warn me. The danger she spoke of was *you* this whole time. Isa should've warned me, and you know what? I think she tried. She never liked being around you."

"Even if she disliked me, she wouldn't remember what I told her," Verla said. "Don't act like you wouldn't have done the same. You've killed people, too."

"To *save* innocent lives!" I countered.

"My sister was innocent, and the priestesses slaughtered her!" Verla shouted.

"So take this up with *them*," I snarled. "You didn't have to involve innocent people."

"There *are* no innocent people! Not in this!" Verla screamed. "I was *relying* on my community to stand up for Nicole, and to save her, and you know what they did? They all *stayed silent.* They allowed the priestesses to do as they wished, as they've always done! You've seen them do it, Nadine, time and again, and by hell you keep holding on to this childish fantasy that people can *do good* and *be better.* Grow up and realize the reality of who you're surrounded by. The coven will keep allowing people in power to do whatever they wish, and no one has the stomach to try and reverse it. No one except me."

"We can still fix this. There can be another way!" I demanded.

"Why should I care what happens to this goddess-forsaken coven? It never cared what happened to me!" Verla hissed. "This town is full of selfish people who only care about themselves, so why can't I do the same?"

"You're right. The coven should've spoken up on Nicole's behalf," I spat back. "That doesn't mean you have any excuse to kill whoever you wish on this sick crusade to bring your sister back!"

I stole another glance at Lucas. He'd picked Marcus up and cradled him to his chest. Our son hadn't made a sound. Lucas reached for a pile of crystals that were still intact. If he got his hands on them while I had Verla distracted, he might be able to use the power within them to cast a spell.

He glanced quickly toward the cave entrance, and I knew he wanted me to distract her long enough to get Marcus out of here. We'd called Professor Wykoff, along with Professor Warren and Miles, after I astral traveled to Lucas and found out where Verla had taken him. They should all be on their way. Then Professor Wykoff could take Marcus far away from here while we dealt with Verla. I'd never let her lay a hand on him.

"The priestesses wanted people to listen, but they wouldn't listen to Nicole," Verla sneered. "You think they would listen to *me?*"

My breath shuddered as I took another step away from her. "I thought the priestesses were bad, but you're so much worse. You got Grammy killed!"

"I wasn't the one who killed her," Verla defended. "I merely convinced her to walk into danger, but it was the Executors who took her life."

"You're deplorable!" I spat. "You didn't kill Grammy by your own hand, but you intended for her to die, and you killed so many other innocent people. How could you give up your own child?"

Professor Daniels told us in Demonology that it was possible to make a demon deal to acquire more magic, but that it would require the exchange of a soul. I never imagined anyone would actually do it.

"Like your parents, sacrifices had to be made." Verla stated it so coolly that it chilled me to the bone. She'd become so detached that she honestly believed she was justified in what she'd done. I understood the detachment grief could cause, and I'd learned that morality wasn't clear-cut, but Verla had taken it so far that I could no longer comprehend her decisions.

I stepped to the side again, luring Verla's attention away from the cave entrance. "It all makes sense now. The Protection Tree was suffering, but it didn't start this. You did. We should've known. The coven divided before, and the Waning never happened during any other divide in history, so it couldn't have been the tree's fault. The tree was dying because it needs magic to live, and the Waning is what killed it, not the other way around."

"Of course it was," Verla replied. "You had so much faith in me that you were willing to accept only the answers you wanted to hear."

"You're right," I said. "I should've connected the dots sooner, and that was a great mistake. The priestesses and I performed a spell to identify the type of magic causing the Waning, and we determined it was demonic. I'd written it off as witch magic, because demon blood runs through our veins. But all this time, that spell was pointing us to the demon deal *you* made."

"You only see the best in people, Nadine," Verla accused. "That's one of your greatest strengths, but it is also your greatest downfall."

I chose to ignore that, because she was clearly trying to manipulate me. "Professor Warren said the explosion at the school the night of the Golem War was more than the potions had in them. It was you who created that explosion against the golems, not the potion stores."

"Yes, I still wanted to protect you, as I always have," Verla promised. "I really was on your side this whole time, and I was honest about my role in The Coven's Shield. I didn't want the priestesses to find the Oaken Wands, because they could use them against me and stop what I'm doing here. But you won't stop me, will you, Nadine? You'll help me."

I was appalled by the suggestion. "Why on earth would you ever think I'd help you?"

"Because I can't do this on my own," Verla said desperately.

Lucas ducked out of the cave entrance with Marcus in his arms. It didn't make me any less scared of Headmistress Verla, but it gave me relief knowing my son wasn't near her anymore.

"I've tried everything, and each of my spells failed," she continued. "If you and your friends help me raise my sister, this can all be over. You can have your magic back, and the Waning will end. Nicole and I will leave town, and you will never hear from us again. Isn't that what you want… to have your powers back, so you can save everyone?"

If only I'd been able to save everyone. Then people like Dean, Grammy, and my parents would still be with us.

Something hit me then, something so appalling I thought it might break me. My voice shook. "The Waning took so many lives. The night of my baby shower when Magnus poisoned me, I tried to use my powers to stop it, but I couldn't, because I was powerless to the Waning. My baby boy was *poisoned,* and I could've reversed that with my powers, but I couldn't because of *you.* It's *your* fault Dean is dead!"

"It was all for the greater good," Verla replied—like I should understand it. "I had to kill my baby, and yours had to be sacrificed. These children never had a chance to live anyway, so they don't know what they're missing. Dean had to die so Marcus could live, so if you think about it, I actually saved Marcus."

"Don't you dare make assumptions like that!" I yelled. "You could've helped undo the poison, and you chose not to. Both of my children could've lived!"

Verla frowned. "It appears I'm not the only one making assumptions."

I recalled something else then, which only made the fury raging within me burn hotter. "The night I gave birth, you told me that some of us have to die so others get to live. You were trying to comfort me, but in reality you were comparing my baby's death to killing your own child. You're disgusting! Losing Dean wasn't a choice I made, but you chose to give up Allyn."

"To save my sister!" Verla screamed.

"From what?" I demanded. "For all you know, you're trying to uproot Nicole from a beautiful life in Alora. You aren't trying to save Nicole from anything. You're trying to save *yourself,* and I'm sorry to say it, Verla, but you're too far gone."

"The coven executed her!" she roared. "They rejected her! You think they'd accept her in Alora?"

"Witches aren't made to bring spirits back from the dead, because to do so would defy the very nature of death," I insisted. "We had to learn that when we gave up our son. Death is a part of the journey. Bringing your sister back is only bringing back the past, and you need to let her move on, just as you need to continue without her."

"That's bullshit, Nadine, and you know it," Verla snapped. "Lucas brought you back from death. You two think you're so special that you're the exception. If he can still have you, then I can still have her."

"That was under extraordinary circumstances that didn't threaten innocent lives or all of witch magic. I hadn't crossed over yet, but your sister has been gone for years."

Verla pursed her lips, like she was frustrated I didn't get it. "It doesn't matter the time that has passed. The rift in our soul is as fresh as it ever was. I was going to raise my sister, then you were supposed to come in and undo the damage with the Oaken Wands. The Waning was never meant to be permanent!"

I was repulsed. "You thought I'd just come in and clean up your mess so you didn't have to take responsibility?"

"I knew you were destined to change things—it's as your prophecy said. I'm not the one who hung all those people! I didn't mean to hurt anyone."

"You caused the Waning, which was the catalyst for the divide," I accused. "You could've ended the witch hunts at any time. You've had magic all along, *and* my grandfather's journal that could've led us to the Oaken Wands sooner. You could've helped us!"

"And given myself away?" Verla demanded. "Nicholas's entries were nonsensical and of no use to you. If you'd have seen the journal, you'd know what I was up to. I couldn't let you end this before I finished what I started."

"You don't have to finish this just because you started it. It's okay to change your mind when you learn the thing you committed to his harming you."

"The only thing that's harming me is being apart from her this long," Verla seethed. "You want to save everyone, Nadine? Save me. Help me bring her back!"

I shook my head. "The blessing you gave on my wedding day was one of courage. I am courageous, and that means standing up for what's right. If we do this, there's no telling what the consequences might be. So no, I'm not going to help you. You can't steal our powers forever. One day, you will die, and your spells will be gone with you. If you have to kill me now so that future generations of witches can live on, then I guess you're going to have to kill me."

I trembled from head to toe, terrified she'd actually do it. She had the power to end me in a second, and I'd just given up the only thing still keeping me alive—keeping us *all* alive. But as much as death scared me, I knew there was peace in it, too. If this was where our journey on Earth ended, then it was also where our adventure in the afterlife began. And perhaps it was a beautiful thing to do it together.

"You don't really want that, Nadine," Verla accused.

Tears beaded in my eyes. "No, I don't. I'd like to stay to watch my son grow up. All the time I expected to have with him, to be his mother, would be lost. Everything Lucas and I dreamed of… gone. But we were never promised any of it in the first place, so maybe in the afterlife we can build something new."

Verla shook her head, looking terrified at the thought of me so easily accepting my own death. As worry fell over her features, I caught sight of the woman I once loved so dearly. Though the mask had come off, there were still parts of her I recognized buried deep beneath the shadows. Verla had chosen some dark, wicked paths I would never go down, but there was still a glimmer of affection in her eyes. She was afraid for me, and I believed her when she said she didn't want to hurt me.

"You don't know where you'll end up," Verla said wistfully. "Alora isn't promised. You could end up in the Abyss, or another realm entirely."

A tear streaked my cheek, and my voice broke. "Are you sure you want to be the one to send me there? You haven't killed me yet, so there must be a reason you're hesitating. In your vision, I saw that you warded this tomb to keep out people you didn't want here, but I got through. You wanted me to come here. You wanted me to stop you. So Verla… please stop."

"I can't." Her bottom lip trembled, and I despised admitting that I felt a twinge of sympathy for her. She didn't appear as an evil villain who'd descended into madness. She seemed more like someone whose grief had consumed her to the point where she was desperately trying to claw her way back to herself. I didn't agree with the means she'd done it, and I'd never forgive her for killing my parents and selling her son to a demon...

But I could see her for what she was, which was a scared, grieving woman who'd given up hope long ago.

"You *can* stop," I pressed. "Doing so is a choice, and I know there must be a part of you that doesn't want to do this anymore, or you would've killed me by now."

Verla hesitated. Then her gaze traveled over to her sister on the cot, and a dark shadow fell over her features. "I have no choice but to finish this, and if you're going to continue to stand in my way, then you can have the death you so desire."

She lifted her hand, and I closed my eyes and lifted my chin as I accepted my end.

"If you won't listen to her, then perhaps you'll listen to me," a deep voice said.

The blow I expected never came. I opened my eyes to find Professor Warren had squeezed through the cave opening and planted himself between Verla and me. If he was able to get through her wards, that meant she wanted *him* here, too.

A glowing death spell died on Verla's fingers. She had completely frozen, and I witnessed a spark of adoration in her eyes when her gaze landed on Professor Warren. She loved me as a child, but she cherished Professor Jonathan Warren as a beloved partner. I recalled what she'd revealed to us in her vision.

I was in love with Jonathan Warren. That was more terrifying than any dark road I could go down, because I knew if I let myself love him hard enough, he just might fix me.

She wanted me here, but I wasn't the one who could stop her. Only the man she loved could do that.

"Clarice," Professor Warren said softly.

I couldn't believe I hadn't seen it before. It was obvious in the way he said her name that was completely infatuated with her. The way she returned his gaze with regret in her eyes told me she loved him dearly.

"What are you doing here, Jonathan?" Verla demanded in a shaky tone.

"I know about Allyn," he said sadly.

Slowly, Verla turned her gaze to her raised hand. She seemed to realize for the first time what she was about to do. Her fingers trembled as she dropped her hand to her side. A sob broke from her chest, and that cold, harsh woman who'd done all those terrible things crumbled before my eyes. "I—I couldn't tell you."

Professor Warren remained surprisingly calm. "I know you couldn't. You tried so hard to bring your sister back, but that's never what you really wanted in the first place, was it? You just wanted to feel whole again."

"She deserved a better life, Jonathan," Verla whispered sadly.

"Of course she did." Professor Warren reached out and took Verla's hands in his. "But *you* deserve better, too. I know what it's like to self-sabotage, to hurt yourself over and over again, but it doesn't have to be this way. You have a chance now to make a different choice, and I know that if you're strong enough to do all *this*, then you're strong enough to reverse it. I can't stand to watch you get hurt, Clarice."

Verla sagged into his arms. "You're right, Jonathan. I said I'd do anything to bring her back, but I've tried *everything*. It's tearing me apart, and I no longer recognize who I've become. I don't know anymore if I can do it… and even if I can, I don't know if I want to keep trying."

"You don't have to," Professor Warren promised. "You've said no to things you deeply love before. You can say no again."

"I did love you," Verla sobbed. "I never should've let you go."

Professor Warren stroked her hair. "I'm here now."

"I hate what I've become," she admitted. Verla stumbled back, curling her lips back in disgust as she stared down at herself. "I don't want this power. Take it, before I destroy everything! Take it from me, please, because I can't stop myself!"

"Lucas, now!" I shouted through the cave opening. He had the Oaken Wands, along with crystals to spark his power. Verla was at her most vulnerable, and if there ever was a time we could overpower her, it was this moment.

All around us, crystals glowed a brilliant array of rainbow colors as the power within them ignited. The colors shimmered and danced off the stone ceiling. It was immensely beautiful and profound. Verla's knees buckled, and she sank to the ground weakly. Her features paled as her power drained out of her.

My friends had done it—they'd overpowered Verla with the Wands.

Outside the cave, something shattered like glass. It had to be Verla's ward.

"Go!" Lucas shouted. "Take Marcus far away from here."

"I will," I heard Professor Wykoff reply.

My friends came rushing into the cave one by one, their Wands raised and pointed at Verla. Miles aimed his pistol at her. Our cats scurried in and hissed at her.

Lucas shoved the Curse Breaker Wand into my hand. "Together!" he shouted.

I didn't understand what he meant. They'd already drained her power—I could see that clear as day. Verla tried to push herself upright, but her arms shook so feebly that she couldn't quite sit up.

Grant and Talia shared a worried look.

"It's not working!" Chloe shouted.

The smell of chamomile and peppermint filled the air. I didn't know where it'd come from, but it made the hairs on the back of my neck stand straight up.

A low, wicked laugh came from behind us, sending my heart plummeting to my toes. Slowly, we turned in unison to see the pale, eerie corpse of Nicole Verla rising from her cot. Her old, tattered nightgown hung from her creepy form.

"Nicole," Verla breathed in disbelief. "The spell worked."

I couldn't believe my eyes. I'd entered the crystal cave while Verla was forcing Lucas to perform her spell with her. I thought I'd distracted her and stopped it, but it was clear now that the spell had finished when I arrived. It'd taken time for Nicole's body to wake, but Verla's final attempt at a revival spell had been successful.

Nicole tilted her head as a sinister smirk crossed her face. "Finally. I was starting to doubt you'd actually pull it off, Clarice."

"I said I'd do whatever it takes," Verla told her desperately. "The Oaken Wands have taken my power, but now that you're back, we can leave the coven together!"

"Oh, honey," Nicole taunted with an evil laugh. "The thing about twin flames is that we share a soul connection... and that connection is *incredibly* powerful. While you were plotting to bring me back all these years, I was planning my own revenge. *They* didn't steal your magic—*I* did. The demon deal you made and the power you amassed flows through our soul, which means now that I'm back, this magic is mine as much as yours. I'm going to use the power of the coven to make them pay for what they did to me. And I'm going to force you all to watch as I finally bring the Miriamic Coven to its miserable end."

LUCAS
TWENTY-THREE

Bang! Bang!

The sound of Miles's gun rang through the cavern. We all panicked at the sight of Nicole's corpse rising from the dead. I grabbed Nadine and yanked her to the farthest corner of the cave. Grant threw himself in front of Talia, and Chloe took a cautious step back. Verla clung to Professor Warren.

Miles pulled the trigger again and again, emptying the magazine into Nicole's chest. Bullet wounds opened in her skin, but they didn't bleed.

Nicole gave an evil laugh as she stepped forward. The wounds healed before our eyes. "You think your little pistol is going to stop me? Clarice didn't know how to control her powers, so allow me to show you what witch magic is capable of."

Nicole lifted her hands. In an instant, a portal opened beneath our feet. My heart lurched as we tumbled through it. Nadine's shocked scream followed behind me, and our cats screeched as they too were sucked through the portal.

My feet landed on solid ground, and I stumbled forward to catch myself with my hands, still clutching the Mortana Wand. My friends landed beside me, but the screams didn't stop. Shocked cries came from all angles. There were so many of them that I couldn't identify who they belonged to.

I lifted my head to see where Nicole had taken us. The air was cold, and stars dotted the night sky above us. Brick buildings surrounded us on all sides, and a fountain flowed in the area between them. Nicole had portaled us to the center of Octavia Falls—straight to the town square.

Ours wasn't the only portal she commanded. Hundreds of other portals had opened up, and coven members tumbled through them. As soon as one portal closed, two more opened to bring more members of the coven to the town square. Within moments, the square was crowded with thousands of people who looked around in confusion.

"What's going on here!?" townspeople demanded.

I glanced around the crowd frantically, but my friends—along with Verla and her sister—had disappeared into the sea of people. I didn't see Professor Warren anywhere. Chaos erupted around us as people screamed for their loved ones. I shoved my way through the crowd, until my eyes landed upon Nadine, who was being dragged back by a disorderly crowd.

"Lucas!" she cried.

"I'm here!" I yelled back. I desperately reached out, and Nadine's fingers found mine. I shoved past a few more people until I curled Nadine in my arms. Her racing heartbeat pounded against my skin in sync with my own.

"I don't see Nicole or Verla anywhere!" Nadine panicked.

"Over here!" Grant's voice carried over the crowd. I turned to see him standing on the edge of the fountain and waving his arm above the townspeople's heads.

Nadine and I pushed through the crowd until we reached the fountain. Talia had climbed onto the concrete ledge beside him and was searching the square for the others. She must've spotted them, because she whistled loudly to get their attention. Miles and Chloe saw her and shoved past people to get to us.

Only when they found us, they'd brought others I never expected to see again—a woman with black hair and porcelain skin; a goth girl with purple hair; a young woman dressed in all black who looked strikingly similar to Talia; and a girl with sleek dark hair and bracelets all over her wrists.

"Monica, Onyx, Tate, Mandy..." I said their names out loud, but it still didn't seem real that they were here. Monica hadn't been seen in Octavia Falls since we faked her death and sent her to *Hok'evale*. Tate and

Mandy had moved there last year, too, and Onyx had been in Paris for weeks.

A woman's terrified scream tore through the night. I turned to see Meredith standing a few feet away from us. Her features had gone stark white as she stared at Monica, who she believed to be dead. Meredith had been less than kind at her sister's funeral, as she believed the lies the priestesses told claiming Monica had been behind the Hearse crash.

"You… you're dead," Meredith stammered. "I put you in the ground!"

Monica's features softened when she looked at her sister. "I'm here in the flesh. There's much to explain, but I assure you I never died. I've only been in hiding."

"You caused The Hearse Tragedy!" Meredith sneered.

"I didn't, and I can explain that," Monica started.

She stepped toward her sister, but Meredith scurried backward, knocking into a few other people. "Stay away from me!"

Then she whirled around and shoved through the crowd. Monica's features fell in complete disheartenment.

"A lot has happened since you left," I told her. She hadn't been awake to hear the awful things her sister said about her at her funeral, and I hoped she'd never know.

Onyx shot a worried glance around the crowd. "What's happening? One second I'm sleeping in my bed, then I feel myself falling through a portal."

"Same," Mandy said. "Tate and I were out to dinner, and then we were suddenly here."

Tate placed a hand on her hip. "Lani's not going to be happy if we dine and ditch."

"Last I heard, the Miriamic Conflict was over," Monica added. "The priestesses were killed, and our magic faded completely. The Miriamic Coven no longer exists, so how is it possible that we're all here?"

"Because your magic never died," Nadine explained quickly. "It was stolen."

"By Headmistress Verla," Talia sneered.

"Except her sister has all the power now," Chloe added. "She's the one who brought you all here."

Monica's eyebrows pinched together. "That's impossible. Clarice's sister is dead."

Grant laughed uncomfortably. "Not anymore, she's not."

"More like… undead," Miles said. "She brought everyone back to show off her power, so she can destroy us all."

Onyx turned to Nadine and me. "How do we stop her?"

I gazed down at the Mortana Wand in my hand. "I wish I knew. We have the Oaken Wands, but they're failing to respond to us. Nicole is too powerful. She's taking all the coven's power before we can access it."

"There's got to be a way to take it back," Monica insisted.

Cats screeched as they skittered through the chaotic crowd. Our cats found us, and Isa jumped onto the fountain's edge to let out a loud cry of distress. We followed her gaze to see Nicole raising her arms to levitate herself above the crowd so that everyone in the square could see her. She hovered high above the townspeople's heads.

"Welcome back to the Miriamic Coven!" Nicole boomed. She must've been using a spell to project her voice across the crowd. People turned to look at her, and their shouts turned to confused whispers.

"It's Clarice Verla!" someone called. "She'll save us!"

Nicole gave a chilling laugh and tossed her hair over her shoulder. "Do I look that alive? I'm flattered. Unfortunately, my sister will not be the one to save you all, as she's the one who damned your coven to this pitiful existence."

The whispers grew louder.

It's Nicole.

What's she talking about?

I thought Clarice's sister was dead.

"I brought you all back to witness the final downfall of this coven," Nicole announced. "I warned you all of what would happen, but you didn't listen. Now, you have no choice but to hear me."

Nadine grabbed my hand, then lowered her voice to whisper to our friends. "I know the Wands aren't responding to us, but we have to try overpowering her. It's our only chance."

Talia tore her frightened gaze off Nicole. "Agreed. If *she* can over-power *us*, we can claim that power back."

"Let's do this," Grant said.

Chloe nodded firmly. "We're not going down without a fight."

The five of us joined hands, clutching the Oaken Wands between our entwined fingers. I dug deep inside myself for the magical spark I knew had to be there. It seemed impossible to find, but in our most desperate moment, we *had* to.

"The night I was murdered, I spoke of the witch's fate—*my* fate," Nicole spat. "The moment you killed me marked the beginning of the end for you all. I was trying to tell you the way things would go, but you didn't listen, so now I have to make you pay."

I found no traces of magic within myself, but I'd be damned if I didn't keep on trying.

"Nicole!" A woman shouted her name. The crowd parted to reveal Clarice Verla staring up at her sister with tears in her eyes. "You don't have to do this! This isn't why I brought you back. We can be together again, but we don't have to hurt these people to do it."

Nicole scoffed. "My death changed you, Clarice, but it changed me, too. I'm not the same person I was before I died. Look at what the coven did to me."

"They were wrong to kill you," Verla agreed. "But you're back now. Remember what you said the night you were hanged? *I won't go alone.* And you won't, Nicole. I'm right here with you. So let's go far away from here… together."

Nicole gave a wicked cackle. "You thought I was telling you to come after me, but I was warning the coven that one day I'd get my revenge and take this coven down with me."

"I did this all for *you!*" Verla insisted. "So that we could be together again. If this is what you truly desire, then all my effort was in vain."

"*You* didn't do this for me," Nicole spat. "You did this because I orchestrated it. Our souls are entwined, even across realms, and it was *I* who placed these ideas into your mind. When I found myself in the Abyss, I devised a plan with a Scelus demon—the very one you summoned and sold your son's soul to. I couldn't birth a child and make a deal with a demon, but *you* could."

Gasps traveled around the crowd.

"I've got nothing," Chloe hissed.

"Keep going," Nadine pressed. "It's our only shot."

"You won't get away with this!" a man yelled. I tore my attention from the Oaken Wands for a brief moment to see Lincoln pushing through the crowd. He shoved his way to the front with his back to us. I noticed he held a large stone in his hand that he'd picked up from the ground. He aimed it at Nicole, and he was a pretty damn good shot, too. The stone smashed against her head, snapping her neck to the side.

Slowly, Nicole twisted her head back in his direction, her bones giving a sickly crack as they popped back into place. "You think that's going to stop me? I have all witch magic, and all you have is little stones."

"Stonings have stopped people before, and we can stop you now!" Lincoln seethed.

All around the crowd, people gathered stones and threw them at Nicole. They rained down from all directions. She merely lifted her arms, appearing to welcome them like raindrops. They didn't seem to hurt her at all.

"That's only going to piss her off!" Chloe protested, but coven members continued to throw stones in self-defense.

"You merely continue to prove my point!" Nicole sneered.

She flicked her fingers, and Lincoln's neck snapped in an instant. My stomach lurched as I witnessed his head twist completely around, his lifeless eyes staring past us. His body slumped to the ground. People scurried away from Nicole in fear, dropping their stones at their feet.

"The coven will never change," Nicole hissed. "You'll always be the same hateful, fearful parasites you were when you killed me."

"Nadine," Chloe urged. "We need to try something else."

"We *have* nothing else." Nadine's hand shook in mine as she kept her gaze hopelessly locked on Nicole. I could see it in her eyes that she was racking her brain for solutions, but we were all out of ideas. Nicole was too powerful.

Nicole turned to her sister, looking annoyed that she'd been interrupted. "You did well bringing me back and supplying me with all this power. Now that it's done, I suggest you stay out of my way before I kill you."

Verla staggered back. "How can you be so cruel after all I've done for you? We're *sisters*! Nothing has ever meant more to us!"

"That changed the night I died," Nicole said. "You tried to stop me from destroying the Protection Tree."

"You weren't in your right mind," Verla insisted. "I was trying to save you from the priestesses."

"*I* was trying to save *you*!" Nicole screamed. "But the coven proved that night that their religion is more important than their people. You all thought I was crazy, but I knew what was coming. You were so concerned about this sanctified object that you killed one of your own for defiling it. My life was worth more than your symbol! I'm going to end things, because if you didn't listen then, you'll listen to me now."

Nicole curled her lip back as she stared down at Verla in disgust. "It's your choice whether you want to stay and watch the coven burn."

"You won't kill all these people!" Verla demanded. "I know you, whether you've changed or not. You've never been one to hurt others."

Nicole looked her sister up and down. "I could've said the same about you years ago, yet look at what you've done, claiming it all to be for the greater good. There's no greater good than wiping out the Miriamic Coven once and for all."

"You'll have to live with that guilt for the rest of eternity!" Verla shouted. "Are you sure you want to carry that weight alone?"

Nicole threw her head back and laughed. "You think I plan on doing this all alone? That Scelus demon didn't make plans with me just to collect *one* measly soul. Now that I have access to all of witch magic, he and I will use it together to conquer other realms, and no one will dare to ignore my warnings again. Santos isn't the only demon that can turn women into goddesses."

"You're lying," Verla accused. "You said you needed *me* to make a deal with the demon, but I made no such agreement about *this*. If this demon really wanted to help you, then where is he now? In the Abyss, waiting for you to do all the work for him? He's only going to break his promises and take your power for his own. That's what demons do!"

Nicole smirked. "On the contrary, he hasn't been to the Abyss for quite some time. He's been in Octavia Falls all these years, keeping an eye on his investment and making sure everything went according to plan."

Someone cleared their throat from the crowd, and the square fell silent. The sea of people parted as an old lady in a wheelchair pushed herself forward.

My heart plummeted to my toes when I saw it was *Rose*. She pushed herself to her feet, and a maniacal, demonic laugh erupted from her chest.

Nadine grabbed me tightly, her fingers curling into the fabric of my shirt. It couldn't be. Rose was a little old lady who spent all her time doing puzzles at the nursing home. She'd been a victim of the hospital bombing, and she'd stayed in a guest room at our house for months. When the priestesses arrived, we'd made sure Rose was on one of the first buses out of town, so she'd be safe. She was absolutely harmless.

Then I realized that was exactly why she was dangerous. This demon wasn't like Professor Leto, who'd found enjoyment out of taunting us from a position of power. This demon wanted to live among us and keep an eye on what was happening without interfering. To do that, he'd chosen to blend in and take a form that no one would ever suspect… like a frail old lady living at the nursing home… someone we'd taken into our home.

Rose didn't have any family in Octavia Falls. From what we knew, her husband had died many years ago, and her son had moved away decades ago. Something told me those people didn't exist—they'd only been a cover story for this false character the demon had created.

I didn't know how I hadn't seen it. I'd sensed something was off about Professor Leto the second he arrived in Octavia Falls. Verla had felt it, too, as she admitted in her vision. So why hadn't we sensed this demon?

I realized the answer before I finished asking the question. This was the same demon Verla had obtained her powers from, which meant he had to be stronger than her. To sense him for what he was, we'd have to be more powerful than he was. We weren't even close.

"I'm sick of hearing these people talk," Rose sneered, her voice taking on a deep, otherworldly tone. *"I've waited a long time for this. It's time to get what we came here for!"*

Rose lifted her hands, and before our very eyes the skin on her face melted away, leaving behind only flesh and bone. Four pointed horns grew from her forehead, and her clothes turned to ashes to reveal the bloody muscle underneath. The demon's empty eye sockets glowed red, and he bared a row of pointed teeth.

People screamed and started shoving each other back.

The demon's legs began to elongate, and he grew several feet taller in seconds. I thought he'd stop growing once he reached the size of the Scelus demon we saw in Verla's vision, but he kept growing bigger and bigger, until he was at least a hundred feet tall and towered above all the buildings.

The crowd erupted into chaos. Screams echoed throughout the square as people ran into nearby buildings for cover.

"Go!" I shouted.

My friends and I took off across the town square, but there were so many people trying to escape at once that the street was completely blocked. I saw Professor Warren ushering people through the doors of a nearby restaurant.

"Through here and out the back!" he shouted.

People raced for any exit they could find—streets, alleyways, or shops—but the crowd was so large that all escape routes were congested. We were completely trapped.

I shot a glance over my shoulder to see Nicole levitating herself higher. She landed on the demon's shoulder, smirking proudly down at the panicked crowd.

"Kill them," she ordered the demon. "Kill them all."

The demon swiped his hand at the nearest building, and the bricks blasted apart like a bomb had just detonated. Debris flew everywhere, and dust billowed into the air. Blood from the people who'd entered the building splatter across the street.

The demon stomped his foot against the roof of the neighboring shop, and that crumbled to pieces beneath his weight. Within seconds, multiple buildings that had stood for hundreds of years were reduced to rubble. At least a hundred people were killed inside of them.

The demon charged through the brick buildings, toppling them over like dominoes. He'd nearly reached the hardware store on the corner when a group of witches ran out of the doors with ropes in their hands.

"Now!" a man in the lead yelled.

I caught sight of his mismatched socks, and I realized it was Professor Clarke. He held one end of a long rope, while Valerie from school gripped tight to the other end. They were joined by the Wicked Warlock band members Clay and Carl, who shared a second rope. The four of them ran forward and circled the demon's feet. The ropes wrapped tight around his ankles. Instead of stopping him like they hoped, the demon merely lifted a massive foot, and the ropes snapped.

The demon's infernal laughter echoed across the town. The four coven members who tried to defend the square burst into flames all at once. Their screams only lasted a few seconds before their bodies slumped to the ground. Professor Clarke's charred corpse landed beside a tree growing from a pot on the sidewalk. The flames licked so high that the tree lit aflame. From there, the fire only spread, catching a canopy over one of the shops on fire, before quickly expanding throughout the whole building.

The demon smashed his foot into the ground again, and the entire Earth quaked underneath him. The pavement snapped, and a massive crack traveled through the center of the square in moments.

"Look out!" I screamed.

My friends and I jumped out of the way a second before the crack ruptured into an enormous gorge at our feet. It split open wide, spanning twenty yards in an instant. Several townspeople couldn't move out of the way in time, and they fell into the crevice. Their screams echoed endlessly.

I caught sight of Monica, Onyx, Tate, and Mandy running from the demon on the other side of the chasm. We'd been separated from them.

Debris rained down on us as the demon continued rampaging across the square. I shot a quick glance around to see several tables sitting on the patio of a nearby café.

"Over here!" I called to my friends.

We abandoned the frantic crowd and raced toward the café, where we ducked under the tables. Our cats scurried into a huddle beside us. Bricks and other building material landed over top of us, but we'd reached cover just in time. I crouched down low, dragging Nadine close to me so I could save her from flying debris. My arms shook against her, and her breathing turned ragged.

Nicole cackled in absolute delight. Deadly spells erupted from her palms as she aimed them at people trying to escape. A massive battle orb the size of a truck exploded near the bank, and dismembered body parts flew over us as people were killed in an instant.

She aimed her attention at the fountain. With a wave of her hand, she alchemized the water inside into bubbling lava. The lava spilled out onto the street, claiming several victims as they ran past. Their bodies sizzled as the molten lava consumed them.

Nicole spun around on the demon's shoulder and laughed down at a group of five witches hiding in the bushes. "I saw what the future held, and I had to witness my own fate. Now, you will witness yours."

She must've been using some sort of Mentalist abilities to place images into the witches' heads, because all five of them screamed and sprinted away. They ran into lamp posts and solid brick walls, like they couldn't see where they were going. They tried fighting off things that weren't there. The women shrieked so loud it sounded absolutely torturous.

Any remaining exits were now completely blocked by dead bodies or debris. People tried to escape over the remains of fallen buildings, but the demon lit the rubble aflame, along with the scrambling townsfolk. In under a minute, half the town square had been completely demolished before the demon turned his sights on homes that lined the next block. Past the mounds of rubble, I saw him stomp beautiful houses to dust so quickly it was like they'd been made of sand.

My eyes landed upon a woman in the center of the square. Verla hadn't moved to run away like the others. She'd dropped to her knees where she'd been standing, watching helplessly as her sister and the demon worked together to destroy what remained of our city.

"Why is Verla just sitting there?" Grant demanded. "She's the only one who can talk her sister down!"

"She tried, and it didn't work," Nadine said sadly.

"We have to do something!" Chloe insisted.

"What *can* we do?" Talia asked. "We don't have magic."

I forced down a lump rising to my throat. "Leave Verla. She chose this. She can suffer the consequences. All we can do is focus on making it out of here alive."

Miles frantically glanced around. "Every exit is blocked! We're going to have to find a way over top of the buildings."

Just then, a sound like thunder rumbled across the sky, but it was unlike any thunder I'd ever heard before. It echoed like it was contained within a chamber, the sound bouncing all around us and never stopping. It sent an eerie shiver down my spine.

I looked upward to see a streak across the sky that had completely blacked out the stars. At first I thought it was dark clouds rolling in. Then I noticed a shimmer around the edges of the black mass. I could feel it sucking my energy straight out of me, and I thought I might collapse right there. Whatever it was, it was entirely magical and wholly terrifying.

"What is that!?" Miles screamed.

Before any of us could answer, we witnessed the most horrifying sight. A man called a woman's name, and she turned toward him. The two ran toward each other across the square, but before they could reach one another, they were sucked into the air and disappeared into the inky black streak that marred our sky. One second they were there, and the next, their screams were cut dead silent, like they never existed at all.

Another streak of blackness appeared, only this time, it wasn't in the sky. It opened across the square, and the buildings that once stood there vanished in the blink of an eye.

"They're some sort of demonic portals!" Grant cried.

"No," Chloe said hollowly. "They're black holes."

As soon as she said it, I felt the air suck out of my lungs. A third black hole opened only two buildings down, and the shop it appeared in front of blinked out of existence. Nadine and I were closest to the black hole, and the table we hid beneath began to screech across the sidewalk as it was sucked toward the deadly void.

Nadine screamed as her feet were swept out from under her. My heart lurched in terror, and I grabbed her hand before she could be yanked away, but the black hole sucked us both closer. I pulled on Nadine as hard as I could, rearing away from the empty blackness until I was flat on my back. I tried to find a foothold on the sidewalk, but I was merely dragged along. The skin on my back skidded and tore against the concrete. Behind us, I heard our cats shrieking and our friends screaming in fear for our lives.

"Lucas!" Nadine cried.

I kept hold of her wrist with one hand, then flung my other arm out to catch a lamp post. Nadine's feet lifted into the air as she was sucked toward the black hole. Her terrified gaze landed on mine. She didn't have to tell me what she was thinking, because I felt the same terror grip me from the inside out. We both feared this was the end, and that we'd already seen our son for the last time.

"I won't let go!" I promised.

"Grab my hand!" Grant called from behind me.

I craned my neck to see the four of our friends had created a human chain. Miles clung to a tree on the other end. Straining, I pulled as hard as I could to yank Nadine and myself away from the black hole. I hooked my foot around the lamp post, then flung my arm toward Grant's outstretched hand. He held tight to my wrist and pulled us backward.

Nadine and I landed on the sidewalk outside of the black hole's powerful pull. I clung tight to her as we scurried back. Something flickered within the black hole. I couldn't quite make it out, but I thought I saw buildings. They seemed similar to Octavia Falls, but they were wrong, too… almost like we were peering into an alternate dimension where everything was a mirror image. It was there and gone so fast I couldn't be sure of what I saw.

Nadine noticed the same thing, and her tone wavered. "These aren't black holes."

"Whatever they are, we have to get far away from them!" Miles cried.

We turned and ran for the closest cover we could find, which was an alcove of a nearby shop entrance. We tried the door, but it was locked. Miles grabbed a brick off the ground and tried smashing the shop windows, but they were made with security glass that didn't break.

We all heaved for breath, and I had to steady myself against the building to regain my strength. There was no guarantee another one of those holes wouldn't open up right where we stood, but the square was still in complete chaos with nowhere to go.

"If these aren't black holes, what are they?" Chloe demanded.

Nadine forced her tone to steady. "They're tears in the fabric of our realm."

"Even with all of witch magic at her command, Nicole shouldn't be that strong," Talia insisted.

"I don't think she's doing it on purpose," Nadine said. "We said bringing her back to life could have dire consequences and threaten our magic for good, and we're witnessing what that looks like now."

"Spirits cross realms all the time," Grant pointed out. "Hell, the Scelus demon crossed realms and has been here for years. Nothing like this has ever happened."

"The demon must've never left after Verla summoned it, and that fits within the rules of magic," Nadine suggested. "But Nicole's presence defies all magical laws. By being here, she's draining Alora's power. Witches can't bring people back to life after they've crossed over, and the very fabric of our realm is tearing apart to keep her here."

Miles tossed his brick aside and wiped sweat from his brow. "How do we stop it?"

"We need to claim our power back and send Nicole back to where she came from," Nadine said.

"We've tried everything!" Grant protested.

Nadine stared wistfully across the town square. The screams of terrified townsfolk filled the air, and fires blazed across the city. Rivers of blood ran down the streets. I didn't know how she still managed to hold on to any hope, because it appeared the coven was already done for.

She dropped her gaze to the Curse Breaker Wand still clutched tightly in her hand. "We haven't tried *everything*. There's one last thing. The Law of Love."

"The Law of Love?" Miles asked.

"It's one of the three laws of witch magic," Nadine said. "It's taught in our Magical Theory classes. Our afterlife was born out of the love that Mother Miriam and Santos shared, which means our magic resonates at the same frequency as love."

"What are you suggesting?" Chloe asked sarcastically. "We *love* hard enough and overpower the demon?"

"Love isn't just a feeling, but an action," Nadine replied. "Alongside love is compassion. We can't stop this demon, but Verla can. Nicole stole her power because the two of them share a soul, which stands to reason that Verla can claim it back."

Talia shook her head. "She's not going to fight her sister."

"We have to give her a chance, because the choice is hers now," Nadine said simply.

I knew Nadine always saw the best in people, but it was hard to believe that even now she still thought Verla could change. "Headmistress Verla always had a choice and could do anything with her power, and she chose to go in the wrong direction," I countered. "She's clinging to the past, but when people try to make things how they were, they can't progress. Believe me, I know. Verla had the chance to help the coven with all the magic she had, and her talents could've been put to good use, but instead, she tried to restore something that's gone and keep things as they were. She's been nothing but selfish and chose to divide us by keeping power for herself instead of sharing it. When you're in a position of power, you should be willing to share that power, and Verla didn't. What makes you think she'll choose differently now?"

"Because *we* will choose differently now." Nadine sounded wholly convinced. "The coven has never been there for Verla before. She thought she had to do this all alone, and that's what drove her down this road. The coven keeps repeating this mistake over and over again. We don't take care of our people, so they put their own self-interests first and hurt others for it.

We saw it with Professor Carlisle and the Gingerbread Witches, and again with Professor Daymond and Magnus Knight brewing nightshade. The priestesses did horrible things to get what they wanted. It's a common theme that's plagued our coven for years. If we want to change it, then *we* need to take responsibility for the role we played and commit to changing it."

"You're saying this is all the coven's fault?" Grant demanded. "Nadine, you can't reason with people who do horrible things."

"I'm not saying the coven's at fault for individuals' choices," Nadine replied. "I'm saying that this problem goes deeper than individuals. Their choices are a symptom of our society. Just because Verla was wrong doesn't mean we were right."

"We can't just forgive Verla!" I protested.

"I'm not talking about forgiveness, and I'm not excusing anything she's done," Nadine pressed. "I'm only saying that we can find an explanation for it and understand that Verla's leaving behind clues to the state of the coven. There's more to this than her wrongdoings, because her choices are a symptom of a deeper issue—a reflection of where our society stands. She's showing us where we went wrong, even if she doesn't realize it. There's a part of the coven that's broken, but we can still make it right. I know what it's like to want to tear down the world for the people you love. Her decisions are a plea for help, and if we can recognize that, then we can do something about it."

"We need to save these innocent people, not Verla," I demanded.

"We're all *one*," Nadine insisted. "I said once that we need to care for individuals, because there's no community without them, but I wasn't living up to that myself, because I wasn't caring for my own well-being. I thought it was them or us, and that we were being selfish by taking care of ourselves, but I was wrong the whole time. It's not one or the other. It's *both*. Community doesn't begin or end with just one person, nor does it exist solely as a collective, because both individuals alone and everyone together are all parts of a whole."

Nadine continued. "We've seen what single people can do when they aren't cared for. The priestesses were just a few people who did a lot of damage because no one could help them at their most vulnerable time. They cared until the Waning made them desperate, and we saw how fast they could change. The answer isn't to silence people when we don't like what they're saying, but to listen to why they're screaming in the first place, because people lash out when they're hurting. We don't need to control Verla or take her power right now. We need to listen, so she can heal, because when our individual members heal, we all do."

"What she did was wrong," I argued. "There's no making it right again."

"We've struggled so long with right versus wrong, but life is more complex and nuanced than that," Nadine pressed. "Two opposing sides can be right at the same time, and they can be wrong, too. I was wrong to think I needed to heal so I could give my all to the coven and fix this for everyone. I've learned we can't save everyone. At the same time, we don't have to work alone. It's like how Talia and Chloe helped me find the Curse Breaker Wand. I thought I had to go about it alone, but with them beside me, I was able to accomplish what I couldn't do on my own. We need both community and individualism, because they aren't exclusive. I know now what it really means to heal. As individuals, we heal ourselves so that we can show other people how to heal *themselves*. We aren't here to fix everyone's problems, but to help people help themselves. That's what a community is about—supporting others."

The thought of supporting Verla in any way, shape, or form after she'd royally fucked us over didn't make a damn bit of sense to me. I didn't comprehend how Nadine could think this way after Verla had killed her parents, killed Helena… killed *Dean*.

But I trusted my wife with everything. And if this was the only way to make things right, I needed to put my complete faith in Nadine to turn this around. There was no greater sacrifice for Nadine to make than for her to forgive Verla now, and convince her to fight for the good of the coven that had betrayed her. As the chosen one, it was the most painful— and most powerful—move she could make to reach out to Verla after everything she did. It was the reason Mother Miriam trusted Nadine with this task… because she was the only one who had the capability to do such a selfless thing. We needed to follow her.

Talia seemed half-convinced. "What can we do?"

"We can give Verla a chance to make this right, because if we don't, then this lesson is bound to repeat itself," Nadine said. "We said we'd finish this together, that the coven had to unite. To do that, we need all of us—every single one. If we can come together now, we can prevent this from happening again."

"The coven has proven it can't work together because no one can agree on anything," Grant contested.

"That's not what working together means," Nadine replied. "We aren't all going to agree on everything all the time, but when we care for each other, and consider each other, we can compromise and grow in many different ways. People are stubborn and want things their way to avoid the pain of being wrong, but healing is about learning that it's okay to be wrong sometimes, and to correct your wrongdoings when they've caused harm. We don't have to be right all the time and make the best choices every time, but we learn and do better, and that's what community helps us do. The coven needs healing right now, and we can't do that if this ends the same way it started. We can't keep repeating this cycle."

"You're not wrong about that," Miles muttered.

"When I moved here, Talia told me the Miriamic Coven believes in second chances, but I haven't actually seen this play out," Nadine continued. "If we're to be witches, then we need to *be* witches and give Verla the second chance we believe in. There is nothing that can excuse what Verla's done, but there is also no solution that begins with abandoning her. The only way to help is to help her help herself. She'll be held accountable, but this needs to happen first."

"Nadine's right," Chloe agreed. "Nadine and I were enemies who broke our generational curse together. Neither one of us could've done it alone. Now it's the coven's chance to break a cycle, and just like I couldn't leave Nadine to break our families' curse alone, we can't leave Verla."

Nadine looked around at the rest of us pleadingly. "The priestesses weren't effective leaders when all they did was take, but we weren't effective leaders when we gave everything we had, either. We've been saying for years that this could all be resolved if we just work together, but we're expecting people to rise up and work with us when we aren't working with them. If it takes both an individual and a community, then we need to find the balance between where the community takes responsibility and where the individual does. Right now, this demon isn't ours to slay. This is Verla's fight, but we have to step up and be there for her. If I've learned anything about healing, it's that healing happens through community, but only when the individual is ready. We need Verla, and she needs us, because the coven is nothing without its people, but the people are nothing without the coven."

Talia stepped forward. "I can't forgive Verla for what she's done, but I can show her compassion. I'm with you."

"We've tried everything else, and fighting her didn't work," Grant added. "So whatever you think we can do now to help, I'll do it."

Nadine turned toward me. "In the crystal cave, we tried to take Verla's power, but that's a mistake we've made before. This time, we have to give her the power to correct this herself."

I didn't think Verla could be saved, but I realized that wasn't what Nadine was asking for. I'd learned through my own journey that healing wasn't as simple as it seemed. I thought we could show people how good things could be, and they'd jump on board and work together. I figured that if we fixed everything for them, people would step up and do their part, so we could accomplish this together, but that never was the answer.

Like Nadine had said, healing wasn't about being able to fix things for everyone else. It was a complex, ongoing journey that left ripples behind. Some people would choose to be a part of that, and others wouldn't, and whichever way they went was never up to you to decide.

Either way, you did your greatest work being true to yourself, so that other people could do the same. It was a hard truth to realize that not everyone's healing journey looked the same. You had to do what was right for you and make your own decisions, because while everyone else can be there for you, only you can do the healing. It was a choice to do so.

We couldn't fix what Verla started, and we couldn't force her to make the choices we desired. But we could make our own decisions that left ripples of inspiration behind. The rest was up to her.

I straightened my spine. "You're right, Nadine. We can't save everyone. I couldn't save Ryan. He chose to save himself. We didn't save the coven from the priestesses. They saved themselves. And we can't save Verla. She has to be the one to do this."

I twisted the Mortana Wand around in my hands. "True compassion doesn't hold any expectations. If we give Verla a choice, we have to be okay with the possibility that she makes a decision we don't agree with. Nicole has access to all witch power, and if Verla can't stop her, then the coven will end tonight. So let's make a decision we can stand behind no matter the outcome."

"I'm choosing love and compassion," Nadine said. "Even if it ends us."

I chuckled at the irony. It was so like the Shield Squad's motto. *To hell and back, even if it kills us.* Only this time, we weren't walking into hell. We were simply choosing to show love, in a situation where it didn't look like love would fix anything.

And somehow, that was even more terrifying.

Nadine approached Verla across the square, and the rest of us followed. Screams echoed through the night, and fires raged around us. In the distance, I could hear the crumble of buildings as the demon crunched them beneath his feet.

Verla noticed our approach, though she didn't lift her head. "I'm sorry," she whispered in a broken tone.

Nadine knelt at her side. "We still have a chance to stop this."

"My sister is a curse I brought upon the coven, and you can't stop her anymore," Verla said hopelessly.

Nadine placed the Curse Breaker Wand in Verla's hands. "You're right. *I* can't. I'm a Curse Breaker, and I broke my generational curse, but this one is yours to break."

Verla's gaze locked on Nadine, though she appeared wholly confused. "This Wand doesn't hold any power."

"No, but *you* do," Nadine said. "We don't have any power, and we can't do the work for you, but we can support you."

"I don't have any power, either," Verla countered. "Nicole stole it from me."

"Nicole said this magic flowed through your soul," Nadine pointed out. "If she can overpower you, you can overpower her."

Verla reeled back. "You want me to destroy her. She's all I ever had."

"I know the pain of grief," Nadine said gently. "We want so badly to hold on because we're afraid if we let go, it means we didn't love hard enough. But you don't have to let go, only loosen your grip. And that in itself can be one of the greatest acts of love. Your sister didn't hurt you now, because she doesn't want to see you suffer. You have to love yourself like your sister loves you."

Tears sparkled in Verla's eyes. "Without her, I don't know who I am. I'm nothing."

Talia stepped forward. "That may have been true in the past, but you have a chance to change that. I know what it's like to hold on to people who are bad for you because you don't know things can be any different. You've clung to your sister because you think she's a part of who you are, but there's more to you than her. You and your sister share a soul and a special bond, but you're not the same person. You get to decide who you're going to be moving forward, and you can be whoever you want with or without her."

Talia placed the Seer Wand into Verla's hands, then stepped back.

"I can't ask this of you," Verla replied.

"It's okay to ask for help," Grant said. "We're all taught to be so independent, but that doesn't mean you can't accept support. I tried so long to brew my own potions to keep myself alive, because I didn't trust anyone else to support me in the way I needed. But when I couldn't do it anymore, I crashed, and I was forced to accept the doctors' help. It's not a bad thing to learn and grow on your own, but eventually, you'll find there are things you just can't do without the help of others. You're beyond your breaking point, Verla, and you can't do this alone anymore. Let us help you."

Grant placed the Alchemy Wand in her hand.

Verla shook her head hopelessly. "The coven took everything from me, so I felt justified in taking anything from them to save myself. But now that I accomplished what I set out to do, it didn't make me happy like I thought it would. I took everything from you people, and I still didn't get what I wanted. How can you still have any faith in me?"

"Because people get to change their minds, and that's okay," Chloe said. "I've made a lot of horrible mistakes. I've said and done things I don't deserve to ever be forgiven for. I wish that I could go back to the past and erase the girl I once was, but we don't get to change what's already been done. All we can do is make better choices in the future. I always thought I knew what my future would look like, because of how I'd been raised. But this life I'm living now is nothing like I ever imagined, and even in the midst of the Miriamic Conflict, I'm happier than I ever thought I could be —not because of what my life looks like, but because of who I chose to become in the process. You brought Nicole back because you wanted things to be different, but sometimes changing the world requires *us* to change first."

Verla stared down at the Mentalist Wand as Chloe handed it over. "She's not going to listen to me."

I stepped forward. "All Nicole wants is for you to listen to her. I thought working together meant that we all agreed on everything. We tried so long to get everyone to listen to us, but we didn't need everyone to. We needed to make compromises, and sometimes we needed to change our minds. Working together is really important, but people still get to choose."

I held out the Mortana Wand. "This Wand is bound to my soul, but I'm giving it to you willingly, because I want you to know that the choice is still yours, Clarice. It's up to you to take your power back and finish this. You've been stealing magic from our people for years because you didn't think you had any power of your own, but you've had the power to change this all along. You said you couldn't control the magic, but I think you knew how to. You were only afraid of what would happen if you did."

Verla gazed across the chasm that had split the square in two, staring at the burning buildings shamefully—anything not to look us in the eyes.

Then slowly, Isa padded forward with her head down. She nudged Verla's knee with her nose, then gave a soft meow as she placed a paw on her leg. Verla turned her gaze to Isa, and regret filled her eyes.

"I wish I could take back everything I did. I didn't want to lose my sister," she admitted dolefully. Then she lifted her chin to look at me. "But perhaps you understand better than I do that I wasn't afraid of losing her, but scared of becoming my own person without her."

I placed the Mortana Wand with the others in her hand. "The power's in your hands now. The only question is, what are you going to do with it?"

Verla pushed herself to her feet, clutching the Oaken Wands tightly. "I know I don't deserve any of this, and after what I've done, I won't ask for your forgiveness. But I never intended to destroy the coven, and I can't let you all pay for my sins. My sister was wrong. The coven doesn't deserve to be destroyed. If all of you can show me compassion like this, then the coven she knew when she died has already changed. You're the coven's future, so let's save whatever future you have left."

Verla rolled her shoulders back, and mesmerizing beams of white light began to glow all over her skin. Her body levitated from the ground, and her chin tilted toward the sky as magic poured into her. The earth began to shake, but it was unlike the evil earthquake the demon had caused.

Instead, the chasm that had ripped through the square closed as Verla's power pulsed throughout the town.

Wind whipped around us like a cyclone, and building material rose into the air to circle our headmistress, as if creating a protective shield around her. The raging fires blazing through the town died down, and the townspeople's screams turned to gasps of wonder as they marveled at the brilliant magical light pouring out of Verla. She appeared like a star shining over us.

The demon's angry growl echoed over the rooftops. From blocks away, I witnessed the demon whirl in our direction. The deep red of his eye sockets blazed as his gaze locked on Verla.

"You can't do this!" Nicole shouted, her voice booming over us, projected by the power of her spellwork.

Slowly, Verla lowered herself to the ground, and the cyclone swirling around us calmed. The light emanating from her form dimmed, but there was still a slight magical glow shimmering around her. She appeared wholly confident as she faced her sister.

"I can't let you hold me back anymore, Nicole." Verla's tone was soft, but her voice carried over the town. "We keep hurting each other, and it's time we put an end to it. I never wanted all this power. All I wanted was *you*. But if having you means hurting everyone else, then I need to say goodbye."

"You wouldn't dare steal this power from me!" Nicole raged.

"I can't steal what was never yours in the first place," Verla said. "I'm reclaiming this power, but it's not ours to fight over."

Nicole chuckled, like her sister's attempt at contesting her was merely comical. "You always thought you were better than me. You were Dad's favorite, and that's why he gave you the house. No matter what I did, you always had to one-up me. You were the better student, the better lawyer… always more accomplished."

"That's not true," Verla argued. "Those dreams were ours together."

"*Be serious,*" Nicole mocked. "*Stop goofing around.* That's all you ever said to me. You couldn't stand it when I was happy. I'll show you how serious I can be. You can try to take this power from me, but I'll take *everything* you love from you."

I expected the demon to approach us, but instead, he turned to lead Nicole toward the edge of town.

"Where are they going?" Nadine asked.

"To the only place I love," Verla replied in a shaky tone. "Miriam College of Witchcraft."

As I watched the demon retreat, his form disappeared behind an inky black streak that appeared in the middle of Octavia Falls. Homes continued to topple beneath his feet, and his rampage echoed over the city, but the danger threatening our realm was only getting worse. With each inky black streak that appeared, pieces of our town vanished from existence.

"Our realm is still tearing apart!" I cried.

"Here." Verla placed the Oaken Wands back into our hands. "I can't overpower Nicole completely, but I have enough access to the coven's magic to return power to your hands. I can feel the pieces of our soul fighting for control. I can't do this alone… so will you help me?"

Nadine glanced around at the crowd of townspeople gathered in the square. "Yes. All of us, together."

Our friends readied their Wands.

"Through unity and these wands of oak, we pray to the Goddess to restore what's broke?" Grant asked, reminding us of the incantation we'd come up with for restoring the coven's magic.

I recalled something then, something Nadine had said to me long ago.

"I'm broken," I'd said to her.

"Not broken," she'd replied. *"Just growing."*

If I wasn't broken, maybe I didn't need to be fixed, I recalled thinking. *If I was growing, then maybe the wounds would heal. Maybe it wasn't about putting the shattered bits back together and hoping the glue would stick. Maybe it was about growing new branches.*

The coven wasn't merely a broken town that needed its shattered bits of rubble fitted back together. We were an ever-evolving community, and to truly heal, we couldn't simply restore the broken pieces and go back to the way things were. We had to grow into something new.

I shook my head at Grant. "No. I've got something better. *We hold firm to our roots and honor our truth, to claim our power and start anew.*"

Nadine lifted the Curse Breaker Wand. "To a new beginning."

"To staying true to ourselves and embracing authentic transformation," Talia added as she pointed the Seer Wand to the sky.

"To learning how to be better people," Chloe said as she raised the Mentalist Wand.

"And working together." Grant aimed the Alchemy Wand upward.

I raised the Mortana Wand. "To the growth and healing of all our people."

We spoke in unison, our voices overlaying one another in a perfect chorus. *"We hold firm to our roots and honor our truth, to claim our power and start anew."*

Power surged through us, swelling up through the earth and filling every cell of our bodies with a glorious, transformative energy. All colors of the rainbow swirled around us, then twisted up our arms and together through the ends of the Oaken Wands. The Wands overpowered the Waning, drawing the magic Verla had stolen from the people back into our hands. By working together with her, the magic flowed so smoothly that there was no struggle to control it.

Every particle of my being seemed to connect to one another, until I didn't just perceive myself, but I saw and felt every molecule that made up my friends' mind, bodies, and spirits. Everything they loved and desired, along with all their pain and grief, became mine for just a brief moment… and mine became theirs.

As the spell grew in intensity, my perception expanded outward, until I wasn't just connected to my friends, but I became the entire coven all at once. I didn't know where I ended and others began, nor could I separate myself from the town, our history, and the hope that remained in the heart of the people. We were all one as the power that connected our coven seemed to merge us together, before restoring us to our individual parts.

The Oaken Wands glowed so bright that I had to shield my eyes. Then the most incredible spell I'd ever seen blasted upward toward the sky. A beautiful explosion of colors burst above us like a supernova. Power rained down on the people, and their forms began to glow with the color of their individual magic. On our own, we were monochromatic, but together we were a vibrant, multicolor blaze that left each one of us marveling in complete awe. It was a perfect visualization for the power the Miriamic Coven possessed. Individually, we were each one piece of a whole, but it was our individual strengths that made our community stronger.

"The Oaken Wands have restored the coven's power," Nadine stated. "Now, our people can choose for themselves."

We'd learned a lot since being elected to the Imperium Council just a few short months ago. Among our greatest lessons, we learned that building a community wasn't about convincing everyone to think the way you did. Community wasn't something you could force people to participate in, and your community didn't have to be the one you were born into.

Community was a choice, and not everyone had to be a part of that decision if they didn't want to. That didn't make them wrong—only a part of something different than you. Community was about choosing a path, and then finding the people who wanted to be a part of it. That didn't mean we had to agree on everything, but it did mean that all were welcome.

I raised my voice toward the coven. "We have one last chance to defend this town. You can either join us in the fight or take your families and flee. We hold no judgement in which decision you make, but we will be facing this demon to defend you. Those who wish to join us may follow."

We turned toward the demon, and thousands of coven members rallied forward to join us. Those holding the Oaken Wands led the march, with Miles and Verla flanking at our sides.

Nadine gripped the Curse Breaker Wand tighter in her hand. "Let's finish this."

nadine

TWENTY-FOUR

T he coven marched to the edge of the forest near the school. Our cats scurried in front of us protectively, the hairs on their necks rising as they hissed angrily. The demon had trampled trees flat, and the road leading up to the school had been upheaved by the quaking of the earth. The area surrounding the school appeared completely unrecognizable in the wake of his destruction.

The Scelus demon loomed over the turrets of Miriam Mansion. He swung a heavy arm out and crushed the tallest turret in the palm of his hand. Nicole's wicked laughter rang over us as she stared proudly down at the wreckage. She blasted a spell through the windows of the highest level, shattering them to bits in an instant. From here, I could see the satisfied smirk on her face as he reduced her sister's beloved school to rubble.

It was absolutely devastating to witness. The school had been undergoing renovations after the last attack upon it, and now the classrooms we cherished were being turned to dust.

"Hey, Skeleton Face!" someone shouted to get the demon's attention. "Leave our school alone!"

A powerful battle orb went flying through the air and hit the demon in the side of the head. The demon stumbled to the side, but he shook his head like the spell was nothing but a nuisance. I glanced over my shoulder to see that Gregory had followed us to the school.

He beamed as he stared down at his hands. *"Wahoo!* It feels good to have our power back!"

I shot a glance behind myself to see the forest was filled with at least a thousand coven members. I recognized so many faces, many of whom had fought alongside us before. Our friends who had fled town long ago were back to help—Monica, Tate, Onyx, and Mandy. Beside them, people from school looked poised and ready to defend their home. Professor Richards led a group of students, and I noticed Darcy, Samantha, Brayden, and Alex among them. Professor Warren planted himself in front of Verla. Even after all she'd done, he still wanted to protect her from her sister.

Nearby, Dr. Yonker, Dr. Tracey, and Dr. Mack were all here, though I wasn't shocked that they'd come. What truly surprised me was to see a group of people who had opposed us in the past. Among them, Gwen, Camille, Meredith, and Judge Calloway were standing at our sides.

Every doubt I'd ever had about our coven surviving this conflict melted away at that moment, because I knew that when witches worked together, we were unstoppable. The Miriamic Coven had faced magical enemies, witch trials, and demons before, and each time—no matter how battered and bruised we became—we rose to victory. I always knew the coven could outlive any outside threat, but I hadn't been so sure we could survive when we'd become our own worst enemy. But now we stood together, and that was something we'd never done since this conflict began. This demon may have otherworldly power, but he had no idea what he was up against.

The demon's red eyes blazed with rage. Drawing his arm back, he aimed the debris clutched in his fist at us. He hurled it in our direction, but the bits of rubble transformed mid-air to become hellish weapons. Bricks and shingles turned black, elongating into sharp spikes that looked like shards of obsidian.

I didn't even flinch. My friends and I lifted the Oaken Wands in unison, and an impenetrable shield encompassed our people before the spears could impale us.

Judge Calloway caught my eye. "Give them hell, priestess."

Power swelled through me, and I could tell the rest of them felt it, too. I nodded to my friends, and we began moving as a unit. "Let's show this demon what the Miriamic Coven can do!"

Talia raised the Seer Wand first. Tate took her sister's hand, and several other Seers stepped forward. Miles, Alex, Brayden, and Dr. Mack all joined hands as they worked together to focus their power through the Seer Wand and toward the Scelus demon. Hundreds of other Seers backed them up, freely lending their power to the spell.

A chilling note rang through the air, and ghosts of those who haunted the school flew out of the broken windows and spiraled into the air. A dozen ethereal beings circled the demon, and his blood-red flesh began to turn an icy blue as the ghosts preyed on his energy.

The demon swatted the ghosts away, and because he was a transdimensional being himself, his hands met solid forms. The ghosts gave pained wails as they were thrust aside.

The demon merely laughed, his guttural tone resounding through the sky like thunder. He seemed amused at our attempt to stop him. He stomped a heavy foot, and the earth gave a violent shudder. An entire wing of Miriam Mansion collapsed in an instant. The lawn spanning before us crumbled, falling away into a dark abyss like puzzle pieces breaking off one after the other. The chasm spread within moments, intent on swallowing us all whole at once.

"Oh, no you don't," Chloe sneered.

She lifted the Mentalist Wand, and hundreds of members of her Cast stepped forward. Mandy, Camille, Monica, Meredith, and Judge Calloway all raised their hands to aim their power together as one.

As the army of Mentalists came together, Meredith took Monica's hand in hers. It was profound to witness, because Meredith had been cruel to her sister in the past. But now, after what we all watched in the town square, Meredith appeared ready to turn over a new leaf. She came together with the sister she once rejected, and together, they joined with the other Mentalists to cast a powerful spell.

The collapsing bits of earth paused mid-air at the Mentalists' command. Rocks and clods of dirt rose upward, and the Mentalists shot them straight at the demon like massive bullets. They moved so quickly that the projectiles blasted straight through the demon's abdomen and out the other side.

The demon screamed and stumbled backward, but he wasted no time casting another spell. As he lifted his hands, he overpowered the Mentalists and sent their weapons spinning back toward them. Except they weren't mere rocks and clods of dirt anymore. The demon had transformed them into sizzling black globs of poison that glowed green around the edges.

"We need alchemy!" I ordered.

Grant moved quickly, and a crowd of Alchemists gathered behind him. Verla, Onyx, and Professor Richards flanked him on one side, while Darcy, Dr. Yonker, and Gwen gathered on the other. Together, they thrust out a spell that alchemized the poison into harmless clouds of smoke that drifted away in the wind.

The Alchemists turned their powers back on the demon, and his flesh began to sizzle as they transformed his blood to acid. The demon stumbled backward, crushing trees under his feet as he let out a pained cry.

"Let's finish him!" Professor Warren yelled.

A horde of Mortana stepped forward as Lucas raised his Wand. Samantha, Gregory, and Dr. Tracey joined my husband and professor. A powerful death spell blasted out the end of the Mortana Wand, landing square in the center of the demon's chest.

"No!" Nicole shouted. She swayed on the demon's shoulder, struggling to maintain her footing.

The demon turned his head toward the sky and screamed, but the spell Lucas had cast seemed to shudder against him.

"He's resisting us!" Lucas shouted. "He's not fully alive, so the death spell isn't taking!"

I grabbed Lucas's free hand in mine. "We do this together. All Casts, all at once!"

He nodded firmly. "This coven is ours, and no demon can take it!"

Together, every coven member stepped forward to face the demon. We lifted the Oaken Wands, and the magic of our people blasted out of the ends of them. I could feel the full power of the coven coming together as one as the Oaken Wands took on a united front. Magic of all colors lit up the night sky so brightly it illuminated the whole town as if it were daytime. The Curse Breaker Wand shook in my hand as it funneled the tremendous power of thousands of witches into one spell.

Our magic slammed into the demon in a singular violent blast. He groaned in agony as the power surged through his body, causing his veins to turn from a deep bloody red to a bright white.

"We need to give it everything we've got!" I shouted. "Use your wands, your Cast stars, anything to focus your power. We can do this together!"

"United as one at the end of this war, you will leave Octavia Falls and hurt us no more," Lucas shouted. *"By the Goddess and all her loving, we banish you and restore our coven!"*

We all joined in on the incantation as Lucas repeated it over again. Our magic swelled to epic proportions, until mighty currents of power assaulted the demon from all angles.

A high-pitched, hellish roar shook the skies as the demon failed to resist us any longer. The spell turned his own magic against him, and fiery streams of lava crackled across his skin.

"No, this isn't possible!" the demon bellowed. *"No force can defeat me—"*

A magical blast detonated, and trees toppled over. Coven members huddled together to avoid being thrown off our feet, and our cats dug their claws into the dirt.

The demon erupted into thousands of ashy pieces that blazed through the sky like a massive firework. His screams died as he was reduced to bits. In the distance, Nicole's cries echoed through the forest.

Ashes rained down all around us, and the magic lighting up the sky dimmed to reveal the stars once more. The forest had been demolished, with only the strongest trees still standing. One wing of the mansion still stood, but the rest of our beloved school was scattered over the lawn.

For a moment, all was silent. Then, cheers of victory erupted through the night. Coven members cried out in relief now that the demon was gone.

"We did it!" Gregory cried. "We showed that demon who's boss."

My eyes were still locked in the distance. As the fiery ashes of the demon rained down on us, I witnessed an orange glow ignite deep within the trees. A shadowed figure crossed in front of the fire.

"This isn't over yet," I said.

The crowd began to quiet as all eyes turned on me.

I pointed toward the shadow I'd seen. The glowing orange blaze was only getting brighter. "Nicole's still out there. We've reclaimed our power, but she still has magic of her own. Whether she has a demon on her side or not, she's going to do everything she can to end this."

"Headmistress Verla won't let that happen, will you, Clarice?" Lucas asked.

Verla had been standing here moments ago, but when we looked around, she was gone. I spotted movement through the darkness.

"She's going after her sister," I said. "Come on. We have to stop Nicole before she tears our realm apart completely."

We took off running in the direction of the fire. Coven members followed, and Isa raced beside me.

"Nicole, you have to stop this!" I heard Verla shout in the distance.

"You tried to stop me then, but I won't let you stop me now!" Nicole spat.

Flames roared, reaching high above the remaining treetops. Through the forest, it appeared like a bonfire had ignited. The trees gave way to a wide clearing, and I realized the fire was eating away at a large, gnarly oak tree.

The Protection Tree.

All around the clearing, the demon's ashes lay sprawled, sizzling like papers burning around the edges. The ashes had fallen upon the dry, broken crack sliced through the center of the Protection Tree and had lit our sacred oak ablaze.

We could feel the heat from the flames rolling over the forest in waves. This wasn't any ordinary fire. It'd been ignited by the ashes of a demon and burned a deep, evil red that wasn't of this world.

Nicole shoved Verla toward the burning tree with murderous intent in her eyes. Verla stumbled to the side, narrowly missing being burned by a flaming whirlwind that swirled around the tree.

"Verla!" I shouted.

I ran forward, but Nicole thrust her palm outward, and I slammed straight into a solid shield. Thousands of coven members circled the clearing at all angles, but no one could break through Nicole's shield.

"Nicole, please!" Verla begged. "I just brought you back. Please don't make me force you to stop."

"You're still not listening! You can't stop me anymore, Clarice. This is the way it was always going to end for you." Nicole shoved her sister back again, using a powerful spell to knock her off her feet and across the clearing.

Verla used her own magic to soften the blow, and sparks flashed as she made impact with the ground. Dirt covered her face, and blood trickled down her cheek as she pushed herself upright. She winced as she rolled her shoulder back. Verla's brows pinched together as she eyed her sister up and down, appearing stunned that Nicole would hurt her.

Then something shifted. Verla looked from the Protection Tree, then back to her sister. Her features fell, like something profound had just dawned on her. Verla understood her sister far better than anyone, and it was clear she realized something now that the rest of us hadn't.

"I hear you, Nicole," Verla said gently. "And for the first time, I understand why you did all this."

"What are you doing!?" Meredith shouted at me. "Finish her with the Oaken Wands."

Verla's gaze snapped in my direction. "Nadine, no! I have to be the one to finish this!"

I had no reason to trust Verla after everything she'd done, but I chose to give her a chance back in the town square, and I had to let her take it now. I kept my Wand down at my side.

Meredith whirled toward Judge Calloway. "Silence them, Judge. We need to get rid of her."

Judge Calloway shook her head as she peered upon the scene curiously. "No. We don't have to silence people, only hold them accountable. Let Clarice say what she wants to say."

All eyes turned upon the sisters standing in the clearing amidst the backdrop of a blazing inferno.

Verla pushed herself to her feet to face her sister. "I'm listening, Nicole. When you tried to chop the Protection Tree down the night of your death, you called it a murder tree. Everyone thought you were out of your mind. But then you said something in the square, and it all makes sense now. You said you were trying to save me."

"I *was*," Nicole admitted. "But you acted like you didn't want to be saved."

"I can't be saved anymore," Verla said softly.

I realized then what Verla already understood. The fire Nicole had seen in her vision was this one consuming the Protection Tree right now. Nicole had tried to stop any of this from ever coming true by intending to chop the tree down, but as her own warning foretold, her death would mark the beginning of the end. It was a self-fulfilling prophecy.

"The night you died, you said you saw a fire and noose in your vision," Verla reminded her. "I assumed you meant the return of the witch trials, and I thought I understood that all this time. But you weren't talking about the coven. You were talking about *us*. The noose was your fate, but the fire you foresaw was *my* death. This isn't about these people. It's about me."

Nicole's hands shook as she slowly dropped them to her sides. "I saw that the Protection Tree would be the end of you. I was trying to stop this moment from ever happening, but then you went against me and wouldn't let me save you. You let them kill me, so I came back to finish this and end *you* like they ended me."

Verla lifted her chin confidently. "Then you have this moment you so desire, because like you said, I can't stop it anymore. It was always meant to end here."

"What do they mean, *this moment?*" Professor Warren asked from beside us. He didn't want to believe what he was seeing with his own eyes.

I swallowed the lump rising in my throat. "Headmistress Verla is going to embrace the witch's fate and complete the prophecy once and for all."

I could see it in Verla's eyes. Her mind was already made up.

Professor Warren's features went completely pale as all the pieces fell into place. "Clarice, no!"

Verla turned to look at him. "Don't stop me, Jonathan. This is what has to be done, for the good of all."

"This isn't how I wanted things to end," he said sadly.

"We can't change what's already been done," Verla told him. "I've done horrible things, and I won't ask your forgiveness, because I know it's something you can never give me. I sold our child to a demon, and there's no coming back from that. You have to accept me for who I am, and not who you wanted me to be."

"I know things will never be what I thought they were," he said. "Perhaps there was a future for us at one time, but not anymore. Even so, there's a part of me that will always love you, even if things didn't go the way I planned. I just… thought there was still a chance to get our son back and make things right."

"I will make things right," Verla promised. "But to do that, I can't stick around where my presence is going to keep hurting people. I'm just grateful I get a chance to say goodbye. Believe it or not, I really did love you, Jonathan."

"I loved you too, Clarice," he replied.

Judge Calloway stepped forward. "This doesn't have to be the end. The priestesses didn't listen to Nicole the night they hanged her, but I think we can all agree that what happened here isn't right. We can't keep making the same mistakes, and we have to own up to the role we all played here. On behalf of the entire coven, I am truly sorry. But if Nicole had this vision so she could stop it, then we can still change things."

"I thought that, too," Verla said. "But not all visions are meant to be stopped. Nicole warned of the witch's fate, that her death would mark the beginning of the end. But that doesn't have to be a bad thing. Nicole and I began this conflict, but together, we can end it. All of this happened to draw out what wasn't working in the coven so we could address our problems and work through them. The end isn't an end to the entire coven, but to the old ways of the coven."

"Don't act so noble!" Nicole spat. "I was the one who had that vision, yet here you are trying to overpower me *again*, like you always do! I saw the Protection Tree burning, and I witnessed this fire consume you. I tried to save you, and you turned your back on me. Now I get to turn my back on you. You don't get to *choose* this. That's not how this works. *I'm* going to end you. I'm sick of always coming in second to you."

Nicole blasted a spell outward, but Verla threw up a shield. Nicole held her spell steady, aiming her magic in a powerful stream, while her sister pushed back. Above us, powerful thunder cracked through the sky. Panicked shouts filled the forest as coven members staggered backward. I grabbed tight to Lucas as my stomach dropped from my abdomen.

Another inky black tear in the fabric of our realm split the sky apart. It was larger than the others, spanning miles in both directions. Debris from all across town rose into the air as the black hole began sucking our town into oblivion. Wind whipped around us, and the flames consuming the Protection Tree burned ten times brighter.

Our world was falling apart, and we didn't have long before our town and the rest of our people were lost to our mistakes.

"Verla!" I shouted above the roaring wind. "It's now or never!"

Her eyes sparkled as her gaze locked on me. There was so much left unsaid in that longing stare—so much regret and sorrow I couldn't even begin to understand.

Verla turned back to her sister. "You've never been second, Nicole. I always loved you and looked up to you in so many ways. You think you can only win this by disagreeing with me, but can't you see you've already won, because I agree with you? I agree with your vision, and I'm ready to accept what you've known all along."

Nicole shot a glance toward the darkened sky. "I died because these people put the coven first and didn't care about me, so now they can perish together. If you really want to die with them, then get it over with already!"

"This isn't about them," Verla demanded. "It's always been about us, and you thought I chose them over you. That's why you're still trying to destroy them. It only takes one person to be outcast to destroy the entire group, and I know that, because I lived it. But at the same time, I'm the one who made this choice, and I'm the one who has to fix it. This tree stood as a symbol of protecting the coven, but it's time to change what that means. Each member of the coven is like a branch on this tree, making up part of a whole. But I've been sucking the life from the other branches and suffocating the coven. Now as an individual, I have to decide what I need… and what I need is to let them go, so everyone can thrive."

The rift above us rumbled as it opened wider. I clung to Lucas desperately as screams rang out around us. His arms tightened around me. Trees uprooted and spiraled upward into the black hole.

"I'm the one who brought you here," Verla told her sister. "It's my spell that's sustaining you, and my soul that's tethering you here. Otherwise, the demon could've brought you back himself, but you needed *me* to do it, because only my soul could bring you back. You're already gone, Nicole, and I should've realized long ago that I couldn't bring you back. It's time for me to let go, and once I do, you can't stay here anymore. I don't want to hurt you, but I can't let you hurt anyone else. The hurt ends here, with us."

"What happened to doing whatever it takes, Clarice?" Nicole snarled.

"I did that to bring you back," Verla replied. "And now, it's time to do whatever it takes to bring the coven back."

"Then go!" Nicole shouted. "Just like you left me before, you'll leave me again!"

She charged forward, her arms outstretched as she shoved Verla toward the flames.

Verla's arms wrapped around her sister in an embrace as she stumbled back. "I'll never leave you again. You saw me dying alone in this fire, but visions can be changed. Now we can do this together."

Then Verla leapt into the flames, dragging her sister with her.

The demonic fire burned hotter and brighter. We all scrambled back as red-hot flames shot toward the sky, swirling upward in a vortex toward the black hole. The heat reduced the Verla sisters' bodies to ashes in mere moments. As the fire took their lives, the magical flames consumed their power, too, and tendrils of magic spiraled upward with the fading embers.

Then slowly, the branches of the Protection Tree began to wither to ash. The ashes were whisked away in the vortex, until the trunk of the tree turned to cinders too and disappeared into oblivion. The flames dimmed as the last of the embers drifted away, and the coven was left standing in an empty clearing. The tear in our realm rumbled one last time, before slamming closed with an echoing *boom*.

Lucas's shoulders sagged against me. I looked across town to see the other streaks of black in the sky had vanished. Nicole was gone, sent back to the realm she came from, and the magic that had been shuddering against our world and struggling to sustain her life had receded with her. Verla was dead, and my heart ached for her loss. She'd done horrible things, things I could never forgive her for. But she was still my mentor and somebody I had loved, and her sacrifice had protected us all. Our town had been completely destroyed, but our world had been saved.

All around us, bright white lights began to emit from the heart space of coven members. I looked downward in awe to see that my chest was glowing, too. The ache in my heart turned to warmth, and all the emptiness that we'd felt when the Waning completely took over now disappeared. Instead of an empty, meaningless void in our hearts, magic filled us up and overflowed out of us all at once. The Waning was finally over for good.

It was ironic. All this time, we thought we needed the Oaken Wands to save us. We had used them to return magic to the people and defeat the demon together. But ultimately, the real thing that saved us was trusting our people. We'd shown up for Verla in her most vulnerable moment, and in turn, her sacrifice saved us all.

Cheers rang out around us as coven members drew each other into hugs. Tears of relief fell from my eyes as my shoulders trembled with the release of restricted emotions. All the fear and worry I'd bottled up came flooding out of me all at once, and I felt an immense freedom overtake me. I threw my arms around Lucas's neck, and he squeezed me close as he buried his nose into my hair.

"It's over," he whispered in a calm, reassuring tone. He didn't have to tell me he'd heard their last thoughts, because I could tell by the certainty in his voice. The Verla sisters were gone for good.

I didn't ask him what they'd said, because I knew those thoughts were theirs alone. Lucas would carry them with him to the afterlife so that there, the sisters could continue to heal.

"We've fought for so long," I said. "I can't believe we've reached the end."

"Believe it," Lucas replied gently. "I saw the look Verla gave you before she dragged Nicole into the flames. She wasn't just saving the coven, Nadine. If there was anything left here worth saving, it was *you*."

I drew away to wipe my eyes. "I don't know who the real Verla was, and I don't think I'll ever know, but I'll always be grateful for what she did for us in the end."

To have full access to our magic again felt monumental, because my magic had been unpredictable since the day my powers awakened. I lifted my palm. As if to prove to myself our magic had fully returned, I sent beads of witch lights dancing over my fingertips. Then I formed a large, magical orb in my palm that illuminated the entire clearing. I tossed it into the air, and it hovered above us like a bright, hopeful star.

Talia stepped forward and placed a hand on my shoulder. "Your magic is beautiful, Nadine."

I draped my arm around her. "Yeah, but it doesn't belong on its own."

Talia smiled. She created her own witch light and tossed it upward. It hovered next to mine, and the two orbs swirled around each other in a beautiful dance.

Lucas formed an orb, then Grant and Chloe. Miles and Professor Warren joined in, until everyone gathered in the forest tossed a witch light into the air in celebration. The entire area glimmered with thousands of witch lights, creating our own personal galaxy of independent stars in this coven of connection we'd created.

I never gave much thought to how victory would feel, only how I prayed one day our struggles would end. No one talks about the strange silence that follows your victory cheer, where everyone just looks at each other wondering where to go next. It was an odd feeling to bask in triumph amidst an undertone of melancholy for all the lives we'd lost earlier in the night.

I wasn't the only one who felt it. Talia's smile faded to an expression of sympathy. Then she took my hand and began to sing.

You were the crystal on my altar
And the wand that I had conjured
You were the potion in the cauldron
The incantation I once pondered

It was a traditional Miriamic funeral song, one we'd sung many times before. It seemed all so fitting now, even in the wake of victory, because with defeat came the calamitous reminder of all we'd lost to get here.

It wasn't sad, though, not like this song had felt in the past. This time as I joined her in the song, my heart didn't ache for what we'd lost, but filled with gratitude for all we'd been given. Lucas took my other hand and began singing. Grant and Chloe joined us, and slowly more and more coven members held hands until our entire people united together in song. The witch lights all around us hovered in our midst, representative of all the souls that had gone on before.

I never thought I'd witness people like Gwen and Camille join us, but they too stepped forward into our circle, then added their voices to the verse.

You were all that gave me power
You lifted me so high
Now at this final hour
I bless you with goodbye

This was a goodbye to the old coven, and a farewell to the people who could no longer be here for it. It was a profound goodbye that marked the end of an era and held so much hope for the future. Never did I think a goodbye could be soothing, but there was no part of my soul that ached for this... only pieces that wept with happiness for all we'd done and shared together.

We had a life together
But if it's right with fate
I'll meet you in my spirit
Right at Alora's gate

As our voices swelled over the clearing in perfect harmony, the ghostly image of a woman appeared where the Protection Tree once stood. At first, I thought it had to be one of the Verla sisters, but as the spirit's features took shape, I realized I didn't recognize her. She was my height, with smooth skin and long brown curls. The woman wore a long dress that looked to be straight out of the 18th century.

Lucas, however, seemed to recognize her. He released my hand and stepped forward. "You're Octavia Barrows, aren't you? You're the Curse Breaker who our town is named after. You died to cast the protection spell, and you became the Protection Tree."

"Yes," Octavia said kindly. "I have protected this coven for centuries, but I regret to say that I could not protect us from ourselves."

"You didn't have to," Lucas replied. "It was up to us to figure this out, not up to generations of the past."

"Our mistakes belong to all of us," Octavia said. "Even your ancestors have to own up to the roles that they played in all of this. These problems don't exist among a singular generation, but span back lifetimes. But now the coven has learned from its mistakes, and we can move forward into new times. I cherished my time here, but now my spirit has been released from the Protection Tree, and I too can move on. However, there's one more message I have for you before I go. May I see the Oaken Wands?"

My friends and I stepped forward and presented the Oaken Wands to Octavia. As I gripped the Curse Breaker Wand, I realized something about it felt different. The immense power I felt surging through it at one time wasn't there anymore.

"What's happened to the Oaken Wands?" I asked Octavia.

"Their power has been released with my spirit," she answered. "These Wands were carved from a branch of the Protection Tree, but the tree holds no power anymore, and their spell has been broken. However, the stars are in the right alignment tonight. A member of each Cast lives, and the whole coven is willing to join together. You can recreate the spell that first forged the Oaken Wands if you so desire. The choice is up to you."

I stared down at the Wands. We'd spent so much time searching for them that it didn't seem right to give them up. But this wasn't my choice to make.

I turned to the coven. "The Oaken Wands were designed as a fail-safe to keep other magical societies from stealing our power, but in the entire history of the coven, our greatest enemies were ourselves. We can choose to give power to a small group of people, which could be beneficial in times of war and hardship, but this is the kind of power that started a war that nearly broke us. The choice is up to the coven. Do *you* want this kind of power in the hands of your council, so that they may call upon your magic when needed, or do we place the power in the hands of individuals?"

Professor Warren shook his head sadly. "We saw what power in the hands of too few people can do. If we're to truly step into a new era of the coven, we can't repeat this mistake. Times of war will come again, but the Oaken Wands aren't the answer. We can't risk our power ending up in the hands of the wrong people."

"Jonathan is right," Judge Calloway agreed. "If war should come, we won't need magical relics like the Oaken Wands to save us. We only need each other."

We turned the vote over to the coven, and the decision was unanimous. We wouldn't create a new set of Oaken Wands, because we didn't need their power. Their power was already within us.

"Then the Oaken Wands will be no more," Octavia announced.

She waved her hand, and Oaken Wands began to disintegrate in our palms. I watched curiously as the tip of the Curse Breaker Wand crumbled to ash and drifted away in the wind, returning to join the ashes of the Protection Tree it once came from. The Wands continued to deteriorate inch by inch, until all that remained in our palms was mere dust.

Lucas turned back to Octavia. "Whenever you're ready, I can help you cross over to Alora."

A light smile crossed her ghostly features. "You don't have to take me anywhere, because I'm already home."

The forest began to morph before our eyes. Ethereal wisps swirled around us, until they began to form large, solid shapes. The pointed turrets of Gothic homes appeared around us, though they had a ghostly glow to them. They were slightly see-through and not quite *here,* as if the town that appeared around us was layered directly upon the forest.

As the vision became clearer, we found ourselves standing in a town square with brick buildings surrounding us on all sides. It looked like a replica of Octavia Falls, where the buildings the demon had demolished were still standing. At the same time, it seemed even more magical and spellbinding than our town could ever be. Overhead, a full moon shone silver light down upon us, creating an ethereal glow that shimmered around each shopfront. Gentle flames danced from jack-o-lanterns in each window display, and leaves in mesmerizing fall colors of bright oranges, reds, and yellows drifted over the cobblestone. The night air was warm, enveloping us like a warm hug. Everything about it felt like home, down to the sweet scent of spiced apple cider that filled the air.

"What's happening?" I asked, glancing around the square. It had to be some sort of vision from a Seer, or a projection by a Mentalist. Except I couldn't explain the profound feeling of *love* that came with it.

Professor Warren's eyes watered as he took in the town. "It's the Law of Love. It's as I teach in my classes; *Mastering the vibrations of love will allow you to tune into Alora's magical frequencies with astounding accuracy.*"

I realized what that feeling meant. We were witnessing Alora, here with us in real-time. The coven's power was so strong it resonated through the realms and manifested Alora here with us now.

I went completely breathless. "Alora has been layered upon Octavia Falls this whole time, on another plane. Our loved ones really are with us all the time."

As I said it, spirits began to take shape before us. Hundreds, if not thousands, of our ancestors had come to witness the miraculous moment.

Meredith must've recognized someone, because she blew a breath of disbelief, like she couldn't believe what she was seeing. "Scott?"

A man with blond hair stepped out of the crowd. I'd seen him once before, the night of the Festival of Santos. The priestesses had dragged him on stage and forced him to disavow his marriage to Meredith because they were from different Casts. Meredith had agreed to marry another man, as she believed it was what the Goddess desired. Scott resolved to the priestesses' will because he didn't have any other choice, but they later executed him anyway.

Meredith began to weep. "My dear husband. I'm so sorry for everything that happened. I was wrong to follow the Chosen blindly and give my life to them when I loved you so much. I believed the lies, and I'm ashamed that I ever let any of it come between us. Can you ever forgive me?"

Scott wrapped his ethereal arms around her. "I wish we had both seen the truth then, and maybe things would've turned out differently. I know you were scared, and I see now that what I thought was cruelty was only you trying to protect us both. If you'll still have me, Meredith, I will be waiting for you in Alora."

Tears streamed down her face. "I will, Scott. There is nothing I want more than to be given a second chance so I can make amends. I treated others so terribly, and I wish I would've trusted myself instead of the priestesses. I know things can never go back to the way they were, but I will spend the rest of my life, and into the afterlife if I must, making things right again."

Meredith turned toward her sister. "And Monica, I'm sorry about how I treated you. I don't know what truly happened to you, but I'm willing to listen to your story. I hope that you'll accept my apology."

Monica wiped tears from her eyes. "Meredith, there's nothing I want more than to be with my sister again."

The sisters embraced.

"Shane!" Alex shouted. He'd spotted his brother in the crowd of spirits and ran over to him. Shane had died in the Dungeon of a nightshade overdose our sophomore year. They looked identical, except Alex appeared slightly older and more worn down. The twins pulled each other into a tight hug.

"By golly, you did it!" A short, plump man stepped in front of us. He reached out to shake my hand, and I was surprised to see that his form was nearly solid. He wasn't quite *all* there, but our fingers didn't fade through one another, either.

"Hector?" I asked. I hardly recognized him at first, because the lines on his face seemed smoother, and his hair was thicker than I remembered.

Hector had been the head cook at the Cat-fé here at school. The priestesses had been threatening his family to get him to work for them using the Alchemy Wand to brew poison, before Verla's poison meant to target the priestesses had killed him first.

Beside him stood an older man. It was William Connor, one of our allies who'd been supporting us against the priestesses and had lent us the safe house we'd lived in for over a year.

"You've all done well," William said with a kind nod.

"I can't apologize enough that your lives were caught in the middle of all this," I told them.

"You don't have to apologize," Hector assured me. "We knew the risk we were taking on when we joined your movement."

"We were happy to lend any assistance we could," William added. "Even if it meant our lives. The coven has been saved, and so, our deaths are not in vain."

As I gazed around the surrounding spirits, I realized I recognized so many people we'd lost in the midst of the Miriamic Conflict. A group of people from school watched us from the edge of the crowd. I recognized Professor Daniels, a woman who'd taught Demonology and Journalism, whom the priestesses had hanged for a murder she didn't commit. Beside her stood Professor Perez, who'd been a victim of the demon the priestesses had summoned, and Professor Poppy, who'd died of a viral infection less than a year ago.

Then there was Professor Ward, who'd perished on the pyre the night of the Burning. She stood beside two girls from school I'd only met a few times—Ashley and Christine. The three of them had been researching the Oaken Wands, and the priestesses had burned them at the stake to silence them.

Other familiar faces appeared before us, including Felicia and Stacey, who were students that had been killed the night the school was attacked and the space-bending spell collapsed.

Nearby, Professor Loren lifted a hand and waved to us. I could still picture the image of her frail corpse lying on the battlefield in the wake of the Golem War. She stood beside her daughter, Autumn. The last time we'd seen Autumn, she'd fallen into a pit to the Abyss while fighting off the *nuckelavee* the night at Octavia Hall. She must've found her way out of hell and ascended to Alora. The two beamed happily as they were once again united.

Autumn wasn't the only one who'd ascended, either. As my gaze roamed the crowd, I spotted Priestess Charlotte standing beside Priestess Stella. The last time we'd seen them had been in the Abyss, when Priestess Charlotte had ascended to Alora and Priestess Stella had stayed behind.

We couldn't help Stella back then, but I saw now that she had progressed on her journey and made the choice to ascend.

I thought all these people might be angry or bitter that their lives had been cut short, but they weren't. They smiled and waved at us, appearing wholly at peace.

Two kids smiled our way like they knew us. I didn't recognize them at first, but only because they weren't the same age as I remembered them. The younger of the two boys, who looked around eight or nine years old now, carried a plastic toy dinosaur with him.

"Caleb?" Lucas asked breathlessly.

The boys rushed forward, laughing as they ran across the square. Caleb stopped in front of Lucas, and he placed his toy dinosaur in Lucas's hands.

"Thank you for giving my mom and dad peace," he said.

It was Caleb Thomas and Isaac Miller, the two boys who had been murdered by the Gingerbread Witches. They'd grown up in the time since their death.

"I wish I could've saved you both," Lucas told them.

"In a way, you did," Isaac said. "We know our families will never stop mourning our deaths, but now that they have answers, they can live their lives knowing that one day we'll be together again. In the meantime, we've got people here to love and take care of us."

The boys turned, then ran over to a man with a thick beard. I recognized Jude Bennett, who'd lost his life on the battlefield during the Golem War. He'd left behind a wife and son of his own, but as the kids ran over to him and he took them in his arms, I saw that he'd become a father figure to them, too. He'd been a friend of their parents, and the kind nod he gave to us told me he vowed to care for them until their own parents crossed over.

A woman with tight curls and a purple shawl came forward.

"Everly!" I cried. She'd been one of our greatest allies, who had stood up for us and was beaten beside us in the town square for it. She'd died of a curse I hadn't been able to break.

Everly drew me into a hug. It felt so warm and comforting, even though she wasn't entirely there. "I am so proud of you all. Seers aren't like prophets. When witches make a prediction, the outcomes can change. But I knew when I gave my prophecy that you had what it took to fulfill it. Even though I died in the process, I'm happy to have given up my life so that we could reach this moment."

The prophecy she'd given played back in my mind.

By fire and noose
The coven will fall
Division and suffering
Destruction to all

Great power of the chosen
The coven be made whole
By the only witch of her kind
And a reaper bound to her soul

"You called me chosen," I said. "Mother Miriam once told me I wasn't chosen by someone else, but that the prophecy was given because it was the path Lucas and I had already chosen ourselves. But we couldn't have brought the coven back on our own. This choice was all of ours. Thank you for being a part of it."

Beside me, Talia sniffled as she caught sight of someone else in the crowd. "Tyler...?" Her voice wavered.

Tate grabbed her sister's shoulder to steady herself. "Is it really him?"

Tyler approached his sisters and took each of their hands in his. "It's really me."

"Tyler, you ass!" Talia slugged him in the shoulder. "You weren't supposed to die. You promised you'd be my best man at my wedding, and I'm not even engaged yet!"

Tyler chuckled, and tears streamed down Talia's cheeks as the three siblings started laughing together. Their laughter was like a song, so full of joy and reunion.

"Yeah, you jerk," Tate teased. "What about that song you promised me? You never finished writing it."

Tyler smiled. "I did. I wanted to visit you in *Hok'evale* after the war was over and sing it to you. I left a recording of it on my computer, in case anything happened to me. Ask Mom and Dad. They'll be able to find it for you."

"In case anything happened to you?" Talia repeated. "Tyler, were you planning on sacrificing yourself?"

"Only if I had to," he admitted. "I'm sorry I had to go. I didn't want to leave either of you behind, but I died that night trusting that my sacrifice would be worth it. I don't want you to be sad that I'm gone. Listen to our songs, and know that I'll always be with you."

The girls embraced their brother in a group hug.

A young woman cleared her throat, and we all turned to see a girl with a jet-black ponytail and almond-shaped eyes wearing a Miriamic College hoodie.

"Amy!" Mandy cried. She ran forward, throwing herself into Amy's arms. Mandy sobbed as she pulled her best friend close.

It was hard to think about Amy without remembering the sound of her screams the night of the Burning. Amy had been one of my dearest friends, and I missed her a lot.

She laughed as Mandy squeezed her tighter. "I know I'm a ghost, but I think I can still be suffocated."

"I've missed you so much," Mandy said. "I'm never letting you go. Ever again."

I stepped forward. "It's really good to see you again, Amy."

Mandy stepped aside, and I pulled my friend's spirit into a close hug. She smelled of vanilla, just like I remembered.

"I've missed you all," Amy told me. She drew away to embrace Lucas, then did the same to Talia. Miles gave her a light hug, even though the two hadn't known each other well.

When Grant hugged her, he leaned back to lift her up in his arms. "I've missed my favorite lab partner."

Amy laughed. "It seems you've been brewing potions just fine without me."

Grant set her down. "It's not the same. You're a brilliant Alchemist."

"She's a brilliant person," Tate said longingly. She drew Amy into a hug, but as they pulled away, her hands lingered in Amy's a moment. "I wish you could've stayed."

"I had to go," Amy replied gently. "My death pushed you all to change things, and you finished what you set out to do. I'm in a better place now, but so are all of you. Even though it seems we've been separated all this time, I've always been with you."

Chloe approached Amy. "I know we weren't friends, but I want to tell you I'm sorry for the way I treated you. It was wrong of me to threaten your cat and use you to try turning Mandy into a toad. I said really mean things I wish I could take back. Can you ever forgive me?"

"I'm in Alora now, Chloe," Amy said, gesturing around. "Those feuds of the past mean nothing to me here. Of course I can forgive you, because all I want for you is healing."

Lucas grabbed my shoulder, startling me. I followed his stunned gaze to lay eyes upon a man with a similar build and features to my own husband. I'd seen pictures of him before, and I knew instantly that it was Lucas's brother, Eric.

Tears beaded in the corners of Lucas's eyes. "I never thought I'd see you again. Not in this life, at least."

"Believe it, brother," Eric said as he strode forward. "This was always meant to happen. You know I'd never leave without saying goodbye."

Lucas dragged his brother close, and they clapped each other on the back as they lingered in a long overdue embrace. Lucas squeezed his eyes shut tightly as tears free flowed down his cheeks.

He didn't look sad, though. With the tears came a smile, and his immense gratitude was clear as day.

"I used to be so angry at you," Lucas whispered. "I thought you left me alone. But I want you to know whatever I said back then, I don't mean it anymore. I'm not mad at you, and I hold no resentment. All I ever did was love you, and I was only sad to let you go."

"It's okay that you were angry with me," Eric said gently. "I just wish I could've been there to help. I should've told you how much I loved you before I left."

"You didn't have to," Lucas assured him. "I already knew."

"Except I love you *more* than you will ever know," Eric said.

Lucas pulled away and glanced around the square again, marveling at all the familiar faces. "How is all this possible?"

"Your song resonated with so much power and love that it brought us here," Eric explained. "It takes a lot of spiritual energy to bring another realm like this to Earth, but the coven is healing, and that's the most powerful spiritual energy of all. We don't have much time, as this kind of spell can't be replicated. So enjoy every moment, Lucas... here, and every moment after."

"I will," Lucas promised, before dragging his brother back into a tight hug.

I was happy for Lucas, but I knew that if his family could come back, then so could mine. I looked around for them, but I didn't see anyone I recognized.

Then I noticed a man and a woman approaching me. They appeared only a few years older than me, and wore clothes that were decades outdated. The woman gave me a kind smile, but only when she said my name did I recognize her voice.

"Nadine," she said with arms spread wide.

"Grammy!?" I cried. I ran to her, then fell into her arms. All her age lines had smoothed out, and her white hair had turned to brown waves that fell to her shoulders. That kind smile, though, was exactly as I remembered it.

As I pulled her close, I could taste the savory flavor of her brisket melting in my mouth, and I inhaled the scent of jasmine that followed her wherever she went.

"I don't understand," I said. "You look so young."

"Spirits in Alora are not bound by physical age," Grammy explained. "We take on the appearance of who we feel we are internally. When witches first die, they appear as they did in death. With time, however, they can age forward or backward, but our spirits are never stagnant. And, well..."

She took the man's hand beside her. "Nicholas makes me feel so young."

"You're my Grampy," I said in astonishment. "It's so good to finally meet you."

"I've been *dying* to meet my granddaughter," he joked as we embraced.

I laughed. "I see Grampy has a sense of humor."

Grammy beamed. "I wouldn't have married him otherwise."

"By the Goddess, you look so much like Faith," Grampy said.

I'd been looking around for her, but I didn't see her anywhere. "How is Mom?"

"Why don't you ask her yourself?" Grammy stepped aside, and I swore my heart sang so loud everyone around me could hear it.

My parents stood in the center of Alora's town square, my father rocking a baby in his arms. Tears sprang to my eyes as they approached me. "Mom, Dad!" I cried.

I'd seen them once in a vision during my Evoking Ceremony, but it wasn't the same as them truly being here. They'd appeared the night of my wedding to give their blessing, but they'd been there and gone in a moment. Just looking at them now was more time than I'd ever gotten with them since their death.

"Nadine," Mom said with a bright smile.

She barely finished my name before I'd thrown my arms around her middle. She smelled of freshly baked bread, and the sweet taste of chocolate chip cookies filled my mouth. I could feel the high-frequency buzz of her Alchemy magic resonating through her.

"I've missed you both *so much*," I cried.

My mom drew away to push my hair behind my ears. "I know, honey. And we've missed you."

Isa inched forward to smell my mother, then began rubbing her nose against my mom's leg. My mother smiled as she bent to scoop Isa into her arms.

"I came back, though," Mom said. "She may be only a fragment of my soul, and she's not the mother you once knew, but know that I am her, and she is me. Our love for you is one, and equally eternal."

"Thank you for being here, Mom," I told her. "I've needed you so much, and even when you couldn't be here the ways I wanted, you came in the ways you could. I will always love you both."

"You don't have to worry anymore, honey," Dad said. "Your family is together here, and we'll be waiting for you when your time comes."

I gazed down at the bundle in his arms, and sobs broke from my chest when I stared down into the eyes of a child that looked strikingly similar to Marcus. He wasn't the tiny baby I remembered, though. Dean looked several months old now, an identical copy of Marcus. He smiled up at me and reached his hand toward my cheek. Dean was growing up here in Alora, and I couldn't imagine his spirit being placed in the care of anyone better than my parents.

"Can I hold him?" I asked.

"You're his mother," Dad said. "You don't have to ask."

Dad placed my son into my arms, and Dean stared up at me with wonder in his eyes—like he knew me on a deep soul level that no words could ever explain.

Lucas came up behind me and wrapped an arm around my waist. He reached over to stroke Dean's cheek. "He looks so at peace here."

"He's a very happy baby," Mom said.

As she said the word *baby*, I heard the soft cry of another infant. Lucas and I both looked up to see a woman in her thirties carrying a swaddled infant across the square. She was beautiful, with soft skin and a long, twisted braid down her back, but I didn't recognize her.

Professor Warren appeared to know who she was, though, because he'd completely frozen in place as he stared shell-shocked at her.

"Roberta," he whispered.

I realized then it was Professor Warren's deceased wife.

"You don't have to say anything, Jonathan," Roberta told him gently. "I already know how you feel, and I know how hard it is to talk about."

It occurred to me then that Professor Warren hadn't really talked about his past. His wife seemed to understand that his silence was intentional and exactly what he needed. Everyone's trauma was different. Even two people who experienced the same event could feel very differently about it. If our trauma was unique, that meant that we all healed in our own way, too.

Some people found comfort in talking about their experiences to find answers, while others harmed themselves by replaying it. Some people healed by mending the relationships that had hurt them, while others—like Onyx and Lucas—found their greatest healing in walking away. Everyone's path was different, and that was beautiful. Professor Warren didn't seem like the kind of person who had to talk about his past to face it.

"We had a wonderful life together, and I will cherish those moments forever," Roberta continued. "You don't remember, but our souls made an agreement before we came to Earth. We only promised each other a short time. I left this world when my spirit chose to and not a moment sooner. Don't let this reunion hold you back from the life you have yet to live. You have a love yet to experience—the love of a father."

Roberta placed the child into Professor Warren's arms, and as the corner of the swaddle fell away, I noticed something in the child's features. He wasn't like the other spirits surrounding us, who were all slightly translucent with an ethereal glow about them. This baby was solid, as if it belonged not in Alora, but on the physical plane.

"This is Allyn?" Professor Warren asked in disbelief. "I don't understand. He was sold to a demon and taken to another realm. How is this possible?"

"The coven killed the demon, so his contract is null and void," Roberta explained. "Allyn never died, merely crossed realms. We were able to retrieve him from the demon's realm so that your son could be returned to you."

Tears streaked Professor Warren's cheeks. "It's been years, yet he still looks newborn."

"Time moves differently from one realm to another," Roberta explained. "From Allyn's perspective, he's only been gone a few hours. Seeing as he never truly died, he belongs with you in Octavia Falls."

Professor Warren bowed his head and lightly pressed his lips to his baby boy's forehead. "Thank you."

Roberta stepped aside, and as Professor Warren lifted his gaze, his eyes went wide. We all turned to see what he was looking at, only to come face-to-face with the spirit of Headmistress Clarice Verla.

She looked around in confusion. "How did I get here?"

Lucas wore a curious expression, and he approached Verla slowly. "You aren't like the other spirits here. I can feel energy signatures and sense which realm a soul belongs in. You haven't crossed over yet. The choice is still up to you."

"I should be in the Abyss, with my sister," Verla said. "Why didn't I go with her?"

"Because you're your own individual," Lucas said. "Even though you and your sister share a soul, each reincarnation is unique. You get to choose who you are without her. She'll always be a part of you, but this version of you can move on without her, if you so desire."

"After everything I did, I don't deserve to return to Alora." Verla gazed around the crowd, and her eyes flickered from one familiar face to another, lingering on the people she killed. "Hector, William, Everly… you all died at my hand, and I can never express how sorry I am for what I've done. I thought I'd do anything for love, but I realize now that the love I was desperately holding on to wasn't the love I wanted. I wish I understood that then, before anyone got hurt."

Her gaze turned to Professor Warren, then down to the child in his arms. "Nothing I can do will take back what I've already done, but I hope that in trying to make things right, you and our son will live a better life. I'm so sorry, Jonathan."

"I know you would've loved him, if you could've stayed," Professor Warren said. "I'm going to take good care of him."

Shimmering tears streaked Verla's ghostly cheeks as she turned to my parents. "Faith, Nathan. I know an apology cannot fix the damage I've caused. I took you away from your daughter, and I hurt your family beyond repair. I loved you so dearly, Faith. I wish I could change what I did, but I must acknowledge the choices I made, even if they were wrong. I thought I was protecting my sister, but I should've protected you."

"I hold no ill will toward you," Faith said gently. "I only wish I could've been there for you while you were grieving. I never meant to leave you behind when I fled Octavia Falls."

"You had your own curse to bear," Verla countered. "I never blamed you for leaving. We can sit around for the rest of eternity wondering what might've happened, but ultimately, it won't change what really did. All I can do is say I'm sorry, and hope that your future is filled with peace and love, because I never meant to take that away from you."

"You didn't," Mom said.

Then my mother walked forward and drew Verla into a hug. Verla hugged her back, and their magic resonated with one another, creating a bright white glow that emanated from their chests and through their entire spirits. I'd never seen forgiveness in physical form, but by the Goddess, it was the most glorious radiant light in all the universe. Verla hadn't asked for forgiveness, and she'd even admitted she didn't deserve it, but my mother honored her with it anyway.

As the women drew away from each other, a shadowed figure beyond them caught my eye. My heart stalled in my chest. I curled Dean's spirit close in one arm, then grabbed Lucas's shoulder with the other to steady myself.

A woman in a black velvet hooded cloak came forward, flanked by a tall creature with the head of a ram. She dropped her hood to reveal her pale skin and red lips. Her hair fell in dark waves around her shoulders. Gasps traveled throughout the coven, because each one of us recognized them.

It was Mother Miriam and Santos.

Mother Miriam approached Verla and took her hands in hers.

Verla drew back in confusion. "Goddess. I don't deserve to stand in your presence."

"I am not a Goddess who judges you," Mother Miriam said softly. "*All my children deserve to stand in my presence. I will love and guide you, as I have done for each of my children before.*"

Verla's voice cracked. "I wish you would've stopped me, so I wouldn't have hurt so many people."

"I tried," Mother Miriam said. "I sent friends to help you, and I gave you a child. But you were always going to make your own choices in the end. As a mother, it's my job to let you learn your lessons through your own life experience. I do not step in to control your decisions, because whatever you decide is a lesson you must learn. I can give you options, and I can show you different paths, but the paths you choose to walk are yours."

"I didn't know you were there," Verla stated sadly. "I thought I was alone."

"I never left you, and I never will," Mother Miriam said. "You are welcome in my home, if you are willing. I can take you with us to Alora, or Santos will take you to the Abyss. It's up to you where you want to go."

"I've always dreamed of returning home to Alora, but I'm not sure that's where I belong anymore." Verla hesitated. "Is this a decision I have to make on my own, or can I ask the coven to decide? They're the ones I did wrong, so it seems only fitting that my sentence should lie in their hands."

Mother Miriam gave a kind nod. "If that is what you wish, then you may ask them for guidance."

Verla turned to Judge Calloway. "You have delivered many verdicts in your time as judge. What sentence do I deserve for my crimes?"

Judge Calloway shook her head, like Verla was asking the wrong question. "If I were to sentence you the way I have in the past, then the coven hasn't learned anything. When the new Imperium Council was formed, they suggested a reform program for criminals, as they believed coven members had a chance to rectify their behavior by receiving the proper care. I see now that I judged their suggestion too soon. Perhaps our coven doesn't act out in violence because they seek to hurt others, but because they themselves need help. I don't think you deserve an eternity in the Abyss, Clarice, but if you are still asking the question, then I don't think you're ready for Alora, either."

"I will serve my time in the Abyss, then," Verla stated. "And when I've rightfully learned from my wrongdoings, I can ascend."

"You misunderstand," Judge Calloway said. "Those are not the only two options."

Judge Calloway's gaze flickered to the charred dirt where the Protection Tree once stood, and I understood what she was saying.

"Stay here with us," I offered. "When a witch sacrifices herself for her people, her spirit can grow into a tree. Our Protection Tree is gone, and the protection spell surrounding our town has fallen. Octavia's spirit has been freed, and we need a new guardian to protect the coven from outside threats. If you want to atone for your mistakes, then stay, and protect us the way we should've protected each other when this conflict began."

Verla gazed around at the people. "Do you all really want me to stay?"

"You sacrificed yourself for us," Miles said. "I think you deserve another chance."

All around us, coven members nodded in agreement.

"If that is what you wish, then I will accept my role as guardian," Verla agreed. "But if I'm to truly change, I must commit to doing things differently. I won't ever let anyone make wands from my branches, and in protecting this coven, I will prevent anyone from summoning a demon to do what I did. No witch or warlock will ever take your power again."

Mother Miriam held her head high. "I am proud of all my children. It is time for us to go now, but know that we are always near."

Lucas and I kissed Dean one last time, then I placed our son back in my mother's arms. Coven members stepped back from our ancestors, and our cats followed to circle the clearing. We joined hands once more as Verla's spirit took her place among the charred remains of the Protection Tree.

Mother Miriam began to sing a song I'd never heard before. Or, I thought I hadn't. Not in this lifetime at least. But when I heard her voice, it was like hearing a mother's long forgotten lullaby that she once sang while you were sleeping. I couldn't recall where I'd heard it—perhaps in another lifetime—but my soul knew every lyric.

Candles burn
And cauldrons rust
Broomsticks break
And turn to dust

But there's no end
To my sacred vow
This promise that
I leave you now

Wherever you go
Whatever you do
I will eternally
love you

A harmonious chorus rang over all of Octavia Falls as coven members living and dead joined in song. Slowly, Alora began to fade around us. At the same time, Verla's spirit glowed a bright white as the coven's magic flowed through her. I could feel our magic swirling together as one.

Above us, the sky lit up purple and teal as our magic began to form a protective shield around the town. It started high above our heads before raining down in an arc that spanned miles. I recalled what Grammy had told me about the significance of these colors. In the Miriamic Coven, purple symbolized spiritual connection and teal symbolized peace. It seemed wholly fitting now.

The light was so magnificent that I had to turn my eyes away from its brilliance. As the radiant light faded, I looked back to see that a tall oak tree stood in the center of the clearing. It wasn't as large as the old, twisted Protection Tree, but one day, it would grow to be even bigger. The leaves shuddered once, as if Headmistress Clarice Verla was letting out a sigh of freedom.

I looked around the forest for any signs of Alora, but all the spirits and buildings that had been here moments ago were gone. The coven was left standing amongst the remains of our desolate town, but somehow, the destruction didn't terrify a single one of us.

We'd fought so hard to bring the coven together, but we knew now that fighting had never been the answer. We had to learn that lesson together, and now that our coven was united, our suffering was over.

That didn't mean there wasn't more work to do. Healing wasn't something that happened in a singular moment, but it had started here with all of us, and there was no going back to the way things were. We were stronger than ever, and we could never be divided again.

I understood then why we'd struggled so hard in our position on the council. We'd been trying so desperately to cling to what was left of the coven and build upon a foundation that was no longer working.

I saw now that in order to rebuild the coven like we wished, it had to be completely destroyed so something new could take its place. When I looked around Octavia Falls, I didn't see the buildings that had been crushed. I saw the people who had prevailed.

From this moment forward, none of us would ever be the same. The coven had changed. The Miriamic people witnessed the birth of a new age, in which together we'd created something we hadn't had since the coven first formed…

Unity.

EPILOGUE

Three Years Later

Life in Octavia Falls had never felt more joyful. The Miriamic Conflict was over, and our coven was a prosperous community again. The dark magic that had once shadowed our town had been phased out by the light of thousands of witches.

Octavia Falls looked nothing like it did three years ago. After the demon's assault, a handful of shops were still standing, and an entire section of residential houses had remained untouched, but most of our city had been demolished. The historical society had preserved what they could, and we rebuilt from there. Still, the windows of these old shops along Main Street seemed to reflect the summer sun brighter than ever before. I inhaled a deep, refreshing breath as I strolled down the street, the sunlight warming my face.

"Catch me, Daddy!" Marcus yanked his hand out of mine and took off running down the sidewalk.

"Not so fast!" I teased playfully as I chased after him.

I caught up with him quickly and looped my arm around his tummy, then flipped him over my shoulder. He was three years old now, and I couldn't believe how big he was getting. He could talk in full sentences, and if I didn't keep a close eye on him, he'd go running off and disappear like a little escape artist. This kid marched to the beat of his own drum, that was for sure. Marcus let out a high-pitched squeak when I caught him, and the most glorious sound of my son's gleeful laughter filled the air.

If there was anything that shone brighter than our magic, it was my family. They were the most brilliant light in all my life, the very song that made my heart sing. I tickled Marcus, and he giggled happily.

Marcus gasped when he saw something that caught his attention. "Put me down, Daddy!"

I set Marcus back on the ground, and he ran over to a shop painted to look like a pumpkin. Plastic jack-o-lanterns sat on a display outside, and Marcus shoved himself between them.

"Take my picture!" he begged, flashing a big, cheesy smile.

I conjured my phone and snapped a few pictures. He struck a few poses like he was modeling for a fashion magazine.

It was early morning, and the shops were just opening. The lock on The Jolly Pumpkin's front door slid open, and Hattie stepped outside to place a sign on the sidewalk. Everest barked as she followed behind her Elementai.

"Priest Lucas," Hattie greeted. She'd spent some time in *Hok'evale* after the evacuations, but Hattie had been back since the end of the war. She spent the summer and autumn here in Octavia Falls and the rest of the year in California with her tribe.

"Please, just call me Lucas," I requested.

"It's an official title, and an important one at that," she countered. "When your term expires, we can all stop calling you priest."

After the end of the Miriamic Conflict, my friends and I told the coven it was time for us to step back from the Imperium Council, as our place running the coven was always meant to be temporary. Now that the power had been returned to the people, it was their choice on whether to keep the Imperium Council as it was, or to dissolve the council altogether and install a new system. We told them that Octavia Falls was theirs, and if we weren't welcome anymore, we wouldn't stay.

"This coven is yours as much as ours," Judge Calloway had said. *"You are the ones who brought us all together to end the Waning and save our town. We want you to stay. I do not believe that we need to abolish the Imperium Council system, but perhaps we can change the way in which we approach it, with elections every four years."*

We agreed wholeheartedly. Everyone in the coven deserved to be listened to, and we would all get a voice now.

When it came time to hold an election, the coven voted us back onto the council. Talia and Grant had politely declined, as they wished to return to school full-time to finish their degrees. I agreed to serve one term until the coven got back on their feet, when another Mortana could be elected and take my place on the council. Personally, I wanted to get back to focusing on journalism. Nadine and Chloe were natural leaders, and they had no reservations about sitting on the Imperium Council for as many terms as the coven would have them. Something told me they'd be running this town for quite a long time.

In place of Grant and Talia, Professor Richards had retired as a history professor to serve as the Alchemy priest for the time being, while Dr. Mack had stepped up as our Seer priestess. Like me, she agreed to serve for only one term. She wanted to help the coven, but I didn't think her heart lied in politics. She talked about leaving the coven after the next election so she could reconnect with witches who'd left for good, and help counsel those coven members living in other societies.

Most of the coven had returned to Octavia Falls when our magic returned, but there were others who couldn't bear to ever come back. I understood that and respected their choices, but I wished they could see how much things had changed.

We'd rebuilt so much of the town in the past three years. Even the Imperium Council wasn't the same as it once was. We were no longer overworked, and while it was still our job to make sure everything in town was running smoothly, we didn't need to have a hand in everything anymore. Committee members managed their own sectors, and they did it better than a few singular council members ever could. When people were given creative freedom, they were passionate and motivated about their jobs, and they were proud of the work they'd done. The rate at which homes and businesses had been rebuilt was astounding, and our economy was thriving.

Hattie turned to Marcus. "I see you like my pumpkins, my dear."

"Jacker-lanterns are cool," Marcus said, not quite getting the word right.

"I have jack-o-lantern candies inside," Hattie offered. "They make your eyes glow orange like a pumpkin. You can have one if your dad says it's all right."

Marcus yanked on the bottom of my shirt. "Please, Daddy!"

"One candy," I agreed. "We don't want to spoil your lunch. Mommy's at home making your favorite."

Marcus gasped dramatically. "Apple pie!"

"Yes, and that will be enough sugar for one day," I teased.

Hattie went inside and returned with a jack-o-lantern lollipop. Marcus tore off the wrapper and popped the sucker in his mouth. He crossed his eyes as they started glowing orange, as if he could look at his own eyeballs.

"I hear the big ceremony is today," Hattie said.

"Yeah. Construction has finished on Miriam Mansion, and we'll be unveiling it at a ribbon-cutting ceremony this afternoon," I told her. "Marcus and I came into town to pick up the last of the items we need for the ceremony. It's a big day. The mansion has been one of our biggest projects these past few years. It wasn't easy piecing back together the remains of the building, but our construction crews are very talented, and they've managed to reconstruct as much of the original structure as possible. There's a new wing that's brand new, but most of it is material from the original building."

"I drove by the school last week," Hattie said. "It's amazing what they've been able to do."

"It really is," I replied. "You should come to the open house. We'll be casting a space-bending spell during the reopening to expand the classrooms again. The college really needs the extra space."

"I bet the students will be happy to get out of the community center and back into a real school building," Hattie said.

I nodded. "Grant and Talia have continued their classes, and there have been times when they have to rush from the community center to the courthouse to get to their next class, because we don't have the space to keep classes in one building. It will be good for everyone to get students and professors back in one location. Students will be able to move back to the dorms this fall."

"Will you or your friends be staying there?" Hattie asked.

"No. It wouldn't make sense for Nadine and me now that we've started a family. We don't live too far from campus now, so it's not a problem for us to get to classes."

"You must be graduating soon," Hattie said.

"Within the year," I replied. "Nadine and I have been taking classes part-time to finish our degrees. I have only one semester left until I graduate with my Journalism degree, and Nadine will be done next summer with her degree in Criminal Justice. Miles accelerated his schoolwork and already graduated from his Criminal Justice major, and Chloe just got her degree in Public Administration. She graduated with Grant, who got his degree in Culinary Arts, and Talia double majored in Music and Counseling. Grant and Talia are talking about buying a house soon now that they're done with school."

"That's lovely," Hattie said. "I'm so proud of you all. Well, I won't keep you long. It sounds like you have a big day ahead of you. I'll see you at the open house."

Hattie waved goodbye, and Marcus and I continued down the street. As the town came alive in the early hours of the morning, lively chatter began to fill the air. A café door stood propped open, and a beautiful melody from a woman playing the flute spilled onto the street, backed by the distant twinkle of wind chimes hanging from a shop a few doors down. Witches and warlocks gathered on patios and conversed kindly over morning tea. The smell of burning cedar filled the air as shop owners cleansed their doorways to ward off bad energy, before whispering prayers to bless their shops with good fortune for a profitable day.

We passed by shops where skeletons who were dressed in long, flowing dresses danced in the window displays, then past a pet shelter where kittens pawed at balls of yarn while waiting to be adopted. A nearby bookstore had leatherbound journals in the window display that flipped their pages on their own.

We walked past the visitor center, which was something our town had never had before, as it was unusual for Octavia Falls to welcome visitors. Now, we had a center set up to help guide visitors from other supernatural societies during their stay here. Our protection spell still kept out those who wished us any harm, but we now welcomed more visiting professors and supernatural tourists than ever before.

All kinds of flyers were hung on a bulletin board near the visitor center entrance, advertising community festivals, group dance classes, and assistance programs. I noticed a flyer for the health clinic, and my heart filled with pride for all the coven had done together. With our magic back, the economy was booming, and we were able to use the money flowing into the coven to restore our healthcare system. More than that, we'd set up a new walk-in clinic that provided free resources to witches and supernatural refugees alike.

Marcus finished his sucker, and the orange glow faded from his eyes. I helped him toss the stick into a nearby garbage, and he got a big smile on his face when he turned.

Marcus ran over to the window of a wand shop. He banged his tiny palm on the window and jumped up and down excitedly. "The dragon man is here!"

The owner of the shop caught sight of Marcus, and he hurried outside to greet us. A miniature cat with dragonfly wings fluttered beside him.

The old man tipped his newsboy cap at me. "Lucas. Good to see you."

"Beau," I replied kindly.

Beau Blankard was the half-fae, half-warlock friend of Helena's whom we met in *Hok'evale*. He'd been the one to tell us about the Warlock's Trial. Beau had been driven from our town decades ago when the coven found out what he was. They'd poisoned his mate simply for existing in Octavia Falls as fae. Beau had talked about returning to Octavia Falls to reopen the wand shop he'd run for twenty years when he was younger, and that's exactly what he did once the Miriamic Conflict ended. He'd managed to purchase the same building he once owned all those years ago.

Marcus yanked on my pant leg. "Daddy, can he shift?"

I chuckled lightly. "That's something you'll have to ask *him*."

Marcus dropped his gaze and slowly stepped up to Beau, bashfully skidding the tip of his shoe across the ground. "Can you do the dragon?"

"Why, of course, Marcus!" Beau said happily. "Anytime you ask, although you may want to stand back."

Marcus scurried backward, but his eyes stayed locked on Beau.

Beau cleared his throat and loudly announced, "I'm going to shift into a dragon now!"

All down the street, children ran over to watch. You'd think they were all witnessing Santa Claus on Christmas Day. In Octavia Falls, a fae shifter like Beau was equally mystical, and the kids absolutely loved him.

Beau stepped out further onto the empty street to make room. Then his limbs began to elongate, and his nose turned into a snout as he shifted into a dragon before our eyes.

All Marcus's shyness melted away as he threw his hands in the air and giggled. The pure joy of a child never ceased to amaze me.

Beau was a relatively small dragon compared to other fae shifters, but he was still bigger than any vehicle parked on the street. He was entirely black, though his scales shimmered a dark purple. Even in dragon form, he looked like the Mortana he was. Two black horns protruded out of his head, but those were the only sharp spikes on him, as he had a smooth spine and tail.

Beau spread his leathery bat-like wings and kicked off the ground. He flew above the buildings and spiraled one rotation through the sky before landing back on his feet. Then Beau turned his snout upward and breathed fire that rained harmless embers down on the crowd of kids. The children clapped and cheered in absolute delight.

Beau shifted back into human form, hobbling a bit as he returned to the front of the shop. "By the gods, I'm getting too old for such tricks."

"You don't have to fly on my son's account," I told him.

Beau laughed. "If I'm going to die, I'll die happy. These kids love it!"

"One day, I'll be a shifter," Marcus claimed.

"Is that so?" Beau entertained.

"Yep," Marcus stated proudly. He got down on his hands and knees and bared his teeth at Beau. "Rawr!"

I didn't get this kid. He had a weird obsession with the fae.

Beau jumped back and placed his hand over his heart to play along. "Oh, my! You'll make a very fierce shifter indeed."

"I'll be scarier than you, but pretty, with feathers on my head like a peacock!" Marcus ran his fingers through his dark waves to make them stand straight up.

He was always making up stories that didn't make a whole lot of sense. I couldn't always follow where his imagination took him. No one had ever accused my son of being anything less than theatrical, that was for certain.

Beau cocked his head toward the door. "Come on in. Your order's all finished."

Beau led us inside the wand shop. Hundreds of expertly crafted wands lined displays on the walls. They were all different sizes, shapes, and colors, and each one was entirely unique. Beau only sold wands he'd made himself, and each one was more incredible than the last.

A TV played a news station quietly behind the counter. Marcus scurried behind the register and climbed onto a chair to make himself perfectly at home while he stared mesmerized at the television.

I sighed. "Marcus."

"It's okay," Beau said kindly. "He's more than welcome to sit. It's just a supernatural news station based out of Malovia. They're doing a segment on the royal family. I like to know what's going on back in my home country. Makes me think of Sebastian…"

Beau got a faraway look in his eyes when he mentioned his late mate.

He quickly snapped out of it. "Right, your order. I have it right here."

Beau pulled an intricately carved wooden box from under the counter. It was beautiful, with all kinds of Miriamic symbols twisting together, along with depictions of crystals and the moon phases.

I ran my fingers over the carvings. "It's beautiful. You really didn't have to do all this."

Beau waved his hand like it was nothing. "The coven has been nothing but kind to me since I returned to Octavia Falls. Lending my talents is the least I could do."

"Thank you. The coven will cherish this for quite some time," I told him.

"It's already been paid for, and I know you're in a hurry, so I'll let you get back to your day," Beau said. "Thank you for letting me do this for you."

I took the box under my arm. "It's no problem at all. We're grateful for your contribution."

I turned to my son, who was completely glued to the TV. The newscast showed a faraway shot of the Malovian royal family leaving the palace in Dolinska, though I could hardly make them out.

The angle shifted, and it focused on a little blonde girl that looked around Marcus's age. I guessed she must be the child of someone important.

"Princess!" Marcus cried, pointing at the television.

"Yes, she does look like a princess," I told him.

Marcus hopped up on his knees and growled at the TV like he was playing shifter again. He started barking at the girl on the screen, letting out a wolfish howl.

I sighed. "Usually he pretends to be a cat, but I guess he's a dog today."

Beau laughed. "He's adorable."

"Most of the time," I agreed. "I try to support his imagination as much as I can, but it can get away on him—like the time he cut holes in his bed sheets so he could play with the ghosts inside his closet."

"Real ghosts?" Beau asked.

"Imaginary," I said. "We had the sheriff check the whole house, and there's nothing but a ghost cat living there."

"Hmm…" Beau eyed Marcus curiously. "Don't discredit his imagination and stories. Children can be very perceptive."

Marcus barked at the TV again.

"Perceptive, or maybe just a bit fantastical," I said. "I'm not sure. Marcus, time to get home to Mommy. We don't want to miss apple pie."

At the mention of apple pie, Marcus seemed more alert. He climbed down from his chair and followed me out of the wand shop and back to the car.

I drove toward the edge of town, past the school and to a long driveway lined with trees on all sides.

"Where are we going, Daddy?" Marcus asked from his car seat.

"We're going home."

The trees gave way to a large clearing, and the most beautiful home in all of Octavia Falls stood before us. A wall of green ivy grew up the side of the house, and the large arched doorway stood propped open.

After the Miriamic Conflict ended, Nadine and I had returned to our special place at the abandoned mansion behind the school. Turned out the old headmaster's family still owned the property, but they didn't wish to return to Octavia Falls and were willing to sell it at a low price. They didn't think anyone would be interested in sinking their money into restoring the building, but this place had always been our safe haven, and we didn't care what it took to restore it to its former glory.

We made a respectable salary serving on the Imperium Council, so we'd been able to remodel the front of the house so we could live in it while we worked on restoring the rest of the property. The old, cracked stone steps had been repaired, and the roof had new shingles. We'd removed overgrown weeds and dead shrubs, and now the lawn flourished with fresh-cut grass and colorful flowerbeds. It was everything I could've ever dreamed and more for us.

I recalled the first time I brought Nadine here. She'd seen so much beauty in this house, even in its former dilapidated state. I'd struggled to see that and had called it *just a house*. I couldn't have been more wrong. There was so much beauty in the detailed crown moldings, and an elegance to the carved mantle in the living room. I once struggled to see the beauty in the world, but Nadine inspired me to find the good in everything. I used to be so unsure of myself, but I wasted so much time looking at the bad. Nadine fell in love with me here in this mansion because she saw all the good I couldn't see, and I was grateful to finally be witnessing it myself.

That didn't mean we didn't have hard days. Nadine and I still had disagreements from time to time, and I could slip back into depressive episodes, but we knew how to communicate through those moments so that even when things were tough, we didn't have to suffer through it. I attended weekly therapy appointments, and Nadine joined me in healing therapies that had helped us both immensely. We practiced yoga together every morning before the kids woke up, and on the weekends we attended breathwork classes and sound bath therapies at a local studio. We found that when we connected with our bodies, we could create our own kind of magic—in the bedroom and out of it.

When slowing down didn't work, we strapped the kids in a stroller and took them down to the park, where we played disc golf together or pushed the kids on the swings. Every day was different in our family, but we found that as long as we spent it together, we could get through anything.

As I pulled into the driveway, Nadine stepped onto the front porch with our daughter propped on her hip. She lifted Erica's hand and helped her wave. The two wore matching dresses that were casual enough for summer, but professional enough for the ceremony today.

"Mommy!" Marcus cried happily.

I parked the car and helped Marcus out of his car seat. He tore across the lawn with his arms spread wide. Isa, Oliver, and Rishi had followed Nadine outside. Rishi ran toward Marcus, but the cat tripped down the stairs and face-planted into the dirt. Isa rushed over to lick Rishi's ears.

Erica pointed a tiny finger at me. "Dada."

I hooked the wooden box under my arm, then climbed the porch steps. Nadine and I traded kids. I took Erica in my arms while Nadine scooped Marcus into a tight hug.

"Oof, you're so big," Nadine told him. "You've only been gone an hour, but I think you grew two inches!"

"Yeah, I'm three inches!" Marcus held up three fingers.

"I think you're three years old," Nadine humored him. "And maybe three feet tall."

"I'm three," Marcus said. "Three of everything."

Erica mumbled a string of words I didn't quite catch. Then she shouted, "Two!"

"That's right," I told her, stroking her brown pigtails. "You're two years old."

We found out shortly after the war ended that Nadine was pregnant. Erica had been born a few weeks early, though not dangerously early like the twins. She was seven pounds at birth, which was large for a baby born at thirty-six weeks, but now she was a petite little thing that I didn't think would ever catch up to her brother. She was fourteen months younger than Marcus, but looked significantly smaller.

Nadine leaned forward to peck me on the lips. "We have guests."

We carried the kids inside, and our cats followed. I hung my keys on a hook near the door, next to Nadine's set. The modern brass key I'd found upstairs years ago, which I'd given to her on her birthday, dangled from her keychain. It fit into all the locks in the house.

I recalled when she first saw the key, she asked why I'd give it to her.

"*It's our special place,*" I'd said. "*And this is me promising you we'll be making lots of memories there.*"

I'd fulfilled my promise, and I continued to do so every day.

Nadine led me past the living room, but I paused for a beat outside the doorway just to take it all in. Sometimes, I still couldn't believe this was my life. The peeling wallpaper that had once sagged from these walls had been replaced by new drywall and a fresh coat of paint. We'd kept the original hardwood floors but had them refinished. Now, the room was full of our furniture, and children's toys scattered across the floor.

Above the mantle, the chariot card we'd pulled from Talia's deck at our wedding hung framed. A taxidermy mouse Gregory had gifted me a few years ago stood on display. We'd found the mouse dead in the house after Oliver caught him, and I remembered what Gregory had said about wanting to do taxidermy art, so I'd given it to him. He came back with this reaper mouse he'd made special for me. The creature was dressed in a black hooded cloak Gregory had sewn himself, and the mouse held a white wand carved out of bone.

Laughter rang down the hall from the direction of the dining room. I tore my gaze off the mantle and continued down the hall, where I found Grant, Talia, Miles, and Chloe gathered around the table. Tall stacks of programs for the ceremony lay in front of them, and they worked together to fold them and pack them away in boxes to take to the school later. There must've been hundreds of programs, as we expected a large audience.

Nadine situated Marcus at a kids' table set up in the corner. She laid sheets of paper in front of him and opened small containers of washable paint. He was already sticking his fingers into them and smearing the colors across the page. If there was anything Marcus loved more than making up stories, it was painting.

I placed Beau's box next to a stack of papers on the dining table, where Gus, Bella, Kiki, and Marley were lounging. Then I set Erica in a chair at the kids' table and scooted her close so she could craft with Marcus. Instead of paints, she opted for crayons. Even at two years old, she was more poised than Marcus, sitting straight up while she ran the crayon over the paper intentionally. Marcus, on the other hand, hunched over his painting and smeared colors together frantically. Erica was intentional with her lines, but Marcus understood color, and he avoided mixing anything together that would muddy his painting. Somehow, everything he made turned out looking really good—better than a three-year-old should be able to make.

"Is that what I think it is?" Miles asked, gesturing to the stack of papers on the table. He was dressed in his sheriff uniform, as usual. When the elections took place, the coven had voted him back on as sheriff, and the townspeople loved him.

"That depends," I said as I sat beside our friends. "What do you think it is?"

"I'm *hoping* it's the finished draft of the guide Nadine's been working on," Miles said. "She says she won't come to work for me until that's done."

Nadine grabbed a stack of programs to start folding. "I said my Curse Breaker guide *will be* finished before I come work for you. That still stands, but I need to finish my degree first. We're busy enough with council duties, classes, and parenting that I can't add another job into the mix, even if it's only part-time."

"I need a good detective on the police force," Miles begged. "No one has the attention to detail that you do."

"Call me when there's a murder," Nadine said playfully. "Until then, I have my family to focus on. Once the kids are a little older and in school, I'll have more time to be a cop. You can count on that, because it's literally all I ever dreamed of being, but I'm not in a hurry."

Nadine had always been a high-achiever, and that hadn't changed. She was still aiming to become a priestess *and* a police officer, and she didn't give a damn if anyone said that was too much, because it was her dream. It wasn't one or the other, because she believed she could serve the coven best as priestess by working closely with law enforcement, and many of the duties overlapped anyway, so it was worth following her passions.

"If that's not the guide on Curse Breaker magic that Nadine's been working on, what is it?" Chloe asked as she packed a pile of programs into a box.

I slid to the pages closer to me. "I was waiting to tell anyone until it was done. I wrote a reaper guide."

Grant's gaze snapped up from the programs he was folding. "Lucas, that's great! Why didn't you tell us?"

"I didn't want to feel any pressure to get it done," I said. "We still have time until a new Reaper's Apprentice awakens their powers, and I wanted to give myself that time. But as it turns out, I loved every second of working on it, and it's as complete as I can make it for now. I've transcribed everything from Autumn's Reaper Records, and I've added in my own observations, insights, and experience to teach the next Reaper's Apprentice about their powers. I'll keep adding to it as I learn more, but for now, this is the first edition."

"That's really awesome you did that," Chloe said. "You could have it printed and sell copies in the local bookstores. This history and these principles aren't just for reapers. All Mortana should have access to this information. It could help fund the newspaper you want to open."

Nadine and I exchanged a glance.

Talia narrowed her eyes at us. "You two are hiding something, aren't you?"

"It's not official yet," I admitted. "We've been in touch with the owner of the *Miriamic Messenger*, and she's hiring me to do a feature on the Hawkei tribe. I'm really excited about it, because it perfectly aligns with my mission as a journalist. It's important our people understand more about other supernatural cultures so we don't cause harm. I'll get a chance to visit *Hok'evale* again and learn more about the Hawkei."

"Chief Cauac has already agreed to do an interview and help in any way he can so that Lucas portrays the Hawkei accurately and respectfully," Nadine added. "It's going to be a really fascinating piece."

I nodded. "That said, the owner of the *Miriamic Messenger* wants to retire in a few years. She insists the business needs to go to someone who she trusts to report impartially, so she's offering a really good deal to the right person. If all goes well with this piece on the Hawkei, she wants me to take over the paper once my term as priest expires."

Talia squealed. "Lucas, that's amazing! Can I see your reaper guide?"

"Sure," I said. "If you want to read it, I'm open to feedback."

Talia reached across the table with her left hand.

"Hold on. What is *that*?" Nadine cried, pointing at a ring on Talia's finger—yes, on *that* finger.

Talia and Grant burst into a fit of laughter together.

"We were waiting to see how long it'd take for someone to notice!" Grant exclaimed. "I wasn't sure how much longer I could hold it in!"

"We're engaged!" Talia cried happily.

"Congratulations!" Nadine sang as she stood to give Talia a hug.

Chloe shot out of her chair. "Are you kidding me? We're going to be sisters-in-law?"

Talia nodded enthusiastically. "Yes!"

Chloe rushed around the table and practically shoved Nadine aside to throw her arms around Talia. "Finally!"

Miles leaned an arm over the back of his chair. "Took you two long enough."

"I've been waiting to propose until we could settle down," Grant explained. "Now that we're done with school and I'm making good money as a cook at The Pie Shack, I could afford the ring. And Talia's thriving in her job at the counseling center, so it felt like the right time for both of us. I'm still going to open my own restaurant, after we get settled down. I wanted this moment marking the beginning of the rest of our lives to be perfect."

"And it was," Talia gushed as she showed off the ring. It was a small, dainty ring with an oval diamond in the center and smaller pointed diamonds made to look like leaves. "Grant rented out The Pie Shack after hours and decorated it with the most beautiful witch lights. He set up a table with flower petals and romantic music. The candles even sparkled from this alchemy wax he created that made the flames glow different colors. Then he made me the most delicious chocolate silk pie. When he brought out my slice, the ring was propped up on the whipped cream, sparkling so beautifully."

"That sounds *so* romantic," Nadine said dreamily.

"It was," Talia replied. "I love how much of himself and his magic he put into it. A girl couldn't possibly say no."

Grant leaned over to stroke her hair. "*You're* the magical one, because you said yes. I've never been happier."

"Hear, hear!" Miles exclaimed, raising an imaginary glass.

We all agreed. None of us had *ever* been happier, and I didn't go a day without marveling at the joyous life we woke up in. It was certainly not something to take for granted.

My friends continued laughing, telling jokes, and reminiscing on good times while we finished folding the programs for the ceremony. Nadine served lunch—a delicious stew with a side of homemade bread and apple pie for dessert—then we cleaned up and gathered our things to head to the school.

"Daddy, look!" Marcus yanked on my hand and guided me over to the kid table, where his painting had been drying during lunch.

I looked down at it to see he'd painted a bunch of dark blobs with strange faces. Some of them had a dozen eyeballs, and others had sharp teeth. I was amazed at what he could do with finger paints at three years old, but at the same time, the picture gave me pause. These blobs looked a whole lot like… monsters.

I worried about Marcus a lot. It was common for parents to do, but Marcus was… special. We'd tried to break his curse with the Master Wand, but that had backfired on us and the Master Wand snapped in two. The Oaken Wands hadn't been any more capable of breaking his curse.

After the Waning ended and we got our magic back, Nadine was able to perceive Marcus's curse again. The curse the priestesses cast on Marcus—which prevented any witch or warlock from telling him about his demigod powers—was still active, and we hadn't found anything strong enough to overpower it. Furthermore, his curse prevented us from creating another Master Wand, so we couldn't try that again.

Professor Wykoff had been searching for solutions for years, ever since the night the Master Wand broke. She had yet to find a viable solution.

Marcus was a happy kid *now*, but I worried what exposure to this curse would do to him long-term. We'd already seen how a curse from infancy had affected Nadine and Chloe, and Marcus's was stronger yet.

As a father, all I wanted was to let Marcus be a kid as long as possible, but when he showed me pictures like this, I worried there was a darkness buried deep inside of him that I may be unable to save him from.

"That's lovely!" Nadine told Marcus as she came up behind us. "The purple monster's my favorite."

"The black one's *my* favorite," Marcus said proudly. He snatched up the painting and romped off down the hall.

I turned to Nadine. "Do his paintings not bother you? This is the third monster painting in the last week."

"It's not unusual for kids to imagine monsters in their closet," Nadine said with a shrug.

"Yeah, but what if *his* are in his head?" I worried.

"I simply told Marcus to make friends with his monsters. He seems to be doing well with that advice."

"Marcus isn't just some ordinary kid," I insisted. "He's got a curse he can't break, and on top of that, he's my son."

Nadine frowned. "Lucas, we've talked about what it means to be the son of a reaper. I don't believe the bullshit about the Reaper's Shadow curse—that Samael Davis killed his mother and cast the curse because he was born with some darkness carried down from his Reaper's Apprentice father. Witch magic doesn't work that way, so that part of the story can't be true. Something else happened to that kid who cast the Reaper's Shadow curse, and whatever it was isn't going to happen to our son."

"I agree with you," I said. "I used to think reaper powers were dark and dangerous, but I don't believe that anymore. What happened with the

Reaper's Shadow curse was some sort of cycle of generational trauma, and we've stopped that cycle in our own families. But that doesn't mean Marcus won't have trauma of his own. He's already gone through so much, with a curse we can't break on top of it. I want to be able to help him, and if we can't tell him what he is or what he's capable of, we can't prepare him or help him properly process any of this."

I'd tried telling Marcus of his demigod powers before, experimented to find loopholes and workarounds, but every time I tried to talk to my son about anything remotely related, I choked up against my own free will. I'd tried writing it down, and the ink would fade before he could look at it. There truly was no way to tell him, and so, he would always be left in the dark. This wasn't something I wanted him to figure out on his own.

"But I wasn't talking about Marcus being the son of a reaper," I clarified. "I meant it'll be hard for him because neurological conditions can pass down genetically. I have multiple mental health disorders, and Marcus could've inherited similar neurology."

"We can handle that," Nadine promised. "We know how to get him the care he needs if he requires support. All we can do in the meantime is give him a good life. Besides, we don't know that this curse is going to last forever. Professor Wykoff has been away all summer researching Marcus's curse, but she'll be back this afternoon for the ceremony. We'll talk about this with her then."

"All right," I agreed. "Let's get to the ceremony. We don't want to be late."

I grabbed the carved wooden box from the table, and our friends carried the boxes of programs out to the cars. We loaded the kids in their car seats and the stroller in the back, then drove down the road to Miriam Mansion.

School officials had already lined rows of chairs at the front of the school. There was also a podium set up, along with a wide red ribbon stretched before the doors. I dropped my box off at the podium, then my friends and I helped distribute programs to each seat before coven members started arriving.

As cars began filling the parking lot, Nadine, Chloe, and I went to find our spots up front with the rest of the Imperium Council. Miles stood near the podium with his hands on his hips, keeping watch for any threats. His position as sheriff was pretty easy these days, but it was his job to stay on high alert. Grant and Talia went to find a seat with our kids in the front row.

"Priest Anthony, Priestess Linda." Nadine greeted the other council members kindly. It still felt strange to call them anything but Professor Richards and Dr. Mack. "Have you seen the headmaster?"

"He should be around here somewhere," Professor Richards said as he peered through the crowd.

I followed his gaze, but I didn't see the headmaster at first. Instead, my eyes landed upon a woman with purple glasses, and a man pushing her wheelchair. He helped her into a spot near the front reserved for wheelchairs, then sat in the row beside her. In her lap, she held a young child. The kid was the same age as Marcus, but he looked a bit younger, with a rounder face and shorter limbs. He wore glasses with a strap, though I knew he couldn't see well out of them.

Lydia and Quentin had returned to Octavia Falls once the conflict ended, and they'd brought their son Alistair with them. He'd been born with achondroplasia, a form of dwarfism, and though he wore glasses now, his vision was quickly deteriorating, and he'd been diagnosed legally blind. We got together with them for play dates, and he and Marcus always had a blast. Alistair was nimble on the playground, but walked with a cat on a leash otherwise to help him get around. The first time I'd seen his cat, it'd been a kitten, but the cat was always eating and getting fatter by the day—hence the name they'd given it, Pig. Alistair had started using a cane as a secondary assistance device.

Quentin and Lydia had been some of the few people we knew personally who'd moved back from *Hok'evale*. Monica, Tate, and Mandy had all established a good life there and returned to *Hok'evale* after we killed the demon. Monica had reopened a music shop, and Tate was working at the rehab center there. Mandy worked with a jeweler making all kinds of beaded trinkets. She'd sent a beautiful beaded rattle for Erica's birthday a few weeks ago, and our daughter hadn't stopped playing with it since.

Onyx was also notably missing from the ceremony. After things settled following the conflict, the United Supernatural Union reached out. Our previous representative had perished the night of Nicole's attack, and as part of our treaty with the Union, we were required to appoint a new representative. Onyx had already been working with other supernatural races and making alliances in Paris, so the coven appointed her our Union Representative. We rarely saw her these days, but I was glad she was living her dream. The last time we talked, she seemed enthusiastic about the work she was doing, and I'd never seen her happier.

Among the crowd were other friends who had survived the conflict. Samantha and Darcy sat next to each other, shooting glances over at Alex, who was standing near the back in his police uniform.

"If you like him, you should ask him out," I heard Darcy say loudly.

"Shh…" Samantha hissed. "I didn't say I liked him. I just said the scar on his face is hot."

"You didn't *have* to say it," Darcy said. "I know a girl in love when I see it. Plus, he looks at you the same way my boyfriend looks at me. He clearly likes you."

"You think?" Samantha squeaked. She glanced over her shoulder again, and Alex caught her eye and smiled. She went beet red under his gaze, then giggled as she turned back to Darcy. "All right. I'll ask him out after the ceremony."

Professor Richards pointed to the crowd. "Ah, there's the headmaster. He's with Allyn."

Headmaster Warren knelt at the edge of a row of chairs, talking to a young child that sat between Gregory and Brayden. The kid was Marcus's age, with light hair and the complexion of a ghost. Headmaster Warren made a funny face, and the child let out a full-belly laugh.

For as strange as it was to call Professor Richards *Priest Anthony*, dropping the *professor* title off Warren's name felt entirely natural. Headmaster Jonathan Warren suited him quite well, and he was really good at his job.

But his job didn't leave much time for family, and after everything that happened, Warren decided that what was best for his family was different from most. He'd been too stricken with grief to raise a child. He didn't talk about it often, but he opened up to me once to say that every time he looked at Allyn, he saw Clarice Verla.

"I knew I couldn't be a good parent to my son," Warren had admitted to me. *"The best thing for him is to be raised by someone else. I still want to be a part of his life, but I can serve him better in the role of a grandfather than his only dad."*

Gregory and Brayden had stepped up to raise Allyn as their own. The couple had gotten married at a nearby courthouse after the evacuations.

Everything had felt so uncertain then, and they wanted to tie the knot before they lost the chance. After they returned to Octavia Falls, they assumed it'd be a few years before they could adopt a child, but Allyn had needed somewhere to go, and Warren had chosen them. Legally, Gregory and Brayden Walker were Allyn's dads, but Warren was still around to help.

Nadine and I walked over to Warren. He noticed us and got to his feet.

"Nadine, Lucas. It's so good to see you," he said as he shook each of our hands in turn. "I have to say, I don't know if we would've been able to salvage the school without the two of you. From the bottom of my heart, thank you."

"We couldn't have done it alone," I said.

Nadine gestured toward the podium. "It's time to get started, Headmaster."

"Yes, of course." Warren turned back to Gregory. "I'll see your family tomorrow night for dinner."

From what I heard, Gregory and Brayden brought Allyn over to Warren's house every Sunday night for dinner. Their arrangement was unconventional, but the four of them had become a family of their own, and that was beautiful.

Professor Warren stepped up to the podium, and the crowd quieted as his voice rang through speakers. "Welcome to the Miriam College of Witchcraft Grand Reopening! I'm Headmaster Warren, and we're thrilled you're here today to share this historic moment with us."

Krista Thomas, little Caleb's mom, knelt near the podium and started snapping photos with her professional camera. The pictures would go in the *Miriamic Messenger* next week.

Professor Warren went on to give some history about the college, as well as thank members of the community who had donated their time or money to rebuild the school. It was quite a long list, as it seemed that everyone had chipped in some way to help restore the building to its former glory.

"Before we open the school for tours, our Imperium Council welcomes you to be a part of this historic event by joining hands, so that together, we may perform a space-bending spell to expand the school to accommodate our staff and students' needs," Warren announced. "We join together with the following incantation: *What once lay broken is now revived. We expand this school to its former size.*"

All around us, hundreds of coven members joined hands and began speaking the incantation. Power surged around us as I linked my hands with Nadine on one side and Chloe on the other. Nadine's eyes began to glow a bright white as the power of the coven filled her up. She brought our power together and guided tendrils of magic to circle the entire building and swirl upward, until the whole school was encompassed by a massive spell.

From the outside, it appeared that nothing was happening, but through the front windows, I witnessed the walls of the Main Foyer stretching and expanding to our will. The grand staircase sank back into the school, and sconces doubled before our eyes as the walls tripled in size. Even the large fireplace seemed to grow under our spell, and I could've sworn I saw the painting of Mother Miriam above the mantle shimmer, like she herself approved of our spellwork.

The school absorbed the power, until all the shining tendrils of magic seeped into the walls of the building.

"Now, the Imperium Council will join me to cut the ribbon and welcome you back to our school!" Headmaster Warren announced.

He withdrew the box Beau had carved from beneath the podium and carefully opened it. Inside sat a long ceremonial wand that Beau had crafted by hand. The wand was even more beautiful than the box that held it. The handle had leaves and flowers carved into it, with vines that twisted around symbols from all Casts. The ceremonial wand looked like something antique and from another time, though it was brand new.

The Imperium Council gathered together, and Headmaster Warren stepped between us to hold the tip of the wand to the ribbon. Only when I got a look up close did I notice that Beau had engraved something else into the blade—an inscription that read *Unitas*. It was a Latin word that meant *unity* or *oneness*. It was the perfect touch.

"Smile!" Krista shouted.

Her camera clicked in quick succession as we leaned in to place our hands over Headmaster Warren's. Together, we cast a simple spell that sliced the ribbon in two. The ribbon fell away, and the crowd erupted into ceremonial celebration.

"Welcome back to Miriam College of Witchcraft!" Headmaster Warren shouted.

As the ceremony ended, people began flooding into the school to tour the new classrooms. I was amazed at the Main Foyer when we entered. It was a lot like I remembered, but it was somehow more beautiful. The red carpet that spanned up the staircase was brighter and softer than ever before, and the black chandelier that hung over our heads shined brilliantly.

Our friends met up with us in the Main Foyer. "This looks amazing!" Chloe raved as she spun around to take it all in.

"Miriam College of Witchcraft has never looked better," Talia agreed. She pushed the kids in a stroller. Erica was passed out, but Marcus twisted his head in every direction to take in the expansive room.

"How big is the pool?" Grant asked eagerly.

"I made sure to give the pool a little extra magic, just for you," Nadine joked.

"Anything else that's changed?" Miles wondered.

"I funneled more magic into the kitchens because they always seemed a bit too small," Nadine said. "However, there's one thing I decided *not* to change. Follow me."

Nadine led us around the back of the grand staircase to an elevator there. When the school was being rebuilt, we worked closely with construction crews to ensure the new school was entirely ADA-compliant, even when accounting for the space-bending spell. Nadine had insisted on tons of elevators and ramps, accessible sinks in the restrooms, braille signage, and all kinds of other accommodations in the buildings and class curriculum. Disabled kids deserved to enjoy and love this school just as much as everyone else did.

We took the elevator up to the second floor, and Nadine led us to the far end of the hallway. There was another elevator there, but where I expected to see a staircase, there was merely a blank wall.

"What's this?" Chloe asked.

"It's the Vanishing Stairwell, of course!" Nadine exclaimed.

Grant took a few steps back. "Ah, hell no! I'm not getting stuck in there again."

"It's not really vanishing," Nadine said. She pressed her palm to the wall, and her hand went straight through it. "I bent the space to make it look like a wall, but it isn't. It's a trick stairwell that's entirely safe."

"I like it," Talia said simply. "Miriam College of Witchcraft wasn't just about our classes. It's about the history of this building and the stories it tells. Believe me, finishing our coursework at the community center wasn't nearly as fun as roaming these halls with you guys. Nadine's keeping the tradition going."

"That's exactly what I wanted," Nadine stated proudly. "The next generation will grow up with legends of their own. I thought it'd be nice to have something to share with them."

I wrapped an arm around her waist. "It's perfect."

"Yes, it will be a joy traumatizing the next generation of students," Chloe teased. "Remember the time you pushed me into the Vanishing Stairwell, Nadine?"

Nadine laughed. "That's not fair. You trashed my room *and* tried to frame me for defiling Mother Miriam's painting."

"Oh, kiss already!" Miles exclaimed. "I don't care if Chloe's my wife. You two have the ultimate enemies to lovers story, and I'm sick of watching you two flirt and never getting to a climax."

Nadine smirked. "You want me to make your wife climax, Miles?"

Chloe rolled her eyes. "Don't listen to him. He just likes the idea of me making out with other women."

"Let's not and say we did," I suggested.

Nadine laughed. "Sorry to disappoint you, Miles. I'm gonna have to go with my husband on this one."

Chloe draped an arm around Nadine's shoulder. "We may not be lovers, but we do make very good friends."

Nadine looped one arm around Chloe's waist, and the other around mine until we were all gathered in a group hug. "Friends forever," Nadine promised.

"*Friends forever.*" We spoke in unison, as if the words themselves were an incantation sealing our life and our stories to one another.

After everything we'd been through, there was no taking it back. We were united as one, in this life and the next.

We continued through the halls of Miriam Mansion, touring dorm rooms and classrooms. Even the Grand Ballroom seemed bigger and more vibrant than it'd ever been before.

We finished our tour in the cafeteria, where there were refreshments laid out for the open house. Our friends gathered around a big table, and Marcus and Erica nibbled on fruit and crackers. We were almost finished eating when I caught sight of Professor Wykoff entering the cafeteria.

I nudged Nadine. "Professor Wykoff is back."

"We should go say hi," she suggested. "Tal, can you watch the kids?"

"Sure, but if your son starts finger painting with applesauce again, I'm not cleaning it up," Talia replied.

Nadine quickly moved Marcus's plate of applesauce away from him.

We approached Professor Wykoff, and our former teacher dropped her shoulders in relief when she saw us. "Lucas, Nadine. It's wonderful to see you!"

We exchanged hugs, but when we drew away, I noticed a hint of worry in her eyes.

"Is everything all right?" I asked.

"Everyone is safe for now," Wykoff assured me, though I didn't like the way she said *for now*. "I finished my research."

I shot a glance at Marcus. He was laughing at Grant, who'd placed two pieces of salami over his eyes and made faces at the kids. Marcus tried copying him by putting a pepperoni on the end of his own nose, but it fell off his face and onto the floor.

A lump rose to my throat. "We should talk in private."

"Yes, of course," Wykoff offered.

She led us out into the Main Foyer, which was all but deserted now. We gathered around a private seating area near the crackling fireplace. I took Nadine's hand in mine, and she squeezed back tightly.

"I do wish I had better news to share," Professor Wykoff began. "I've been working closely with the Demigod Guardians, and we know now why the Master Wand couldn't break Marcus's curse."

"There must be something that's stronger," Nadine insisted.

Professor Wykoff shook her head regrettably. "That's what I have to tell you. There's nothing that can break his curse."

My stomach dropped, and Nadine's features went pale.

"I've never run across a curse that can't be broken," Nadine pressed. "Even if it takes time."

"I'm afraid even time can't change this," Wykoff replied. "In our research, the Demigod Guardians have learned that a spell a demigod casts upon themselves cannot be reversed. In this case, your son's curse was cast using the Master Wand, which was born of his own power. Magically, it's as if Marcus cast this curse upon himself, and so this magic is locked in. There will never be anything more powerful that can break it."

"There has to be something else we can do," I insisted. "If he finds out he's a demigod through other means, then the curse will have no hold on him anymore, right? The curse says that no witch or warlock can tell him about his powers, but what if we get one of our allies to talk to him?"

"It still won't work, because indirectly, we're still telling him," Wykoff said. "Marcus is going to have to figure out what he is on his own."

"How do we prepare him for that?" Nadine asked. "We know Marcus is going to be involved in some sort of supernatural battle when he's older. Talia saw a vision of him with the Seer Wand, headed into battle on a wolven shifter's back. Talia said he was more powerful than any warlock she'd ever seen."

"You can teach him theory, but his magic won't fully awaken until he's older," Professor Wykoff said. "The best you can do for your son is to nurture his mind and spirit, so that when his powers do awaken, he's ready for it."

"So there's *nothing* we can do to help him with his magic?" I asked.

Professor Wykoff sat up straighter. "I know you want the best for your child, but you must understand that you can't physically be there for him through everything. His destiny is his alone, and there will come a time when you have to set him free and let him fight battles in which you're unable to stand beside him."

The thought of my son fighting anything like we had made me sick to my stomach. I leaned back in my chair to peer into the open doorway of the cafeteria. Marcus caught my eye, and he jumped out of his chair to come running into the Main Foyer. Talia tried to catch him, but he was out of her reach in a second. I waved to her to let her know not to worry about it.

"Daddy!" Marcus cried as he ran across the foyer toward me.

I opened my arms to him, but he tripped a moment before reaching me. My heart leapt into my throat as he went tumbling toward the active fireplace. I swooped down to catch him around the belly before he fell face-first into the fire. Nadine gasped in surprise, but it took everything I had in me to swallow down my fright. If I let Marcus know I'd been terrified for his safety a second ago, he'd have a full-on meltdown.

Instead, I tossed him over my shoulder like I had this morning and tickled his belly. "What are you up to, silly goose?"

Marcus giggled in my ear. "Daddy! Tickle me more!"

I plopped back down in my chair and cradled Marcus in one arm while I tickled under his chin with the other. Nadine playfully grabbed his feet and tickled his ankles.

"Mommy!" Marcus screamed in delight.

His laughter filled the room. It was a sound that melted my heart each time I heard it. It occurred to me how wonderful it was for Nadine and me to be holding our son here in the place we fell in love.

At the same time, I couldn't shake the fear saying these beautiful moments were temporary—at least for our son. He was going to have to find what beauty looked like to him, and sooner or later, I would have to accept that his path wasn't going to be the same as ours. What he found along the way, and the beauty he discovered in the end, would be his alone.

As I turned my gaze toward Nadine, I let my features fall. I kept tickling Marcus while I took a moment to catch my breath. He didn't notice. I resolved never to let him see me fear for his future, because I couldn't teach him to be afraid of it himself. Instead, I had to show him he was capable of anything.

Wherever Marcus's destiny took him, and whatever it meant for him to be a demigod, we would be there to support him. We'd already fought a war, and whatever the visions Talia had seen with the Seer Wand had meant, they were not our fight, but our son's. We could try to protect him from that, but there was no stopping fate. No matter where he went, it was up to us to make sure he knew his family, and his coven, would always be behind him.

As much as we wanted to take this destiny from him and fulfill it ourselves, this was something even magic couldn't stop. Perhaps in some way we'd already done all we could, that by fulfilling our prophecy, it paved the way for the coven to continue on, so that our son could grow up to conquer his own destiny.

Our prophecy was complete, and we weren't the chosen ones anymore. We were parents now, and that meant our job was to do our damndest to raise our children to the best of our abilities. To be a parent meant that when the time came, we would have to step back and let Marcus pursue his own destiny—with or without us.

Nadine and I drew away from our son, but a wide smile remained plastered on Marcus's face.

"Mommy, Daddy," he said. "I love you."

I leaned down to press a kiss to the top of his head. "We love you too, pumpkin."

Nadine entwined her quivering fingers in mine. "More than you will ever know."

Greater than the fear was the love between our family. Nadine and I had found our happy ending. In it, all we could do was believe in our son and share as many beautiful moments with him as possible. I was a Death warlock, but I'd given my son the one thing I could give no one else.

Life.

I made my choices, and I couldn't imagine any better life. What my son did with his?

That was his to decide.

END OF BOOK SIX

Thank you for reading the College of Witchcraft series!

Marcus's adventures begin in The Villain Institute (Hidden Legends: Prison for Supernatural Offenders Book One).

Now available! Turn the page to read a special excerpt.

HIDDEN LEGENDS

Read more from the Hidden Legends universe! Each Hidden Legends series takes place within the same world, but in separate and unique societies. Every series stands on its own, and they can be read in any order.

☾

ELEMENTALS, DRAGONS, & MORE

Academy of Magical Creatures by Megan Linski & Alicia Rades

☾

SHIFTERS, FAE, & SORCERESSES

University of Sorcery by Megan Linski

☾

SUPERNATURAL PRISON

Prison for Supernatural Offenders by Megan Linski & Alicia Rades

☾

Never miss a new release! Join our newsletter at www.hiddenlegendsbooks.com/fanclub

THE VILLAIN INSTITUTE
SNEAK PEEK

Charlie

"Well, Oberi," I said to my Familiar. "We have some time before our next class. What should we do?"

Oberi barked, and his wagging tail hit my leg repeatedly. He started leading me back the way we came, then stopped at the rec room.

"What is it, boy?" I asked. "You want to go inside?"

Oberi barked and ran away from me, but he came back a few moments later.

I furrowed my brow. "I don't understa—"

Oberi shoved his nose into my hand. I felt something furry and round and grabbed on to it. It fit easily inside my palm. "A tennis ball? You want to play fetch?"

Oberi barked happily.

"Where are we going to play?"

Oberi didn't hesitate. He rounded on me and pressed his head into my leg, pushing me forward. As soon as I started walking, he came back to my side and led me through the rec room. We stopped at a wall, and I reached my hands out to feel my surroundings. My fingers curled around a door handle, and I twisted.

Hot, humid air met my skin, and Oberi and I stepped outside. I could feel the expansiveness of the open air, but my magic seemed to hit a block hundreds of yards away. It felt a lot like when I'd stepped on the bus, though not as strong, since we weren't in confined quarters. I noted the feeling as noxite and assumed that was the fence Ava had mentioned that surrounded the property. Though it was hot out, I couldn't feel the sun on my skin, as if thick clouds covered the sky.

Voices filled the yard— so many that I couldn't make them out. A twang sounded each time a basketball connected with the pavement, then came the clink of chains as the ball sank into the basket.

In the distance, someone yelled, "Hut!" Bodies collided together with hard thuds.

Ouch. Football sounded like a good way to get beaten inside the prison. I couldn't believe the guards allowed it, to be honest.

"So you've taken me to the prison yard, Oberi?" I asked, stroking his head. I lowered my voice and muttered, "I am not looking forward to this."

Oberi whimpered, and I knew I couldn't tell him no. Even magical huskies couldn't be expected to be cooped up inside all day.

"Fine." I sighed. "But only because I care."

I avoided the basketball players and headed to the other end of the prison yard, where the voices were far off. I tossed the ball toward the fence, and Oberi took off running. He yipped happily, then returned a few moments later and dropped the ball into my hand. It was coated in saliva and smelled of dog breath.

"Ew, Oberi," I complained. He barked again and panted. "Hell, why do you have to be such a good boy?"

I drew my arm back and threw the ball farther this time. Oberi went tearing across the yard so fast that dirt flew up from where his paws dug into the grass. Chunks hit me in the leg.

Oberi returned less than a minute later, and I threw the ball again. I heard the football players too late. Someone came sprinting toward us just as I tossed the ball. Cheers followed behind him.

Thwack. The tennis ball hit somebody square on.

"Touchdown!" someone yelled, but it was too far off to be the guy I'd hit.

"What the fuck?" a deep voice roared. That was definitely the guy who just took the blow from my tennis ball. Shit.

The man stepped toward me. Oberi threw himself in front of me and growled, the tennis ball totally forgotten.

"Who the fuck do you think you are?" he snapped.

I opened my mouth to respond, but I never got a word out. A heavy fist cracked into my jaw, and I was thrown sideways.

"What the hell!?" I growled as I steadied myself. My head spun. I pressed my fingers to my lip, and they came away covered in a warm liquid. "It was an accident."

"Bullshit," the guy growled. "You did that on purpose."

Oberi barked as the man reached out to grab me. His hands landed on my shoulders, and I noticed they were huge. "You want to pick a fight with a vamp?" he snarled. His chilling breath crossed the top of my head. The guy must've been a whole head taller than me. "Be my guest, but your sorry ass is going to lose."

Air rushed toward my face, and I ducked his fist. A chorus of oohs rang out from behind him. He moved faster than I could react, though, and I didn't have time to dodge the next blow. He swung an uppercut at my jaw, and my feet left the ground as I went flying backward. I slammed to the ground hard, and breath whipped out of my lungs. I gasped. Oberi rushed over and licked my face. I used my magic to force air into my lungs, but it only helped a little. My ears rang, and my sense of balance was shot.

"Go Mad Dog!" someone shouted.

Mad Dog must've been encouraging them, because several others joined in on the cheers, and they only grew louder.

"Get up!" a boy hissed from above me— someone different than the others. His voice was smoother, not quite as rough and angry as the vampire gang. He placed his hands on my shoulders, but they were smaller and softer than Mad Dog's. Whoever it was wasn't gentle, though. He yanked me to my feet. A cat mewed lightly beside him. "You have to fight back!"

"Fight back?" I balked. I was still trying to figure out which way was up and which way was down. That punch had nearly knocked me out. "Who are you?"

"I'm Marcus. I'm the guy who's gonna make sure you don't get killed," he said in a rush.

"I can't fight back," I argued. "He's huge! And a vampire, no less. This isn't a fair fight."

"So he's faster and stronger than you," Marcus said, like it wasn't a big deal. "Use your magic against him."

"What for?" I demanded. Something lurched in my guts. I doubled over, feeling like I might hurl.

Marcus caught me. "You're new here, aren't you? If you want to survive in this prison, you can't let anyone walk over you. You win this fight, you win every fight afterward. This is the only chance you've got. Now get back in there and finish this."

Marcus clapped me on the back, and I stumbled forward toward Mad Dog. I didn't know who my new ally was, but he was right. This wasn't a street fight I could just walk away from afterward. I was locked in here with Mad Dog, and losing this fight meant I'd be marked as an easy target. If I walked away, I was inviting him to come after me again. And not just him, but anyone who was hungry for blood. Winning was the only way to show everyone they couldn't mess with me. I had to do this— not just for myself, but for Oberi. I wouldn't let him become a target, too.

"You throw a good punch," I said, wiping the blood from my lip.

The chorus of cheers died down, and Mad Dog let out a low chuckle. "You must have a death wish."

I shrugged. "Something like that. So, is that all you've got?"

"There's a lot more where that came from," Mad Dog snarled.

I quickly realized Mad Dog liked to fight with his fists, because a punch came rushing toward my face again. I felt it by the change in the air. I ducked out of the way and reacted before he could get another punch in. I thrust my arms outward, and the Air followed my command. I felt the resistance as it slammed into him. The thud I expected from his body hitting the ground never came. He barely even stumbled.

Use my magic… not as effective as it sounds.

How the hell was I supposed to fight a vampire? It's not like I could suck the air out of his lungs. He was undead, and didn't need to breathe. It wouldn't affect him… right?

Hell if I knew.

Mad Dog approached me again, but before he reached me, Oberi darted in front of me. He growled and snapped his jaw, but the vampire was faster than he was. Air swirled by me as Mad Dog swung out a foot.

Oberi whimpered as it connected with his gut. I heard the thud as my Familiar landed in the grass a few feet away.

Pure, unadulterated anger rushed to the surface. I didn't think. I just reacted.

I flung my hands out, and Air magic blasted through them. I felt it streaming around Mad Dog's body, and though he resisted, he couldn't fight the wind gusts enough to get close to me.

"Nobody hurts my Familiar!" I screamed.

My rage came bursting through, and Air magic unlike anything I'd ever used began to circle around Mad Dog. My magic felt like a rope, tightening around the low life and pinning his arms to his sides. I might as well have been summoning a tornado, because that's how strong the winds felt. Dirt swirled through the air, sending particles bouncing off my skin and into my eyes. Trash and other debris could be heard tumbling across the pavement near the basketball courts, and the hoops rattled. Screams filled the prison yard. The guards began yelling to get things under control, but it was nearly inaudible over the winds.

"I'll make you sorry you ever touched my Familiar," I sneered.

I threw my arms upward, and the air followed. The mini cyclone I'd created blasted upward, taking Mad Dog with it. His screams could be heard echoing in the distance as he fell from a great height. I heard a splash, but I could barely process it. I just stood there, shaking.

"Holy shit, man," Marcus said as he returned to my side. "Right in the lake! A classic."

I furrowed my brow. "There's a lake?"

"Hell yeah." He sounded pleased. "Mad Dog is siren food. He won't be messing with you again."

"Holy shit. Did I kill him?" My stomach hollowed at the thought. I hadn't meant to take things that far.

"No, he'll be— get down!"

Marcus grabbed me by the neck and shoved me to the ground. We landed side-by-side in the grass as something small whizzed above our heads. I nearly crushed Marcus' cat, but the creature wiggled out from under my arm.

"What the hell—?"

"Noxite darts," he breathed. "The guards will shoot at anyone! Let's get out of here."

I grabbed Oberi's scruff and scurried to my feet. I kicked up another whirlwind around us to throw any noxite tranquilizers off their course. I followed Marcus and Oberi around the side of the building, and we ducked into the school. The entrance was narrow, like a long hallway. I heaved heavy breaths, but it hardly felt like there was enough air in here.

"Holy shit," I gasped as I leaned against the wall.

"Holy shit is right," Marcus agreed. "You beat Mad Dog! Good job, man."

"I'm not talking about Mad Dog!" I cried. "I'm talking about the guards. Did they see us?"

I hoped not. The last thing I needed was to head to Cellblock 9 my first day of class.

"With that whirlwind you created?" Marcus panted. "I couldn't see anything through that. I think you're safe. You've got some crazy skills, though. I've never seen elemental magic like that."

"Mad Dog's gonna want revenge," I stated.

"Nah, you did good," Marcus said. "I got in a fight with one of his buddies my first day here. Won it like a champ, and they haven't bothered me since. Anyway, good luck at the Institute."

"Wait!" I stopped him before he could walk away. "Why'd you help me? Are you an Elementai like me?"

Marcus chuckled. "What, because of my cat? Nah, Rishi's not a Familiar. My tattoo marks me as a warlock. I'm surprised you didn't notice."

I didn't say anything. Marcus hadn't caught on that I was blind, which was a good thing. I didn't want anyone in this prison thinking they could take advantage of me.

I shrugged. "I'm new."

"Well, it was a good thing I was out in the yard when I was," Marcus said. "You have to be careful here, new guy."

I scoffed. "Believe me, I know. Thanks for the help."

Marcus chuckled. "Seeing you kick Mad Dog's ass was worth it."

"This might sound dumb, but..." I wondered how to word the question. "I thought vampires couldn't be outside during the day. Shouldn't Mad Dog and his crew... I don't know, burn up in the prison yard or something? Or is that just a myth?"

"Nah, it's true," Marcus said. "But the cloud cover on Darke Island is so thick vamps don't have to worry about the sun."

Damn. I had so much to learn about this world.

"See you around," Marcus said.

"Yeah," I replied. "See ya."

After Marcus and his cat walked away, I realized that he never told me why he helped me. It was like he'd avoided the question all together— like he was hiding something.

Prison wasn't the place to go poking into people's secrets, but I'd be damned if I didn't want to know what Marcus was hiding.

Read more of Marcus's story in The Villain Institute!

BONUS OFFERS

Find coloring pages, games, quizzes, and bonus content at hiddenlegendsbooks.com.

Join the *Orenda Academy: Hidden Legends Fan Group* on Facebook for all things Hidden Legends!

Check out the *College of Witchcraft Official Playlist* on Spotify!

Never miss a new release! Join Alicia's email list at aliciaradesauthor.com/newsletter.

ABOUT THE AUTHOR

Alicia Rades is a USA Today Bestselling Author of young adult and new adult paranormal novels. Her stories follow characters in equal-dynamic romantic relationships and feature themes of discovering one's power and overcoming limitations. When she's not dreaming up magical stories, she's either binge-watching paranormal TV shows, meditating, or making crafts and cooking with her family. Her favorite tropes are small-town mysteries, witches, and magical academies set in the modern world. She has an unhealthy obsession with psychic characters and writes with a deck of tarot cards next to her computer.